A NEW WORLD

"This country,"—Chad's eyes glowed and his voice took on the tone of a man speaking of a much-loved person, caressing her with words—"This is where the future is. A man can make a kingdom for himself out here. Start a dynasty." He looked at Hallie. *"Our* dynasty, Hallie. Something we shall create together."

The fields of high grass were golden after the dry winter. Birds flapped up from the grasses and flew away. Black and white magpies of incredible beauty sat in the gum trees, singing their melodic tunes. The air was soft against Hallie's face.

"It seems like summer," she said.

"Winter here is warmer than summer in England," Chad replied. "Spring and autumn are as perfect as you can get."

"Doesn't it ever snow?" She couldn't believe it would never be dreary and cold.

"Never." Chad turned to look at her, and a grin spread over his face. "It's so different from England. You'll think you've died and gone to paradise."

"No," she said, as though to herself. "I've come to paradise and just begun to live."

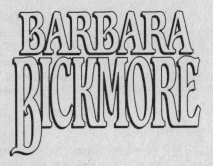

BARBARA BICKMORE

THE MOON BELOW

ZEBRA BOOKS
KENSINGTON PUBLISHING CORP.

ZEBRA BOOKS are published by

Kensington Publishing Corp.
475 Park Avenue South
New York, NY 10016

Zebra and the Z logo are trademarks of Kensington Publishing
Corp.

Second Zebra Books Printing: February, 1994

Printed in the United States of America

DEDICATION

I dedicate this book to my most beloved daughters, who have allowed me always to be me. From them I have learned far more than I taught. No words can express what they mean to me, the beauty they have added to my life, and the happiness and vision they have given me. For many other reasons, I thank:

DEBRA CLAPP, *for inviting me to wander around China with her for two months in 1985.*

LISA CLAPP, *for offering me the original idea for Australia at the time in history of which I write.*

The three of us spent the summer of 1988—in a constant state of awe, wonder, and delight—traveling through 5,500 miles of Australia.

And to

MEG RULEY, *my agent, a true Wonder Woman, who has made miracles come true.*

CON SELLERS, *loving teacher and friend and the first published writer I ever met, who brought me to Meg, and who has tried to give me faith in myself by constant encouragement and inspiration.*

and I wish to thank

BOO BOO CHEATHAM, *for reading this as I went along and often calling me from six hundred miles away with encouragement, with willingness to brainstorm ideas to help me out of corners I might have painted myself into, and for always being willing to read what I write.*

JOËLLE DELBOURGO *and* SONA VOGEL, *for editing the final manuscript and for Joëlle's continued faith in me.*

The Eugene, Oregon, Public Library, which has never failed me.

One

Hallie had cried until there were no tears left.

Her father took two steps forward, bending over to pick up the shovel; he tossed earth into the fresh grave, on top of the casket that had just been lowered into the earth.

Danny, her twin, reached out to put an arm around her black-clad shoulders.

The procession began its slow march out of the cemetery, along the cobbled streets, through the gray haze of New-castle.

Hallie was more angry than anything else. Angry at a life that demanded this from them, at its terrible sense-lessness. She looked at the head of the funeral cortege; her mother and the now-widowed Ruth walked stoically, their backs ramrod straight, their shoulders nearly touching. It was Dada whose shoulders sagged.

Three days ago, on November 28, 1809, Philip, her oldest brother, had been alive. Along with Dada and her other brothers he had gone down in the mine in that time right before night became day, as the men did every morning six mornings a week, fifty-two weeks a year.

"It's so unfair," Hallie whispered to Danny, the biting wind blowing tendrils of her long blond hair across her face. Her brother reached out for her hand again, holding it so tightly that it hurt. "I'm sick of it."

She didn't realize her voice was so loud until Danny went, "Shh."

The procession moved more quickly now; those who were close friends would come home to the Thomases', to sit together trying to console the inconsolable. Hallie stared at the people ahead of her. "I can't go on this way," she said, jagged desperation in her voice.

"But you will," Danny said, his face solemn. "You'll marry George and live with his mother and have babies, and life will go on."

Hallie stopped so abruptly that the couple in back of her tripped. She pulled Danny to one side of the dispersing crowd. "But I don't have to do that, do I?" she pleaded. "Marry George and live like I've lived forever?"

Danny shrugged. He had no answer, just as she had no choice.

"And watch him and you and Dada go down to the mines every day, and wonder whenever the whistle blows if it's one of you? Raise sons to go down to the mines and die?"

"Oh, come now, Hallie," Danny said patiently. His blond hair and clear blue eyes were exact replicas of Hallie's, but there was a solidity to his features that hers did not possess. "It's not like that all the time. Phil is the first of our family—"

"The first, but probably not the last." Her voice held bitterness.

"Life hasn't been that bad, has it?" he asked.

Her eyes looked at the line of gray houses, all alike. The stench of stale urine mingled with that of boiled cabbage. "I'm nearly eighteen," Hallie said. "What will I ever experience, except having babies, that I haven't already experienced? Name one thing, just one thing, that could be different from anything we've known."

Danny looked at her, puzzlement reflected in his eyes. "You've never been like the others."

Yes, she knew that, had always known it.

"You weren't content to marry Walt or Richie, or any of the boys who wanted you. Now you don't want to marry George Burnham. What's left for you?"

Hallie sighed so profoundly that Danny stopped to look at her. "Haven't you ever wanted more, Danny?"

Danny just looked at her, as if the question had never occurred to him before. "What do *you* want, Hallie?"

"I don't know. But I know that there *has* to be something more than this." She gazed around at the soot-covered houses, at the streets raw with sewage, at everything so grey, so worn . . . all of it dead before its time. "There have to be places where coal dust doesn't cover everything, where there's more to life than a wedding and babies and worrying about husbands and sons dying in mines. There has to be a life that offers more than *this*." She waved her arm in a wide circle.

They had arrived home at the small, dark four-room

8

house that was just like every other house in sight. Hallie and Danny and their brothers and sisters had been born in this house. Mum and Dada had moved to it the day they married, and their world had been circumscribed by it ever since.

"I can't bear to think of continuing a life that leads to such tragedy—and monotony," Hallie went on.

"Don't you *want* to get married?" Danny asked, curious.

"Of course," answered Hallie, who couldn't imagine a woman not marrying. "But there *has* to be something in addition to that."

"Well, there's work," said Danny, not understanding her. Everyone he knew worked in the mines, had families, perhaps stopped at the pub Friday nights, went to church on Sunday. What else was there?

Hallie shook her head. "Not everyone works in coal mines."

"They do in Newcastle."

"I know. And die here, too."

Hallie left him there to greet their neighbors while she went into the house to help her mother and sisters feed the dozen people who would soon squeeze into the small dwelling. She could not remember a day when her mother had not dusted the furniture and swept through the house; nevertheless, every day of all of Hallie's eighteen years, a film of soot had settled over the furniture and windowsills. Over the years, it had settled on the walls, and even the monthly scrubbing and yearly whitewashing could not remove the grime that had implanted itself there.

Hallie's mother, Sophie, stood in the kitchen doorway, a teakettle in her hand. She looked disoriented, as though she had no idea where she was. Philip had been the first of her grown children to die. Hallie walked across the room and reached for the kettle. "Here, Mum," she said softly, "sit down and let me."

Her mother shook her head. "No, it gives me something to do. You look to Ruth."

Philip's widow sat as though in a trance. Her three-year-old son held onto her skirt, his face sticky with jam, crying for her attention. Hallie lifted him up into her arms. "Come on, Kevin. Let's go wash your face and see if we can't find a bit of cake for you. Would you like that?"

Somehow they all got through the next hour. When the

door closed behind the last visitor, Ruth didn't move. No-body said anything. Hallie and her mother collected the plates and cups that cluttered the small room. Dada lit his pipe, while Danny and Harry stared at nothing, and Ruth rocked back and forth, holding her eighteen-month-old daughter in her lap.

"I don't want to go home," she said in a flat voice. "I'm scared to be alone."

"We'll make up the sofa," said Mum, walking over and putting a hand on Ruth's shoulder, "and Kevin can sleep with Hallie. You don't have to be alone."

"Yes, I do," said Ruth. "I'll be alone the rest of my life." She was twenty-two years old.

Dada coughed, the deep, hacking rattle that had been with him ever since Hallie could remember. She looked at him. He would be forty-six come January; he looked sixty-five.

Gathering Kevin in her arms, she went up the stairs to her bed under the eaves. It really was too narrow for two, but Kevin was so slight he'd hardly make a difference, she thought, climbing in next to him and curling her arms around the little figure. She could feel his body relax as he drifted into sleep; heard the even breathing, and won-dered what life held in store for him. Maybe Ruth would have to go to the woolen mill to weave fourteen hours a day. Mum could take care of the children, though she was getting too old for that. If I marry George, I can take care of them while Ruth goes out to work, she thought. It tilted the scales toward George. Yet she knew that marrying George, or any of the others who had asked for her hand, would doom her forever.

There is no hope, she thought, and a wildness seized her, a despair.

From the attached house next door, through the thin walls, Hallie heard Mrs. Munson crying, the pitiable sound that bordered a shriek, the noises Hallie heard two to three times a week. And then drunken laughter and a clap that sounded like wood cracking. Hallie knew Mrs. Munson would have a black eye come morning.

The next day, tired from too little sleep, Hallie went through the motions of doing the wash. Every morning she washed for those ladies in the big houses, the ones who weren't quite wealthy enough to hire their own laundresses but who were rich enough to send it out. By the time she finished hanging it on the line, she saw it already yellowing as it flapped in the smoky haze. At noon she prepared dinners for Dada and Danny. An elevator would take the lunch pails down to the men, and they would eat in the damp darkness, as they had during the thirty-two years Dada had worked down there, and as they had since each of her four brothers had turned fourteen and followed him down. Then, since this was Thursday, she stopped at Mrs. Adams's and cleaned her house.

It was dusk when she finished, the same time the miners headed toward their homes. Exhausted boys, old men at age fourteen, trudged along with grown men, doomed forever onward to the only life they knew. Lights flickered on in the houses fronting the street as Hallie arrived home. Ruth and her children had not left, but tonight Ruth was helping Mum with tea. Reverend Macauley was there.

Dada sat in his chair, shirt sleeves rolled up. They all looked at her expectantly as she walked in, but no one said anything until she started for the kitchen.

"No, Hallie, sit down," said Dada.

It was so unexpected that Hallie stared at him.

"Reverend Macauley has come to see you."

"Me?" That did make her sit down.

She had known the minister all her life. He was stern enough to command respect but was never frightening. His thin, soft voice held warmth even though he seldom smiled. Hallie thought maybe he had seen too much pain, too many Philips, too many stillborn babies.

"Hallie, do you remember Chadwick Morgan?"

Hallie searched her memory without success. "Should I?" she asked, wondering if she'd done something wrong.

"You haven't seen him since you were a child, about seven or eight years ago." The minister leaned forward, studying her.

"Morgan," said Dada. "Would that be kin to *the* Mr. Morgan?"

Reverend Macauley nodded.

The Mr. Morgan owned the mines.

11

"How would Hallie ever have known kin to the Mr. Morgan?" asked Dada.

Reverend Macauley looked at her and waited for an answer. "He remembers you, Hallie." The reverend's thin lips curved. "He says he met you in church many years ago."

"Oh, Chad!" she said, suddenly recalling clear gray eyes. "Yes, of course." The one bright spot of her childhood. The fleeting moments . . .

Turning to Dada, the minister said, "As a boy, Chad was one of the most endearing children I've known. He loved to ride horses as fast as they could go; he was fearless. After graduation from Eton, Chad told his father he didn't want to attend a university. He never was much of a student, though I always thought he was smart as a whip."

Hallie struggled to recall what Chad looked like, but all she could summon to mind was the white blaze on his horse's face.

"That was fine with his father, who thought it none too early to begin training Chad in the mining business," Reverend Macauley continued. "But Chad refused. He knew the mines would never be his. He would not inherit them. His older brother would. The law of primogeniture, you know . . . Besides, Chad never liked the mines or Newcastle. He wanted to see the world. There was quite a row. I know, because his father came to see me and asked me to talk with Chad. I always liked that boy. But his mind was made up. He told me he'd known all his life that he had to get away."

How lucky, thought Hallie. And now a few memories of him came tumbling back.

"When he accepted a commission in the army, it broke his father's heart. He has been home only once in these last seven years," said the reverend.

The room was silent, waiting, expectant. Hallie's memory focused on a tall young man astride his beautiful black horse, and she wondered what he, who had disappeared so long ago, had to do with her.

"Chad is in New South Wales now," Reverend Macauley went on. "He has written and asked me to deliver a letter to you and to speak on his behalf."

"Where's New South Wales?" asked Hallie. She, too, dreamed of faraway places.

12

"I'm not rightly sure, but it's on the other side of the world. Down below. Chad writes that it takes eight to nine months to get there by ship."

The other side of the world. Underneath . . . Hallie wondered what that was like. If you could fall off someplace and drop down.

The minister fished in his breast pocket and brought out a letter, which he gave to Hallie. She stared at the envelope; there was her name in big sprawling letters in black ink. She turned the letter over in her hands. The only other time she could remember anyone getting a letter was years ago when Mum's brother, Uncle Edward, wrote to them from America.

Hallie carefully opened the letter, trying not to tear it. She sat down at the table at which the family ate dinner and, while everyone looked on, spread the pages out in front of her.

My dear Hallie . . .

She looked up as Mum suggested, "Read it aloud, Hallie."

"It's been so many years, you may not even remember me. You may be married by now. But I remember your adventurous spirit, and the blue bow you wore in your hair the day I first saw you. It matched your eyes. You must have been eight years old, and I was sixteen. I came out of church and saw you standing by my horse, talking to it and reaching up to touch it. When I came near, you smiled at me and said you hoped I didn't mind, but it was such a beautiful animal you just had to talk to it. You'd never been near a horse before."

Memory inserted itself into Hallie's consciousness. A big black horse with a white blaze on its face and white band around its ankle, and the tall young man smiling at her, holding a hat in his hand.

"And maybe a year later, when I was out riding, I nearly ran over you, do you remember that?"

Hallie raised her eyes from the letter and stared into

space. Yes . . . She'd been walking on the hill outside of town, already yearning to get away from the grime of the city, when a horse and rider had come out of nowhere, flying past her so close she could feel the wind. Later, they had come back across the field, the beautiful ebony horse and the young man. He had stopped when he saw her.

She forgot what he had said, but he'd given her a hearty laugh, and his eyes had twinkled. She remembered reaching up her hand and being pulled up onto the saddle in front of him. "Hold tight!" he'd cried, and off they'd gone, galloping so fast the scenery was a blur. Her hair had flown behind her, and she'd felt the warmth and safety of his body against her back. For the first time, she had tasted freedom.

Her eyes returned to the scripted black letters on the page in front of her.

"We didn't see much of each other, though I do remember turning around every Sunday in church to see if you were there. And you always were. I knew it, even if we didn't talk."

Yes, whenever she'd seen him, she had hoped he'd take her for another ride.

"Once, when we stood talking on the church steps for a few minutes, I remember we agreed that we hated Newcastle, and yearned for a place where one could see the sun and smell the air."

She must have been eleven by then, and was running around that same meadow when he and his horse had walked up to her. He was on foot and said, "I was hoping to see you. I'm going away." He didn't know where, he'd told her. He'd joined the army and hoped to be sent far away, to Egypt or India, perhaps.

"Or to America?" she'd asked. Her Uncle Edward was there, which lent it some credibility.

"No," sighed the young man. "Twenty years ago that would have been fun; I could have fought for the honor of England. But we don't have troops there now. I don't really care where I'm assigned."

14

"Is your horse going, too?" Hallie had asked.

The young man had laughed. "I'm afraid not." Then he'd added, "I wish I could give him to you."

But he couldn't. She couldn't have fed such a magnificent animal anyway.

"I am in such a place now, where the sun shines and where it is warm and there are trees and animals like none you've ever seen, where the sky is so clear you feel you can touch the stars.

"New South Wales is a land waiting to be developed and civilized. I have cast my lot here, resigned from the army, and petitioned for land. The governor has granted me five hundred acres.

"I want a wife and family, Hallie. There are very few women in this wild land. And lately I have been thinking of your adventurous spirit and your desire to leave Newcastle. Do you still feel that way? If you do, I would be very happy if you will come to New South Wales and be my wife. Reverend Macauley can make the arrangements.

"Chadwick Morgan"

Hallie had difficulty swallowing. The fire crackled as a log broke in two.

"What's that mean?" asked Dada, as though he couldn't believe what he'd heard. "*The* Mr. Morgan's son wants to marry my Hallie?" The expression on his face, his raised eyebrows, indicated he was both concerned and perplexed.

"He was a fine lad when I knew him," said the minister. "She couldn't do better."

Couldn't do better? thought Hallie. Couldn't do half as well.

"Well, I dunno," said Dada. "Half a world away . . ."

"He tells me he thinks your daughter will be excited by this new raw—yes, that's his word—raw land. He promises you she'll have a far better life than if she remains here." When Reverend Macauley saw the dubious look on Dada's face, he interrupted himself to say, "Mr. Thomas, your grandsons will have the chance to be more than miners when they grow up, forever dwelling in the bowels of the earth." He coughed self-consciously, then continued, "Chad will be pleased if you will consent, Mr. Thomas."

"Well, I don't know," said Dada again.

But Hallie knew already. Chad was offering her salvation; a land where the sun shone—a new way of life.

No George. No coal mines. No gray.

"I do consent," cried Hallie, unable to control the quiver in her voice. "I do."

Two

MUM. DADA. DANNY . . .

Never again.

Her family had faded over the horizon, never to be seen again. But she would miss nothing else. She knew what she had left behind: darkness, dirt, conformity. She had left behind hopelessness and gray despair.

Hallie breathed deeply, inhaling the salt sea air as though it would cleanse her lungs. These last five weeks at sea, despite the tossing of the winter Atlantic, seemed to have cleansed her soul, too. She stared at the endless horizon, at the place where sky met sea so indistinguishably they melded into one.

I'm breathing in blue, she thought, and smiled to herself.

The gentle tossing of the ship lulled her into a peace she'd never known, and she stood there for a long time. Night descended and she stared into its endlessness, feeling the velvet softness of the trade winds, mesmerized by unknown stars. I don't even know where I am, she thought.

For the first time in her life she was filled with hope. . . .

They had set sail from London the day after New Year's, barely a month after Reverend Macauley had presented Chad's letter to her. The minister had volunteered to take her to London and make sure she boarded the HMS *Charleston* safely. There had been much wringing of hands by Mum, and a catch in Dada's throat, and looks from Danny designed to inflict guilt upon her ("I want you to be happy, you know that. But I can never again be as happy with you gone").

Yet it had not been enough to hold her. She was heading to a life which, in her inner core, she'd felt was her destiny. She had no idea where she was going, but she knew, she just knew, that she had been created for this faraway land that she had not known existed six weeks before.

Hallie had hugged her other brothers and Danny, who was the part of herself she was leaving behind. Her sisters, Myrna, Hester, and Kate, all cried a little, and Kate had said, "You might as well be dying. We'll never see you again."

The tears had come when Dada put his arms around her and whispered, "My Hallie . . ."

No one could understand why Hallie had chosen to leave . . . except her mother, who was dry-eyed. Hallie could tell from Mum's red eyes that her crying had been done in the night. "I know you're going to something better," Sophie said. "I know you were never meant for this life. But it doesn't hurt any the less." She'd handed Hallie a packet, around which was tied a piece of ribbon. "It's not much," she'd said. "But it's important to me for you to have."

Hallie had opened it to find a baby's blanket inside. "Someday you'll have my grandchild"—there was a tremor in Sophie's voice—"and I want to be a part of it." Also included were the wooden knitting needles with which she had knit the blanket. "You'll be knitting yourself sometime." They were the same needles Hallie had heard clicking in her mother's hands nearly every evening of her life, worn smooth from so many years. She didn't think her mother owned anything else that was just hers.

She'd kissed her mother's cheek and felt the arms around her, not wanting to let go, had felt the fingers clutching her tightly. Yet she had known that never would she question her decision, never would there be any doubt about the rightness of what she was doing.

She had felt no qualms watching Reverend Macauley waving from the dock, knowing that as his figure grew smaller, her life was growing larger. . . .

The *Charleston* was part of a flotilla of four of His Majesty's ships. The *Theseus* and *Tigard* held mainly prisoners, over 260 of them. The *Wyckliffe* was the ship that carried supplies for New South Wales, food for the prisoners already there, and clothing and furniture that had been ordered by the residents. It carried no passengers or convicts.

Hallie's ship carried all the paying passengers, along with forty-seven convicts, thirteen of them women, four of them with children.

For the first three days Hallie was dreadfully seasick, like nearly everyone else. The whole ship smelled of vomit. The paying passengers weaved onto the deck and, gripping the rail, threw up into the sea. From the hold, where the prisoners were jammed together in darkness, the smell of urine and regurgitation floated up to choke the passengers. When the choppy gray seas grew smoother, the prisoners were allowed on deck, by twos and threes, to exercise. By then the smell had abated, though it never completely disappeared.

By the middle of February the ships pulled into the Canary Islands. While in port, the prisoners were not even permitted on deck for their exercise, but the passengers disembarked to wander around the sweet-smelling gardens and quaint streets and to bask in their first taste of tropical weather. Hallie had no idea where the Canaries were, but she hoped New South Wales might resemble them. They took on fresh water, and vegetables and fruits designed to ward off scurvy; meat was hoisted aboard, as was Madeira wine by the boxload.

Wanting to avoid being caught in the doldrums that were inevitable along the western coast of Africa, the captain headed to Rio for the next stop. The weather became intolerably hot, and the humidity rendered passengers comatose. All the bilges stank. Rats, lice, and cockroaches crawled out of hiding places. Seawater in the lower hold mixed with excrement and traces of urine and the odors of rotting food; convicts, in their steaming holds, fell ill from the effluvia.

Six people, five of them convicts, had died since they'd left England. Hallie, however, flourished. Her pallid northern England complexion turned golden. Her blond hair had bleached under the equatorial sun, and tranquility was reflected in her eyes.

She was now turning into a beautiful woman. Captain Dunsmere often invited her to sit at his left at dinner. She found herself drawn up to the deck, beside the wheel, where the captain spent many hours. He knew the background of this land to which they were headed, and she listened to him by the hour, drinking in his stories of criminals he had transported.

In 1788, he told her, the government had founded New South Wales as a penal colony. No one had seemed to know of its existence until thirty years ago, when Captain Cook, the famous explorer, had stumbled upon it. How large it was, whether or not it was connected to the mainland of Asia, whether it was an island or not, still remained a mystery.

"Why a penal colony?" asked Hallie. She remembered the jail in Newcastle, a big, old, dirty brick building with tiny barred windows. She'd always run past it as fast as she could.

Because, explained Captain Dunsmere, there were not enough prisons in all of England to contain its criminals. The worst ones, the murderers and repeat offenders, were hanged. But the others were sentenced to jail terms, usually seven years. The jails were bulging at the seams. When America had been a British colony, that vast uninhabited land had served as a dumping ground for England's criminals. Thousands of prisoners had been transported to America every year. For 150 years prisoners had helped to populate that underpopulated land. Their sentences were reduced, and after a few years they were released from jail with the understanding that they were never to return to England. In this way England had helped to colonize America and at the same time relieved itself of suffering the consequences of released felons. It had also been far cheaper to send prisoners three thousand miles away than to feed and house them in England.

But the American Revolution had changed all that. Now, ships that were no longer seaworthy, ones that were rotting hulks at the London and Liverpool docks, served to house those prisoners who spilled over from the jails. The majority, when released, soon showed up in jails again. They were a menace to the good citizens of Great Britain, the captain told her.

When the king had sent the first shiploads of prisoners to New South Wales, Dunsmere explained, he had encouraged soldiers to travel there, too. He'd offered enticements of land, that they would bring their families with them so a decent civilization might serve as a model basis for prisoners when released.

"Are there Indians?" asked Hallie, knowing that much about America.

The captain didn't think so, though there were very black people who were stranger looking than any people he'd ever seen, and whom he heard ate insects and worms.

"Ugh," said Hallie, grimacing.

"Exactly," replied Captain Dunsmere, flattered by this young woman's interest in his conversation.

The stop in Rio bolstered their spirits. The crew spent three weeks washing the ships, taking on fresh lemons, limes, and fruit that those from the northern latitudes had never seen before; clothes were washed and the ship repaired.

Hallie found Rio exciting. She had never seen dark-skinned people. Their laughter filled the streets. The young barefoot women of Brazil wore their hair in long braids. Unbraided, it trailed on the floor. Hallie never saw it unbraided, but many of the sailors did.

The captain bought bags of flour, mainly for the burlap, which could be converted into rough clothing for the thirty-two women prisoners, whose clothing had nearly disintegrated. Every morning that they spent in Rio, the majority of able-bodied seamen had hangovers. The *Charleston*'s surgeon left the ship in Rio, himself too ill to continue.

It took them six weeks to reach Cape Town, the southernmost tip of Africa. There, the crew spent several weeks preparing for the last and most difficult part of the voyage. Unlike Rio, though as hot, Cape Town was dusty and unfriendly. This stop would be their last vestige of European influence before the long emptiness of the Indian Ocean.

Over four hundred animals were loaded; since there was no more room on the store ship, sheep, cattle, horses, hogs, and poultry were crammed into the already inhumanely crowded prisoners' quarters. Seed was purchased and fresh water taken aboard hopefully to last through the tropical doldrums of the next few months, when no land would even be sighted.

None of the passengers was prepared for the seas of the Indian Ocean. They were overwhelmed and sometimes panicked by the monstrous swells that tossed the ship first

21

high in the air and then into the valleys, where they were surrounded by water that rose in glasslike sheets around them. Fear paralyzed them, and enormous gray whales, which seemed like phantoms, accompanied the ship for days on end.

It was the first time Hallie had been seasick since the initial days of the voyage. And what started as an intermittent dull ache on her right side became a searing, stabbing pain. She doubled over in agony, vomiting on the floor beside her bed. Nausea overcame her, and she lay, head hanging over the narrow bunk, until dry heaves took over.

Finally one of her cabin mates, Mrs. Ellison, returned from luncheon and grimaced as the sour odor of the cabin assaulted her. Then she saw Hallie, moaning, her head hanging from the bunk.

"Oh, my dear!" she cried.

Within minutes she had found a mop and bucket and was wiping the floor clean, a look of distaste on her face. When Hallie kept retching, Mrs. Ellison put a hand on her burning forehead. "You're not just seasick," she pronounced. "You're ill. I'll call the captain."

The world spun around, the cabin disappearing into a vortex until Hallie could see nothing, her mind caught in the blankness before her. She heard the door open and Captain Dunsmere's voice saying, "She's feverish, all right," but her eyes wouldn't focus and she couldn't see him. Their voices came as from a great distance, from some long, hollow place.

She heard Mrs. Ellison's birdlike chirping. "Well, something must be done."

And then all was quiet.

The rolling of the ship surged in and out of Hallie's consciousness, interspersed with moments of black pain. She didn't know how much later—whether it was hours or days—she heard a man's voice she had not heard before, near her ear: "Does this hurt?" And though she could tell the cold fingers tried to be gentle, she also heard her own voice screaming as the tormented area was prodded.

The same soft voice, one she would never forget, said, "Her appendix is about to burst. Unless she's operated on immediately, she'll die. I mean now, within the hour."

Die? Hallie struggled to hold on. I'm too young to die. . . .

The same voice, again close to her ear, asked, "Can you hear me?"

Hallie forced her eyes open. Kind, dark eyes were but inches from her face. "You're going to be all right. I'm going to help you."

He had been kneeling next to her; now he stood, and she saw he was bearded. His dark hair, dirty but combed, reached his shoulders. His shirt was in rags. How could anyone who looked like that save her?

But his eyes, she thought. I trust those eyes.

"I'm going to take you to the infirmary." He bent over and picked her up. The movement sent fresh pain surging through her. "It's going to be all right," he murmured. As he held her close in the narrow passageway, Hallie was aware that he smelled.

"Are you a doctor?" She was surprised at how weak her voice sounded

"I am," he answered as he walked, bent over in the cramped passageway. "And I promise to save you. You will be sore after the operation, but just for a little while. It will not be the pain you have now." He stooped to enter a room.

Hallie closed her eyes as he laid her on a table. She heard voices, heard the stranger say to her, "I'm going to wash up, and then I'll be back and I'm going to take out your appendix."

Mrs. Ellison held a cool, damp cloth against Hallie's forehead. When the captain and doctor returned, she heard low voices. Mrs. Ellison said, "Oh, I can't do that."

The doctor's voice was no longer soft; it had an edge to it. "You not only can, you will." And then Hallie heard his voice, low, in her ear. "You're going to sleep . . . what's your name?"

Her eyes fluttered open again. "Hallie Thomas . . ."

"You're going to sleep, Hallie, and when you wake up you'll be better, and I'll be right here with you. Don't be afraid. I'm going to put this cloth over your face now, and you'll find yourself swirling into darkness. I'm going to help you."

Hallie inhaled the strange-smelling mandagora that Mrs.

Ellison held on a rag across her face, and as she lost consciousness she wondered about this ragged-looking, smelly man with the soft trustworthy eyes. But aloud she said, "He's going to save me," though no one understood the garbled words.

Three

When Hallie awoke, she saw nothing except the dark ceiling; it swirled around and around. The dizziness disappeared when she closed her eyes. There was a throbbing ache where the stabbing pain had been, and she was no longer nauseated. She heard waves sloshing against the bulkheads, swaying the ship. She felt disembodied, far from reality, far from the ship, far from herself. She slept again.

The next time her eyes fluttered open, she saw a face with warm brown eyes—so dark they were almost black—staring at her with both fervor and what she believed to be infinite kindness. A hand touched hers. She closed her eyes again but did not sleep. The hand stayed curled around hers.

If she opened her eyes and stayed awake, the hand would go away, she knew. She was incredibly weak; it would take all the effort she could muster to open her eyes and keep them open. So she lay there, her mind empty, the hand comforting.

She didn't know how long it lasted. When the hand unfurled itself and left her, she inadvertently called out, "Don't," and then her eyes flew open.

The man sitting beside her had the same eyes as the man who had asked her to trust him, but he was not the same man. "Don't what?" he asked.

She looked up at him, seeing him as though through a mist. "Nothing," she whispered.

But as though he understood what she had meant, he put his hand around hers again. "You're going to be fine," he reassured her.

"Who are you?" she asked.

"Tristan . . . Dr. Tristan Faulkner."

Now she realized why she hadn't recognized him. His hair and beard were not only washed, but trimmed, and he wore clean clothes. Since she had not seen him the entire

25

six months of the voyage, she sensed that he must be a prisoner.

"You saved my life, didn't you?" she asked.

"That I did." His voice gentled. "And you rescued me." He smiled at her. "It's already a mutual association." He squeezed her hand.

Hallie thought him the most beautiful person she'd ever seen. "I don't understand," she said. "How did I rescue you?"

"They rowed me over from the *Tigard*. And Captain Dunsmere will keep me here the remainder of the trip. Your needing me saved me from a fate worse than death." There was a faraway sadness to his eyes; the hardness of his expression thinned his lips. Then, as though guilty of feeling sorry for himself, he forced a smile again and said, "See, clean clothes. I've even had a bath, such as it was. Got the lice out of my hair. I feel quite human."

"What—What did you do?" She couldn't believe that this man was a criminal.

He rose abruptly from his chair, nearly knocking it over. From the rigidity of his body she sensed his anger. "Treason. They say I am guilty of treason."

"Treason? . . ." It was beyond Hallie's understanding. "Are you guilty?" She could have bitten her tongue off.

He looked down at her. "Yes," he replied, his voice low. "If you consider love of my country a crime."

"Were you a spy?"

He laughed, though there was a brittleness to the sound. "Nothing like that." He sat down again. "Do you know anything about Canada?"

Hallie shook her head. "It's someplace near America, isn't it?"

"In a way . . . I'm Canadian," he explained. "But I went to the United States to school, to Harvard. And when I came home, I tried to urge my fellow Canadians to rebel, like the Americans had; to be a free people."

"That's all?" she asked.

He permitted himself a grim smile. "More or less."

She wanted to know more but was too tired to continue. Instead she reached out and, placing her hand in his palm, closed her eyes again. She felt his hand enclose hers; he sat keeping vigil while she slept again.

When Hallie next awoke, the doctor was across the room, standing by the door. The captain was looking down at her. "Ah, there you are," he muttered when he saw her eyes open. "How are you feeling?"

Her abdomen ached; she knew she couldn't possibly raise herself. The dizziness was passing, but she still felt lethargic. "Thirsty," she murmured.

"I'll get her a drink," the doctor volunteered, and disappeared.

Mrs. Ellison and the captain were not her only visitors. Every paying passenger on board visited Hallie. And of course Dr. Faulkner came often. Hallie loved his visits; even when they lasted hours they seemed far too brief.

Tristan, as he had suggested she call him, had been assigned the room next to the infirmary, with the first mate, Mr. Edwards. In the beginning Edwards had showed irritation at sharing his cabin with a prisoner, but he soon changed his mind; over evening chess he quickly formed a fast friendship with his new cabin mate. He saw immediately that this was no conventional prisoner, and found himself enjoying the physician's company.

Because of the ship surgeon's departure in Rio, Tristan now attended to ailments. He made it clear that if he were going to treat the *Charleston*'s patients, the prisoners in the hold were to receive equal attention. Captain Dunsmere was pleased with the turn of events.

One of the first questions Tristan had asked Hallie was why she was braving this hazardous journey so far from home. She had answered honestly that home was not where her heart had been, that she was going to marry a man she had not seen since they were children, that she wanted to raise her own children where there was sunshine and no coal.

"Funny," mused Tristan. "You think you're going to paradise, and I think I'm going to hell. The end of the world means different things to us, doesn't it?"

Hallie was permitted to stay in the infirmary long after she could have moved back to the cabin she shared with Mrs. Ellison and four other women. She thought it was partly because Tristan enjoyed their private talks as much as she did. But the day came when there was no reason at all for her to play invalid, even a recuperating one, and she moved back to her cramped quarters.

Now, she sat up on deck, enjoying the sunshine even when the ship foundered in the tropical doldrums. It never seemed too hot for her. And when there were no patients, her savior came up to sit with her. For this she was happy, as she knew it would not have been seemly to visit the infirmary to talk with him.

She told him what she had learned of Australia, what Newcastle had been like; she described her family. And he told her what being in prison was like: he had been transported for trial in England, then kept for over six months in a dank dungeon with sixteen other prisoners. He must have lost much weight, he told her, because he had never been so thin. He thought that after his release, in five and a half years, he would head toward America. He wanted nothing more to do with anything British. Yet as he said this his voice softened, and, nostalgically, he recalled the Canada he had so loved—sledding down the hills outside of Quebec and skating on ice in the long, cold winters; maple syrup time in the spring; the reds and golds of autumn. His father had died the year he had returned from Harvard. He thought that the British would never have dared to imprison him if his father had still been alive. Yet of that he could not be sure; admittedly he had been an agitator, a rebel.

"Would you do it again?" Hallie asked.

"No," he shot back instantly. It was obvious that he'd given the matter a great deal of thought. "Knowing the consequences, I would not."

Hallie thought of him every night when she lay on the narrow, hard bunk. She had never witnessed such passion, tenderness, and intense caring in a man. She closed her eyes, and his face, with those dark eyes tinged with sadness, dominated the darkness. When she opened her eyes, his face still floated in her mind's eye. She stretched out to touch him, but he was always just beyond her reach.

As time went by, Tristan became the center of her universe. She could no longer keep her mind on conversations with other passengers; Captain Dunsmere's continued tales of Australia held little of the allure they'd had before Tristan entered her life. She shivered, even in the warm latitudes of the Indian Ocean, when she pictured him in a jail cell, rats running over his feet.

He had not touched her since she had left the infirmary, but she remembered his large hand cradling hers. Often he did not look at her as they talked, but stared out at the horizon. Sometimes they would stroll around the small deck. Meals, of course, were out of the question. The captain, in deference to the sensibilities of the paying passengers, did not permit Dr. Faulkner to eat in the dining room; his food was sent down to the infirmary. Otherwise, however, Tristan was given the run of the ship. Passengers who had been all too ready to criticize Captain Dunsmere gradually accepted the doctor, with his fine manners and obvious skill and compassion.

One day Hallie returned to her cabin after the noon meal to find a young girl—she couldn't have been more than fifteen—huddled on her bed, shaking uncontrollably. As Hallie walked into the room, the girl gasped, her eyes wild with fright. Her burlap clothing was shapeless and torn, her hair matted, and there were scratches down her arm where the blood had already caked. Despite her obvious filth and her look of desperation, Hallie could tell she was a pretty child.

The girl burst into tears as Hallie stood observing her. Hallie walked over to embrace her, but the girl crouched farther into the corner. "I won't hurt you," Hallie said, kneeling down next to her.

"Don't let them get me, please!" the girl cried.

"I won't," said Hallie, managing to wrap an arm around her. Gradually, the shaking stopped. She knew the girl must be a convict, escaped from the hold. Yet she wondered how someone so young could be capable of a crime? "You'll have to tell me what's wrong if you want me to help," she said, brushing matted hair off the girl's face.

The girl stared at her with such terror that Hallie wondered what could have happened to inspire such feeling. "Don't let them get me again, please!" She curled herself tightly against Hallie, feeling the safety net of the arm around her. Hallie wondered what to do.

"I can't stand it one more night," the girl whimpered.

Hallie frowned. "Stand what?"

"The sailors. What they do to me." The girl's teeth still chattered.

"What do they do?" A feeling of doom settled over Hallie.

"You know . . . use me. Every night. I'll throw myself overboard if I have to do it one more night."

Use her? Hallie had only vague intimations of what that meant. She recalled her mother's tentative, embarrassed admonitions about the "things men like to do to a woman . . . that are part of a woman's duty in marriage. You won't always like it, but you'll get used to it. And you have to do it to have children."

Something told Hallie that this "it" was what the young girl was referring to. Tristan might be able to tell her. Certainly he could take care of the scratches on the girl's arm.

Hallie stood up. "I'm going to get a doctor. I'll be right back."

A strangled sound escaped the girl, and her eyes widened with terror. "No, no, no! Don't tell anyone I'm here."

Hallie said, "You can't hide for the rest of the trip. I promise I'll take care of you. But you need a doctor. I won't be long."

The girl began to cry, mewing like a wounded kitten. "Not a man," she whimpered.

"Yes," said Hallie. "A very nice, kind man who, like yourself, is also a prisoner. He will want to help you. I promise."

She did not wait for another objection but hurried out of the cabin and began to run down the hall to the infirmary. Tristan was mixing a liquid and looked up when she entered. "Come with me, and don't ask any questions," Hallie said.

Tristan immediately followed her down the corridor and into her room. He took one look at the girl and then glanced inquisitively at Hallie.

"She's hiding. She's been hurt. And she's scared." In a lower voice she said, "I don't understand what's happened. I thought you might."

With stark terror rounding her eyes, the girl tried to disappear into the corner. Tristan glanced at the dried blood on her arm and said, "I'll get medication."

He was back almost instantly. Murmuring reassurances, he approached the girl, who was hypnotized by his voice.

30

She stared at him and let her arm lie limp as he cleansed it. She gasped when the medicine stung.

"Now, tell me what happened," he said.

The girl remained silent. Tristan turned to Hallie. "What did she tell you?"

"That the sailors 'used' her and she couldn't stand it one more night."

Tristan shook his head as though he understood what Hallie was talking about. "We have to do something about this," he said to the girl. He looked around the tiny cabin. "We could put a pallet on the floor, but just barely. Still better would be the infirmary." And then, as though musing aloud, he continued.

"I think I'll tell the captain she's too ill to stay crowded with the others. I'll also tell him she has . . . oh, something that would be contagious to the sailors. Tell him she must stay in the infirmary and that you're willing to nurse her."

He looked up at Hallie. "You are, aren't you? Willing to?"

Hallie nodded. If he had asked her to climb overboard and try walking on the water, she would have attempted it.

Then, in a soft voice, he asked the girl what her name was. "Beth," she answered, trembling. "Elizabeth White."

"How old are you?"

"Fifteen."

Exactly what Hallie had reckoned. How could a girl of fifteen be sentenced to seven years in prison and sent half-way around the world?

Captain Dunsmere did not even reproach the prisoner once he saw her wounds. He did thank Hallie for her willingness to minister to Beth. And so she moved back to the infirmary to care for the fifteen-year-old felon.

When Hallie went up on deck that afternoon to watch the sunset, Tristan followed her. They leaned against the rail and watched the rays slant from gold to purple as the sun sank behind the ocean. For a while neither talked.

Then, gazing out at the horizon, Tristan asked, "Do you believe in God?"

Hallie looked at him sharply. No one she knew ever questioned such an idea. No one had ever asked her if she believed; in fact, no one had ever asked her how she felt or thought about *anything*.

31

"I don't know," she answered slowly. "I've been afraid often of going to Hell, because sometimes I do doubt."

"People don't go to Hell for that, Hallie." He turned to her. "What kind of faith is it that can't be questioned?"

"I thought faith should be taken on faith." This had been an issue that had confused her for years, but she had never voiced it before, never dared.

Tristan sighed. "I'm confused, too. If there is a God, He certainly works in mysterious ways. He seldom seems to be on the side of what I consider right, or moral."

One elbow resting on the ship's railing, Tristan reached over with his other arm and took Hallie's hand, raising it palm upward, studying it as though it might unlock the secrets of the universe. Then he lifted his eyes to hers. "If there is a God," he said, his voice so low she had to strain to hear, "why do you think He had us meet at this time in my life?"

Hallie's eyes locked with his. They stood that way for a long time, and she found all thought suspended, nothing else in the world but the look in Tristan's eyes and the feel of his hand around hers. Then, his gaze never leaving hers, he brought her hand to his lips and kissed it, his lips brushing her palm and lighting fires within her.

Just then they heard voices, and though no one approached them, Tristan dropped her hand, turning back to lean against the railing and stare out at the darkening horizon.

Hallie didn't want this moment to end, and sought some way to continue the conversation. "If there is a God," she said, wanting to let him know she cared, "how could He let you be sentenced to seven years' imprisonment for doing what you thought was right?"

Tristan was silent for a long time, not moving. Then he said, "Job."

"What?"

"The Book of Job in the Bible."

But he didn't explain, and Hallie didn't understand. Reverend Macauley had either not illuminated his congregation about Job, or Hallie's mind, as usual, had wandered during the sermon.

"Do you read?" asked Tristan.

"Of course." Hallie was insulted. "I've read all my life.

All the children in my family went to school until we were twelve. Dada said we had to learn to read the Bible." She wanted to tell him that she had been the smartest one in the class, boys included.

"Ah, education . . ." She could tell Tristan was smiling, even though it was now dark. "The scourge of Christianity. For how does one stop reading with the Bible? How does one stop the desire for learning when one truly tastes it? And if one begins to read other things than the Bible, one learns things that make one question."

He sounded a bit scholarly, but Hallie enjoyed listening to him. He was more interesting than her teacher had been. When he turned to her, she had to stifle the urge to reach out and touch him.

"What do you believe in, Hallie?" he asked softly.

The question surprised her. She thought for a few minutes and then said, "It changes. I used to think life was hopeless, but now I don't. I think, though, that you can't just wait for life to happen. You have to be ready when opportunity comes and reach for it."

"What else, beautiful Hallie?" He reached out and twisted a finger in a tendril of her long hair. "Do you believe in . . . love?"

Love . . . "I love my family. I love them dearly."

"But what about a man? Do you believe in that kind of love?"

"I hope I can respect and like my husband enough that I will love him . . . that he will become my family." But she already knew she was feeling something for Tristan to which she could not put a name. It was strong right now. She would have liked to reach out her hand and put it on his arm, place her hand in his again and feel his warmth. She would have liked him to look deep in her eyes, put his arms around her and hold her close. She had never known these feelings. Did that have something to do with love? She thought so. But she could not tell him that.

Instead, she changed the subject. "Why are you a doctor?"

There was a bitter edge to his voice. "Love for humanity, Hallie. Plain and simple." His laugh, though quiet, was harsh. "But not appreciated. From here on I tend to physical needs only, not try to help with the political; aye, the

33

so-called spiritual. I think, should I ever live through incarceration, I shall allow myself to be involved with only the simplest pleasures, the purely aesthetic, like tending rose gardens."

"Roses smell lovely. And they add such beauty to life."

Tristan laughed. "Maybe that is my mission, after all." He reached out, and she felt his hand enclose hers. He turned her toward him. "You know, don't you, how I feel about you?"

Hallie's heart hung suspended . . . beating so violently she thought he must hear it. He tilted her chin back, looking deep into her eyes. "You would never marry Mr. Morgan were I free to ask for your hand," he said softly. His face came closer, moving slowly toward her until she had to close her eyes. His lips were soft on hers.

He pulled her close, his arms encircling her, his lips feathering kisses on her eyes, down her cheeks, on her neck. Her body came alive at the nearness of him, at the touch of his lips on a vein in her neck, at his breath in her ear.

"Oh, my love," he murmured. "There will never be anyone to compare with you. Hallie, beloved . . . I am yours, forever. Wherever I am, there you shall be also."

"Yes," she cried, her arms around his neck.

His hand touched her breast, cradling it as he leaned over to kiss the fabric that enclosed it. "Know that you have enslaved my heart, Hallie," he said. "I shall be a prisoner of love more than of politics. I shall dream of you every night, carry you with and within me forever. Oh, Hallie . . . my love, Hallie." His hungry lips met hers again. "Love me, too," he whispered.

"I do," she replied. "And I shall forever."

"I can't bear to let you go," he said, bringing her hand to his lips. "But I must."

The hunger he awakened in Hallie that night did not die. Later, when she lay trying to sleep, she heard herself say aloud, "I love Tristan." It was a wonderful feeling. At that moment it did not enter her mind that she was soon to be married to another man.

She heard Beth sobbing in her sleep, and reaching over the side of her bunk, Hallie took the young girl's hand. Holding tight to one another in the darkness, they slept.

The following day land was sighted—New South Wales, barely a line on the horizon.

"There"—the captain pointed—"that's where we'll enter the harbor. Between those two rocky crags. They call it the Heads. See, they protect—nearly hide, wouldn't you say?—the harbor entrance." It was their first sight of land in almost four months.

Captain Dunsmere announced, "We'll anchor here tonight and proceed into Sydney Cove in the morning."

The land lay darkly green in the evening sunlight. On either side of the jutting rocks strips of narrow sandy beaches dotted the shores as far as the eye could see. Scrub trees hugged the low-lying hillsides under blue skies that Hallie loved. Despite an awareness of the immense loss that landing would mean, she could not control the surge of adrenaline that coursed through her. After more than eight months at sea, she was about to embark upon life in a new world.

"Welcome sight, isn't it?" the captain said, smiling at her.

Not as she had imagined it would be. Hallie gazed out at the land.

The captain puffed on his pipe and muttered, "He's a fine one, he is. Not like the others." Hallie felt blood rush to her cheeks.

"If it were up to me . . ."

"I know, sir," she said, looking at him. "As it is, you've been very kind."

"It's easy to be kind to you, Miss Thomas. We don't get many women like you."

When the captain walked away, Hallie stared out at the harbor entrance. Tomorrow, she thought, I shall enter that passage into an unknown world and leave behind not only all I left England for, but love, too.

She stood watching the bloodred rays shadow into purple against the paling sky.

Four

Two days before the *Charleston* lay at anchor outside the Heads, Chad Morgan shook himself, drops of water spraying into the sunshine. Gooseflesh covered his body as he dried himself with a coarse towel. His early morning bath in the cold stream had invigorated him.

After he had dressed and pulled on his boots, he paused to stare at the nearly finished house. Finished for now, anyway. He saw it eventually two stories tall, with at least five or six more rooms joining the two already there. Even now, he thought, there was a graciousness to it that was lacking in the homes of the other farms. Built of native sandstone, in the Georgian style of architecture so prevalent in England, the structure was long—over sixty feet—with high ceilings. An entry hall divided the drawing room–dining hall from the bedroom. Admittedly the kitchen was tiny and relatively airless, but most of the cooking was done outdoors. As was the custom, the kitchen, hardly six by eight feet, was not attached to the house. If Hallie wrote that she would come, he would build a kitchen more compatible with the hours a woman would spend there.

If Hallie wrote . . . He should be hearing soon. It had been a bit over a year and a half since he had written to her, just time enough for her to have received his letter and responded, if she had answered immediately. If she wasn't already married. If she had the courage to come halfway around the world.

Walking through the meadow toward the house that gave him such pride, Chad remembered the Hallie of his youth, the young girl with fiery eyes. Yet her manner had always been feminine. The only sign of restlessness she had re-aled was a yearning for faraway places, to be out of Newcastle. She had been a rather pretty girl, if thin. He had thought of her often, though seen her little. She had made him long for a younger sister, someone to teach and mold, someone with whom to share his interests.

Her quick intelligence had been obvious, and he'd sensed in her a desire for adventure, though he had not put that name to it then. She was a child to his teenager, so he'd never thought of her as a woman, but as someone it would be fun to teach to ride, someone who would flower as he opened the window of the world to her.

At the time, friendship was out of the question. They came from different worlds. But here, in New South Wales, where he saw promise in his future, he had begun to think of her, to wonder what she had become as a woman, whether she was married and had children. He wanted a wife who was not afraid of work, so that ruled out all the women he might have married at home. He would like a wife who had enough intestinal fortitude to travel halfway around the world for a new start, a wife who would give him many children. He knew, too, that he wanted a wife who wanted what he wanted.

After he had decided to cast his lot in life here, he had spent two years searching out all the new arrivals as potential wives. Most of the women, of course, had been sent as convicts, and he would not think of that. The other young women were the daughters of officers, or relatives who had come searching for husbands, women generally given to airs and seeking a softer life than what they had known back home. After looking at most of them, Chad could not even imagine a quick roll in bed with them, much less sharing his life. And then, two years ago, he had begun to think of Hallie Thomas; remembering, at first, the blue eyes that matched the ribbon in her golden hair.

He had first seen her when she was eight and he sixteen. The little girl had been reaching up as his horse lowered its head, and had run her hand down the horse's face, murmuring softly to it, her eyes filled with wonder and tenderness. His heart had melted at the sight, thinking what a pretty picture it made. At the time, it had not dawned on him that this was a girl; he'd merely seen a child and a horse.

Over the years, the few times he'd seen her, he was aware of the disparity between the haves and have-nots. Hallie wore the same dress until she outgrew it. At first it would be far too large for her, giving her an ungainly, awkward air. She would wear it until she nearly burst its seams. It was always clean, and Hallie always looked neat and on Sundays had a ribbon in her hair, but the people he knew did not wear the same clothing day in and day out until they no longer fit. His older sisters had closets full of dresses and sometimes changed clothing two and three times a day.

When they had talked of faraway places, lands in perpetual sunshine where there were no coal mines and where life was an adventure, Hallie's eyes had sparkled with desire. He had been attracted to her, he thought, because he could voice his own dissatisfactions with his world and find a kindred spirit, albeit not of his class. When he'd finally thought of sending for her, he'd imagined how grateful she would be—not only to leave Newcastle, but to marry far beyond any hopes she might have had. That is, if she weren't already married. Chad realized he could not yet offer her much more than she would have as a married woman in Newcastle. She would have to work hard, but there was gold at the end of his rainbow. She might have to feed his ten convicts every day, but someday she would know more wealth and comfort than she could ever have dreamed of in England. And she would have the sunlight and clean air she had yearned for as a child, the beautiful countryside that lifted his spirits daily. He knew with certainty that if she were the woman the child had hinted at, she would find this land and this climate part of her dream's fulfillment.

He was not sorry he had left India for New South Wales, not sorry he had relinquished his commission in the army to become a landowner, hard though these last years had been. Building the house had been fun compared with clearing the land. Looking at it now, he was filled with pride.

The land he had chosen was farther from Sydney and Parramatta than most had chosen. He wanted not only fertile land, but the vastness into which he could expand. He envisioned far more than his present five hundred acres, which had grown even in the last four years from an initial 250. And now that William Bligh had been sent home in shame, the new governor, Lachlan Macquarie, appeared to be a man of vision and generosity of spirit. It was time for this country to be assigned a governor who could lead it to greatness. Chad intended to be part of that greatness.

Behind the house was the barn where he kept the horses that were his pride. His own, which he had trained himself, had been foaled during one of New South Wales's spectacular thunderstorms, so he had named it Thunder—a big bay stallion that could outrace any horse he had ever known. A horse with spirit and soul, a horse he loved.

He smiled to himself. Perhaps that's what he wanted in a woman, someone with spirit and soul. He did not expect love, or even deep companionship. The latter he could find with men far more easily than with any woman, but it would be pleasant to have a woman around who could understand what he wanted, what he liked, what his dreams were. He had men with whom he could gamble, but he found it pleasant to picture playing whist with a wife of an evening, watching her smile with pleasure when he brought her a present. He needed for her to understand that he intended to found a dynasty that would be part of this world a hundred, even two hundred years from now. He smiled to himself as he pictured her holding a child in each arm, in a rocking chair in front of the fireplace.

He would like to find her attractive enough that bedding her could be pleasurable. He had been initiated into the joys of sex by his mother's best friend, Lady Amelia Spencer, when he was just fifteen. That liaison had lasted for well over two years, the naive young boy turning into a knowledgeable lover. In no other woman since had Chad ever found the abandon and excitement of his first experience, and he did not anticipate such in a wife. Part of the thrill and the fire of first love was of mysteries unveiled. His two years in India had added to his expertise, and there he had had experiences that had amazed and delighted him, ones he knew would never have been possible back in England but they had not touched his heart as his initiation with Lady Amelia had done. At fifteen he had not been able to separate love and infatuation. At the time, his mind as well as his body had been consumed by the fires she lit. He could do without that now. He wanted nothing to divert his path, no woman to devour and drain him today. He felt that two bodies meeting had nothing to do with two souls coming together, but he also believed that it was not a part of anything he expected, or even yearned for, in life.

Yet that which he could not see ruled him far more than he imagined. After breakfast he found Archie, his convict foreman, who had been with him from the beginning. Like almost all other immigrants, Chad had known little of farming before his arrival in New South Wales. There *had* been sheep in the countryside around Newcastle, but he knew nothing of them. What he'd learned of them had been through word of mouth here and in the animal husbandry text he'd sent for. Already he was taking exception to several of its precepts.

Archie, on the other hand, had grown up on a farm just outside London, and he shared his knowledge of haying and growing crops. As to horses, Chad knew as much about raising and training them at fifteen as most men learned in a lifetime.

Together the two of them had done all the work until Chad had qualified for more convicts two years ago, and since then Archie had managed the prisoners. He and Chad had built a barracks for them, not the usual sod hut or tent that most farmers supplied. It had been ready and waiting for the prisoners when they arrived, as well as real beds and a fireplace for cold winter evenings. Some of them had never had such a comfortable place to lodge.

Chad remembered how he had gathered them together the first night they'd arrived, seating them around the long trestle table he and Archie had built. He'd waited for them to finish their first dinner on the ranch, and then, after he had personally served them coffee, he stood before them and said, "I know that none of you has ever farmed. I know that none of you wants to be here." There was a murmur of agreement, and he'd wondered what he had let himself in for. They looked like a sullen, randy group.

He'd continued, "You know that you are to labor from sunup for eight hours and do exactly as I order you. After that you need not work at all, or you may do extra work for which I shall pay you either in cash or rum. You may find someone else to work for in your free time, for extra money." He was reciting their rights, but he knew there was no one nearby for whom they could work. Sydney was a hard day's ride on a good horse, or a bit more than a day and a half with a wagon. Parramatta was half that distance. "But you will be back here, in your barracks, by sundown. You know, and I know, that you can receive floggings for failure to follow my orders." He'd stopped, looking at the men. One of them had sounded a bitter laugh. The lantern flickered, sending dancing silhouettes of the motley group against the wall. I'll make them shave every day, Chad had thought. Make them begin to care about how they look.

He'd sat down on the end of the table, swinging one leg back and forth. "I have never known a beating to be a deterrent. I shall not flog you." He'd seen the men grin at each other. "But I expect a good day's work. I will not ask you to work harder than I do. But if your work does not satisfy me, I shall return you to the superintendent of prisoners, and you will no doubt be assigned to some master who does flog." For a moment he'd wondered if he was making an idle threat.

"What I will give you is knowledge of how to farm, and how to work hard, and how to clear land and plant, how to build, and how to be proud of yourself, so that when the time comes that you are free men, you can accept your fifty acres and succeed, never to return to the life that led you here."

Chad had admitted to himself that he'd probably wasted his breath, but he so ardently believed in what he said that he could not resist saying it. If this colony was going to be founded by convicts and their labor, he felt one of his missions was to bring them up by their bootstraps. He had never known anything to be accomplished without self-pride, and he intended to instill this in anyone willing to work hard. He had no idea that he was a dreamer. In his mind, and to those who knew him, he was a sensible, hard-headed realist.

Not all the original prisoners had worked out, of course. One had escaped, to be caught ten days later by soldiers and flogged into unconsciousness, then assigned to Norfolk Island, from which escape was impossible. Another was averse to work of any kind, and had an ill temper to boot. But of the original ten, eight were still with him, as well as Archie, and a sort of camaraderie had evolved. Chad ate lunch and dinner with them, but he enjoyed his breakfast

41

in solitude. At mealtimes there was much laughter, and no one objected to the swearing that was an inherent part of their conversation. Since there were no women available to them, Chad suspected they had their own ways of relieving sexual desire. Archie had told him he preferred not to sleep in the barracks, but chose to spend his nights in the barn, where he made a bed of straw next to the cow's stall.

Now, as he saw Archie and the other convicts emerging from the barracks after breakfast, Chad hurried over. The men were splitting up into separate groups—one to build more fences, another to clear a field of its trees, one to plow a field and prepare it for planting, another to the brick kiln. Chad took Archie aside and said, "I'm going in to Sydney." He did not feel compelled to explain. He himself did not realize that there wasn't an explanation. He told himself he was going to see if there were a letter yet from Hallie, but he also thought he'd take the wagon and oxen rather than his horse so he could bring back supplies if any had arrived. He had ordered various necessities in the last two years, and so far none had appeared.

As he started out toward Sydney Cove, Chad was at a loss to explain his exhilaration. What if Reverend Macauley has written that she's already married? he wondered.

Gray-green, wide-spreading dwarf trees, like none Hallie had ever seen, forested the low-lying ridges, swooping down to the shores on either side of the harbor. Even this early in the morning, the sun danced silver on the choppy sea. Screeching gulls circled overhead, following in the wake of the *Charleston* and her sister ships. The blue sky was so clear that Hallie wondered if she were seeing through the universe. One small white cloud skittered southward.

It was all so beautiful, she reflected—and so empty without being able to share it with the one you loved. Never could she have imagined a feeling as powerful as what she felt for Tristan, not even for her family. She would have changed places with him were it possible. Last night she had wanted to cry out that she would wait for him. In five and a half years he would be free.

But how could she support herself for five years? Even in England she couldn't have done that. Besides, she knew he would not have listened to her pleas. It was a romantic impossibility.

Even as her thoughts centered on Tristan, ahead of her she glimpsed buildings nestled on a hillside and realized she was beginning a new life. Another life. Certainly she had begun and ended one in these many months on the ship. Though torn by the loss of Tristan, she could not control her excitement as she gazed upon this exciting new land. On either side of the harbor were rocky, wooded hills, thick with dark green scrub growth. To the left was a narrow sandy beach, and to the right, sandstone cliffs. Here and there were tiny islands, and inviting coves snugged close around every bend. The harbor widened and narrowed without regularity. Hallie guessed the rocky cliffs that hugged the shore were from ten to twenty feet in height; then there were grasses and stubby trees, with an occasional softly swaying palm. It was seven miles from the harbor entrance to the circular quay around which Sydney Cove had sprung up.

As the ship rounded a promontory, Hallie saw an imposing mansion nestled on a hillock to her left, surrounded on either side by woods and sloping green lawns. It was the largest and most majestic home she had ever seen. Though she did not know it, flora from England and South Africa had already impregnated itself with a marvelous adaptability into the soil of this new country, and native Moreton fig trees were so large that they resembled banyans, with long wide-spreading branches covered with thick green leaves. She had never seen trees like these. The vast majority, as was the case all over the immense continent, were varieties of eucalyptus, called gum trees here: tall, silver-green trees whose stringy bark peeled from their trunks and hung in raggedy ribbons. Hallie did not yet know they were evergreen trees, never leafless and always looking slightly unkempt. The air smelled of them, a clean, camphorated smell that defied description, not at all like England. In the distance long, rectangular red-roofed buildings hugged ridges above the town. A windmill towered above them to the right, its canvas spinning in the breeze. If anything could have looked the exact opposite of Newcastle, it was Sydney Cove, she thought. Nearly two hours after plowing between the Heads, from the open Pacific into the sheltered harbor, the *Charleston* veered to the left, past the point that jutted out into Bennelong harbor, named after the aborigine who had learned some English and had already visited London.

Hallie didn't know what she had expected, but it was not what she saw. Sydney, in its thirty-second year, already looked decrepit. Buildings not yet twenty years old were in various states of decay; streets ran haphazardly, in no organized pattern. Citizens of the new land had early learned that its sandstone soil was not fertile; any farms had moved a dozen miles upriver, at the western end of the harbor, to Parramatta. Original trees had been cleared, and sandstone—found on cliffs all along the harbor—and trim brick buildings and whitewashed wooden houses with red roofs had been built, generally in the Georgian style. However, the town looked shabby and dusty. Here and there a lone geranium straggled through weeds in yards of the houses that Hallie saw. On the far shore decaying, ramshackle warehouses gave the impression of slums. Most development hovered near the harbor or nestled within sight; Hallie could see trees and rolling hills beyond the town.

In the thirty-two years that New South Wales had been populated by white men, five settlements had sprung up. Sydney and nearby Parramatta were the centers for government, as well as having been founded as convict settlements. The new governor, Lachlan Macquarie, having arrived on the first of January, this year, 1810, spent time equally between his homes in these two towns. A farming settlement with a population of 937 was already established to the north on the Hawkesbury River, and a smaller, pastoral settlement at Camden lay half a day south of Parramatta. Far to the north was the penal colony at Coal River. In 1810 the population of New South Wales was 10,454, of which approximately fifty-three percent were adult males. Of these, 1,132 men, 151 women, and 154 children were convicts.

I must put Tristan aside, Hallie told herself, or I will ruin my new life. They both had known that it could not be. I must not give in to my heart, thought Hallie. I must tell myself that this is a new life from this day forward. This is what I have come for. What she had with Tristan had been brief

44

and temporary. She knew she could never feel as strongly for anyone again, but she also tried to be sensible. There was no sense in torturing herself over what could not be. She had come out here to be a wife and mother and she would be a good one. She would not let emotion interfere with her purpose in life.

Her heart was not cooperating as well as she wished it would. Yet the excitement of the approaching land, of a new continent of which she would be a part, could not fail to arouse her. A throng of people gathered on the shore. For the first time since she had agreed to come, Hallie felt a twinge of fear. There was no turning back, no security, no familiarity. This was it for the rest of her life.

The *Charleston* cast anchor, and behind her the three sister ships sailed slowly into sight. The prisoners would be kept in their holds until the paying passengers had disembarked and the store ship had been emptied of its cargo. Already small boats were being lowered to take the passengers ashore. Hallie wondered what she should do if Chad was not there to meet her. How would she get word to him, where did he live? Would he know that the ship was arriving and whether she would be on it?

"Want to be one of the first ashore?" Captain Dunsmere asked. "We'll send Mr. Edwards along to protect you."

Why should she need protection? Hallie wondered.

She and five of the other women passengers, along with two married couples, were in one of the first three boats to row ashore. People thronged the beach, waving and calling out indecipherable greetings. In front of bushes to the left, Hallie noticed three black men with spears. Was this what she needed protection from?

She scanned the crowd as the boat neared the wharf, looking for any sign of recognition. The cove was alive with small sailing ships, with rugged canoes being paddled out to the still oncoming *Tigard* and *Theseus*. A barge was headed toward the store ship.

Despite the worn appearance of the town, Hallie thought it an exciting sight. Cleared green strips of land, surrounded by clumps of trees, delighted her. Buildings and houses had space between them, and everything looked sparkling clean—there wasn't a sign of dust or soot. The

45

sky, unlike that in Newcastle, was visible and starkly blue; the sun shone with a brightness unlike that of England.

A gaudy red bird, its beak and crest a bright green, startled Hallie by careening too close to her, and she jumped, nearly landing in the water as the small boat pulled in toward shore.

I'm halfway around the world, she thought. I don't know a soul in all this land, and if I had sense, I'd be scared. Nervous, at least. Instead she tingled with excitement and a sense of adventure.

At the last minute men rushed out to haul the boat up the beach so that the women could disembark without getting wet. Two men ran from the throng toward their women. Hallie and the other young women stood in a semicircle, their eyes scanning the crowd.

Suddenly she saw him. Until that moment she hadn't even been able to remember what Chad looked like, but the minute she saw him, she knew this was the man with whom she had cast her lot, her life. He was taller than the others, his wide, powerful shoulders and tanned leathery face visible above the crowd. In fact, he was one of the biggest men Hallie had ever seen. She didn't remember that about him. But she recognized the face that had erased itself from her memory.

She saw his gray eyes move slowly from woman to woman, rest momentarily on her, then continue to the others. His glance tunneled out to the ship again and the other two boats that were bringing passengers ashore. Again he looked at her, and again turned back to the incoming boats. He didn't recognize her.

Perhaps it's not Chad, she thought, but every instinct told her it was. She didn't know how she recognized him. He didn't look like anyone she'd seen before. His tanned face, already creased from years spent in the sun, was craggy, as though his profile should have been carved in rock. He didn't look like the pale, proper English boy he must have been when she knew him. He donned a well-worn, wide-brimmed hat to shade his eyes from the sun, and Hallie saw him squint again at the boats that were now pulling ashore. Six more women climbed down onto the beach.

Hallie noticed his gaze dance briefly over that group and then return to her. This time he lingered as their eyes met. There was no sign of recognition, but he smiled and touched his hand to his hat. Hallie felt pleasure. He didn't recognize her, but she could sense his admiration. She would stand quietly and wait for him to realize who she was. She would stand and stare at him so that every time he looked her way he would have to acknowledge her.

Of course he didn't recognize her. He hadn't even received word that she was coming, that she had accepted his proposal. He had no way of knowing, with any certainty, that she would be on the *Charleston*. And certainly, at almost eighteen, she couldn't bear any similarity to the eleven-year-old girl he remembered.

Suddenly, in one large rush, the crowd pushed toward them, men reaching out their hands, making lewd suggestions, grabbing. Mr. Edwards tried to push them back. In the next group down the beach, one of the young women began to cry. Hallie shrank back, and a long arm reached in front of her, its elbow jabbing into the face of the man leering at her, forcing him back upon the others. She looked up. Chad smiled down at her, the grin lopsided but friendly. Still he gave no sign of recognition.

"Here . . ." He grabbed her hand and began to shove his way through the throng. Once past the mob, but still standing on the beach, he released her hand and doffed his hat. Bending over slightly, he said, "Chad Morgan, at your service, ma'am."

She smiled. "Chad, I'm Hallie."

He stared at her a minute and then broke into uproarious laughter. Raising his eyes heavenward, he saluted briefly. "I didn't expect you," he said. "I'd hoped for a letter telling me you'd be coming." Then a grin covered his face. He took her hands and stepped back to look at her. "I'd never have recognized you."

She could tell he was pleased. She was, too. Suddenly, shyness overcame her. Here was the man with whom she had chosen to share her life, and she didn't even know him. His chivalry charmed her, but his size intimidated her. He was well over six feet, two inches, and his shoulders were broad. He looked rugged, not like a British gentleman. Yet the sparkle of his eyes was reassuring, though they lacked the gentleness of Tristan's. . . . Hallie shook her head; she must not do this to herself.

Chad noticed. "Is anything wrong?" he asked.

47

"No," she said, though even she realized her voice sounded small. "I recognized you even as I was coming ashore. And I hadn't thought I remembered you."

"You didn't remember me?" he asked, chagrin obvious in his voice. "Yet you came?"

"Oh, I remember your horse and your taking me for a ride."

"My horse!" he said as though to himself. Then he laughed as at a private joke. "I thought you might already be married."

When she made no response, he said, "Let me take you to the hotel, then I'll come back to get your luggage."

"I only have one bag," said Hallie, walking along with him.

The street swirled dust around the hem of her skirt, but the dress had not been washed in so long that it didn't matter. Hallie felt herself swaying, and reached out to touch Chad's arm, steadying herself. Chad said, "You'll feel like you're still on the ship for a while."

The crowd on the beach was still raucous as rowboats continued to bring in passengers. "I should apologize for the hotel, but it's the only one in Sydney," Chad said as they walked along the nearly empty street to the west bank.

The hotel room was indeed dingy, but it was the first time in her life that Hallie had had a room to herself. The sheets were clean and very white. The small window looked out on the harbor.

Chad left her to return to the ship for her bag, and by the time he returned it was well after noon. "I came to town to do some shopping," he explained as they lunched in The Boar's Head. Hallie had never been in a pub before. "I had no idea a ship was due. So I have the wagon with me. We can't get home in a day." Averting his gaze, he looked down at his plate and said, "Would you like to wait awhile to get married, get to know me, make sure you want to do this?"

Oh, thought Hallie, had I never met Tristan, there's no one I would rather marry. She liked the way he took charge. She liked the looks of him. She liked his voice—it sounded like water running over stones in a creek. She knew she could never care for anyone as she did for Tristan, but that kind of love had nothing to do with marriage. She could

48

never have Tristan. She had come around the world to marry this man.

"I came to marry you," she said. He raised his eyes from his plate. "I see no reason to delay it. I'm ready."

Five

In the afternoon he took her shopping with him. They went to the coopersmith's, where Chad bought nails and some tools. He thought it would be best to wait until morning when fresh supplies had been unloaded from the ships before completing his purchases. With luck, the animals and the seeds he had ordered would be on board.

Chad explained that, by wagon, the farm was a day and a half away, among some of the "prettiest country in the world. The house isn't much yet, but it will be. It's just two rooms now, but"—his eyes gleamed—"someday it's going to have two stories and lots of rooms. Each of our children will have a room, and there will be a dining room, and a kitchen, and a library, and a room for dancing . . . But right now, it's not much. Though it's not a sod hut, as so many of the others are. For a year or more Archie and I did live in a sod hut, though."

"Who's Archie?" Hallie asked, devouring the last of her dinner. Chad might not think it very good, but after nearly a year of ship's stale victuals, she found it—if not delicious—at least satisfying.

"Archie's a convict," Chad told her. "I've had him for four years. He's my foreman." After a moment's hesitation he added, "And my friend."

"What do you mean, you've had him? Aren't convicts kept in jails?" *Oh, Tristan, where will you be?*

"Up in Coal River and over on Norfolk Island they are. But settlers need help. The most dangerous criminals are jailed, like those convicted of murder—"

"What about treason?" interrupted Hallie.

"Treason?" Chad's fork stopped in midair. "I don't imagine they'd be sent here. They'd be hanged in England. But certainly they'd go to prison. It'd be dangerous to have them around." He continued eating. "A settler can petition for convict help. Just as he can petition for land. The governor has the final say. I own five hundred acres now, so I'm permitted a number of convicts. I have nine, including Archie."

"What if they run away?" asked Hallie. She wondered why a convict would stay around voluntarily, with no bars to impede him.

"There's no place to run to. No place where there's food, no places for shelter. And besides, if he's caught, his term is extended, and he'd probably be sent to Coal River or Norfolk Island. Or Van Diemen's Land. No one wants to be sent there."

He cut his chop, and Hallie noticed he had elegant, expressive hands. Long, slender fingers that looked like they belonged in a drawing room, rather than doing hard manual labor. "Besides," he continued, "life isn't too bad here as a prisoner. Certainly better than in England. Rules are that a convict labors from sunup for eight hours. Then he can either work for wages or be lazy. I have to house and feed them, clothe—take care of them. When their time is up, they can either go back to England or—more to their advantage—petition for fifty acres and eighteen months' supply of food and seed and become emancipists—free men."

"Do many do that?"

Chad looked at her, studying her eyes, his gaze lingering on her lips. Hallie felt self-conscious and lowered her glance to the table.

"It's too soon to tell," Chad said quietly. "I certainly would."

She looked up again and met the level gaze of his clear gray eyes. She noticed a pulse beating in his neck.

"I wouldn't want to go back to England," he continued, "where there's not much of a way to earn a living for these unskilled men. And this country"—Chad's eyes glowed, and his voice took on the tone of a man speaking of a much loved woman, caressing her with words—"is just waiting to be developed. This is where the future is. A man can make a kingdom for himself out here. Start a dynasty." He looked at Hallie. *"Our* dynasty, Hallie. Something we shall create together."

Hallie felt the blood surge within her, carried along as part of his glorious dream.

51

"That's what we're going to do—start a dynasty. A hundred years from now the name of Morgan will still be a name to be reckoned with, just as it will be ten years from now." His eyes had the look of a visionary. "It'll be hard work. But neither of us is afraid of that."

How did he know what she was afraid of? A moment of irritation coursed through her, interrupting her pleasure in listening to his grand scheme of life. Then she relaxed. It was true: she'd never known anything but hard work. And she wouldn't mind it out here, either, where the sun shone and no smog drearied life.

She looked across the table at this big man with whom her life would be entwined, and thought, I made the right decision. None of the boys I knew at home had dreams like this. And she did not doubt that Chad's would become fact. Never for a moment did she question his success—*our* success, she thought as a deep feeling of satisfaction welled up within her.

Chad's room was across the hall from hers. After dinner he walked her upstairs, stood awkwardly by her open door and said, "I . . . I hope you won't be sorry you came, Hallie Thomas. Good night—and sleep well." Then he turned and entered his room, closing the door quickly.

In her room, Hallie leaned her back against the door, smiling. She danced a little two-step and then fell backward onto the bed, hugging herself. She pinched her arm and laughed aloud, crying, "Ouch! It must all be true."

And then her thoughts sobered. She became aware of the hardness of the bed, no harder really than the one she had slept on aboard ship, but it brought her thoughts back to Tristan. She felt ashamed of herself for having enjoyed the day, for being pleased with Chad, and guilty that her life was going forward and Tristan's was going to hell. She wondered if he were going to a jail or whether some settler would claim him as a servant. She couldn't imagine Tristan being a servant, but she could imagine him wasting away in jail, could imagine his being beaten by sadistic jailers, could imagine him eating food with flies in it, could see him pacing back and forth in a tiny cell, with no release from the boredom and frustration. She began to cry at the pictures she painted in the darkness. It was a long time before she fell into a troubled sleep.

* * *

Chad lit a cheroot, then walked over and stared out the tiny window into the darkness. He did not light a candle.

"By damn," he said aloud, grinning. He had used all his willpower not to take Hallie in his arms a minute ago. He wanted to feel her against him, touch the softness of her lips, run his hand through her hair.

He would never have recognized her. The thin little girl, almost pretty, had become a beautiful woman. When their eyes had met across the beach, he could see the sapphire blue shooting to him through the crowd. Her hair, unstylishly long and loose, was streaked by months under the sun; her skin was golden. It had not dawned on him that this could be Hallie. The most he'd hoped for was a letter saying she would come. Yet he'd searched the landing boats and understood he was wishing.

Again and again his glance had flashed back to her. It was not just her beauty that captured him. It was the way she stood, not quite with the others, with a mixture of self-assurance and innocence. What the hell, he had thought, she's probably . . .

Then the crowd of men had pushed forward, yelling out offers of employment, of sexual favors, bargaining lewdly and loudly. The newly arrived women had cowered back, frightened and bewildered. Without realizing he was going to do it, Chad had elbowed through the unruly mob and grabbed her hand, leading her away from the group.

"I'm Hallie," she had said.

His whole body was so alive now with the thought of her that he couldn't sleep. He knew what he wanted to do. He wanted to knock down her door and take her in his arms and make love to her. Instead he crushed out his cigar and went to find a card game. That always took his mind off other things.

When he returned, long after midnight, he smelled of rum and tobacco and was two hundred pounds wealthier. He was always richer after a game of cards.

Hallie thought she'd barely been asleep when she heard Chad's awakening knock. Hurriedly she dressed and ran a

53

comb through her hair. When she opened the door, he stood there in the same clothes as yesterday, but his boots shone and he was freshly shaved and barbered. His eyes skimmed over her.

"After breakfast," he said, "we'll buy you a dress to get married in."

Hallie had never owned a new dress. Chad apologized for the dearth of choices in the shop he took her to, but Hallie was surprised at the number of pretty dresses. There were at least a dozen to choose from, and she simply couldn't make up her mind. Finally Chad reached out and said, "This," of a pale blue one with ribbons at the neckline. She had never had a dress cut so low in the front.

"But that's too pretty," she protested. "I can't wear that to work in."

"We'll take this," Chad told the clerk, "and a dress to work in. How's that, Hallie? What other one do you like?" She was overcome—two new dresses in one day, more than she'd had in her whole life.

When they returned to the hotel, Chad said he had to leave her but would be back in an hour, after he rounded up his supplies from the store ship—a number of his ordered items had arrived, to his relief and pleasure. The minister would be ready to marry them at eleven.

When he did return, there were pigs in the back of the wagon, a cage of chickens, squawking like mad, and five sheep—"rams from South Africa that I'm using to cross-breed with mine; see if they're better in this climate"—as well as barrels and burlap bags bursting at the seams. Two enormous oxen pulled the wagon, which creaked under the weight of so much cargo.

Though he said nothing, Hallie could tell Chad approved of her looks. He helped her onto the wagon as though she were entering a liveried carriage.

The marriage ceremony was brief. Chad drove just a block, to a small, neat, white clapboard house. "The justice lives here," he explained, jumping down and reaching up to help her down. With his hands around her waist, he waited a moment, looking down at her, searching her eyes. "Are you sure?" he asked.

She liked the feel of his hands on her and wanted to touch them, to reach out for his strength. "I'm positive," she answered. Flashing him a smile, she asked, "And you? What about you?"

He grinned and let go of her. "I've a feeling this is the luckiest day of my life." He bowed, and she preceded him up the walk. No one had ever done that to her before. He makes me feel like a lady, she thought. I like it.

The door was opened by Mrs. Service, a short pudgy woman with graying corkscrew curls. She wore a white frilled cap upon her head and a matching apron over the skirt of her dress. "Oh, Mr. Morgan," she gurgled, "do come in." She ushered them into the main room, which had shining white wainscoting and cupboards.

"Ah, there you are, Chad." The justice peered over glasses that rested on the end of his nose. "And this is the future Mrs. Morgan?"

Mrs. Morgan. Hallie Morgan. She rolled it over on her tongue, tasting the sound of it. Will I lose Hallie Thomas? she wondered.

Chad introduced Hallie to the Services and said, "I'm afraid we're in a bit of a hurry."

Mrs. Service giggled and handed Hallie two flowers, yellow ones that Hallie had never seen before. Then she turned and walked over to a spinet in the corner. Sitting down, she coughed slightly, turned to them, and with a childish smile began the "Wedding March."

Hallie thought, I want Mum. Mum should be here to see me married. And Dada to give me away. Tears caught in her eyes, and she looked at Justice Service as through a veil of gauze. Then Chad reached for her hand and she felt his strength flow into her.

"Will you take this man . . . to love . . . to honor . . . to obey, so long as ye both shall live?"

She heard her own voice answer, "I will." *So long as ye both shall live. . . .* Such a long time, she thought. And I scarcely know him. What will our life be like?

As soon as it was over, Chad said, "Let's get going. We'll be lucky to get past Parramatta today."

So, in her pretty new blue dress, from which peeked her old black shoes, Hallie Morgan climbed on board, with the pigs and chickens, and sat next to her husband. He flipped a bark switch, called out to the oxen, and the wagon lurched forward.

It was early spring, late September. A warm breeze caressed her in the heat of noon. Chad told her they had to go by way of the Parramatta Road because they couldn't cut across fields with such a big load. But he did not want to stop in Parramatta; he wanted to reach home by the next afternoon. "On horseback," he told her, "it's a hard eight-hour ride. But that's bypassing Parramatta and coming right across the hills. This way, with this load, it'll take a day and a half."

The fields of high grass were golden after the dry winter, and as their wagon approached, birds flapped up from the grasses and flew away. Black and white magpies of incredible beauty proliferated. Hallie watched them as they sat in the crotches of gum trees, heard them singing their melodic tunes. "It seems like summer to me," she said.

"This *is* superb. And winter here is warmer than summer in England, most of the time. Spring and autumn are as perfect as you can get."

The air was soft against Hallie's face.

"Does it ever snow?" She couldn't believe it would never be dreary and cold.

"Never." Chad turned to look at her, and a grin spread over his face. "It's a life so different from England. You'll think you've died and gone to paradise."

"No," she said, as though to herself. "I've come to paradise and just begun to live."

Chad's hand left the reins and reached out, and for a moment she thought he would touch her but he stopped just short of that, pulling his hand back to the reins again. His smile touched her, however, and she felt warmed.

The road, skirting the river's inlets, ran like a ribbon through the tall grasses. Towering around them were smooth silver gum trees, their strips of bark waving gently in the breeze. Hallie loved their smell.

"They're never without leaves," Chad told her. "They lose their leaves all year long, but get new ones at the same time. There are never gray, leafless winters as there are in England."

Suddenly two large, brown, furry animals leapt in front of the wagon, jumping in tremendous arcs off their back feet. They showed no fear and bounced down the road ahead of the wagon. Hallie sat up, astonished.

"Kangaroos." Chad said to her. "Hallie, this is the damnedest, most wonderful country in the world. There are animals like no other place in the world, trees like nowhere else. It's like it has no connection with the rest of the world. Look!" He pointed to a tree that seemed to be feathered with white blossoms. "Watch."

Chad whistled, and a flock of cockatoos, their bright yellow crests like flecks of sunlight, wheeled into flight, circling together, then returning to roost in the tall gum trees.

"They're beautiful," she breathed.

They drove in silence for a while, Hallie absorbing the landscape: low, undulating hills forested everywhere by gum trees. It was not like the thick forests of England, which she had glimpsed on the carriage ride from Newcastle to London. There were no thick evergreens, no dense undergrowth.

"It looks lazier than England," Hallie commented.

"Lazier?" Chad laughed and turned to look at her.

In late afternoon he turned off the road, following ruts instead of the smooth dirt. "There." He pointed from a hillock to the prettiest village Hallie had ever seen. "We don't have time to stop, but that's Parramatta. It's an aboriginal word, meaning 'head of the river.' The governor's there now, and what a governor he is. Just what we need. After Bligh, we nearly gave up hope. Macquarie is going to be to us what Washington was to the United States.* Mark my words."

Hallie wasn't too sure what Washington had been to the United States.

It was well over an hour to sunset when Chad slowed down the oxen. Hallie gasped at the beauty of the spot where he stopped. Water lilies floated in one corner of a pond, whose water was so still that the reflection of the tall trees seemed but extensions of the reality.

"We'll camp here for the night," Chad said, jumping down. He came around to Hallie's side and stretched up to catch her. As he set her on the ground, he held onto her waist for a moment. "Mrs. Morgan," he said. "I didn't know if you'd come. It's not an easy life for a woman out here."

---

*See Historical Note, page 615.

"You didn't warn me of that," she said, but he could tell she was teasing. The loveliness surrounding her was worth the whole trip, she thought. Never again to inhale coal dust. Never to wipe soot from walls. Not to be hemmed in by narrow streets and dark houses, all alike—one after the other. The open space, the trees dripping their bark, the wildly colored birds flitting from tree to tree had already touched something deep within her. She hadn't been in this new land thirty-six hours, yet already she felt more at home than she ever had in England.

"Ever made a fire outside?" Chad asked as he reached into the wagon for his rifle.

"Of course not." He must know that.

"While I go find our dinner, you collect some small twigs. There should be plenty of thin dead branches for kindling. Pick only the ones at the bottoms of trees, or dead ones on the ground. See"—he stooped to pick one up—"most of them won't be thicker than your finger. Then"—he reached into the wagon again and brought out a pail—"fill this from the billabong."

"Billawho?"

Chad laughed. "They are no freshwater ponds out here. The land doesn't have any underground outlets. Billabongs are what remains after the floods, and they rise and fall with the rain. No tides, no nourishment of their own, although they sometimes serve as channels to rivers—and some of them do have fish."

Hallie nodded. "Are they safe to bathe in?"

Chad cocked an eyebrow.

"I haven't had a bath since I left England," she explained. "The water looks very inviting."

"Yes, it's safe," he murmured. "And you will be, too, while I hunt. There aren't any dangerous animals, except for occasional snakes, but they'll be more scared of you than you are of them."

"I doubt that." She shivered at the thought of snakes. But the idea of immersing herself completely after all the months with little water outweighed her fear.

"I've never found a dangerous animal," Chad reassured her. "May be the only land on earth where one can sleep out in the open and not be afraid of wildlife. It's the tamest land in existence." He shouldered his rifle. "You'll be safe in the billabong."

He marched off toward the far stand of trees, and Hallie watched him go. He was not really graceful, but he was light on his feet. His was an easygoing gait, as though he had no direction or purpose, yet Hallie already knew otherwise. He did not seem to be in a hurry, yet he covered the ground quickly.

For all their conversation, they had not said a personal word. He had not even asked her about the trip, or of what her life had been like since they had last seen each other, and he had volunteered little about himself. Yet he conversed easily and often amusingly. He seemed to have a good nature and to know what he wanted. Hallie hoped he wouldn't be disappointed. She could tell he liked her looks, but how would she stand up in this vast, lonely country? Would she be able to do the work he'd expect of her? Would he like her cooking? She felt she had so much to learn, but it did not dismay her, however. I can do it, she thought. I can do it all, given time.

After she had gathered what seemed like a mountain of twigs, she took the pail to the billabong. She said the word aloud, enjoying the feel of it on her tongue, liking the sound of it. The lilies were gathering themselves up for the night as she stripped off her clothes and slid into the cool water. She could feel the grime wash away, although a cake of soap would have helped immeasurably. Ducking her head under the water, she clawed her hands through her hair, trying to cleanse it. The water was so clear she could see her toes. Ducks sailed back and forth in the water lilies. She saw two beautiful graceful black birds and swore they looked like swans; their long necks arched in the fluid, elegant way endemic to the swans she had seen on the pond in Newcastle, but the beaks on these birds were an impossibly bright red.

A shot reverberated through the air and echoed. Just one: Chad had their dinner. Sometimes in the fall Mr. Tilson, their neighbor, had gone hunting, taking his gun to fields outside of town. Hallie recalled that he had usually come home with a deer. Since there was just Mr. Tilson and his wife, he always gave the Thomases a large portion, and they'd had venison until Christmas. But Hallie had never actually seen a gun or a freshly killed animal. Idly, she wondered what Chad had shot.

Paddling around, she luxuriated in the water, which no longer felt cool. So many months of dirt were washing away, she was surprised the water was still clear. She stayed on the opposite side from the waterfowl, hoping not to disturb them, glad that Chad hadn't aimed at them.

She hadn't realized how long she'd been immersed in the water until she noted the bright red, purple-rimmed clouds to the west. The sun was setting, more spectacularly than she could recall seeing in England. she rushed into her clothes, savoring the newness of her wedding dress, feeling the chill of the cool evening air.

Chad had built a spit and was roasting rabbit. A coffeepot gurgled over the coals. Hallie thought, I don't know this man, I've never seen trees like this, or swum in a billabong— she grinned inwardly every time her mind touched the new word—and everything I'm doing is new to me, yet I have never felt so at home anyplace. She wanted to tell Chad, but he interrupted her thoughts with, "Ever eaten rabbit before?"

No, she hadn't. And she'd never felt so clean or heard such birds or felt so alive. "Over on the billabong," she said, "there were beautiful birds. They looked like swans, but they're black."

"They are swans, black ones. No place else has them. Hallie, this country is another world. It's the most exciting place on earth."

After they'd devoured the rabbit, it was dark. And cold. As Chad pulled blankets from the wagon, throwing them on the ground, he tossed one to her. Draping it around her shoulders, Hallie wandered over to an enormous eucalyptus. The last red rays of the sun had faded, and thousands of stars were visible. Raising her arm, she said, "They look close enough to touch. Maybe there's never been a more beautiful night."

Chad followed her. "Do you know anything about stars?" he asked, standing beside her.

"One could hardly see them in Newcastle," she reminded him. "I know I like them. But I was hardly ever outdoors at night. And my bedroom had no window. When we were on the ship, I felt they were my friends . . . like they were a part of me, or I of them. I could never figure which."

He moved nearer to her, so close she could feel his breath. "I'll teach you about stars," he said, his voice low. "If you know the stars, you can never get lost."

Hallie felt flustered. She didn't know what Chad was going to do, but she was certain that he was going to do something.

His hand touched her shoulder. "Look straight up," he told her. "See those two bright stars next to each other?"

When she had located them, he continued. "Now, look over there to the right. It looks like a kite or an elongated diamond—four stars. The one at the far right, in the middle, it's so faint sometimes you can't even find it. But it's there now. Do you see it? Pretend to draw a line through the middle of that diamond *and* down through the center of those two bright stars to the left. Where it meets is due south. If you can locate that, you'll know what direction to go if you're lost. It's called the Southern Cross. For over a hundred years navigators have sailed their way around the southern hemisphere with only that as a guide. You can't see it north of the equator."

"Maybe we're upside down," ventured Hallie. "If everything's so different, maybe we're looking down. Maybe the moon's below."

She felt the length of his body move next to hers. "Maybe it is." His laugh was a whisper. Again she wondered what he was going to do. "Your hair smells good," he said, feathering his fingers through it.

When she didn't say anything, didn't even move, he asked, his voice hardly audible, "Do you know anything about being married, Hallie?"

Was this what her mother had meant? "I don't know," she answered, aware of the tremulous quality of her voice.

His hands on her shoulders, he turned her to face him and then leaned down to kiss her, his lips touching hers gently. "Have you ever been kissed, Hallie?" he asked.

The memory of Tristan's kiss was still within her. She nodded.

"I mean properly kissed?"

"What does 'properly kissed' mean?"

"Like this." The urgency of his lips on hers, the closeness

61

and warmth of his body against hers, awoke sensations in Hallie similar to those she'd felt when Tristan had kissed her. Chad's hand twisted through her hair, then his lips left hers and feathered kisses down her cheek, along her neck. She heard his choked voice whisper, "Oh, Hallie," before he picked her up and walked with long strides to the blankets by the wagon.

Six

The eastern sky showed only the faintest pearl-gray. What woke Hallie up were the birds—a melodic chorus, as though they were singing to her. Hallie's back ached from sleeping on the hard ground. She lay with her eyes closed, enjoying the serenade. When she did open her eyes, the stars were still bright. She wondered why she didn't feel stranger. She had slept on the ground of an unknown land, next to a man she had known not quite forty-eight hours, a man with whom she would spend the rest of her life. Her husband.

She did not roll over to look at him but lay perfectly still, listening to the evenness of his breathing, feeling the warmth of his leg next to hers. She wondered what it was that had happened last night. Was this the "it" her mother had warned her might be unpleasant? Was it what Beth had meant by "men have used me"? And why would Beth have had blood on her arm in connection with it? Why had no one ever told her about this?

Hallie located the Southern Cross and concentrated on it, proud to figure out that they were heading south by southwest. Then she closed her eyes and relived last night—. Chad's hands touching her, his lips brushing her neck, moving onto her breasts. Her mother had told her she could just lie there, that a woman didn't have to do anything. But Hallie had found that difficult. Her body had moved as though it had a life of its own. She'd felt warmth when Chad had run his hands down her body, when he'd removed her dress and moved his naked body over hers, when his lips had forced hers open and his tongue touched hers. As Chad had kissed her, as she'd moved in response to his urgency, her eyes found Tristan in the stars overhead, imagined the outline of his face in the twinkling lights. Closing her eyes, she'd felt Tristan's hands on her body, imagined Tristan kissing her breasts, Tristan pushing her legs apart, Tristan whispering into her neck and finally moaning softly, sighing, "Hallie, Hallie, Hallie . . ."

This morning she knew it had not been Tristan. It had been this man with whom her life was now irrevocably entwined. She suspected that what had happened last night was what it meant to be husband and wife, that this was a part of something shared with no one outside of marriage, with no one else ever. It certainly had not been unpleasant, as her mother had indicated. She had enjoyed the feelings that surfaced, the touching, even though she hardly knew this man to whom she was married. Though it was Tristan's hands and lips she had fantasized last night, what had happened made her feel closer to this man who was her husband.

She was Hallie Thomas Morgan. Hallie Morgan. Mrs. Chadwick Morgan. She who had been Walter Thomas's daughter was now Chad Morgan's wife. Pale pink began to streak the horizon as she wondered if the only way she had any meaning was to belong to some man, be his daughter or his wife. If so, she was glad she had chosen Chad Morgan. She would be more than if she'd been George Burnham's wife, that she knew. Though she couldn't verbalize it, she sensed she would have the opportunity to find more within herself as Chad's wife than if she had remained in England.

A flock of birds with bright pink breasts and silver-gray backs landed in the field beside them, chattering raucously. Hallie turned on her side to watch them, amazed at the bright colors.

"They're galahs," she heard Chad say in a sleepy voice. He gave himself no time to wake up gracefully but was pulling on his clothes by the time Hallie turned around. He did not look at her as he jumped up and stamped into his boots.

Breakfast consisted of cold hard bread and hot tea. "I hope you can cook," Chad said. "Archie and I need some good cooking."

Hallie considered herself an excellent cook, but she didn't know how to cook rabbit. Maybe she wouldn't know how to cook anything they'd be eating in this country, but she could bake better bread than that which they had for breakfast. Food was something that was never stinted on at home; clothes, yes, but food, never. Men needed their strength in the mines.

When she could see through the trees, Hallie thought it a gentle country. Low hills, alternating with fields of grass and stands of trees, undulated on either side of them, yet she glimpsed far horizons from the valleys. A narrow stream meandered beside them. Aside from eucalyptus, there were large cylindrical trees and some smaller light green ones, indicating new leaves of spring. Golden fields accentuated the dark green forested hills. The sun beat down so relentlessly that Hallie wished aloud for a large hat.

"I'll buy you one next time I'm in Parramatta," said Chad. "I should have thought of it in Sydney. You can't go around without a hat. You're going to get burned."

Hallie had tucked her wedding dress away and was wearing the other new dress Chad had bought her. It was prettier than any she'd had at home. Home . . . this is my home now, she told herself. A herd of kangaroos—perhaps two dozen of them—darted from a grove of trees, forcing Chad to bring the oxen to an abrupt halt.

"No other place in the world that I know about has animals like these," Chad commented while they sat watching them. "They're called marsupials. There are others, too, that do the same thing—give birth to babies that are scarcely ounces in weight. By some freak means, they crawl, frail and blind, to find their mother's pouch, which is like a suitcase attached to her belly, and they crawl in there and stay, nursing for months and months, until they're able to exist by themselves. She can't give birth while she has one nursing, though she can conceive. Once the nursing one leaves the pouch, the conceived egg begins to grow."

Hallie was fascinated but also embarrassed to hear a man talking of birth.

Late in the morning they came to the first dwelling since passing Parramatta. Hallie would never have known it was a home. It looked like a small hill, a mound of dirt with grass as a roof. But it had a door. "It's a sod hut," explained Chad. "They're thrown up until a farmer has time to build a house. Or, if there's no woman, sometimes the man'll just live in it until he gets one."

"One what? A wife?"

"A wife, or some woman."

"You mean a servant?" Someone who lived in one of those could afford a servant? Hallie thought only someone very poor would deign to live in a place that was covered with earth, that didn't look like a real home.

Chad looked at her out of the corner of his eyes. "Or a convict lass."

And then Hallie understood. Beth might be assigned something like this, and whether she liked the man or whether he was kind or whether she wanted to or not, she would be forced to do what she and Chad had done last night. Hallie tried to imagine doing it with someone other than Chad . . . or Tristan. Someone who might not take the time to be gentle, someone who might "use" her without kindness. True, it had hurt her for a moment last night, but that had passed. So, she thought, it was not something that happened only in marriage.

"Whoa," Chad called, reining in the oxen. "We'll stop and introduce you to a neighbor."

"Neighbor? Are we close to home?"

"Not for another few hours." Chad jumped down from the wagon and called loudly, "Hallooo," heading toward the hut.

From it emerged a filthy man, his scraggly beard reaching to his chest, scratching at his crotch. His clothes fit poorly, his hair was greasy and matted. He looked as though he'd just awakened.

"Gawd, Chad, give a man a little warning when you're bringing a woman, woncha?" He ran a hand through his hair, but it didn't help.

"This is my missus," Chad said. She thought she heard pride in his voice. "Hallie, this is Edgar Littleton."

Hallie nodded. She didn't see any cultivated fields, no animals, nothing to indicate this land was being farmed.

When they had pulled away and left Edgar staring after them, Chad said, "Edgar's emancipated."

"What does that mean?"

"I told you. He came over as a convict. When his term was up he chose fifty acres and enough victuals and seed to last eighteen months. He'd have been a fool to return to England. I think he was guilty of stealing food from a bakery. Most of the prisoners don't know a thing about

66

farming. They've never been away from the center of London, or Liverpool. Nearly all your convicts are from cities. Most of them have been sent here for minor crimes. Many have neither the energy nor the know-how. Some would accuse them of lacking intelligence, but I want to disprove that. I think it's lack of opportunity. I teach mine to work hard and to learn how to do it well and be successful. There are exceptions, of course. I suspect Edgar's not one of those destined for success.

"Yet you seemed friendly to him."

"Hallie, this is a big empty country. It pays to be nice to people. I don't hold it against someone because he's been in jail. Oh, I would have in England, I'm sure. But this is a new land. If a man pays for his mistake and wants to start over, I'm going to do what I can to give him encouragement. I intend to live here for a long time, and I see no reason to make enemies."

She looked at him, a smile forming on her lips. "What a nice man you are."

He smiled back at her. "Do you think so?" he said, and reached out to cover her hand with his.

Early in the afternoon they approached another dwelling, this time a small wooden house situated at the foot of a hill. A flourishing garden was fenced, and a single rosebush—not yet in bloom—stood sturdily by the front door, which was ajar. A dog's barking brought a woman in a sunbonnet from behind the house. Her hands were covered with dirt from digging in the soil, but she was neat, and her eyes filled with delight when she saw them.

"Mr. Morgan," she said, wiping her hands on her apron. Her eyes were question marks as she looked at Hallie, though her smile was welcoming. "Enoch's up plowing the field." She pointed behind the house, where Enoch, at work, was hidden.

"Mrs. Bond"—Chad jumped down, going around to Hallie's side and raising a hand to help her down—"this is my wife, Hallie." Again, Hallie could hear pride in his voice.

"Oh, my dear," said Mrs. Bond, reaching out both hands. "Ignore the dirt and let me hug you. It will be wonderful to have another woman around." She turned to Chad. "Why on earth didn't you tell us?"

"I wasn't sure myself," he answered. "I didn't know ships

were landing when I went in to Sydney. And I hadn't heard if she was even coming."

"When did you ever meet such a pretty woman when you've been out here all these years?"

Chad's eyes softened as he looked at Hallie. "I knew Hallie when she was a little girl."

"And you remembered her all these years? Isn't that sweet. Welcome, my dear. You're probably in a hurry to get home, Mr. Morgan, but you must stop for tea. Let me have the pleasure of another woman's company for just a bit."

She ushered Hallie into her small house while Chad went out to find Enoch. There were just two rooms, as Chad had warned her their home would have. One was the kitchen, where any living apparently went on. At the far wall was a large fireplace with a heavy iron pot hanging down the middle of it. There was no fire there at the moment, but Hallie thought it looked cozy. The walls were whitewashed, and the furniture was obviously handmade, crude yet attractive. Pots and pans hung from nails on one wall, as did a square spinning wheel. The floor was earthen but worn hard and swept clean. One small window let in what light there was. There were two chairs, a straight one and a rocker with a bright red cushion on it. Mrs. Bond's pride and joy was a cast-iron stove, which she lit under the teapot. "Won't take a minute," she said, bustling about with the tea things. "Oh, it's good to see you! I get starved for another woman."

So far, Hallie hadn't been able to say a word. Suddenly Mrs. Bond turned to her. "Do you like our country?"

"Oh, I do," Hallie replied eagerly. "I think it's quite the loveliest place I've ever seen. It's so clean and big, and there are so many trees and birds."

"Oh, it's big all right. Big and empty. And sometimes I love it; I love the sunshine and blue skies, I love having my own house, and even my own garden. But it can get awful lonely."

Hallie didn't know what to say.

Just then Chad and Enoch stomped in. Enoch looked to be about the same age as his wife—mid-thirties, Hallie guessed. She wondered why there were no children. He nodded his head at her and stood awkwardly. "It'll be nice for Margaret to have company." To both of them that seemed the main benefit.

They asked her about her trip, and Hallie, knowing all three had made the same journey, simply said that she had enjoyed it, that the eight months did not seem interminable. She did not say she wished it had lasted longer, that she had wanted to sail on forever with Tristan.

"Enjoyed the trip?" Margaret echoed. "Mr. Morgan, you've got yourself some woman, I think."

Chad looked at Hallie and grinned. "Looks that way," he said.

Later, when they were continuing on their journey, Hallie asked, "Why weren't there any children? I'd have thought there would be."

"Mrs. Bond has lost three," Chad told her. "Miscarriages all. No doctors out here." Hallie, who didn't know anyone who had doctors at birthings, wondered why that should make a difference.

Several hours into the afternoon, when the sun's rays began to slant on the golden valleys and the dark green hills, Chad said, "We're nearly there." He stopped the wagon and jumped out. "I want you to see it from the hilltop." He helped her down. Reaching out, he took her hand and began to lead her up the hill. It was not high and it rose gently. Nevertheless, by the time they neared the top of the incline, Hallie was breathless. To the west, far away, she saw ridges of purple mountains.

"No one's crossed them yet. We've no idea what's beyond," Chad told her. "Someday, maybe . . ."

Then he pulled her the last few steps, saying, "There."

"Oh . . ." Hallie let her breath out softly.

A silver stream meandered through the valley. Light green fields, on which a few dozen sheep, some cattle, and two horses grazed, were dotted with clumps of darker trees. A pool shone azure under the sun, mirroring a cloud that hung, all alone, over it. Beneath a towering gum tree, reflected in the stream, stood the house.

It was not a hut like the Bonds'. For one thing, it was painted a cream color and looked, from here, far larger than two rooms. Furthermore, there was a grace to it that Hallie was unaccustomed to seeing in homes. The scene was idyllic, and she started down the hill, mesmerized.

Chad stretched out to hold her back, but she was beyond his reach. "I just wanted you to see it from here." He had been studying her reaction.

"It's beautiful. You go drive the wagon. Let me walk down."

He smiled and turned to go. Then he stopped. "No, I'll walk down with you. I'll send Archie back to get the wagon."

But she had already started running, dancing down the hill, her arms raised up into the air as though welcoming all that she saw. He stood and watched her and then began to run after her, jamming his hat on his head as he raced.

Hallie sprinted through the fields, not stopping until she was in front of the house. Winded, she stood as still as a statue. The main building was at least sixty feet in length. She hadn't expected this. Four long windows, two on either side of the front door, stretched eight or ten feet in height. On closer inspection she saw they were French doors, though she didn't know the name for them then. It would be a marvelously light place in which to live.

From behind her Chad said, "I started working on this the day I wrote you the letter. I wanted to be ready in case you said yes. It's taken over a year and a half to do it. Someday, Hallie, it will be much bigger."

Her eyes shining, she turned to face him. "You built this yourself?"

"Well, I had some help." He was pleased with her response.

She started eagerly toward the two steps, but he put out a hand to restrain her. "Wait a minute, Mrs. Morgan," he said, and picked her up. "I have to carry the bride over the threshold." He kicked open the door and entered the house. Once inside, he held her for a moment, but she was too busy surveying the house to notice. When she was on her feet again, she realized they were in an entrance hall, with ceilings higher than any room she'd ever been in, except the church back in Newcastle. She guessed the house was twenty feet deep, and followed Chad into a large room.

"I'll order wallpaper someday," Chad said, watching her. At the far end of the room was a giant fireplace. There were no curtains or drapes at the windows, and there was so much light, they could have been outside. Chad walked along the outside wall, opening the French doors.

The walls, like those of the Bonds, were whitewashed, and Hallie was reminded of church. She walked on thick, wide, polished wooden planks, much more elegant than the earthen floor of the Bonds' home. Two large chairs, covered in a wine-red tapestry, were arranged on either side of the fireplace. Against the wall was a long table with three cane-bottomed chairs. "Archie built the dining room furniture," Chad told her. "He just finished the third chair last week, and none too soon." It was not a home she could ever have imagined.

Chad walked back to the entrance hall and said, "Come see the other room. I'm afraid it's lacking in comfort."

Though not as large as the first, the bedroom must have been twenty feet square. It was nearly the size of the entire Thomas home in Newcastle. The wooden floors were polished to a high luster in here as well. Against the far wall, next to another floor-to-ceiling French window, was a smaller fireplace. There was a writing desk adjacent to the hearth, complete with an upholstered straight-back chair. On the floor was a pallet, longer but almost as narrow as the bed on which Hallie had slept at home. When her eyes flicked over it, Chad said, "Perhaps we can find someone to make us a bed."

Hallie could scarcely believe it. She had come around the world to what she'd imagined would be a deprived life in an undeveloped land, and found more luxury than she would have dreamed of in her lifetime. Once again she thought she should pinch herself to make sure she wasn't dreaming.

As Chad started across the room toward her, a man appeared in the doorway. "Thought I heard voices, but I didn't hear no wagon."

Chad stopped. "She came," he said to the man in the hall. "This is my wife."

Archie, who must have been nearly the same age as Chad, doffed his hat, and his eyes, a faded blue, crinkled as he smiled at her. One tooth was missing. "Ma'am," he said. His reddish hair went every which way, and his body was as thin and lean as a post. Hallie liked and trusted him immediately, even though she knew he was branded a thief.

71

"I left the wagon beyond the hill," Chad said.

Archie must have wanted to ask why, but he didn't. "I'll go get it," he said though he stood looking from one to the other of them before he left.

Hallie walked over to the long front window and opened it. The coolness that indicated the setting of the sun stole into the room. "It's still chilly enough for a fire evenings," Chad told her. "But come, I'll show you the kitchen. It's out behind the drawing room. You can start dinner."

Thus Hallie was brought back to reality.

Seven

The phosphorescence of dawn awoke Hallie. Gradually, streaks of rose-hued salmon, like ragged shards of broken glass, split across the pale turquoise heavens. Stretching, she smiled and looked around her, aware that she was outrageously happy. She was already in love—with this beautiful country and its bright skies and green hills, with its towering gum trees and its flamboyant birds. In love with the wide-open skies and this wonderful house, more gracious than any she had ever been in.

Dinner last night, her first as a married woman of the house, had been enjoyable despite the fact that, after the long trip, cooking for so many had tired her. Two of the convicts had come to the kitchen to carry dinners for themselves and the others down to the barracks. But Archie had eaten with her and Chad. There had been no time for anything elaborate, no real chance to show off her culinary skill, but Archie told her he hadn't eaten such a meal since . . . "well, maybe never." She'd noticed that he did not act subservient toward Chad, but in fact called him by his first name. She'd seen, too, that Chad treated Archie more as a compatriot and confidant than a convict servant. Yet when Chad suggested something, Archie did it. Often he did not even have to ask Archie to do something; Archie thought of it before being told to do it—like offering to go for the wagon.

Chad acted as though he and Archie were working together, as though his plans were theirs. They talked of fencing in an area behind the barn for the pigs, of putting the Afrikaans sheep in the new paddock.

Chad had asked Hallie if she'd ever gardened. No, she replied, certainly not in Newcastle. He'd turned to Archie. "The seeds arrived."

Archie responded, "If we get the ground ready, Mrs.

Morgan can plant within the month. The timing couldn't be better."

"I'm determined we'll be as self-sufficient as possible this year," Chad vowed.

It all sounded exciting to Hallie. The idea of growing their own food was something she'd never thought about. One of the first things she wanted was a decent kitchen. The one at home was so large that it had become the room the family lived in. The one here was like a cell—dark, with one tiny window. She could tell that a kitchen was not something to which a man gave any consideration. If she were to spend a good part of her life there, she hoped she was not fated to spend it in a tiny dark hole.

She sat up, wide awake. So many things to do, so much to learn . . . Last night, after dinner, when it was time for bed, Chad had walked into the bedroom with her, then gestured at the pallet and said, "I hadn't realized. That really isn't large enough for two, is it? If I'd known you'd be here . . . I'll sleep outside. I did last night." And he'd left her alone. She wondered if this would be the routine. She knew from her parents' and her brothers' and sisters' marriages that they slept every night with their spouses. Wasn't that part of marriage? Yet she agreed the pallet was too narrow for two.

And how often did "it" happen? Just when you wanted children, or more often than that? Did children result every time? Did she automatically have a baby starting to grow within her? She shook her head, exasperated. There was so much she didn't know, so many important things that no one had told her. She wished she could ask Chad, but felt she didn't know him well enough. Tristan could tell her; he was a doctor. He probably wouldn't laugh at her questions.

When she went outside, no one was in sight. Archie, she knew, slept in the barn, which she had not seen last night. This morning, since it was chilly, she found a shawl in her bag and threw it around herself. Behind the house, at the edge of the meadow, she saw the barn. Hallie thought it nearly as pretty as the house. It was larger, and had a wide door through which she was sure a wagon could be driven. As she approached she heard a horse neighing. Pacing

74

around its stall, which was securely locked, was a bay stallion so massive that she shied away from it.

She liked the smell of the barn, the smell of hay, even of manure. It smelled like country should smell, she thought, so unlike coal dust. A door on the opposite side led to a fenced paddock, where two more horses roamed. Archie was already at work there, hammering a fence at the side of the barn. He muttered a greeting through the nails he held between his teeth.

"I'll call you when breakfast is ready," Hallie told him. She could not understand his reply.

Chad was not in sight, but a fire had been started over coals, and a pail of cold water had been left for her on the kitchen table. Hanging from the roof of the kitchen was a side of salt pork; Hallie decided to make bacon from that. Actually, it was a well-stocked kitchen, she thought; there were flour and several other basics. But she made mental notes, as she went along, of things she would ask Chad for if he wanted her to cook the kinds of meals she was used to.

When she was ready, she went to call Archie—and bumped into Chad. His hair was wet, and one lock hung in a curl over his forehead. His complexion was ruddy, and he was filled with vitality. "Just washed off in the creek," he explained. "When you need water, get it above the waterfall. I'll show you—it's right over there. When we bathe, we go downstream. Not far."

"Tell Archie breakfast is ready." He looked so nice that Hallie almost put out a hand to touch his arm, wanting to recapture the security she had felt with him that first day. He smelled like the trees.

When he and Archie came to breakfast, Chad laid a little yellow wildflower by her plate but said nothing. She touched it and was about to thank him, but he spoke first. "Do you know how to ride?"

"The only horse I've ever been on," she answered, smiling, "was yours, when I was little."

"Oh," he said, and grinned as though making fun of himself, "that's right. That's the horse you remember, isn't it? Well, we'll have to teach you to ride."

"Real good," said Archie, his mouth full of biscuit.

"Archie, have one of the men hook up an ox to the plow

and work on the field. I'll give Hallie a riding lesson. You can't live out here without knowing how to ride." He didn't make any comment about the breakfast.

A few minutes later, when Hallie headed out to the barn, Chad emerged leading a horse much smaller than his. "She's gentle," he said, stroking its forehead. Reverently, Hallie rubbed her hand along the satin flank.

"Don't stand in back of her. Ever." Chad was pleased with Hallie's lack of fear. "First, let me show you how to put on a saddle." He threw a blanket over the horse first, then tossed a saddle on top of that. As he started to tighten the cinch, he stopped. "Damn . . ." There was a sheepish expression on his face as he said, "I forgot. This isn't a sidesaddle. We'll have to wait and get you one."

"I don't want to wait," she said. "Can't I learn to ride like you do?"

"Your skirt would split."

"I'll hold it," she said, already hiking it up. "Please, Chad, don't let's wait. Let's start right now."

He looked at her, standing with her skirts pulled up to her knees, and all he said was, "We'll have to get you some boots." But he was grinning so much that it looked like it might split his face. He held out his hands and indicated she should step on them so he could hoist her up.

Chad was pleased at how easily Hallie took to riding. Aside from her riding lesson, the chores of the day were like the chores of Newcastle. She cooked meals and washed clothes, but she did the clothes in the creek below the waterfall—in the midst of trees and water tumbling over smooth stones—instead of in a wooden bucket out back. She walked along the creek and picked more little yellow flowers like those Chad had brought her, and some purple ones that looked enameled, they were so perfect. In all her life she had never picked flowers. She thought it one of the nicest things to do in the whole world. She stuck one behind her ear and gazed at her reflection in the creek. "I feel like a fairy princess," she said, and smiled to herself. "I fell off the real world and dropped down here to a place not quite believable."

A kookaburra swooped down from a tree branch to study her. Its orange and gray striped tail contrasted with the tips of its wings, which were shades of turquoise. When she reached out, it flew back to the tree limb.

Returning to the house, she laid the wet clothing out on the grass to dry and went to prepare dinner. She'd need a dinner bell, she thought, something that could be used to summon the men to meals. One of the convicts was still plowing a large rectangle, leaving big broken clods of earth indicating where he and the ox had been. She didn't know where Chad was.

In the kitchen lay five chickens, warm blood still oozing from where their necks and feet had been. Hallie had plucked the feathers of many chickens; the sight did not bother her. She took them to the creek, stripping their feathers as she walked through the tall grass, gutting them and washing them in the cold rushing water. What luxury to have an endless supply of water, she mused.

She would make dumplings, too, in the stew pot. Dumplings for twelve, she thought, wondering only momentarily if she were up to the task. After all, she told herself, when all the children had been at home, Mum cooked for ten every night. I'll get used to it, too.

There were carrots in a burlap bag outside the kitchen door, and onions, too. She'd baked two pies in the morning, from still-crisp apples she'd discovered. If Archie thought he'd eaten a good meal last night, she thought, grinning, just wait until tonight. Maybe even Chad would praise her tonight.

But, again, he said nothing about her dinner. He let Archie belch and say, as he wiped a hand across his mouth, "I may get spoiled. Yesterday I thought he married you for your looks. Tonight I think it's your cooking."

Chad laughed. "That may be the longest speech Archie's ever made to a woman." Then he stood, pushing back his chair, and said, "Come, let's introduce you to the men. They're curious."

She followed Chad down to the barracks, where he called out to the men. As they emerged, Hallie noted that they all stood erect. Aside from that, she thought them the most motley-looking group of men she could remember. So far she'd only met the two who'd come up to collect the dinners. This time Chad went down the line, introducing them by name—Sam, George, Brian, William, and then she lost track. She couldn't remember eight new names at once. Except for the tall dark one, Brian, she thought they looked interchangeable. Their faces were all lean, and most of them had thin, tucked-in lips. Their eyes all seemed to be pale blue—a washed-out blue, except for the big dark man, whose eyes were black. She wondered how she would ever tell one from the other. These were men whose names she must learn, men whom she would be living in proximity with for years. A couple of them stared at her, but the others shuffled their feet and looked at the ground or at some invisible spot directly behind her.

It wasn't that she didn't like them. She simply felt uncomfortable. She thought she would never find anything to talk with them about. If Chad had a voice in what prisoners he chose, she wondered what had made him choose this group. Still, she forced herself to smile, grateful that she had no direct contact with them, that Chad and Archie would serve as her buffers.

His hand on her elbow as they started back toward the house, Chad said, "Before it gets dark, Hallie, I'd like to take you for a ride, to see my property." She smiled and nodded. She already knew she felt passionately about his land, and now he wanted to show it off.

He helped her up on Thunder, jumping after her, throwing his leg across the saddle where she sat sideways. Putting his arms around her, he grabbed the reins. Immediately the horse started trotting, easing gracefully into a canter. Hallie loved the feel of the air on her face, the feeling of speed that gradually increased, the warmth of Chad next to her back. As he urged the horse into a gallop, she remembered when they had sat exactly like this so many years before, remembered how it had felt to go so fast that the scenery was a blur, remembered how safe she had felt next to Chad.

When they reached the top of a hill, he slowed the horse down, walking it along the ridge. "Down there—see those trees?" he said, pointing. "My land goes out to there. But someday I'm going to own all of this, all we can see, and all that can be seen from the next hill. I'm going to own as far as the river."

"Is that far?" She liked sitting there with his arms around her.

"A couple of miles. I'm going to own thousands of acres and thousands of sheep, and I'll be more important to New South Wales than any Morgan mines have ever been to England."

So, he needed to prove something to himself, she thought. His brother would inherit the mines, but he would create an empire of his own, on his own.

"Sheep?" she asked, filled with the wonder of the land she saw rolling before them. "Why sheep?"

"Because England's woolen mills need them. Napoleon's deprived her of Brittany sheep, and she's going to have to find another source."

"Won't that be expensive, to ship them around the world?" She had to force herself to concentrate on what he was telling her, so overpowered was she by the closeness of his body.

"It'll be worth it. That's going to be our destiny. We're going to make a fortune in the most fortunate land in the world." His lips brushed against her hair. "Have you ever seen anything prettier, Hallie?"

"No," she said. "Never."

His arms tightened around her, though he held the reins lightly. "We're a part of history, Hallie. If you'd stayed in England, you could never have been a part of history."

"I'm glad I came," she said, leaning against him.

There was a moment of silence. "So am I. . . ." She felt his breath in her ear, felt his body next to hers.

Turning the horse around, Chad let it walk slowly down the hill. The sun was beginning to set, sending up jagged lavender and gold splinters from the horizon. They did not talk on the way back.

Later, after the kitchen was cleaned up and Archie had gone to the barn, while the fire in the hearth was dying down, Chad said, "I don't think I'll sleep outside tonight." He did not look at her, merely banked the glowing embers.

Hallie gazed out the window, where she saw a pale sliver of moon. The sky was alive with stars. "It would be nice to live outside, wouldn't it?" she said softly. "Go to bed under stars every night."

Chad did not respond, just stared at her from across the room. He put the poker down.

She took a candle and went to the bedroom. He did not

follow. She blew out the light and began to undress. It was never dark in these rooms with their long windows. Lacy shadows from the gum leaves danced between her and the moon. Even though it was chilly outdoors, she opened the window and stood there in her nightgown, listening to the faint rustling night sounds.

"You'll catch cold," he said in a low voice behind her. She had not heard him come into the room. The length of his body moved against her back, his hands on her shoulders. Gooseflesh coursed down her arms as his lips brushed her neck, as his breath tickled her ear. With sudden insight, she knew "it" wasn't done just to have children. She could feel the heat of her blood as his hands cupped her breasts. Her heart quickened as he turned her to face him, tilting her head back and bringing his mouth to hers.

His lips still on hers, he began to unfasten his shirt. This, she thought, is what makes one married. This is what makes people close. This is what married people share that is denied to the rest of the world. Without even thinking, she reached down and lifted off her nightgown so that she could be close to him, could feel their flesh together. She heard him laugh softly and say, "Oh, Hallie," before they lay down on the narrow pallet.

He touched her in places she hadn't known existed. He took her with an urgency that propelled them onto the wood floor with a thump. Again he laughed, loud this time. They rolled over on the floor, never breaking their rhythm. She arched her back, and it was as though the stars exploded into a thousand fragments.

When he stopped, when it was over for both of them, she clung to him, not wanting him to leave, wanting to lie like this, enfolding him, forever. But he did leave.

And he was gone when she awoke, curled in the fetal position, before sunrise. He was gone all day, gone with the oxen and the wagon.

By noon she worried. Had he left her? Was the magic of last night not felt by him, too? The washing done, she didn't know what other chores to do. Finally, in the afternoon, she went out to the barn and asked Archie if she could help him finish the chicken coop.

"Nope," he said. But when she just stood there, he told her she could hand him some nails.

"Maybe I could hammer something," she offered, feeling useless and worried.

"Nah," he said. "This isn't woman's work."

What is? she wondered.

Chad still wasn't home by nightfall. Hallie went through the ritual of dinner, but she ate little. At least Archie cleaned his platter three times. He wasn't worried.

What if something had happened to Chad? What would she do out here alone? Why had he left without a word?

It was after dark, long after dinner, when she heard the wagon approaching, her ears alert to the slightest sound. The tension in her body dissolved. At least he was safe, even if the cause of his disappearance might be a bone of contention between them.

His voice called out, "I hope something's left over from supper." He was bent over, unable to stand erect. "I've been to Parramatta and back." On his back was a double bed. He dragged it into the bedroom, tossed his hat on a chair, and said, "Now, woman, something to eat."

He was grinning.

Eight

The sun blinded her. She tried to listen very carefully to Chad. He held a small seed, then dug a thumb into the earth, now broken up in fine pieces and raked smooth. "Space these about six inches apart, and make the rows eighteen inches apart. Barely cover these with earth, but those, over there, the corn, bury a thumb's depth, and plant them eighteen to twenty-four inches apart in little mounds. The smaller the seed, the closer to the surface."

In the six weeks since Hallie's arrival, the ground for a plot of vegetables had been hoed, its thick clods at first broken into large lumps and then crumbled into such fine particles that they resembled sand. Chad told her the looser and finer the soil, the more the vegetables would be able to breathe and absorb water.

She had laughed. Vegetables breathing?

They had waited to plant seeds until a new moon inched its way toward fullness. Archie believed in the pull of the moon on the earth. "As the moon gets bigger, it pulls seeds above the ground," he'd said.

Now she kneeled with Chad as he attempted, with infinite patience and as though she were a child straining at her lessons, to explain the procedures involved in tending a garden. The sun glinted off the tool he held in his hand and knifed behind Hallie's eyes. She nodded as he spoke, but even though he had gone over it all three times, she still wasn't sure she understood. It sounded so simple, yet the sun made her light-headed. She fought to keep the world from whirring around.

Watching her, Chad reached out and put his hand on her arm. "Are you all right?"

"Of course," she answered, squinting at him. Obviously the large sun hat he had bought her in Parramatta was not doing its job. "It's just the glare of the sun. I'm not used to working outside in it. I'll be all right."

82

He looked at her skeptically, then stood up. "Archie and I are going to the upper pasture. We think the cow is calving up there, so we'll have milk at last, if we can find her and bring them back. Will you be all right?"

Hallie nodded. "The smaller the seed, the nearer to the surface."

"That's right. This row is carrots. When you get to the end of the seed, tie this colored thread on a stake and plant it at the end of the row." He stood up, wiping the dirt from his fingers against his pants leg. Striding across the field toward the barn, where Archie awaited him, he turned, once, to look back at her.

Hallie poked her finger into the warm, sweet-smelling earth, then gazed at the vast expanse of plowed field. Squinting, she tried to visualize the results of her labor, to imagine corn, potatoes, peas, green beans, yams, cabbage. But she couldn't. She concentrated, trying to picture a large golden sweet potato, and as she did so, she fell flat against the earth, vomiting into the seeds she had just planted.

She lay there, waiting for the dizziness to pass. With certainty, she realized she must be pregnant. She heard the clip-clop of horses walking, heard the urgency with which Chad called her name, felt arms picking her up, heard him saying, "Hallie . . . Hallie. . ."

When he laid her on the bed, she found herself wishing there were drapes at the window, to keep out the sun, to keep it away from behind her eyes.

"You're sick. . . ." Chad sounded concerned.

Hallie opened her eyes, the vertigo having passed. "I don't think so." She smiled weakly. "I think I'm going to have a baby."

Chad knelt down beside her, excitement leaping from his eyes. "Do you think so?"

She nodded. Chad gathered her in his arms and pulled her against his chest. "This is what I've wanted," he cried, exultant. "It's the beginning of my dynasty."

Not just yours, she thought. Mine, too.

The sickness came in waves and at different times of the day. She always felt better in the evening. But sometimes it would hit the moment she rose in the morning, and she could not prepare breakfast. She was disappointed not to be able to continue her morning riding lessons with Chad.

While she lay languidly in bed, Chad and Archie disappeared for the day, fencing not only their land, but the land beyond it, still unowned, so that the sheep would not wander too far.

The sickness lasted only six weeks. Along with Hallie's realization of her pregnancy, it seemed the whole world gave birth. Spring lambs began to arrive. Hallie had never seen a newborn animal. When a lamb could not take colostrum from its mother, Chad told her to feed it cow's milk in a bottle. One sheep died in the throes of giving birth to twin lambs, and Hallie's job was to nurse them with the cow's milk. She enjoyed this part of her day enormously. The lambs cavorted, racing across the fields on wobbly legs, looking surprised but not dismayed when their frail legs collapsed beneath them. She could have spent hours at each feeding time just watching the lambs and laughing at them, but there were other chores that needed her attention.

When she stopped feeling sick, Chad taught her how to milk the cow, which she had named Amanda. Milking required using muscles she hadn't developed, and the first week she thought her hands and arms would break right off. But gradually she caught on, and aside from having to get up so early—before dawn—she came to enjoy this chore. She liked the early morning best; there was no rush. Birds began to call out then, as the sky streaked itself awake. She liked the smell of the barn, and she and Amanda grew accustomed to each other. Amanda would turn around and moo, rubbing up against her when it was all over. Hallie didn't even have to call Amanda in the early evenings: the cow came home voluntarily to be milked. After Hallie had taken all the milk that she could use, she let the calf, which Chad had whimsically named Titus, have the rest. Then she would sit and watch as he nuzzled his mother. It was a time that filled her with contentment.

She was surprised to see sprouts peeking out of the earth in her garden. Somehow she had not really expected these green shoots that fought their way sunward as the warm days gave way to heat.

"They'll be crowded out if you don't weed them," Chad warned her. She didn't enjoy that part so much. She wondered why he didn't volunteer one of the men for that.

Chad whistled as he worked, and he worked all day long.

The fencing never seemed to be done. Once Hallie's queasiness disappeared she began taking lunch to him and Archie, and sometimes stayed to picnic with them. She loved riding through the meadows, under the giant trees where she heard the twittering of finches and the raucous chorus of kookaburras. She began to study the land, to know its hills and valleys, know where a spring unexpectedly created a pool. Taking lunch pails to Chad and Archie, she thought, was vastly different from taking lunch pails to Dada and her brothers in the mines, through the gray, grimy streets of Newcastle.

Because she tired more easily with her pregnancy, she would nap when she returned after lunch and then—in the late afternoon—do her weekly chores. On Mondays she washed the clothes downstream. Other afternoons she weeded and found great fun in hunting for eggs that the chickens delighted in hiding. She asked Chad to teach her to fish, and at least once a week caught their dinner in the creek.

Chad was always patient, whether teaching her to ride or to fish or in answering her questions about gardening or the land. Yet he was different. He had stopped touching her. He no longer turned to her in the night, though often she caught him staring at her across the candlelit room. He did not take her for rides at night or put his arms around her. He kept his distance.

So, thought Hallie, that was "it" after all. He only did it to conceive a child. Not for desiring her, but for a dynasty. She missed his touches, his kisses, his desire—missed also the passion she had discovered in herself.

One night, as Hallie sat darning—it was too warm for fires in the evening now—Chad said, "Can you think of some things you need for the kitchen, or anything else? I'm going to Parramatta tomorrow. Maybe on to Sydney. Ships may have come in with things I ordered."

"May I come?" she asked.

Chad looked up from the notes he was making. "Whatever for? I'll buy anything we need. I'll be gone two, maybe three nights."

Hallie went over and sat on the floor beside him. "I haven't seen anyone else or talked with anyone the five months I've been here. I'd really like to go." She had never asked him for anything.

He reached out and touched a tendril of hair that curled by her ear. "Your hair is like spun gold," he said, as though not even talking to her.

She gazed up at him. Take me, she said silently. Take me.

"Poor Hallie . . . Are you so lonely?"

"Not really," she answered, her eyes not leaving his. "But once in a while I think it would be nice to see other people, talk with another woman . . ."

"Ah, that's it," he said. "You need some gossip."

No, she thought. Gossip isn't what I'm after. "I'd like to talk with some woman about birthing," she said, though she had another six months to go. "I'd like to know what to expect. I'd like to see Parramatta. I haven't seen a town in months."

"My city girl. . . ." He put a finger under her chin. "I hadn't realized I'd been depriving you."

"I don't feel that way," she protested. Why had he taken his hand away? "It's just once in a while . . ."

"Never mind," Chad said. "I understand. What's enough for me isn't enough for you."

"That's not it at all!" Hallie replied, and realized it was the first time she'd raised her voice to him. "I'm happier than I ever knew I could be. But now and then I'd like to talk—woman talk. I don't know a thing about having babies, do you?"

Chad's eyebrows raised at the vehemence in her voice. "Not much."

Hallie continued, "You've given me more than I ever dreamed of having. And I do appreciate it, I really do. But that doesn't mean I can't yearn, does it? I don't ask for things that cost money. You've given me two dresses," she acknowledged. "That's two more new ones than I ever owned in the rest of my life. I don't complain about that terrible hole of a kitchen, do I? Even in this hot weather, when it's a furnace in there? I try to show you I'm grateful. I do everything you tell me to do, and I enjoy doing it. I never knew that keeping house could be enjoyable, but I even love doing the wash in the creek. I hated doing it in Newcastle. I get a thrill out of seeing food forming into actual shapes, and digging radishes right out of the ground. I love the lambs—I'm so happy it scares me. But it doesn't stop me from wanting to see someone, anyone. Talk with a woman and hear about . . . oh, you know."

Chad didn't say anything. Then he took both her hands in his. "Of course you shall come with me, Hallie," he said, his voice soft. "You're right. You never ask for anything." He leaned over and kissed her forehead. "Not even a new kitchen." His voice teased her.

Chad had not been to Sydney since he'd first met Hallie. One never knew when provisions that had been ordered over two years ago would arrive. Or if they would come at all. So, hoping to find the remainder of the supplies he had sent away for long before Hallie had arrived, he took the oxen and wagon. It would make for a longer trip by several days, but with Archie taking care of the farm, they were in no great hurry.

It would be nice to ride next to Chad all day, Hallie thought. Usually she hardly saw him, except for evenings, after the sun went down. She told herself she didn't mind, that life was much fuller than if she'd stayed in an English city. Yet sometimes the urge for woman talk overpowered her. She wanted to ask what it was like to have a baby; she wanted to know what she should have in readiness for it. But it was more than that. She wanted to laugh about nothing in particular, to be able to smile with understanding with another woman, hear a voice that wasn't always imperative.

Not that Chad ordered her around. But it was obvious that he expected his wishes followed. He expected and received it so consistently that he never had to give orders, even to Archie. She didn't feel she shared with Chad. He talked of "my dynasty," "my farm," "my dream." But then Dada had been like that, too, she reflected, except he never seemed to have had dreams: "my family," "my wife," "my house," even though it was the company's. She wondered if Chad would think of the baby as "my child." As she pondered this, she felt the first kick, the faint stirring of life within her, and was startled. It's my child, she thought. It's not his yet, not even ours.

* * *

Chad didn't talk much as they traveled. They started out as soon as Hallie had finished milking Amanda, when it was barely light. The pale sky gradually darkened to a bright blue, cloudless and endless. The valleys were greener than when she'd come, for it often rained at night, so the ground would be drenched mornings, but the sun soon burned it dry. The blue-gray of the gum-tree leaves contrasted with the bright summer green of the oaks. "Their wood is soft," explained Chad when Hallie asked why such a strange name.

Quails, with their broods marching behind them like little soldiers, darted through the grasses. Sparrows twittered from acacia trees. Parakeets dazzled Hallie as they flew from tree to tree. She called attention to a soft, gray fuzzy animal, sleeping, high up in the branches of a eucalyptus.

"It's a koala. They're nocturnal. Sleep all day," said Chad. Hallie had been so enchanted with her surroundings she had not realized that it had been hours since they'd talked. She tilted her hat and leaned back, looking at her husband.

Dada and Mum had sat most evenings without talking, Dada chomping on his pipe and Mum knitting. Now and then one would say, "My bunions hurt. Guess it's going to rain." Or, "Mrs. Eddington is expecting again." So Hallie didn't expect much conversation in marriage. And, indeed, once Archie left for his bed in the barn, she and Chad seldom had much to say. But Mum had had other women, and Dada had probably talked and listened all day to the men below. She had no one.

The nights were the worst for her. Once in bed, Chad went right to sleep; he never held her, never touched or caressed her. Whenever they shifted against each other in bed, he rolled away. It was only later, after he was asleep, that she would feel his body touch hers when he turned.

Her belly had begun to swell, and she thought he had not noticed. She did tell him, however, that she had felt the first movement, the first faint kicking. And once, in the middle of the night when he thought her asleep, she'd felt Chad's hand on her stomach, not moving, just resting against the flesh. She had smiled to herself, knowing he, too, wanted to feel the first stirrings.

But aside from that, he had not put a hand on her since

she had told him of her pregnancy. It seemed that he had stopped desiring her. And that was what she missed, just as much as the companionship and conversation of other women. She missed the touching that Chad had supplied so liberally the first few months of their marriage, the kisses with which he had devoured her, the excitement of their two bodies together. . . .

Now, without realizing she was doing it, she reached across the wagon seat and placed her hand on his arm.

He turned to look at her. "Yes?"

"Nothing," she said, but did not remove her hand.

They arrived at the Bonds' homestead, where Hallie appreciated the welcoming hug. Mrs. Bond insisted they have lunch, even though the sun was not nearly overhead. It couldn't have been more than mid-morning. While Chad and Enoch talked out back, Mrs. Bond took one glance at Hallie and said, "Oh, you are, too."

Mrs. Bond and Hallie were expecting at about the same time. Mrs. Bond said that she felt better this time than she had with the others, was experiencing no bleeding, and was most optimistic.

"Does it always hurt when it comes out?" Hallie asked.

Mrs. Bond answered, "Always."

"Does it leave a scar?"

"A scar?" Mrs. Bond echoed, frowning.

"You know, across the belly button."

Mrs. Bond looked at Hallie with incredulity and then laughed, although there was kindness in it. "Oh, my dear, it comes out in the same place it went in."

Oh, thank goodness, Hallie thought. Thank goodness I learned this. "What does one do then?"

"You cut the cord with scissors or a knife that has been boiled in water."

"Cord? What cord?"

Mrs. Bond delighted in being the one to teach Hallie about childbirth. She told Hallie what to buy in readiness, suggested things she could make—little swaddling blankets, for instance. She told Hallie how to nurse a baby, though her own babies had never lived long enough for that. She told her what to do with the afterbirth.

"Won't it be wonderful?" said Mrs. Bond, beaming. "Our children will be playmates. No doubt you're hoping for a boy, what with Mr. Morgan, but I'm praying for a girl, someone to keep me company. Enoch, he wants a boy, of course, so I don't tell him I'm praying for a girl. Girls are such company."

"It's funny," Hallie mused aloud, "I hadn't even thought about whether it will be a boy or girl. It doesn't seem real to me yet." At home, she thought, boys only went out to work, to die or be crippled in the mines. Girls kept the homes. Here, it didn't matter. They'd both work on the farm, and besides, she expected to have many children. She wanted Chad to touch her many times; she wanted to help him with his dynasty. The thought of populating a new land with her children, hers and Chad's, filled her with excitement and anticipation, something she would never have known in Newcastle, where her children would have been just like others in crowded little homes. Here, they would be part of the future of this land she had grown so quickly to love. How lucky women were to be able to bear children.

"Stop by on your way back," called Mrs. Bond as Chad pulled the wagon away. Hallie felt infinitely content. Talking with Mrs. Bond had satisfied a need within her. Maybe, after the baby came, she could ride over once a month and stay overnight, even if the Bond house was tiny.

In mid-afternoon Hallie spotted the church spire of Parramatta above the trees, in the distance, and thought she had never seen such a pretty village. She had not fully appreciated it her first day, so filled was she with both Chad and looking forward to her own home.

To Hallie, Parramatta looked like villages she had imagined in fairy tales. The gently rolling hills wound around a slow-moving river where swans and ducks glided, and trim houses dotted the countryside. More populous than Sydney—it was already a town of over two thousand—it nevertheless lacked the bustle associated with its smaller harbor neighbor. The wide avenues were lined with trees, and Hallie laughed to see a cat chasing a dog across a street. The houses were built of homemade red brick which was sometimes plastered white, or constructed with the larger, tan sandstone blocks that could so easily be cut out of the river cliffs. Residences were spaced far apart, and the undulating hills were covered with tidy fenced yards. All in all, Parramatta looked clean and neat and spacious.

The soil, welcoming aspect of the town was broken by the mill, where eighteen women, chains wound around their ankles, walked continually up a wheel. As the wagon drew nearer, Hallie could see the pain on their faces, see the sweat sticking to their ragged dresses. "Heavens, Chad!" she gasped.

"The women's prison is in Parramatta," he said. "They're prisoners. It's called a treadmill. Instead of a windmill or animals grinding the corn and wheat, these convicts do it. In all the towns hereabouts, prisoners are assigned to the treadmill. They work in shifts. They can't last very long." He stared straight ahead. "Their Achilles tendons break, they develop leg tumors, the chains cut into their legs."

Hallie's hand clutched her chest, and a strangled sound escaped her. The women could barely continue. Stripes of dried blood showed through the back of one woman's dress. Another slumped and keeled over, but the treadmill kept moving, and her neighbor leaned over to pull her up. When she could not continue the terrible pace and hold the sagging woman at the same time, a jailor appeared and cracked his whip across the woman's back. She collapsed, and he jerked her off the treadmill. The other women, their eyes averted, continued pacing.

Hallie felt the gorge rise in her throat. "Dear God," she whispered, clutching Chad's arm.

"The price of crime." Chad's voice was dry.

Hallie imagined the scene had affected him also. By now they were past the treadmill, but Parramatta no longer looked so pretty to her.

Nine

Hallie could scarcely believe she was dining at the governor's while they were in Parramatta.

Government House was a large two-story mansion constructed of the sandstone so prevalent nearby, and cut into large blocks. Right now scaffolding covered the exterior of the residence. "When I arrived last year," Governor Lachlan Macquarie told Hallie by way of apology for the clutter and disarray, "the house was in great disrepair."

She thought Lachlan Macquarie the most imposing person she'd met. Partly it was the uniform he wore, with ornate gold epaulets at his shoulders and a high, stiff black collar that necessitated holding himself erect. His wide-spaced dark eyes accentuated what she thought could only be called a regal nose, long and sharp but not unattractive. His upper lip was thinner than the bottom one, and his smile was gracious and frequent.

His wife nodded and in a soft voice said, "Yes, it was uninhabitable, really. I've sent for new furnishings." The governor smiled at her with pride and open affection as she led the way into the dining room.

Six ornate candelabra positioned along the length of the long table lit the dining room so brightly that Hallie was dazzled. The silverware sparkled, so she knew that it must be sterling and that the china decorated with tiny hand-painted flowers was fine porcelain, even though she had only read of such finery.

The lovely Mrs. Macquarie had set Hallie at ease immediately. They had only been in the colony nine months more than Hallie, so much of the evening's conversation was spent making comparisons between New South Wales and England, always to the latter's detriment.

Dinner itself was a more elegant affair than Hallie had ever experienced. Servants—convicts in claret-colored knickers and jackets that had white, lacy frilled collars—stood at their elbows, filling glasses, unobtrusively removing plates, retrieving a dropped napkin. There was veal in a wine sauce, tiny succulent peas, new potatoes sprinkled with parsley, large loaves of freshly baked bread, and, for dessert, a pudding that Hallie thought heavenly.

"From all I'm told," Macquarie said at one point, turning to Hallie, "your husband is going to be one of this colony's greatest assets."

Hallie smiled demurely. It took no courage at all for her to say, "Not just in the future. I think he already is." She looked across the table at Chad. He did not smile, but his eyes met hers.

"Lucky man, Chad," the governor murmured.

"Yes, sir," Chad answered, his eyes still on Hallie.

After dinner, while Chad and Governor Macquarie remained at the dining table talking over brandy and cigars, Mrs. Macquarie led Hallie into what she called the withdrawing room. She smiled as she explained, "It's called that because it's where the ladies withdraw to while the men talk business after dinner. In England, of course, they're drawing rooms. I expect the new furniture to arrive any day now." And, indeed, the enormous chamber with twelve-foot ceilings held no more than a curved settee and two straight-backed chairs, though a patterned carpet covered the wide-planked flooring. "Next time you see it," the governor's wife continued, "I hope you'll find it beautiful."

Mrs. Macquarie, Hallie decided, was a gentle, attractive woman of great spirit. When enthusiasm and a sense of adventure lit up her face, it was imbued with beauty. "I'm his second wife," she said at one point. "He'd been a widower for eleven years when I married him four years ago, in 1807. He had, for all practical purposes, he told me, withdrawn from life. I know that by marrying him, *my* life began."

"I feel that way, too," Hallie admitted. She wondered whether it was this country or the men they had married that made them feel this way.

Later, when she and Chad were getting ready for bed in the Macquaries' guest room, she told Chad, "I like her. Like her lack of airs, her ability to make people feel like instant friends." Chad agreed.

They retired early, for it had been a long day. In the

morning Chad asked, "Would you rather stay here than go into Sydney with me? I'll be back tomorrow."

"I'd like to go with you," Hallie said.

"There's no need to rush, particularly if half the things I ordered have come in."

This time, while Chad busied himself, Hallie wandered the streets. She dared not enter the area known as the Rocks. From the landing quay she observed the wattle-and-daub convict huts, which had no glass windows and looked dark as well as dirty, even from this distance. For the first time in many days she thought of Tristan. Was he in one of them? Was he here in Sydney or up at the prison in Coal River? Was he walking a treadmill? Chad had loomed so large in her life, and she was so caught up in new experiences—as well as with her pregnancy—that she had thought little of Tristan of late. The treadmill had brought him back into her memory.

At a neat, small, brick shop she saw a sign that read SEAMSTRESS, and she went inside. A Mrs. McCracken sat at a large table, bolts of cloth on a shelf, her needle whipping through flowered muslin. Hallie introduced herself and explained that she did not want anything sewed but was interested in fabric. Mrs. McCracken showed her flannel as soft as a lamb, just perfect for the kind of blanket Mrs. Bond had suggested. Hallie decided to ask Chad to buy her some. Mrs. McCracken also had skeins of yarn, and Hallie thought of her mother's knitting needles clicking far into the night. She would knit her baby a jumper, too, if Chad would buy her some yarn.

When she met him at the hotel and told him of her desires, he shoved some coins across the table at her and said, "Yes, of course. We may not be back in town before the baby comes. Buy what you wish and then go on to bed. I'll be late."

Hallie waited up as long as she could, long past the time she usually fell asleep, and still Chad had not returned. It was nearly dawn before she was awakened by his clambering into bed next to her. Within seconds he fell asleep, his breathing deep and regular. She lay there until hearing a rooster crow, wondering where her husband had been all night.

Though his eyes were bloodshot, Chad was in fine humor

94

when he awoke barely two hours later. He whistled as he shaved, and ate a gargantuan breakfast, volunteering no information. Then, telling Hallie that he had to attend to an errand before they would be ready to leave; he disappeared. Three hours later, when he returned, he was smiling. "Let's go," he said. "The wagon will be so heavy it'll take a long time to get home."

He bubbled with conversation on the way back to the farm. When at one point Hallie again voiced the horror of the treadmill she had seen, he explained the penal system to her,

"Hallie, my dear, up until the American Revolution, over a thousand of our English convicts a year were sent to America. Nearly a quarter of a million of them. What were we to do when that outlet was no longer available?"

"But what do they do, so many of them, that is criminal?" she asked.

"Let's see," said Chad, trying to recall. "I know that the crimes that are punishable by death are . . . let's see—shoplifting anything worth over five shillings—"

"Death? For that?" Hallie was astounded.

He nodded. "And for stealing over forty shillings from a home, stealing someone's cow, horse, or sheep . . ."

"Do you mean if I stole someone's sheep, I'd be sentenced to death?" Hallie could scarcely believe such severe punishment.

"Exactly. Also highway robbery, forgery, arson, destroying a ship, setting fire to coal mines, and destroying machines that manufacture textiles."

These were crimes so alien to anything Hallie knew that she had difficulty comprehending them. She wondered what happened if the "crime" was unintentional, what if your family was starving and you stole a loaf of bread?

Chad looked at her. "Not very charitable people, the English, are we, Hallie?" His voice took on an intensity that was becoming familiar to her. "Ninety-five percent of England's people have no rights at all. Do you know that the poor of our beloved mother country can be conscripted to work in mines, can be impressed into the army or navy, or even be jailed for being unemployed? About a quarter of the English people live on the edge of starvation. No wonder they become criminals. Stealing a loaf of bread, for

God's sake, is punishable by either seven years in prison or transportation to New South Wales and indenture."

Hallie started to speak, to cry out, then closed her mouth and sat still, astonishment evident on her face. Finally all she could do was whisper, "Oh, Chad," horrified with the injustice of life.

Chad saw the look on her face and reached out to cover her hand with his. He was silent for a minute, the creaking of the overloaded wagon the only sound. Then he turned to her. "Hallie, England is not a country for the average man. This country is. This, and America, are places where there's hope. Oh, I know, I never came from an average family. But what would have been my destiny had I stayed? My brother would have put me on a dole. I would have spent my life on a reasonable allowance, doing what? Some administrative job for the mines? England holds little hope for anyone but the eldest sons and nobility."

He had never talked this way with her before. Hallie noted the bitterness in his voice, the way his hand tightened around hers. He looked over at her, and as her eyes met his, his voice softened. "I'm not really against England, Hallie. It has the finest educational system in the world, for the upper classes. It's probably the most civilized any society has ever been; it has vision. I have no desire to be anything other than an Englishman, but I'd have had no hope of changing in England, no hope of being anything other than a brother waiting for a handout. But here . . . here I can rise as far as I'm capable. It's not just the poor and the uneducated who are limited in England."

He was silent for a bit, and a chorus of kookaburras joined the creaking of the wagon. The sky was overcast, a milky blue. Though she really did not need the wide-brimmed straw hat Chad had bought her now, she was glad he had chosen that rather than a sunbonnet.

It was late afternoon when they came to the same place where they had spent their wedding night. Again, Hallie saw the black swans gliding in the clear water. Again, she gathered twigs. This time Chad shot a duck. As she bathed in the billabong, he appeared. He stood on the edge of the pool, under a tree whose bark dripped in long tattered strips, watching the ducks circle in and out of the reeds, watching the graceful, red-beaked swans drift effortlessly.

Stripping off his clothes, he walked briskly into the water, swimming across the billabong with broad, strong strokes.

Hallie, in water up to her neck, watched him, mesmerized by his physical beauty. She had never seen him naked, she realized. She wondered why he no longer desired her as she yearned to reach out and touch him. When he emerged from the water, she studied him. Broad shoulders, strong arms laced with muscles, a slender waist, tight buttocks, long, hard legs. Without realizing she was even doing it, she walked out of the water toward him.

He turned. She stood at the edge of the billabong as the afternoon sun shone rosily on them. Neither of them moved. They might have been frozen statues, so long did they stand, staring at each other. She thought she heard him mutter, "God damn," as he started toward her slowly.

Before he reached her, she felt her nipples tighten, felt her body flow toward him, stretch out to touch him.

His lips on hers, while soft, had a hard urgency. He was not tender, but kissed her with a roughness kindled of anger and desire. He bit her, his arms around her tightening until their bodies seemed as one, the hardness of him exciting her, enveloping her. Her breasts were crushed against him as his hand flowed down her back, pulling her against him until she could feel him between her legs, feel the strength and power of him, hear him murmur, "If you just weren't so beautiful, so goddamned beautiful . . ."

And then he looked deep into her eyes and stopped. Just ceased. Let her go. His hands fell to his sides, and though he was breathing heavily, he turned and leaned down to pick up his clothes. He jammed his legs into his pants, his back toward her.

Hallie—nerve ends raw, waiting, wanting—wondered what had happened. "Chad, wait," she called.

His back to her, he stopped.

She had to ask, though she had tried not to for so many months. "Why?"

Slowly, he turned on his heel and faced her. "Why what?"

"Why did you stop?" she implored.

"For Christ's sake, Hallie . . . because you're pregnant! So I won't injure the baby."

Despite the fact that her entire body was alive with desire, she felt instant relief. "Oh," she breathed softly.

He walked back to her. His finger cupping her chin, he looked into her eyes. "Are you going to tell me you didn't know?"

"All these months"—her voice sounded like a little girl's—"I've thought I didn't please you, that you haven't wanted me."

Chad put his arms around her and drew her to him, so close the roughness of his shirt scratched her cheek. "Sometimes"—his voice was very low—"it's torture. Never, not one night since we've been married, have I not wanted you. And it's not just night. I can be out riding Thunder, or mending a fence, or watching you as you bring me lunch, and I want you, Hallie."

Oh, thank God, she thought. It's only his desire for a fine strong child that keeps him from me. It's not that he doesn't want me. . . .

She threw her arms around him. With his right hand he tilted her head back, looking deep into her eyes. "Want you, Hallie? Looking at you drives me mad with desire. I keep away from you because I know myself too well. I spent too many years womanless; I could not stop once I began. I want you so badly, Hallie, that I ache."

A soothing warmth spread through her, an indescribable sense of peace and well-being. She wanted to go on standing like this, in the cradle of his arms, to feel his heartbeat close to hers. But he backed away, looking down at her.

"I am very glad you came here. I am proud you are my wife. I like your spirit and your willingness to learn. I like"—and this time he smiled—"your body and your mouth"—he kissed it lightly—"and your eyes. I'm sorry if you have not known this."

He turned and walked to the fire he had built, where the duck was roasting. "Dinner's ready," he called.

Hallie pulled on her clothes and ran toward him. The duck was tender, and Chad made conversation through dinner. Serenity enveloped her. When they had finished eating and the sun's golden rays blazed a bright vermilion as it sank behind the horizon, Chad threw blankets on the ground. It was too warm to use them except to sleep on. As they lay, fully clothed, on the blankets, Hallie saw that Chad, too, was staring into the darkening sky.

"There's the Southern Cross," she murmured. He reached for her hand.

"Where were you last night?" she asked tentatively.

"Making money," he answered.

She couldn't believe he'd been earning money during the night. "Doing what?" she pursued, slightly shocked at her boldness in pursuing the subject.

"How do you think we have money for all we buy? The farm isn't a money-making proposition yet."

Hallie thought about it for a moment, then shook her head. "I don't know. I've never really wondered before."

"Playing cards," he said.

"Gambling?" Hallie was shocked into silence. After a few moments she asked, "What would happen if you lost?"

"I don't lose." His hand tightened around hers.

In the morning, after they had started up again, Chad said, "I've bought you a present." His tone was teasing, and though he gazed straight ahead at the oxen, the crinkles around his eyes deepened. "It will arrive later this week."

"A present?" Pleasure spread through her. "You don't have to give me a present." She could never remember being given a present for no particular reason.

Chad laughed. "If I *had* to, I probably wouldn't want to."

What, she wondered, did she need? She thought she had everything. "Oh, Chad," she said softly, "you've already given me so much."

He put his hand on her knee, holding the reins in his left hand. "Two dresses and a trip to Sydney? Hallie, someday I shall give you much more . . . much, much more."

"I don't need more," she said.

The gift came five days later on six wagonloads. It was blocks of sandstone and hundreds of bricks.

"I'll build you a kitchen," Chad said, smiling in anticipation of her reaction. "It will have big windows in it, and a brick floor, and a wall oven as well as a fireplace. We shall build a brick pathway which will be sheltered so that when it rains you'll not get wet."

He watched her face fill with wonder. She recalled telling

him, before their trip to Parramatta and Sydney, that the kitchen was a furnace in this weather. She had not asked for a new one, but she could think of nothing she wanted more. He noticed the single tear that welled in the corner of her right eye. She wanted to thank him, but no words came.

Chad put his arms around her.

Ten

Hallie had taken to doing the washing in the afternoon so she could bathe in the cool stream when that was finished, laze in the water, sit and sun herself on the rocks. It rejuvenated her more than a nap.

"Sometimes," she'd told Chad, "I feel like the sun and I are having a love affair."

He'd gotten that funny expression he sometimes did, and then laughed. "The sun can't love."

"How do you know?" she'd challenged, her voice playful. "It loves me. I think I was made for this country," she'd added, stretching like an indolent cat.

The garden now took such a prodigious amount of time that Chad had now assigned a convict to do the weeding.

Hallie still enjoyed riding out to Archie and Chad, wherever they might be, and bringing them their lunch. One afternoon in early February—the hottest part of the year—after days of muggy humidity, the sun shone clear and hot, and Hallie did not stay to lunch with Chad and Archie. She wanted to hurry back and immerse herself in the creek, up to her arms and knees with the washing, and then lie soaking in the sun. But she had hardly arrived when she heard laughter and shouting from beyond the bend in the creek.

Cautiously, leaving her laundry on the bank, she walked through the trees and down the curving stream. Nearly a dozen very black women and several children were cavorting in the creek. Hallie heard herself gasp. They looked like no human beings she had ever seen before. Several of the children had very blond hair. To her, with their jutting jaws, thick lips, and coarse features, they seemed more animal than human, yet that they were humans she had no doubt. They wore no clothing at all but were not in the least self-conscious about it. Except for two young women, their breasts all sagged. She thought them exceedingly ugly.

After her initial surprise, she was frightened. Running back to her laundry, she was ready to pick up everything and race to the house. But then she heard the laughter again—a joyous, abandoned sound that drew her in spite of herself. She crept back to spy on them, inching forward without realizing it, trying to hear what they were saying. Suddenly one pointed directly at her from across the stream. There were looks of disbelief and cries, as all the women fell back, clutching their hands over their breasts, not so much in modesty but in fear. Only one little child, probably about three or four, with hair so pale it looked platinum, ventured toward her. One of the women screamed, and ran to catch the child before it could reach her.

They stood on the other side of the creek, jabbering, pointing. It was Hallie who felt exposed, naked. Gradually they grew quiet and looked at her. She stared back at them until she felt she was intruding. Forcing a smile, she backed away until she was hidden by the bend in the creek, then slowly washed her clothes. She did not stay to sun herself, did not even bathe in the stream, but as she walked back to the house, she experienced a lonesomeness she had not felt since coming to this new land. The sight of women playing together, of women in company with other women, the sound of carefree laughter, made her feel lonely.

At dinner that night she said, "I ran into a band of black women today, down at the creek."

Both Chad and Archie reacted as though she had just announced that the cavalry had come marching through. "Where?" asked Chad.

The tone of his voice was so sharp it startled Hallie. When she didn't answer, he repeated his question.

"Why?" Hallie asked. "Are you going to shoot them?"

"I'm going to tell them to get off my property."

Courage rose in Hallie's breast. "Less than a dozen women and children swimming in our creek . . ." It was the first time she had used "our," but neither of them noticed. "What harm is there in that?"

"If there are women and children, there are men," ventured Archie, who looked as alarmed as Chad.

Defensively, she said, "They were perfectly harmless, laughing and playing in the water. They did look strange, and some of the children had very light hair. I've never seen people like them."

"Abos," said Archie.

Chad nodded, spearing a chop. "Haven't seen any around here all these years," he said. "They've no right to the land now. It's mine." A frown creased his forehead and his body stiffened.

"Do they know that?" Hallie asked, laying her fork on the table.

"They have no sense of ownership," answered Chad. "They never stay in one place. They're dirty and disgusting. Why, they even eat grubs and insects. Catch fish. Hunt roos." He shook his head as though ridding himself of an ugly image.

"They didn't seem dirty to me," Hallie said slowly. "They were bathing in the stream."

"Foul it," Archie muttered.

Chad pointed a finger at her. His voice was sharp. "Don't go near them, Hallie. If I hear of them coming any nearer, if they hurt you—"

"Why in the world would they hurt me?" She did not tell them she had been frightened. She was angered at his treating her like a recalcitrant child.

"They're savages," answered Chad, as though that explained everything. "If they come any closer, we'll run them off." His voice and the squaring of his shoulders held a threat.

"I admit I didn't feel comfortable seeing them. But what harm are they doing?" Hallie pursued. The sound of their laughter echoed in her heart.

That night, as they lay in bed, Chad reached out and put an arm around Hallie's shoulders. "I don't want anything to happen to you. Or the baby. Those abos make me nervous."

Hallie was so unused to any gesture of affection from Chad that she lay very still, hoping he would not withdraw his arm. He didn't; he fell asleep with his arm still around her. She laid her head on his shoulder, liking the feel of him, the closeness.

It was a long time before she, too, fell asleep. She ached

103

for her mother, for her sisters; Myrna, Hester, and Kate. She longed for Danny, for Dada—the women at the creek had evoked memories of home, bringing with them a keen awareness of the lack of companionship she'd endured these last months. She wanted to hear their laughter, see them splashing in the creek and jumping off that big log. She wanted, she realized, to see them again.

Over the course of the next two months, Hallie did see them again—daily. Every day she moved a bit closer. And every day the women looked at her and then pretended to ignore her until they had become used to her. Then one day one of the younger women beckoned to Hallie, and she walked over to join their splashing and their laughter. They poked her skin and patted her rounded belly, shaking their heads knowingly. Hallie did not know that they were still in the Stone Age, that they did not connect intercourse with babies. They related swelling bellies with babies, and one of the women, closer to term even than Hallie, patted herself and patted Hallie as though to express that they were sisters.

When they offered her a witchety grub collected from a tree, Hallie wanted to refuse, but she could not. She ate it but never told Chad. It was a small price to pay for companionship. They didn't understand each other's languages, but in ways known from time immemorial they communicated. Hallie sat naked on a large branch that overhung the river, her feet in the slowly moving stream, filled with contentment. She joined in their laughter and watched as they played together. These women never seemed in a hurry, never felt compelled to stop their afternoon abandonment for work. They never spanked their children; in fact, Hallie could not tell who was the mother of any of the children.

They invited her back to their camp, back in the woods. One afternoon she stayed so late that their men began to return with the kangaroos and wallabies they had killed with sharp-looking curved instruments Hallie hadn't seen before. When she tried to explain them to Chad, he said, "I think they're boomerangs, hangovers from a prehistoric age." But then everything about the aborigines was from a prehistoric age. "Hallie, don't go to their camp. That's an order." When he saw the stubborn look on her face, he squared his shoulders. Then he gentled his voice and said, "Please."

One afternoon, on her way to the swimming hole, Hallie heard a moaning. In a cleared thicket, alone, was the young aborigine who was also expecting a baby. Her legs wide apart, she knelt on the ground, panting loudly but regularly, moaning softly to herself, gasping now and then as pain seared through her. Hallie stopped at the sight. No one else was around.

She knew nothing about alleviating the woman's pain, but here was a chance to witness a childbirth before her own. She pressed herself against a tree, trying not to move, hoping not to alert the native to her presence. Suddenly the woman took in an uneven breath and withdrew it in a ragged, pain-filled sigh and Hallie could tell from her arched back that she was pushing, hard. She clung to a stout branch and bit into it once, her whole body shaking. Her cries had turned to sobs, and then she moaned as a head burst between her legs. She looked down, grunting with another heavy push, and a baby slid down onto the earth, connected to its mother by a string.

Hallie stared, fascinated. That must be the cord Mrs. Bond told me about, she thought. The baby was covered with blood. The woman did not move it, but kept grunting and pushing hard until something that looked like liver or the entrails of a pig came slithering out. It fell next to the baby, and Hallie realized the woman had twisted to the side so that it would not fall on and smother the baby. She knows more about childbirth than I do, thought Hallie. Then the black woman let go of the branch. Lying down on her side, she picked up her baby and cleaned it off with some leaves. She cut the cord with a shell and gazed down upon her child.

It did not look as Hallie would have expected. Its hair was light, but then so were the other children's. But this baby did not have the typical aboriginal features. It had the slanting jaw, but it did not have the wide nose or the thick lips. It was far paler than Hallie would have believed possible. The mother stared and pushed it away, a look of horror on her face.

Other women came out of the woods. They must have been there all the time. When Hallie left, no one paid the slightest attention to her. She didn't know whether anyone had even seen her. But she had seen childbirth. She could bear the pain, she was sure. As long as she knew it was temporary, she thought she could stand anything. So, she should kneel and push. That was it. But she would have no branch to hold onto or to bite into when the pain became too intense.

How would she cut her cord? And what would she do with it then? For the first time in her pregnancy she was scared. Not of what might happen to her, but because she felt so unsure of what should be done. She hated being so ignorant, resented knowing so little. Mrs. Bond had told her to nurse it, that it was like a lamb getting colostrum, but now that Hallie had personally witnessed childbirth, she realized Mrs. Bond had omitted much. She thought she ought to return, to see what happened next.

The women were standing around in a circle, piling dry branches onto an already crackling fire. Flames leapt from the logs piled high. The new mother was holding her infant above the flames. Though the flames did not sear the child, the baby's faint cry trailed through the air. The invisible waves of heat danced above the fire. Hallie wondered what kind of dreadful ritual this must be.

The mother turned the baby over and over, as though roasting it on a spit. The other women chanted in low monotones. Oh, mother of God, they're trying to brown it! Hallie realized in horror. And suddenly she understood why the baby did not look exactly like the other aborigines. It had a white father.

Hallie wanted to run into the circle and snatch the baby from the fire. Instead, she turned and fled.

She could not even cook dinner that night. When Chad and Archie came in from work, she was not in the kitchen. She was in bed, under covers, even though it wasn't cold. She could not control her shivering. Her teeth chattered, and she sat with her arms around her knees.

When Chad came in to inquire about her absence, he took one look at her and asked, "Hallie . . . the baby?"

She shook her head and began to cry. Though she omitted telling him about witnessing childbirth, she did tell him about the women burning the newborn baby. She couldn't stop shaking until well after he had gathered her into his arms and stroked her hair.

"Could I be right, Chad? Could a white man have fathered that child?"

"Yes, of course," he said, holding her close. "It happens all the time."

"Why—Why on earth would a man do that?"

She heard him sigh. "Some men don't care whom they bed. They don't care about the woman, about whether she's clean or pretty or intelligent or . . . white."

Hallie looked up at him. "Why do they do it?"

Chad gave a short laugh. "How to explain? . . . Men, my dear, have different needs from women. And, at times, they will use any outlet to satisfy that need."

"Have you?" Hallie's eyes were wide and round.

Chad cradled her head against his chest. "Not with an abo. But yes, with women I have not cared about, though I like to think I have been somewhat fastidious."

"With women who have not wanted you?" Hallie was so fascinated, her shivering had stopped.

Chad was silent for a moment. "Once." She could hardly hear his voice. "A long time ago." He stood up, letting her go. "A man does not always expect a woman to want sex, Hallie. Most wives do not respond like you do. A man takes for granted that a woman will not want it."

"And you force yourself on them?"

"Christ, this is not a conversation I ever expected to have." His voice held amusement as he lit a cigar. "Yes, I suppose so." He walked over to the open window.

"How awful!" Hallie shrank back upon the bed.

"And what should I do to have a son if you had turned me away?" He turned to face her, to confront her.

"Do women do that?" she asked, feeling like a child.

"Some do. Others make it perfectly clear that they suffer the humility." He ground out his newly lit cigar in a tray on the table.

"Humility? I don't understand."

"Thank goodness for that, my dear." Chad smiled, his gray eyes amused. "That is my good fortune, and, I hope, yours. Come now and get dinner. I'm starving."

The next day the aborigines were gone. Hallie missed

them; she had had companionship for over eight weeks. Chad was relieved.

By now her kitchen was finished. And it was a good thing, too. In her ponderous condition she could barely have fit in the original kitchen. She could no longer ride, and she waddled when she walked. Everything she did was an effort. At least twice every night she had to get up and feel her way out to the privy in the darkness.

When her time did come, the labor pains started in mid-morning, when the men were out in the fields or beyond the hills. Hallie sat down, the pain tempered with elation as she wondered how long it would be before the baby came. Maybe in time for her to be able to have dinner ready. At home, her sisters and sisters-in-law had stayed in bed for days. She hoped she would be more like the aboriginal woman, who was standing within minutes.

She wondered whether she'd have a boy or a girl. Would Chad be disappointed if the baby were not a boy? Men put such a store in sons, she reflected as another pain surged through her, maybe because men accomplished things and women lived through them. Women didn't have the dreams, didn't have the capacity for work, didn't have the freedom of choice. Women didn't make history, except by being with the men, by being the mother of men.

Yet I dreamed, Hallie reminded herself proudly. It was a man who had to make my dream come true, but at least I had the courage when my chance came. Not many of the women she had known would have chanced what she had. Not to dream, not to chance—how dull. And how lucky I am, she thought as another pain quickly followed the last.

When it had passed, she forced herself to stop daydreaming and concentrate. Mrs. Bond had told her to boil water, so she lumbered into the kitchen. But the native woman had had no water, Hallie thought, and she had cut the cord with a shell.

Hallie had just started heating water when a contraction seared through her so sharply that she could not stand up straight. Water rushed down her legs; Mrs. Bond had warned her of this. Weak, she sank to the kitchen floor, sweat beading on her forehead.

After a moment she struggled to her feet and, bracing herself against the wall, managed to walk out of the kitchen

108

just as another pain shot through her. Outside, there was nothing to hold onto, but she willed herself to stand up straight. The pains had come upon her so suddenly; there had been no warning. The little twinges she had felt that morning had not alerted her. She tried to remember what Mrs. Bond had told her, but all she could see was the aboriginal woman in the woods.

The next pain was so intense, it knocked her off her feet. She wondered if she should try to crawl to the woods, to find a tree to cling to, like the abo woman. But she knew that white women had babies in bed, not in the woods. White women in England, she thought. Who knows what they do here?

At that moment she heard Chad call, "Hallie!"

She felt him pick her up, carrying her, murmuring, "I knew it. I felt it. Something made me stop work and come back. I knew you needed me."

But she didn't. He was a man. He could not help. Yet she clung to him as he laid her on the bed, kneeling down beside her. "My darling," he whispered, wiping her forehead with the sleeve of his shirt. "What can I do?"

In his enthusiasm at impending fatherhood, Chad had not given much thought to the actual childbirth. He had watched Hallie knitting in the late evenings or hemming flannel squares. He had assigned one of the convicts who showed expertise in carpentry to make a cradle, which swayed gracefully on a pedestal. It stood now in their bedroom, in readiness. When he would awaken mornings, he sometimes caught Hallie rubbing her belly and smiling across the room at the cradle. But he had thought that he'd seen enough animals give birth that he should know what to do when Hallie's time came. It had never dawned on him that he would feel this nervous.

"I wish I had a branch," she said.

"What do you mean?"

"A thick branch."

A look of incredulity flashed across his face. "A branch?"

Hallie nodded.

Chad did not ask why, but, "How big?"

Hallie tried to remember the size of the strong limb that the aborigine woman had clung to. Using her hands, she made a circle.

"That big?" he asked. When she nodded, he disappeared, returning in less than fifteen minutes carrying a branch about six inches in girth.

Her laughter had a touch of hysteria to it. "That's no good," she said. "It's not attached to anything."

Chad leaned over her, brushing a lock of damp hair from her brow. "Hallie, what did you want the branch for?"

She told him about witnessing childbirth, about the abo woman clinging to a tree branch, about her biting into it. She wished the headboard had something she could hang onto, something that would give her leverage when she had to kneel and push.

"I'll be your branch, Hallie," he said, stripping off his jacket and rolling up his sleeves. "Hold onto me."

She didn't want Chad here, didn't want him to see her this way. He was always talking about how beautiful she was, and she knew she looked dreadful now. She certainly didn't want him to see the baby come, see the private parts of her. But she also knew that what was important to him now was the baby, the beginning of the Morgan dynasty in New South Wales. She was the instrument for that path to immortality, and she had no false illusions about that. It satisfied her.

"What should I do?" he asked.

"I'm not sure, Hallie answered. "I think . . . I ought to be left alone. You shouldn't be here."

Chad looked at her. Her face was pinched from discomfort, her brow was damp again, and he saw fear reflected in her eyes. "Nothing in this world would make me leave you alone," he said.

"Men don't know anything about childbirth," Hallie protested weakly.

"Tell me exactly what you know," Chad responded.

When she'd told him all that Mrs. Bond had told her and all that she had seen in the woods, he took her hand in his and smiled. "Now," he said, "we know exactly the same. Maybe I know more. I've helped bring colts and calves and lambs and puppies into this world. I won't leave you, Hallie."

Another contraction surged through her. If Chad had not been there, she would have screamed in agony.

"I'm going to go wash my hands," Chad told her. "I'll be right back."

While he was gone he allowed himself a stiff drink of whiskey, even though it was before noon. He also added water to the nearly empty kettle. While drinking, he stood in the doorway and gazed out toward the river, at the horses in the far field, at the hills, at the greenness that surrounded his homestead. Today he would add a son to his list of accomplishments. He did not deny to himself that he was unnerved, that when Hallie clenched her teeth in pain, when she moaned and balled her fists, he felt helpless.

He started to put the glass back next to the whiskey. Then, smiling, he filled it half full and took it in to Hallie. "Here," he said, "drink this. It will help ease the pain."

Hallie had never had spirits before; she grimaced at the taste and wanted to spit it out. But Chad talked to her softly, telling her stories of his years in India, of his first years here—and gradually she downed the whiskey. His voice lulled her and his tales held her attention. He had never talked of his struggles here, of clearing the land, of his first trials with the breeding of the horses which now brought such sums of money.

"But horses are only temporary," he told her. "The future is sheep. Horses are for fun, but the need for excellent fleece will be what brings us riches." He realized he was talking to keep Hallie's mind off herself, but he found he enjoyed sharing his dreams with her. When he saw from her face that a pain seized her, he would reach out and tell her to grab his arm, as she would a branch. He could tell from the pressure how intense her pain was, and he took some pleasure in sharing it, as though he, too, were giving birth.

It was mid-afternoon before the baby came. "Hallie, you have to take off your dress," Chad told her. "It's in the way."

She hesitated, even now. "And your undergarments," he added. "Here, let me." He raised her up and undressed her, permitting her to retain her chemise. He wondered if he might be sick when he saw blood, which he knew accompanied childbirth. When he had been forced to kill a man in India, the blood had not made him ill. But then

111

anger had carried him on its wings. This was different; this would be Hallie's blood. He went to get another drink, and brought Hallie a small one, too.

When he returned to the bedroom she was moaning. Her eyes stared at the ceiling, but he could tell she didn't see it or anything else. The covers were twisted and her teeth were clenched.

She wailed, knifing her legs and spreading them apart. He untwisted the sheets and saw the damp fuzziness of a head pressing against her vagina. Oh, God, he thought. My son. My firstborn child. A ragged scream escaped Hallie as her whole body shuddered. Searing pain blackened her vision. For a moment she saw nothing, feeling only an agony that was unbearable and not realizing she had screamed. She had to get rid of it. She pushed hard, and the baby's head burst out.

Chad reached down and gently held the head in his hands. It looked like nothing so much as a chipmunk. Another gigantic push by Hallie and the baby spurted into his hands, covered with a clear liquid. Immediately he reached for a towel, wrapping his son in it.

Hallie's eyes were closed. "Is it alive?" Her voice was barely audible.

Chad didn't know. It had made no sound. He couldn't tell if it was breathing.

As though her voice came from a great distance, he heard Hallie say, "Mrs. Bond said to hold it upside down and pat its back."

As Chad did so a little cry escaped the baby. "He's fine, Hallie!" Chad cried, a grin spreading over his face. "I think he's fine!"

Hallie thought another baby must be there, too. Twins. She pushed again, and the afterbirth slithered onto the bed. Chad thought for a moment that Hallie's insides had fallen out.

Eleven

James Chadwick Morgan flourished, as did his father and mother, and their farm. In fact, 1811 was a banner year for them.

Hallie recuperated from childbirth quickly. In less than two weeks she was once again cooking for everyone. The convicts found ways to visit Jamie daily. They pretended coincidence, but the ones who came from the barracks to the kitchen to get their dinners peeked into the cradle and even made silly little noises at the baby when they thought no one was looking. Others managed to find errands to do around the house or messages filled with nothing to be delivered, questions that needed no answers. Chad and Hallie laughed about it, finding it all quite endearing.

Though Chad would never consider changing a diaper, and though he was as naive as Hallie about handling a baby and they both looked awkward at first, Hallie was surprised at the attention he lavished on Jamie. Back home, though her brothers and the neighbors always welcomed children, she had seldom seen any of the men hold their babies or rock an infant. Pride evident, the men had nonetheless left parenthood to the women until the children were older.

Not Chad. When he was around and Jamie cried, he picked him up from the cradle, nestling his son in his arms, walking around in a rocking motion, sometimes even singing him to sleep. In the evening, while Hallie tended to the mending, Chad would hold Jamie and tell him stories. Hallie loved to listen.

"Are these ones you heard as a child?" she asked. Both of them knew Jamie understood not a word.

"Some," he answered, scarcely able to take his eyes from his son. "Others I make up."

They were stories of how lambs strayed from the ewes and how terrible things nearly happened until the rams rescued the lambs; or about foals and how, upon listening

113

to the stallion's advice, they grew up to be the fastest horses in the world. They were stories of jumping kangaroos and of fish in billabongs. Hallie was amused by Chad's fertile mind and storytelling ability.

They were good times, filled with contentment and satisfaction. They were as families should be. Chad loved to sit and watch as Hallie nursed Jamie. All of her thoughts centered around Jamie. Was he breathing in the night? She took him everyplace—down to the creek when she washed, into the kitchen when she cooked, out to the garden; she even tried to fashion a sling so she could take him riding. Chad advised her not to ride yet. "Wait until Jamie's a month old. I've heard that you should take care of yourself for that long."

When Jamie was not quite a month old, Chad took off for Sydney. He said he wanted to see the governor and "do some other business." He told Hallie he might be gone five or six nights. This time he didn't take the wagon, but rode off on Thunder right before dawn. Hallie wondered if he would play cards every night.

When he returned, she heard the charging hooves and looked out to see him racing down the hill from which she'd first seen this land; even from a distance she could tell his mood. Dashing down the hill, just slightly behind Chad and Thunder, was a pale gray streak. Hallie stood in the doorway, holding Jamie, watching. Her heart quickened; the emptiness disappeared.

He pulled Thunder up so short that the horse reared. The other pale gray horse, having no such signal, went pummeling on, stopped abruptly by the rope around its neck.

Jumping from Thunder's back, Chad barreled toward Hallie and Jamie. For just a moment Hallie thought he was going to kiss her. Instead he reached out, taking Jamie from her, and nodded at the silver horse.

"See if you like her," he said, unable to control a grin.

Like her? She was the most beautiful horse Hallie had ever seen, as light as the pearl-gray of dawn, with a mane as black as Newcastle's coal. And it was not even breathing heavily after the downhill race. Although she was not a connoisseur of horses, Hallie was still able to realize that the lines of this horse indicated superb breeding, better even than Chad's horses. Flung over its back was a woman's sidesaddle.

Holding Jamie, Chad walked next to her, his body touching hers. "She's yours. She's a thank-you, Hallie. Thank you for my son."

Hallie was so mesmerized with the horse that she did not respond with, "He's my son, too." But it flitted through her mind. Chad leaned down and kissed her neck, something he hadn't done since she'd become pregnant. Jamie gurgled.

"What's her name?" Hallie asked, her eyes still on the horse.

"That's up to you. She's barely broken, and so may be a bit wild. I'll work with her."

"No," she said. "Let me."

Chad raised his eyebrows but said nothing. When Hallie approached it, the horse neighed and pawed at the air.

"Don't move," called Chad.

Hallie stood still. It took over ten minutes, but as soon as she was able to touch the mare, when she ran her hand down the horse's nose, and its eyes at last met hers, Hallie's emotions were similar to those she'd felt when she had first held Jamie.

"Oh, Chad," she said. "We have so many horses. Why?"

"We didn't have any like this. And Jamie's mother should have the best. I guess it's a birthday present, Hallie. You gave me Jamie. I give you . . . what shall you name her?"

"Princess."

He waited to tell her the other news until they were in bed that night—until after he had touched her for the first time in so many months, until after he had reached out for her. She had known he would from the way he'd looked at her during dinner and afterward, after Archie had left, and they sat in front of the fire, after she'd finished nursing Jamie.

Chad reached out to put his hand over hers. "Hallie, I can't tell you how happy I am." The candlelight flickered between them.

Understanding the feeling, having experienced it ever since she'd arrived in New South Wales, Hallie smiled at him. "My cup runneth over, too."

Chad pulled her up, his arms encircling her. When his

115

lips met hers, it was with a desire and a hunger that he had denied himself for many months. Hallie felt her body spring to life, felt his hand on her breast ignite fires deep within her.

He picked her up and carried her into the bedroom. There, he whispered, "Let me undress you."

With each piece of clothing that he removed, he lingered; kissing her breasts, stroking her nipples erect with his tongue. He laid her on the bed, kissing the backs of her knees when he removed her stockings—things he had never done before. He did this slowly, rhythmically. Though no candle was lit, the moon danced through the shadows. Chad stood, ripping off his own clothes until he stood naked, silver in the moonlight.

As he drew off the last of her undergarments, his tongue ran up her leg, lingering on her thighs until she thought she would cry out in ecstasy. His tongue flicked its way up her body until he lay on top of her, his mouth melting into hers. Rolling over, he pulled her on top of him, his lips touching her breasts, his hands pulling her buttocks into him. She rose on her knees, feeling him gently biting her nipples. His hands guided her onto him. She moved up and down, drawing away from his mouth, sitting erect, her arms raised in the air. His hands moved from behind her, cupped her breasts, rubbing back and forth in tandem with her rhythmic up-and-down movements. Prisms of light broke in her head. Closing her eyes, she hoped the tempo would never stop. Shivering waves washed over her, and she heard herself moan. Chad, hearing her final sigh, quickly turned her over, covering her with kisses as he plunged deeper within her, whispering, "Don't move."

When it was over, he lay upon her for a moment before moving to her side.

After a while Hallie reached down to pull the covers over them, curling herself inside the circle of Chad's arm. They lay there for a long time, watching reflections of the leaves dancing against the walls. He reached down and kissed the top of her head, murmuring something unintelligible and soft.

She'd just begun to drift off into sleep when he said, "I bought eight hundred sheep this time, Hallie. Half of them

116

Bengals, and the other half from Cape Town. I'll send the men to get them tomorrow."

Hallie looked up at him, suddenly wide awake. "Eight hundred? My heavens, Chad, where in the world will we graze that many?"

He had been waiting for this. Even in the dark she could tell that he smiled. "That's why I went to see the governor. I bought another fifteen hundred acres."

She sat straight up. "Fifteen hundred acres? Mercy. How much is that?"

"Beyond the river," and she heard his sigh of pride. "It's selling for five shillings an acre. Captain Standish is giving up his land grant and returning to England, so I bought his sheep. They're prime. And they should nearly double their number come lambing time."

She wondered where all the money had come from. Gambling, as well as his horses, she imagined. Princess must have cost a pretty penny, too. Oh, this could never have happened to her back in Newcastle. How dull life would be married to George Burnham, in that dark, cold, dreary city. And how exciting it was here.

She lay down next to Chad again. His breathing became more even and his arm around her shoulders relaxed. Before he fell asleep, she asked, "Did you see Mrs. Bond? Is her baby alive this time?"

"She's dead" His words were slurred. "She died, along with the baby."

It was a long time before Hallie fell asleep.

It took her several months to feel truly energetic again. She was nursing Jamie, who was four months old, feeding the lambs, preparing meals for eleven of them three times a day. She asked Chad to assign milking the cow to one of the convicts, but she still churned the butter. There never seemed to be enough hours in a day. Chad took for granted that she would plant the kitchen garden again, but he and Archie had also discussed having a really large garden this year, in order to sell vegetables in Sydney and Parramatta. Chad thought he might even be able to sell to the commissary—ships that docked were desperate for fresh vegetables—so he assigned two convicts to this new project.

117

No matter what else, Hallie found an hour every day to ride Princess. She raced up the gently rising hills, where she stopped to view her land, sometimes seeing the blue mountains in the western distance. Now that their acreage spanned the river as well as its tributary creek, Hallie loved riding to it. When she took Jamie, she strapped him on her back, and then they would ride gently, no faster than a slow canter. If he was fussy, a mid-afternoon ride always soothed and put him to sleep.

This year, for the first time, shearing was a big operation. Chad and Archie tried to train some of the convicts to help, but the convicts always nicked the sheep, until Hallie could not watch for all the cuts. One day she asked if she could try, but Chad told her, "No. You need a strong back for this. It's not easy." Still she watched, in fascination. They had built a shearing shed, and the greasy fleeces piled up high.

She was not surprised to discover she was pregnant again.

Chad insisted she give up riding. He allowed her to ride in the wagon but forbade her Princess. When he told her he'd heard they had neighbors three miles to the south, they set out in the wagon one morning to meet them. Hallie took a picnic lunch and some early lettuce and radishes from the garden, as well as a pail of milk and a dozen eggs.

It was late November and hot. The morning sickness she'd experienced in her first pregnancy had lasted barely a month this time, and except for a constant tiredness, Hallie felt good. It had been a long time since she'd even talked with anyone who didn't live with them. It was as long ago as the trip to Sydney, last summer, since she'd been off their land. She hoped the new woman would be someone she liked.

The neighbors' house was made of logs, sturdy and tight and not at all attractive. There was only one window, and it was much smaller than their house. A lean-to out back served as a barn. A couple of pigs wandered unfenced; a horse was tied to a stake. It was easy to see that someone was trying to start a garden but lacked a plow.

They're just starting out, Hallie rationalized. I've no idea what our place looked like when Chad was just beginning, by the time I saw it he'd worked it for four years and had labor to help build the house and barn.

A slim young woman, wiping her hands on her apron and reaching up to push her hair out of her eyes, came to the doorway. When she saw visitors, her dark eyes lit up and she greeted them with a welcoming smile. Hallie thought her beautiful. Her sable hair fell in waves to her shoulders; her complexion looked like cream. With her high cheekbones and generous wide mouth, she was a woman men stopped to stare at.

Chad jumped down from the wagon. "Chad Morgan, and my wife. . . ." He nodded toward Hallie. "We've come to welcome you and see if there's anything we can do to help." He took his hat off and bowed slightly.

"Oh, my, my, I didn't expect visitors," the woman said. "How nice." Her eyes found Jamie, and she walked to the wagon. "A baby!"

Chad helped Hallie down, and the woman's eyes devoured Jamie. Proudly, knowing the woman must think Jamie the most beautiful baby in the world, Hallie offered, "This is Jamie, and I'm Hallie."

Now the woman looked at her. "Oh, yes. How nice." The three of them stood staring at one another until the woman wiped her hands on her apron again and said, "I'm Henrietta Colton. My husband's around someplace, for sure."

"I brought a picnic lunch," said Hallie. "And some produce from our garden, some eggs, and fresh milk. . . ."

The sudden sound of hammering indicated where her husband must be. "I'll go find him," Chad said, and walked off.

"Come inside," said Mrs. Colton, gesturing to Hallie.

The inside of the cabin was as dark as the one window indicated. There was just the one large room. The earthen floor was swept clean, the bed neatly made with a quilt covering it, and a rough table and two chairs fronted the fireplace. Aside from a trunk near the bed and what must have passed for a cupboard, the room was bare. How depressing, thought Hallie.

But she liked Henrietta. "Etta, please. Everyone calls me that." In a quiet, breathy voice, Etta asked, "May I hold the baby?" Hallie thought she looked like the Madonna, holding Jamie. "I want a baby more than anything in the world," Etta said softly.

"It will come," said Hallie, who knew all too well how easily they came.

Etta, it turned out, was a mail-order bride. While they waited for the men, she told Hallie her story. She had never known her parents; at the London orphanage they told her they'd found her on the doorstep when she must have been but days old. That was eighteen years ago. She had never known any other life. Though she was never treated cruelly, according to her definition and knowledge, she had no schooling, had never slept in a room with less than a dozen people, worked a loom ten hours a day six days a week. Until she was fourteen she had never left the orphanage, never seen anything of London or met anyone outside the orphanage.

But when she was fourteen she had been sent up to Yorkshire as the servant at a vicarage. A year ago, in church, the vicar had read a letter to his flock from the church in Sydney, imploring young women to come to New South Wales and marry the men who needed women. Fifty young men had banded together to pay the passage for any young women willing to come. They wanted rural girls, and had sent letters asking ten village churches for five young women each. It seemed like such an exciting adventure. When her vicar asked for volunteers, Etta had jumped up. Although he had tried to talk her out of it, his wife had said, "She's bound to marry sometime." So Etta had come around the world.

When the young women arrived, all fifty of them on the same ship, they had been met at the dock by the minister, Mr. Cooke, who—along with his wife—escorted them in five wagons to a warehouse. There they were allowed to freshen up, and were told that there would be a mass wedding in five days. In the meantime, the men who had paid for their passages would meet them. There would be suppers, and a picnic, and a dance, and a barbecue. They would have five days to get to know each other, these hundred young people. At the end of those five days a lottery would be held. The man with the lowest number would have first choice; the women had no choice. The fiftieth man, of course, had no choice either.

The girls thought it very exciting. Most of them had never been to a dance before and spent their days learning

120

the steps. For most of them it might be not only their first, but their last dance. Many of the men had land grants and intended to try their hands at farming. A few worked in stores; one ran the ferryboat from Parramatta to Sydney. Others were bakers, potters, carpenters, masons. They had come to New South Wales as soldiers, and elected to stay after their term was over, or they had ventured to this land so far away to see what kind of new life they could begin. Their reasons were varied.

"Mr. Colton's number was three," Etta said. Hallie couldn't tell whether or not Etta was pleased. The woman's dress was old but clean, and it clung to her voluptuous body. Hallie would have ventured to guess she might have been the number-one choice. She certainly was a beautiful woman, with her eyes almost purple, and high color in her cheeks.

When the men came in, Hallie couldn't have been more surprised. William Colton was of medium height, with sandy hair and pale green eyes, and he was the skinniest man she'd ever met, all angles and bones. "This is right neighborly of you," he said. His lips curved in greeting, but Hallie noticed that the smile did not reach his eyes. "Have you offered the missus tea?" he asked Etta.

"Oh, I've brought a picnic lunch," said Hallie. "I thought we could celebrate having neighbors."

There wasn't room inside, so Hallie suggested they eat out under one of the plane trees, which would shade them. No breeze cooled the hot noon.

Chad offered to lend his plow, saying that one of his men could bring it over on the wagon. Will Colton said again, "That's right neighborly of you." He offered no information about his past, agreed that this was the land of the future, and had Etta run in and out of the house a dozen times on trivial errands.

"How do you get water?" asked Chad. Colton had not built near a stream.

"Didn't think about that when I built," admitted the thin man. "We have to go about a quarter mile beyond them trees."

"Dig a well," Chad suggested.

Will was silent.

Jamie slept most of the time, and that's where Etta's gaze

stayed. Every time Will told her to fetch something from the house, she jumped and ran. She hardly said a word once the men had joined them. Hallie didn't understand why, but she found herself feeling sorry for the woman.

As they were returning home, she said so to Chad. He hadn't noticed anything, just thought the woman quiet, but "that man doesn't know the first thing about farming. I bet he doesn't even know how to dig a well." Nevertheless, the next morning he sent Brian Daugherty, a convict he particularly trusted, down the valley with the plow. "Stay and help him, if you must," Chad told him.

Brian was gone overnight. When he returned late the next afternoon, he told Chad he'd done the plowing. He had a strange look on his face.

"Something happened over there," Chad said to Hallie and Archie at dinner that night. "I don't know what."

It would be many years before they found out what.

Twelve

Two months after Hallie's daughter Alexandra was born, the Macquaries gave the grandest ball the country had yet seen.

Chad and Archie visited Parramatta several times a month and went all the way into Sydney twice a month. Ostensibly, they went to sell the vegetables that grew to such prodigious sizes. They also took with them eggs that Hallie had gathered and butter she'd churned—all more than they needed. It was the only time Chad ever made a show of money. He and Archie usually returned bleary-eyed from drinking and gambling, but invariably in good spirits. Chad always laid the coins from the garden enterprise on the table, and it never ceased to impress Hallie. She suspected she never saw any money he had received from gambling. He always brought a keg of rum, too, as a reward for the convicts. He saved it to give to them on Saturday night, and the next day most of them weren't good for much.

When he and Archie went to Parramatta, they stayed overnight. The alternate weekends, when they were Sydney-bound, they were gone three and sometimes four nights. Hallie understood the two men enjoyed the social aspect of the trip too. And she envied them. Aside from the trips she took once a month to visit Etta, she saw no visitors. Not that she'd have time for them anyhow, she told herself. It was just that she desperately missed having a friend, someone with whom to share . . . anything.

Aside from missing female friendship, Hallie was immensely content, if always tired. She thought that soon she might ask Chad for a woman convict to do the kitchen work and the laundry. But she kept putting it off, realizing she should be grateful for the life she had. And she was.

She compared her life with Etta's. Her neighbor had become pregnant shortly after Hallie and Chad had visited them, but though she had wanted a baby so desperately, her eyes had a haunted look. Even when her swelling belly burst the seams of her one dress, she wore it. Yet Hallie felt sure that the poverty in which she lived was not the reason for the look in Etta's eyes. Etta smiled when she saw Hallie and the babies coming, but each time it seemed as though she might burst into tears.

It wasn't that Hallie received what she needed in friendship from Etta, but she felt duty-bound to visit this woman who always looked so unfortunate. Will had twice more asked Chad if he might borrow Brian for a day's work. Brian got such a strange look in his eyes when asked to go over to the Coltons that Chad said, "Brian, if you'd rather not go, I'll send someone else."

Brian hesitated for a minute, scratching his cheek, and then said, "It's all the same to me." But, after Brian returned, somehow Chad felt it wasn't.

Brian was a strapping dark man—his hair and eyes were as black as a Spaniard's, but his complexion was pale as the Irishman he was. He had been caught fishing in a river that belonged to a duke, a crime punishable by deportation. He had to leave behind a wife and four-month-old son when he'd been shipped overseas. Much liked by the other convicts, he never fought and always worked well. On Saturday nights he, alone among the convicts, never drank himself into oblivion, but elected himself arbiter of the peace among the men. His overriding passion was to send for his family and make a new life here. He had had another master before Chad and had run away, which had added a year to his sentence. But Chad had known the previous master, and swore that Brian had reason to run. Rather than have Brian deported to Norfolk Island, Chad had requested him—and he'd never had reason to regret his decision. Brian was someone whom Chad thought would succeed when emancipated. Both Brian and Archie would have served their time in another two years. Chad thought each had already learned enough about farming and had enough perseverance to do well on their own.

After Brian's last visit to the Coltons, Chad approached him. "Brian, I've a proposition for you." He had remembered the strange look in Brian's eyes. "In almost two years you'll be a free man." Brian nodded. "I'll pay passage for your wife and son. If you send for them now, they'll be here when you're free, when you can petition for land. But you must promise to stay on here, for wages, for at least two more years."

Brian stared at Chad, who lit a cigar, adding, "I'll even have the men help build you a house, wherever your land will be."

"Don't send me back to the Coltons," Brian said. "Never again."

Chad doted on Alexandra, named for his grandmother, but it was Jamie who continued to be the center of his attention. Before the boy began to walk at ten months of age, Chad had bought him a pony and held him in his arms as they walked the pony around. Sometimes, in the evening, he would sit with a child in each arm—they were scarcely a year apart—and tell stories as though they could understand. Hallie had never known a man to be so demonstrative with his children.

How generous he was, she thought, looking at him holding their children. How kind. Maybe Dada would have been as generous if he hadn't always been straddling the edge of poverty, so tired from fourteen-hour days in the mine.

Hallie had written to Brian's wife for him, for the convict could barely read or write. However, she did not know that Chad had a reason for making his offer to Brian—until she learned of it on the night of the ball. . . .

Hallie had never been to a dance before, or to a fancy dress dinner. Chad told her of the invitation when he returned from a trip to Sydney, grinning and holding up a gown he'd bought her. It was breathtakingly beautiful, a rich sapphire-blue satin. With it came a pair of matching slippers. He smiled as he opened another box—new undergarments. "And a matching ribbon for your hair. Maybe this one doesn't match your eyes, it *is* darker, but it's close enough."

Chad and Hallie, along with a dozen others, had been invited to dine at Government House before the ball. "Why," asked Hallie, "with all the important people in the city, are we singled out?"

She had just put the babies to bed for the night. Chad

125

walked over and put his arms around her. "We're very important people."

She turned to ask him why, and he kissed her. "Your husband," he said, holding her waist, "is one of the richest landowners in this country."

"Richest? We're rich?"

Chad laughed. "Do you know how many sheep and horses we own?"

"Hundreds of sheep, I suppose." She wasn't interested in sheep while she fingered the luxuriousness of the satin in her hands.

"Yes, well, hundreds." He realized then that she wasn't really listening. "Hallie, each time I go in to Sydney, the governor begs me to accept some assignment or other. I don't want to. I want to farm, I want more land. I want to chart the course of history in this country."

"How are you going to do that?" She held the dress up in front of her and tried to see her image in the window.

"I've told you a dozen times—sheep."

Hallie pirouetted in front of the window, her fingers caressing the smooth fabric against her. She wondered what more they needed. It seemed to her they had everything anyone could want.

Chad smiled as he observed her pleasure, but he was intent on what he was saying. "Sheep are going to build you the biggest house in the land, Hallie—a baronial estate. They're going to get us a town named after us, and our names in history books a hundred years from now. They're going to assure Jamie of the chance to do anything he wants, and permit Alexandra to marry anyone she wants. They're going to allow you"—he kissed her—"to do anything you want."

"I am doing what I want." She put her arms around him.

"Let's do it in bed," he suggested.

With Chad by her side at the ball, it did not dawn on Hallie to feel uncomfortable, even though she was not exactly sure what to do. For the nights they were in Sydney, they were staying in one of the bedrooms at the governor's Sydney residence. Servants came and went without making a sound. Hallie had a bath drawn for her and, for the first time, sat in a cast-iron bathtub with hot water. She found it the most luxurious experience she'd ever had. A maid kept pouring warm water over her when her bath cooled.

The rooms were wallpapered, which was also a first for her. Deep mauve wallcoverings, accentuated by a beautiful oriental rug, harmonized with the forest-green sofas. The furniture was massive. There was a teak desk in the governor's office that was larger than Chad and Hallie's dining table. Straight-backed mahogany chairs gleamed with polish. Large framed paintings—several of English scenes and one of a sailing ship—hung on the walls. There were heavy pewter candlesticks everywhere; Hallie was unaccustomed to such brilliance.

If they were as rich as Chad said they were, why didn't they have some of these things? she wondered. When she asked him, he answered, "Someday. Right now our fortune is all in land and sheep." Then he looked at her. "Would you like all this, Hallie?"

"Oh, it seems very nice," she admitted, "but what would I do with myself if I had servants to wait on me and nothing to do but take baths and pour tea?"

Chad smiled. "We're going to have so many children that you will never have a problem with time."

"How many are we going to have?" Hallie liked being a mother.

"How about a dozen?" He took the ribbon from her hand. "Let me tie it in your hair," he murmured, and leaned down to kiss her neck. She was surprised. He seldom kissed her unless it was going to lead to lovemaking. "Now, let's go down. I have no doubt that you are the most beautiful woman in Sydney tonight."

What actually impressed Hallie the most as they entered the enormous dining room was the hanging chandelier in the center. She thought a hundred candles must be flickering there. The massive table easily seated twenty, with mahogany chairs whose seats and backs were covered in rose brocade.

A large bowl of flowers in the center of the table lent a heavenly fragrance to the evening. Hallie had not seen blooms like them before. How charming, she thought. I'll have to try that. But she didn't know what to do with all the forks and spoons. Everyone else seemed to take them for granted; certainly no one else was glancing around with a bewildered air. So she watched Chad carefully and did what he did. He had already told her, when she'd expressed her nervousness about the affair, that "if you use the wrong silver, they're not going to ostracize you. This isn't England. Besides, you're my wife. Whatever you do is all right. At least"—he'd smiled at her—"it's all right with me."

The dinner table conversation ranged far and wide. After nearly three years in country isolation, Hallie found herself so stimulated by all the talk that she was scarcely aware of the roast beef and Yorkshire pudding, of the baby limas that melted in her mouth, the browned potatoes and preserved peaches.

"England still thinks of us as primarily a penal colony," commented one guest, wiping his mouth with a linen napkin. "Odd, eh? Life is more exciting than anyplace I can imagine. Perhaps not as comfortable . . ."

"Well," one of the women said, "I do miss some of the niceties. The theater, for instance. More shops. Musicals."

"They're coming," someone else chimed in. "I do think the world considers us a dull backwater, but we'll show them!"

Hallie was pleased and surprised at the attention paid to her. She had thought no one would bother to converse with her, that it would be Chad to whom people aimed the conversation. But both the women and the men included her in their conversation. To any questions about life on the farm, she gave direct answers. "Fancy helping to deliver lambs!" cried a young, pretty woman across the table from her.

Her name was Susan Langley, Hallie learned, and she appeared to be Hallie's age, perhaps a year or two older. Her dark brown hair had auburn tints, and her eyes were green with brown-gold flecks. Every move she made was fluid. Her apricot dress reflected her complexion, high color in her cheeks and skin as smooth as Hallie's new dress. She laughed frequently, and the sound reminded Hallie of tinkling bells. She was an extraordinarily charming woman.

Her husband, Harry, was the banker in Parramatta. He didn't look like any banker she imagined, but then she'd never known one. He had rusty hair and a great bushy mustache and was almost as tall as Chad, though he lacked her husband's grace. Although he tended to portliness, he was a natty dresser. His manner was, in general, congenial. But thus far in the evening, he and Hallie had exchanged no more than a polite "good evening."

"Chad, here, claims he's going to bring us into the larger world of commerce and put us on the map," the governor announced, bringing Hallie back to the conversation in progress. "He's going back to England next month to get orders for our fleece. He's going to stop in Spain and get some of their merinos to interbreed with the Afrikaans sheep. The French merinos, you know, are no longer available, what with the war and all."

Hallie stared. She heard the conversation, but it made no sense to her. And then Chad's eyes met hers.

As if from a great distance, she heard someone ask, "Why will crossbreeding merinos and Afrikaans put us on the map?"

"I'll let Chad answer that," said the governor.

"Merinos aren't used to our heat or our grasses," Chad explained. Hallie had seen his eyes flick to her, but she didn't hear the rest of his answer. All she had heard was, "He's going back to England next month."

She stared across the table at her husband, saw his mouth moving and his hands gesturing, but she heard nothing. All noise had ceased for her. *"Chad's going back to England next month."*

Was she going with him? Were she and the children accompanying him? Who would run the farm? Was she staying here? What would she do?

Chad had not asked her.

Chad had not told her.

"Chad is going back to England next month."

She didn't remember the rest of the dinner or much about the ball. She recalled seeing smiling faces and nodding heads, so she knew she must have participated in the conversation. When they were alone in their room, with the world closed out, Chad took off his handsome coat and said, "If I'd known you didn't know how to dance, I could have taught you."

"You're going to England."

129

He walked over to her and put a finger under her chin. Smiling down at her, he said, "I'm sorry you heard it so publicly. I'd wanted to wait until closer to the time to tell you."

She brushed his hand away and turned from him. He said nothing but continued undressing. When he slid between the sheets and saw her still standing by the window, he blew out the candle. After a while she undressed and lay down. When he reached out for her, she lay still and said, "No." She had never said no to him in their three years of marriage, not for any reason.

He started to say something, then thought better of it. He lay on his back, his hands pillowed under his head, for a long time. The room crackled with silence. Then: "Hallie, I'm doing this for us."

Silence.

After several minutes she said, her voice pinched, "You could have told me."

Again, silence.

They had not brought the wagon into Sydney for the governor's ball. This time they had ridden their horses, just the two of them, over the open fields. Hallie had loved the experience. Now, going home, they had no chance to talk over a leisurely journey. She could enjoy neither the scenery nor the sense of freedom riding a horse usually gave her. Instead she pushed Princess. Her anger and hurt had become palpable, her clenched jaw a reflection of the numbness she felt by what she considered treachery on Chad's part. The whole world had known before she had.

It wasn't until the next day, at breakfast, that she said, "How long are you going to be gone?"

Chad reached out and put his hand over hers. She pulled hers away. "Hallie, it's something I must do. It will lead to our fortune. I want to show the woolen mills our fleeces, I want to bargain with them, I want to get long-range orders from them, ones on which we can live for years to come. I don't trust anyone else to deal with them. I know just what I want to do."

"Why haven't you ever talked this over with me? Why didn't you ask how I felt? Why didn't you, at the very least, tell me yourself?" She tried not to cry, but her voice cracked.

"Because I knew how you'd feel."

"Isn't that all the more reason to talk it over with me?"

Chad was silent for several long moments before he spoke. "Hallie, your feelings would not stop me from going. Were *you* not my wife, I might have some hesitation, but you are. You and Archie, between you, can handle anything."

She doubted that.

"I've talked with Archie," Chad said. "He's due to be emancipated next year, but he'll stay on here as foreman, with pay, at least until I return. And, hopefully, for much longer than that. He knows everything about running this place. I have faith in the two of you together."

So, she thought, he had talked it over with Archie, but not with her.

Chad continued, "When the present convicts are emancipated, you and Archie can choose others. I shan't be gone that long."

"How long?"

"Well, it takes a year and a half just to come and go, of course. I'd guess two years."

Two years! Tears of frustration welled in her eyes. "That's not what I came so far for, Chad—to be left alone. That's not why I came to New South Wales."

Chad reached across the table and held her hand in his. This time she did not draw away. "I *should* have told you." He tried to look at her, but she avoided his eyes. "I see I was wrong in not doing so. Perhaps I feared an argument. . . ."

Now her eyes flashed at his. "When have we ever argued? I simply would have liked some consideration. I thought we were in this together, that it's *our* life, that we've been a team, a family. And now you . . ."

His hand tightened around hers and he said, "Hallie, this trip may mean the end of our being known mainly as a penal colony. Don't you see, it's not only a chance for you and me, but for this land? A chance for greatness. A chance for a different breed of people to emigrate here, people who want and know how to work hard, people—"

131

"I don't care about them. . . ." And now the tears did come. "How can I possibly manage here for two years?"

Chad's voice held no emotion. "But you will. And very well. Remember, you have Archie. And by offering to bring Brian's family over, I have assured you of his loyalty." Ah, so that was the reason, she told herself. He had been planning this all along.

"There are a few things I should teach you before I leave. One is how to shoot. Come," he said, rising. "We'll have a lesson now."

Hallie was terrified of guns. But she had a keen eye and a steady arm. Despite the forlornness she felt, pride swept through her when Chad told her she'd be an excellent hunter before he left.

He spent evenings teaching her what he thought she'd need to know. He explained that if Archie took the vegetables into town, there should be enough money to support them in the growing months. Archie knew how to shear, and though it had become too large an operation for one man alone, Chad was going to teach Brian before he left and thought the two of them could handle it. He trusted both men. Archie would handle the convicts, so Hallie didn't have to worry about that. There'd never been any trouble, and Chad couldn't envision any. The men were treated fairly and knew they had a good deal here.

What he admitted he could hardly bear was the thought of absenting himself from Jamie and little Alexandra. "Jamie will be three when I return, scarcely able to remember me. I wish I could take him with me."

Hallie listened carefully to all Chad's advice, but she could hardly talk to him. Her anger became an implacable part of her. It did not dissipate; she carried it around within her. The night before he left, after he had spent the evening with the children, he reached out for her. "Hallie, my wife . . . I shall sorely miss you." He leaned over on the pillow and kissed her neck. "What will I do for two years without your beautiful body, without sleeping next to you and touching you, without making love to you? I shall miss that as much as anything, I think."

I'll show you what you'll miss, she thought. And they made love with a vengeance, with a fury that gave vent to Hallie's anger, with a passion that was meant to last for two years. And when she saw the streaks her nails had made on Chad's shoulder, she understood the blood on Beth's arm a little better. Her fierce intensity took them to regions they had not approached before. When it was over, they lay spent, unable to speak, breathing heavily.

After a while Chad said, "If ever I doubt God, coupling with you shows me the wonder of His ways. I shall never forget you, Hallie. Nor tonight."

Their lovemaking that night impregnated her again. Hallie did not discover it until a month after Chad had left. And then she felt despair. How was she to cope with his absence and pregnancy at the same time?

Thirteen

With Hallie's third pregnancy, there was no morning sickness. In fact, she didn't suspect a thing until she realized she was two weeks past due. Maybe it gets easier each time, she thought. Sometimes she thought Chad only had to look at her and she got with child.

She knew that was what he wanted—children for this dynasty of his dreams. That's what was important about her— mothering his children. She suspected he had sent for her because women of his own class would never have worked as hard as she did, would never have been willing to go months on end without company, without new clothes and society. Hallie asked for none of that, and Chad had known it before he had sent for her. When he bought her a new dress, she was delighted. She would wash the windows until she could see her reflection in them, and then pirouette in front of them. The night of the governor's ball there had been a mirror in their bedroom, and she had stood for long moments in front of it, gazing at herself.

"I wonder if this is really me?" she'd asked herself. Chad had told her she was beautiful. If she were the same person underneath, but not as pretty, would he still desire her? she wondered. Was it only the part of her that the world saw that drew him to her? Or was it mainly that she was the avenue to his dynasty that aroused him?

She knew she had pleased him. He'd never criticized her. He had invariably been patient with her, but didn't ordinarily share himself with her. He would tell her *after* he bought more sheep, or *after* he had bred a horse, or *after* he had sold it. He had not even told her that he planned to leave her for two years.

She missed him—missed his warmth next to her in the night, missed hearing him telling stories to the children. She missed his laughter, and his boundless energy, missed the security his presence offered.

Still, she was angry at his leaving her. Damn him, she thought. Am I to see no one for two years? With Chad gone, there was no one to talk with, no one to share with. And, she realized with a sinking heart, no one to help her when it came time to have her baby. How could she possibly manage alone?

Though she had no morning sickness with this pregnancy, she did tire easily. She wanted naps in the afternoons, but Jamie did not permit it. Alexandra, at four months, spent most of her life sleeping. On the other hand, Jamie at sixteen months was a handful. He was curious about everything. Just as Hallie thought she had him asleep for the afternoon, he was up and running around the room. He did sleep twelve hours at night, but he didn't close his eyes during the daytime. And, come night, Alexandra awakened, fussing to be fed and changed. Thus Hallie was continually exhausted. And pretty soon she would have to oversee the garden; it was nearly time for planting.

She didn't know what the convicts did all day. That was Archie's concern, and Chad had told her to rely on him. He knew what needed to be done and did it. Right before he left, Chad had surprised Archie with his ticket of leave. The governor had granted it when Chad explained that as overseer Archie would command the convicts' respect more easily if he were free. Now Archie worked for pay.

He ate dinner with Hallie, though he didn't talk much. Every night she asked, mainly for conversation, what he had done during the day and what was going to be done the next day. With two thousand acres, work was spread out. And in another two months it would be lambing time. When Hallie asked, Archie said he anticipated close to two thousand lambs. Dear God in heaven, thought Hallie. How will I care for all the little ones that will need bottle feeding? But she was too busy with each day to worry about how to handle whatever would develop in a couple of months.

One day after Chad had been gone three months, she had just finished cleaning up after lunch and was contemplating taking Jamie for a pony ride when she heard the beating of a horse's hooves. Walking to the front door, she gazed down the valley and saw a dark speck racing toward her, the horse flying as though on wings.

135

She walked several paces from the house and shaded her eyes so that she would not have to stare straight into the noonday sun. As horse and rider approached, she saw it was a woman. It's Etta, she thought. Something's wrong.

But it was not Etta.

Crouched low on the saddle was the dirtiest woman Hallie had ever seen, her hair matted flat against her head, her eyes wild with hysteria. She slid off the horse and, barely able to stand, whispered, "Oh, thank the Lord . . . Hallie."

Hallie stared for a second, then took a step forward. "My heavens, Beth," she said, astonished, and walked toward the girl she had not seen in three years. Beth collapsed into her arms. The horse stood there, frothing at the mouth.

Hallie dragged Beth into the house, settling her on a chair and going into the kitchen to find leftovers and some hot tea. When she returned, Beth's eyes were closed and her breathing was more regular. Jamie stood staring at her, thumb in mouth.

As Hallie approached her, Beth jumped. Staring around wildly, as though she expected danger at any moment, she gulped the food that Hallie offered her. When she finished, she said in a voice of jagged desperation, "Hide me, Hallie. Let me stay here, please." And again, "Hide me."

Hallie knelt beside the young woman and put her arms around her. "Of course, Beth," she said. "You're safe here with me." She pulled the girl up and kept hold of her hand. "Come on. Jamie and I were just going bathing in the creek. You'll feel refreshed when you're clean." She took soap with them, and when they were all splashing around in the cool water, she herself washed Beth's hair. Jamie continued to stare at her. When Beth reached out for him, he eluded her and laughed. It would have been a charming sight, had Beth not been so constantly and overwhelmingly terrified.

When they were back in the house, Hallie lit a fire. She wrapped a blanket around Beth and then said, "Tell me."

Beth shook her head. She would not talk.

"Is somebody after you?"

"I . . . don't know."

"Did anyone follow you?"

Again Beth shook her head. And when Hallie pressed

her further, she just kept on shaking her head. No, she wouldn't—or couldn't—tell Hallie anything.

"Well, no matter," Hallie soothed. "I'll take care of you." She went to fetch the fretting Alexandra, who was waking from her nap. When she reentered the drawing room, Beth took one glance at the baby and reached out for her.

"Oh, please . . . let me hold her!" Hallie handed her daughter to Beth, who clutched the baby to her breast and rocked her back and forth. She did not release Alexandra—except to let Hallie nurse her—until it was time for bed. She said nothing else.

When Archie came in to supper, Beth jumped, frightened. Hallie put a hand on her arm and said, "He won't hurt you. This is Archie, our foreman." In a soothing voice she made simple, first-name introductions, having forgotten Beth's last name. Beth didn't speak even then. She continued to hold Alexandra, who made gurgling sounds of contentment, but she would not look at Archie.

When it was time for bed, Hallie said, "You can sleep with me." And as Beth fell asleep, clutching Hallie's hand, Hallie wondered, how did she find me? And what put such terrible fear into her?

At last, another woman, she thought. A friend.

Though Beth did not speak again for several days, Hallie felt joy at her coming. She talked to her as though she received answers. Jamie wound himself around her legs, and when Beth wasn't holding his sister, he climbed onto her lap and fell asleep.

At the end of a week, when Hallie awoke, Beth was gone. She flew up, wondering what had happened. But Beth had not gone away; she was in the kitchen preparing breakfast.

"What luxury," Hallie said, smiling. And when she started to clean up, Beth shook her head vigorously. She would do it instead.

So Hallie fed the children and, putting Alexandra back in her cradle, took Jamie with her to find Archie, who was just assigning the last of the men their duties for the day. "Where's Brian?" she asked.

When she was together with the two men, Hallie said, "I swear you to the strictest secrecy. No one—and I mean no one, not the other convicts, not visitors—no one else is to know this. The woman who arrived last week was a convict. She came over on the ship with me; that's where I met her. Whether or not she is still a convict, I don't know. If so, she has escaped and I am harboring a fugitive. If she is no longer a convict, she has had some experience which has so frightened her that she cannot talk about it. You are to tell no one she's here. I imagine some of the men will see her, but if anyone asks, she is an old friend from England who has come to join me. When you hear anyone coming to visit, warn us. She must be hidden."

Archie and Brian looked at each other and nodded.

When Hallie returned to the house, she found the bed made and Beth sweeping out the house. Looking at her, Hallie realized her friend was skin and bones, even though she swept with great energy.

When Alexandra murmured, Beth ran to fetch her and sat holding her as the morning sun flooded in the windows. Hallie smiled. No one could have too much love, she thought. Holding the baby seemed to calm Beth enormously. Jamie reached for his mother's hand.

"We'll go do the washing," Hallie said to her son, leaving her friend and daughter in contentment.

When the clothes were drying out on the grass, Hallie found that Beth had found apples and was baking pies. The wonderful aroma drifted to her even outside. Hallie scarcely had time to bake sweets anymore.

Hallie fell into the habit of telling Beth everything. That Beth did not respond verbally in no way indicated she was not listening. Hallie told her of Chad, what he was like, what his dreams were, how kind he was, what he had given her, how much land they had. She told Beth of how she had been called to deliver the Coltons' baby. Now she could appreciate what Chad had gone through when he'd delivered theirs. Far better they should have sent for Chad, she said, for he had more experience than she did.

Will Colton had embarrassed Hallie while she'd worked with Etta to deliver her baby, which had turned out to be a girl, Mary Ann. He'd wanted to watch the entire process, and had practically hung over her shoulder. It was not so much that he'd been worried about Etta, Hallie thought when she looked back on the experience, or that he'd wanted to hold the little girl when it was born; it was as if he'd been hypnotized by the process. Hallie laughed, telling

138

Beth that before she had set out to be midwife, she'd had to ask Chad what needed to be done. "There seems to be nothing Chad can't do," she said.

Nevertheless, her affection was still tempered by her anger at his leaving her and the children alone. But if he were here, she thought, as the days rolled into weeks, where would Beth sleep? Would he even permit her to stay at all? She found that with Beth, she was freed from many of the household chores. Gradually the younger woman took over more and more responsibility. She baked their bread and, after weeks of asking Hallie what she would like for dinner, finally began to plan the meals herself.

When she talked, it was usually to ask a question. Hallie soon became used to Beth's silence and even felt comfortable with it. She found herself chattering as though involved in a dialogue.

This time, when the lambing started, Hallie was free to participate. She had always found it exciting. Without Chad, Archie needed her help. He showed her how to pull recalcitrant lambs from their mothers, how to wriggle her hand into the animal's vagina and straighten cramped legs, how to help slide out the lamb once its head appeared and its body was slow in following. She loved seeing the newborn lambs shake themselves, and couldn't help being amused by their attempts to stand immediately, watching them totter and fall and try again. Observing a lamb blindly try to find its mother's teat within minutes of its birth made Hallie aware of the miracle of creation.

Although Beth refused to leave the house for any reason, except for the kitchen or the privy, Hallie forcibly pulled her to the barn one afternoon. "You *have* to see this, Beth. You love babies so much. Come see a lamb being born." Beth finally let herself be led to the barn, looking around fearfully. Hallie always said it was because the ewe wanted to show off for Beth, that it gave birth to triplets, one of them as black as Newcastle's coal. One of them would have to be bottle fed.

Now that Beth was here, taking care of the lambs was not as formidable as Hallie had feared. She and Beth spent hours of every day bottle feeding lambs whose mothers had died giving birth or had rejected them for unknown reasons. Since there were just so many hours in a day, however, they had to let some of the weaker lambs die. Hallie tired of the repetitiousness and wondered if her time couldn't be put to better use. But Archie, along with Brian and the other convicts, had everything else under control.

With Beth around to take over household chores and help in feeding the lambs and care for all of Alexandra's needs except nursing, Hallie's energy crept back. By her fourth month of pregnancy she felt better. She had begun to forgive Chad. She did not find life much harder without him, and discovered she enjoyed making the few decisions required of her. Between Beth and Archie, her life flowed smoothly. And she enjoyed Beth's company. Jamie loved Beth and never seemed to find her silence unsettling. He, like Hallie, chattered away to her all day.

Jamie gathered eggs with Hallie, and now that she wasn't as tired, she could make a game of it. She left Alexandra with Beth when she paid her monthly visit to the Coltons, but took Jamie with her, riding over on Princess, though she knew Chad would have disapproved. He didn't think she should ride while pregnant, any more than he thought she should be bedded.

The small garden Will Colton had planted was beginning to bear. He had bought another pig and had a litter of piglets. Scrawny chickens scurried around, and Etta had trouble finding even two eggs a day from them. On a previous visit Hallie had brought her some receiving blankets and knitted a sweater for the infant Mary Ann, but aside from these, the child had almost no clothes. Hallie had also brought Etta a dress she said she no longer could fit into, for Etta's one dress—the one whose seams had burst with pregnancy and age—was still her only dress. The bodice was a bit too large for her, but Etta wore it every day and used her old one as a pillow for the baby, placing it in an old crate she used as a bassinet.

"Why don't you get a convict to help you?" Hallie asked Will. "You could get a lot more done. Convicts can be a big source of cheap labor."

"Don't own enough land to qualify," he replied, whittling down a branch to a sharp end.

"Would you like me to speak to the governor about it?" Hallie asked. "I know him. I could tell him you need help."

"Won't do no good," he answered. "Got no place to bed him down or no way to feed him."

"But if you have help, you can get more done and be able to do those things. What about it, Will? I'll be glad to ask him."

Will shrugged his shoulders.

Hallie's first opportunity to get to town to see the governor came when Archie announced they were beginning to accumulate more produce than they could use. They had planted close to two acres, not counting the wheat and maize. It was time, he said, to begin weekly trips into Parramatta.

"I'll come with you," Hallie said. The thought of staying in town overnight, visiting with people, even buying supplies, delighted her. And she could talk to the governor about the Coltons.

Archie objected. "Not a job for a woman."

"I'll let you do the bargaining, if that's what bothers you. But I'm coming."

"Chad wouldn't approve."

"Chad's not here," Hallie replied stoutly, emboldened by the independence she'd experienced in the five months since her husband had left.

She had such a wonderful time in Parramatta that she bubbled for days afterward. She took some of the money and bought fabric so that Beth could make herself a couple of dresses, and enough for one for herself. She bought shoes for Beth, and undergarments. She had never in her life bought presents for anyone before, and she loved the feeling. Although Beth never left the house, Hallie also bought her a sunbonnet. Someday, she thought, Beth will come out.

Chad had instructed her to pay Archie each month, but Hallie—in an expansive mood at the heady experience of spending money for the first time in her life—bought him a pipe and tobacco also. She had heard him say once that he thought nothing quite as satisfying as a good pipeful of tobacco. Archie bought a keg of rum for the convicts. They still had money left over, even after Hallie bought flour and ground corn at the mill, as well as tea and candles and other staples they needed.

Governor and Mrs. Macquarie were not in Parramatta,

141

so Hallie couldn't petition him about a convict for Will Colton. Instead she stayed overnight with the Langleys, whom she'd met at the governor's ball.

Hallie became fonder of the Langleys each time she saw them. She felt she had found friends. She loved the joy they constantly milked from life. Harry had served in the army in Bombay before being assigned to Sydney. Two years ago he had resigned his commission to open Parramatta's first bank, privately owned and financed by friends of his from England and India.

Susan, the daughter of an army officer who had been stationed in India most of her life, had been born and met Harry there. Though she had been to England four or five times, she never considered it home. In India she had been used to servants and a social life far more active than New South Wales offered. Here she did have a woman convict servant, but no liveried carriages, no afternoon teas, no brightly lit salons, no fancy dress balls, none of the pomp and circumstance she had been accustomed to in India. It had taken her time to become acclimated to the new land, but her love for her husband—always obvious in the way she looked at him—made her determined to adjust with grace.

Harry was jollier than most bankers, of that Hallie was sure. He teased his wife, but always with kindness. She invariably laughed and tickled him under the chin at such times.

They made a great fuss over Hallie, and Susan told her that she would really enjoy visiting their farm, seeing what life was like "way out in the country." Hallie invited them to come anytime, and then could have bitten her tongue. No one must see Beth.

She gave Archie the pipe and tobacco on the ride back. He didn't know how to accept a gift and stammered. Hallie waved away his thanks, pleasured with the feeling of being able to give. She wondered if Chad would have scolded her because of her spending spree, but she doubted it. He was a very generous man. And it was such a wonderful feeling, one she hoped to experience often in the future.

I'd probably never have known it, she thought, had Chad not chosen to go away and leave me on my own.

142

Fourteen

"Will you find me a wife?" Archie asked Hallie.

Startled, Hallie looked at him. "Find you a wife?"

He nodded, keeping his eyes averted.

She brushed her hair back from her forehead and smiled. "Why can't you find one yourself?"

A razor-sharp sound zapped through the air as he cut yet another tail off a lamb. Running away from them, the lamb let out a little bleat. Hallie grabbed for the next one and held its head as Archie approached the other end. No matter how many times she participated in this gruesome chore, Hallie never got used to it.

"I don't know nuthin' about courtin'," Archie answered after a silence of several moments. "You could tell which would be a good woman for me. I been long enough without one. Figure only a woman convict, or an emancipated one, would even consider me. Now that I'm free, I thought you might not mind if I built a little house over the hill. She could be of help to you, you know. Cook for the convicts, maybe, or anything else you want doin'."

Hallie didn't know if she was up to this responsibility. "What if I choose someone you don't like?"

"I ain't choosy," he said, snipping another tail. "Just don't have her look like a horse, and see if she's got a bad temper. I don't want someone yelling at me all the time." He grabbed the lamb Hallie was holding. "I'm thirty. It's time to have some young'uns."

"I'll see what I can do," Hallie promised.

The opportunity occurred sooner than either anticipated. The following week they took their usual trip into Parramatta, where Hallie heard from the ferryboat captain that a ship was due to land in Sydney that day. It had been sighted below Botany Bay two days ago.

"Why don't you go ahead with the selling," she suggested to Archie. "Here's a list of things to buy. I'll catch the ferry up the river to Sydney and be back tomorrow, maybe with a bride."

"Oh, God . . ." Archie turned pale.

"You better get a shave," advised Hallie. "And buy yourself some new clothes with some of the money. A whole new outfit, you understand."

"I d-don't have no p-place for her to live," he stammered.

"Maybe we don't have to rush into it," Hallie mused. "If I find someone, you two could get to know each other. Maybe she could work at the Langleys' or with someone else here in town for a while, and you could have time to build a little house and time to court. How about that? Then if either of you changes your mind, you won't be beholden to each other." And, she thought with relief, you won't spend the rest of your lives blaming me.

At the same time, she could also petition the governor for a convict for the Coltons.

At seven months Hallie looked very pregnant. She felt beautiful, radiant, not self-conscious at all. She could not walk with grace, but she did move with serenity. She reminded herself to instruct Beth in the ways of midwifery now that Chad was gone.

Susan Langley voiced disappointment that Hallie was going on to Sydney instead of staying to visit. "You could come with me," Hallie ventured. "It will be fun."

Susan didn't think she could, but Harry, her husband, disagreed. "Of course you can," he said. "I'll go, too. Just put on your bonnet and we'll catch the next ferry."

"I want to talk to Governor Macquarie about help for some farmers out near us, as well as see about a wife for Archie," Hallie told them.

Harry laughed. "Hallie, you do beat all. We'll make a party of it. Two ladies in your condition"—Susan was pregnant also, but not as noticeably as Hallie—"need a man around. Sydney's not safe for any woman alone."

Though they'd been married for nearly five years, this was the first time the Langleys were expecting a child, and they were filled with a happiness that Hallie found contagious. She loved being with them, and for their part, Harry and Susan always acted as though Hallie's visits were the most pleasant diversions they could imagine. Whenever she arrived, they put aside whatever else they might be doing and invited other people to dinner. Hallie didn't know how Susan always accomplished it so quickly. In this way she gradually came to know the Parramatta community.

Although she had not directly passed any new settlers on her way to town, Hallie learned that the valley was attracting newcomers. Aside from the Coltons, whom no one in Parramatta had met, seven other families had moved to land grants within the last six months. Hallie decided that after her baby arrived, she would take time and ride around to visit each of them.

It would be late afternoon, nearly dusk, before Hallie and the Langleys arrived in Sydney. The ferry ride was beautiful. Hardly a breeze stirred, and the river reflected the blue sky, mirroring trees by the water's edge. Ducks swam in every cove, pretty little beaches dotted the shoreline, and soft green hills rose in the distance. Hallie loved watching the massive-winged pelicans zoom in for a landing, amazed at the gracefulness of such awkward-looking birds. Silvered fish jumped in the water, and the pelicans would swoop down and try to catch them with their long bills. The way they gathered, in groups, staring at the ferry as it glided through the water, delighted her.

Gradually the river broadened and islands dotted the harbor, which widened considerably in irregular patterns. Fingers of water jutted out of sight around curves. Hallie, who hadn't seen water other than their creek and the slow-moving idyllic river since she'd landed, was captivated with the meeting of sky, trees, and water, with the inlets that looked as large as lakes.

"Aren't we lucky," she said, "to have come to such a beautiful country."

It was the first time she'd really relaxed in a long while. For once there was nothing she *had* to do except enjoy herself and chat with the Langleys and the other passengers—and she gave herself up to that willingly. However, among other bits of local gossip, Hallie heard one piece of unsettling news: apparently it was becoming unsafe to take the road between Parramatta and Sydney once twilight set in. Convict gangs were at work to improve the road, and they often waylaid travelers, carousing with women convicts who

145

were being sent to the factory. There were tales of drunken orgies, robberies and beatings, human depravity. Hallie made a mental note to alert Archie to the disturbing turn of affairs.

When at last they arrived in Sydney, it was nearly dark, and the sails of the ship sighted two days ago off Botany Bay were visible around Bennelong Point. But passengers would not be allowed to disembark until tomorrow, when it was light.

Harry registered them at the hotel, insisting on adjoining rooms so that he could act the part of Hallie's protector. They dined and laughed far into the night. The Langleys' tales of India seemed terribly exotic to Hallie, and they were equally interested in Hallie's life. Susan could hardly imagine a woman living far out in the country, coping with life alone. Hallie enjoyed the socializing that living in a town offered, but coming in several times a month and meeting so many new people satisfied her enough. She felt disloyal when she thought that if Chad were here, she would not be making these trips to town, and certainly never into Sydney.

In the morning, though, when they strolled down to the landing quay, they discovered rowdy crowds, almost all men. The male prisoners were landing first, chains being thrust around their legs as they were shackled together about ten at a time. They had not shaved, changed clothing, or washed since they had left England. They were thin, and though they glanced around them in hope or fear, their eyes looked dead. Officers of the New South Wales Corps prodded them with sticks and marched them away, single file.

The women prisoners were another matter. Those interested in hiring them were rowed out to the ship, and Harry insisted on accompanying Hallie. What Hallie saw shocked her. The men who had come to bargain for their services poked the women, leered at them, even tried to fondle them. Some of the women didn't mind, and themselves made lcwd signals. But the majority shrank from the men, frightened at the horde that suddenly surrounded them. Some of the women were sickly; some had children in their arms or clinging to their burlap skirts. They were as dirty and unkempt as the men.

Hallie was immediately attracted to one young woman who slapped a man who touched her. Her oval face was appealing. She was young, a year or so younger than Hallie herself, it appeared. Her light brown hair was grimy, but her spirit was alive.

When a man crossed a jailer's palm with silver, the jailer wrote down the name of the prisoner he'd chosen and to whom she was now assigned. "It's slavery," said Hallie.

"It's prostitution," Harry replied, grimacing.

Hallie saw a man of medium height, a nice enough looking man, eyeing the girl who had attracted her. She decided she didn't want him to take the young woman. Walking over to her, Hallie introduced herself. She asked the young woman of what crime she had been accused. "I stole a loaf of bread and a pair of stockings," the woman replied. Though her attitude was belligerent, Hallie liked the fire in her eyes, the softness of the voice that nevertheless yielded not an inch.

The man who had been staring at the girl tried to elbow Hallie out of the way, but she stood her ground. She was the only free woman on board. Surely not all these men plan to misuse the women, Hallie thought. Some of them must be looking for maids for their wives or nannies for their children. Still, it was obvious that the vast majority wanted a woman—any woman. To clean house, to cook, to do the work demanded of her, to bed with. Hallie imagined that after the woman's term was up, the man would throw her out and find a new one. Maybe he'd do that long before the term was up—find someone new. And the discarded woman would then have no future. Certainly no one would want to marry a woman who had been so used.

Hallie was horrified. Women who were not spoken for would be assigned to the Women's Factory in Parramatta, there to weave all day long and, she remembered, be punished—if necessary—with the treadmill. She wondered which was the worse fate—what these men were offering or the prison.

"Come with me," Hallie said to the young woman when she could make herself be heard over the rowdiness of the crowd. She hadn't told the woman that marriage was being offered. She wanted to speak up for her before some man did, wanted to get off this ship. She was very glad Harry had insisted on coming.

She turned to him now and opened her purse. "How much money, do you think, for . . ." She smiled at the young woman. "What is your name?"

"Molly. Molly Conway."

"I've no idea," Harry answered. "I'll pay whatever is necessary, and you can reimburse me. Can't be more than five shillings, the cost of an acre of land."

When they were back on shore, Hallie untied the rope that had been thrust around Molly's waist. Molly had said nothing, but Hallie was pleased to observe that she regarded her new surroundings with interest. Hallie asked Susan and Harry to find clothing for her new charge while she went to petition the governor for a convict for the Coltons.

She had to wait nearly two hours to see Governor Macquarie. Mrs. Macquarie was out, so Hallie strolled through the gardens that the governor's wife was developing with such tender loving care. When at last she was shown into his impressive office, the governor rose from behind his big desk and put his hands around hers.

"Hallie, my dear, I wish I had known you were here! I'm sorry you had to wait."

He agreed at once to assign a convict to the Coltons, even though Will did not own enough land to merit one.

"With help, I think he can make something of the land," Hallie said. "The convict will have to build himself a sod hut, I suspect. But that seems far preferable to being on a chain gang."

"I'd think so, too," agreed the governor. He scribbled something on a piece of paper and said, "Have Colton deliver this to the superintendent of convicts in Parramatta."

Mrs. Macquarie arrived before her meeting with the governor ended, and she made Hallie promise to come and spend a few days after the baby was born. She and the governor both remarked that Hallie was a plucky young woman to be running a large farming operation all alone. Hallie did not explain that it really was Archie who ran it.

After his wife excused herself, Macquarie personally escorted her to the front door. "If I can be of any help, let me know," he said.

"We may need more land," Hallie said, surprised to hear herself speak so boldly. "We had almost two thousand lambs this spring and pretty soon will run out of grazing land."

"If only all settlers had the ambition you and Chad have. You are the future of this country, my dear."

Hallie smiled. Up until now she had thought that her only role was as the bearer of Chad's children.

"How much more land do you think you'll need?" asked the governor.

Hallie thought about it. She had no real sense of how much an acre of land amounted to. She had heard Archie say that pretty soon there'd be too many sheep for the pastureland they had. "Oh, several thousand more acres, I think," she replied at last. "I hear it's selling for five shillings an acre." She had no idea how much they could afford. The only money she ever saw was from the sale of vegetables, and that went for their living and for seed, although she had managed to acquire a few luxuries.

"Do you need any more prisoners?"

"I don't know," she said. "The ones I have seem to be enough. I'll let you know if I need more. Most of them are due for emancipation within the next two years, so I'll have to replace them." She did not realize she had begun to use "I" instead of "we."

"It might be a good idea," the governor mused, "to train some before the older ones leave. You have room for them, don't you?"

Hallie smiled. "I'd like you to see for yourself—after the baby is born. I'm very proud of what we're doing there."

Actually, she thought, *I'm* not really doing much of anything.

Hallie met the Langleys and Molly at the ferry dock. Susan had taken Molly to the hotel and given her a bath, and the young woman was much improved, and really quite attractive.

Hallie explained the situation to her. The Langleys had agreed to keep Molly with them for a month, so that she and Archie could meet each other weekly and see if they were compatible. Hallie thought Archie would be most pleased.

149

Hat in hand, Archie was waiting for them when they docked at Parramatta. It was not quite dark, and Hallie was glad they'd had time to clean Molly. Archie stood awkwardly, looking as though he were unaccustomed to his new clothes. Hallie had never noticed before how funny-looking he was. Probably because he had never really been a stranger to her, he had always looked reliable and solid. But seeing him now in new clothing came as something of a shock. His red-ginger hair was sparse and looked ridiculous slicked down. Usually it stood straight up and frizzed out in all directions. He was not as thin as he used to be, but he was still lean and muscular. His nose was a hook and his thin lips looked tucked in. Unfortunately, his reliability was not reflected on his face, or in his eyes, which were small and an almost yellowish hazel. Well, she thought, Molly may not be impressed, but it's a far better fate than she could have hoped for.

Archie didn't know what to say. Molly eyed him levelly.

The Langleys housed Molly with their maid, in the loft over the barn where they kept their carriage. In the morning they kindly invited Archie and Molly to join them for breakfast. The would-be husband and wife looked each other over warily, but only when they didn't think the other was looking. Neither smiled during the meal.

Hallie said that she and Archie would be back the following week. Once they had started for home, later in the day than was usual for them, Hallie asked, "Well?"

Archie didn't answer immediately, his hands on the reins. Then he took time to light his pipe, tamp it, and spit over the side before he said, "She's nice-looking."

"Yes," agreed Hallie, "but what else?"

Archie looked at her, his eyebrows raised questioningly. "What—what else? She don't seem ill-tempered."

What else matters? thought Hallie. Is that how Chad felt? How all men felt? If a woman was nice-looking and not ill-tempered, that was enough? It made her feel insignificant, and she didn't like it.

Susan had had a lunch packed for them, and when they came to the billabong that Hallie remembered with such fondness, she suggested they stop and eat under one of the giant gum trees. There were the black swans. If only Archie hadn't been along with her, she'd bathe. It was hot and she hadn't bathed since she'd left the farm. The water looked so inviting.

"Archie," she called out to him. He was sitting on the wagon, not under the tree with her. He never knew how to act when alone with a woman, even though they shared supper every night. "I'm going to bathe here. Move the wagon, will you, beyond those trees?"

"No need for that," he answered. "I'll just take a walk. Call when you're finished." She knew he'd respect her privacy.

Slipping out of her clothes, she waded into the billabong, its clear water covering her body with a coolness that refreshed her. She paddled around, humming to herself. She was pleased with Molly and thought Archie was, too. Would Molly like him? She supposed it didn't matter too much. Better to be married to Archie than used and discarded as most of her shipmates would be. Better than working in the Women's Factory.

Slowly she inched her way toward the reeds, where the swans' red beaks glittered. But the closer she came, the farther they retreated. Not wanting to disturb them, she turned to go back to shore. She wanted to get home before dark.

Standing by her clothes, legs spread wide apart, hands on hips, was a man. "Well there, sister," he said. "Fancy meeting you here."

She did not like the tone of his voice, nor his looks. His ragged clothes were torn and filthy. He was nearly bald, but had an immense bushy beard. His small eyes glittered. He stooped down and took her clothing in his hands. "Ain't this purty." He held up one of her undergarments and laughed. "Want it?" he asked. "Gotta come get it."

Hallie's heart was in her throat. "Put that down and get out of here while I dress." She didn't feel nearly the authority her voice evidenced.

"Oh, no mealy-mouthed one here." The big man smiled. "I like 'em that way, with fire in them. This is gonna be fun." When he grinned, Hallie could see that a front tooth was missing. His clothing suggested he was a convict.

"I'll report you," she threatened.

He laughed loudly. "Lady, by then it'll be too late."

Too late? Too late for what? she wondered, her mind

151

trying desperately to function. "Please . . ." She changed tactics. "Please go away while I get dressed."

"You gonna come out or shall I come in?" He held her clothing up high and ripped it slowly, the sound searing through the air like chalk on a blackboard. He flung the two pieces to either side of him and began to wade into the water.

Hallie screamed.

From behind the man Archie flew out of the woods. In one fluid motion he jumped on the big man's back, shouting, "Get to the wagon, quick!"

Hallie didn't even hesitate at the thought that Archie would see her naked. While the stranger tried to shake Archie from his back, Hallie ran from the water and up the slight embankment to the wagon. The gun, she thought wildly. The gun Chad told us to always carry under the front seat. She heard the men scuffling but did not turn around. Had Archie remembered to put it there? She could not run quickly in her seventh month of pregnancy. Damn, she thought. Please God, help me. Let me run faster.

She reached the wagon and tried to lift the seat. It wouldn't budge. Oh, why hadn't she watched how Archie had done this? Adrenaline pumping through her, she tore off the seat and ripped the boards from the floorboard. And there it was, the pistol. Hearing steps behind her, she reached for it, but a strong hand clasped around her wrist.

"Well, well, a baby in that purty body . . ." The man was breathing hard. "Never done it with a woman like this before." His hand tightened around her wrist with such a viselike grip that the gun dropped. Gathering all her strength, Hallie turned and pushed him back. His long arm reached out, and the knife in his hand, bloodstained, raked open the length of her arm. She felt no pain but saw the red blood ooze down her body. It was warm. She kicked, aiming for his groin. With a scream he clutched himself, which gave Hallie time to climb down and try to reach for the gun. Pain made his face ugly. "Bitch!" he hissed. "You'll pay for this."

He threw her to the ground so hard that a sharp pain shot through her head. Flinging himself on top of her, he pinned her and slapped her across the face. Her teeth bit into her lips, and she tasted blood. His knees kept her from moving as he knelt directly on top of her. The pain was immense, yet Hallie made no noise. With one hand he yanked at his pants, freeing himself. Hallie felt him against her as his knees pressed her legs apart. Her hand still groped for the gun, but he was too busy trying to enter her to notice. One of his hands held a wrist in a scissor grip; the other was busy trying to force himself into her. With all the strength she could muster, Hallie wrenched her arm from under his weight, clutching the gun at last. She aimed it directly at him. He laughed again, a big wide openmouthed laugh as he began to enter her.

She pulled the trigger.

His eyes looked surprised for the fraction of a second left to him before his whole face exploded in a hundred fragments of skin, bones, and blood, all over Hallie. The force of the explosion sent his body, headless, reeling backward. Hallie looked at what was left of him and vomited, shaking uncontrollably all the while. It was a minute before she wondered where Archie was. Doubled over with stomach cramps so severe she could hardly walk, she half crawled to the billabong.

Archie, stabbed in at least half a dozen places, lay face-down in the water.

Fifteen

Hallie recalled looking down at her naked body, watching the blood—still dripping down her arm—begin to coagulate. Her clothes had been ripped to shreds. Turning Archie over, seeing his eyes blank and empty, she began to cry. At the same time, she inched the trousers from his new suit down his legs and pulled them onto herself.

Doubled over with stomach cramps, shaking so convulsively that her fingers scarcely functioned, she unbuttoned his bloody shirt. As she did so, she kept patting his face, sobbing "Archie" over and over, as though calling him would bring him back to life. Tears fell onto his shirt as she wrested it first from one arm and then the other.

Somehow, dragging him by the feet, slowly—pausing for breath—she got him to the wagon. Pushing, pulling, crying so hard she could scarcely see through her tears, she managed to maneuver him on top of the wagon and left him sprawled, palms stretched up, legs spraddled. He looked disjointed.

"I can't help it," she wailed as though he could hear. "I can't move you any farther. I'm sorry. . . ." She patted his face again.

His shirt did her little good, for the knife wounds left blood-ringed holes throughout and it flapped around her. She took his belt and wrapped it around her arm, stemming the flow of blood. Then she climbed up on the wagon, feeling a sticky warmth running down her leg.

My baby, she thought. I'm losing it, too. She couldn't force herself to look at the headless body lying faceup. There was no recognizable sign of his head anyplace, except an ear hanging from a limb of a gum tree, trapped in the hanging bark.

Hunched over, Hallie said, "Giddyap," and wondered how it was that the sun still shone.

Of the trip home she had no memory—until the house

154

came into view and she recalled wondering if she'd make it. She remembered Beth came out from the kitchen, wiping her floured hands on an apron, and Hallie heard herself say, "Archie's dead," before dizziness overcame her and the world faded away.

Later, Beth told her she'd been afraid Hallie was dying, too. She'd toppled from the wagon into the dirt, and Beth had rushed out to her. "I dragged you into the house and got you onto the bed," she said. "I had to cut the shirt off you, it was so caked solid with dried blood. Oh, Hallie, I don't know what I'd do if you died!"

Although Brian had never ridden into Sydney—had never been alone anywhere in New South Wales, in fact, except for the visits to the Coltons—Beth sent him for a doctor. "I didn't know what I'd do about facing someone, what I'd do about being seen here," she told Hallie. "I didn't let myself think about it. You were all I cared about."

Hallie knew it would take two days for a doctor to arrive, if one could be found who was willing to come so far. In the meantime, her arm became infected, her fever rose, and she began to hallucinate. Late the second day she lost all consciousness and remained blacked out for three days. The doctor arrived at midnight of the second day.

She lost her baby. She nearly lost her arm. She almost lost her life. All this Hallie heard about later. What she remembered was opening her eyes and thinking she was back on the *Charleston*. She recalled so clearly seeing the dark eyes staring at her with such infinite compassion. She remembered saying, "Am I dead?" and the kind face saying, "No, you're going to be fine."

The same sympathetic face now watched her intently, the same warm hand encircled hers. She closed her eyes. It couldn't be. But she felt pressure on her hand, felt it being squeezed. "Hallie," said the gentle voice.

When she opened her eyes again, he smiled. She stared at him, then looked beyond him, at the wall. It was not the *Charleston*. It was her bedroom at the farm.

"Tristan . . . ?"

He was clean-shaven now, though there was a three-day growth of stubble. The beard he wore when Hallie had known him was gone. His clothes, which he had not changed since Brian had called for him, were rumpled, but

155

they fit beautifully, and Hallie could tell they were expensive.

"How in the world—"

"Later," he said, still holding her hand. "I'll tell you about me later." Instead, he told her how Brian had found him, and how the minute he'd heard her name, he'd run for his horse. He had been watching over her for the last three days.

"Archie?"

"Dead."

Yes, she knew that. She remembered him lying facedown in the billabong. How had she ever lifted him, in her condition?

Her hand flew to her stomach. "My baby?"

"Gone, Hallie." Tristan held her hand tightly. He told her that Archie had already been buried, that the remains of the escaped convict, headless, had been found. "He tried to rape you, didn't he?"

Hallie nodded, remembering that laugh through which she had shot, the bullet that had splattered him all over her. She began to cry, and Tristan gathered her in his arms.

Archie . . . her baby . . .

Gone.

Whenever she moved, pain seared down her left arm, which was covered in bandages. "It became infected," Tristan explained, stroking her tenderly. "You'll always have scars."

Hallie gave him a wan smile. "Every time I see you, you save my life."

Tristan lowered her to the pillow, then let her sleep. She dreamed of the face with the big round O of laughter splintering in front of her, fragments of his skin stuck to hers. When she awoke Tristan was still there, though this time he was clean-shaven and Beth stood beside him.

"The children?" Hallie asked.

"They're fine." Beth looked tired. "Don't worry about them."

"Not if you're taking care of them, I won't."

When Beth turned to leave, Tristan said to Hallie, "I know. I know about her. Your secret is safe with me."

Hallie never doubted that. "Tell me about you," she said.

"Let me get some tea into you first," he said. "You need

156

nourishment." The tea tray sat on the table beside the bed. He poured a cupful and held it to her lips. The warmth comforted her. "Drink it all," he ordered.

"Now," she said when she had finished it, "tell me all about you."

"I spent next to no time as a prisoner," he began. She noticed his ruddy complexion, reflective of time spent outdoors, noticed his slightly stooped shoulders, his long slender hands. "As soon as it was discovered that I'm a doctor, I was assigned to the Women's Factory in Parramatta. But I was scarcely there two months when the governor sent for me. There are just two other doctors in the whole of New South Wales. He offered to pardon me completely if I'd promise not to leave the country. He gave me a house in Sydney, which is also my office. I treat prisoners, too—that was part of the understanding. But he set me up in private practice, obtaining the medical tools and medicines needed. I go to Parramatta twice a month—more, if necessary. I have a horse. Actually," he smiled at Hallie, "life is not much different than it would have been for me in Canada, except the clientele is more varied."

Hallie felt weak and empty, as though she might never again have energy. Yet the sight of Tristan calmed her. She watched him as he sat next to her, holding her hand, looking into her eyes. "So you've been a free man these past years?"

Tristan nodded. He did not tell her that he had become one of Sydney's more respected citizens in a very short time. He did not say that he served Sydney's society, delivered Sydney's babies, that he was one of the main forces behind the big hospital now being built. He did not tell her he dined at Sydney's finest tables.

She noticed the calm set of his mouth, noticed that his eyes were no longer filled with pain and anger. "You look like you've made peace," she said. "Are you happy?"

"Happy? Ah, that elusive state of being. Happy, when I know this entire continent is my prison? Not that I have an immediate desire to leave, but knowing I can't . . ." His eyes took on a faraway look, and unconsciously he shifted on his chair, drawing away from her. "On the other hand, I have never found a land more conducive to . . . hope. Here is a chance for civilization to start over again, rectify its mistakes, learn from the past, and in the most equable climate and scenery imaginable."

Hallie, not realizing he hadn't answered her question, said, "Oh, the hours I could have saved worrying about you. I had terrible visions of how you must be faring in a damp cold cell."

"I'm not sure there are many of those around here," Tristan said. "In Van Diemen's Land, yes. There are still some on Norfolk. But as long as cheap labor is needed . . ."

Hallie searched for any question to keep the conversation going, to keep him with her, yet it was difficult to summon the energy needed to actively participate. "What about the chain gangs I see along the roads?" she asked finally.

"They're hard-core, Hallie. Ones whom no one dares to hire, ones whom the government won't even consider allowing any modicum of freedom. Even I, an ex-prisoner, have little sympathy for them. They're incorrigible."

They looked at each other for a long time. Then she reached out for his hand. "Oh, Tristan, I've wondered about you so often," she said softly.

"I've known where you were," he said.

"And you never came to visit? Never came to see me?" He didn't answer.

"Are you . . . married?" she asked.

His eyes left hers. "No." Letting go of her hand, he stood up. "I'll tell Beth to prepare you something to eat." He walked out of the room.

Hallie closed her eyes. Did all this have to happen for me to see him again? she wondered. Did Archie have to die, did I have to lose my baby, did I have to kill a man? She heard herself sigh.

When Tristan came back, he was carrying Alexandra. "What a beautiful child you have here," he said. "But then I've always known any children of yours would be beautiful." He placed the little girl on the bed next to her mother. Alexandra cooed and wouldn't let go of Tristan's thumb.

Beth followed with a bowl of soup, Jamie trailing behind her, holding onto her skirt. He stared with large round eyes at Hallie. She held her good arm out for him and he ran to her, asking, "You not go 'way?"

"No, darling. I'm getting better, and I'll be up and run-

158

ning around with you before you know it. I hope you're taking good care of Beth."

Looking at Tristan, Jamie smiled shyly.

"We'll go for a pony ride next week," Hallie promised.

Beth drew Alexandra into her arms so that Hallie could sip the soup. She could feel energy seeping back into her—not much, but some. "Who's doing the work?" she asked Beth. "What are we going to do without Archie?"

"The ones who were building fences are doing that, and the ones who were clearing trees out of a field . . . I mean, I really don't know what any of them are doing." There was a note of apology in Beth's voice. It was a long speech for her.

Hallie handed her the empty bowl. "No, of course you don't." I don't either, she thought. Archie took care of it all.

When Beth and the children left, Tristan said, "Your husband has gone to England?"

Hallie nodded. "He's probably not even there yet. He left—what month is this?"

"April. Late April."

"Yes, I should know that. The rains are ending. He left in August."

"My God, Hallie!" he cried. "How could he leave you alone?"

Why was Tristan shouting at her? It wasn't her fault. "He went on business, to get orders for our fleece."

"He should never have left you alone for all this time." Tristan paced around the room. "God almighty, it will be another . . . How long before he comes home?"

"Maybe a year and a half, perhaps not quite." Hallie felt like crying. "It depends on how long it takes him to get the orders he wants."

Tristan stopped and pointed a finger at her. "He should have taken you. He had no right to leave a woman alone with two children . . . None of this would have happened if he had been here."

Tears filled Hallie's eyes. "I know."

Tristan came to her, reaching for her hand again. He sat down beside her. "What will you do now? The dead man was your forcman?"

Hallie nodded. "He took care of everything. He had worked with Chad for several years before I arrived."

As if he could barely contain his frustration, Tristan stood again and resumed pacing. "My God, what will you do? What needs to be done?"

"I don't know," she said, feeling desperately weak. "I don't know what needs to be done." And she began to cry.

Tristan handed her his handkerchief and let her sob, stroking her arm as she blew her nose and wiped the tears away. Then he said, his voice gentle, "I wish I knew how to help. Do you have much livestock? Much land?"

"A couple of thousand sheep, and as many acres."

"Thousands?" he echoed, surprised.

"Well, shearing's over for the year."

"How many convicts in your employ?"

"Eight, aside from Archie."

"What kind of work do they do?"

Hallie began to sob again. "Oh, Tristan, I can't think of it now! I don't know what I'll do. . . . I don't know what needs to be done."

Quickly he sat on the bed beside her. "I'm sorry. Look, try to sleep, Hallie. I have to return to Sydney; I have patients there. Now that I know you'll be all right . . . But I'll come back in a week or ten days. I don't want you up and doing anything. Let Beth wait on you. You've had a very bad experience, both physically and . . . otherwise. You can wait to think what to do when your energy returns."

Hallie reached over for his hand. "I'm glad I found you again."

Tristan looked down at her, an indecipherable look in his eyes. "My dear Hallie . . . you are going to have to be so strong."

He would not leave me, she thought. Not if he were my husband.

Beth managed all the household chores while Hallie convalesced. She cooked for the convicts, yet she never looked up to meet their eyes when any came to the house. She told one to gather eggs, another to see that the garden was weeded, another to make sure the horses were fed, another

160

to milk the cow—all chores which they were used to but had declined to do once they had no leadership. Except for Brian. Quietly he roamed the land, seeing where fences needed mending, changing pastures when one was overgrazed.

Ten days after the accident, when Hallie forced herself out of bed for several hours, she sent for Brian. "You have to help me now," she told him.

"I don't know what to do," he replied, startled.

"Neither do I, so we'll have to learn together."

"Well, I think it's time to let the rams out of the far pasture." Brian half smiled. "I think it's that time of year."

I don't know when it's time to breed anything or how to go about it, thought Hallie. She assumed Chad had talked with Archie about which stallions to breed to which mares, but she had no idea of either how or when. She knew that in order for the cow to continue giving milk, it had to be bred. But when?

Thank goodness shearing time is over, she thought. At least I don't have to think of that until next spring, another six months or so. She didn't allow herself to wonder how in the world they'd do it. She'd face that when the time came.

Damn Chad, she thought. How could he do this to me? And then she found herself smiling for the first time since the attack. If it weren't for him, she'd be in Newcastle, with no challenges at all.

She walked out to the kitchen for a cup of tea; there was always a kettle boiling for just such a purpose. Beth was up to her elbows in flour, preparing to bake biscuits. She went ahead with chores now without consulting Hallie, and for this Hallie was grateful. She put an arm around Beth's shoulders. "Thank God you came," she said, echoing her thoughts.

Pleased, Beth smiled. "Maybe He does work in mysterious ways."

It took Hallie longer to recuperate than she could believe. Even after three weeks she tired easily and could find few reserves of energy. But when Tristan visited again, saying, "I can stay overnight but no longer," he pronounced

161

himself pleased with her progress. He sat and listened to Hallie ponder what needed to be done and question how to do it.

"Let me talk to the men," he suggested at last. "I'm in a unique position."

Hallie didn't know what he'd told them, but when he returned he said, "Let me ask Governor Macquarie, on your behalf, for Brian's ticket of leave. The other convicts will work more willingly for a free man than for one of them. I'm pretty sure I can talk the governor into it. Tell Brian you'll make him foreman. I'm rather impressed with the man."

It was wonderful to be able to lean on Tristan. "Chad paid for Brian to send for his family when he's free, which would be in about another eighteen months," Hallie told him. "I quite like him, too. I'll talk with him. I think he'd do anything for Chad."

The light faded from Tristan's eyes.

At that moment Jamie came running into the room. At two years old, he had begun to test his freedom daily. Beth was too busy to discipline him, and besides, she adored him and let him do anything he wanted. She never chastised him. Now he raced around the room, stomping his feet as loudly as possible. "Whoa," he called at nothing, and reared up, snorting like a horse.

Tristan turned to him. "How about a ride?" he asked. Smiling at Hallie, he asked, "Have you any idea where the limits of your property are?"

"I could show you, but I can't tell you," she said.

"Well, I don't want you on a horse yet, so Jamie and will just take a ride. Would you like that, young man?"

Jamie jumped up and down. Alexandra was far too young to play with, and the boy's considerable energy was limitless.

Hallie watched them ride off on Tristan's roan gelding. It was a nice horse, but she could tell it couldn't compare with the ones they were raising. They rode down the valley, next to the creek, and she gazed after them even when they'd mounted a hill and disappeared beyond the crest.

She had not allowed herself to think of her feelings at

seeing Tristan again. Now they surfaced as she watched him carry her son out of sight.

There was no doubt that she was happy to see him again. But the love she had felt for him had been effectively sublimated. The years of not seeing him, of living with Chad—a man who was kindness itself, who carried her along on his dream, who challenged her, who gave life and delight to her body, who fathered her children—had dimmed Tristan's memory. With Chad, she was so busy living that she had had no time to mourn Tristan, even though his memory had resurfaced now and then—a memory, she told herself, that had no part of reality.

Now, here he was, a tangible part of her life, having saved it again. Here he was, helping her to sort out her life, giving her needed advice, trying to show her paths to which even he did not know the routes. If he had no answers to what needed to be done on such a large farming operation, he was, at least, a willing listener. A shoulder to lean on. A rock.

Life is certainly strange, she thought.

She would not let herself think more of Tristan. Better just to accept his presence. There was too much that needed thinking about to wonder about him.

That night he slept in the barn, taking over Archie's stall. "I like the smell of it," he said.

Afterward it became his habit to ride out to the farm now and then and stay overnight. After the initial horseback ride with him, Jamie would begin to jump up and down as soon as he saw Tristan coming, and would not let Tristan alone until he was taken on another ride. Whatever Tristan asked of him, Jamie was eager to do. Whereas Hallie sometimes had to raise her voice to command her son's attention or stop him from some forbidden act, all Tristan had to do was speak in a quiet voice and Jamie listened. Also, Tristan was the only man at whom Beth would look directly. He had earned her trust years ago.

"If I could do it without alerting the authorities, it might be nice to find a husband for Beth," Hallie said during one of his visits.

Tristan looked at her strangely. "Don't. Not everyone is destined for marriage. Beth has wounds, I suspect, that need healing. I don't think she much likes men."

163

"She likes you."

Tristan shrugged. "Leave her alone with her emotions. She's doing just what she needs to be doing. You are her salvation."

"As you are mine?"

"Well," he smiled, "I admit I've saved your life a couple of times, but your incorporating Beth as part of your life is saving her sanity. I imagine you're the first person she's ever loved."

Hallie gave him a questioning look. "Funny, using the word 'love.' I've always saved it for family," she mused. "But you're right; Beth is part of my family now. I longed so for another woman—a friend. And now"—her eyes were soft as she gazed at him—"I have found two friends."

Tristan acknowledged the compliment with a nod. "Someday Beth will tell you what happened to her—but in her own time. I don't think it's that she doesn't trust you. I think she has effectively blocked it out of her memory. Her present life began when she rode out here. . . . What are you going to do about protecting her? What if someone comes out before she can hide?"

"I've wondered about that," Hallie admitted. "I keep telling myself no one rides out here. But she did. And you did. And someday Governor and Mrs. Macquarie have promised to come out, and the Langleys."

Tristan was startled. "The Langleys? Harry and Susan are friends of yours?"

She nodded. "Dear ones. I stay with them whenever I go into Parramatta. How do you know them?"

"I'm going to deliver Susan's baby," he said, and his face grew soft. "Susan Langley's one of the loveliest women I know." Hallie felt a pang of jealousy. "And Harry's the best friend I have here. I dine with them often."

Suddenly Hallie gasped. "Molly! I forgot all about Molly! Oh, Tristan, Archie was going to marry Molly, who's living with the Langleys. I must get word to them that Archie is dead. What will be done about Molly?"

Tristan had no immediate answer to that question. He sat and watched as Hallie began pacing, her arms closed over her breasts.

"Molly was put into my custody until she could marry

164

Archie. The Langleys must have wondered what happened to me. I'm surprised they haven't tried to find out."

"Everyone in Parramatta, and Sydney too for that matter, knows," said Tristan, reaching for his cup of tea. "I've let it be known that you were in no shape for visitors."

From across the room, Hallie tried to face him. "Well, we must do something about Molly. It was terrible, just terrible the way women were treated on that ship. A woman alone, especially a convict, is doomed before she even leaves the ship. Some of the men were making the women lift their skirts, some were pinching them . . . Oh, Tristan"—she rushed over to him and knelt beside him—"they were doing revolting things—so insulting. I don't want Molly to go through that."

"No one should have to go through that," Tristan agreed, his eyes tender as he looked at her. "Perhaps you ought to talk with her. Maybe I could bring her out with me next time I come. Could you use another hand here?"

"Of course. And we always have enough food." Hallie was suddenly reminded that she hadn't been in town to sell vegetables for weeks. What would they do for money? Well, if she didn't go into town, she couldn't spend any, either. "How long before I can ride again?"

"I would say whenever you feel up to it. Are you afraid to ride into town?"

"No," she said, her voice taking on a hard edge. "I'll just always carry a gun close to me. Even having a man with me didn't help last time." Her eyes narrowed. "But, I'm not going to let myself be intimidated. From now on, I'll be prepared."

Tristan gazed at her with undisguised admiration. "But we digressed. What are you going to do to protect Beth?"

"I haven't given it much thought. Up till now she's hidden when we've heard anyone coming. Under the bed, once." Hallie grinned.

"I suggest the loft in the barn," Tristan said. "Or, if Molly comes, build them a little house of their own. You needn't show anyone to the servants' quarters, certainly."

Hallie's hand flew to her throat. Not to have the warm comfort of Beth next to her in bed at night? Not to have Beth bounce out of bed, before she herself was wide awake, when Alexandra cried? Not have Beth sit listening to her chatter about the day's events before the fire at night, or out on the lawn on summer evenings?

"I'll think about it," she said. But she wasn't sure she would.

Sixteen

Harry Langley rode out alone one day. Beth saw him coming and ran to tell Hallie, who was out in the shearing shed. "Someone's coming," she cried. "The children are in the house." And with that she left for the barn and climbed up to the loft. As it turned out, Tristan's suggestion proved sound: Beth would have no trouble hiding behind so much hay.

Hallie's hands were greasy from fingering thousands of fleeces. Wiping her hands on her apron as she walked toward the house, she smiled at Jamie, who was playing a game under the overhanging gum tree and saying "No" to Alexandra in a loud voice. He did not seem unduly concerned about whatever his sister was doing, however.

Hallie recognized Harry as he neared the house and slowed his horse to a trot. "Harry, it's good to see you!" She called out as he dismounted. "Where's Susan? Nothing's wrong, I hope?"

"Not at all," he replied, smiling. "But she's too near term to risk the rough ride, even in a carriage. We've been wanting to come see you ever since the accident, but Tris said you weren't up to company. Finally, we decided to wait no longer. We want to see for ourselves how you are. And I'm the official envoy."

He held Hallie's hands in his and grinned. "I'm ready for a cuppa," he said. Then he knelt down next to the children. "And these are those amazing children you tell us are so perfect."

Hallie laughed. "Well, I realize I have no others with whom to compare them." She left him to bring a cup of tea from the kitchen. When she returned he said admiringly, "So this is where you hide. It's certainly beautiful. Not at all as I'd pictured it. Don't know what I expected, but not this." Without waiting for an invitation, he walked through the front door, balancing his cup of tea nicely in one hand. "Who designed this, Hallie? It's really lovely."

Since she'd arrived, Chad had added a curving sofa, not all that comfortable to relax on, but elegant, thought Hallie, familiar with no furniture other than that she'd grown up with. The drawing room was unusually attractive. She guessed she'd grown to take it for granted, but she recalled how thrilled she had been upon first seeing it.

"Someday, Chad says, he's going to add on and we'll have more rooms. But this is just fine for now. I'm happy here."

Lowering himself to the couch, Harry sipped his tea. "What are you going to do now?"

She understood he meant now that there was no Archie. "I'm not sure, Harry. Find out what needs to be done, first of all."

He was silent for a minute. "How're you going to do that?"

Hallie shrugged and her hands flew in the air in a hopeless gesture. "I don't know."

"What can I do to help?"

She laughed. "Oh, Harry, you don't know the first thing about farming!"

"That's true." He set the cup on a table. "But I'm fairly good at organizing. I thought together we might put our minds to what needs doing." He pulled a sheaf of papers from his pocket. "Now, first of all, let's pick your brain. We'll make a list of all the things you know or you think need doing here in the course of a year."

Hallie reflected for a moment. "There are so many things, Harry. I don't even know them all."

"Well," he suggested, "let me jot down ones you know about. Not in any order. For instance, shearing . . ."

"Yes," Hallie frowned, "certainly. And after that, lambing, cutting their tails off. Castrating the young ones. Culling old or infirm sheep to sell for mutton. Changing the pastures so that overgrazing doesn't permanently damage the land. Worming the sheep. Inspecting their feet for foot rot. Selling the fleeces."

She tried to recall conversations between Chad and Archie, when they'd plan chores for the following day. "Deciding which stallion to breed to which mares. Keeping track of dates so preparation can be made for the foals' births. When to sell them."

She stopped. It sounded like more than she could face.

"Go on," urged Harry, his pencil poised in midair. He pulled a pair of spectacles out of his pocket and perched them on the end of his nose.

"Breeding the cow. That's easy." She laughed. "There's just one bull. But when is a question."

She stood up and walked over to one of the open, long French windows. Leaning against the sill, she gazed out over the fields and murmured, "Deciding what to plant where. Preparing the fields, buying seed, planting, weeding, hoeing, thinning—"

"My heavens, Hallie!" Harry had stopped writing and was staring at her, his mouth half open. "You can't do all this."

She went on enumerating, as if she hadn't heard him, and after a moment he rushed with his writing to keep up with her list. "Cutting hay. Storing it. Planting wheat. Harvesting. Butchering chickens, pigs"—her voice was slow, as though she were wrenching each thought from some distant memory—"gelding a male calf, if there is one. Keeping the buildings in good repair."

She turned to him, and her laugh had a hopelessness about it. "That's not even accounting for any emergencies." Dear God in heaven, she thought. Harry's right. I can't do all this alone.

After they had made the list, Harry handed it to Hallie. "Look this over and see what you think you can do. I'll come out again soon and we'll talk over your plans. Maybe I can be of help in that way. I certainly don't have the answer to any of these questions. Talk with your men. You can't do it all, certainly."

"Maybe I can," she said. "But I'll need more help than I have now. What about Molly—do you want to bring her out with you next time?"

Harry nodded. "If that's what you want. But it's not more women you need. It's men who know how to do what needs to be done."

"Let me talk with my men now. Give me a week or so to make some plans. See if you can find a convict for the

Coltons." Hallie found the piece of paper the governor had given her, permitting Will Colton one convict.

"Trouble is," said Harry, "those settlers who start out with just the land grants and don't have enough money or labor to develop them almost invariably fail. It takes an inordinate amount of hard work to become self-supporting, and it takes money beyond that to make the ventures profitable. I don't hold out much hope for your Coltons."

"That may be true, but a convict will give him a chance. He can't do it all by himself."

"I'd think you own enough land that you could request more help."

"Yes, the governor offered me more. But let me think. Let me decide what I want to do and ask Brian how they've done it in the past."

"You're plucky, Hallie." Harry reached for his hat and got up to go. If he rode hard, he'd get back to Parramatta just at dusk. "I'll give Susan your love. She's not due for a month, so I'll get back out in a week or two and we can talk again. Make a list of things that I may be able to help you with."

Hallie took hold of his hands. "Harry, your friendship is one of the nicest things in the world."

"Include Susan in that, too." He smiled down at her. "Her heart's here today even if she isn't."

She watched him ride off, into a fast gallop by the time he hit the hills, thinking how lucky she was to have such friends. Then she went out to the barn to fetch Beth, and told her about bringing Molly out. Beth's eyes darkened.

"I'm going to tell her you came out from England, that you're free. She won't know anyone to talk to, so your secret will be safe."

"Where'll she sleep?"

Hallie heard the jealousy in Beth's voice. "I've thought about that. What I'll do is add a room to the house. Then, when company does come, you won't have to run to the barn. I'll just say it's the servants' quarters, and no one will need to see it. We'll build it behind my bedroom, with a door between the rooms. Molly can stay in there. And," she added, "you can, too, when Chad comes home." It seemed as though Chad had been gone forever, not just nine months.

In fact, his ship should just about be reaching Southampton. Hallie closed her eyes and tried to remember what he looked like. His image was hazy, undefined, a series of dots shimmering in front of her. Well, she thought, at least I'm no longer damning him for leaving me. But she did sigh, with the weight of all that was now thrust upon her. And there he was, on the other side of the world, not knowing Archie was dead, not knowing that the future of his precious dynasty lay in the hands of someone who didn't know what to do, in the hands of the woman whose only destiny was supposed to be bearing his children and keeping his house. She was aware of her responsibility—that all his dreams and all he had worked for, all he was hoping for, were on her shoulders.

While Beth prepared dinner, Hallie sat down at the dining table with a large sheaf of blank paper and a pen. She got nowhere, no more than the lists she had made out with Harry. After dinner she told Beth to put the children to bed while she went out to talk with Brian.

It was a warm evening, with just a hint of autumn in the air. Even though this was the beginning of Hallie's third autumn in New South Wales, she was not yet used to May being fall. And fall being warm. Tristan had talked to her last time of planting fruit trees, of lemon trees and oranges. Not far to the north, he told her, banana trees grew luxuriantly.

Automatically, as she did whenever she was outdoors at night, she located the Southern Cross. Identifying it always gave her a feeling of knowing where she was. She knew that was a ridiculous concept, but it was there nevertheless. Walking across the field to the barracks eased her nervousness at how much she was now responsible for. The crescent of moon silvered its pale light onto the leaves, still so green, always so green, never leafless. She had heard some disgruntled wife in Parramatta saying, "What kind of country is this where trees don't lose their leaves? It's unnatural."

Not to her it wasn't. She loved the softness of the night air, the faint rustle of leaves. At this quiet hour she could hear the rushing of the creek, swollen after the winter rains. This land is mine, she thought. This is the land I was created for.

Lights were on in the barracks, since it was just after

171

seven. She knocked on the door, for she had never been inside. Laughter silenced; the door opened. Tim, one of the younger men, peered into the darkness.

"I've come to see Brian," Hallie said, trying not to stare into the long rectangular room. She had long ago told Archie to make sure it was swept out and that beds were made each day. Now she saw that the habit had continued even with Archie gone. Brian came to the door.

"I'd like to talk with you," said Hallie. "Come on out."

When he did, they walked over to the table and benches set up about twenty feet from the barracks. Hallie sat down on the table, her feet resting on the bench.

"Brian, I want you to talk with the men. Can you write?" He shook his head.

"Can any of the men?" she asked.

He didn't think so.

"Well, ask them to think about all the chores they've done individually over the years," she said. "Think about how they were done, and when. I'll come back over in the morning, after breakfast, and write it all down." There were five men among them who would be freed within the next year to year and a half. "Tell them I'll keep them on and pay them when they're emancipated, if they help out now." How she'd pay them, she didn't ask herself. She had no idea where money came from; she'd worry about that later. "On the other hand, if any of them want to accept their fifty acres, I'll do everything possible to help them get started." Hold that carrot in front of them, she thought. "If any of them have families," she told Brian, "I'll send for them. I can't replace these men with people who haven't worked here.

"I'll get more convicts," she continued. "Ones to help. Tell the men if they'll help me now, I'll help them when they're free."

Brian smiled in the darkness. "Ma'am, I've been thinking lately that maybe the luckiest thing that could ever have happened to me was to be sent here."

Hallie smiled, too. "I agree. And one of the things you can start thinking about, Brian, is where you want to build a house for your family. If you want fifty acres, I'll give you fifty of our acres. And you can farm them if you want, as long as you stay on here as foreman. When I get more

172

men, I'll assign some of them to start building you a house."

The one thing no one seemed to know about was when to breed the cow. Finally, the bull was tied on a long leash in the paddock next to the barn, and each day the cow was sent in there. After a short while nature was bound to take its course.

Not one of the men tried to escape. Not one of them shirked work. Hallie told them they would be in charge of the new convicts. With luck she'd get another eight, and each of the men would be assigned one as a helper. "You'll be the boss," she said, wondering if she was committing a foolishness. "But if I hear of any of you mistreating the new men, if I ever hear of you making them do something that you yourself would not willingly do, you've cut your own throat. Do you understand me?" She sounded far sterner than she felt.

Somehow, it worked. When Harry came out the next week, Tristan rode with him. Hallie had made out a list of all that needed doing, saying she also needed more men. She wanted to choose them herself, however. She thought perhaps it was time to get the governor out here to see what they were accomplishing. She was coming into town soon to buy bricks to expand the barracks, she told Harry, and she wondered what to do about sandstone to add onto the house.

She thought she should wait until hearing from Chad before she sold the fleeces, but another shearing would occur before then, and she didn't know where they'd pile them all. But she'd think about that come spring, she said.

Harry asked, "Have you thought of how you'll finance all this, Hallie?"

No, she had never had to deal with money. There wasn't so much growing in the garden now that winter was approaching. Chad had left her with that as her source of income, never assuming such emergencies would arise.

Tristan looked at Harry, who harrumphed. "I'll make you a loan," he said. "You don't even have to put up the farm as collateral." Hallie had no idea what collateral was. "When you have room ready for the new men, come in and

173

stay with us and I'll go over to the prison with you to see about them."

"No, let me," said Tristan, who had remained silent through this conversation. "I think that's one of my areas of expertise."

"Oh, fine, fine," Harry agreed. "In the meantime, Hallie, if you'll cull the old biddies, I'll see about selling them for mutton. Van Diemen's Land is always yelling for meat. Though the going price isn't tops, it will still bring you income and help you out. And if you've extra hay, I know people who are crying for it."

"I don't have this year, but I'll make sure I do next."

He smiled. "Yes, I'm sure you will. And now, my dear, I'm off. Shall I wait to send Molly out until you have a room readied?"

"If it's not too much trouble."

"No, not at all," Harry assured her. "She can help with the baby. Susan's due any day now."

"I'll stop and see her again on my way back to Sydney," Tristan told him as they all walked outside. "I'll be through tomorrow."

"Righto," Harry said, and was off with a friendly nod and a wave of his hand.

Once he'd cantered away, Beth and the children appeared in the doorway. Jamie ran to Tristan, pulling at his pants leg until Tristan reached down and lifted him up.

"Have you been good?" he asked the boy. "No, don't answer that question. I've a present for you whether you've been good or not. Just because you're you."

"A present?" Presents were such a rarity that Jamie looked around in anticipation.

With the boy in his arms, Tristan strode to his horse. Reaching inside the saddlebag, he withdrew a square box and put it on the ground. Jamie wriggled out of his arms, laughing up at Tristan as he knelt to examine the contents. Several holes had been poked through the sides, and Hallie guessed what it was before Jamie even saw it. His face a study in wonder, he gently lifted out a spotted ball of fur.

Tears stung Hallie's eyes. She lifted a hand to wipe them away, knowing she would preserve forever the image of the tall, stoop-shouldered man and the young child, staring at each other across the puppy.

174

Alexandra, who had been standing between Beth and Hallie, waddled toward the puppy, her arms outstretched even though she had never seen a dog before. Hallie thanked God that Jamie did not push his sister away, did not grab the dog possessively. Instead he cried, "Gently. Touch gently." From then on Alexandra called the dog Gently. It never had another name.

Tristan turned to Hallie. "I brought you a present, too. Since the ground never freezes here, since nothing ever freezes here, you can plant these and they'll be dormant until spring. But I found them now. You need flowers around here." He held out two thorny plants, nothing but green spiked stalks.

Hallie remembered his saying so long ago on the ship, "Should I live through incarceration, I shall allow myself to be involved with only the simplest pleasures . . . like tending rose gardens."

"From such thorns," he said, "comes beauty. And from my jailing has come you."

Gently barked and chased its tail around in a circle.

Seventeen

After dinner Hallie and Tristan sketched ideas for adding a room onto the house. Hallie wanted it to adjoin her bedroom. Beth tucked the children into bed and, as Hallie went in to kiss them good night, said she was going out to the barn to look at the new foal. She took a lantern with her.

"I'd suggest making it large," Tristan advised as they talked of the addition. "Pretty soon the children are going to be too big for all of you to share your bedroom, even if it is spacious."

As he sketched with a pencil, Hallie walked over to him, watching over his shoulder. It was so good to have him here, have a man around again. Have this particular man here. She watched his long fingers holding the pencil as it flew across the paper. Looking down at his dark hair, she noticed flecks of gray, though he was barely into his thirties.

She heard him say "You smell good" as he stopped writing momentarily. He did not look up at her.

Just then they heard a scream.

Tristan jumped up and strode to the door. Opening it, he listened. There was no sound, except the crackling of the fire.

"It was a woman's voice," said Hallie, pushing past him. "Beth's in the barn." They both began to run.

Another cry, this time a man's. As they neared the barn, a figure barreled out of the doorway, catapulting into Tristan and nearly knocking him over.

It was Beth, her eyes wild and her bodice torn down the front. Facing Tristan and Hallie, she whispered, "I done it again. . . ."

Tristan put his arms around her. "Done what?"

Beth began to shake. "Killed a man," she said, her teeth chattering.

From inside the barn a man's voice called, "Bitch! Low-down goddamned bitch! I'm gonna bleed to death."

Tristan let go of Beth and raced into the barn. Beth's lantern lit only a corner of the barn. "Where are you?" he called.

Outside, Hallie gathered Beth into her arms. The girl couldn't stop shivering convulsively. "He tried—he tried . . . you know."

Hallie suspected she did know. She called to Tristan, "Are you all right?"

She heard a muffled yes in response. He had found Josh, one of the convicts, sprawled against a post, holding his bleeding arm.

"Jesus goddamn bitch," the man was muttering. "I'm gonna bleed to death."

Tristan, whose eyes were becoming accustomed to the dark, knelt next to him.

"It's me arm," the man said. "She took a hay rake and come at me, she did."

"You're not going to bleed to death." There was no sympathy in Tristan's voice. "Come on. We'll wash your arm and bandage it. No, don't come. You better stay here, away from her, and I'll bring water and bandages out here."

"I weren't goin' to do nuthin'," moaned the young man. "Just wanted a kiss or two."

"Did you ask her about it?"

The man looked at him with a blank stare.

"Then it serves you right," said Tristan, standing. "You should've stayed away if she didn't want it."

"Aw, come on, guv'n'r. What's a man to do? Wait till a woman wants? Come off it. Damn bitch."

Tristan made a sound of impatience. "Maybe this will serve as a lesson."

"Who's she think she is? She don't give the time to no man here. Acts high and mighty, and she's nothin' more'n a scullery maid, from all I can see."

"I'll be back," said Tristan, leaving.

Hallie was walking Beth back to the house, one arm around her shaking shoulders. Tristan caught up with them. "Are you all right?"

Beth burst into tears. "Is he dead? Have I done it again?"

"No, he's going to be fine. What about you? Are you hurt?"

"Not so's you could see," Beth sobbed.

"Get her to bed," Tristan told Hallie as he went to find his medical bag. By the time he returned, Beth was tucked in bed, holding a cup of tea in her still-shaking hands. Hallie sat on the bed beside her.

"I'm so cold," Beth said, chattering. Hallie found another quilt.

"I told him if I ever hear of his taking advantage of a woman again, I'd see he's returned to jail." Tristan sat on the chair and studied Beth. He leaned forward and asked, "Do you trust us, Hallie and me?"

Beth nodded.

"You said you'd 'done it' before. Killed a man?"

Beth stared at him.

"It might be a good idea for you to tell us your story so that we can help you. You can't—shouldn't—keep it inside forever. Share it with us, my dear. We want to help you."

Beth stopped shaking. Terror faded from her eyes and a dullness replaced the fear. "I've known my days were numbered, but I've felt so safe here, as though this is where I belong."

"You do belong here, Beth," Hallie said. "I need you." She put her arms around her friend.

"If I tell you—you might not want me to stay. Then what?"

Hallie looked at Tristan before she spoke. "Nothing you could tell me would make me feel that way. Nothing."

Beth looked from one to the other, and all three of them were silent. She finished her tea and handed the cup to Hallie, who moved onto the bed and sat next to her, holding her hand. Tristan sat at the foot of the bed.

"I never knew my father and my mother died when I was thirteen," Beth began. "So I became a maid, in a grand house, it was. Had nearly a hundred rooms. When I wasn't in the kitchen, I'd dust the rooms. A different one every day, they was so splendid.

"It was outside London someplace, I didn't even know where. They'd come to pick me up in the fanciest carriage. They had about a dozen servants, and I was the newest and youngest. It was there I learned to sew, and cook, and clean.

178

They made me take a bath every week, I who had never had a bath a year."

Hallie and Tristan smiled at each other. Beth's eyes were focused in some long-gone time.

"Lady Margaret, a widow she was, spent most of her time in London, but we kept busy even when the family wasn't there. They were real nice to me. When the family was there it was wonderful fun. Lady Margaret's daughter, Lady Rosalind, had the two sweetest and most beautiful babies. They had such beautiful clothes. Then there was the lady's youngest son—he was nineteen. He was the most beautiful man I'd ever seen, and I used to sit on the stairs and stare at him when he didn't know it."

Oh, God, thought Hallie. Don't tell me she killed *him*. But she could already sense what was coming. She held Beth's hand tightly and looked at Tristan, who was watching intently and listening to every word.

"Mr. Gregory, he was nice to me, so polite. He treated me like a lady, he did. Shortly after my first Christmas there—and I didn't know there was such a thing as Christmas before that, they even gave me a new pair of shoes— well, maybe a month after they'd all gone back to London, the young son, Master Gregory, the beautiful one, came down from the city all by himself."

Tristan stood up and moved to the window, looking out into the darkness. Hallie could tell he knew what was coming, too.

"When I was cleaning the rooms the next day, Master Gregory appeared at the door, and it was a while before I saw him there, humming as I was and dusting the beautiful vases and stuff like that.

" 'You're a pretty girl, you know,' he said, and his warm voice washed over me. I jumped, wondering how long he'd been there.

" 'Do you like me?' he asked. I couldn't talk. I just stood there. He walked over to me . . . Beth turned to look at Hallie. "I can still see him," she said. "He was dressed so nice, not like men I'd known, in a brown velvet vest and tan-colored pants, with a shirt that had ruffles. He didn't have a jacket on." Beth's voice took on a dreamlike quality, and Hallie could tell she was back in that room with the young man. "The collar of his shirt was open, like he'd just been getting dressed or undressed. His eyes were like his vest—velvet-brown. A sweet look was on his face, and he put a finger under my chin and made me look straight into his eyes and said, 'It's too bad someone your age has to work. You should be playing. Have you ever played?'

"I didn't know how to answer anything. He was so close I was scared, but I kept looking at him. 'I shall teach you how to play,' he said, his voice real low, and then he leaned down and kissed me."

From the window, Tristan said, "Oh, God." An angry frown creased his face, and he did not turn to look at the women on the bed.

"I'd never been kissed before, not by my mum, not by anyone. It was a real nice feeling. I opened my eyes and he was smiling at me. 'Did you like that?' he asked.

" 'Yes,' I answered. Then he walked out of the room. I was no good for work the rest of the day. My mind was with Master Gregory. I still felt his touch. His lips had been so soft.

"After I'd finished my work, I slipped outside without anyone seeing me and ran across the big lawns, out to the woods, and just sat there, staring into the trees. I remember seeing a deer, and we just looked at each other for the longest time. Everything was beautiful that day." Beth looked at Hallie and said, "I kept hugging myself.

"All the next day I wondered if I'd see him alone again. Cook asked what was wrong with me because everything I picked up, I dropped. And then it was that hour right before darkness sets in, when it's time to light the lamps, and Cook told me, 'The young master wants you in the library. What've you done? Nothing to upset him, I hope.'

"I hoped not, too. He was standing with his back to the fire, one arm stretched across the mantel. The big black dog was sitting beside him, and the way he looked at me, I thought he saw into the very bottom of me.

" 'Come here,' he said. When I stood in front of him, he wasn't smiling, but in a real low voice he asked, 'How can a young girl like you bewitch me?' I didn't know what he was talking about.

" 'Did you know I came down here just to see you? I haven't thought of anything else since Christmas.' " Hallie sensed that Beth had relived this scene many times over the

180

years. Her voice had gentled, and from the way she spoke, she might have been alone in the room. "I didn't know what to say, but I felt funny inside. He reached out and put his arms around me and pulled me close to him. It was a lovely feeling. He smelled clean, like the woods. He kissed me again, though this time it was longer and I found myself kissing him back.

" 'Ah, my little witch,' he said, and I could feel his breath in my ear. 'Pretty Beth, did you think I haven't been aware of you every minute? I have,' and he kissed me again. Then he pulled a ribbon out of his pocket and said, 'This is for your hair.'

"Except for the pair of shoes at Christmas, no one had ever given me a present before. 'Here,' he said, 'let me tie it.' He pulled me over in front of a mirror, and I stood there while he tied a bow." Hallie saw the scene, saw herself reflected in the mirror, saw a handsome young man tying a bow in her hair, felt his closeness, his breath on the nape of her neck.

"Then he said, 'Go upstairs and wait for me at the top of the stairs, near my room. I'll be up in a moment.' It was more than a minute, and I stood there shaking, wondering what was happening. Then I saw him, walking across the marble floor in the big hall, heard his heels clicking on it. His hand moved up the smooth wood railing, and he started up the stairs toward me—ever so slowly, his steps muffled by the carpeting. When he reached me, he took my hand and led me down the long hallway to his room."

Hallie found herself holding her breath. She knew what was going to happen and hoped it wouldn't. Yet the young man's look and his breath were upon her, too, and she knew it would have been impossible to resist.

Beth, still caught in her memories, continued, "Closing the heavy door after us, he drew me to him and gazed down at me for the longest time. Then he began to untie my collar and unbutton my blouse. I didn't know what he was doing, but I didn't care. I have never had anyone single me out. I had never been held or kissed or made to feel important. And he was so gentle.

"He took off all my clothes. . . ." And now she looked at Hallie and then at Tristan's back, searching to see whether she found disapproval from either.

"Of course," said Tristan, still gazing out into the night. He sounded angry.

"Go on," Hallie urged.

"He took off all my clothes, and when he had undressed me he knelt down and put his arms around me. 'You are beautiful,' he told me. 'So beautiful I ache. You are a flower, and these are your buds.' He reached up and kissed my breasts, which *were* just buds. It felt so good."

"Yes, it does." Hallie didn't realize she'd spoken aloud until she saw Tristan start and whirl around to stare at her. She was so embarrassed she wanted to rush out of the room. Instead, she squeezed Beth's hand even harder.

"Then he picked me up and laid me on the bed. I was so surprised at the difference in us. He started at my feet, kissing me. He kissed me all over until gooseflesh covered me. It was the nicest feeling. His fingers explored me and his tongue darted in and out of me and I began to cry because it felt so wonderful. Then he said, 'I have to hurt you for just a minute. It will never hurt again, but I have to for a minute.' "

Hallie remembered that night by the billabong. Yes, that's all it hurt, just for a minute, and even then not much.

"When he got off me, Master Gregory went over to his bureau and took a shiny piece of glass from his drawer. It had a chain on it and he held it out to me. 'This is for you,' he said. 'Wear it where no one can ever see it, but whenever you touch it or look at it, think of me.'

"Cook looked at me real peculiarly when I came downstairs. She said, 'I hope you know that the more you please the young master, the better you'll do here.' "

"Of course," Tristan spat out.

"Master Gregory slept late every day and then went riding. But after lunch we always went up to his room and played. We played we were riding horses, and we played we were elephants, and we played we were all sorts of animals. He told me he was making up for all the years I hadn't played. It was the only beautiful time of my life." Beth wrenched her mind back to the present and looked at Hallie. "Until now."

Hallie let go of Beth's hand and put an arm around her shoulders. "Then what happened, Beth?" she asked softly.

Beth sighed. "Well, when he left to go back to London,

I was miserable. I'd never known what loneliness meant before. I couldn't do anything but think of him. I'd sit at night, by the light of my candle, and finger the pretty presents he'd given me. The ribbon, the shiny glass stone, the pretty silk scarf, the linen handkerchief. I'd put them in my hand and feel them, and that's how I kept him with me.

"When I was with him he always wanted me to wear the shiny necklace, even when I wore nothing else. He stayed in London a few weeks and then came back down to the castle. He took me out in the woods. Spring was coming on, and we'd undress and dance around a little spring that was there, and splash each other, and laugh. My life was like music—the world sang for me. I had never known anyone so gentle, so kind. He made me feel important and beautiful, and I laughed all the time.

"Then his mother arrived and we couldn't spend afternoons together, and we'd look at each other every time I passed and it was awful. Being in the same room but not touching. Three days went by and I cried myself to sleep with wanting him so bad. Then he whispered to me in the hall when no one was around, 'Come to my room this afternoon. The family's going visiting in the village.' After I'd seen them drive off in the carriage, I ran—I could scarcely bear to be away from him. That day he wasn't gentle. We wanted each other so badly and knew we didn't have much time, we just tore our clothes off and fell to the floor, behaving like animals. Not the kind we had pretended to be and had fun being, but rutting pigs or dogs, going at each other with a fierceness neither of us could control. When he was done this time, he flung me aside on the floor and jumped up to put his clothes on.

" 'Get up, hurry up. I hear the carriage,' he said.

"I pulled my pantaloons on, but it was too late. The door to his room burst open and his mother stood here. The look on her face I have never forgotten."

Hallie's arm tightened around Beth, and Tristan turned from the window and walked back to the bed, sitting at the foot of it.

"Master Gregory had just finished buttoning his vest. His coat lay across the bottom of the bed. But I stood there

183

with nothing on but my pantaloons and the glass necklace at my throat.

"Lady Margaret looked at me, and then at him, and asked, in a voice that sounded like she was strangling, 'Gregory, do you have an explanation for this?'

"Acting like he didn't really know me, his face innocent as could be, he said, 'Now, Mama, it's not at all like it looks.'

" 'I should hope not,' Lady Margaret said in a stern voice she used only occasionally.

" 'I found Beth in your room, acting suspiciously. Immediately, I thought she must be trying to steal your jewelry. When she denied it, I didn't believe her, so I've been searching her and voilà! See! I would never have found it had I not demanded she remove her clothes.' He pointed at the shiny glass on the chain around my neck."

Tristan reached out to cup the blankets around Beth's foot.

"Lady Margaret walked over to me. 'My diamond necklace . . .' I could hardly hear her voice. 'The one your grandfather gave me when I married your father. The family heirloom.'

"She pulled it so hard the clasp dug into my neck before it broke and fell into her hand. She clasped it against her breast and looked at me. 'To think I trusted you, sweet young thing.'

"After I dressed, she put me in the carriage and rode into the village with me, handing me over to the constable, telling him I had tried to steal her diamonds."

Hallie found herself crying, but Beth stared straight ahead, dry-eyed.

Eighteen

Only Hallie's sobs broke the silence.

Beth stared straight ahead, seeing nothing. Her body was in the room, but she was not.

Hallie and Tristan looked at each other, pain reflected in their eyes. Finally Tristan urged, "Go on, Beth."

When she didn't, he leaned over and, his voice so quiet it was not much more than a whisper, said, "You killed a man. . . ."

Without acknowledging their presence, Beth began to talk. It was as though she spoke more to herself than any kind of explanation.

"I thought it was the end of the world. But it was only the beginning, the beginning of a life so terrible that I wished I were dead every night of my life." Then her eyes began to focus, and she looked directly at Tristan. "They threw me in jail, not in the village but down in London, and put me in an old ship, where there was never daylight. Rats ran across us, they fed us gruel once a day, but that wasn't the worst of it. At night the jailers would come through with lanterns, studying which women they wanted that night. Lots of the women pleaded to be taken. They thought they'd be treated better. And it's true, those that were chosen were offered extra tidbits of food. But it wasn't worth it. Once, when the superintendent chose me, I got a bath, but that was the only time."

An "Oh . . ." escaped Hallie. She had to bathe when she came in from the fields, hot with sweat. Not bathing for months on end . . . Even on the ship she'd managed a pitcher of water each night.

"It was never like it had been with Master Gregory. Never gentle and sweet and fun. They made me do terrible things, they poked me and seemed to like hurting me. When I'd cry out, they'd smile as though that was a reward. Some-

185

times two or three of them would be together. Some liked to chain me to a bed and do all sorts of terrible things."

Hallie tried to imagine what they'd done to her, but her mind didn't function that way. She was left with no clear picture, one she didn't want to become clearer. Beth turned to her and grasped the hand Hallie now had in her lap.

"I wanted to be dead." There was a desperation in Beth's voice, and Tristan moved up the bed, reaching for her other hand. "I never wanted another man near me again. However, I knew this would continue for seven years. I also thought I'd be dead before that. I couldn't stand it another seven years.

"I was fourteen when they put me on the boat to come here." Hallie thought of the security she'd felt at fourteen, yet she'd been desperate about her life, wondering if washing clothes and cleaning houses were to be her destiny. She felt guilty to have been dismayed about that kind of life when she listened to Beth.

"I didn't know where I was going and I didn't care. I didn't care about anything. I'd sit in corners and cry. Sometimes I couldn't eat. I threw up a lot."

"Who wouldn't," said Tristan.

"But there was hope. I was leaving that jail, and maybe out where I was going, life would be worth living. But, on board, it was the same all over again. Each night, to reward the sailors who had been good that day, the captain allowed them to choose women. And the rest of the sailors would watch while whoever had you that night would do it in his hammock. Sometimes they'd share you with the others. One night fourteen men used me. I remember because I thought, One for each year of my life."

Hallie shuddered. "Did you know that was going on?" she asked Tristan.

"Of course." Tristan's eyes were sad as he studied her. "It always does."

Beth went on, glancing for a moment at Tristan. "Until I met you, Dr. Faulkner, I never knew a man could be nice without wanting to do things to me. I never knew a man could be kind and gentle and . . . Oh, I thought Master Gregory was that way, at one time. But he wasn't really, was he?"

"No." Hallie squeezed her hand. "He wasn't." He was evil, she said to herself. To cast a young girl into this kind of life for his own temporary pleasure. She hated him. If he'd walked through the door, she could have killed him.

"I never had a night's peace, from the time I was sent to jail until I hid in your room on the ship. And then when I met you, Doctor, I thought maybe this country *would* be better, that maybe jailers and sailors were the only ones who were mean."

"And young masters of the manor," added Tristan.

Beth sighed, so deeply that it seemed to trail across the bed. "When I arrived I was sent up to the Women's Prison Factory in Parramatta, but I was only there for a few weeks. A man, Able Norton, came looking for a servant. Lived up north on a small farm. Said his wife had died and he needed a woman to keep house. When he saw me, he laughed. 'You're no woman, you're nothing but a child,' he said. I hoped he'd pass me by. I'd rather have stayed and worked at the loom, been with other women. Though the guards beat you if you couldn't keep up with the tread-mill, and they kept food from you if you didn't weave your quota each day, they didn't come in every night and do disgusting things.

"But he took me, Able Norton did. Took me up the coast to one of the prettiest places I'd ever seen. It sat on a bluff overlooking the ocean, and there were pelicans on the beach, and gulls. It was a nice little house, and I thought maybe my luck had changed."

But it hadn't, Hallie could tell. She suspected that the worst was to come. She wanted to reach across Beth and take Tristan's hand. She wanted some comfort when the worst came. How could Beth stand more? she wondered.

"For a couple of weeks Mr. Norton was real nice. He told me how he liked his food cooked, and he wasn't too particular about how the house was kept, because it was real sloppy when we arrived. I cleaned it up, and mended his clothes and washed them, even without his asking me. I went out and helped him in the garden. We didn't talk much, but it seemed like heaven to me after the rest of my life.

"But then he went to town to get supplies, and he came

back with some rum. And after dinner, when he got to drinking, he looked at me with his little black eyes and said, 'Tonight you're going to sleep with me.' I'd been on a pallet, near the fireplace."

"I asked, 'Do I have to?' "

"He asked, 'Why does that scare you, girl? Ain't I been good to you? Look, don't pretend with me. I know that all women convicts sent over here are whores. I know you been used. You been lucky I let you alone a couple weeks. I been without a woman since my wife died. I don't aim to live my life that way.'

"He got up and came across the room, standing over me, outlined against the flames from the fireplace, looking like the Devil that comes to bad children in their dreams. He said, 'Come on, girl, maybe you'll like it.'

"I thought maybe he'd be nice like Master Gregory was. But I guess no one's like that. Able Norton did awful things to me, even worse than I'd had done before."

Hallie looked at Tristan and knew she could not ask even him about what Beth might have gone through. It was too terrible to imagine; what must it have been like to endure?

Suddenly Beth's hand left hers and she ripped open the buttons of her nightdress, revealing two dark red welts on her breasts.

"My God," uttered Tristan, staring at the disfiguring ugly marks, "he burned you."

Hallie let out a cry, bringing her hands to her head, covering her eyes. Beth turned to her and said, "They don't hurt anymore.

"The skin's dead." Tristan sounded like a doctor, yet Hallie could tell by his voice that he, too, was pained.

After a few moments Beth resumed. "He didn't burn me till the end. But he wasn't ever kind to me. He'd just been biding his time, I guess. He couldn't stand it that I didn't like it. After dinner he'd start in on his rum, and I knew what was coming. Yet when anyone stopped by, he was nice as punch. He'd tell me to fetch tea for them and act like he ran a nice home. But it got so, after a while, it didn't even take rum for him to beat me. He'd hit me if I charred a steak or if his eggs was too runny.

"He kept telling me if I'd just smile, if I'd act like I liked him, he'd be nicer to me. And I swear I tried. I'd try anything. But I just couldn't do it. Sometimes just looking at him, I'd begin to cry. I kept hoping he'd take me back to the factory and find another woman. But he didn't.

"When he'd go off for town for a couple days, or hunting, he'd chain me to a big ball; I couldn't lift my leg. I could hardly move. I couldn't get to the privy, or get food or water, or move anyplace. Once he was gone so long I thought I'd die of thirst. He treated his dog nicer'n he did me."

Tristan got up and began to pace around the room, his hands jammed into the pockets of his pants. Hallie thought she heard his teeth grinding.

"Once he rubbed cold gravy over me and let the dog lick it off. All he did was laugh the whole time. 'My two pets,' he said. I hated him with every ounce of energy I had. I hated every man I ever knew. I'd lie in bed nights after he was done with me and plot how I could kill him. I don't know why I didn't."

"Neither do I," Tristan said in a hard voice.

"When he really got into drinking, he was so mean to me he could've been the Devil. One night he had a bottle and began drinking even before dinner. He hardly ate but kept drinking and staring at me. Everytime I started to get up, he'd grab my wrist and say, 'You don't move until I tell you to.'

"He kept asking why I didn't like him. He was smoking a cigar, and he reached over and touched my neck. Then I heard the sound of my dress being tore off me; he just pulled my blouse so hard it ripped, and he had this terrible grin on his face and he said, 'Don't move.'"

Beth closed her eyes and her chest began to heave. Tristan walked around the bed and sat next to Beth, gathering her in his arms. She began to cry, great gulping sobs that shook her. His arms tightened around her. Hallie was crying, too. Through her tears, Beth continued, "That's when he burned me. Ground his cigar into me. If there'd been neighbors, they could've heard my screams. I screamed bloody murder.

"He threw me to the floor, and as I fell, the bottle broke, sloshing the rest of the rum over me, running into my burns. I could hardly see for the pain, but as I looked up, he was taking off his belt, and he began beating me with it, standing there above me, laughing down at me with those devil eyes."

"Stop!" cried Hallie. "I can't stand it."

But Beth did not stop. "He began to take his clothes off, and I saw this evil giant leering down at me, grinning. He said, 'Look up at me, girl. Look at my male parts. Don't act like I'm some kinda freak. See them. I'm going to push them down your throat till you gag on them. I'll show you.' He started to fall to one side because he was so drunk, and I grabbed that bottle with the broken top and pushed it up at him as hard as I could until I felt blood over me. It was warm and sticky and he was screaming like I'd been, and I saw one of his balls hit the floor and roll across the room.

" 'You bitch!' he shrieked. He fell to the floor, clutching himself, screaming so loud I thought I'd go deaf. I looked over at him. I was in pain, too, but I heard myself laugh, and I couldn't stop. His blood became a puddle, and I kept laughing.

"I think the rum all over my burns was a help. I grabbed a dress that wasn't torn and my cloak and ran out of that house. I saw his horse standing by the shed. I threw myself on it, grabbed the reins, even though there was no saddle on it. I'd never ridden alone on a horse before, but I kicked that horse and we took off, me holding on for dear life."

Hallie had stopped crying now and was staring at Beth in open-mouthed astonishment. Tristan was still holding her close against his chest, in the circle of his arms.

"My only thought was finding Hallie. I had no idea where I was, even though I'd lived there almost two years."

Two years, thought Hallie. God in heaven.

"I didn't stop for a whole day, but then there weren't many houses up north there. I hid in the woods when I'd see a house, and waited until I saw a woman alone. The first woman had three children, and once she saw my burns, she was real kind to me. By then my burns had festered, and she soaked them in some solution and fed me. I told her what had happened. She wrapped food in a handkerchief and told me to take it easy or the horse wouldn't last. She gave me a blanket, and warned me not to tell my story to anyone, not anyone ever, or I'd be sent back to jail and hanged."

Beth took another deep breath and sat up, back against the pillow. "She pointed the way south. Along the way, every single woman I asked helped me. One warned me to be aware of escaped convicts. But no escaped convict could do more to me than what had already happened.

"Each morning I'd look at the sun and figure where south was and start riding, always in woods and away from houses. Sometimes I'd go half a day without seeing a house.

"But I went too far south. I got to a cabin and waited until I saw two men leave and go out to the fields, and then I knocked. The lady there knew you." She turned to Hallie. "She told me to come back north a couple miles, pointing me toward here."

"Must've been Etta Colton," Hallie said, feeling that the life had been drained from her. She was exhausted.

"I was scared all the time, but I wasn't sorry about Able Norton. I was only sorry I hadn't done it to all the men who had done that to me, maybe even Mr. Gregory. I'd killed a man, and it felt good. But now, I wanted to live. For the first time since I'd been sent to jail, I wanted to live."

She lay there in silence, rivulets of tears drying on her cheeks. After a few minutes she turned to Hallie and asked in a tremulous voice, "Do you want me to leave?"

Hallie threw her arms around Beth, crying, "Never! You are safe here forever." And then she pulled her head back and looked into Beth's eyes. "I love you," she said. "Perhaps more so now than ever."

Long afterward, as she fell asleep next to Beth, her arms flung across the young woman, Hallie thought it was the first time she'd said "I love you" to anyone in the new world. She resolved to say it aloud to Jamie and Alexandra in the morning. Such things should not be left unsaid.

The image of Tristan holding Beth and comforting her went to sleep with Hallie. Thank goodness Beth knows not all men are bad, Hallie thought, never having known even one man like the many her friend had encountered.

In the morning she said to Tristan, "It will be a good

idea to add a room to the house so that Beth will have a place to sleep when Chad returns." She never noticed the veil of darkness that fell across Tristan's eyes when she mentioned her husband. "But I will have to make other arrangements for Molly. Beth doesn't want her here."

"I'll make them, if you'd like," Tristan offered. "I'm sure I can easily find a place for her."

"Make sure she isn't put with someone like Able Norton."

Tristan reassured her.

When he came back the next time, more than a week later, it was with the news that Susan Langley had given birth to a fine boy, Christopher Tristan Langley. He did not tell Hallie that this was the tenth boy in the Sydney-Parramatta area to have the middle name of Tristan.

"Molly has already proved valuable," he told her. "By the time I arrived, Susan had been in hard labor for hours. The baby was caught sideways, and I had to turn it around, an arduous task. Molly helped me and calmed Susan better than I could have. I showed Molly how to administer the mandagora, and she acted as though she'd been doing it for years. Nothing seemed to upset her. Later I learned it was the first birth she'd attended, but I couldn't have told that at the time. When Christopher finally did emerge, she took over his care as though she were a born nurse. Susan won't let her out of her sight. Her recovery is slow, and I think Susan has come to rely on Molly. She'd be sore put if you wanted the girl."

Tristan also informed her that if it was convenient, Governor and Mrs. Macquarie wanted to ride out with him in another two weeks.

"Oh, my," said Hallie, flustered. "What will I do? They'll have to stay overnight, of course. I'll give them my bedroom, and the children and I will sleep in the drawing room." She laughed. "I'll have to think of how to feed them. Beth will just have to stay out in the barn the entire time they're here, and I think I've forgotten how to cook."

"Tristan, Tristan!" Jamie ran into the house. "Want ride."

Tristan held out his arms for the little boy. "I think that's a reasonable request. Then we'll try and teach that dog of yours some manners. You'd like a well-behaved dog, wouldn't you?"

Trailing behind Jamie was Alexandra. "No," she said. She wasn't talking in sentences yet, and "no" prefaced everything. "Want ride, too."

Tristan looked at Hallie. "Come on. Let's all go together."

"Let me saddle Princess up," said Hallie, delighted with the idea.

"Let me unburden my horse first," Tristan said. Across the saddle and in saddle bags were all manner of strange-looking twigs and branches. He pulled one out and showed it to Hallie. "This one's a peach tree," he said. "And along in here someplace are some other plants to pretty up the place. Not that it needs prettying, really. But I don't have anyplace in my little yard in Sydney to indulge my passion for gardening, so thought I could do it here. Perhaps it's my only path to immortality."

Hallie looked at him. He did say the queerest things at times.

It was a beautiful winter's day. The sky was clear as a bell, and the sun warmed the afternoon to the high sixties, despite a soft breeze. Alexandra was beside herself with the delight of being included. She pointed at every tree, at every sheep, at cattle wandering in the far pasture. Hallie felt a surge of pride when they crested the top of the hill from which she could view the river, tumbling more rapidly than it ever did at other times of the year, wider than she had ever seen it. This land was so beautiful that sometimes she felt an actual ache with the grandeur of it.

Tristan was watching her. "You love it, don't you?" he said softly.

"I love it like it's a person," she responded. "It's part of me. Or I'm part of it. I'm never sure which. I think I was born for it. If there *is* predestination, I know I was destined for here."

"And if there is no such thing?"

She laughed, happiness brimming over. "Then I'm just lucky. Luckier by far than I could ever have dreamed."

"Let's get down so the children can run around," Tristan suggested.

Jamie and Alexandra dashed down the hill, charged with energy known only to children under five. Alex, trying to keep up with her brother, kept falling, but giggled in good humor every time and was soon trying to catch up with him again. Their shouts filled the air.

"I love all this vast emptiness," Hallie said.

"I wonder how long it will remain empty," said Tristan. "Three more families have moved into the valley."

"Sometime I have to go meet all these newcomers," she said. "But I'm too busy now. I couldn't sleep for nights wondering how to get everything done and wondering what it was exactly that needed doing. But ever since I decided to tackle one thing at a time, I've felt better. Or," she smiled, "I could never have taken the time for this ride. It was a lovely idea, Tristan." They were sitting on the brow of the hill, watching the children zigzag in the field below.

"When I'm in Sydney I spend half my time thinking of coming out here." His eyes didn't meet hers. He picked a blade of grass and studied it.

"You make a difference to Jamie. He so looks forward to your visits. You're very nice to my children, Tristan." Hallie smiled at him as he turned his head to look at her. "And the thing with Beth . . . Oh, Tristan, I don't know how I'd ever have stood that all by myself. And she—I'm so glad she knows that not all men are . . . untrustworthy."

They were quiet for a minute, looking at each other. He reached out for her hand. "And you? What about you? Are you glad I came?"

His hand, enfolding hers, was warm. "I don't know what I'd do without you. The only reason I can face all this is because I'm not alone. The world out there may think I'm a woman alone trying to do all this, but I'm not. I have you."

He drew her hand to his lips. "Years ago"—and now he did not look at her, but down at the river, at the horizons beyond it, at the faint jagged splashes of purple mountains westward—"you asked me if, knowing the consequences, I would have done what I did—committed treason, so they say—and I said no. But I would, Hallie. I would have done

194

anything—anything—had I known it would bring you into my life."

Just then, arms outstretched in the air—Jamie came flying up the hill, Alex far behind him. "I'm an eagle!" he shouted, running over and jumping on Tristan.

Nineteen

Before the Governor arrived, Hallie and Brian spent days trying to figure out what had to be done. Hallie had spent most of a morning with all the men, asking them to try to remember what chores they'd done over the years, no matter how small. Some of them even had ideas of what needed to be done. She made a long list.

She felt guilty that she had no time to get over to the Coltons. She always had the idea that her visits brightened Etta's life. Will's should be easier now that a convict had been sent out to him, she reflected, although she had no idea how that was faring. She suspected Will had never given orders to another man before. He was always so obsequious, she wondered if he would keep the upper hand. Yet Etta always rushed to do his bidding, always keeping her eyes on him to see if he appeared to want anything. Was it love or fear? Hallie wondered. She couldn't imagine feeling either for Will Colton.

He ignored the baby and never seemed to be aware of Etta's needs. Hallie wondered if the convict would end up sleeping in the woods and if he'd be fed halfway decently. If not, she'd feel partly responsible. Well, she would just *have* to get over there. Not that she could do anything if all was not well.

Tristan had decided that Beth could not hide forever. Sooner or later some unexpected company would turn up. After hearing Beth's story, he had spent several weeks investigating the death of Able Norton, but he could find no records of the man's existence, much less his death. He did not think there was a warrant out for Beth; he could find no record of one.

He suggested inventing a story that seemed most reasonable. In this land, he doubted that it could be challenged. No one else, except Harry Langley, had even been out to visit in the three years Hallie had been at the farm. So no one would know when Beth had arrived. He suggested changing her name. Say that she had come over as a free woman looking for a new life, and Chad, during one of his trips to Sydney, had found her while still on the boat and taken her immediately, long before he had returned to England. Beth had been with them for at least two years.

Hallie and Beth agreed with this idea, but Beth said it would still be difficult for her to meet with strangers. Tristan thought she would be safer if people saw her and took her presence for granted. But she should have a new last name at least. What new name would she like?

"On records your name must be Elizabeth. So our calling you Beth should be safe. But not White for a last name. How about . . . Stillwell? Good British name."

"Elizabeth Stillwell . . ." Beth turned it over on her tongue. "It sounds far more elegant than I am."

"You came on . . . well, I'll have to investigate and see what ships came two years ago," Tristan told her. "I'll go through their manifests, if I can, and see what I can come up with." He smiled at her. "It will take courage, Beth, but I think if we start right off with Governor and Mrs. Macquarie, who won't question your presence at all, it will soon be taken for granted that you have lived and worked out here for a long time."

So it was a nervous, seemingly demure Elizabeth who silently served dinner to the governor. Neither he nor his wife paid any attention to her, except to compliment Hallie on her cook. The governor was more interested in the convicts.

"Within the next two years," Hallie told him, "they'll all be free. I've promised that if they want, I'll keep them on and pay them, build them houses if wives are what they want—if they'll pull together and help me now."

"She also told them," added Tristan, "that if they want fifty acres but also want to work here, she'll give each of them fifty acres from her land."

"How will you pay them?" asked the governor. "I'd think the only way you could afford to farm here is with free convict labor. Most people just replace the convicts they have with others."

Hallie nodded. "I know that. But I need these men now. I need their help. If they help me, I'll help them. I'm left in a difficult situation without Archie. I can't do it all alone. As you know, Brian's been granted his ticket of leave, and I've made him foreman. But neither he nor I knows half of what Archie knew or a quarter of what Chad knows."

"You have such courage," Elizabeth Macquarie said, her voice filled with admiration.

Hallie smiled at her. "It doesn't seem to take courage. What else is there to do? Chad spent years building this up. I can't let it go just because I'm not sure what to do. I have to learn. And besides, I love this country. I love our land. I have a chance here that I'd never have had in England."

"Don't we all," mused Tristan.

"Including me," the governor said, nodding.

Hallie and Governor Macquarie rode out the next day along the boundaries of the farm, most of which were fenced into the pastures where sheep were rotated after they'd grazed the land.

The governor was impressed. "Chad is sure, of course, that sheep are the future of New South Wales. But what *really* is the future of this country are the people—people like Chad and you . . . and Tristan . . . and even the convicts. The people who come here are its richest resources, even though at the time it often doesn't seem it."

They turned and headed back to the house. "In Newcastle," Hallie thought aloud, "I'd not have made a decision in my whole life. And here I'm not only allowed to *do* things, but required to. I like it."

"Visionaries, you and Chad," said Governor Macquarie. "And I'll help in whatever way I can."

"I need more convicts, as you suggested a couple of months ago," Hallie told him as they reined in their horses by the barn. "Brian and I think nine or ten more would be about right. And in the spring, come lambing time, my land won't be sufficient for all my sheep." She stroked Princess as the governor dismounted. She decided he was as interesting as he was distinguished-looking.

"How much do you need?" He looked beyond her, out over the rolling land.

"It's going at five shillings an acre. Harry Langley said he'd lend me money for land. I'd like five thousand acres." Hallie wasn't even sure how much five thousand acres was.

It would almost triple their present holdings. "I want it out there." She pointed southeast.

The governor looked at this young woman, not yet twenty-three, whose eyes burned with fire, and he never doubted her success. "I'll see to it," he said briskly. "And tell Harry there's no hurry for the cash."

As the men built another barracks, Hallie drove into Parramatta to interview the convicts Tristan had selected. He wanted her final approval. She wanted carpenters and masons and potters as well as field hands. Of course there were no field hands; there never were. Nearly all the convicts were from cities. None of them looked particularly promising, and certainly there was no Brian or Archie among them. Maybe she'd take just a few from this lot, then wait and see what subsequent ships brought in.

Harry didn't like the idea of two women living way out in the country with so many male convicts, but that was the least of Hallie's worries.

She spent one evening admiring Christopher, who was indeed a beautiful baby. When she told Susan that she would need Molly after all, that with ten new convicts, eighteen in all, it would take a woman all day just to cook for them, Susan said, "Don't take Molly. She's become Christopher's nurse. I couldn't bear to part with her. She's wonderful." And Hallie agreed that anyone Susan wanted so badly should be left with her.

Now that Molly was dressed neatly by the Langleys and was happy being Christopher's nurse and Susan's confidante, she glowed. The dancing eyes gave life to her pretty face, and her hair—washed often and curled lovingly by Susan—shone in ringlets around her face. When there was no company for dinner, Susan told Hallie, Molly dined with them. She had become family.

Hallie decided to wait to find a woman until they could build a place for her to sleep. She also forced herself, one beautiful day, to take Jamie and ride over to the Coltons'. She wanted to see how they were faring.

Etta was dreadfully thin, but she wore a dress Hallie had not seen before. Her hair, once gloriously waved, hung limply, clinging to her neck in strands. Mary Ann was fat and clean, waddling around, often falling, her black hair curling around her cherubic face. The impish dark eyes were in sharp contrast to Etta's. Jamie stood staring at Mary Ann with his fist balled up against his mouth.

Hallie noted that despite her emaciated condition, Etta was obviously pregnant again. That, at least, must please her; she wanted babies so. When she mentioned it, Etta simply said, "Yes," evidencing neither delight nor dismay.

It looked as though the convict had brought improvement to the Coltons' standard of living. He—Hallie did not know his name—lived in a sod hut at the edge of the woods. A barn had been thrown up, and Hallie noted there was hay in it. There were also a cow and a few chickens, so she needn't have brought the eggs and milk. At the last minute she had also brought flour and cornmeal, freshly milled in Parramatta, which she offered as a neighborly gesture.

Hallie saw no sign of Will or the convict. She knew that her visit buoyed Etta, and thought if she were really nice, she'd have stayed longer. But she found the visit depressing and could hardly wait to leave. She asked Etta if there were anything she could do, any way to help.

"Oh, no," Etta said, not looking at her directly. "I don't need anything."

"Don't you get awfully lonely?" Hallie asked. Etta had not left the farm, except for two visits to the Morgan's, since she'd been there.

Etta merely turned and stared at Hallie. Finally Hallie averted her eyes, realizing Etta would not answer.

Riding home on Princess, with Jamie in the saddle in front of her, Hallie was saddened. She wondered why Etta acted so mournful. Outwardly, at least, the Coltons were prospering. Hallie wanted everyone to be as happy in this new world as she was, wanted everyone to seize the opportunities on their doorsteps.

It's made me stronger, she realized. This land has done that. And so, she concluded reluctantly, had Chad's leaving, though she had been happy when her husband had run everything, when she'd been taken care of. That's part of it, she thought. I'm not being taken care of for the first time in my life. Independence no longer frightened her.

She did the best she could each day, and had decided that was the most anyone could do in life. She did not worry about not being able to take care of Chad's land. She knew, now that lambing time was approaching, now that Chad had been gone nearly a year, that she and Brian and the other men would muddle through as best they could.

Though Tristan could not help with the farm chores, he listened to her. Her heart quickened when she saw him coming. On his periodic visits, he always brought presents. He advised her when she asked, but did not offer suggestions when she seemed in control. She thought the look she often saw in his eyes was admiration.

And Harry—dear Harry. He had such faith in her that he had said, "I don't want the farm as collateral, Hallie. After all, that's in Chad's name. You're my collateral, your spirit."

Hallie knew with certainty that she and Brian could never shear all the sheep. They had spent a week riding out to the far pastures, culling those that were not lambing, which would then be sold for mutton. Only last month in Parramatta she had heard that the prison in Van Diemen's Land would take all the meat she could supply. The army commissary here preferred lamb and beef to mutton. It was understandable, of course: most of the officers of the New South Wales Corps had their own land spreads and had gotten rich in this country by selling their own livestock. Many of them had intimidated, and even destroyed, some of the governors who'd dared legislate against what would make them wealthy. Chad had told her he thought them arrogant. She seemed to remember his use of the word *evil* in connection with several of them. They had become the single most powerful financial and political force in the country—until Macquarie had arrived.

Many of them lived in luxury, with convicts as house servants. Their wives put on airs they could never have affected in England. But, unlike in India, they had no natives over whom to lord their status, and the ex-convict or newly arrived settler was not bedazzled by the rigid manners from which they had escaped. The officers' wives had no one to impress but each other.

Hallie felt sorry for them. They were trying to live British lives halfway across the world and were missing out on the marvelous differences of this continent. They seldom strayed beyond the city boundaries, bemoaning the lack of culture, even though some of the convicts from the Sydney prison had begun to present amateur theatricals. These women were afloat in a strange world, and nothing they did—though Hallie thought they did not try very hard—solidified the mores of London in Sydney. There were too many whores seen publicly on the streets, there were too many pubs, too many convicts or day laborers paid in rum rather than coin. There was too little city and too much vastness to make for a cohesive society. And that, thought Hallie, was one of the marvels of this land. It bred rugged individualism.

When she voiced her thoughts to Tristan, he said, "I find it most interesting that the children of these convicts are growing up, generally, to be law-abiding and hard-working."

"Any ideas why?" Hallie loved their evening talks. They so stimulated her to use her mind, challenged her to live in the world of the metaphysical.

"Yes," he answered. "They don't grow up in crowded slums. They're not lost as just one among many. There's no real established gentry to look down on them. They don't grow up feeling inferior. They have enough to eat, and they run around in sunshine. And though there are, certainly, the pickpockets and whores of London and Liverpool, they tend to remain in places like the Rocks in Sydney. These children, on the other hand, are growing up out in the country on fifty acres or in a place where their fathers can find jobs. And where they, themselves, are seen as individuals. They're not lost, as they were back in England. They're part of society here. They belong.

"The scum of the earth, which Mother England hoped might drop off the end of the earth, are rising to the occasion. Not all of them," he amended. "But certainly a good majority. You haven't been to Sydney lately, have you? Where scraggly weeds proliferated a few years ago, there are tidy gardens with flowers. People are taking pride in their surroundings."

"Why, do you think?"

"Hope."

Hallie digested that. "Would you go back to Canada now, if you could?"

Tristan looked at her. "If there were no other mitigating circumstances, you mean?"

He so often used words she didn't understand. "What does that mean—'mitigating'?"

"It means"—his voice was low, and he stared into her eyes—"if you weren't here. If I didn't have to consider how far I'd be from you."

She looked over at him, at the unreadable dark eyes. She could seldom see what was behind them. Months would go by without a personal word between them, words about their relationship. And then suddenly he would interject something like this. It always confused her.

She was a married woman. She had told herself she would not resurrect the love she had felt for Tristan aboard ship. He had become her friend—with Beth, one of her two best friends, though she knew she could not sleep in a bed with Tristan as she did with Beth. She knew that when she and Tristan brushed against each other, her skin came alive. When she and Tristan sat talking like this, she was aware the air was charged with an electricity—sometimes virtually crackling—that was lacking when he was in Sydney. But she did not let herself dwell on it. And then he threw statements like this into the conversation.

"Yes . . . if you didn't have to consider your friends here." Certainly he had a multitude of them. When she'd traveled into Parramatta, she'd discovered he was one of the most popular people in the community, so he probably was in Sydney, too. She was not the only one for whom he did kind things. Kind seemed to have become his middle name.

"My friends?" He raised an eyebrow. "No, Hallie, I would not return. Nor would I go to America. I used to think I would not stay anyplace under the Union Jack. But I have fallen in love."

Oh, dear, she thought. How will I handle this?

But he said, "Passion has entered my soul . . . not only

for the beauty of this land, but for its grand possibilities. I am planting my roses not only at your doorstep, Hallie, but all over New South Wales."

"Goodness, where do you get so many roses?" asked Hallie, relieved yet disappointed that the conversation had not gone the way she'd feared.

She couldn't understand why.

Tristan laughed.

Twenty

"I don't know anything else but sheep," said the man with the bleary eye. One was a bright blue, the other milky and unfocused. "But I wanted no more of the moors." He smiled at his own joke. "I'm sick to death of cold weather and chilblains. I dinna know whether they raised sheep in America; I dinna want to go to a country where I could'na understand the language and which is Papist, too." Hallie decided he was referring to Spain. "Before I even touched foot on land Mr. Langley grabbed me and told me I had a job."

Hallie simply stared at him. He had come out of nowhere, riding on a spavined horse. Now, at least, she knew that Harry had sent him.

"He said to give you this." He held out a wrinkled piece of paper, and Hallie took it, brushing the hair out of her face. If this man really knew sheep, he couldn't have come at a better time. There were thousands to shear. Not that one man could be that much help; she needed dozens. The crinkled paper read:

My dear Hallie,
   This will ensure your being in my debt forever. More than any monies the bank has loaned you, this man will help your entire operation, if what he has told me is true. He has been a shepherd all his life. Shepherds enjoy loneliness. (Or maybe they are not lonely when they are alone.) Put Jock McTavish in charge of your sheep, give him whatever he asks for in the way of added labor, and listen to him. Fix up a wagon for him as he wants and give him a good sturdy horse. The wagon will be his home.
   He doesn't shear. He can, but he says that's not part of his job. He can probably help train some of those lads of yours, however.

I suggest that aside from a wagon for housing (he travels from pasture to pasture with the sheep), you pay him a percentage of your fleeces each year. That kind of incentive will work wonders, I believe.

Susan joins me in sending her love. She and Chris and I shall be out before long. She reminds me she has never seen . . . You really ought to have a name for your place, Hallie, now that you are such a large landowner.

Harry Langley

Hallie looked at the man; probably as old as Dada, she thought. He had a white stubble for a beard, and he was wiry and thin, about her height. She held Harry's note in her hand and, nodding at it, said, "This says you won't shear. Why not?"

"Too old," he said without apology. "Back can't take it."

"I have several thousand sheep that need shearing, and only two of my men know how to do it."

Jock McTavish scratched his ear. "Got other men?"

Hallie nodded again. "Eighteen in all."

"I kin teach 'em," said Jock, "so long's I don't needa bend over all day."

"What's wrong with your back?" She wondered if he was too infirm to be a shepherd.

"Nothin' if I don't lean over all day." He gazed out at the fields and rolling hills. "Might pretty. And it never freezes, that the truth?"

Hallie smiled. That had been one of the first things to delight her, too. "You don't have any family, Mr. McTavish?" she asked.

He turned his watery eye on her and studied her a minute. "Not on this earth." His voice was quiet. "Wife and two sons died in cholera epidemic five years ago."

"Oh . . ." Hallie's heart went out to him. "Five years?"

"Five years, four months, and twenty-two days," he said.

Hallie looked at him. "I'll have the men ready for shearing lessons tomorrow. Then you can tell me what kind of wagon a shepherd needs. Meanwhile, you'll have to sleep with the other men, out there." She pointed toward the barracks. "Do you know how to ride?"

"Watch me," he said by way of answer.

There was something about Jock McTavish that Hallie already liked and trusted. She hired him, then ordered the convicts to build him a wagon—with a canvas cover, the old shepherd insisted. While four of the men—two new convicts and two of the older ones who lacked the rebellious lethargy of the new ones—worked on building it according to his instructions, Jock said, "Give me six men and I'll make sheep shearers of them."

Thus began Hallie's sheep-shearing business. When all of their sheep were sheared, Harry suggested sending them out to other farms where shearing was needed and charging so much per sheep. It was an immediate success. Hallie decided to take reservations for next year, as it brought in good revenue. When farmers couldn't afford to pay her in cash, she accepted a percentage of their fleeces, wondering what in the world she was going to do with the mountain she already had.

The only time she saw the children was at dinner. From shortly after dawn until dusk she was up and out in the fields, riding Princess, overseeing work, conferring with Brian. Jamie and Alexandra turned to Beth for their needs before looking to their mother. Hallie didn't know what to do about it. Any day now, she thought, the work load will lessen and I'll have time to be a mother again.

This year, she told herself, I'm not going to grow food for Parramatta. We'll have a garden big enough for us, but the men can better spend their time on farm work. Hay had to be cut and dried; there were three foals that spring. Lamb tails needed docking. Only the most splendid males were saved as rams; the rest had to be castrated. And there was the never-ending task of building and maintaining fences.

In the midst of it all two other new arrivals appeared on the scene. Harry and Susan did ride out, with Christopher, as promised. They brought Molly along with them and a pale, very wan-looking young woman of about twenty-five, in a neat dress that looked newly purchased. She had a boy of about nine with her, a slender child with liquid black eyes, round and huge under his unruly mop of black hair. He was the most beautiful child Hallie had ever seen.

Though she had had no warning, one look at the boy told her that he and the woman were Brian's family. How pleased he would be! she thought. Then she realized that there was no place for them to sleep. She had not expected his family yet; in fact, she had forgotten all about the letter, which had been mailed over a year and a half ago.

There was a flurry of greetings, of introductions, of Susan saying, "No wonder you don't come into town more often," gazing around her at the beauty Hallie had come to take for granted. "Harry told me your house is lovely. And oh, it does have such graceful lines."

Mrs. Daugherty sat in the wagon with her hands folded, timid and fearful of this wide-open space, looking around for her husband. But the boy jumped down and exclaimed in a lilting Irish brogue, "Look at all the horses! Does me dad have one?"

Hallie liked him immediately. "Indeed he does. One that only he uses."

Gently ran barking from behind the house.

"Where's he, me dad?" the boy said, kneeling down to gather the dog in his arms.

All the men were working away from the house. Hallie looked at the young boy, so eager, and said, "I'll take you myself." She turned to the Langleys. "Do you mind? We won't be long. I want to see the look on Brian's face."

Harry said they'd make themselves at home and he'd show Susan and Mrs. Daugherty around. Molly took charge of Christopher. They really needed more room, Hallie reflected. She'd have to have the men set to building the Daughertys a little house and then get that extra room added behind her bedroom. Oh, so much to do!

"Come with me. . . ." She reached out for the boy's hand. Brian must have mentioned his son's name, but she couldn't recall it. "I bet you've never ridden on a horse, have you?"

He shook his head, dark eyes shining with excitement.

"We'll ride out together and find your father." She led him to the barn, where she saddled Princess. Showing him how to straddle the saddle, she climbed up after him and, putting her arms around him, held the reins loosely. "Don't be afraid," she said. "I won't let you fall."

"I'm not afraid." And he wasn't; she could tell.

As she cantered over the fields, it reminded her of the first time she'd been on a horse, sitting sheltered in front of Chad as the wind whipped her face and the trees raced by. She had loved the feeling.

In less than ten minutes Brian's work corps came into view. Hallie's heart began to pound as she imagined what Brian would feel, how the whole family would feel. She wanted to watch him when he spied his son, wanted to give him this moment.

Stopping a short distance from the group, she called to him. He turned to face them, shielding his eyes from the sun with his hands. He said something to the men, who continued working, and began to amble over to Hallie. She slid from her saddle and held up her arms for the boy.

"Is that me dad?" His voice was a whisper.

"Yes."

He stood watching as his father approached. Brian's gait was firmer, more confident than when Hallie had first met him, his face bearded and dark, his eyes images of his son's. It was not until he was nearly twenty feet from them that he hesitated, then approached more slowly. His eyes had been fixed on Hallie, but now they shifted to the boy . . . the son he hadn't seen in six years. There was no way they could have recognized each other after all that time, except that both were so dark. Except that they looked so like each other.

Then Brian stopped. Dead in his tracks.

Hallie's hand went to her throat and she felt tears prick the back of her eyes. She gave the boy a slight push, which was all he needed. He began to move—slowly and tentatively—toward his father, who stood staring at him, his long arms hanging at his side. Hallie felt her lips puckering, was aware of difficulty swallowing.

"Robbie?" Brian's voice touched the boy, who started running, gathering speed until he hurled himself into his father's outstretched arms, nearly knocking him over.

Hallie thought she should look away, should let the two of them have this moment together; but their happiness was hers, too. She wondered if Jamie would react that way to Chad when he came home. Would he even remember his father?

That made her think. Chad had been gone more than a year. He'd be home in less than that, she guessed, yet she didn't feel anything at the thought. She remembered the fun they'd had, his kindness, his enormous zest for life, but she couldn't see his face or hear his laughter.

So much had happened to her of which he was not a part. Tristan shared those parts. Beth was integral to them. The Langleys shared some of them, as did Brian. But Chad was a universe away, not even aware of what had happened to the world he'd left behind. He didn't know that it had increased and multiplied, and that there was no Archie. He did not know she had lost a child—did not even know she had been pregnant.

He did not know she was running the farm, that she helped to deliver sheep and foals, that she knew how to mend fences and had driven the wagon while men pitched forks of hay high onto it. Did not know . . .

"What my life is about," Hallie murmured, finishing her thought aloud. It was as though the man she had married were no longer a part of her life.

She rounded up all the blankets she could to prepare pallets for the Daughertys, and decreed that Brian and his family should stay in the drawing room until a house could be readied for them. That first night she thought they should be afforded privacy. Insisting that Susan and Harry and Christopher use her bedroom, she and the children, along with Beth and Molly, took themselves out to the barn and bedded down in the hay.

Hallie couldn't remember when she'd had more fun. Beth laughed until it sounded as though she were crying. The three young women, nearly of an age, giggled like schoolgirls until late into the night. Hallie had never seen Beth so uninhibited. Jamie and Alexandra stayed awake far later than was usual but fell asleep long before the women tired. Hallie could see why Susan so enjoyed Molly. She was sorry Susan wasn't out with them. Molly was full of fun, devilish in such a nice way, and she told story after story in the most jolly manner. She said she'd steal bread and anything else all over again, commit murder if necessary, to be sent here instead of staying in "that dreary dark country."

She said someday she guessed she'd marry, when her time was up, though she thought the Langleys would assure her ticket of leave, through the governor, had she any prospects in mind. But she hadn't met anyone she wanted to give up her present status for—"except the doctor. He's the kindest man I ever met, as well as one of the nicest-looking. But he never pays me no never mind—as a woman, that is. He's merciful nice to me as a nanny, though. Treats me like a real human being."

Hallie felt her heart turn over. Somehow she never thought of Tristan marrying. If he had a wife, he wouldn't come out regularly to visit, wouldn't bring her plants, and wouldn't take Jamie riding, stay overnight, and spend hours talking with her. She would miss that sorely.

As she drifted into sleep, she imagined Tristan kissing Molly, and sadness overcame her. She had never contemplated such an event. Why not? she asked herself now. He should not be denied a family, denied love. But we're his family, she told herself, knowing the unfairness of such a thought even as she clung to it. When she dreamed, she saw Tristan kissing Molly, kissing Beth, kissing Susan Langley, kissing women she had never seen. Don't! she cried out to him. Don't kiss them! Kiss me. It's I who love you. I have always loved you.

In the morning she did not look at Molly as kindly, though she was angry at herself because of it. Even after Molly and the Langleys left, Hallie talked to herself, realizing it was unfair to be jealous of Molly. Just because Molly was attracted to Tristan—and what woman wouldn't be?—did not mean he was attracted to her. It was she, Hallie, with whom he spent time. It was she, Hallie, to whom he brought presents, whose children he loved. It was she, Hallie, whom he must love. As she loved him.

There. She had not dared to let herself say it aloud, to think it in the here and now. But there it was.

Clear as day.

Bright as the stars at night.

The rains did not come that year. The sun shone in a sky so blue that there were never clouds. Hallie did not realize the lack of rain until Phil, the convict in charge of the garden, said, "The corn's not growing high. Some of the vegetables are drying up."

So a bucket brigade was formed. Three times a week,

early in the morning, all the convicts lined up from the creek to the garden and watered it.

The absence of rain did not bother them in any other way. In fact, Hallie enjoyed the weather. When it was sunny and warm, she was aware that her soul expanded. She felt nicer; she was a flower unfolding, having been given warmth and sunshine. She liked herself better than she ever had in England. Sun and warmth, she thought, made her more generous. So she considered the lack of rain a boon.

What did bother her was a letter from Chad. She had been expecting one at some point, but its contents disturbed her deeply:

My Dear Wife,
The first news is that I will not yet be home. There are two reasons: One is the great good fortune the quality of our fleeces is bringing. The woolen mills to which I have shown the fleece are enthusiastic about the quality. I think it best if I wait until you send all that we have, so that I may bargain even more forcefully now that the war in Europe seems to be ending. I do not want the eventual availability of French wool to jeopardize us.

Oh, my God, thought Hallie, calculating quickly. That means at least another year and a half. Eight or nine months for the fleece to get there and—if he sells them immediately—another eight or nine months for his return passage.

I trust you and the children are in excellent health. I have such faith in Archie that I do not worry about you, though do miss my family. It is already far too long.
There is another complication. My father is dying, the doctor says. His days are limited. Since I have not seen him in over a dozen years, and he begs me to stay, I feel I must. My conscience, it is true, is torn. My duty lies not only here with Father, but with my family, with you.
I know this will work hardship on Archie. Pay him

more and promise him whatever you think he would like. I think our friendship is such that he will be willing to stay as foreman. I count on that.

In the event that emergencies arise, I am transferring 300 pounds to the Bank in Parramatta. With luck, you will not need to use it, but I do not want you living in poverty or need. I hope you will indulge in a few extravagances. Certainly we can afford them.

I hope you can arrange for the fleeces to be on the next ship. It's the quality of our breeding program that has produced such superior wool. I have ideas for an even more superb product. The contacts I am making here assure us of a successful future. Tell the other farmers that, and reassure the Governor on that account, too. Everyone here is interested in our island Continent. It is becoming known as something more than just a penal colony.

I visited your home, introducing myself to your parents. They were most interested in hearing about you and of all details of their grandchildren. Your brother Danny is expecting his second child shortly. Tess, his wife, is a comely lass. I shall call on them again in order to know your family better *and* to reassure them that you are still a part of their world.

I am sorry, dear Wife, to be kept from my family for so much longer. I wonder if I can really bear that.

I hope that, along with the fleeces, you will enclose a letter, telling me what is happening on your side of the world, up there where you look down at the Moon. Isn't that how you think it might be? I've decided you must visualize the Moon at the Equator, and here in England we look South to it, while there, where you are, you look North to it, down—isn't that your reasoning? I smile when I remember that. When you look "down" and locate the Southern Cross, remember me.

I am thinking of you and the children. Tell them I will teach them all about the Heavens when I return. Talk of me to them, Hallie, so that they will not forget me. I fear that. Fear that you will forget me, too.

Chad

So they will not forget you, mused Hallie. How can they remember you when I find it so difficult?

"Let's bundle up the fleeces and get them to Sydney," she said aloud to herself. She had discovered that she enjoyed having issues to solve, and so far she'd been able to unravel all the logistical problems.

It was questions of the heart she had trouble with.

Twenty-one

Belinda Daugherty relieved Beth. The day after she and Robbie arrived, she was helping Beth in the kitchen. Though it was relatively spacious, the kitchen really was inadequate for preparing three meals a day for two dozen people. By the time the two-room house was finished for Brian's family, six months later, Hallie decided to build a kitchen between the two barracks before adding a bedroom onto her own house. If Chad was not going to be home for almost two years, her bedroom was adequate for Beth and the children as well as for herself. The addition to the house could wait.

A combination kitchen/dining hall was readied, and Belinda took over that aspect of the work. She prepared three meals a day for the convicts, thus relieving Beth of more than she could handle. Although Beth had opened up with Molly, and liked Belinda, she was still shy with strangers. She could not make herself smile at any of the men, even Brian. Only with Tristan did she relax. She talked little and never initiated conversation except with Hallie and the children. Hallie never had to think of domestic chores now. She never cooked, never did the washing, never swept the house, never built a fire, never made a bed.

Sometimes, she thought, what I do is men's work. Not only did she do the physical work usually relegated to men, she also made decisions, spent evenings with a pad and pencil, making plans for the future, estimating needs, projecting schedules. She had bemoaned the fact that her lack of knowledge with figures kept her from understanding money and acreage.

Tristan said, "That's easy to remedy." When next he came out he brought an elementary arithmetic book and set to teaching Hallie addition and subtraction. It became a ritual of learning, with Tristan leaving problems to be solved between his visits. Before long both Beth and the nearly four-year-old Jamie joined them around the table. Alexandra, not wanting to be left out, tried to listen, but she couldn't concentrate and settled for running around the table and pulling on an old towel with Gently.

Jamie and Robbie Daugherty, despite the six years' age difference, became inseparable. Robbie was excited about everything. Belinda said, "We never knew there was so much space. I was scared to come, because we'd never been out of Dublin. But alone, I couldn't take care of Robbie. Sometimes we didn't have enough to eat. My sewing didn't bring in that much." The two of them adjusted far more easily than even Brian could have hoped for. Belinda said, "Mornings, after I clean up from breakfast, I walk up that little hill behind our house and stare out over it all. I think I've died and gone to heaven."

Brian taught his son to ride. Hallie's heart turned over every time she saw the look in Brian's eyes when he studied his son.

Robbie began to attend what had become the nightly math lessons, and showed startling aptitude. They saved the really difficult problems to work through with Tristan, who told them he imagined they were the most eager and intelligent class anyone could have. They smiled smugly. It did not bother Hallie that she was on the same level as ten-year-old Robbie. She was thrilled to be learning. A school, she thought, that's what we are.

And, indeed, that's what the evenings were like. In order for Beth, Jamie, and even Robbie to understand arithmetic, they had to learn to read. Hallie was able to help them with that. When Brian realized his son was learning to read and write, he also began to frequent the house evenings and edged around the crowded table. Tristan had to bring out more pencils and paper.

The time came when Hallie decided she wanted to meet her neighbors. By now, Harry informed her, over two dozen families were in the valley. True, some were nearly half a day's journey, but he drew her a rough map when she visited the Langleys and told her also that Chad's transfer of funds had arrived so that Hallie was able to pay for the building materials she'd need.

She set out one week to meet her neighbors, although she couldn't get to all of them. In this way, too, she became

216

familiar with the country in which she had lived for nearly four years. What she saw made her realize that this was mainly a man's country. Over half the women were not wives, but convicts serving their time—in bed mainly, thought Hallie. Used, with no consideration of their needs or wishes. They were dressed in tattered clothes and worked in dark one-room huts, for the most part. They didn't talk unless spoken to, and then monosyllabically. Hallie wanted to shake some of them, but realized this kind of living was probably preferable to actual jail. She thought these women must feel so alone. Men who were not their husbands probably didn't share anything with them. Then she was reminded of Chad, who hadn't shared his inner self, either. He told her *after* the facts, never sharing his hopes and dreams. She knew, from Tristan and Harry, that not all men were like that, however.

One evening she was telling Tristan—and the weeks (sometimes more than a month) between his visits seemed to stretch into eternity—about her trip around the countryside. "These people feel so isolated," she said. "And they're so busy just trying to eke out a living that they can't take a day off to ride into Parramatta when they run out of flour or sugar or tea."

"You manage," he said. The children were bedded for the night, Beth had retired, and they were sitting at the table drinking coffee. Bird sounds had become mere twitters as darkness descended.

"You can't compare what I have here with a man on his own—or a man and a woman, sometimes one or two children. Work goes on here even when I go into town. A couple of them have a convict or two, like Will. But they can't afford more. They can barely feed themselves. And they're lonely out here . . . especially the women.

"If we had a store out here," she continued, rising and walking around the room, excited, "it would save these people a lot of time. If they ran out of supplies, it would take most of them just an hour or two—at the most, three—to come shopping. The women could even ride over alone, it would be so close to home. It would be a place not only to shop, but to visit with others."

"Here? You want a store here?" His voice told her he thought she was jesting.

"Why not?" she replied defensively, as though prepared to do battle with him. She stopped pacing and stood with her hands on her hips.

She could tell he was trying not to let her see his amusement. He bit his lip, but she saw the mirth in his eyes.

"I mean beyond the hill over there." The hill from which she'd first seen her home. "We could bring out milled flour and maize, even stock tobacco and rum. I think it wouldn't hurt to have a few ribbons and yards of fabric. And for those farms without cows, we could sell milk. And eggs, though everyone seems to have chickens."

Tristan smiled at her. "My little entrepreneur," he said. *My* . . . As though she were his. "What does that mean?" she asked.

"Businessperson. Hallie, you do beat all." He put his cup down and, rising, walked over to her. "Why don't you talk to Harry about it. I don't know a thing about business."

She knew that, but she loved talking her ideas over with him. He never seemed impatient and always acted as though whatever she had to say was the most interesting idea in the world. Even when he looked as though he might laugh, it was with an attitude of laughing with her, never at her . . . unless it was to laugh at her intestinal fortitude. You know"—he reached out and took her hands in his— "you carry more excitement and energy in your little finger than most people exhibit in a lifetime."

She loved it when he touched her. She felt it all over. "Is that why you come out here all the time?"

It was summer. Although it was after nine o'clock, the sky had not yet darkened completely, and the stars were not yet visible. No lamps had yet been lit. Tristan stood up and walked over to the door. He paused there a minute and turned his head to look at her. Then he walked out the door, into the warm twilight.

Hallie followed him, standing in the doorway, watching him walk until he stopped under the gigantic silver gum with its drooping leaves. She could see that he was staring into the creek, from which rose the reflection of the new moon in the pale sky.

The honeysuckle he had planted last year near the front door scented the air. Though there was no breeze, leaves in the tops of the trees rustled. Gently rubbed her leg,

218

having followed her to the doorway. Absentmindedly she leaned down to rub his back. She watched Tristan for the longest time. When he turned at last to face her, it was dark.

She began to walk toward him. As she reached him, he said, "I come here because . . . I pretend that Jamie and Alexandra are mine; I fantasize that the shrubs I plant here make this place partly mine. I come here because I see minds come to life here. I come because I, too, come alive here." He reached out and put his hands around her waist. "I come here, above all, because this is where my heart is."

He had not mentioned the word "love," but Hallie understood that was what he was talking about.

When he left the next morning, she said, "I'll ride into Parramatta with you and talk to Harry about my idea."

All the way into town she was aware of Tristan, conscious of being alone with him. For the first time in a long while she thought, damn Chad. He has no right to stay away all these years.

Several houses dotted the valleys. Two were ones Hallie had not yet visited. Tristan, who seemed to know all about anyone anywhere, informed her, "That's where Tim Jenkins, an emancipist, lives, with his woman and their two children."

"Woman? Not his wife, you mean?"

Tristan shook his head. "No, though they live as man and wife. She was a convict, too. They're hardworking, but all these men who start with just fifty acres stand so little chance. They scrabble from sunup to dark just to eke out a subsistence."

"Still," said Hallie, "isn't it better than what they had back in England?"

"I venture to say it is. But most of the emancipists give up and work for others, or too many fall back into habits of stealing."

"You'd think with such a chance for new starts they wouldn't have to resort to that. Hardly anyone here starves. No one freezes to death."

"Having something in common with ex-convicts, I tend to sympathize. But I must admit"—Tristan said it as though he didn't want to—"many of them are lazy. If they spent as much time on honest work as they did trying to circumvent the law, they—"

"Don't say it," Hallie interrupted. "You know as well as I that most of them never had a chance in England. There aren't jobs, and you can be arrested for being unemployed."

"It's true," admitted Tristan. "It's just that so many don't want to know what an honest day's work is. On the other hand, there are dozens who relish the opportunity to start life anew and work hard for it. They are what I see as the backbone of the future. How many of us are given the opportunity to start anew?"

"Do you think of yourself as an ex-convict?" Hallie asked. His last sentence implied that he did, though she never thought of him that way.

Tristan's expression was sober. "Not often. But I do remember my incarceration too well." By now Hallie had become used to the way he talked. When she didn't understand a word, she tried to figure it out from the context in which he used it. "I do think it gives me an empathy I lacked before. An understanding. I believe"—he turned to look at her as they rode side by side—"now, that everyone should experience some unhappiness. Some pain. I wouldn't wish complete happiness on anyone."

Hallie frowned. "I thought happiness was the aim of life."

Tristan laughed. "Hallie, my dear, I don't think you believe that. Think about it. How shallow you'd be. How, for instance, do you find it within you to dispense love so indiscriminately? If you had been raised in the nobility, do you think for a second that you'd be so kind to all you come in contact with?"

Hallie thought about that. She had never seen herself as dispensing love indiscriminately. Love was a strange word for Tristan to have used.

She didn't know why she felt defensive, but it made her uncomfortable. Inadvertently, she kicked Princess, who began to canter before Hallie reined her in.

"We may be using the word in different ways, Tristan said when they were once again side by side, "but you know more about love than most people I've ever met. You reach

220

out to people. If it's within you, they're not going to be unhappy, not wanting." He was smiling, sitting erect in the saddle, holding the reins loosely.

"Oh." He made her nervous, seeing her this way. He saw her as someone she wasn't. "You mean because I took Beth in?"

"That's just part of it."

"Beth gives me more than I give her." Hallie tossed her head. Did Tristan see a Hallie who wasn't real?

"Because you love her. And then there's Brian's family."

"Chad thought of sending for them. He wanted to tie Brian's loyalty to us. I had nothing to do with that." Tristan prodded his horse to keep up with Hallie.

"Yet it's you who make them feel at home, you who build them a house, you—"

"Tristan! Don't make me out nicer than I am." She wanted him to love the real Hallie, not the Hallie he imagined her to be. "Belinda does her share of work. She's even begun to wash the convicts' clothes. She's the one who knows what love means, if you're using it as giving part of yourself and your time."

"All right." Tristan smiled, amusement reflected in his eyes. "If this makes you uncomfortable . . . But you *do* reach out to everyone, Hallie. It's one of the things I . . ." He hesitated.

"Love about me?" He was using the word in a broad sense; she would, too. "Well, I'm not sure you're seeing the real me. I just try to get through each day as best I can. . . ."

"And ride out to make sure your neighbors aren't in need, and make life for your convicts more livable than most places in the entire world, and treat them as though they're people worthy of consideration."

"Well, aren't they?" Her voice held a note of belligerence.

"If you'd rather, we'll talk of something else. But one final word. This idea of a store is not to make money, is it? It's to help out your neighbors." He stopped his horse. "Yes, Hallie, it is one of the things about you I love."

She pulled Princess to a halt and turned around to look at him. Her eyes met his. "One of the many things," he added softly.

They stared across their horses at each other. "Talking

of loving people," Hallie said, trying to treat the word lightly, "you're the hero of the community. You go out of your way far more than I do."

"It's true. . . ." He didn't smile, just kept staring at her. "I am capable of giving a lot."

"I know that," she said. "So does my whole family. You give us more than the rest of the world put together."

"And would give you more were I allowed."

So there it was, out in the open. Yet neither of them could do anything about it.

"Don't you ever feel it's one-sided, giving? Don't you want to get?" She knew she was treading on fragile ground.

He kicked his horse gently, and they rode side by side again, closely. "Ah, that may be the secret. If only more people knew. Hallie, my dear, by the act of giving, I get."

She thought about that, relieved the conversation was not veering to the strictly personal. By now they had reached the outskirts of Parramatta and slowed their horses to a walk.

"I remember Christmas back home," Tristan continued after a pause. "It was the happiest time of the year. Yule logs on the fire. Always snow. Our home was the largest, so my aunts and uncles and cousins always came to our house. We'd have roast turkey and cranberry and plum pudding."

"Yes, we had plum pudding, too." Hallie thought of her own Christmases past. They had roast goose dinner at noon. Father Christmas always left a toy for each of the children and either a hand-knit muffler or caps for the adults. It was the only time of the year she ever received a toy. One year there was a doll, and another year she and Danny together had received a sled. What fun they had had! When she was older she helped knit the caps and mittens.

"There were never less than twenty of us." Tristan smiled at his reminiscence. "We went to midnight services Christmas Eve, so we slept late Christmas morning. That is, everyone else did. I was always awake at the crack of dawn. We'd have a big breakfast before all the relatives arrived, and my mother would start the turkey roasting. When my aunts arrived, we'd sit around the Christmas tree, always strung with popcorn and alight with candles, and spend hours opening presents."

"Hours? How could it take you so long?" Hallie was relishing this conversation. Tristan seldom talked of his past.

He laughed. "It was wonderful. But it wasn't until I was older, earning my own money, that I really began to enjoy Christmas. The pleasure I got was reflected in the faces of those for whom I had so carefully chosen presents. Particularly my nephews and nieces. I have never found giving has taken from me, Hallie. Giving renews me. I do not think I do it to earn the gratitude of those to whom I give. I think I just enjoy the actual act of giving, of thinking of the present, and thinking that it will add pleasure to the life of whomever I give it to." He mused, "Giving may possibly be selfish on my part."

Hallie thought of the dozens of plants and trees he had brought out to the farm. Of the hours he spent teaching them all to add and subtract, and now even multiplying. Of the time he spent listening . . . That was a form of giving, too.

"You know, Tristan," she said, "you're quite the nicest person I've ever known."

They arrived at the Langleys', and Tristan jumped from his horse. "I hope you'll always think so," he said, raising a hand to help her down.

The Langleys were delighted, as always, to see Hallie. Susan did not invite others to dinner this time, and for this Hallie was grateful. Tristan had gone on to Sydney, and she enjoyed just being with Susan and Harry, relaxing with them and hearing the latest gossip of Parramatta and Sydney. Just looking at Susan was pleasurable. Her dresses were always so pretty, always pastels and so feminine, looking as though they'd just been ironed.

"We're thinking of building a house in Sydney, too," Susan told her. "Harry does so much business there that he's gone several nights a week. So, if the governor can have two homes, Harry says there's no reason we can't."

"I have to be able to compete," explained Harry, "and it looks like Sydney is overtaking Parramatta in size. Business is centering there, even though all agriculture branches out from here. Think we'll open up a branch of the bank in Sydney."

"The colony seems to be growing." Hallie didn't know how she felt about that. She liked not being crowded.

"Now that Captain Flinders has circumnavigated and charted this island continent, he's shown there are thousands of miles across, and thousands of miles north and south . . . limitless possibilities. Since Wentworth and friends crossed the Blue Mountains and found rivers and grasslands in the interior, we may be able to raise enough animals to feed the world." Harry's eyes shone. "There's no end to what can be done with this continent."

"Well, in my small corner, I want to do a little something."

Harry looked at Hallie questioningly. "It's usually interesting when you get that look in your eye." He tamped his pipe and lit it, waving the match as he drew on the pipe, and then sat back, waiting.

"I want to start a store. . . ."

He listened as she told him of her idea and then sat thinking. "Twenty-four families doesn't sound like enough people to support a store, Hallie."

"That's close to two hundred people," she said. "Why, with my family and convicts and hired help, we're close to thirty ourselves."

"That's true," agreed Harry. "I hadn't seen it that way. And certainly the valley continues to grow. Wouldn't be surprised if a township doesn't form out there before too long."

"I've also been thinking . . . not many of them have money for some of their needs. We could take livestock in trade—pigs, chickens, maybe calves. If we build a little stockyard, then when we came to town we could bring them to sell. Those that have vegetables or eggs and milk could do the same."

When Harry didn't respond, Hallie asked, "Is it a silly idea?"

"No, no," he replied. "Quite the contrary. Hallie, do you know anything about business? About ledgers and keeping books?"

"I've learned addition, subtraction, and now I'm learning multiplication," she said proudly.

"I don't think that's quite enough," Harry said, and smiled over her head across the room at Susan. "Let me think some more about it."

Later, as they were going up the stairs to their bedrooms—the Langleys, like half a dozen others in town, had a two-story home—Susan took Hallie by the arm and said, "I'm going to have another baby."

Hallie hugged her. But as she lay in the feather bed, trying to fall asleep, she thought, I should be having more children, too.

In the morning, at breakfast, Harry said, "Build it, Hallie. Let me know when it's done and I'll come give you ideas on stocking it. Also, I'll start looking around for someone to manage it for you, if you'd like. That is, you weren't thinking of doing that yourself, were you?"

Hallie laughed. "No. And you know I need your business advice, Harry."

He pulled at his rusty mustache. "I'm not sure that, once in a while, it shouldn't be the other way around. You have the Midas touch, Hallie."

Hallie looked at Susan, who shrugged. Harry noticed.

"It means that everything you do succeeds," he said, smiling.

Don't say that, thought Hallie. It means something is bound to go wrong.

Twenty-two

"You know that pond, the largest one, in the far pasture?" asked Brian. He had never been able to use the word billabong.

Hallie nodded.

"Well, it's not there."

She looked up at him. "What do you mean, not there?"

Brian scratched behind his ear. "Just that," he replied slowly. "Went up there this morning and found a couple dead sheep. It's 'cause the pond dried up. They don't have water."

"Well, it couldn't have just disappeared."

"Afraid so . . ."

They'd been bucket brigading the garden from the creek for so long that it had become routine. Had they been so long without rain? "It must have dried up," she said at last. Dead sheep . . . A shiver ran down her back. "Why don't you ride out and find Jock and see if he's noticed anything. See what he has to say."

Brian nodded and turned to go. "Wait," Hallie said. She had an idea that whatever was happening was important. "I'll go with you." It was late afternoon.

"He could be most anyplace," said Brian. "You won't get home tonight. We might have to ride a couple hours."

That's what I get for owning so much land, Hallie thought. "I'll tell Beth, and get us something to eat. I've slept outside before."

It was early November, and the rains—due last March—had barely sprinkled. The ground was always golden in the winter and early spring, before new growth started. As they rode along searching for Jock, Hallie noted that the green shoots that should be crowding together were few and far between. The grass was fawn-yellow and crackly underfoot, not the green-gold of spring.

They found Jock before dark. He had built a fire and

was roasting a rabbit he'd shot. A billy of tea was simmering.

"They're gettin' thin," he said. "There's nigh enough grass. But the crick up here is still running. I don't know what to do if it's drought." The word spread terror through Hallie. Droughts were for deserts. "Never had one in Scotland, leastaways that I can remember. Better change the sheep in that pasture. Find cricks that're running. They'll last longer'n waterholes."

I own a river, thought Hallie. My sheep can't die for lack of water.

Despite the worry now thrust upon her, Hallie enjoyed the trip. She hadn't slept out under the stars since the two times at the billabong five years ago with Chad. She stared up at the heavens, at the shower of stars so close, so clear. I wonder if anyone lives on them? she mused. One shot across the sky, losing itself but leaving a trail. What makes them? she wondered. What *is* a star? Whatever, she was glad for them.

Without consciously trying, her eyes focused on the Southern Cross. Chad can't even see it, she thought, trying to picture his face. She could hardly remember him. She no longer even wondered what he was doing. He was in another world—in a world where swans weren't black, where there were no kangaroos or aborigines; in a world where convicts were not daily topics of conversations, where those born into her circumstances never had a chance. He was in a world so different from hers—a world where women didn't sleep out under stars or run farms, where ponds didn't dry up, where men lived in the perpetual darkness of coal mines, where trees lost their leaves and were no more than branches in winter. Where winter was in December and January rather than July and August, where winter was cold and the homeless froze to death. A world devoid of cockatoos and kookaburras, where pelicans and parrots were unknown. A world so unlike this one. Everything so different, so opposite.

"I wouldn't go back there for anything," she said aloud. She did miss Mum and Danny and Dada, but she felt closer to Beth and to Susan than she had ever been with her sisters. I wish they could see this land, live here, she

227

thought. Breathe freely, without coal dust. See the sun all year long. See these stars. See their grandchildren.

In the morning, as they rode back to the house, Hallie and Brian decided to move the sheep to pastures by the river and the creek, even if it meant refencing some pastures. "Get the men at it right away. Move those sheep from the upper pasture, today, to some place where they can get water."

In the afternoon she rode over to where some of her men were at work building the store. Hallie had thought that a square twenty-by-twenty-foot building would be adequate, but Tristan had advised enlarging it so that whoever managed it could have living space in back of the store. Make it big enough for a family, he'd suggested. So she'd added two rooms behind the original space, for living quarters. They were building a paddock, too, beside a small barn to protect animals from the elements, if necessary. Hallie thought it was beginning to look quite nice. She spent evenings making lists of things she thought should be stocked. She had added pencils and paper after Tristan kept bringing more each time he visited. Last time he had brought some simple books, which she had begun to read to Jamie and Alexandra. He watched as Hallie traced the words with her fingers as she read aloud, and would squint and try to figure out what a word said. Robbie read to Jamie, too, and was as patient as Hallie. Robbie also sat for hours with Alexandra, teaching her arithmetic with marbles; and after she *saw* one marble being added to two, he wrote it down and talked to her about it. Hallie thought him a born teacher.

When the first lambs started arriving, Jock kept all the men busy roaming the pastures, searching for rejected newborns, helping difficult births, culling those sheep that hadn't bred. Hallie always enjoyed this time of year, the season of birth. . . .

And not just of sheep. Belinda had morning sickness. Beth again prepared breakfast for the convicts, until by late morning Belinda felt fine and relieved her in the kitchen. She and Robbie both basked in the open air and sun, in the friendship they found at the farm.

When Tristan came next, he brought a present Harry had sent to Hallie. He brought Ben Lambert.

Ben was a convict, a dour-looking young man about twenty-five years of age. He had arrived in Sydney five days before, looked around him, and yearned for London. He would return to England in a minute, he thought, despite having to face the horrible trip—despite being deprived of baths, despite eating food fit for nothing but animals. Despite the smell. All these trees, all these unoccupied spaces . . . so few people.

Hallie's first impression of him was not favorable. His manners were impeccable, yet he obviously was from the lower classes. His speech hinted of Yorkshire, though he had lived in London all his life. Clean-shaven, he had a luxuriant crop of sandy hair and gray-green eyes that shifted behind smudged wire-rimmed glasses which kept slipping down his nose.

He was obviously not used to a horse. When Tristan jumped to the ground, Ben sat clutching his reins.

"Hallie, this is Ben Lambert," Tristan said. "Harry thinks he's just the man you need for the store."

Hallie looked up at the thin man with the set chin, and Tristan caught the expression in her eyes.

"Ben's just off the boat. Has another six years to serve. Harry says he's smart as can be with figures . . ." Amusement crept into his eyes. "He's up for charges of forgery and embezzlement."

Hallie turned to him. "Embezzlement? Isn't that stealing?"

Tristan nodded, but he smiled as though at a huge joke. "Nevertheless, Harry—and I, I must admit—think that he's just the right man for you. Dealing with figures will be far preferable to a chain gang or field labor, I am sure. Don't you think so, Mr. Lambert?"

"How do I get off this horse?" He was too frightened to move.

As it turned out, Ben Lambert had never been on a horse before. When Tristan helped him dismount, his knees were bowed and he walked gingerly. "Saddle sores, I suspect," Tristan told him. "You'll get used to it. They'll be better tomorrow."

Ben scowled. "Get used to it? I don't intend to ride again."

Hallie and Tristan grinned at each other. "Come in, and

229

we'll have a cup of tea," Hallie suggested. "And talk about this."

She learned that Ben had been an accountant for a large shipping firm. It was there that he had been caught juggling funds, though he did not put it exactly that way.

He answered when asked questions, in a taciturn manner that didn't waste words. Hallie couldn't figure out whether he was shy or ill-humored. Perhaps a bit of both. Though Harry would have known whether or not he'd be good at the books, she thought Ben might inhibit people bent on buying something. He certainly was not outgoing. And a convict left alone at the store? He could run off with money. He might cheat the customers. He might alienate her neighbors.

"No," Ben replied when Hallie asked him if he had a family. It was like pulling teeth to get him to talk.

"Have you ever waited on people before?"

"No. Don't much like people." He reached down, plucked a blade of dried grass, and inserted it between his teeth.

Hallie shot a glance at Tristan. Every instinct told her Harry and Tristan were wrong. Well, they could ride over to the store and he could see it. She had begun to stock it, and after every wagonload of supplies had been delivered, she would stand in the doorway just looking at the goods on the shelves, smiling to herself. The bolts of fabric, few that there were, added color. It smelled not only of freshly sawn wood, but now of coffee and spices as well.

There were large windows across the front, for Hallie loved to let the sun in wherever she could. In summer, at home, she opened the long French windows across her drawing room and bedroom and left them open, inviting the outside in.

Though Ben said nothing about it, they could see it pained him to hit the saddle again. "It's not far," Hallie reassured him. "Just about a mile." He made a little noise that sounded, to her, like a moan.

As they approached the store, Hallie said, "Now isn't that nice-looking?"

"Well, I'll grant you this," Tristan said, "it's certainly the nicest-looking one in . . . Where *is* this, Hallie?"

Without hesitation she answered, "It's Morgantown."

230

Chad had wanted a town named after them. She didn't notice the veil drop over Tristan's eyes or the smile leave his face.

Ben looked around. "Morgantown? This here's just one building."

"The first," Hallie said.

"Where do people live?" asked the bewildered city man.

Tristan answered, "On farms around the countryside. Nearest neighbor's about three or four miles. You'll see them all sooner or later. This is on Mrs. Morgan's property."

Proudly Hallie showed Ben where he would live. A wild look came into his eyes. "You mean I stay out here all by myself? There's no one nearby? I stay alone all night—and all day?" It sounded as though he were pronouncing sentence on himself. "It'd be solitary confinement. I'd rather go back to Sydney and take my chances."

I'd rather he did, too, thought Hallie. She had not taken to the young man. He might know figures, but she didn't think she liked him.

"Hold on," said Tristan. "Give it a chance. Whatever life you lead here is not going to be like any you knew back in London. Here's a chance to do what you were trained to do. A chance to make the most of your life."

"Most of my life?" It was not quite a wail.

"Try it until I come back out in another two weeks' time. Or, rather, give it a month. See how you and Hallie—Mrs. Morgan—take to each other."

Ben looked at her balefully. Hallie didn't think he liked her looks any better than she liked his. It wasn't that he didn't have nice features; in fact he did. But his face was sullen and his attitude anything but cooperative. He'd scare Etta into not talking, she thought. The poor woman would flee before she could so much as ask for flour.

"We're not quite ready to open up yet," she told him reluctantly. "I need a few more supplies, and I have to let the other farmers know the store's ready." They had been enthusiastic when she had broached the subject of a nearby store. "You can come up and stay in the barracks with the other convicts," she offered.

That night Hallie, Tristan, and Ben sat down and talked of whether or not she could afford to extend credit. She

231

didn't know what it meant. When the conversation centered around Ben's area of expertise, he began to talk, if not forcefully, at least with confidence. As he explained what credit meant, about bartering, he came to life. His voice took on a deeper timbre and his hands waved in the air. He talked of ledgers and keeping track of credit, of how much could be extended to each. They made a list of all their neighbors, and Ben chewed on the end of a pencil as he frowned and worked over a ledger.

He said, "I think you should have licorice sticks to give to children."

Hallie looked at him in amazement. "Why?"

He shrugged. "Good idea," was his only answer.

He had not seemed responsive to Jamie and Alexandra, so Hallie didn't think it was because he particularly liked children. "I'll think about it," she said.

It was just dawn when Hallie heard a horse. As the hoofbeats pounded into the ground, she jumped from bed and looked out the window. A stranger pulled up in front, leaped from his horse, and began pounding on the door. She called out to him and quickly dressed.

"I'm Walker," he said, as though that explained something. "Miz Etta's having a bad time with the baby. She said you'd come."

He must be the Coltons' convict, Hallie realized. "Yes, of course," she told him. "And there's a doctor here. Wait a minute and I'll waken him."

She threw on her clothes and ran out to the barn. Throwing the door open, she called, "Tristan!" It was still dark inside.

"What's wrong?" Though his voice was still thick with sleep, she saw an apparition heading toward her, saw Tristan in his nightshirt, and suddenly thought, I shouldn't be here.

"Hallie . . . are you ill?"

"No." She stayed put, going no closer. "Etta Colton's in labor. They need you."

"I'll be ready in two minutes," he said, hurrying back into the darkness.

Together Hallie, Tristan, and Walker rode fast out to the

232

Coltons' farm. Etta lay on the bed, semiconscious. Mary Ann ran in and out the door. Will sat drinking coffee; he had gained weight since Hallie had last seen him. He paid no attention to Etta's cries, which sounded like the bleats of lost lambs. Sweat covered her, and her glazed eyes reflected pain. She had thrown up on the pillow beside her, and Will had just left it there.

Hallie introduced Tristan, who did not waste time talking to Will but headed straight to Etta. Within two minutes he said, "Breech birth. Where can I wash up?"

Will nodded to a pail in the corner.

"Heat it to the boiling point," Tristan said.

But Will made no move to do so.

Hallie grabbed the pail, scooped water into a pan, and set it on the stove, which was not lit. While she built a fire, Tristan took off his jacket and rolled up his sleeves.

"There, now, Mrs. Colton, I'm going to help you." He turned to Will. "Any whiskey around?"

Will shook his head. "Don't touch it."

Tristan said to Hallie, "There's some in my saddlebag, for just such occasions. I'll get it."

From the doorway, Walker said, "I will."

When Tristan had washed and was ready to examine Etta, he turned to Will. "I'm going to examine your wife. This won't be pretty. You might wait outside."

Will shook his head. "She's my wife. I'll stay."

Hallie's eyes met Tristan's. I forgot to tell Tristan that Will watched the whole thing last time, she thought. Tristan looked over at Walker. "You might take the little girl outside and do something to amuse her."

Walker did not have to be told twice. Mary Ann was nearly the same age as Alexandra, but was already taller. Her black hair was uncombed and her dress was soiled. "Want piggyback ride," the little girl said as Walker led her outside.

"I wish I'd thought to bring mandagoro with me," Tristan muttered. "This is going to be painful for her. Here, Hallie, get her to drink this." He handed her a whiskey bottle.

Turning to Etta, he said, "You won't like the taste, but try to drink as much of this as you can. I'm going to have

233

to reach inside you and turn the baby around, and that can hurt mighty bad."

"It can't be any worse than what I feel now." Her voice was hoarse.

Hallie laid a towel over the regurgitation. She would change the sheets after the baby arrived. As she poured the liquor down Etta's throat, Etta reached for her hand and held it tightly. In about twenty minutes Etta was asleep and half the bottle of whiskey was gone.

"Wash up, Hallie, you're going to help," Tristan told her.

Will Colton sat at the table, staring, silent. Tristan lifted Etta's nightdress and jackknifed her legs. He slid his whole hand into her bulging vagina, feeling the baby lying sideways. No wonder she was in such pain. Slowly, he felt his way until the baby's head touched his fingers. Manipulating expertly, he reached up to make sure the baby's arms were at its sides and not stretched overhead. He maneuvered the legs upward and felt the head slide into place. His relief was evidenced in his sigh. Realizing the whiskey had done its duty, he knew he could not rely on Etta to push or help in any way.

He wanted that baby out of there, and now. The tiny head showed fuzz at the vaginal entrance. Reaching to put fingers on both sides of its head, he pulled gently, ever so slowly. Will got up from the table and came to stand over his shoulder. Ah, the head was out, facing down; now he eased one shoulder out, and the other quickly followed. Thus he was able to pull the baby into the world. Quickly holding it up by its feet, he patted its back and a lusty cry escaped.

Tristan smiled, then handed the squirming bundle to Hallie and turned back to deal with the afterbirth.

"Where's a blanket?" asked Hallie. Will was staring at the liverlike placenta that fell into Tristan's hands.

Hallie looked around the room. Nothing had been prepared for the baby. The cradle that Mary Ann had used was nowhere in sight. There were no baby clothes, no blankets, no towels.

"Will!" she spoke sharply. He looked at her. "Where's a blanket?"

He took out a knife from his pocket and cut a corner off the blanket on the bed.

It was then she decided that Will Colton was repulsive.

They waited until Etta was conscious, then Tristan held her while Hallie changed the sheet. When Etta's new son had been nestled in her arms, Will said, "Well, guess I'll get to chores."

Hallie offered to take Mary Ann for a week, until Etta could be on her feet again. Will refused. "We'll manage."

It was early afternoon when she and Tristan arrived back at the farm. He said, "If I leave right now, I'll make Parramatta by nightfall and can be in Sydney by mid-morning."

Right before he left, Tristan shocked Hallie by remarking, "Does Mary Ann remind you of anyone?"

"What do you mean?"

"She's the image of Robbie."

Twenty-three

Weeks passed, and still the rains refused to come. No glorious, dramatic thunderstorms rolled across the hills. No cracking lightning hurled itself against dead trees and started bush fires miles up in the mountains, whose haze rolled coastward, creating the most awe-inspiring sunsets in the world. No rolling gray clouds churned the heavens apart.

Even the gentle, steady afternoon rains Hallie had grown used to had failed to materialize. Billabongs dried up. Grass stopped growing. Sheep and cattle grew thin. Those farmers whose lands were not along the creeks and rivers found livestock dead each day, found that their corn barely poked itself above the ground. Discovered the earth had crusted into sand and crumbled into sterile dust in their hands.

Hallie's bucket brigade assured them of water enough for the garden. They would not be without food. But everyone was aware that the buckets, even when touching the bottom of the creek, came up only half full. It took twice as long to water the garden. And the relentless sun dried the watered fields quickly. Black snakes, in their search for water, littered the fields like long dark waving strips.

Not all of Hallie's thousands of sheep could find access to the river or the creek. Fields were littered with the carcasses of lambs and of the old sheep who just gave up. The smaller farmers, the ones who had few livestock and had relied on well water—the shallow wells that had so easily been dug—stared up at the sky and, if they were praying people, prayed. Sometimes their prayers were answered, in the form of an unexpected, short tropical deluge where the water ran off the parched ground in a matter of minutes. The blazing sun dried the land.

Beyond, toward the mountains, the plains smoldered to a yellow evenness. The atmosphere was overcast for days on end from the high-floating smoke of bush fires, which made breathing labored. In Sydney carbonized leaves from the mountains, buffeted by the circulating currents, landed in people's backyards.

Month after month of unabated sunshine depressed many of those used to the lush greenness of English summers. They yearned for the gray dampness of London winters. The sameness, the dryness, the interminable sunshine drove people crazy. Some farmers left their fifty acres and moved into town to become carpenters, or bricklayers, or any of the myriad jobs that awaited any able hand.

"How much money do you have?" Tristan asked Hallie.

She glanced at him. "I'm not sure. Why?"

"The people in this valley soon won't have money to buy supplies. They'll have no income from their sheep, which will be dead—either of thirst or lack of grass in the fields, or because they'll have to sell them at less than it cost to raise them. There's already a glut of meat on the market, people hoping to sell their animals before they die. I think most could make it through this drought," he said, though to himself Tristan admitted he had no idea how long a drought could last. Neither did anyone else. "But they need financial help. If you could extend them credit . . ."

"You mean let them have supplies for nothing?"

"You could charge interest, perhaps. I see the pain in their eyes, and—"

"Where will I get the money to buy supplies if I can't sell to them?"

"I don't know," Tristan replied. "That's why I'm asking. Some of these people have worked so hard, it'd be a shame to have them forfeit their land when next year there may be water enough and plenty."

"Next year?" Hallie hadn't let herself think it could continue so long. "You want me to *give* these people what I buy?"

She didn't think Chad would approve of that. She wasn't sure she had worked as hard as she had in order to give it all away to neighbors. What if the drought continued even longer than next year? Then where would she be, having spent all her money on provisions for people she barely knew?

"I know it would be a risk," Tristan said, watching her. "I'll help, too. I have money saved. These people need help

237

in order for this land to stay solvent, in order for us to grow and to exist."

When Tristan was able to leave Sydney, he usually arrived at the farm late on a Saturday afternoon, leaving by noon on Sunday. To Hallie, it seemed forever between his visits. She wondered, once in a while, if there might be a woman in Sydney. But the hospital was being built, and the growing population of the town required more of him. She knew that when he had a free weekend, he rode hard across the golden fields to her.

She and Brian had culled every sheep they could, sending them to be butchered and added to the glut of meat on the Sydney market. Much of it rotted, gone to waste.

"Why don't you talk with Harry?" she said to Tristan. "I hardly ever seem to get into town anymore, there's so much needs doing here. Ask him if I can afford to do that—give credit." The only reason she would even consider it was that Tristan suggested it.

With a month between Tristan's visits, Hallie feared their learning would cease—and that if it did, it might never resume for Brian, Beth, and herself, though the children might pick it up again.

But then Ben stepped in. He did not like to stay at the store at night. After dark he rode to the barracks and ate there, helping himself to cold leftovers Belinda left for him. He found it preferable to staying by himself. He looked out the store windows as little as possible. The empty spaces sent shudders through him.

He was gone from the barracks at dawn, back to the store. It was not often that he was alone there. From the very beginning, people rode in family groups or one by one, sometimes a wife alone, sometimes a woman and child, often a man coming ostensibly for a pouch of tobacco, but in reality riding in for conversation.

It was not long before Ben knew who was pregnant in the valley, who was beating his wife, who had new convicts, who had dead sheep, who had sick children. He knew the names of all the children, of most of the convicts, and called even the wives by their first names.

His empty face, so devoid of a smile or any sign of life,

238

mellowed. A perpetual stalk of dried grass between his teeth, he made small talk all day long. He recommended medicine for bunions, for headaches, for gout. He ordered anything that anybody wanted and could pay for.

At first he had been reluctant to climb into the paddock where sheep were fenced, thinking they wanted to attack him. Within weeks, though, each one was named, given special tidbits, and ran up to rub against him.

He never actually *rode* his horse. He never went faster than a walk. He looked upon all horses as his enemies.

Ben stopped Tristan during each visit, drawing him pictures of where Ed Wilkerson had a pain, or asking what treatment Gracie Johnson's burn should have and what might be done to ease a sore throat. He told Tristan who was expecting babies and asked what to do about a child's earache or Tim Jenkins's perpetual diarrhea.

Though Hallie could not warm to him, she came to respect him. It amazed her that her neighbors confided in him and that he was a walking newspaper, up-to-date about all current news in the valley. If he'd only smile once in a while, she thought. She didn't know why he involved himself with everyone; he hadn't an ounce of sentimentality. He never showed empathy, or even sympathy—nor much warmth.

On Sundays she did invite him to dine with them, though she didn't know why. The Daughertys were invited also, and it gave Hallie a sense of community to see so many around her Sunday dinner table. Belinda and Beth worked harmoniously in the kitchen, and that one day a week Hallie told the convicts they could take turns cooking—that Belinda would not cook for them.

At one Sunday dinner they bemoaned Tristan's absence. Robbie seemed to have innate intelligence concerning numbers, and the group asked him math questions they could not solve individually. But the young boy, now eleven, could not answer all their questions. They still gathered evenings, but spent their time learning to read, except when Tristan rode onto the scene. Their mathematical education waned.

"I can help you," said the sad-voiced Ben. "I don't know how good a teacher I'd be, but I can answer your questions."

Hallie looked at him. He didn't ever behave consistently.

He said he didn't like people, yet he wound himself into the lives of those who surrounded him.

And so, two evenings a week, Ben became their teacher. He was not only a whiz at mathematics, but was a walking dictionary as well. There was hardly a word whose definition he didn't know. He also assigned writing lessons to those who were learning to read.

On those nights when classes weren't held around the dining table, he came over to the house after dinner with the sheaf of papers his pupils had written, and placed a lamp on the dining table. Sitting there, his eyes intent and narrowed, he wrote in the margins, talking softly to himself.

One evening he came back from the store with a letter for Hallie that had been left off there by someone passing through. It was from Chad, and it came like a bolt. It had been so long since she'd even thought of her husband. She waited until she was alone, then neatly cut the end off the envelope and withdrew the sheets of paper, recognizing her husband's large, spidery handwriting. The letter, she noted, had been written nearly ten months before.

My Dear Wife,
    I have not had time to receive an answer to my last letter, but I await such anxiously, wondering how you and the children are.
    My father lingers, life slipping ever more through his fingers. And Hallie, my dear, I am afraid for your father also. He can no longer work in the mines. When I have gone to visit, he coughs constantly, spitting blood into his handkerchief. I suspect he has consumption. I shall see that they always have a home. It is sad to see both our fathers dying, one from having worked a lifetime in the bowels of the earth, and the other not having his money help him to health at all.
    Your brother Danny is unable to work, too. I hate to have to write you these things. Rather I could be there to comfort you when you hear the news than that I should be the bearer of sad tidings. Danny, whose second child, a little girl named Pamela, is healthy and well, lost his left eye in a mine accident. Reverend Macauley has found him a job as a clerk in

a store, but Danny champs at the bit, yearning for physical work, and is angry at the world.

I, too, champ at the bit for physical work, for work on my own land. I feel my dream slipping away from me.

I hate the gray English winters, the grime on the streets, the crowds of people. I find I like your family and tend to spend time there rather often. I don't think they quite know what to do with me, but I feel more comfortable there than with my brother and his wife. My sisters, of course, are both in London. I do take turns staying with them when I am in London.

I talk to Danny of home. I think he would return with me were he not afraid to leave your mother, with your father dying. I can see the desire shining in him when I talk of our land. So different from this dismal place. The longer I am here, the more I understand why I left, and why you dared eight months at sea to join a man you scarcely remembered.

When I go down to London, I haunt the docks, hoping for news of Australia. Did you know that's what they're thinking of calling it? It means South. Terra Australis—Land of the South, from the Latin. The whole Continent would be named that, but we will still keep New South Wales for our part of the larger territory. I like the sound of it, don't you?

Tell Archie I depend on him. When I return with the profits from our fleeces, we shall buy more land— and I shall begin an intensive breeding plan wherein we shall raise the best sheep in the whole world.

You had better see about new convicts. By the time you get this, the terms for all those that we had will be up. They will be free to leave. No doubt they will want their own fifty acres, or be free to find jobs they truly enjoy. If any will stay, tell them I'll pay them when I return, and will assure them of both work and a place to stay. I'm sorry to thrust this upon you. I am sure, between household chores and the children, you are busy enough. (And, much as I trust Archie, he does not share my vision or know what experiments I would like to try.)

Buy a pretty dress. Buy the children whatever they

want and need. It's no doubt time for Jamie to move from a pony to a horse. Tell him the first thing I'll do when I come home is find a horse for him.

My body may be here, but my heart is with all of you.

Chad

"My father is dying," Hallie said aloud. "And Danny is blind in one eye." It was more than she could bear at one time. She began to cry.

Finally she got up and walked through the French windows to the outdoors. Damn the mines! Eating her family up. Devouring the men she loved. She walked to the creek, clear under the azure skies. It flowed over the rocks, not rushing as it did when they had rain every year. What was this—the second year without rain? She sighed loudly and walked back to the house, back to Chad's letter, its pages in a pile on the table.

She stared at it for a long time. Certainly by now the fleeces had arrived, and with them the news that Archie was dead. He must be worrying that all he had dreamed and worked for was going to ruin. So, in case he might not yet be on his way back, on the remote chance he would still be in England for another nine or ten months, she composed a brief letter to him, merely to reassure him that all was well.

She did not mention Tristan, nor the store and Ben, nor the hundred and one other things that made up the fabric of her life. It was a formal, stilted letter to a man she could scarcely remember.

Hallie received a second letter the next day, when Tristan arrived. "It's from Elizabeth Macquarie," he said, and handed it to her.

My Dear Hallie,

Do not say no to this invitation because Chad is away. Please come to a dinner we are giving to celebrate the King's birthday and to show off our new furnishings. Government House has finally been refurbished, and the renovations are finished.

You will be a most welcome addition all by yourself. There are so many more men than women that dinner parties and balls always seem lopsided. You promised, years ago, to come spend time with us in Sydney, and have never done such.

Susan Langley and I are fighting over whose hospitality you will accept. If you promise to dine with us several times and tour my gardens one afternoon, I shall contribute to tranquility and be gracious about your making the Langleys your official headquarters. However, we would be most happy to have you stay whatever length of time you can with us.

Even the newcomers whom you haven't yet met have heard of you and will be delighted to meet you in person. I have told Tristan that I will not take no for an answer, so he has my permission to persuade you if this letter is not enough. Do come, Hallie. We never see enough of you. It is only through Tristan and the Langleys that we hear about your accomplishments.

Come brighten up my life. Our lives, says Lachlan.

With fond regards,
Elizabeth Macquarie

"I don't have anything to wear," Hallie said, looking up as soon as she'd finished reading.

Tristan burst out laughing. "That's the first typically feminine reaction I've ever heard from you."

Doesn't he see me as feminine? she wondered.

"Will you trust me to buy you a dress?"

The only new dresses she'd ever had Chad had bought for her. "No," she said. "I want that pleasure. I think I'll ride in with you when you leave, give myself a week's vacation. It will give me a chance to talk over this idea of credit with Harry. And," she smiled, "Chad told me to buy a new dress, so I needn't even feel guilty about it."

This time she noticed the blankness that came over Tristan's eyes when she mentioned her husband. "I'll come into Sydney and do some shopping. I still need a couple of extra convicts. Maybe I can interview some new ones. I'll stay a few nights with the Langleys and a few with the Macquaries. It sounds wonderful. I haven't been away from the farm in far too long. And it will be a treat to go to church."

"I'm not sure that would be my description," Tristan said wryly.

"Don't you go to church when you're in town?" she asked. They had never talked of that. She took it for granted that everyone in town went to church.

"As little as possible. I find men like Reverend Marsden too ready to mete out the justice of the God of wrath they preach about. He's also a magistrate, you know. Called 'the flogging magistrate.' That doesn't seem, to me, what a man of God should be about."

Hallie looked at him. "Do you spend much time thinking of such things?" she asked with curiosity.

Tristan shrugged. "Probably too much. I either solve the world's problems or ask the unsolvable questions as I ride back and forth between here and there."

"What are the unsolvable questions?"

He reached out and put a hand under her chin. "Do you never think of them?"

"I don't know." She didn't want him to move away, take his hand from her. "What are they?"

"Is there a God? Is there a purpose to life? Why are people cruel to each other? What are we doing here? What do I do about you?"

His fingers curled around a tendril of her hair.

What does he do about me? she wondered. And I about him?

Twenty-four

It was late afternoon, nearly evening, when Tristan left Hallie at the Langleys' new house in Sydney. Though it was by no means ostentatious, Hallie thought it beautiful. The furniture they'd ordered from England had not yet arrived. The pieces they had were locally made, and Harry thought them extremely well done. There were no carpets yet, but the wide-planked floors shone.

The rooms were spacious, with high ceilings and paned-glass windows which still lacked drapes. The only room that was really impressive was the drawing room. "You could hold a ball in here," Hallie murmured.

Susan smiled. "We intend to."

Susan was large with her second child, and glowing with happiness. "It's always such a pleasure when you show up unexpectedly. Are you really going to stay for a week? I can hardly believe it."

"I couldn't if it weren't for Beth and Brian," Hallie replied. "But I'm sure they can get along without me for a while. When I got Elizabeth's invitation, it seemed like a good time to indulge myself. I plan to be as frivolous as possible. I've never been frivolous in my life."

"Then it's about time." Her friend smiled.

"Exactly my thought, too. But now, tell me all the news."

"Wait until Harry gets home. He can always add so much more. He has his fingers on the pulse of the colony."

Hallie observed Susan's strikingly pretty face, her clear gray eyes so serene. "You're proud of him, aren't you?"

"Oh, Hallie, I look at him and sometimes I think I could burst with love. I wonder how I'm so fortunate. Proud of him, oh my, yes. He has such . . . vision."

"I remember that's one of the first things that impressed me about Chad. His vision of the future of this land."

"Do you miss him terribly?" Susan asked.

"I—I don't think so," Hallie answered thoughtfully.

"Often I scarcely remember him. Sometimes, Susan . . . sometimes I think if he hadn't gone away, I couldn't have done all these things I do. I was angry with him at first, thinking no man had a right to leave his wife alone to cope with life. But I thrive on it."

Susan studied her. "You *do* seem bursting with exuberance," she said, "though I don't know how you do it all."

"I don't mean to sound disloyal," Hallie said. "But I think I'm a stronger person since he left. I like me. It's not always easy, but it makes me . . . stretch."

"Stretch?" Susan didn't understand.

"Yes, I think that's a good word. Of course, were it not for having help taking care of the children and house, I could never do it all."

"And," Susan sounded tentative, "you do have Tristan." There was a moment of silence as the two women looked at each other.

"I am marvelously lucky in my friends," Hallie said noncommittally. "I not only have him, but you and Harry, too."

Susan sat down and patted the sofa beside her, but Hallie chose to stand. "Hallie, does it make you nervous, like it does me, that life is so wonderful? Do you get scared that it can't last?"

Hallie laughed, and then did sit down next to Susan. "The lull before the storm?" she said. "Sometimes I think that way. But then just enough comes along to keep me on edge. This drought scares me. It gets worse all the time." She paused. "Archie's death was a blow. And my father is dying."

Susan's eyes softened, and she reached out to clasp Hallie's hand. "I'm sorry. You must feel badly. Nothing like that interferes with my happiness." They sat silently for a minute, then Susan said, "I'm glad you're going shopping. I wish I could come with you, but I seem to tire so easily with this pregnancy. I just don't feel up to long jaunts. I feel rather like a vegetable. I don't know what I'd do without Molly; she takes such care of Christopher. You'll get to see them at dinner. Harry will be home before too long, and we'll dine. You got here just in time."

Just then Harry entered the room and expressed delight at seeing Hallie. They talked for a few moments of the farm and store but were interrupted when Christopher and Molly came in.

The hour before dinner passed in a flurry of catching up, and in admiring Christopher. Hallie found it a relief to involve herself with something other than the farm, with people whose conversation was not all about sheep and drought.

After dinner she and Harry sat at his desk in a corner of the drawing room and talked about the idea of "credit." "The way it works, Hallie, is that I extend you credit so you can extend it to the farmers."

Hallie let that sink in. "How do you feel about that?" she asked, trying to sort out all the ramifications of things she was just beginning to understand.

Harry tugged at his mustache, a habit that always accompanied his meditation. "As usual with your ideas, let me churn it around in my mind while you're here, talk to the governor, work some figures over on paper."

"Maybe I shouldn't buy a new dress," Hallie volunteered, although the prospect of not being able to indulge in a shopping spree disappointed her.

Harry smiled. "That, my dear, will have nothing to do with extending credit to your neighbors. Buy a dress and whatever else you're thinking of before the drought gets worse."

"Is it going to get worse?"

"How in the world do I know? None of us knows. This isn't desert country, like the Sahara. We have no knowledge whether or not drought here can go on for years. Any dry spells since we've arrived here have not lasted long enough to be debilitating." By his use of "we," he meant the British. Sometimes he sounds like Tristan, Hallie thought.

"Let me think on this," he continued, rising and escorting Hallie to the drawing-room door. "In a few days we can discuss it again."

The net day Hallie stopped at the new hospital that Tristan had so often talked about. Along the main thoroughfare that would soon be named after Macquarie, the massive beige sandstone building was not far from the circular quay.

Nearly a block long, it looked like it could stand against any storm hurled at it.

The streets now had a mathematical precision to them, laid out in neat rows and with some sense of plan. The Rocks, up by the docks—directly to the west of the quay—was a place to avoid. No longer a tent city for newly arrived convicts, its brick buildings housed ex-convicts and prostitutes. Sewage ran in the streets and bred disease. But the rest of Sydney evidenced planning that had not been obvious when Hallie arrived. Houses were well kept, with the neat English gardens of which Tristan had told her. There was also evidence of the tropics: banana and palm trees grew in gardens, and red hibiscus, creamy frangipani, and purple jacaranda added exotic touches to the olive-green of the always present gum trees. Hallie thought Sydney had become quite pretty.

The New Hyde Park Racecourse, which Macquarie had championed, now drew crowds on Saturday afternoons, and Hallie suspected that once Chad learned of this he would waste no time training horses. She had never been to a race, and there were none while she was in town, but she could imagine the excitement it would engender in people anxious for liveliness and sport. There was nothing of the Puritan about these new Australians.

She had to agree that there was a special excitement to Sydney. It was the first city—if it could be called that yet—that enthused her. There was so much building going on that the sound of the hammer never ceased in all the daylight hours. The new houses didn't even have fireplaces; Sydney's reputation for a mild, pleasant climate was becoming legend.

She felt like a schoolgirl on vacation. Touring the shops, she decided to buy the most beautiful dress in town. It was so wonderful not to be poor. She had no idea how much money she had or how much she owed Harry, but Chad had almost ordered her—and Harry had added his encouragement—to buy some finery. It would be fun to attend the governor's banquet celebrating the King's birthday, coming in from the country to be the best-dressed woman there. Hallie laughed out loud, and several men who had already been staring at her smiled in appreciation. She, who had never cared much about clothing, deciding to be the best-dressed woman at the governor's dinner! She'd show Tristan just how typically feminine she could be!

The minute she tried it on, she knew it had been made for her. It was cream-colored satin, with a tiny bouquet of pink and blue silk flowers accentuating the cleavage of the low neckline, and draped itself against her, falling in graceful folds to the scalloped hemline. It hugged her waist tightly, and as she studied herself in the mirror, she thought, Why, I'm quite nice. It looks lovely.

Without Chad around to remind her of her beauty, she had forgotten how she looked, except when Tristan arrived. Then she would check to see that her hair was not unruly, and pinch her cheeks to make them rosy. Her eyes would sparkle automatically when Tristan appeared. Though he hardly ever commented about her looks, for which she often was grateful—she had become irritated that it was the only thing about her that Chad ever complimented—she could always tell that her looks pleased him.

Now, gazing at her reflection in the dim light of the dressing room, she thought that Tristan couldn't help but be impressed. The saleswoman assured her that this was the latest style arriving from Europe, and eagerly agreed to have the gown sent on to the Langleys'. I'll buy a ribbon that matches the flowers and wind it through my hair, Hallie thought as she undressed. A blue one to match my eyes. And blue shoes. What rank extravagance! But she didn't care: the dress was perfect for her.

She also bought a pale gray dress to wear at the farm on the evenings when Tristan visited; it wasn't fancy, but it would nevertheless let him know she was conscious of her femininity.

But I'm not, really, she mused as she strolled along the street. I'm not really feminine at all. I don't stay home and take care of the house. I hardly even take care of my own children. She did spend time with them, but just in the evening, when they studied together or played games and laughed uproariously. She was not around the house when they cut a finger or scraped a toe or asked whatever questions children asked all day long.

She shook her head, trying to rid herself of thoughts of inadequacy. I can't help it, she reflected. Someone has to take charge.

The city inculcated her with a desire to explore. It wasn't dirty and cramped like Newcastle. There were new streets to explore, new shops, new pubs. Well, she wouldn't go into one of those alone. She noticed a number of women walking along the streets, unaccompanied. Several feet behind, carrying packages for them, were young servant girls—obviously convicts serving out their terms as maids. Men stood on street corners, often in small bands, sometimes calling out lewdly to the women who passed by. The ladies kept their eyes straight ahead and pretended not to see or hear.

Suddenly a thought stopped Hallie right in the middle of the street. She had no idea where Tristan lived. She had often wondered what his home was like, how his office looked, whether or not he had a housekeeper, what he did for meals, if his house was sloppy with clothes thrown willy-nilly or neat as a pin. And who took care of it for him? She always had trouble imagining Tristan in Sydney. When she thought of him, it was either visualizing him at the farm or riding his horse to or from Sydney. All these years—as many spent with Tristan as with Chad—and she had never once seen his house. When he was gone from her, she wondered what kinds of maladies he was treating, in her mind's eye envisioning him entering sickrooms, operating, having social intercourse in the city.

Well, Sydney wasn't yet so big that she couldn't easily locate him. The first shopkeeper she asked directed her to Dr. Faulkner's. Retracing her steps, she found that his house was not far from the hospital and racecourse. It was in a row of attractive cottages, each with a small well-kept garden. But Tristan's rose over them, one and a half stories high. It seemed to take up two lots and spread gracefully. Its brick was whitewashed and sparkled in the afternoon sunlight. What made Hallie break into a wide grin were the bright blue shutters. In front of the windows facing the streets were equally bright blue window boxes with flowers cascading from them. A brick walk curved through the neatly mown grass, and a sign, hanging from a post next to the street, read:

DR. TRISTAN FAULKNER
PHYSICIAN & SURGEON

The door was slightly ajar, so she walked in—into the patients' waiting room. It obviously doubled in the evening as the drawing room, for there was a curved sofa, a piano, polished wooden floors surrounding a circular Persian rug, and three straight-backed chairs lining the wall by a door that seemed to lead to the dispensary. A round mahogany table shone in the center of the room, set off at one end by a large pewter bowl filled with flowers. Hanging over the fireplace was an enormous somber painting of a bowl of fruit. All in all it did not look like the home of a single man.

A man with his arm in a sling sat on one of the chairs. He smiled at her but said nothing. Hallie could tell he was toothless; at least, there were no front teeth, and his mouth caved in as though he were lacking lips.

She sat down, folding her hands in her lap, studying her surroundings, trying for a sense of the Tristan she did not know. When the door to his office opened, a woman and small girl walked out, the mother holding the child's hand.

"Henry . . ." Tristan nodded at the man with the splint, then his eyes found Hallie. It was as though he had not left her just the day before. His eyes lit up and he smiled and said, "I won't be long, Mrs. Morgan."

It was over half an hour, however, and she was relieved that no new patients arrived. When, finally, the man with the splint left, Hallie for a moment thought Tristan was going to put his arms around her, he acted so pleased to see her.

"Come to see me in my lair?" The smile wouldn't leave his face.

"I wanted to see how you live when you're here," she said, not realizing until then that she suddenly was consumed with desire to know everything about him when he was away from her. Why had she never inquired into this part of his life, the part that was the mainstream of his activities and time?

"Come into the kitchen and I'll fix a cup of tea," he said. "It's such a novel experience that *you've* come to visit me."

"It *is* a strange feeling," Hallie agreed, following him. The kitchen ran behind the drawing room, high-ceilinged and bright. Cheerful curtains adorned the windows, and gleaming china plates stood on end on the cupboard shelves. The room was painted yellow, something she had never seen before.

When she commented on it, Tristan said, "Kitchens should be the cheeriest of places, I think. I eat here. I do my accounts here. I write letters here. I like the smells here. My mother sent me that rag rug." It was a large oval of various shades of browns, blues, and reds. "She made it for me."

"It's beautiful."

"I know." He poured water into the kettle, permitting the tea to steep. "But its real meaning is deeper than that. I also know what went into each twist of the rags, each stitch that holds it together." His voice had taken on a tenderness.

Hallie watched him as he busied himself in the kitchen. "Do you miss your family very much?"

"Of course. Don't you? But then, you came voluntarily. I didn't. If I'd had my choice, I'd never have left my family. Yes, I wish my mother could visit, but I wouldn't wish that long voyage on anyone. From Canada it would take her nearly a year. And a year back. Two years out of her life just coming and going to see me. No, I wouldn't let her do that. Besides, except for my absence, she's very happy with the family and all her friends—who are legion. My mother is a very remarkable woman." He poured tea into two cups and handed one to her.

"You've never told me about her," Hallie remarked. "Or any of your family."

Tristan sat opposite her and smiled. "This is where I eat all my meals. Unless I'm entertaining, I never dine at the table in the other room. This is far cozier."

"Do you do your own cooking?" He was surprising her. Most men didn't know how to behave in a kitchen.

"Not all of it. I have a woman come in afternoons, when I'm going to be home for dinner, and she cleans for me and fixes dinner. But I'm only home a couple of nights a week."

Hallie was thinking how little she knew of him. "Where are you the rest of the time?"

Tristan grinned at her over his cup. "I wondered if and when you'd ever get around to questions like these. Sydney

252

is a very sociable place, and they take pity on the bachelor physician. There aren't many homes where I haven't dined."

Especially if there are marriageable girls, Hallie thought, studying him. She'd never seen anyone more handsome. "I've just realized that I know nothing of your life here."

"Maybe you haven't wanted to," suggested Tristan, not looking at her.

"What do you mean by that?" she asked defensively.

"Perhaps *our* world only exists when we are together."

They looked across the table at each other. His eyes were soft, liquid, tender . . . not unreadable, as usual. I love him, she thought, wanting to reach out and touch his hand, feel the pulse in his wrist, his heartbeat. Instead she asked, "Why have you not married, Tristan?"

"You know why." His voice was low, so quiet she could barely hear him.

"Tell me."

He stared at her, into her, for a long time, saying nothing. Then he rose and said, "Would you like to see my office?"

He walked out of the kitchen, through the drawing room, and opened the door to his office. She followed him into a small dark room. There were racks of bottled medicine, pills, a little scale, knives, a drawing of the human body on the wall, a skeleton, and books everywhere. All very neat, tidy. It had an odor to which she was unaccustomed. It smelled like a hospital. Its only window—a small, paned one—overlooked a backyard garden, where yellow and pink flowers nodded their heads.

He saves lives from here, Hallie thought, gazing about her. He repairs broken bones. He tells people they are dying. He performs miraculous cures. He serves humanity from here. She walked around fingering the bottles, touching the pencil on the desk, rubbing her hand across the grain of a table.

"Where do you sleep?" she asked, looking up at him. "I want to see where you sleep."

Without saying anything, Tristan turned and walked back through the drawing room and into a hall beyond it. He began to mount the stairs, which creaked as he climbed them.

There was only the one room, large and airy, whose high ceiling slanted under the eaves but whose long windows made it bright. A window was open to let in the air, and a curtain fluttered in the breeze. In the center of the room was an enormous four-poster bed whose columns rose taller than Tristan, their shining dark wood intricately carved. A flowered quilt served as the bedspread.

"Your mother again?" Hallie touched the coverlet.

Tristan nodded, not taking his eyes from her as she observed everything. On the nightstand next to the bed were a lamp and three books. Hallie walked over and picked them up, studying the titles, ones she had never heard of. The largest was *The Compleat Plays & Poems of William Shakespeare*. She wondered how anyone could read such a big book. Another was *Wordsworth's Poems*. She flicked it open and read, "We come into the world trailing clouds of glory." The third was *Greek Tragedies*. None of them looked particularly interesting.

She put them down and examined the small desk in the corner, under one of the windows. A sheaf of papers lay there, next to a bottle of ink, a feathered pen, and a pair of glasses. "I didn't know you wore glasses."

He didn't respond. She looked at him questioningly.

"Hallie, leave here. Get out of my bedroom. Go away while you can.

While I can? He means before he kisses me. He means before I kiss him, before I feel his arms around me and we do something that we both know is wrong. Before we do something awful.

She brushed by him as she walked to the stairs, feeling her heart beating wildly.

Twenty-five

Men hopelessly outnumbered women at the governor's dinner in honor of King George. There was no such thing as a wallflower. Hallie, in her sophisticated new ball gown, was stunning and found herself surrounded by men wherever she turned. That most of the women were married made little difference. Men were hungry for female companionship, and if the woman were beautiful, that was an added fillip.

Twenty guests had been invited to dine at Government House in Sydney, where the Macquaries were beginning to spend most of their time. Bowls of flowers added not only to the fragrance of the evening, but to the beauty. Again Hallie thought, I must remember to try that at home. Candles blazed so brightly that she thought everybody and everything in the big room glittered.

Governor and Mrs. Macquarie stood by the door, greeting newcomers while a sergeant-at-arms announced the guests. Hallie, who had arrived with Susan and Harry, observed that the women had obviously spent much time and money on how they looked for this occasion. Dressed in pastels, they resembled flowers floating around the room. Where was Tristan? she wondered, anxious to see reflected in his eyes how feminine she looked.

A few smartly dressed young officers stood erect, talking in a group. They did not mingle easily with the civilians. Hallie overheard someone complaining of having to dine in the company of "dubious characters one would avoid on the street." Looking around, she observed no one who matched that description. All were well dressed, well mannered. One young subaltern in the group, whose red curls accentuated his freckles, drew himself up and righteously declared, "I would rather not eat, than dine with such men." Then he found his cap and, startling everyone, left before dinner.

This led to a stimulating conversation. Among the guests in attendance were Simeon Lord, perhaps the most financially successful emancipist. Lord had been shipped to New South Wales after his 1790 conviction for stealing one hundred yards of muslin and one hundred of calico, with a total value of ten pence. After his term—during which he was assigned as servant to an officer in the New South Wales Corps—he remained in Sydney and began dealing in sandalwood, whale oil, and other Pacific islands trade. Before long he was shipping to Canton and America, employing more and more people every year, and was well on his way to becoming one of the wealthiest men in the colony. Macquarie had appointed him a magistrate, and the two men had become friends.

At dinner Hallie was seated between two men she had never met, a Mr. Fulton and a Mr. Grissom. There were two long tables, and Reverend Marsden headed the other one. Hallie could not hear their conversation but found the one at her table highly entertaining and provocative.

The governor said, "I often think the colony consists of those who have been transported and those who ought to have been." He had not been noticeably offended by the young subaltern's conduct. "I view the colony as a settlement *for* the prisoners. After they are released, they should be urged to lead moral, productive lives. It is my responsibility to help them. If there is no hope that they can be treated as equals, as men who have satisfied justice, then they will have no goal—no dream—for rehabilitation. Offering men a chance for acceptance will make them act meritoriously."

What about the women? Hallie asked silently.

Henry Fulton, an emancipist who had been implicated in the Irish rebellion and thus sent to serve a sentence in this colony, was a worthy parson and teacher. He spoke up now, his voice quiet but compelling. "Your humanitarian impulses open you to much criticism."

"That may be why I am the governor," Macquarie said, his eyes flashing, "and they are not."

"It is generally the officers of the New South Wales Corps who react most violently," said a short man with a belligerent air. Hallie learned later that he was Francis Greenway, also an emancipist. The buildings he'd designed

256

and built would immortalize him and color the landscape of New South Wales for hundreds of years. "They have been trying to run this colony since it was founded. To their own benefit, and only theirs."

There was a brief silence following this breach of propriety. The few officers of the corps remained silent, either looking down at their plates or staring with hostility at their antagonist.

But this did not stop Greenway "In order to keep their own superior positions, they want to be assured that everyone else is below them. And what happens to the freed men who have been beaten and dehumanized by these soldiers? Now their equals, don't the officers have reason to be afraid?"

This was not dinner table conversation. This was best saved for after dinner, when the men would sit around the table with brandy and cigars while the women withdrew to the drawing room. But it was too late now.

"Well, certainly, when I arrived," continued the governor, "I did not expect any congress with men who had been convicts." He smiled an apology at the emancipists present. "However, brief experience has convinced me that some of the most commendable men in this colony"—he looked around and smiled at his guests—"those in present company included, who were both capable and industrious, are emancipists. I learned early on that it would be preferable not to hold out hope to a man if ever afterward he would be treated as dishonorable."

Someone muttered, "Hear, hear!"

"What can be so great a stimulus to a man of respectable family and education, who has fallen to the lowest state of degradation, as to know that it is still in his power to recover what is lost and to become a worthy member of society, and be treated as such?"

Susan Langley spoke up. "Governor, I wonder if England realizes the great good fortune this land has in acquiring you for our leader?"

The governor acknowledged the compliment with a smile. "Sometimes I do wonder. But it is myself I must live with. And I can act no other way. This country should be made home—*and a happy home*—to every emancipated convict *who deserves it*. If people are too proud or sensitive to consort with convicts and emancipists, they had better go somewhere else—for this country was founded, after all, as a convict colony."

"And now," interrupted his wife, "could we have sweeter conversation along with the dessert?"

The talk then turned to the Macquaries' recent trip across the Blue Mountains. Listening, Hallie realized how sequestered a life she lived. She knew none of what the Macquaries and others had experienced. Her life was circumscribed by her acres and the people she supported there.

She learned that once the Blue Mountains had been crossed, the governor had decided to build a road over the high rugged mountains that had challenged Sydney's citizenry for twenty-five years. He had heard of the fertility and vastness of the land that lay beyond the mountains, and had offered pardons to any convicts who volunteered for the dangerous and difficult work of building the road, provided it was finished in six months. And when this task had been accomplished—within the allotted time—the governor and his always courageous, energetic wife had set out with a band of men to see for themselves the new vistas, the steep narrow cliffs, that were once the barrier to the great inland of this continent.

Beyond the mountains, he'd designated a site for the first town, giving it the name of Bathurst, honoring the secretary of state for the colonies. Why not in honor of the men who had crossed the mountains? Hallie wondered. Why not a town named after someone who had achieved something here?

Laughing as he recalled a subsequent trip made by someone named Evans, Macquarie recounted how this explorer had come across a river beyond Bathurst and named it Lachlan. That's better, thought Hallie. Something certainly should be named after Lachlan Macquarie. But what the governor found amusing was that Evans and his men had also stumbled upon an aborigine, who had obviously never heard of white men and was terrified. He'd climbed a tree and sat up in a branch, "hollering and crying fit to be tied." Evans reported the abo could've been heard a mile away. The more Evans tried to get him down from the tree, the louder the savage cried.

"I'm still full of hope for these black creatures," the governor said. Hallie noticed that his guests always deferred to him, and it was he who led the conversation. But no one seemed to mind, since he was so interesting. "After all, thanks to us, these people are just emerging from the Stone Age, from savagery. Though their natures are uncivilized—through no fault of their own—now that we are here, they appear to have attributes which, if properly developed, might help them progress to being agricultural laborers or a lower class of mechanical laborers. I do believe it only requires the gentle hand of time, of kindness and patience on our part, to bring these poor unenlightened barbarians to a sense of the duty they owe to their fellow man—to society."

"What you're suggesting," said Fulton, "is that if we teach them a sense of duty as the highest avenue to fulfillment, the acts of hostility they keep committing against us may decrease?"

The governor nodded, though Hallie noted that several of the army officers snorted. One lieutenant laughed aloud in derision and said, "It's not possible. The only way they'll learn is through repeated punishment. They don't want to adopt our ways."

"I agree," said a Mr. Palmer, not connected with the army. "How can you make farmers out of people who don't eat our kind of food, who live on grubs and dirt?"

Hallie saw one of the women shudder and heard her exclaim, "Oh, how awful! What kind of creature would eat worms?" The thought seemed to send shivers through her.

"I have," Hallie said. All eyes turned to her.

"A group of aboriginals stayed on our land a number of years ago," she explained. "They were very nice to me. In being hospitable they offered me some of their food. I couldn't refuse."

Everyone stared at her until she was sorry she'd mentioned it.

"Weren't you scared?" asked the same young woman, eyes wide.

"Not at all. They were great company for me. They laughed a lot and I liked them." She would not tell of their burning the baby.

259

"Well, nevertheless, they're not quite human, in my opinion," said one of the more portly men.

"I think they can be," the governor interjected. "I'm planning on taking a few of the young boys and girls and establishing a native school in Parramatta. Mr. William Shelley will teach them industrious habits and cleanliness. I am also going to grant land bordering the sea at Port Jackson for the adults to cultivate so that they can learn this productive way of life rather than run wild in their usual pursuits in the forests."

Again, without premeditation, Hallie asked, "Why? Isn't there room enough for us all to practice whatever we want?"

Why did silence follow her questions?

After a few moments Governor Macquarie said, "I intend for schools to begin in all the townships within the next year. No longer will people have to send their sons to England to be educated."

Hallie was horrified. Send one's children away to school? Send them all the way back to England, nearly a year of their lives wasted aboard ship in order to go to school in England?

"Yes," said Reverend Marsden, "we really must be sure that every man is capable of reading the Bible. Each man should learn the sacred truths. From such does the fountain of morality flow."

"What about the women?" Hallie asked. "How are we to learn the sacred truths?" After all, she knew how to read.

Everyone stared at her again. "Why, from your husbands, of course," the man of God rejoined.

As if on cue, Mrs. Macquarie rose and said, "Ladies, shall we retire to the drawing room and leave the men to worldly matters?"

Why were the women shunted into the drawing room, Hallie wondered, when she wanted to learn from the men's conversation? This was her first experience of the custom of separating the sexes after dinner. But, then, it also was her first dinner party in society.

Once in the drawing room, Elizabeth Macquarie apologized to her guests for having allowed the conversation to get out of hand, saying she should have jumped in and directed it to more pleasant avenues. Yet left to their own devices, the ladies did not direct their conversation to the pleasant and bland. Instead, discussion centered on the hanging tomorrow.

The same young woman who had been so horrified at the thought of encountering aboriginals said, "I really don't like to attend the hangings. But Trenton"—Hallie imagined that must be her husband—"insists our boys witness the floggings. He thinks they're a deterrent, an example of where evil leads."

"Floggings?" Hallie heard her own voice.

"Oh, my dear," said Mrs. Palmer, "it's obvious you live in the country. Not all of them are public, of course. But when there's a hanging, some of the more hardened criminals who have committed severe infringements are publicly punished also. Boys from the male orphan school are *required* to attend, and most of us bring our children so they can see what comes from disobedience."

Hallie looked across the room at Susan Langley, who held a handkerchief to her mouth. Thank goodness, she thought. I would have been so disappointed to find Susan accepting such a thing.

When the dinner was over, Harry offered Susan and Hallie each an arm, and the three of them walked slowly down the street, the balmy air scented with night flowers.

"Why are executions public?" Hallie asked. The silences that had followed her questions at the governor's dinner had taught her to be quiet. Now, however, she felt safe in the cocoon of friendship.

Harry said, "Picnics are made out of gallows days. Schools are let out, and people come from far and near to witness the event. They're supposed to serve as terrible examples of what can happen if you don't obey the law."

"Do you think it keeps anyone from breaking the law?"

"My dear"—Harry's voice held a note of hopelessness—"you are asking age-old questions that probably can never be solved."

Ah, thought Hallie, one of life's unanswerable questions. Tristan would be proud of her. . . . Tristan! He had not come, after all. Where was he?

"This colony has many hangings and many more floggings," Harry continued. "If you lived in town, you'd see that one of the common children's games is flogging—practicing on trees. Do you mean you have never flogged your children?"

Hallie could tell by the tone of Harry's voice that he knew she hadn't, that neither he nor Susan would even think of such a thing. "I'm not even sure what flogging entails," she replied. "It's beating someone, isn't it?"

At that moment they arrived at the Langleys'. In front of the house, sitting in his carriage, was Tristan. "I thought you'd be home before too long, so I detoured on my way home," he said, jumping down.

He can see the feminine dress I bought for him after all, Hallie thought, smiling to herself.

Harry let go of the women and put a hand on Tristan's shoulder. "Make a habit of it, won't you, when we're in town?"

"Come in for cocoa?" asked Susan. "I've gotten in the habit of drinking some before going to bed."

"Laced with a bit of brandy, it's especially soporific," Harry added.

"I was hoping you'd invite me when you saw me out here," said Tristan. He smelled of antiseptic, his collar was wilted, and his eyes looked tired. "I spent the evening delivering a baby."

He's here because of me, Hallie realized.

As they entered the house, Harry reached out for Hallie and Susan to hand him their shawls. Susan said, "I'll heat the cocoa. It won't take but a few minutes."

Harry disappeared with their wraps, and Tristan and Hallie were left alone. Tristan's eyes absorbed her dress, noted the pink-and-blue nosegay, lingered there. "You're beautiful," he said, his voice low. "You're the most beautiful woman in the world."

She wanted to go to him, wanted to cross the room and have him put his arms around her.

"Hallie, here, has never been to a flogging," Harry said, coming back into the room. "You explain to her why hangings are matters of public interest."

"They're part of Australian culture," said Tristan, not taking his eyes from her.

"You obviously haven't lived in Britain," Harry said,

lighting a cigar. Hallie hated the smell. "They're holidays there, too. People cheer when they hear the neck snap."

"Oh, Harry!" Susan exclaimed as she reentered the room.

Harry went on, "It's society's way of interpreting God's punishment. If you want to understand this country, you should attend the festivities tomorrow."

"For heaven's sake," snapped Susan, "she'll think you mean it."

"Should I? I don't know if I could stand it." Was it the idea of floggings or Tristan's closeness that made her heart beat so loudly?

"Don't go," said Tristan. "There's no need to search for the dark side of human nature."

The dark side of human nature . . . Everyone she knew was nice. The men Beth had known were evil, but Hallie herself had never been introduced to "the dark side." Maybe it was something she should learn about this land that had become hers, this land and its peoples.

"I think I will go," Hallie said. "I know I won't like it, but I think perhaps it is something I should do." She wasn't sure just why.

In the morning Susan tried to dissuade her. Harry had already left for the bank by the time she and Susan breakfasted. But Hallie was adamant. If this was a strong part of the culture of the land she had adopted, she wanted to witness it, even though it might sicken her.

"I don't want to hide from things just because they're not pretty," she said, pouring cream on her porridge. "I write home and tell Mum and Dada how perfect everything is here. I tell Danny he should come, that life is so different from back home." She looked across the table at Susan. "What if it's just *my* life that's different? What if there really is an ugly part of life that I'm unaware of? Shouldn't I know about it if this is my country?"

"Oh, Hallie, you can know of it. You don't have to see it."

Hallie held up her hand. "I've made up my mind, Susan. You and Harry have told me what it's like, but I can scarcely believe it. You've never seen it, have you?"

"No, and I don't want to."

"Well, somehow I feel I should. You tell me about it and tell me not to go, yet you don't *really* know, do you? Do you think we should ignore something like this, pretend it doesn't exist in this country we love?"

Susan shook her head. She knew Hallie was determined to go. "Just follow the crowd. You can walk up either Pitt's Row or Chapel Row, out past the racecourse. Personally, I don't think you'll want to eat lunch, but Cook can fix you a picnic if you like."

The sun beat down, not so much hot as bright. Couples with children, men in groups of three and four, were heading toward the gallows. Hallie seemed to be the only woman alone. Susan was right: follow the crowd. She gazed around as she walked, thinking again how pretty Sydney was becoming. Susan had loaned her a parasol, "to fend off sunstroke." Hallie, who spent all her days outdoors, thought it fanciful.

She had lain in bed that morning hardening herself. After all, she had seen dead people before. Her brother, Philip—she had even helped wash him. Her grandmothers, both of them—she had watched one of them die; only one grandfather. She had seen a dead baby. She even told herself that she believed in capital punishment. True, she had not given it much thought. But if someone were dangerous to society, if they might kill again—she condoned Beth's action in killing her tormentor. Some people should die, she thought. They should not be allowed to harm the people who did obey the rules, who did practice brotherly love, or at least harmed no one else.

So she persuaded herself that she would be witnessing the execution of justice. Something that the law mandated, that made the rest of the country safe. None of the convicts sent to New South Wales was sentenced to death. It was only if they escaped and repeated their crimes—if they killed after arriving here, if they compounded their criminal tendencies—that they were executed. So it was not as if they had not been forewarned.

The convicts who wanted to rectify their mistakes and be given second chances were in the vast majority, like the men in her employ. Rules, she decided, were created for the minority. The rest went along with consciences firmly intact, or else had no desire to do harm anyhow.

Later, Tristan would ask her, "But do you never take into account the backgrounds of the prisoners, that they grew up unloved or even without a home and guidance?"

What did lack of love have to do with murder, Hallie wondered, or robbery, or violence in any form? She admitted she thought being poor led one to acts of desperation, to stealing in order to live. And then she thought the government too harsh in its sentences. One of her convicts had been sentenced to seven years for stealing a loaf of bread. Look at Brian, trying to catch fish in some nobleman's pond or river so that he could feed his family!

By the time these thoughts had flitted through her mind, she was at the parade ground. Drumbeats and a fife provided the musical background to the macabre drama being enacted. Already three men and a woman had been flogged, and Hallie would only be witness to the last. It was so crowded she could hardly see anything. A man, taller than she, stepped aside and gestured her to a place in front of him.

Hallie saw three wooden staves, resembling a triangle. About seven feet in height, they were fastened together like a painter's easel. A young man was being led toward it. Even from this distance Hallie could see he was trembling. He was forced to lie in the dirt, facedown, while his feet were fastened with leather thongs to the bottom of the triangle. His wrists, bound together above his head, were fastened to the apex. His body was then stretched so that he no longer touched the ground. His shirt was torn from him, leaving his white skin shining in the bright light. Hallie stared at its whiteness so long, it began to blind her. Thus, she did not notice the jailer raise his arm.

The whistle that cut through the air made her jump. A knotted cat-o'-nine-tails slashed onto the white back, striping it with six scarlet ribbons. The young man made not a sound, but his body stiffened. So did Hallie's stomach.

The crowd was rowdy. "More!" someone cried.

Hallie looked questioningly at the man behind her. "He's been sentenced to fifty lashes," the man explained.

Hallie gasped. "Fifty . . . my God!"

Blood beaded on the prisoner's skin with the next stroke.

His hands clutched the staves; the muscles in his arm quivered. The third blow thudded, as though it had struck raw meat. The scarlet became violet. The prisoner screamed.

By the fifth blow his body collapsed and sagged, the ropes holding him up.

Tristan emerged beside Hallie, his hand cupping her elbow. "I didn't think you should go through this alone."

She put her hand through his arm, not realizing she clenched it so tightly it hurt him. "He'll be dead at fifty," she whispered, unable to find her voice.

He put a hand over hers but did not look at her. "They'll stop it before that. And then bring him back another day for the remainder." His eyes were glued to the young prisoner.

Hallie felt the bile rise in her throat.

The scream that followed the tenth blow trailed the ground, sounding like the last gasp of a wounded animal. The young man's back was now bulging into a swollen mass, the red stripes merging into one pulpy tuft. His head had dropped, indicating he had lost consciousness, for which Hallie was grateful. A man walked over and examined the prisoner. His thongs were cut and two soldiers carried him off the field.

"Who was that?" asked Hallie.

"That was a doctor, advising them that any more would kill him."

Hallie looked up at him, her hand pressing her mouth. "A doctor? Oh, Tristan, do you ever have to do that?"

He was silent for a minute. "I did. Three times. But no more."

Hallie did not ask why. She couldn't have stood by and permitted such action to continue, either.

"This man's relatively lucky. Sometimes, if there is a sadistic jailer, the gashed flesh will be rubbed with salt."

Hallie wondered if the lump in her throat was going to bubble out.

"It hurts less if the tails are knotted like they were, and the blows showered in quick succession. This was a comparatively merciful flogging. The longer the time between cuts, the sharper the agony." His voice held no emotion. Hallie was aware that he was not showing his usual compassion, and she wondered why.

In retrospect, the hanging did not overwhelm her as

much as the flogging did. Tristan told her, "This is a man who escaped from the prison up in Coaltown. He not only killed his jailer, but rampaged the countryside, hacking women and children and stealing. I must admit to no sympathy for him."

The condemned man refused a hood, standing and looking defiantly at the crowd, his hands bound behind his back. A minister exhorted him to atone for his sins so that he could find his path to heaven. The rope was looped around his neck, and even then his eyes shot angry sparks of electricity into the crowd. He was filled with a hate that only death would eradicate. At the same moment the rope was pulled, a sharp snap ended the malevolence. The man hung in the air, his legs flopping.

Where did he go? Hallie wondered.

She was amazed to see the crowd, in a festive mood, break into bands and seat themselves on the ground, opening picnic lunches. Some of the little boys ran around pretending to flog each other, shouting loudly.

"Let's get out of here," Tristan said, his voice rough. "Let's walk down to the harbor and watch the gulls and pelicans."

It was a silent walk. Tristan's eyes looked like thunderclouds, and he made no move to take Hallie's arm or touch her in any way. Finally, after they had passed through Elizabeth Macquarie's gardens and were out on the point, watching the birds swooping into the sparkling water, Hallie spoke up.

"Tristan . . ." she put a hand on his arm, and he turned to face her, the look on his face softening. "I've only just realized, on this visit, how much I don't know about you."

He stopped, picking up a smooth round stone and, aiming it well, shot it into the water, where it skipped along the surface. "I was assigned, as are all doctors, on a rotation basis, to determine when the prisoner had had too many lashes to survive. I stopped the flogging after the first whip. After I'd done that three different times, the governor relieved me of that duty."

Hallie put her hand in his. "You have such compassion," she said, thinking no one she knew was nicer.

"It's not that," he said, his eyes on the horizon. "I was flogged myself, once. Fifty lashes."

Twenty-six

Not everything that next year was bad.

Tristan delivered Belinda of another son, much to Alexandra's dismay. She'd hoped there would be another girl, even though Jamie and Robbie seldom excluded her from anything. But being a year younger than Jamie made some things impossible for her. She was still riding a pony when Tristan decided it was time for Jamie to train a colt.

Hallie never understood how Tristan knew so much. He was not confined to his medical practice but had become a horticulturist. He seemed to have the solutions to so many problems; she guessed it came from his insatiable love of reading.

In some ways she was relieved that he knew little of carpentering and nothing of raising sheep. On the other hand, his aesthetic sense was far more developed than hers. But then, so was Chad's.

It amazed her when she even thought about Chad, who had written to her about being further delayed. He was someone from the long-ago past, even though it had been only four years. Her parents and Danny, whom she hadn't seen in over six years, were far clearer to her. In the letter she received from Chad, she hungrily devoured the news of her family.

The war with France was over. He was anxiously awaiting the fleeces, which he knew must be on the way. Her father was bedridden, and Chad—when he was not in London—visited her parents several times a week. He had become quite fond of Danny, "probably because he is your twin, though you are worlds apart in more ways than geographically," Chad wrote her. "Danny opts for security always, angry as that makes him at himself. He is mad at the world because he has no left eye. He sees himself as so limited now. I try to expand his horizons." How, Hallie had no idea. What Chad could do to perk Danny up was beyond her understanding. "But he looks like you, and that is a magnet to me." Those words irritated her; Chad had never seemed to see anything in her beyond her looks. When Tristan had said, "You are the most beautiful woman in the world," she'd understood that it meant far more than her external being.

It was ironic to Hallie that Chad wrote of wanting to help Jamie ride a big horse, but it was Tristan who took it upon himself to do so. One day, watching Jamie ride the pony, Tristan said, "You're becoming much too big for that pony. You need a horse the size of Robbie's." He looked at Hallie. "What about that colt you have? That two-year-old. It's ready to be trained. Want to let us have a go at it?"

"Us?"

"Jamie and me." He noticed the look in Robbie's eye. "Robbie can learn along with us. There's an art, you know, to training a horse." He smiled at the boys.

Tristan should be a father, thought Hallie, yet her heart turned over at the very thought. No, no other woman can bear his children. I don't want him to marry. Let him be a father to my children. They need one. They need him.

Brian heard of the proposed training and managed to be present when Tristan began. He knew how to ride well, but he had never trained a horse. No one at the farm had. Only Chad knew how. Now, their colts ran wild. Hallie had sold three foals to neighbors because she didn't know what to do with them. Chad would have spent time with them and sold well-trained horses for large sums of money.

"I'm glad Brian's taken an interest," Tristan told Hallie that night after the others had retired. "That means that in between my visits he can oversee the boys practicing what I've taught them."

He liked the Daughertys. And, next to his father, Robbie admired Tristan most of all. When Tristan visited, Jamie and Robbie dogged his heels. Alexandra trailed along, never seeming to feel left behind. Indeed, she was included in all the activities, even if only peripherally. Watching Tristan training the colt mesmerized her. She sat and watched every minute, never tiring, until Tristan would become conscious of the little figure by the fence and say, "Come on, Alex, take a turn." She would run out to him, her hands held high so that he could grab them, and with everyone laughing kindly at the small figure, she would try to emulate what the older boys had seemed to do so easily. She adored them. Jamie and Robbie were her brothers, her friends, her protectors. They never tried to play games without her, never ran away from her. Hallie would often look up to see the three of them, off to some place in the woods or down to the creek, holding hands—Alex in the middle. The picture never failed to warm her heart.

Belinda and Brian named their new son Morgan. When Belinda was busy getting meals for the convicts, she brought Morgan to the house for Beth to look after. Beth was never happier than when holding a baby.

Now, twice a week in the evenings between Tristan's visits, Beth, Brian, Robbie, and Jamie took turns reading aloud, albeit haltingly, from the books Tristan had brought them. Once in a while Alex settled herself on either Hallie's or Beth's lap and listened, but generally she sat beside the reader and traced her fingers along the words as they were recited. They were evenings Hallie wanted to capture forever.

Two other nights each week they would all crowd around the table with their pencils and paper and work out math problems that Ben set for them. Tristan had relinquished this task when Ben proved such an adept teacher and was consistently available. Brian and Robbie were nearly as quick as Hallie. But they arrived at the same conclusions by different methods. Brian and Robbie sat and logically penciled a rational progression to the correct answer. Often Hallie could not tell how she arrived at the answer. It was usually at the same moment that the others did, but her hen scratchings did not reflect her mind's progress. It drove Ben batty.

He had come up with an idea that Hallie liked. Sometimes a whole day went by when no one appeared at the store, and he couldn't stand not having company nearby. He might think he didn't cotton to people, but Ben was not an isolate. "We could stand a blacksmith in town," he said.

In town? One store? Yet she had named it Morgantown. No one but Tristan and Ben was aware of that yet. "Did you know Everett was a blacksmith?" He was referring to one of the emancipated prisoners who had stayed on to work for pay.

She *did* recall that. She had learned, over the years and in subtle ways, of the past lives of her convicts. That they had pasts, women in their lives, children and parents, dreams and hopes, were things she had set out to learn. Of them all, only Brian had been married. But what about Ben? She knew next to nothing about his life before she met him, only that he had been an embezzling accountant.

"Were you ever married, Ben?" she asked.

He squinted his eyes behind the glasses that were always low on his nose, always smudged, wondering what that had to do with having a blacksmith. "No."

He had been here nearly a year. What, she wondered, did men do without women? She had long ago heard that women did not have sexual appetites like men did, that men could not do without women easily. Yet all her convicts had been womanless for the nearly six years that she had been here—and probably longer than that. The more recent ones had been deprived of female company on the ship, and probably for a while in England before that. And the men who had been here with Chad, most of whose time was already up, had been without women for a long time. Did Ben never yearn for a woman, dream at night that he held a woman? Hallie could not even visualize Ben kissing a woman. Were there people who did not need other people? She had not yet realized that Ben never asked for anything, never gave the impression he cared about anything one way or another; nevertheless, wherever Ben was, there were people. He had not yet passed a night alone in the rooms behind the store. He spent at least two evenings a week at the house, teaching math, and managed to wander by several other evenings. She did not know it was he who organized card games in the barracks, or that it was he who broke up fights among the men when tempers flared.

She had begun to take him with her on her bimonthly trips into Parramatta to purchase supplies for the store and to cart the chickens and pigs and sometimes a calf that had been bartered. It was Ben who decided what the store needed, taking along a list of requests. In this way he became a familiar figure to the merchants in Parramatta.

The drought had worsened to the point where it weighed

271

upon Hallie's mind night and day. It created panic among some farmers. Wide awake at night, Hallie stared into the darkness, wondering what might become of them. She felt responsible for so many people—and for Chad's dream. She realized that it had become hers.

They had enough food to last. But what if *all* the sheep died? What if the pastures lay brown and sterile? If the river dried up? If the drought lasted for years? Forever?

Harry had said, "Go ahead and grant credit, Hallie. If these farmers go under, so does the country. If Australia does, what happens to the bank? We're all in this together. Having these farmers leave the land will not help the country."

Ben spread the word. In his neat, minuscule handwriting, he kept accurate records in a large ledger. In the opalescent dawns he walked his horse from the barracks, munching cold biscuits left over from the night before. From the store's big front window he watched the sky silvering into pink, presaging the fiery burst of orange from the edge of the eastern horizon. And, once the sun had risen, he sat making entries in the ledger, remembering every cent and every item charged from the previous day. There was no one to check his figures, but he never made a mistake, never forgot an item.

It was he who first learned any news. He never shared tidbits of gossip that he found really personal, but let harmless news, or information he thought might be helpful, slip out in his laconic conversation. And he listened. Aside from his mathematical ability, or perhaps even surpassing it, Ben was one of the world's best listeners—which was probably the reason Hallie never appreciated him as much as the farmers and their women around the valley, or the other convicts. The only things she ever shared with him were concerns about the store. She did not tell him her personal thoughts, as she did Tristan and Beth. Nor did she tell him her worries about the farm, as she did with Brian. Nor her plans for the future, as she did with Harry. She did not require that Ben listen, so she remained unaware of his principal asset.

Ben never asked anyone to listen to him, yet in no way did he think this unfair of life. It was his own choice. When he talked, it was of harmless news. No one knew what lay in his mind. The only one who ever wondered was Tristan, and he did not voice that to Hallie.

Even the daily bucket brigade could not save all the corn. It took two hours to water the garden, and by the end of that time the thirsty earth had consumed what water had been sprinkled on it, and the sun baked the land again in its hard bright glare. But because of the creek, Hallie fared better than most of the valley's farmers. Because of the river beyond the hills, her sheep did not die in such great numbers.

Hallie had told Brian to have the pasture refenced, so that at least three thousand of their sheep were in narrow pastures along the river. Jock had taken the great majority of younger, sturdier sheep up into the hills where springs still gurgled out of the meadows, where it was not as hot, though the grass was dried and there was little to eat. Neither he nor Hallie had given up yet, and did not want to slaughter the sheep that were growing thinner each year. Many of the lambs born that spring died, their mothers lacking milk because of insufficient diet. Every day some sheep were found rigid in the meadows, the birds already devouring their entrails.

There was enough hay stacked in barns, left over from the previous year, so that the horses and the cattle felt no famine, but it was not enough to feed nearly ten thousand sheep. Hallie petitioned the governor for more land, asking for pasture that went far up the river, where it rolled from the hills and there was still green on both sides of the now turgid water which resembled a creek more than a river. The governor told Hallie she needn't wait to pay for it: "Go ahead and use it." But there were no fences on it yet. She knew that if she just let the sheep loose there, she might never find them again.

"Miss Etta's pregnant again," Ben announced one evening after the math class had disbanded and headed for bed.

"How nice," answered Hallie. She hadn't seen the Coltons since the birth of Etta's last baby.

Ben looked at her, one eyebrow cocked. "You seen her lately?"

Hallie looked over at him. He did not usually remain after the others were gone. "No."

"She don't look good." He scratched an ear.

"In what way?" Hallie closed her ledger and listened. She realized he had stayed to tell her something he considered important.

"Can't rightly tell. She never comes in alone. She's always with those runny-nosed kids. The little girl's uncommon pretty. But there's no life in them kids." Ben's voice reflected his puzzlement. He did not look at Hallie as he spoke.

"Maybe they're not getting enough to eat," Hallie said, thinking she could certainly cart some food over to them.

"It's more'n that. And something's wrong with Miss Etta's ear."

She frowned. "Her ear? What in the world do you mean? Has she gone deaf?"

"No." Ben shook his head, a perplexed look on his face. "I can't figure what. It looks funny. Will Colton comes in the store and he won't charge a thing. Unless he's got cash, he won't buy it."

"What's so strange about that?" She thought that quite normal.

"He doesn't have anything." Now Ben looked at her, uncrossing his legs and leaning forward. "He looks around, spends maybe an hour looking everything over, while Miss Etta and the kids sit in a corner and never say a thing, never even move. Then he buys *one* thing—something like coffee one month, flour the next, a hoe the next. Trades a piglet usually. Never seems to run outta piglets."

"I think that's honorable," said Hallie. "If they can make out without other things when they can't be making much money with this drought—"

"No, it's something strange," said Ben. "I don't like it."

Hallie saw nothing strange about a man willing to do without something if he couldn't pay for it.

"It's like he's teasing Miss Etta." Ben looked as though he were visualizing the scene. "He holds something up and grins and says, 'You'd like this, wouldn't you?' And it's a tin of tea or some cornmeal. Something real simple. Or a yard of fabric, when the dress she's wearing is barely holding together. Or a piece of flannel for the baby. And then he grins, a mirthless, silent grin."

"I've never liked Will Colton," Hallie admitted, "and I've never quite known why."

"He's mean," Ben said. "Mean-spirited. I worry for Miss Etta and them kids."

Hallie looked at him. She had never imagined him worrying about anyone. "I'll ride over and see them," she said. "Do you want to come?"

"No." Ben got up and shook his head. "Got no need to. I see them at the store."

Hallie decided at last it was time to get started on building the additional room to the house. Now that Jamie was five and Alexandra four, the bedroom was crowded. While she sat sketching plans, she thought, Why stop at just one room? One will be for Beth. Another for the children, though they can't stay together forever. Two rooms there. And what about when the Langleys or the governor come to visit? And it's just terrible to let Tristan sleep in the barn. It's a wonder he comes at all. Though the one time she and Beth and the children and Molly had spent the night in the barn, she had thought it very cozy.

It wouldn't cost her much, she calculated. They already had the brick kiln. Since there was no hay to cut, no far pastures whose fences needed mending, and since so many ordinary chores were in limbo thanks to the drought, she had men and time enough to lend to the building project. She would ask Tristan if he had any architectural suggestions, things she hadn't thought about before executing her plan. It excited her to think about building onto the house. Chad had said he would, in the future. But she needed it now. He was not here to consult, not here to put any plan he might have into action.

When Tristan came out, he brought Susan, Molly, Christopher, and Kara, the three-month-old baby, with him.

"I know it'll be crowded," Susan said gaily as Tristan helped her down from the carriage. "But it's so hot in the city, and I had this awful urge to get out to the country . . . and I hoped you'd think it was one big picnic rather

275

than feel that hordes had descended on you!" She looked as pretty as a picture.

Tristan said, "I had the temerity to tell her I didn't think you'd be dismayed. In fact, I had the feeling you'd welcome company."

Hallie threw her arms around Susan. "What a wonderful surprise! Of course I'm thrilled. And you give impetus to my new project."

Tristan did have some suggestions about the addition. So did Susan. They spent that evening poring over and revising Hallie's plans until she didn't know which were her ideas or which her friends'.

Again Molly was the only person other than Hallie and Tristan to whom Beth opened up. Molly said she didn't mind sleeping in the barn at all, and Christopher and Jamie begged to sleep there with her. Kara slept in a box in the room with Susan, and Alex was content to stay in the house.

Though Tristan left the next day, Susan's visit was a two-week-long picnic. Hallie didn't remember when she had spent such a space of time just giving herself over to un-structured enjoyment. They packed lunches, rode out into the hills, and picnicked under trees. They bathed in the creek in the hot, lazy afternoons. They rode as far up the river as Hallie had ever been. Susan never stopped exclaiming about the beauty of the land, though brown and dry. The river, even as sluggish as it had become, was a silver ribbon when viewed from the tops of the hills. And in the distance, when the sun was just right, they beheld the jagged purple ridges to the west.

"They don't look from here as though they'd be so difficult to cross, do they?" Susan murmured.

They spent the afternoons talking, reminiscing of their pasts, of other lands, of parents and families. While everyone else read or studied math, they spent evenings outside in the warm night air, talking of things that Hallie was aware she had not discussed with anyone. They talked of being pregnant, and what it was like to give birth. Kara having just been born, Susan relived the experience while Hallie recalled Chad's delivering Jamie. She told Susan about it, and Susan urged her to talk about Chad. But it was difficult—it was so long ago. "He's a blur to me," Hallie admitted. "I scarcely remember him."

"I'd remember Harry if he'd been gone a hundred years," Susan said softly.

"I think"—Hallie tried to understand as she talked it out—"that it's because I've had to do so many things on my own. If I had sat around waiting for him, letting life whirl around me, I think I'd be yearning for his return. But I've been so busy ever since Archie died, and it's been such a challenge."

"Harry's and mine is a love match. We know we're luckier than most."

Hallie wondered what it was she'd felt for Chad.

"I could never do what you do," Susan said, changing the topic.

"If you had to, you could. I find I like it. I don't sit around letting life happen to me, don't wait for someone else to make decisions."

There was silence for several minutes, then Susan added, "How will you feel when he returns?"

In the dark, Hallie pondered the question. He seemed a stranger whom she might never see again.

"What's going to happen when the decisions are no longer yours to make?" Susan's voice was soft, but her questions hard. They were sitting outside, Susan leaning next to a tree, Hallie sprawled on the ground. The lights from inside the house shone in a glow, and the women smiled when they heard the sudden sound of laughter.

Reacting to the feeling of the moment, Hallie said, "Susan, I'm so happy! I want life to go on like this forever. Not the drought, mind you. I'm scared to death about that. It seems like it's been here forever. And I worry that it'll go on forever."

"Nothing goes on forever," Susan said, her voice level.

"I know that," said Hallie. "But I've never lived through a drought before. In the Bible they talk of seven years of famine before seven years of plenty, and I wonder if we have another four years to go before it's over. But when I'm not thinking of it, I'm so happy. Never more so than right now, with my family around me and you here. I don't think I've ever felt more content than I do right this minute."

277

Susan reached over and took Hallie's hand in hers. "I'm so glad we came. It's a perfect way to spend the summer."

And that's what it ended up being. When Harry came to get them, he said he'd stay several days, giving himself a vacation. He wanted to ride around the countryside and participate in picnics, and bathe in the creek and forget his work.

Hallie insisted on sleeping on the sofa, and Harry and Susan took Hallie's bed. Susan was curled in her husband's arms, and while they talked, he feathered kisses on her eyelids and down her cheeks.

"I want to stay, Harry," she said.

Kissing her ear, he murmured, "Somehow I sensed that." Susan went on talking, trying to defend herself. "I miss you and I love you, but I want to stay longer. Christopher is having a wonderful time with calves and dogs and piglets. He's never before been on a pony or slept in a barn. And Molly and Beth seem to be having a wonderful time together, like two schoolgirls. They and Belinda sit up till all hours of the night, giggling. Belinda has even slept a couple of nights in the barn with them, with her new baby. Everybody's relaxed and happy, and I feel like I'm on vacation.

"Hallie promises to take me to meet farmers in the valley, and one of the horses is expecting a foal almost daily, and Hallie and I haven't even begun to be talked out. Tell me you don't mind!"

Harry smiled and took her hands in his. "Of course I mind. The house is like a mausoleum when you're not there."

"Oh, you can't possibly have time to be lonely. You're at meetings three and four nights a week!"

"That may be, but I hate returning to an empty house. It's so silent. No one to put my arms around when I come to bed."

"Put them around me here," Susan offered, leaning her head on his shoulder. "Make love so that it will last us for a few weeks. Memorize me so that when you get in bed you will just have to close your eyes to have me there."

"I don't have to do anything to memorize you," Harry said, kissing her neck. "I always carry you with me. Wherever I am."

Harry liked Hallie's plans for an addition, too.

"It won't cost me any money, either," Hallie reassured him, though he'd asked for none. "We have everything else here. I'm going to use brick instead of sandstone, and I think I'll even add a brick courtyard. Something I'm surely going to add is a porch, one that spans the entire length of the house."

"I've been thinking," Susan ventured, "that it should extend like an L around the end of the house, so you can walk out of either the front or side of your bedroom, and there's also access to it from the back bedroom."

"What a wonderful idea!" said Hallie, excited by the thought.

Work on Jamie and Alexandra's bedroom had just commenced; the next one would be for Beth. All were to be spacious, with wide, high French doors to let in the light. It was going to be a sprawling house, and Hallie hoped it would not look like the new rooms had been thrown onto it haphazardly. Tristan's and Susan's suggestions had given it a cohesiveness, she felt.

Susan and her children, along with Molly, ended up staying for the summer. Harry rode out every other weekend, and once a month Tristan accompanied him.

Tristan . . . Hallie's heart quickened when she looked at him. What did he do every day and evening in the city? What did he write about at his desk at night? With whom did he dine, and what did they talk about? What did his mother say in letters to him? Did his mother know about her? What had he meant when he'd said he was planting roses all over New South Wales? She didn't think he was talking of plants. He never told her, she suddenly realized, when he was happy or sad, when a patient died, or when he had performed a cure. He didn't tell her when he had dined with the governor or stopped in late at night at the Langleys'. He didn't share with her ideas from those books he read. He didn't tell her what it was like to live alone in Sydney.

She stared at him as though never having seen him before. Is he wearing a mask? she wondered. Or do I see only the part of him that he feels it's safe to show me?

Except that she never had time alone with Tristan, it was the happiest summer Hallie had ever known. She let work slide and abandoned herself to the enjoyment of having her friends there.

The one jarring note was the trip Susan and Hallie took to the Coltons. The land was so parched that dust rose around their horses' ankles. But they played games, like schoolgirls, and raced across the valley with the hot air blasting their faces like a furnace. Yet it was not the aridity of the land or the heat that unsettled Hallie. She had packed food in their saddlebags and even taken several yards of fabric from the store. She had coffee and sugar and cornmeal and finely ground flour. She had tea, a dozen fresh oranges, and a bunch of bananas from a tree Tristan had brought her years ago. She brought turnips and potatoes from her root cellar; just a few of many things, thinking Will could not complain of the amount of anything. She hoped he would not even be around.

For a while he wasn't. Hallie was unprepared, despite Ben's warning, for Etta's looks. Even her eyes did not light up with welcome this time. She did put her arms around Hallie and held onto her tightly, but no life sparked in the dark, hollow eyes. Susan could scarcely believe it when Hallie told her later how beautiful Etta had been when she'd first met her. Etta had a pasty, pale look despite her tan.

Mary Ann, who had run around so enchantingly when Hallie had last visited, cowered in a corner until her mother called to her. Then she shyly came toward Hallie and Susan, twisting her fingers in her skirt, which was far too short for her.

Etta did cry with delight when she examined the parcels Hallie offered her. When the baby—David, whose eyes were the color of a winter sky—cried, Etta ignored him. It was Susan who finally went to him and changed his diaper. "Can I feed him?" she asked. "He seems hungry."

Jumping like a frightened mouse, Etta said, "Oh, of course. I was so busy with Hallie that I . . ." Her voice trailed off.

But eventually she began to talk, proudly showing the jars of food she was putting aside for the winter. The house was so neat that Hallie would not have been offended to eat off the floor. Of course, there were just the two tiny rooms.

But Etta really had nothing to say, despite prattling on. Her life, Hallie decided, was contained within these four walls. She had no horse on which to ride into the country, nothing to do outside, no one to talk with year in and year out. Nothing to think about. And she did nothing about it.

In the middle of the afternoon, just as Etta had touched Hallie's arm and said, "Don't go yet. Please don't go," Will and Walker came riding in. Will was laughing, obviously in good humor, but Walker was silent. His clothes were ragged and dirty, and it was obvious Will was not spending money to clothe him. Yet it had been nearly four years since he'd come, Hallie mused. She took time to study him. On the one occasion she'd seen him, she'd been too involved with helping Tristan bring Etta's second baby into the world.

He had eyes as blue as gemstones, and his light brown hair was flecked with gray, even though he was young. Of medium height, he was a stocky man hiding behind a blank stare.

How awful to be a convict, Hallie thought, with no way to make a choice about anything. For seven years having to do what someone else told you and only what they told you. How is it, she wondered, that I never think that way about my men? There was something infinitely sad about Walker. She noticed his eyes kept turning to Etta, who never looked at him at all.

Hallie introduced Susan to Will, saying that it had been so long she was ashamed of herself for not coming over sooner. "Why, I didn't even know you'd named the baby David." She laughed, wondering why she suddenly felt so self-conscious.

Will's eyes traveled the length of Susan. "You got no need to bring all this stuff, Hallie. We don't need it."

"Oh, Will, I hope you'll accept it whether you need it or not. That's what this country's all about—sharing. We have more than enough, and when I visit neighbors, I like to share."

She thought she had never sounded so stupid in her life. She jumped up on her horse and leaned down to touch

Etta's shoulder. "You send word when this baby's due," she said. "I'll come over right away."

As they rode back home, neither of them willing to race this time, Hallie felt depressed. Susan noticed it and divined the cause. "Hallie, that woman is in pain."

"I know it," answered Hallie. "But I don't know what to do about it."

"I suppose there's nothing to do. Don't you wonder what goes on there? I think that man, their convict, is in love with her. He's in pain, too."

Hallie glanced at her observant friend. "I was thinking that, too. Do you think Will knows, if we guessed?"

"I think so. Did you see her ear?"

Yes, the one Ben had mentioned. It looked mangled, as though it had been drawn through a wringer; in fact, it looked more like a head of cauliflower than an ear.

"I think he beats her," Susan said. "I think he hits her over and over, and that's what's happened to her."

"Oh, God," said Hallie, surprised that she had not figured that out herself, surprised that she wasn't more surprised. "You know what Tristan told me when he was here delivering David? He thinks Mary Ann and Brian look like each other." She felt unfaithful to Brian even to say such a thing aloud.

Susan was silent for a long time. Then she said, "Was Brian over there at all?"

"Yes. Chad lent him to Will for some chores. But then Brian refused to go. When Chad offered to send for his family, Brian begged not to be sent back to the Coltons."

"Oh, Hallie, do you suppose . . . ?" Susan's face was white.

"I don't know. Let's not think about it."

"Is Will punishing her for that? For a moment with Brian? God, who wouldn't prefer Brian to that ugly man?"

But Hallie was thinking silently, thinking that as black as Mary Ann's eyes were, David's were as blue as sapphires.

Twenty-seven

There were two days of warning.

The first hint came from lightning far to the east, out at sea. Then clouds, dark gray swirling masses, swept over the land. Low growling thunder reverberated from the heavens. The barometric pressure sank so low that older people had difficulty breathing. The humid air crawled along the ground.

But joy charged through most of the people, who ran from their homes to stare up at the boiling gray ceiling, at the spectacular mass that smelled of rain. Hardly anyone could sleep that night. Toward dawn, bolts of lightning shot into the mountains, followed by cracks of cannon-loud thunder. In the western distance, on the mountaintops, small fires were ignited, dancing into wide-spreading arcs. The more religious thought it sounded like the wrath of an angry God. No one had ever heard such noise from the heavens, nor seen more fury.

The deluge started toward twilight of the second day. Raindrops bigger than anyone could remember began to fall, slowly at first. Their splatter could be heard everyplace, the welcome sound of water pummeling against the earth. Even city people imagined roots of plants sucking hungrily at the life-giving water.

Horses neighed and welcomed the big drops on their dusty backs. Lambs who had never witnessed rain nestled close to their mothers. People stood outside, laughing, letting themselves get soaked, hopping up and down, calling to each other, grinning like fools. Only the abos ran to the hills, climbing trees as though they were koalas. Only their song lines had the history to warn them.

Hallie lay in bed, listening to it pour. She thought she had never heard any music more beautiful. It might be her imagination, but she even thought she could hear the creek gurgling into new life. The rain hit the rock-hard, parched earth and bounced off it. It rolled across the land until it found water and funneled into it. By morning any stream that had had even an inch of water was swollen and bursting over its banks. The river, with water pouring down from the hills and from tributaries, was readying itself for action.

It poured. Like bullets, rain struck the ground. From the house they could see neither the barracks nor the barn. They had neither the boots nor the clothes to keep themselves from getting soaked.

The creek inched above its bank as they watched, and it crawled inexorably toward the house.

"What will we do?" asked Beth, clutching Alexandra's hand. Jamie's nose was glued flat to the window.

"The first thing is get the men to herd the horses up to the hills," Hallie said, trying to think what needed to be done. "Get them to take the animals in the barn as far from the creek or the river as possible." If the creek was rising this quickly, she could barely imagine what the river must be like. "Fix breakfast," she told Beth. "This meal may have to last us a long time. Here, all of you, get out to the kitchen. Stay there until I get back. Do you understand?"

They had to fight the wind and the pounding rain just to walk to the kitchen. In just twenty paces they were drenched. "The fire will dry you off and warm you," Hallie said. "I've got to get up to the barracks."

She took off her shoes and wrapped a shawl around her head and shoulders. Squinting into the downpour, she waded through mud, her feet making sloshing noises as they sucked out of her footprints. It took her twenty minutes to travel what ordinarily took less than five.

Men's faces appeared at the barracks windows. They were not braving the storm. A door opened and a hand pulled Hallie in.

"The creek's rising," she said. "But I think we have time."

"Time for what?" someone asked.

"I'm not sure," she admitted. "I don't know any more about floods than you do. But I think this could be one. I don't know if it'll come up as far as the house. I'd think back here you might be safe, but I've no idea. But I want the horses, any of the barn animals, away from here—up in the hills. I want some of you to round them up and take them up into the hills. Not toward the river, but southeast. It won't be easy. I don't want any of you to stay here. I want some to go over by the river and cut the fences so the sheep can get out of their pastures. Then I want you to take off—take off for the hills and stay there until the rain stops."

No one moved.

God almighty, she thought, feeling fear prickle along her skin, touching nerves that were not yet raw. Do they need further instructions? And then she realized they were waiting to be told who was to do what. They hadn't made decisions for so long, they'd forgotten how. "You, Charles, you and Tom there, and Henry—go to the barn. Clyde, you go, too. Four of you should be enough. Let the chickens free and the pigs. But try to herd the cow and calf, the horses, all of them . . . no, leave mine and leave one for Beth. Leave—let's see, leave Princess and . . ." Better leave the one Jamie had been training. They might need horses to travel quickly to the hills themselves. Oh, God, it was easier to do things oneself. "I'll come with you and take the ones I want back to the house. But get all the others and take them up to the hills." She couldn't tell them exactly where. They'd have to use some collective intelligence.

She turned to the others. "Percy, you and Arthur ride along the lower pastures to the east. We'll have to forget the western ones, you won't be able to cross the river. Cut down the fences so the sheep can get out, away from the river. Lawrence, get someone from the other barracks, get all the men you can and work along the river as far as you can, cutting those fences. Then you get to the hills yourselves, do you hear? Stay there until the rain stops, until . . . until you see that the land isn't flooded."

Maybe it won't flood, she thought.

"The rest of you—help if you can, then get to the hills." She turned around and headed toward the barn. The horses were prancing around, sensing danger. Chad's stallion, Thunder, was neighing loudly and trying to smash his gate. Hallie decided to take him with her. Beth could ride Princess and she'd get on Thunder. Chad would never forgive her if something happened to his horse. She'd let Jamie ride Dancer, the horse he and Tristan were training.

"Here," she said to the men. "Help me saddle these

285

three. Then saddle your own horses and free the others."
She didn't think there was any need to rush, but neither
did she want to waste time. For the first time she noticed
that Ben had followed her to the barn. He was already sad-
dling the horse he walked to the store each day.

"I'm coming with you," he said, as though it were not
open to debate.

Between the two of them they led the horses to the house,
tying them around the big tree out front. The creek had
risen several inches, sweeping branches and debris in its
fast-flowing, muddy route.

It might not come up to the house, she told herself. But
the pelting rain made her realize the hopelessness of that
idea. Would the house be destroyed? Would it reach the
barn, the barracks? She prayed that all they had worked for
would not be swept away. If drought had lasted nearly three
years, might it rain that long? Except for the Bible, she had
not heard of droughts and floods. The soft rains of England did not allow for either.

"You go to the kitchen," she told Ben. "Get some breakfast." She stopped in the house to find warm clothing,
packing it in a bag. She changed her own wet clothes and
then went out to the kitchen. Beth had baked biscuits, and
the children's fingers were sticky with honey. They were
laughing at something Beth was saying, but Hallie could
see fear in Beth's eyes, though her voice was calm and reassuring. Gently, unaware that anything was amiss, lay in
front of the oven, comfortable in its warmth. Hallie ran her
fingers through his fur, then moved next to him, trying to
dispel the chill she felt despite the dry clothes. Ben poured
himself a cup of coffee.

"Let's pack up some food, enough for several meals,"
Hallie told Beth. "Then we'll ride over to Belinda's and all
go up into the hills." She hoped Brian realized that his
first responsibility was to his family.

Hallie devoured the eggs and biscuits Beth set in front
of her, then opened the door to take a look at the creek.
The water was creeping up steadily; she knew they must
get to higher land. But how high? What was safe? She
couldn't imagine the water would rise to cover the hills.

By the time they reached Brian and Belinda's house, they
were soaked through to the skin. The blankets Hallie had

286

thrown around them were useless. Alexandra rode in front of Beth, and the child's closeness was all that warmed her. Brian's house was farther from the creek, at the foot of a hill.

Belinda nearly wept with relief when she saw the forlorn-looking group. But she had hoped Brian would be there. He had left over an hour ago, headed for the barracks. Robbie was chomping at the bit to be doing something useful. His excitement intensified when Jamie and Alexandra arrived. Belinda didn't even say anything about Gently muddying up her floor.

"Maybe we're safe this far from the creek," Hallie said. "Maybe we don't have to go any farther."

But Brian returned home before long, to report that the creek was rising rapidly. He and Hallie agreed they ought to head to the southeastern hills, away from running water. So, early in the afternoon, the little band set out to the south. Hallie tried not to think of all that might be destroyed, of all the buildings and animals and food. That she and her children and friends were together, heading toward safety, was what she kept foremost in her mind.

None of them knew that the torrential rain was running off in sloughs as though scarcely touching the earth, rolling across it to commingle with the rivers. The billabongs had risen to merge with the creeks, which became rivers, which joined the rivers to become seas, tunneling out of the hills in waves, surprising and drowning animals before they were even aware of what was happening. The tidal wave uprooted trees and swept through houses; it caught people and tossed them around like toys before sweeping them into its vortex.

None of them knew the violence that was rampaging over the land.

It was late afternoon before Hallie and Brian decided they could stop. They had not crossed any creeks, seen any water at all from the top of the hill on which they came to rest.

"Looks like it's lettin' up," said Ben, staring up at the heavens. And, indeed, it did. The deluge had settled into a soft steady rain, the kind they had once been used to in late summer. Hallie felt more comfortable. Maybe the worst was over.

287

And it was, as far as the weather was concerned.

Shivering and soaked through, they munched on the cold biscuits and chicken that Belinda had brought. There was no way to make a fire because the leaves dripped water everywhere. Jamie and Robbie disappeared for a few minutes, and Hallie called for them. For God's sake, she thought, don't get lost out here.

"Gently's gone," cried Jamie, panic in his voice.

"When's the last you saw him?" Ben asked.

Robbie spoke up. " 'Bout half an hour ago, I guess. He was right in back of us."

"In back of you where?" asked Belinda. "You two have been running around in circles, in and out of everyplace the whole time."

"I don't know." Jamie balled a fist and rubbed his eyes, trying to stem the tears.

Ben stood up. "C'mon, I'll go with you. C'mon, both you boys." Hallie stared at him. He usually did anything to stay off a horse, and here he'd been riding all afternoon.

"Ben, you might get lost." Just because he was older didn't mean he knew his way. Since he'd arrived, he hadn't been off the farm except for trips into Parramatta with her. He didn't even know where the Southern Cross was, not that anyone could see it in this weather.

He pulled out his watch. "We'll be back before dark. Less'n 'n hour. We'll just go down the hill and call."

As Jamie and Robbie bounded onto their horses, Alex began to cry. "Gently," she called. Hallie picked her up and held her close.

They were back before dark, but without the dog. Alex fell asleep crying. Jamie lay staring into the darkness. Ben sat up, leaning against a tree, looking as though he were lost in thought.

Despite shivering from the dampness, they did fall asleep. All but Ben.

Hallie was awakened by the silence. No raindrops. No bird songs. In half an hour the sun would light up the sky as though a million sparkling jewels had split open the heavens. But at the moment it was just a faint pink line on the eastern horizon. Her first thought was, it's over. She stared down at the valley, and as far as she could see, steam from the damp earth rose to meet the morning air, but there was no water in the lowlands. She lay there, in the silence, letting relief flood over her.

Sitting up, she realized she was still damp, though not chilly. It was warm. Alexandra was cuddled close to Beth. Brian lay with an arm thrown around Belinda, who nestled Morgan in her arm. Robbie was asleep several feet from them, and Jamie . . .

Where was Jamie? Fear knotted Hallie's stomach. She knew where Jamie was: he was out looking for Gently, out getting lost in this vast land. Ben . . .

Ben was gone, too. And so were their two horses.

A strangled sound escaped her and awoke everyone else. "They're gone," she cried. "They've gone to try to find Gently."

"They wouldn't go without me!" exclaimed Robbie, standing up and looking where Jamie had gone to sleep, running over to where the horses were hobbled.

Hallie turned to Brian. "If they left in the dark, they wouldn't even know in what direction they were heading. Ben's a city man, and Jamie—Jamie's just five!"

They all just stood there, each gazing out in a different direction, sensing they would not see what they hoped for.

It was a mournful group that began a homeward journey. As they rode along, periodically one or the other of them shouted, "Jamie!" But there was no answer. Hallie felt paralyzed. How could she find Jamie in this vast land? And damn Ben. God*damn* Ben! Why would he and the boy go off together in the dark of night, neither knowing where they were or where to go? He should have had more sense. She should have stayed awake, knowing that Jamie would be as wild with worry about Gently as she was about him, that his own safety would be secondary to his concern for his dog. But she didn't expect a five-year-old boy to have the common sense she expected of Ben. Suddenly she burst into tears. How would she ever find her son?

By late morning they reached home. If her thoughts had not been so centered on Jamie, she would have been dismayed. All the buildings were standing, but a layer of mud covered everything in the house and barn. The barracks and Brian's home had escaped, but water had crept up from the creek and inched under the doorsills and lingered there still, having deposited silt over everything. The legs of all the furniture were wrapped in mud, and the whitewash on the walls was muddied up to nearly six inches. Shallow water sloshed all over, muddying everything it touched.

It had, for reasons no one could fathom, stopped at the kitchen door and not entered there.

The creek, still high, tumbled over itself in its rush. But it had receded back beyond the big gum tree and was no longer a threat. Broken branches and carcasses of dead sheep swirled by quickly. Hallie knew they must be hers since no one else lived farther out. It didn't matter. Nothing mattered.

Where was Jamie? Was he wandering someplace, hungry, lost—perhaps the opposite way, now miles and miles from home? Ben would be useless, she knew. She doubted he could even tell direction, even if he saw the sun come up. City people paid no attention to such things. She knew. She had only become aware of the sky and its portents over the last six years. Seven, if you counted the journey on the *Charleston*.

Hallie saw that Beth, who had been holding on to Alexandra the entire time, had been crying. Jamie was as much son as Beth would ever have, and Hallie understood that. They looked at each other helplessly, hopelessly.

"I'll clean up here," Beth said, though they couldn't do anything until the water that covered the floor dried. Even then it would be a Herculean task. "First, I'll get us something to eat." Staying busy would keep her mind off Jamie.

Hallie didn't know where to begin. I can't just sit here, she thought. But I don't know what to do, where to look. Jamie and Ben could be out there anyplace, with no food, nothing. They could be wandering around in circles. They could be dead.

There was nothing to sit on, so she pulled a chair outside so she could at least sit without getting her feet wet. But the harder she tried to concentrate, the more difficult it became. She couldn't eat any of the lunch Beth prepared. They couldn't brew tea, for the creek water was muddy.

Brian rode down in mid-afternoon. "I know you can't

think of anything but Jamie," he said, "but you better come look."

She followed him on Princess, across the valley and up the hill that overlooked the winding river, along which she had fenced the sheep so they'd have access to it in the drought.

To Hallie, it looked like the aftermath of war. It looked like God had rained anger upon the land and heaped destruction on it. Tall trees were upside down, their roots dangling in the air. Dead sheep by the hundreds were heaped in piles at the bottom of hills. Others must have been swept away. Any fences had been smashed and their debris strewn across the muddy earth.

They could not know that the river was the result of dozens of streams that flowed down from the mountains, that up in the mountains a big lake with fingers that reached out into smaller rivers had spilled out of its boundaries. They did not know that beyond them, two rivers—each of good size—met to form the one river they knew. They did not know that all of these fingers, all these tributaries, these two major rivers, the lake with its numerous inlets, had joined together to roll in driving force on a relatively narrow path many feet high along their river's course, destroying everything in its way. There had been only two people up the river to hear the terrible noise that presaged the giant wave that washed down the valley early in the dark morning. Like the hand of God, it balled itself up and sped on its narrow path, wreaking havoc on its way north before it turned toward the sea, breaking down at last and flooding the land.

All that Hallie and Brian saw, all they knew at that minute, was what had been done to this land and these sheep. All that Hallie could think of was Jamie. What if her son was there? What if one of those broken figures down there was not a sheep, but Jamie?

Twenty-eight

Hallie slept that night, but she was awake before dawn, riding out on Princess, calling, "Jamie!" There was no rhyme or reason to where she rode. Jamie and Ben had not been between here and where they had camped.

Toward mid-morning the men, in pairs or small groups, came riding back. Those who had been assigned to cut free the sheep by the river reported they'd been unable to save the sheep. Hallie, whose mind was not concerned with livestock, did not realize that meant that between three and four thousand of her sheep were gone. She did not care about anything except finding Jamie.

In her inner core, in some place deep in her guts, she knew her son was dead. She knew that the boy she so loved would never be seen again, at least not alive. Part of her envisioned his lifeless little body being hurled toward the sea, though how far that might be, she had no idea. Part of her saw Jamie and Ben wandering over unsettled land, going first west, then south, then east, and never north. Her hope was that, if they did head north, they would at last run into Parramatta or even Sydney, or the river that could guide them to either city. But would they die of hunger first?

Hallie wanted to hear nothing of lost sheep. She sent the men out to fan out over the countryside in pairs. She wouldn't have cared if all the sheep, the horses, if everything had died, if only Jamie were safe. But she knew he wasn't.

Robbie and Brian rode together. They came back at night, as did the other men, with no sign. Hallie broke into uncontrollable hysterics. She sobbed as Beth put her arms around her and cried with her. Nothing could stop them.

Her emotions having exhausted her, Hallie slept, but fitfully. Beth, in a frenzy of activity designed to keep her mind off Jamie, swept out the house, but the floors were

292

still caked with mud, whose dankness permeated sleep. The days were warm and rain fell gently, sinking into the ground now, nurturing plants, feeding the hungry earth.

The third morning after the flood, from far away she heard the echoing of horse's hooves. It was past dawn, the sky was gray, but a pearly gray—not the gray of storm clouds.

Jamie! was her first thought, but she could tell by the speed with which the horse was coming that it was not Jamie. She rose, still dressed—she had not undressed since the morning they had left for the hills. Not wanting to waken the others, she crept from the bedroom and opened the front door. Jumping from his horse was Tristan. He saw her in the dawn's light and reached out. Striding to her, he put his arms around her and murmured, "Oh, God, you're alive. You're here."

She held onto him tightly. "Jamie's missing," she said, and the words tumbled from her as she told him the story.

She saw the barracks door open and several men came out, heading toward the barn. They were already going out to resume searching.

While Beth fixed breakfast, Tristan and Hallie mapped out plans. "I couldn't even think," said Tristan. "The hospital was never busier. I didn't have a second, yet all I could do was think of you, wonder if you'd been flooded out, if you were safe. I rode all night to get here. Even in the dark my horse can probably find its way here with no help at all, after the numerous trips we've made."

Hallie was glad he didn't try to reassure her, patting her arm and saying, "Everything's going to be all right." No one knew if it would be all right.

Alexandra cried from the moment she awakened. "Gently," she would moan. And then, "Want Jamie." Tristan took her on his lap, but nothing calmed her. Or Hallie.

They ate in the kitchen, the only place not covered with mud. Hallie couldn't even choke down a piece of warm bread, although she did sip the coffee.

A horse neighed, weak, high-pitched sounds. Hallie wondered what was wrong with it. Though she could think of nothing but Jamie, she got up and said, "I'll go see what's wrong in the barn."

But it was not in the barn. Even from here she could see

what it was. Dancer stood in front of the barn, his saddle bare, whinnying.

Hallie screamed. Tristan, still holding Alexandra, ran out from the kitchen. Hallie just pointed. Setting Alex on the ground, Tristan ran toward the colt. Hallie trailed after him, her fist balled into her mouth. She bit her knuckles so hard they bled, but she was unaware of either the pain or the blood.

They stared at each other.

Dancer danced. He pawed at the earth and lifted his head, nodding as though beckoning them. When Tristan reached out to touch him, Dancer snorted and jerked his head again.

"Hallie . . . my God, Hallie, I think he's trying to tell us something." Tristan looked around as though Jamie might be here, too.

Gooseflesh ran down Hallie's arms. "Do you think . . . Oh, Tristan . . ." She peered at Dancer as though trying to divine some message.

"Hurry," he said. "Saddle Princess." Dancer had walked several paces away and was looking over his shoulder at them.

Hallie didn't wait to saddle her horse. She led Princess from the barn and jumped onto her. "No," said Tristan, stopping her, "we don't know how far we have to go. Saddle her. Get blankets, too, and some food. Is there any boiled water anyplace? I'll get rope."

Twenty minutes later they were following the nervous Dancer. Every few minutes he turned his head to make sure they were following him, an anxious, twitchy look in his dark eyes.

Neither Hallie nor Tristan doubted that he was taking them to Jamie. Dead or alive.

The horse led them to where the creek joined the river, where a mass of debris and mud littered the earth. The river, still engorged, tumbled swiftly along its charted course. Here, Dancer turned upstream, to the left. The horse's hooves sank into the mud and made thick sucking sounds, slowing it down.

Hallie and Tristan did not talk. Every now and then Hallie would cry out, "Jamie!"

Two hours after they'd left, Dancer stopped. The river

roared here, not the usual slow-moving silver ribbon that wound peacefully through the valley, but a churning muddy mass. Nevertheless, the water was confined within its banks.

Hallie and Tristan reined up behind Dancer. They looked around, seeing nothing of what they'd been searching for.

"What is it? What do you see, boy?" Tristan's voice soothed. Dancer pawed at the earth and shook his head, his nose high in the air. They both looked up. All they saw were the enormous eucalyptus trees, their silver bark muddied.

"The water must have come through here like a tidal wave," observed Tristan. "It's gone at least fifty feet up these trees, look at the mud. . . ."

They both saw the boy and Ben at the same time. Sitting in the crotch of one of the big trees, at least fifty feet up, were Ben, Jamie, and Gently. Jamie was holding Gently, and Ben—leaning against the main trunk—had Jamie encircled in his arms. There was no way they could climb down from the tree. And it was on the other side of the river.

Ben waved his arm and yelled something, but they could hear nothing over the roar of the water.

"How are we going to get across?" Hallie asked, so relieved that she began to shake until her teeth chattered. Tears covered her cheeks.

"We aren't. You stay here. I'll go upriver and see if I can find a way across."

"Oh, no," said Hallie. "I'm not going to stand here waiting for you, wondering if you've drowned. I'll come see you to safety on the other side."

It was another half hour upriver before they came to a place where the river, still swollen, did not tumble over itself. "Here," said Tristan, handing Hallie one end of the rope. "Hold onto this." He jumped from his horse and took off his boots and jacket, jamming them into his saddlebag.

They had to shout to be heard over the roaring river. "Fortunately, I am one of the world's best swimmers," Tristan said, grinning. She didn't believe him and could not force a return smile. Now that she knew Jamie was alive, her immediate concern was Tristan. Could he possibly swim across the river? It wasn't wide, thank goodness, but she could never have made it, especially when it was moving so swiftly.

"When I get to the other side—" He started into the river, then stopped.

Silently Hallie interjected, *if* you do.

"We'll head downriver, each of us holding onto the rope. When we get down there, somehow I've got to figure a way to get them down from the tree. When they do get down we've got to get them across the river, of course. You tie one end as high as you can on a tree on this side of the river, and I'll do the same on mine, and we'll have to haul ourselves over on our hands, clinging to the rope."

"What about Gently? He can't do that."

"I'll think of something. On the other hand, if I give the rope a big jerk, let go of it. I may need it on that side of the river. If so, you ride back and get some of the men and bring more rope. I doubt that Jamie or Ben will be in any condition to hike, so we'll wait there."

With the rope around his waist, Tristan waded into the water. He looked over his shoulder at her. "You may have to pull me out," he said, and let himself be caught in the swiftly running current. His strong strokes were as nothing in it. Quickly it pulled him downstream, but by a Herculean effort he inched across, so that by the time he had been pulled forty feet downstream he was on the other side.

Hallie thought, I don't know how he did that.

He threw his arm up in the air in a victory gesture and started jogging downriver with the rope still around his waist. Hallie, with Dancer and Tristan's horse beside her, kept pace with him on her side of the river. It was noon by the time they returned to the tree.

From her vantage point, Hallie could see Tristan gesturing and shouting up to Ben and Jamie. Jamie's fist kept rubbing his eyes and Hallie could tell he was crying. Tristan walked around, studying nearby trees, shaking his head. Finally, he jerked the rope and Hallie thought, How will they ever get back to this side? But she let go of it, and Tristan gathered it up into a coil. Then he began to assault a nearby tree that had lower branches. First he threw the rope, several times, until it caught on a low branch. And then, holding onto it, he climbed up to the branch, his bare feet flat against the trunk. From there it was easy to proceed upward. When he was nearly at Ben's height, he threw the rope to Ben. It took a dozen tries before Ben caught it.

Hallie could see them shouting to each other. Ben tied the rope around his thick branch, then Tristan climbed down his tree trunk, sliding down the last twenty feet. Even from across the river, Hallie could tell hitting the ground hurt Tristan's legs. He reached over to rub an ankle. Then, standing directly under Jamie and Ben, he began to climb the rope, hand over hand. In the meantime, Hallie watched Ben take off his shirt. Wrapping it around Gently, he made a sling of it.

When Tristan arrived at their level, Ben tied the shirt around Tristan's neck. Hallie hoped it would not choke him. Then, slowly, with the dog hanging down his back, Tristan began his descent. His toes twisted around the rope while his hands, one under the other, gripped it cautiously.

After he'd reached the ground, he shouted something, and Hallie could see Ben talking to Jamie. Wait, she wanted to shout, wait for Tristan to come get you. But Tristan was not making any move to do so. He stood, rope in hand, waiting.

Jamie, his small body hanging in the air, clutched the rope, his feet twisted around it. Not looking down, he moved first one hand and then the other below it until he was within Tristan's reach. Hallie's heart was in her mouth.

Tristan reached up for the boy and held him tightly, kissing his hair and his forehead, holding him as though he might never let go. Jamie clutched his savior tightly. From across the river, Hallie stifled a sob.

In a minute Ben joined them. But the rope was lost. One end was still tied fifty feet up in the air.

Tristan turned toward her and gestured widely. He was telling her to go get men and rope. She tied Dancer and Tristan's horse to a tree and took off. She did not ride through the mud, but traveled far enough inland that the sloggy earth did not impede her. She was home in less than an hour.

Seven men came back with her. Each had lengths of rope, as well as axes and tools that would be of no earthly use. One of them, Percy, who had been on the farm even before she'd arrived, upon hearing how Tristan got to the other side of the river, insisted upon being taken there and then swam across with a length of rope himself, so they would have something with which to connect. He trotted down on the far side of the river while Hallie rode along her side with the rope held above the rampaging river. When Percy reached the small group, they tied his end of the rope around a large tree. One of the convicts beside Hallie climbed a short way up a tree and laced the rope tightly.

With the rope tied between two trees, not far above the churning water, Ben was the first to come across. Tristan made Jamie watch every move of Ben's, study how he grabbed onto the rope. Oh, God, thought Hallie, don't let any of them fall. Don't let them drown now that we're this far. Ben's feet touched the water as he twisted hand over hand along the heavy rope.

As soon as he had passed over the river, he let go and fell to the ground. Hallie threw him a blanket, still too furious with him to be gracious. Her eyes remained on her son.

Tristan lifted him into the air, holding him while the boy made fists around the rope. Putting one hand in front of the other, he began to inch across the river. Hallie held her breath the entire time. Every man there was ready to jump into that swirling water if Jamie let go of the rope. At last he dropped into Hallie's waiting arms.

He hugged her, but he was grinning. "I made it! I did it all by myself!"

Hallie would not let go of him. She wrapped him, protesting, in a blanket. By then Percy, with Gently in the sling around his neck, had dropped to land. All their hands were bloody. "There's a break in it, right in the middle," he informed the men. "I don't know if the doc will make it."

Of course he would, but Hallie couldn't take her eyes from Jamie. And then, even over the rumble of the river she heard the tearing sound, and looked up to see Tristan swinging into the air before he hit the water, being carried downstream, his body disappearing. Two of the men grabbed the rope. Fortunately Tristan had not let go, and within seconds he was pulled ashore, drenched but grinning. He reached up and one of the men pulled him out.

"Thanks," he said, shaking water from himself like a

spaniel. He walked over to Ben and Jamie. "Nothing like a bit of danger to get the adrenaline going, is there?"

"Do I have it, too, the adrenaline?"

Tristan smiled at the boy. "I'm sure you do." He sat down, exhausted.

Hallie wondered how he could act so chipper. "Let's get going," she said. "We should be home before dark."

"Just a minute." Tristan reached out and put a hand on her arm. "Let's let these tree climbers have some food and water. They haven't eaten in three days."

Shivering, Jamie was jumping up and down, first on one foot and then another. Hallie reached out for him and enfolded him in her arms. She wanted to hold him close forever. Her first instinct had been to scold him, tell him what a foolish thing he had done. She wanted to scream at Ben, tell him he was an idiot, an irresponsible idiot. But he was shaking, too.

Hallie had brought food and gave them cups of boiled water. Jamie wolfed his down, but Ben just nibbled at his. "I didn't think we'd ever get down from that tree," he said, his voice barely a whisper.

"That's not true," accused Jamie. "You told me you knew they'd be along to rescue us.

"I lied," Ben said.

"I'll let them tell you what happened," said Tristan.

"I'm too tired," said Ben, and lay down on the damp ground.

"I'll tell, I'll tell!" Jamie cried. "I wanted to find Gently. I knew you wouldn't let me, so I waited until you were asleep. And then real quiet I got Dancer and we tiptoed down the hill."

"I heard 'em, though," Ben muttered from his prone position. "I wasn't goin' to let the boy roam around the countryside hisself, so I ran down the hill to stop him."

"But I wouldn't stop," Jamie said, munching the last of the food. "I began to run, but Ben ran faster and jumped up on Dancer . . ."

Hallie's eyes widened. Ben jumped on the running Dancer? Ben hated horses.

"And he said, 'If you're going, I'm coming, too,' " added Tristan.

Jamie had kept calling for Gently, and an hour or so later

they heard him. He came running out of the dark, wuffling, glad to see them. But now they were lost. They didn't know how to get back. Ben had thought if they just kept going, they'd get someplace. If they could find a stream or creek or river, they could go downriver. After a couple of hours they heard the river and headed toward it. They didn't know that at that very minute it had gathered into a ball ten stories high and was hurling itself down the valley, that they and the maelstrom of spiraling water would hit that spot on the river at the same moment.

It had been nearly dawn, and they'd seen the silhouettes of trees that lined the river. Ben knew to keep back from the flooded banks. They had heard what sounded like thunder intensified a hundred times. It was a shaking of the earth, the roar of a thousand lions. The terrain moved as though a herd of elephants were rampaging. And then it hit them. But not before Ben screamed, "Hold the goddamned dog!" and put his arms around Jamie. Together the three of them slammed into a tree, and Ben—still holding onto Jamie—reached out and grabbed a branch, the one that had caught him and Jamie across their stomachs, bending them across it.

The water had rolled on, leaving them clinging to the tree. And there they had remained for the three days, too far from the ground to drop voluntarily. So high that Ben's acrophobia rendered him catatonic until he realized that only he could keep Jamie calm, could keep him safe and alive, with the hope that somehow they would be found.

Later, after Beth had stuffed dinner into Ben and Jamie, after the children were asleep, after Ben had collapsed into a sleep from which he would not awaken for twenty hours, after Alex and Beth had told Jamie over and over how much they loved him, and Alex had drawn Gently into bed with her, Hallie stood in the doorway. Her insides had not stopped trembling. She had not been able to eat any dinner.

Tristan sat in front of the fireplace, enjoying the warmth of a fire, looking over at her.

"You saved a part of me again," Hallie said, her chin trembling. She began to cry, soft sounds of relief, of exhaustion, of gratitude.

Tristan crossed the room, circling his arms around her. She sobbed into his shoulder, into the rough grain of his shirt. "What would I ever do without you?" she asked, trying to smile. "You are always saving either my life or that of someone I love."

He looked down at her, at her glistening eyes and her disheveled hair. "I hope you'll never find out what life is like without me." He lowered his head and kissed away her tears. She raised her face, and as his lips touched hers the years of desire gave way and they clung to each other, their mouths ripe with wanting.

"Tristan," she sighed, winding her arms around his neck. "Hold me forever."

"My darling . . . my dearest darling. Would that I could," he murmured into her hair.

They stood that way for a long time, until the waxing moon peeked in and out of the clouds, until the clouds had gone and a halo surrounded the moon.

And then Tristan headed for the barn. But this time he looked back and waved. Hallie stood in the doorway long after he had gone from sight.

It was the first time that she consciously hoped Chad might never return.

Twenty-nine

Two days after Jamie's rescue, Hallie settled down to evaluating her losses.

She thought of apologizing to Ben for the thoughts she had had concerning him, but since he had never known them, she kept silent. She did, however, see him in a new light.

Beth said, "He saved Jamie, you know," and, in some imperceptible way, began serving dinner half an hour later so that when Ben left the store, he came directly to the house. In this way he became a part of the family dinner every night. And he stayed on for the evening even when it wasn't math night.

Generally he sat in silence, puffing on his pipe while Hallie kept accounts. Now and then she stopped to ask him something. After explaining the concepts of bookkeeping to her, he'd say, "Here, let me do that," until he was managing all her accounts, until he kept track of all aspects of farm life. He took the books to the store and attended to them when business was slow. He began to know more about the financial aspect of her farm than she did.

Hallie knew she owed Jamie's life to Ben, and she appreciated his work, but she still couldn't warm to him. She liked him well enough, but she felt none of the familiarity and trust she experienced with Brian. Partly, she decided, it was because Ben so seldom smiled. He didn't know how to make small talk, either. He never put his arm around her children's shoulders as the other men did. He never seemed to participate in an easy spirit of camaraderie with the others. Yet along with Brian, he seemed to be the most respected. Other men brought their troubles and hopes to him. This was an aspect of him that Hallie knew nothing about, because he never repeated anything that was told to him.

Hallie faced the fact that a few thousand sheep were irrevocably gone. She and Brian had ridden up into the hills to discover that over seven thousand of the youngest and strongest sheep were still safe with Jock. He and the two convicts assigned to him—Ralph and Edward—had not lost a single sheep to the storm. They had not even known there had been a flood. They were just glad that the rains had come.

But what Hallie could not adjust to was the disappearance of Clyde and Henry, whom she had instructed to lead some of the horses to the hills. Her first reaction was that they had been drowned. The men were from the group of newer convicts, but they had been with her over a year. They had never shown dissatisfaction, though Clyde did tend to rile easily and got into fistfights more readily than any of the others. But both of them laughed often, and though neither worked as hard as the others, they were neither complainers nor whiners. And both knew horse-flesh.

It was not until they had been gone for two weeks that Hallie admitted they had disappeared for good, along with one of her two best stud horses and two of the most promising mares. This did not include the two horses that had been assigned to them and on which they had ridden away. Though dismayed at the loss of such fine horses, Hallie was so upset by the loss of thousands of sheep that further financial disaster was not what disheartened her the most. Two men in whom she had put her trust had stolen from her and run away.

For those two weeks, before falling asleep, Hallie would try to tell herself the men were out there, lost someplace on this big continent. She told herself there was no way for them to get food, that two men and five horses would be suspect wherever there were people. She would have preferred her fiction that the men had drowned and the horses were running wild, but knew from the looks Ben and Brian gave her that she was being deliberately naive.

This dilemma weighed her down every day. She engaged in self-debate: should she inform the authorities or not? Should she hope for a while longer, or alert the police about escaped convicts, who had compounded their crimes not only by escaping, but by stealing valuable property? She felt betrayed. When she was in Parramatta, after getting

Harry's advice, she did inform the authorities of the men's disappearance.

The countryside blossomed. Farmers could till the land now, lush from the autumn and winter rains. Animals could forage, hope and courage returned to hearts, and people again took life for granted.

That spring, for the first time, Hallie's sheep had over five thousand live lambs. A few lambs died, to be sure, but more had twins or triplets than had ever done so. Though there would be only half the fleeces they normally had—since lambs were not sheared—they now had close to twelve thousand sheep, and the flood had not affected them permanently. All sheep owners experienced the same thing: almost one hundred percent live births. The land seemed more fertile, wildflowers bloomed where there had been none, kangaroos jumped over the land in herds as thick as locusts.

And Tristan brought Emil Schumacher out to the ranch.

Hallie and Tristan had never repeated and never mentioned the kiss. Hallie wondered if they would kiss again—if life would become impossible, or impossibly beautiful. But when he came this time it was as though no kiss had been exchanged, as though nothing were different.

Emil Schumacher was a patient of Tristan's, a German who spoke with an accent so thick that Hallie had trouble understanding him. Tristan at first did not explain why he had brought him. Instead, he and Emil rode around the farm, spending hours at the foot of the hills, digging into the earth with a long stick. Emil smelled the earth and crumbled it in his fingers. Each time he said, "Yah . . . yah," in his sober manner.

While they were so engaged, Hallie read the letter from Chad that Tristan had brought; He had written to tell her that her father was dead.

Dead.

That meant he had been dead for months and months, and she had not known. He wrote: "Your mother is holding up well, under the circumstances." His own father couldn't last much longer. "God willing, I shall be home within the year."

Dada gone . . . She had known she would never see her family again. But just knowing they were there, even if half

304

a world away, had given her a sense of security, of immortality.

"My father's dead," she said aloud, an emptiness welling up inside her.

Beth looked up from her darning and walked over to Hallie, bending to put her arms around her friend. Hallie reached up to grasp one of her hands and began to cry. "Dada," she said aloud, although she was really talking to herself. "He had no dreams. How sad his life must have been. The same thing day after day all the days and years of his life. To have no more hope in life than to wish the same thing upon his sons. I'm the only one in my whole family to realize more to life than in those little houses in Newcastle. You know what the company will do now?" She looked up at Beth. "Now that Dada's dead, they'll make Mum leave the house she's lived in all the years of her marriage, and she'll have to go live with one of my brothers. Or take turns with them." Her mother's future loomed impossibly pathetic.

"I'm glad Danny lost an eye," she continued bitterly. "He can't live out the days of his life in the bowels of the earth. His lungs won't collapse like Dada's did, even if he is angry about it. But what will Mum do? Live out the rest of her life knowing that there's not enough room for her in any house? Not have her own kitchen, but always have to be a guest in her daughters-in-law's kitchens? She won't belong anyplace." Hallie sighed.

Beth's hand tightened on Hallie's shoulder and she knelt down to rest her cheek against Hallie's.

"Oh, Beth, you're such a comfort. Don't ever leave me."

"Leave you? Oh, Hallie . . . all that I love in the world is right here. I've even begun to feel safe again. You may think that this is your house and they are your children. But they are all mine, too. And so are you. You are my sister, my mother, my friend. Until you came into my life, I never knew what the word 'love' meant. Only by knowing you can I understand how you feel about Mum and Dada. Only by having you and the children in my life have I been able to make peace with the world." Her eyes filled with tears.

Hallie went into the bedroom and threw herself on the bed, letting herself cry until there were no tears left.

The bedroom next to Hallie's had been finished for over a month, and the excited children had moved in there. It was an enormous room, with French doors that opened onto the side veranda. Now, behind the drawing room, another large room was nearing completion. Soon, Tristan would have a room in which to sleep. It was shameful, thought Hallie, that in all these years he had been relegated to a stall in the barn—one of Sydney's leading citizens sleeping in her barn. She had had a bed brought out from Parramatta, so at least he no longer slept in the straw. Next she would begin two more rooms, behind the large bedroom in back of hers. The house would be three rooms deep and have a total of six rooms. When the Langleys came out, there would be plenty of space; any visitors could be accommodated. Even when Jamie and Alex needed separate rooms, there would be enough.

It was dinnertime when Tristan and Emil returned. As they all sat on the porch, waiting for Beth to call them in, Tristan said to Hallie, "I want you to taste some wine." With a flourish he uncorked a dark green bottle, pouring golden liquid into the water glasses that were all Hallie had.

Hallie remembered the Madeira the captain had introduced her to on the *Charleston*. She had had wine at the governor's dinner last year, just a sip of dark burgundy, a slightly bitter taste that warmed her nevertheless. She had not known wine could be golden.

"Smell this." Tristan was smiling. "Inhale the aroma. Then take just a sip, and don't swallow it immediately. Roll it over on your tongue."

Hallie obeyed him.

"Now you can drink it, but don't hurry. Enjoy it slowly."

It felt like ambrosia on Hallie's tongue.

"Nectar of the gods," said Emil, his square head nodding, his bushy mustache gleaming with drops of the wine.

"It's wonderful," Hallie breathed. "I've never tasted anything this good."

Tristan's excitement could hardly be contained. "You tell her, Emil."

Though Emil appeared to be in his thirties, he was already balding and made up for his lack of hair with the biggest mustache Hallie had ever seen. He had serious blue eyes that lacked humor, but he brought a passion to his conversation.

"Emil," continued Tristan before Emil could begin, "is from the Rhine Valley in Germany." That meant nothing to Hallie.

"This country is perfect for the growing of wine grapes," Emil announced. Hallie had to concentrate to understand him. "There are certain conditions necessary for good vintage, and you have them all. Soil close to perfection, and just the right slopes to your hills, where hot summer air won't linger."

Hallie, while she listened, tried to figure out why she was being told all this. "Why won't it linger?" she asked, wondering why it mattered.

Tristan answered, "Warm air rises. The heat can't just lie in a valley, but is forced to rise up a hill. That means the air is constantly circulating."

Emil took over. "I have a little farm north of Sydney. I raised the grapes and made the wine that is in that bottle." He reached out and poured each of them more wine. Hallie studied the sparkling fluid, caught in the glass like liquid sunshine. "We have all the right conditions in New South Wales. Sufficient spring rains—we shall not take into account the previous years of drought." He permitted himself a little smile. "Spring rains are necessary for bud burst and shoot growth." He paused. Hallie continued to look at him as she sipped her wine.

"The heat allows for good berry set after flowering," he continued. "We do not usually have heavy rains, which encourage mold and fungi growth. Our rains are quite moderate.

"Dryness and temperate climate are necessary at vintage time, which here is the end of January till mid-March. All of which means"—he paused dramatically—"that Australia could eventually equal France and Germany in the excellence of its wines." He stopped and beamed triumphantly at Hallie, who sipped the ambrosia and glanced at Tristan.

"Yes?" Hallie still didn't understand.

"I want to be part of this." Tristan's eyes blazed with excitement. "And here's where you come in, Hallie. I don't own land. Sure, I could easily buy some. But I don't have

307

time for all the work involved. My main mission is to save lives, but that doesn't mean I can't expand my horizons. I want to participate in a horticultural experiment new to this vicinity—vineyards. I brought Emil out to look over your land. Hallie, I want us to go into business together, to be partners."

Ah, she thought. So that's it. Something to tie us together, something more than a midnight kiss months ago. Something that is ours. "Go on. Tell me more," she said. Was it the wine that was making her so warm?

Tristan poured them another drink. "You have the perfect land for raising grapes, and the help that could be trained to do it."

Emil interrupted. "A blacksmith can be trained to repair winery and vineyard equipment."

"How are we going to make wine out of the grapes we raise?" asked Hallie.

"A winery," Emil said. "Build a winery."

"You supply the work and land," Tristan told her. "Emil will supply the vines and expertise. I'll come up with the necessary financing."

"But"—Hallie turned to the German—"I thought you had a small farm of your own."

"Ach!" he said. "I do. But I cannot afford the help and enough land to build a winery of the size that Dr. Faulkner is talking of. He wants to send wines back to England. Instead of digging into the earth myself, instead of trying to pick each grape by myself, instead of doing all the labor by myself, he wants me to superintend a real winery."

Hallie couldn't tell whether the gleam in his eyes was visionary or fanatic. She gazed at Tristan, who looked as though he were waiting for an answer. Anything he asked of her, she would do. She had fantasized his begging her to take the children and run away with him; she had given free rein to her imagination, seeing Jamie and Alex and Tristan and her on a boat, landing in America. She had visualized the four of them crossing the Blue Mountains and making a life for themselves where no one could find them and judge them. His asking her only to share in a vineyard with him made for an easy answer.

"Of course, Tristan," she said. "It sounds exciting."

"I mean this to be a real business partnership," he said.

"You will own the land and supply labor. Emil will own the vines. I will build the winery and buy anything necessary. We will have to wait years for the first fruits of our collective endeavor. It may be three or four before we need a building to house a winery, but we shall have it in readiness and store the casks and crushers and whatever else Emil will have to send for. And then it must be aged. This probably will not bring in its first remuneration for seven years, Hallie."

What do I care? she thought. I shall have Tristan for seven years, at least. As my partner.

Perhaps it was as a reaction to the years of drought and the havoc of the flood. Maybe it was because the fecund earth seemed to sprout everything it was offered that spring or because the smell of roses wound itself along the length of the porch. Possibly it was because Hallie took immense satisfaction from enlarging the house. Whatever the reasons, at times Hallie thought she might burst from happiness.

The flood had shown her that her children mattered more than anything in the world, so she conscientiously took time from overseeing farm work to spend it with Jamie and Alex. She had Beth pack picnic lunches, and the two women, with Jamie and Alex, would ride far into the hills, until they knew what each bend had in store for them. She took the children into Parramatta so they could see life other than that which isolated them.

Robbie was twelve by now, and Brian took him out to work with him. He was no longer allowed to run in carefree boyhood with Jamie, though he still came over evenings. He was doing man's work now, and Jamie's childish interests were no longer Robbie's. But Hallie noticed that on Sundays they raced the fields together and played patiently with Alex, and she could hear their cries of exultation when they splashed water at each other in the creek.

Robbie told them before Brian did that they'd spied a band of abos. Jamie wanted to see them, so when Hallie heard they were upriver, bothering no one, camped on land she had not yet fenced in, she said they could ride out to visit them. She wondered if they were the same tribe that had visited so long ago, when she was pregnant with Jamie.

They were not, and they greeted Hallie and her children with suspicion. Some of their members had learned a smattering of English, and when they realized Hallie was welcoming them and telling them they were free to use her land, they relaxed, even though the one who spoke English best informed her that this was not her land. It was the land of anyone who wanted to use it. It was land they needed to visit, for water. They called it *cowarra,* which she thought he told her meant land "by running waters."

She did not argue with him. Jamie, full of the curiosity of a five-year-old, asked why the very black little children had "nearly white hair." Hallie couldn't answer that. He and Alex held back, astonished at seeing nearly two dozen black people.

"Why don't they wear clothes?" Alex asked.

"It's hot," answered Hallie as they rode back toward the house. "They have no need of clothes."

"It's hot for us, too," Jamie said. "We wear clothes."

"They have no cloth, I guess." Hallie laughed. "They have different customs than we do."

"They're ugly," said Jamie.

"Are they people?" his sister asked.

"Yes," answered Hallie. "They are human beings, like you and me." But she was not sure of the accuracy of her answer. All she really knew of them was that she had laughed and bathed in the river with the black women almost six years ago, and they had been kind to her. She had been horrified when she heard recently that some of the men in Parramatta spent Sunday afternoons in the sport of going out to hunt "roos and abos." She was sure she had not understood correctly.

But she had understood the word *cowarra.*

By running waters.

Harry was always telling her she should name the farm. And their winery certainly would require a name.

She rolled the word across her tongue: Cowarra. An Australian name.

Cowarra Wines. By running waters. Where the river and creek met.

Cowarra.

Thirty

Although Hallie had trouble understanding Emil, she understood that he hated living in the barracks, and until his little brick house could be finished, he chose to bed in the empty room behind the store, cooking his meals there, too. "I need to be alone," he said.

But not when working. He explained each step, sometimes several times. Hallie trailed him, listening—sometimes fascinated, and once in a while bored at his repetitiveness. "Here, in Australia," he said, "where the sun is fierce, the best place for vines is above the first quarter of the hill, on sloping land to the southeast or west."

"Why?" Hallie seldom comprehended something unless she understood the reasoning behind it.

Emil relished explanations. "On clear cool nights, when the earth's heat is radiated from the ground, the air near the soil is cooler than the air above it, and collects in pools.

"Now, when we plant, we must follow the contour of the hill to prevent erosion. Sunlight on soil between rows causes less acid in grapes, while sunlight on the leaves produces higher sugar in the grapes."

Hallie wondered how he could tell that.

"In places where there's enough sugar but too much acid, we need higher temperatures. Here"—by which he meant Australia—"I think we'll space the rows seven feet apart rather than ten as they do in Europe. The earth stays warm all year."

Hallie had to concentrate hard. She began to bring a notebook with her and jotted down notes so she could remember the encyclopedia of information that Emil tossed out so confidently.

He had asked for two convicts, whom Hallie had no trouble sparing in the fall, but she wondered how she would manage at spring planting and lambing season. The two men trotted along with her and Emil, but Hallie had no

311

idea whether or not they were absorbing all the things Emil was spouting in his thick Teutonic accent.

"We must cultivate the soil more than thirty inches." Thirty inches, thought Hallie. That'll take a lot of muscle power. "Some places up to seventy inches," Emil continued. Hallie could tell the men understood, for they looked at each other and rolled their eyes. Digging seventy inches would not be easy.

Emil acted as though he were teaching children. "We'll dig a trench three feet wide by three deep. Break up, loosen the soil. Then we'll refill the trench with the soil and let it sit over the winter. In the spring we'll plant the vines."

Emil and his convicts spent weeks digging the trenches he required. And then they concentrated on building his little two-room brick house.

Winter passed quickly. Emil's little house was completed, and the additions to hers were nearly finished. Just one room was incomplete, and even that had a roof and walls.

Hallie realized she would need more labor, not only for the planting of grapevines as spring approached again, but because of an increased garden and additional acres of hay and so many more lambs. After petitioning the governor, she received five more convicts.

She tried to be present when Emil gave instructions on how to plant the vines. What she really needed, she thought, was to be five separate people.

They walked along single file, she and Emil and the two convicts who'd now been assigned to the vineyard permanently. Emil knelt down, and the two men hunkered down by him, looking and listening.

"First-year grapes need to be tied up off the soil on these trellises," he said. "After a few years the trunk itself will support the vine."

He talked to them of mold and rot and fungus, which—as yet—none of them understood. He painted frightening pictures, which he made sound like the end of the world, of the diseases that could render all their labor worthless. "I prefer two-wire trellises for cabernet sauvignon," he said, and Hallie figured that must be a kind of wine. "We'll keep the ground turned up around the grapes, though I don't think keeping the soil warm will be a problem here." He glanced up at Hallie. "It's a big problem in Europe."

One day she even knelt down and dug in the dirt herself, planting a few vines, while he stood over her, supervising. "Trim the roots no more than six to eight inches." Then he knelt down beside her. "Here, let me. This way. We want to encourage root production." He showed her what to do, guiding her small hands with his huge ones. "Like this. Spread out the roots and rest them on this center mound. These—these are buds—should be two inches above the soil. Yes ... good. Good. Now fill the hole."

After she had, he told her, "Step on it. . . . Yes. Quite firmly. Don't be afraid. Sink your foot in, leave a little dish to catch extra water."

Then he told her to cut back the newly planted vines to two or three buds, "not just one, because we might lose it, and then where would we be?" But next year, he said, they'd prune it back to one bud, "because by then it'll have a large root system and will speed toward the top wire of the trellis . . . as though exploding." He laughed happily.

The rest of that first year of planting, Emil and one other man would be able to handle all the vines. They would allow a cover crop to grow in the beds, which would help the grapes to slow down and give the fruit and wood a chance to mature. Until fall, that first year, the vineyard would not require enormous amount of work, yet Emil and Homer, the one convict who had become fascinated with the project despite the hard physical work it required, were out in the fields, on the hills, daily. Hallie left them alone. She'd come back to learn what needed doing next fall.

In late November, when Hallie and Ben made a quick trip into Parramatta, Susan and Harry asked if they might come out, without the children this time and just for overnight, to see the new additions.

"We haven't been out since before the flood," said Harry.

"I was rather hoping Susan and the children might spend a good part of the summer with us again," Hallie said.

"I was afraid you were hoping that." Harry smiled, his eyes seeking his wife.

"I'm pregnant again," Susan told her.

"Well, that shouldn't stop anything," Hallie responded.

To herself she thought, If you're going to be away from him, now's as good a time as any. "Tristan can keep watch over you. He manages to get out about once a month."

Susan looked at Harry. "Let us talk it over. I'm not due until late June."

"You can sit on the porch and look at the scenery, and bathe in the creek, and you needn't go riding or anything strenuous at all. I do wish you'd think about it. We had such a wonderful summer the last time you were there."

"*You* did." Harry's voice was accusatory. "I was lonely."

"Harry, I saw more of you then than the rest of the year put together. I think you might have been lonely, but you enjoyed long weekends out at Cowarra, too."

"We'll talk it over and give you an answer next week when we come out."

"All but one of the rooms is finished," Hallie told them. "If you're planning to come by carriage, perhaps I can talk you into taking a wagon instead, and I'll order a bed. I'm sadly lacking in them."

When they came, they brought not only the bed, but an invitation from the governor. He and Elizabeth Macquarie were throwing a New Year's Eve ball. Susan and Harry had decided they would invite a dozen people to dinner the night before, and they hoped Hallie would come to both the ball and their dinner. They could go to the racetrack New Year's Day, and the whole holiday promised to be very festive. Susan said she would come spend a month at the farm over the summer *if* Hallie would bring Alex and Jamie with her when she came for New Year's and let them spend two weeks in the city with them after she returned to the farm. They thought the children would be fascinated with Sydney, they'd take them to Parramatta on the ferry, and liked to think they'd help expand the children's horizons. Then Susan would come out with the children and stay for a month.

"What wonderful ideas!" Hallie threw her arms around them. "Yes to all of them. Yes, yes!" What a gay time. She wouldn't even have to buy a new ball dress. She had not only the one she had bought, hoping to dazzle Tristan, but the blue one that Chad had bought her years ago. She had worn each of them only once.

Susan and Harry both thought the additions to the house

were not only impressive, but carried the grace of the original house throughout. Harry commented on her taste, but Hallie said, "Any taste and grace, I feel, were acquired from Susan and Tristan and their suggestions." Though the bed they'd brought with them was the only piece of furniture in the still unfinished bedroom behind the drawing room, Susan and Harry chose to sleep there so no one would be displaced from their usual beds.

"You weathered the drought far better than most," Harry said. "The other farmers are coming back, but more slowly. They're behind where they'd hoped to be at this time, but the yields this year should be tremendous. Ben tells me people are beginning to catch up on their bills at the store, too."

Funny, he hadn't thought to tell her that, Hallie mused. But then she seldom thought of the store; that was Ben's bailiwick. Ben even paid the Parramatta merchants' bills due them. He and Harry got together once a month to go over accounts. Every so often Hallie would ask, "Are we doing all right?" and Ben would nod.

"Is Ben trustworthy?" Hallie asked Harry as they sat on the porch. Susan was napping.

"Do you have reason to think otherwise?" he responded.

"No," she shook her head, "but I never question his accounts."

"I do. Ben's fine." When Hallie didn't respond, Harry added, "You're lucky to have him, you know."

"He's even taken to doing my accounts about everything—the sheep, the horses. He keeps records of who's bred to whom, and how many pounds of fleece we get, and how much we sell it for, and to whom, and what date it leaves Sydney, and all that sort of thing. He knows more than I do about my finances."

"I said you were lucky to have him. He or I will tell you if you need to worry. As it is, Hallie, you're one of the wealthiest women in New South Wales." Harry lit a cigar and smiled at her.

She looked at him and leaned forward in her chair. "I am?"

"Well," he amended, "you and Chad are two of the richest landowners. Maybe not in money you can lay your hands on, but before too long, Hallie . . . even that will not be a

315

problem." He had to light his cigar again. "Your thousands of sheep back in the hills left you in an enviable position. The prices of both fleece and mutton have soared because so many were lost to the drought and the flood." He gave up on his cigar and tossed it into the grass.

Hallie nodded. "I know I'm already selling breeding stock far and wide. I've had more visitors in the last three months than all the previous years—all wanting breeding stock in both sheep and horses.

"I can't keep up with the horses, but it's nice to be sought out. And I'm having the men fence our land even far up in the hills." She stood and walked to the edge of the porch, putting her arms around a pillar, looking out at the peaceful scene. Everything was going so well.

Harry walked over to stand beside her. "Fine idea to send your blacksmith down next to the store. Farmers don't have to limp their horses into Parramatta now."

"It was Ben's idea," Hallie admitted. "But it's beginning to be a town of its own, Harry. I've already named it, and when I'm in Sydney at New Year's, I'm going to offer to put up buildings for any merchants willing to come this far out. And houses for them, too."

Susan, who had appeared in the door and was listening to them, spoke up. "Hallie, I don't know where you get your ideas, much less your energy."

Hallie turned to smile at her. "I've had no choice, Susan. I was left here alone."

"Ah," Harry twitched his mustache, "but you did have a choice. You could have just sat by."

"The choice," mused Hallie, "wasn't mine. Given the person I am, I've acted in the only way I could."

As always, Tristan had promised to come for Christmas. But the first weekend in December he told her, "You have a choice to make. I'm scheduled to work on Christmas. However, if you prefer, I will come out to Cowarra then, but in exchange I'll have to work the next weekend, when you will be dining at the Langleys' and at the governor's ball."

So, here I do have a choice. Somewhere, deep inside, Hallie felt that what happened about this one small choice

316

might make a difference to her whole life. She had no idea why she had this premonition.

They had just returned from riding, and Hallie slid off of Princess before Tristan could help her. "And the alternative?" She looked up at him.

"Dine with you at Langleys', dance with you at the ball . . ."

She laughed. "You make it sound enticing. Will you come to the races, too?"

Tristan laughed. "We'll create quite a scandal. But, yes, of course. Have you never been to a race?"

Hallie shook her head. "Nor ever danced."

She walked up onto the porch. He reached out and, taking her hands, stopped her. "Poor Hallie. Never danced? It's about time, isn't it?" The touch of his hands melted her.

"Here," he said, "look at my feet, and do what I do." He moved his right foot to the side. Hallie felt awkward, but she followed him with an unaccustomed shyness. "Place your left hand on my shoulder," he said, "but watch my feet. There, one-two, one-two-three, one-two, one-two-three . . ." They circled slowly, until Hallie began to feel a rhythm established. "Do you feel the pressure of my hand there? When in doubt, concentrate on that. Any decent dancer should be able to indicate where you're to move next by the pressure of his hand."

Hallie liked the pressure of his hand. She wanted him to pull her closer, feel him against her, but he kept over a foot between them, repeating, "Watch my feet."

Just then Alex came running along the porch, shouting, "Me, too!"

Without breaking the rhythm, Tristan kept one hand around Hallie's and opened the other so that Alex could hold it. "We're going slow," he said to the little girl. "Watch my feet and do what I do." The three of them moved in tandem. Hallie thought her daughter picked it up more quickly than she did.

At that moment Robbie and Jamie rounded the side of the house and clamored to be included. The five of them spent the rest of the afternoon dancing, amid much laughter. When Beth heard all the frivolity, she emerged from the kitchen but refused to join them.

Before Tristan left the next morning, Hallie said to him, "I'll spend Christmas here at the farm, or Beth would never forgive me. We'll have Christmas dinner with Brian and Belinda and invite Ben. I'm giving the men two days off. They've all been wonderful this year." He looked at her. "You stay in Sydney. And the day after Christmas, the children and I will come into town. Susan said they'd be in Parramatta until the twenty-eighth, so we'll join them and come into Sydney when they do. I'll spend a week or so there, before leaving the children with Susan and Harry."

"Will the three of you come dine at my house?" Tristan asked as he mounted his horse. "The children have never seen where I live. I'd like to show Jamie my office."

"He'll enjoy the skeleton." Hallie laughed. "Of course we'll come. The children and I'll do all sorts of marvelous things, like taking the ferry to Manly. I've never done that, either. Maybe you'll give us a hospital tour, too. And I have some business things Harry can help take care of. I won't feel guilty about taking a week away from the farm if I know I can combine business with pleasure." She patted his horse's flank.

Tristan leaned down. "Why do you feel guilty about enjoying yourself?"

Hallie looked up at him sharply. She hadn't realized that was what she felt. "I don't know. . . . It's not that I feel guilty enjoying myself. I like everything—well, most everything—I do. I enjoy life. But I guess . . ." She searched for an explanation. "I feel I must always be doing something productive."

"Why?" Tristan looked at her.

She shrugged. "I don't know. Maybe because at home we never had time or money to do anything that was just fun. Everything had a purpose."

"We must change that in you, Hallie." He reached for her hand. "Just once in a while you must abandon yourself to fun. I agree with you because I, too, must feel I am doing something for humanity most of the time, but I don't hesitate to take time in life just for me."

Whenever he touched her nowadays, a fire ignited. "When do you ever do that?"

"When I come out here." His eyes were locked with hers.

She wanted to say whatever would keep his hand around hers.

"But you're always busy doing things for all of us. You're always busy here."

"But that I do just for me. And you don't see me, you know, for weeks on end. I take time, now and then, when I do absolutely nothing for anyone and I don't feel guilty. It feels good. I need to give to me so that I replenish myself and can continue to give to others."

"What do you do then?"

He let go of her hand and sat up straight. "Sometimes I read all day long. Or I take a boat and pretend to go fishing. Once in a while I even catch something, but I do it to just sit out in the harbor, away from everyone, listening to the gulls, watching fish jump in silver streaks, studying cloud formations . . . thinking. Finding myself."

Hallie stared at him. She didn't understand this man whose touch set her afire.

He smiled. "When you come to town, I shall take time to dance and to cheer at the races, and wine and dine you. I shall indulge myself and let nothing interfere with pure pleasure."

After a Christmas when Hallie permitted herself more extravagance than she could have imagined back in Newcastle, she and the children headed toward Parramatta.

They had had a wonderful holiday. Hallie gave the men two days off and an extra keg of rum, but she wanted to do more to express her thanks for their help. She bought each of them new shirts and pants, and asked Brian to purchase new underwear and socks for the men, and she gave them all wide-brimmed hats to protect them from the sun. She gave them tobacco and had two geese slaughtered for their Christmas dinner. Belinda and Beth worked all of Christmas Eve day preparing dinner for the men so they wouldn't have to work hard on Christmas itself. Hallie spent time preparing plum pudding as she had had it at home, and stuffed a goose so she could give Belinda and Beth the day off. It was the first time in years she'd spent time in the kitchen, baking.

She bought Ben a suit. Not just work clothes, but a suit.

She couldn't think what else to get him, except tobacco for his pipe. Now he could look like a merchant, instead of a convict. She let Jamie give him a wide-brimmed hat, and Alex gave him a ruffled shirt. He didn't look directly at them when he thanked them, and Hallie couldn't tell whether or not he was pleased.

She showered playthings and new clothes on both Brian's children and her own. To Brian and Belinda she gave a table and chairs, along with the promise to add another room for their expanding family. To Beth she gave a four-poster bed, with a feather mattress. Beth burst into tears, but it was not until later that she asked, "Does that mean I have to go sleep in the new room all by myself?" Hallie had thought she'd be pleased to have a room of her own, something she had never had in all her life.

Hallie enjoyed being Lady Bountiful. She had no idea she'd get such exquisite pleasure from the giving. Never had she spent a happier Christmas. After they'd stuffed themselves with the dinner, they went down to the creek to bathe—the men going farther down beyond the bend by the trees. Laughter filled the warm afternoon air . . . laughter and contentment.

When night fell, and Brian and Belinda and their children had taken off for their home, Ben stood by the door, on the porch. New hat on his head and his suit in hand, he shuffled his feet back and forth and and, staring at the ground, mumbled, "I never believed in God before. I never believed in love before. I never believed in nothing before." Then he looked up at her. "But I believe in everything now." Turning abruptly, he took off into the night.

Hallie gazed after him in surprise.

Jamie and Alex were beside themselves with the excitement of spending several weeks in the city, two of them without Mother. Molly took them under her wing and they set out to explore Parramatta and its creeks and avenues. They stared into store windows, their noses pressed against the panes of glass. The schoolhouse stood empty for the holiday, but Jamie stared at the desks and books and later told his mother, "I'm going to be a doctor like Tristan."

"Do you even know what a doctor does?" she asked, smiling.

"Whatever it is, I want to be just like him." He could hardly wait to visit the hospital and see Tristan's office.

After dinner Hallie said to her hosts, "You have three days to help make me socially adequate. Teach me to dance." The idea delighted Susan and Harry. After the children were bedded down, they called Molly in so they could make two couples, and Molly joined Hallie in absorbing one aspect of social adequacy. Susan hummed and took turns with Harry in being Hallie's partner. Then Harry and Susan would dance together so the two women could observe them. While the children were out the next afternoon with Molly, Hallie practiced dancing in her room. She wanted to surprise Tristan, wanted to be able to dance with him all night, be held by him, be in his arms all evening.

The ferry trip up the river to Sydney delighted the children. Alex followed the flights of the birds with single-minded intensity. Commonplace to her were the galahs, cockatoos, magpies, parrots, and noisy kookaburras that surrounded the farm, but she had never seen pelicans or gulls. These big-billed water birds enthralled her. On the shore at one point they saw black men with spears, and children playing on a sandy beach farther along.

"Someone should be with those children," Susan commented. "To see they don't go in the water. Sharks, you know." No, Hallie didn't know. She was surprised to hear sharks were so far up in the harbor, such a distance from the sea.

Once in Sydney, Susan left them on their own, for she had dinner-party preparations to make. Sydney was alive with social events on this holiday week, and a festive air pervaded the entire town. One afternoon Molly and Hallie took the children to a puppet show; another day was spent going back and forth to Manly on the ferry. Hallie pointed out the rocky promontories called the Heads to her children, telling them that was the first she'd seen of this new land of hers. "Beyond it," she explained, "all that water out there, is the ocean. And eight months away"—though she knew that meant nothing to them—"is England, where I grew up."

No one said, "Is that where Father is?" Neither of the

children remembered him, and Hallie scarcely talked of him.

From the dock in Manly they walked across the narrow strip of land that led to what would become one of the world's famous beaches, but was now just a beautiful crescent of sand where waves broke gently.

"C'mon," cried Molly. "Take off your shoes, children, and let's wade in the ocean. We won't wade far out in it, just get our ankles wet. It's fun. You can try it, too," she said to Hallie.

Hallie watched the children splashing and crying out, waving their arms like birds and zooming around the beach. Molly herself picked up her skirts and ran barefoot in the little waves up the beach. Hallie thought her graceful as a bird.

She sat down in the sand, removed her shoes and stockings, and waded into the gentle breakers. The water was warm, far warmer than the creek. Sand squooshed through her toes. Molly and the children were by now far up the beach. Gathering her skirt in her hands, Hallie ran to join them. She cried out to nothing or nobody, raising her voice in the joy of freedom and abandon.

On the way back on the ferry, as they rounded a bend and saw Sydney around the next curve, Molly said to them all, "Now, don't go tellin' them you've been in the water. Only poor people and abos go swimming in the ocean. Ladies and gentlemen have nothing to do with it."

"Why?" asked Jamie.

"Heaven only knows." Molly smiled, patting their heads. "But let's keep it our secret." She winked at Hallie.

Tristan was seated across from Hallie at the Langleys' dinner party the night before the governor's ball. She had never seen him in formal dress, and thought him quite handsome. Next to him were women Hallie had met briefly before, and Tristan treated each of them as though whatever they were saying were the most interesting topic of conversation in the world. One of the women was Mary Reiby.

Later, Susan told her about Mary. "She's quite a remarkable woman. She arrived here, so the story goes, as a convict at fifteen. Shortly thereafter she married the captain who had brought her here. He owned his own ship and made trips to the Spice Islands and to China. Sometimes Mary accompanied him, but they built a house here, and it was here they considered home. In 1811 he died—I think it was of sunstroke—in Calcutta, of all places.

"Mary returned here as the ship's owner, and set up as a wine and spirit merchant.

"She lives over her headquarters, on Macquarie Place, with the strangest, biggest servant woman I've ever seen. A woman who's not quite black, but certainly colored. A woman from the Fiji Islands, named Fee-Foo. They're always together on the streets. It's a humorous sight. Mary presides over many activities; she's famous for getting the best in arguments with sea captains. She buys whole cargoes and sells to settlers, managing to get rich, but at the same time she doesn't gouge her customers. She deals in wool, and sandalwood, and whale oil, and I don't know what else."

"How in the world could a woman learn all about that?" Hallie asked in wonder.

Susan reached out to put a hand on her arm. Smiling, she said, "How in the world does a woman raise thousands of sheep and acquire thousands of acres of land and start stores and smithies and build houses and barns and raise horses and oversee two dozen convicts?"

"You do make it sound formidable," Hallie mused, grinning. "Yet it seems so simple, really. Time-consuming, but not really terribly difficult."

"To you, maybe," said her friend. "To others, male or female, impossible."

"It's fun. I like doing it. I can't think of anything I'd rather be doing."

"Not even having more children?"

Hallie hesitated. "Not if it means giving up what I'm doing." Besides, no one was here to give her children.

Hallie did not believe in Fate. In truth, she had never given it much thought. She did not yet know that Fate played strange tricks.

Thirty-one

To the Langleys' dinner party Hallie had worn the cream-colored gown she had purchased last year, hoping to impress Tristan with her femininity. To the ball she wore the blue dress that so nearly matched her eyes, the one Chad had bought her years ago. Tristan invited her and the Langleys to a light supper before the ball.

"I so seldom entertain, but this seems like an appropriate occasion," he explained.

Alex and Jamie watched Hallie ready herself. This was not the mother to whom they were accustomed. "You look beautiful," said Alex, hugging her.

Hallie studied her reflection in the mirror. Molly had played with her hair, brushing it until it shone like gold. She had wound a ribbon through it and caught it up into a chignon, letting tendrils escape into curls over her ears. Tanned from years spent in the open, she needed no pinching to bring out the roses in her cheeks. Her eyes sparkled. She was enjoying her vacation in the midst of Sydney society.

"Are you going to dance tonight?" Jamie asked.

"Yes." Hallie was excited at the prospect. At the last ball she had attended, she'd remained on the sidelines and watched the dancers, where she was always surrounded by men wanting to converse with her. But this time she could be part of the mainstream, and she was always happier acting than observing. She wondered if she could dance without stepping on her partners' toes, if she would be able to follow the dance steps, if she would look as though this were her first dance. Would Tristan ask her to dance every dance?

On their way to Tristan's for supper, Harry rode his horse beside the carriage, which only seated two comfortably. Susan asked, "Hallie, do you ever think of Chad?"

"Of course I do," Hallie answered defensively, because she thought of him so little. "Why do you bring that up?"

"Have you thought what you'll do about Tris when Chad comes back?" Susan reached out and took Hallie's hand.

"Whatever do you mean by that?" Hallie realized her innocence was feigned.

"Oh, Hallie, you don't have to pretend with me. Harry and I can see how you feel. I worry so about you. I *do* understand. You've been alone, without a husband, for over five years. And Tris is quite charming. Every woman I know is in love with Tris. Even married ones. There's no one else like him. Why wouldn't you respond to him? But I worry so about your being hurt."

"Hush, Susan." Hallie pulled her hand away. "Don't talk that way."

"You can't be blind," Susan pursued. "He's come out to your place every month for years. The way he looks at you when he thinks no one's looking. . . ."

"I'm not blind, Susan," admitted Hallie. "It is rather hopeless, isn't it? I think we ignore our deeper feelings and content ourselves with friendship."

"You're in an awkward situation, my dear. And people talk so. *Do* be careful."

What could she say . . . when at night she dreamed of dancing with him; when tucked in her heart, she carried the memory of the two times he had kissed her; when what she wanted most of all tonight was to be in his arms . . .

When at last they arrived at Tristan's, Hallie experienced a tingling anticipation that set every nerve to dancing; it was as though she had not known him for years, spent so many days with him. From the moment he opened the door, electricity coursed through her. In formal dress, on formal behavior, in Tristan's house instead of hers, something was different.

Tristan's eyes flicked appreciatively over both Hallie and Susan. Harry noticed and said, "Aren't we lucky to be escorting the two prettiest women in New South Wales tonight?"

Tristan smiled but said nothing. His hand brushed Hallie's bare shoulder as he took her shawl. She thought his

325

touch must have burned her, leaving a scar for everyone to see.

Though past eight o'clock, it was still light outside in what were the longest days of the year. Tristan lit the candles and disappeared into the kitchen, returning a moment later with a bottle of wine.

When he had poured each of them a glass and they were seated at the dining table, and after Harry had praised the quality of the wine, Tristan said, "You know, Hallie and I are in the wine business together."

"Sounds capital," Harry said with characteristic enthusiasm. "Tell us about it."

While Tristan talked, Hallie could not take her eyes from him. And when the Langleys were speaking Tristan stared at Hallie blankly, as she stared at him across the table. With a shake of his head, as though calling himself back to reality, Tristan continued talking of Emil and what they envisioned as a major enterprise for Australia.

Hallie watched his mouth, and the way one eyebrow was slightly higher than the other, something she had not noticed before. She observed his fingers around the stem of his wineglass, and the way his lips curved when he smiled—and she wanted those lips on hers, wanted . . .

"You're going to be an industry all by yourself, Hallie," Harry remarked.

"I'm only a partner in this. I don't know anything about it." *As long as I'm his partner, everything else is secondary,* she thought.

"I'm sure you will, though," continued her banker, "by the time it's in full operation."

"Ah, here comes Martha," said Tristan. The woman who cleaned for him and cooked his dinners had come in for the party. The rock pigeon, baked with herbs, was so tender it fell from the bones at a touch. Small new potatoes sprinkled with parsley and carrots in a dill sauce completed the dinner.

"Martha's a gem," said Susan. "No wonder you treasure her."

Tristan grinned. "I do appreciate her, but I prepared the meal."

Hallie stared at him, astonished. Harry said, "Careful, there, old man. You'll give these women wrong ideas."

326

Conversation then turned to tomorrow's races. Horses from all over the colony had been arriving in town ever since Christmas. Everyone was wagering it would be the biggest race Sydney had seen, and it looked to be a first-class event.

"I think betting and horses have already become the national pastime," Harry commented. "I'm thinking of wagering on the Coombs boy's horses. They're training the best horses in the colony."

"I'm going for the underdog," said Tristan. "Fair Weather."

Harry grinned. "That's like you. No one knows much about that one."

"Exactly why I'll bet on him."

By the time dinner was over Hallie realized she had participated in very little of the conversation. They had talked of things unfamiliar to her, so she had listened and tried to learn. But it was mainly because Tristan filled her head. Much as she loved Susan and Harry, they might just as well not even have been in the room. She was surprised when it was ten o'clock and time to leave for the governor's.

Susan and Hallie rode in the carriage, and Tristan and Harry rode their horses ahead. By the time they arrived, carriages already lined the graveled driveway and were spilling over into the street. They had to park over a block away.

Hallie, following the example of Susan and Harry, placed her hand lightly on Tristan's arm as they strolled up the pathway. He put his hand over hers. "Looking the way you do, I shall be lucky to have even one dance with you," he murmured. "Will you save at least the first and last dances for me?"

Hallie was dismayed. "Only two? I want—"

His hand pressed down on hers. "Hallie, what I want is you. You are so beautiful tonight that I haven't even known Susan and Harry . . ." His voice trailed away as they reached the door.

Susan turned around and said, "May I make a suggestion? Enter separately and be announced individually. And, Tristan, why don't you ask me for the first dance?"

Hallie held onto his arm tightly. "No," she whispered.

When the sergeant announced them, "Mrs. Chadwick Morgan and Dr. Tristan Faulkner" rang through the air.

Elizabeth and Lachlan Macquarie greeted them warmly. "You must save a dance for me, Hallie," the governor said graciously.

"You promised me the first one," Hallie whispered to Tristan. "Pay no attention to what Susan said." She wanted him to see how much her dancing had improved. She wanted his arms around her.

When the New South Wales Corps band struck its first note, Tristan turned to Hallie and held out his arms. "You'll be so popular that I may not see you the rest of the evening. Let us, at least, have this."

Hallie saw people looking at them, saw the look in men's eyes as she moved toward Tristan, and for the first time in her life she was happy to be beautiful.

"You've practiced," he said after a few moments.

"I hoped you'd notice." She smiled as he spun her around.

"I notice everything about you." Their eyes locked. "That dress you're wearing is the color of your eyes, and you are wearing blue satin slippers under it. I notice that no one in this room can hold a candle to you. I notice that your hair is spun gold and your skin has been kissed by the sun."

His hand on her back guided her along. Hallie floated on clouds. "I don't want to dance with anyone else," she said.

"You'll have no choice," Tristan replied. "Every man in this room will want a turn with you. They are all probably wondering how soon they can hold you in their arms. And I must make the rounds with Susan and Elizabeth, and dozens of women whom you don't even know."

"I shall be jealous of every one."

"Don't be. My body will be with them, but my mind—and my heart—will be with you." They seemed to glide across the dance floor.

Hallie watched him over the shoulder of the captain of the Guards, who claimed the next dance.

There was no doubt that the phrase "belle of the ball" had been coined for Hallie that night. Not until supper was announced at midnight was Hallie reunited with Tristan.

He appeared at her elbow as the announcement was made. "I want to make sure no one else will claim you for supper."

Hallie's eyes were sparkling. "It's such fun! I had no idea dancing could be so invigorating. But I'm tired. I want to sit down someplace."

Smiling, Tristan began to lead her away. "Let's walk out on the porch." Outside, the evening air was soft and warm. The wide porch offered a balcony above the green lawns and Mrs. Macquarie's gardens, which filled the air with the scent of roses and jasmine.

Tristan took her arm and guided her down the stairs. Across the gardens, in the distance, the moonlight was reflected in the harbor. Tristan led her to the pebbled paths. The sound of laughter from the party filled the air. Couples strolled out on the porch, but Tristan and Hallie left them behind. It was not until they reached a big Moreton fig that Tristan stopped.

"I hear every woman in Sydney is in love with you," Hallie said, aware that she was flirting with him. She felt like a girl.

"That must be an exaggeration." Tristan did not let go of her hand. He smiled at her, though she could not read the expression in his eyes.

"I understand how they feel," Hallie said as he turned toward her. He let go of her her hands but stood so close to her that she could feel his breath.

"I care only about one," he said, his voice low.

"I love you, too. You must know that."

His arms were around her, and as he pulled her close, he murmured, "I do know that." His lips touched hers, gently at first, soft velvet kisses that brought her whole body to life. When she wound her arms around his neck, he crushed her to him as though he could not get close enough. His mouth moved hungrily over hers, his tongue flicking in and out, exploring, urgent, demanding. He rained kisses, like butterflies, on her eyes. Leaning down, he bent her backward and feathered her neck with his lips. She heard herself moaning softly. He held her so tightly, her breasts were crushed against him.

"I want you," he whispered. "I have wanted you for so long and so badly that sometimes I think I will go crazy with desire."

"Take me," she said, wanting his lips on hers again, hoping he would never let her go.

"Oh, God, Hallie!" He buried his face in her hair.

"I want you, too, Tristan. I have for a long long time."

"Beloved, darling Hallie." Again his lips sought hers, and this time they were not gentle.

Other couples, having finished their supper, strolled out onto the porch and down the stairs to the gardens. Tristan pulled away from her. "I'm as much a prisoner now as I would be in jail."

Don't let go, Hallie thought, alive with the desire she had sublimated all these years. She was nearly twenty-seven years old and had not been made love to in over five years. But others were wandering the grounds, and she knew they could not stay like this.

"Here," said Tristan, reaching out to smooth a tendril of hair by her ear. "You mustn't look as though . . ." He didn't finish, but began to lead her back to the mansion. Abruptly he said, "Funny, isn't it? All the times we've been alone together, and we choose this moment, surrounded by half of Sydney, to—"

"It's because . . . it's safe," suggested Hallie, nodding to a couple strolling by.

"We've never been safe," Tristan said. "Not from the moment we met."

Hallie wanted no supper. She couldn't eat, although she did accept a glass of champagne. The bubbles filled her throat and made her giggle. "This is wonderful. We must make champagne, too, when we get around to it."

Tristan laughed, though she could tell he was controlling himself as much as she was. When the music began again, the governor walked across the room to Hallie. "My turn," he said, bending a bit from the waist, formally chivalrous. "I'm not going to be the only man in this room to be denied a dance with you."

And he whirled her away. Tristan stood on the edge of the crowd, asking no one to dance. When Hallie looked for him, he had disappeared.

A few minutes later Harry sought her out and told her that since Susan was tired, they were leaving. He had talked with Tristan, who promised to bring her home. "So you mustn't consider leaving with us," he concluded. "I'll send the carriage back as soon as we get home."

It was not until the end of the evening that Hallie, breathless from all the dancing, saw Tristan again. He stood with a group of the older men, who seemed to be engaged in serious conversation. The governor was not among them; he was still dancing his way through the evening.

The band played one more song before the ball was officially over. Even though it was two o'clock, Hallie was not tired. She thought herself capable of climbing the Blue Mountains, or of racing up the coast a hundred miles to Coal Town, wherever it might be. Tristan had found her shawl and was waiting for her. When they had thanked the Macquaries and walked down the driveway to the waiting carriage the Langleys had left behind, Tristan tied his horse behind it, and Hallie could hear the clip-clop of its hooves as they began to move down the street. The moon was barely visible over the tops of the trees. Neither of them spoke, until Hallie said, "Tristan, don't take me home yet."

He turned to look at her.

"Susan and Harry are asleep by now. Don't take me back."

His hands held the reins loosely. "Where do you want to go?"

She sighed and looked at him. "In all the world, if you had your choice of what you wanted right now, where would we go?"

His eyes sought hers. "Are you sure?"

"I'm surer than I've ever been of anything in the world."

He reached for her hand and softly urged the horse on. When they arrived at his house, Tristan helped her from the carriage. Once inside, still holding her hand, he started up the stairs.

"I've lain in bed nights dreaming of you here," he said quietly.

Before they reached the top of the stairs, he sat on the steps and pulled her to him, kissing her throat, her eyes, her ears, running his tongue lightly down her neck. His hand caressed her breast, and she thought her heart beat so loudly he could hear it. "I am yours," he whispered. "I always have been."

He gathered her into his arms and, standing, continued up the stairs. The sinking moon sent its last rays through his western window, and he stopped in the crescent of light that danced in the center of the room.

He kissed her, his lips hungry. Her head fell back and she thought she was drowning, aware of nothing but his lips upon her, of his arms holding her, of his saying, over and over, "I love you. I love you, oh God, how I love you."

As she stood in the moonlight, his fingers began to undo the buttons on the back of her dress. Slowly, tenderly, he undressed her. She felt herself swaying as he knelt to draw off her stockings. Closing her eyes, she ran her hands through his hair and pressed him against her stomach, felt him kissing her, his teeth nibbling at her soft flesh, felt his fingers on her thighs, heard rather than saw him begin to undress himself. He stood, then, and their bodies met and melded together. "I may burn up right here," she whispered as he pulled her to the bed and bent over her.

She wanted him in her, so deep within her that he could never leave, that he would be a part of her forever. His lips sought her breasts, and his tongue circled her nipples, first one and then the other. Her body began to move as though it were an entity of its own, divorced from all else in the world. He bit her and she cried out in ecstasy, "Don't stop!" But he had waited too long, wanted her too much.

His hands surrounded her buttocks and pulled her to him as he thrust into her with a passion that burst like skyrockets across the western horizon, that did not fade as the moon sank out of sight, with a desire so deep that it seemed he had reached the core of the earth. Above her, he shivered, great shakes over which he had no control. He fell against her, breathing hard, silent for several moments.

At last he said, "Darling, I'm sorry . . . I couldn't wait. I've wanted this for so long."

And then he began to make love to her. They made love until nearly dawn, gently at times, at others with unbridled passion, talking words of love, spending their passion with such abandon that they thought they could not be aroused again . . . then lying with feet entangled, whispering in the darkness, only to have desire awakened anew, to have the magic surround them, to feel their spirits invoked. Even

332

then they knew this was a night neither would ever forget. Hallie wanted to devour and be devoured.

Before the first faint pearl of dawn gave hint of day, Tristan, stroking his fingers along her belly, said, "I must take you back."

"And if I refuse to go?" Hallie asked, bringing his fingers to her mouth and kissing them one by one.

"Your reputation would be ruined forever."

"What if I don't care?"

"Someday you would."

"But I don't want to let you go."

"I shall never go." He rolled to the edge of the bed and sat up, beginning to pull on his clothes.

Hallie sat up. "Tristan, I don't want this to be all there is. I want you. I need you. I love you. I love you so much I may burst."

When he didn't say anything, she continued. "How will I act at the races with you today and not let the world see how I feel?"

"We've felt like this for years and hid it rather well." He stood up and pulled on his shirt. He grinned. "The big question is how we'll stay awake at the races." He reached out and drew her to her feet. "Hurry, or the dawn will arrive before us."

"I don't care," she said, dressing. "Do you think everyone who looks at us today will know how we spent the night?"

"The only reason I care"—he leaned down to kiss her lightly—"is for your sake. Come, before neighbors wake up and see the Langleys' carriage outside my door and ruin poor Susan's reputation."

It was still dark when Tristan and Hallie reached the Langleys' and tied the carriage to the post. He watched as Hallie tiptoed up the porch and opened the door. Fortunately her room was downstairs, where she could reach it through the drawing room without discovery.

The sun had begun its ascent into the bright blue sky before she fell asleep. She wanted to purr with contentment, with the happiness of passion consummated. Closing her eyes, she imagined Tristan's lips on her breasts again, relived the sensation of their bellies pressed hard against each other, trembled at the memory of his kisses on the inside of her thighs.

And then her eyes flew open and she stared at the ceiling. "Tell me," she implored an unseen being, "tell me I won't get pregnant from this one time."

Yet the thought of carrying Tristan's child within her, the idea of having a part of Tristan be hers forever, appealed to her.

Thirty-two

Despite just three hours' sleep, Hallie was energized. She did not suggest aloud that good sex made one feel wonderful for days afterward, but she was aware of a heightened capacity for physical activity as a result of the marvelous energy that could scarcely be contained.

She had a vague idea from the way that Susan looked at her that her friend knew what had happened, but nothing could interrupt Hallie's joy. She wanted to walk to the races rather than drive in the carriage, and had to stifle the impulse to run and play tag with the children. Molly volunteered to walk with her and the four children. The youngsters were too young to attend the races, but they all kept Hallie company on the way to the racetrack.

Hallie had to agree that the Langleys were indeed fortunate to have Molly. She enjoyed Molly, too, though something kept her from being as uninhibited with her as she was with Susan or Beth or even Belinda. But she liked Molly's exuberance and her earthy sense of humor, and she appreciated Molly's sincere affection for the children, her own included. The young woman never acted like a convict, never played the martyr or was sullen. She seemed honestly to delight in the role Fate had assigned her. She never deferred to Hallie, but treated her as a friend. When Hallie had said, "I need exercise. I'm going to walk to the racecourse," Molly had immediately clapped her hands and cried, "Oh, good! The children and I will come as far as the gate. We haven't been out at that end of town in quite a while." Not that "that end of town" was far; it was just a matter of minutes from the Langleys' house, at the end of the block where the hospital was. Actually, any place in town was within walking distance.

Susan and Harry had already arrived and were saving her a seat by the time she arrived at the track. It seemed as though the entire populations of Sydney, Parramatta,

335

and Windsor, as well as all the inhabitants of the outlying farms, had descended for the New Year's Day race. They were fortunate the day was more like spring than filled with the hot humidity typical of January. Parasols dotted the crowd, protecting city women from the sun's glare, preventing sunburn and freckles and the appearance of outdoor labor. One could tell which women had come in from the outlying districts, women who worked outside with their men.

Hallie would have enjoyed the races more had Tristan been there. Even the women screamed and clapped as the horses rounded the curves, jockeys bent low in the saddles. Hallie wanted to give all of her attention to this new experience, but she was distracted by searching for Tristan's arrival. She wasn't even embarrassed when Susan leaned over and squeezed her hand, whispering, "He'll be here, don't worry."

And he was. He arrived by the fourth race and sighted them immediately, making his way through the crowd, stopping every few steps to shake hands with some man, smile and say something to a woman. It was all Hallie could do to keep her hands at her side when he finally reached them.

"Appendicitis doesn't know when doctors have other plans," he explained.

"I hope all went well," Susan said.

"Fine . . ." Tristan hadn't yet looked directly at Hallie. "I hope Fair Weather hasn't run yet."

Harry laughed. "Care for a bet on that one?"

They shook hands on an amount, and then Tristan turned to look at Hallie. "Well, your popularity last night doesn't seem to have done you in. You look as though you slept well. I take it for granted you enjoyed the ball." He turned to Susan and said, "I do think she danced every single dance. You'd think she'd be exhausted. Instead, she looks as fresh as spring."

"Oh, I had one of the loveliest nights I can remember." Hallie smiled.

"See what learning to dance can do for you!" Tristan sat on the seat beside her. "I hope you were saving this for me."

Hallie tingled at his closeness.

"Of course, old man," Harry answered. "Oh, here comes *your* race. Fair Weather doesn't stand a chance."

"I agree," said Tristan. "I'm betting on him to give him courage."

Hallie felt his leg brush hers before she, too, was caught up in the excitement of the crowd, watching the horses race faster than she thought any living thing could move. Fair Weather lost; in fact, he was third from the last.

Tristan reached in his pocket and brought out a bill, which he handed to Harry. "See, he might have been last had I not had some faith." They all laughed.

Hallie tried to look at the races and not at Tristan. At least I know I have willpower, she thought. It is an act of great self-restraint not to throw my arms around him. Not to kiss him right here in front of hundreds of people. Not to stand on the top of my chair and shout to everyone, "I love this man!"

"You'll come to supper, won't you?" Susan asked, leaning across her husband to speak to Tristan.

He reached out to touch Susan's hand and grinned. "You saved me the embarrassment of inviting myself. Of course. I must admit I was planning on it."

Hallie rode back in the carriage with Susan, but couldn't look at her friend. At the house there was no time for Tristan and Hallie to be alone. They stayed on opposite sides of the room, sat across from each other at the table, and studiously avoided direct looks.

"Susan and Harry have invited the children to stay with them for two weeks," Hallie said, "and then Susan will come back to the farm for a month. I don't know what I shall do without them for that time." She knew she had told him this before, but she wanted to make sure he remembered. Did he understand? "I'm leaving tomorrow," she continued. "I'll take the ferry to Parramatta, stay overnight, and ride Princess home the next day."

"Sorry you couldn't stay longer," Tristan replied in a formal voice. "Sydney quite approves of you, you must know that. You can't spare us more time?"

"No, I've been away a week now. I feel lost when I'm not working. I keep telling myself they can't possibly do without me for so long."

"I think you'd have made a good Puritan, Hallie," commented Harry.

Not if you knew what I did last night, she thought.

On the ferry to Parramatta, Hallie chatted with everyone. She was a flower expanding, blossoming under the warmth of affection. The sky was bluer than it had ever been, the birds sang directly to her, the coves and inlets that disappeared like long fingers from the harbor held untold delights, she was sure. The water sparkled in the sunlight. Australia was the most wonderful country in the world. Her fellow passengers were among the world's nicest.

The Langleys' Parramatta cook had prepared a perfect dinner, and she ate alone for the first time she could remember. Magpies sang to her until dark. She strolled through the garden, inhaling the fragrance of the summer flowers. The sunset was the color of pale roses.

When she went to bed that night, Hallie hugged the pillow, imagining it to be Tristan. She hummed to herself and was unable to sleep. She was completely in love and could think of nothing but Tristan. Would he have understood her hints? They could ride out into the hills, away from everyone, and make love again. She could sit across a table from him and gaze into his eyes without hiding her feelings. She could reach out and touch him when she wanted to. How could they manage to sleep in the same bed? She had only Beth to answer to, and she knew that nothing she ever did would alienate her friend. But she did not want to see disapproval in her eyes.

Yet wouldn't it be worth it? She didn't even feel she had a husband any longer. Five years was such a long time. Morality had nothing to do with what she and Tristan had done, with how they felt.

When she did sleep, she dreamed that she and Tristan and the children were climbing the Blue Mountains. From the peaks they saw grassland stretching forever, silver streams of rivers nourishing the land and far off, towns that needed doctors dotted the landscape. Near morning she dreamed of disembarking from a ship in New York. Places where no one would know them, where they could start life together.

But when she awoke, she knew she could not leave the land that had become part of her. She might possibly leave the farm—though even that thought wrenched her—but she knew she could not leave Australia. Maybe they could move north, up beyond Coal River, where it was tropical and where new communities were growing. Or they *could* go beyond the mountains. She could leave the farm, but not the country.

Or could she?

Later that morning, as she cantered along on the now familiar road, she felt a thrill at every turn, for she knew exactly what she would see. She loved the bird songs, the roos jumping along on either side of her up in the hills. The eucalyptus trees, with their bark hanging like silver ghosts, never failed to move her. Of all the trees in the world, she thought, they are my favorite. A red-and-blue parrot flew directly in front of her. Cockatoos whitened a tree with their nesting. Kookaburras made her smile with their crazy laughter.

She spurred Princess into a gallop and told herself to stop thinking of running away with Tristan. They would just have to face each day as it came, milk the most they could from life, find what happiness they could. There was time enough to talk of the future.

She arrived home by mid-afternoon. Beth hugged her, saying, "I've missed you." Brian stopped by at dinnertime and recited a list of things he wanted to call to her attention. Nothing major. He thought the mare was due any day, and he was watching her carefully. She'd only been gone a week, Hallie told herself. There was no reason for anything to be different.

Beth held dinner until Ben arrived, then they dined out on the porch. Hallie recounted the highlights of the week, amusing them until bedtime. Once in bed, she asked, "Don't you ever yearn to see any of it, go into the city, see other things?"

Beth shook her head. "I never want to leave here, not for a minute of my life."

If I did go north with Tristan, Hallie wondered, or over the mountains, would Beth come?

* * *

Tristan arrived just before dinner the next evening. He said to Beth, "I hope there's enough dinner for me. I've been able to take a bit of vacation, a few days free."

As soon as Beth disappeared into the kitchen, he gathered Hallie into his arms. "You knew I'd come, didn't you?"

"I hoped so."

He kissed her, holding her as though he would never let go. "I can stay for a whole week," he whispered into her ear, and his warm breath made her shiver with delight.

At dinner Hallie found it impossible to act as she always had with Tristan. She was sure that Beth or Ben noticed the difference.

Tristan asked Ben, "Now that your smithy and pub are successful, what are you thinking of next?"

Ben gave a crooked smile and looked down at his plate. "Hear talk 'bout a school."

Hallie stared at him. Would he ever have told her had Tristan not asked? "Ben, you do beat everything," she said. "I think you're becoming real civic-minded. I bet not one single person said anything about a school. You put it into people's heads."

"Don't you think they should learn? Where would Jamie and Alex—and Robbie, for that matter—be if we didn't have our classes here? You want a new nation of illiterates?"

Hallie gazed at him with admiration. Perhaps she had underestimated him.

Beth merely said, "Have another piece of pie, Ben."

Obviously enjoying himself, Ben stayed late at the house. And even after he left, Beth sat around for a while. Hallie wanted to tell her to go to bed. Instead, when she suggested a stroll to the creek in the deepening twilight, Beth said, "That sounds lovely." So the three of them wandered down the creek until it became too dark to see. The lights from the house guided them back.

At last Beth said, "Well, I'm off to bed," to Hallie's great relief.

When they were finally alone, Tristan smiled at her and said, "Come to the barn with me, Hallie."

"The barn?" She laughed.

"I've waited so long, that now that I have you, I don't want to keep away from you."

340

"Don't," she said, kissing the palm of his hand as they started toward the barn. "Don't let me away from you at all. I want you just as much. You're all I've thought of."

He turned to kiss her and said, "My body's ached for you. I can't get to sleep at home for the fragrance of you that lingers, for the indentation your head left on my pillow, for the echo of your voice that bounces from my walls. I've dreamed of your being there, I've wanted you to leave parts of yourself there that I can never erase, and now that you have, I can't sleep."

When they were in the barn, he lit the lantern next to the bed he always used. The barn smelled of sweet hay, and at the other end the cow mooed and a horse snorted. "Let me watch you undress," he said. "Let me savor every inch of you. Do you mind?"

No . . . she would glory in it, she thought. With each piece of clothing that she tossed away, she would offer herself to him, until she was all his. Until their bodies joined together as one, until the stars shone down upon them locked in each other's arms, until their souls intertwined in ecstasy. Until they were consumed by fires that she knew could never be extinguished.

The light from the lamp flickered as Hallie stepped from her dress. She wanted to excite him, make him wild with desire for her. Stepping out of her slippers, she took off everything but her stockings. When she began to roll them down, he said, "No, let me." But before he came to her, he stood by the lantern and undressed. It had been dark when they'd made love in his bedroom, and she had not seen him naked. She loved the look of his hard lean body; Greek gods could be no more beautiful.

Then, slowly, he walked to her and knelt in front of her, kissing her belly, reaching up to caress her breasts, bending down to slip off her stockings. And she saw the wounds, the terrible raised welts that shone white and dead even in the dim light from the lamp. She gasped and reached down to touch the longest one.

As she ran her hand along it, he said, "I can't feel anything there. The tissue's dead." Still kneeling, he looked up at her. "I would have it done again a hundred, a thousand times, if it meant you. Had that never happened, I

341

would not be here, in this country, in this place, at this moment, with you. And you are worth anything—everything." His arms around her, he pulled her close to him, burying his head against her, teasing her with little kisses, his tongue feathering across her belly.

I will make it up to him, she thought. I will make it up to him tonight and every night, I will love him forever so that it *will* have been worth it.

She pulled him up and led him to the bed. Slowly, luxuriously, with strokes and kisses that excited beyond belief, they made love to each other.

Afterward she would not let him leave her, but held him within her, clasping him tight and tracing her fingers across the dead tissue on his back. Later, when they lay next to each other, she said, "I want to kiss them."

"The scars? I won't feel it."

"It doesn't matter." And as she kissed the hard, raised welts, she wept at what he had endured.

Magic is ephemeral.

They both knew the sorcery of the week could not last, that soon there would be hard questions to face. But neither was willing to risk the bewitchment of their week together.

They packed a picnic lunch and rode far out to the southwest bend of the river. There they made love under a tree along its banks while sheep, with a complete lack of curiosity, munched grass.

On another day they rode farther than Hallie had ever gone, up into hills that were not yet hers. They had ridden up the crest of a hill, from where they could see hills and valleys rising for miles, from where they could see the blue haze shimmering above the Blue Mountains. And where no white man had ever set foot, they took off their clothes and made love, with a mixture of tenderness and frenzy. Afterward they lay naked while shadows from the leaves danced patterns on their bodies. Tristan, staring out at all the land below them, asked, "How many acres *do* you own?" His face was resting on his hands, one on top of the other.

Hallie felt decadent, lying here with no clothes, warmed by both the sun and Tristan's love. "I never quite keep

342

track," she said, and turned on her back, kicking a foot up in the air. "Over fifteen thousand, I think. Since so many sheep died in the flood, I'm not going to need more pasturage for years. But we'd have had about twenty-five thousand if that flood hadn't come just at lambing time and killed so many pregnant ewes."

He looked over at her. "You never seem beaten by adversity." Admiration filled his voice as he reached over to run a finger down her shoulder.

Hallie laughed. "Because what I do have is so much more than I ever dreamed of. Because no matter how little I have here, it is still so much more than I could have expected in Newcastle. Because I never seem to have little. Everything that happens to me amazes me." She laughed and turned on her side, reaching over to kiss him. "Including you."

In a lazy voice he said, "You seem to thrive on responsibility."

" 'It's true. I love making decisions, even if they're not right." She was happy he understood. "Of course, not all my decisions have been good ones. I was the one who ordered the sheep narrowed into pastures along the river so the drought wouldn't kill them, and they ended up drowning. But I love being able to make the decisions."

"Makes you feel powerful?" he asked, squinting his eyes against the sun's glare.

"No . . ." She thought a moment. "It's not power, I don't think. It's being in charge of my own life. Not just waiting to react to what someone else decides should happen in my life. My mother's life depended always on what my father decided, what he chose. Except to decide what food to buy, I'm not sure Mum ever made a decision, was ever in control of anything about her life, ever. Thank goodness I escaped that fate!"

Each night they spoke words of love, telling each other how they had felt at certain moments of their togetherness over the years, of how hard it had been to try to mask their feelings. Tristan told her that his mother knew about her, knew that his heart had no room for other women in his life, and had sent him something he wanted to give her. Thus, really, he told her, the gift was from his mother. It had been given to her by his father's mother when she married. It had been in the family for generations. He brought from his pocket a handkerchief in which were a pair of tear-shaped sapphire earrings.

Hallie stared at them and then at him. "But Tristan, they must be worth a fortune."

"What they are worth is immaterial financially, for they are never to be sold. They are given to the women the Faulkner men will love forever. My mother thought it time for you to have them. I've carried them around with me for years, waiting for the right moment to give them to you."

Without thinking, Hallie said, "You should wait to give them to your wife." Then she looked up at him with stricken eyes.

Tristan put his hand over hers, pressing it hard. "If there is a God in heaven, you are my wife."

"Someday . . ." she said, her voice barely a whisper. "But where can I wear this?"

"While we're together. At night, when you sleep. Keep them in a safe place and think of me when you touch them."

"I don't need anything to remind me of you." Tears gathered in her eyes.

He kissed her. "Hallie, I love you more than anything in the world. More than life itself."

And they came together, in the barn filled with sweet-smelling hay, on this last day of his stay.

Tristan could not extend his visit longer than a week. Hallie knew it was time for her, also, to return to work, to reality. No one had brought problems to her all week, so she supposed that Brian and Ben and Beth and probably everyone else were aware of what was happening; but she didn't care.

"Let's run away," she suggested, leaning her head against his chest. "Where can we go?" They had not yet dressed, and though their passion was spent, they lay close together.

Tristan put his arms around her and said, "Don't think of that now."

She threw a leg over his, wanting to be so close she would be a part of him. "I love you so much. I want the whole world to know."

"I can't wait a whole month to see you again," he said, kissing her neck. "I'll be back in three weeks."

"In other words, in an eternity." Her lips brushed his.

"We shall talk then." And he kissed the top of her head.

The next day, as she watched him ride away, Hallie thought she heard laughter in the distance. She didn't know its name was Fate.

Thirty-three

A peaceful euphoria descended on Hallie. Life passed in a languid unreality. When she rode out with Brian to see the sheep or inspect the fencing, or when she helped deliver the mare of its foal, nothing seemed quite in tempo. She saw the world as though through a gauze curtain. At three in the morning, as they watched the foal being born, she said to Brian, "I'm sorry the children aren't here to see this." But she didn't think of the children, and she wasn't aware of what she ate.

She enjoyed the cold dinners Beth served out on the porch, while she, Beth, and Ben sat and talked of nothing in particular in the long evenings. Ben stayed until nearly dark on these summer nights, and when Hallie tried to remember what they talked of, she could recollect nothing.

She was aware of the sky, and of the silver-green trees, of the lush greenness of the fields, of tomatoes ripening on the vines, of corn growing a foot a day—or so it seemed. She felt the whole world ripe, and smiled as the calf suckled its mother's teat. She found contentment in watching Robbie ride along with his father, going out to work each morning.

Long after Beth had gone to bed, Hallie sat out on the porch, sometimes strolled through the fields by the light of the moon, finding herself once dancing with arms outstretched, alone in the meadow. She became intensely aware of the waxing moon, low in the western sky. Studying it carefully, she deduced that it rose an hour earlier each afternoon and set an hour later each night until, at the half moon, it was visible in the sky from noon to midnight. Hypnotized by it, she stayed up until it sank beyond the trees, leaving a haze of silver behind. The moon became a part of her.

When Susan and Molly and all the children arrived, Hallie looked upon them as intruders for the first day. But the second day, when everyone had settled in comfortably, life returned to its normal pattern. Hallie no longer had time to live in her daydream world. Harry stayed for two days and promised to come out the following weekend, and the yells and cavortings of four children filled the air.

Susan, whose pregnancy was beginning to show, was content to stay around the house, bathing in the creek on warm afternoons or sitting on the porch fanning herself. She would come out to the barn, and she and the children delighted in the young animals. Beth and Molly disappeared after the children were in bed; Hallie didn't know where they went or what they did, but it left her free to talk with Susan in the evenings.

It wasn't until near the end of the second week that Susan said, "If you want to tell me it's none of my business, I won't be offended. But what are you going to do about Tristan? And don't act like you don't know what I'm talking about."

Hallie looked at her friend. "Do you think it's wrong?"

Susan reached out and put a hand on her friend's arm. "Hallie, don't you know me better than that? Who am I to say what's right or wrong for you? But it has portents of tragedy, and I fret. For both of you. I love you and worry so for you."

Hallie placed a reassuring hand on Susan's arm. "Don't worry. I'm happy. I'm so happy I might burst."

"My dear, that's obvious. But what happens when . . ." She did not continue.

"I don't know," answered Hallie, standing and walking down the path. "I haven't gotten that far in my thoughts."

"Well, you'd better soon." Susan fanned herself.

"Is everybody aware of it?" Hallie turned to face her.

"It has been a topic of conversation in Sydney ever since the governor's ball." The expression on her face, the half smile she offered Hallie, was enigmatic.

"Do you have any suggestions?" Hallie asked, returning to her friend.

Susan shook her head. "I want you to stop right away so that you won't feel the inevitable pain."

"I'm not going to feel pain." Hallie smiled. "I'm happier than I imagined it possible to be." Really, she thought, it didn't matter what anyone thought.

347

Susan looked at her until Hallie began to feel self-conscious.

"We'll figure something out," Hallie said. "Tristan will know what to do."

"I wouldn't bank on that. Tristan has—"

Hallie interrupted her. "I'm willing to risk . . ."

"What?" Susan's voice sounded brittle. "What are you willing to risk? Are you willing to give up all this?" Her arms gestured wide to indicate all the land, the house.

Hallie, too, looked at this land she loved. "I'm willing to risk everything," she said finally.

"Your children?"

Hallie's heart stopped. She had not considered that.

"You're going to hurt, Hallie, and I can't bear it." Susan's eyes were filled with sadness.

At about the same time, Hallie was beginning to suspect she might be pregnant. Her period was four days late. She was not surprised: all Chad had ever had to do was look at her, she thought, and it happened. Why wouldn't a whole week of constant lovemaking do it?

She tried to sort out her feelings. She was not dismayed, though she realized she ought to be. How scandalous. A husband who had been away over five years . . . The thought that part of Tristan might be growing inside of her, attached to her, that she and he had created a human being who would unite them forever, made her incredibly happy.

Still, she wasn't sure. It would mean that she and Tristan must decide what to do immediately. She had never known anyone who was divorced, but she had heard of such things. Would it brand her as a scarlet woman forever? What would that mean? Part of her didn't care. Maybe, she wondered, I hoped this would happen. Perhaps it brings things to a head. Certainly I cannot stay here, masquerading as Chad's loyal wife.

Gazing out the window at the bright morning sunlight, she was surprised by the sadness that suddenly enveloped her. Divorce would mean leaving this house, this land. So much of herself was here. It had become an integral part of her.

Well, she was not quite twenty-seven. She could start over. There were many beautiful places in this country. She and Tristan could start their winery someplace else, someplace north of Sydney. But what of Tristan? Would he want that? Could he exist that way, away from a hospital, treating just the few people who would inhabit the countryside, changing his life so radically? Of course. What more did they need than each other? He would not even fear being ostracized by Sydney society, what there was of it.

What about Jamie and Alex? They didn't even remember Chad. They loved Tristan. But what would Chad do if he came back? Hallie had begun to believe he would never return. What if he didn't? What if something happened to his brother and he had to stay in England and direct the mines? What if his ship was wrecked at sea? Couldn't she then go on as she always had, only she would be free to marry Tristan?

Her head ached. There were too many things to think about. Thank goodness she wasn't feeling the dizziness and sickness she had felt with Jamie. But then again, she told herself, maybe I'm just late because I'm getting older. Or because of something else.

She would wait until Tristan came out next weekend and ask him.

But when he came, Harry came with him, and there was no way they could be alone. Molly was sleeping in the room with all the children, poor soul, and Beth was in her usual place next to Hallie. With so many people around, Hallie simply couldn't sneak out of bed to go to Tristan. She lay awake for hours, unable to sleep, until she finally threw caution to the wind and slid from under the sheet, stepping barefoot out the open French door and running in the moonlight to the barn.

Tristan was asleep. She leaned over to kiss him, and in a drugged voice he murmured, "I'd given up." But he pulled her to him and they made love. Afterward he would not let her go. "This has been the longest three weeks," he said. "All I could think of was you, wanting to get back to you."

"I'm half sorry now that I invited Susan, if it means being denied you."

"I know." Holding her in his arms, he kissed her nose.

She took a deep breath. "I'm not sure," she said, "but I think I'm with child."

He let go of her then and sat upright. "Oh, dear God. Jesus! I did consider the possibility, but have refused to let myself think of the consequences."

"Don't you want it?" she asked, her heart sinking.

He looked at her and gathered her in his arms. "The thought of having a child with you—oh, darling, if you only knew how often over the years I've dreamed of such a thing."

"Then let's go away. Let's go make a life for ourselves some other place. We'll take the children and Beth."

"Hallie, what about this place? What about Chad?"

She looked into his eyes. "I don't know anything about it, but can't you investigate what divorce involves? Do you care what people say?"

"No . . . Yes. I care what they say about you. How it would hurt you." His arms tightened around her.

"Oh, Tristan, don't think of that. We'll go where no one knows us. We could go to America."

"No." He held her so tightly she thought he might crush her. "I can't. A condition of my pardon is that I never leave New South Wales." A desperate quality crept into his voice. "But it's a big place. We—"

"We could start a winery someplace up north," she suggested hopefully.

He held her away from him and looked into her eyes. "I'm a doctor, not a vintner."

"Wouldn't you be willing?" She needed reassurance from him.

Instead of an answer, he asked, "Are you sure you're pregnant?"

"No, but I can't imagine what else it could be." She frowned. "Can you tell?"

"Not yet. It's too soon. Oh, love, beloved. . . ." He crushed her to him again, and she could hear the beat of his heart.

She kissed him. "I want us to spend the rest of our lives together."

"Yes, darling," he whispered. "I'll think of something."

He and Harry left in the morning.

* * *

Three days later Brian reported that in the far northwest pasture he had found six dead sheep.

In mid-afternoon Susan and Hallie, while bathing in the creek, heard shouting from far off, from the direction of the store. It sounded as though several people, in unison, were calling, "Hallie!" The voices seemed to be coming closer.

The women looked at each other and waded out of the water, dressing as quickly as possible. By the time they reached the house, a wagon was visible in the near distance. It was piled high and there were a number of people on it. Hallie could see two children sitting on top of the baggage. Two women, two men—even from afar she could tell that. They were all waving, and Hallie walked down from the porch toward them, shading her eyes against the sun's glare.

One of the women stood up, in stark relief against the hazy blue of the sky, and Hallie's breath caught in her throat. It was a mirage; her mind was playing tricks on her. Even though she could not see the woman's face, she knew who it was. Was it possible . . . ?

Susan was looking at Hallie, watching the incredulous look on her face. "Who is it?" she asked.

Hallie didn't answer. She heard the familiar voice call out, "Hallie?" and knew then that it was not an illusion. Her face crinkled, her mouth puckering as tears formed in the corners of her eyes. "It's my mother," she said, her voice scarcely audible. "It's Mum."

As she began to race toward the wagon, she caught a glimpse of the other woman, whom she did not recognize. But sitting next to the driver, whose face was hidden by his large hat, was a man . . . was—"Oh, my God," cried Hallie. "It's Danny!"

The driver reined in the horses and jumped from the wagon, not waiting to help the ladies.

"Oh, heavens," Susan said to herself.

Arms open, ready to greet his wife, Chad ran toward her, calling, "Hallie, I'm home!"

Thirty-four

He was even bigger than she remembered. He caught her up in a bear hug and swung her around. But all she could think to say was, "Mum's here."

Grinning, Chad let her down. She scarcely looked at him but ran to the wagon, where Danny was helping his mother down, circling her slender waist with his big hands. Mum was grayer, but she looked no older than when Hallie had last seen her. Daniel stood behind her, a black patch over the eye he'd lost, but smiling as though all the world were gathered within him.

Unable to speak, Hallie threw her arms around them, beginning to sob so hard that she couldn't see them. Mum started crying, too, and Danny hugged them both. Looking at them, Chad said, "This is supposed to be a happy reunion." Walking over to the wagon, he helped Danny's wife down. The two small children wriggled on top of the baggage, until Chad stretched up and caught them, plopping them on the ground. They stood grinning shyly, and cringed back against their mother when Gently came rushing from behind the house, wagging his tail and barking.

Staring at the house, Chad walked over to Susan, who had stood observing all this, her heart beating wildly and her eyes filled with tears at the reunion of Hallie and her family. But even if she was not aware of it, she was thinking, Just in time. Thank God—just in time! Holding out her hand, she said, "Mr. Morgan."

"Mrs. Langley, isn't it?" he said, bending at the waist and taking her hand. "How nice to find you here. It's grand to be home." He looked around, still holding Susan's hand. "Though it doesn't look the same. This porch is new."

"You'll find it greatly enlarged," said Susan. "There are many changes."

Chad turned to look at Hallie. "She's grown even more beautiful," he said as though to himself.

"She's the most remarkable woman I know," said Susan. And her heart bled for Hallie. She herself was glad Chad had come home, but she knew Hallie would be torn apart. And knew, too, that Hallie would have to hide her pain.

Danny was introducing his wife, Tess, and his children, Roger and Pamela. Through it all, Hallie couldn't let go of her mother's hand.

Hearing the commotion, Beth ran out from the kitchen. Not knowing who they all were, she simply stared at the lot of them and wondered how she would ever feed an extra six people on such short notice. Then she saw Chad and shrank back in the shadow of the porch. She didn't know who he was, but his size intimidated her.

Molly, along with Jamie, Alex, and Christopher, came bounding from up the creek, where they had been cooling themselves off in the hot afternoon. They stood observing, trying to figure out where so many people had come from.

Watching Chad stare at the three children, Susan smiled and said, "The smallest one is mine."

Chad walked over to them, but Alex held onto Molly's skirt and Jamie took a step backward. Christopher, far more used to strangers than either of the Morgan children, stood his ground. Chad stooped down in front of Jamie.

"Don't you remember me?" he asked, though he knew there was no way they could recall him. "I'm your father." He stretched out his arms, but neither child came to him.

Molly looked down at him. "Begging your pardon, sir, but I'd suggest you go slow. Let them get used to you before you demand a kiss."

He gazed up at her, seeing her brown curls, damp and tousled from playing in the creek, saw the merry green-brown eyes, and asked, "Who are you?"

"I'm Molly, Christopher's nanny. And you must be Mr. Morgan, Hallie's husband." She smiled at him. "I thought maybe you were a figment of imagination. But you're real, after all."

Chad didn't smile back at her. Hallie's husband?

"Don't force yourself on the children," Molly cautioned. "They're rather shy. Not used to strangers. Wait a bit."

Chad looked at her as though wondering who she was to tell him what to do with his own children. Susan, at his elbow, said, "Come sort this all out. Everybody just seems to be laughing and crying." He allowed himself to be led away from his children, who stared after him in confusion.

"I hope you're glad to see us," said Danny, "because you're stuck with us. Mum will never make that voyage again, that's certain."

"Me, neither," said his wife, who stood on the fringes of the group.

Beth, who'd finally ventured outside, mumbled something about fixing lemonade and went back to the kitchen, but she churned inside, suspecting her life was about to be turned upside down, that the peace and tranquility she had known these last five years was about to disappear. She was afraid, too, that she was about to lose Hallie. Silently she reemerged with two pitchers of lemonade and all the glasses she could find, set them on the porch table and returned to the kitchen to see about adding to the dinner she was preparing.

"I never dreamed you'd leave home," said Hallie, still not letting go of her mother's hand. But her mother was staring over at the children.

"Which ones are ours?" she asked.

Hallie called to them, and Jamie and Alex shyly disengaged themselves from Molly, who started for the house to check on the infant Kara. Hallie knelt down beside them. "This is your grandmother and your uncle," she said. "And your aunt and cousins."

"And your father," added Chad. Hallie glanced up at him. She had hardly acknowledged his presence.

"Yes, this is your father," she said, putting her arms around her children. She didn't know if they'd understand. "Come, you must all be hot and tired. I see Beth's put lemonade out for us."

"Who's Beth?" Chad asked, disgruntled not to have been greeted more effusively.

"I'll explain everything, but give me a couple of minutes," Hallie answered as she introduced her family to Susan, Christopher, and Molly, who had returned to the porch with Kara in her arms. Hallie poured them all drinks and then said, "I can't believe it. It's something I never even dreamed of."

Mum looked at Chad affectionately. "Neither did I, but

he talked us into it. I thought I was too old to leave Newcastle."

Chad smiled at Hallie, his eyes searching hers. "I knew it would make you happy."

Danny said, "He convinced me this was the land of opportunity. He said I'd never have to clerk in a store again and could work out in the open all year long, and my children would grow up healthy and happier than ever at home. He promised we'll build me a home, and," he looked at his sister, "we can be together again."

"This porch is new," said Chad.

"So are many other things," Hallie said, hugging her mother again as though still unable to believe in her presence.

"I know we'll be crowded until we build Danny a house," Chad said, "but it's summer. After conditions on the ship, sleeping in the drawing room won't seem so bad. We'll get to work right away on a place for him and his family."

Hallie calculated quickly. Molly and the children were already in the room behind hers. Maybe Mum could sleep with Susan, and Danny and his family could sleep in the back bedroom; it was still unfinished, but at least the walls and ceiling were up. Chad could sleep on the couch in the drawing room or even out in Tristan's bed in the barn.

"There's enough room for everyone," she announced. "We have bedrooms for all."

Chad gave her a questioning look, to which she responded, "There are three extra bedrooms."

His mouth was agape. "Yes," Susan said, "I even have one of my own." She was nervous.

"You live here now?" Chad asked, cocking an eyebrow.

"Mercy, no," she answered, laughing. "But I come out for a month or two in the summer. Harry and I call it our country home." So much he doesn't know, she thought.

"It's all beautiful, Hallie," said Mum. "I never believed you lived in such a big house, and it's so handsome. Even Chad with his bragging didn't do it justice."

Like Dada had been, Mum looked old before her time, Hallie mused. Wrinkles fanned out from her eyes and creased her cheeks when she smiled. Her hands were rough and red, and though physically she appeared frail, there was pride in her erect stance. Hallie wanted to hold her close, to take care of her forever.

"It is beautiful, isn't it," Chad acknowledged proudly. "I forgot myself just how special it is. Show me, Hallie. Show me the new rooms." He reached out a hand and pulled her up. "We'll be back in a minute."

Hallie didn't want to be alone with him. She didn't know what to say, couldn't sort out her feelings; too much was happening. She didn't know whether she was terribly happy or achingly sad. She felt shy with Chad, as though facing a stranger.

They entered the coolness of the house and he followed her through the hallway, to the guest bedroom. "This one isn't finished yet. It needs plaster and—"

Chad looked around. "It's big."

"It's the smallest," Hallie said. "What with Beth and the children growing up and a goodly amount of company, we needed more room."

"There are more?"

Why did she feel he was silently criticizing her rather than overflowing with the joy of being home? Or was it something within her that squelched the joy? She thought he ought to be pleased with the additions. After all, she had kept to the style with which he had erected the original structure.

She moved through the door at the side of the room, into the room that had become the children's. There were three narrow beds and a crib for Kara. Hallie had moved in a bed for Molly, too. Chad walked out the opposite door, onto the veranda. "The porch goes all around the house?"

"No," she said, feeling defensive. She couldn't look directly at him. He was a stranger, and she was in shock. "Just this side and the front. It's lovely and cool in the summer, and protected in the winter." She did feel it had a certain amount of charm. Susan had helped her choose furniture for it. Did Chad think she had spent too much money?

He started toward her, reaching out. "And the third bedroom—don't you want to see it?" she said, evading him. She walked through her bedroom, back through the hall and drawing room, to the room that Susan made her headquarters. Hallie and Beth had made drapes and a coverlet for

356

the four-poster. She thought it the prettiest bedroom in the house.

"Who's Beth?" he asked abruptly, following her.

Hallie took a deep breath. "Beth's been here since shortly after you left. She and Susan are my two dearest friends in the world. If it weren't for Beth, I wouldn't have been able to do all the work I've done. After Archie died . . ."

She had written him that Archie died but had not given details or told him of the second batch of prisoners. She had not told him of the land acquisitions or of Ben and the store. She had not told him how many sheep they had, and he wouldn't have had time to get the last bundle she'd dispatched, the last shearing. He also would not know of the damage wrought by the flood, though he did know that Belinda and Robbie had arrived and that Hallie had had a house built for them. She had not even told him of her miscarriage, or of the balls at the governor's. When she had written, it was to accompany the annual shipment of fleece, simple notes telling Chad that Brian was foreman and she had seen to his emancipation, telling him how the children were growing. She did not tell him that Tristan had already made sure Jamie was becoming an expert horseman, or that a group of them were learning math, or that Harry had extended her credit. She didn't know how to tell all that to someone a world away.

But she turned to him and smiled. "How thoughtful of you to bring Mum and Danny."

He reached out for her hands. "Does it make you happy?"

"Of course," she said, feeling awkward at his touch. "I can't imagine how you talked Mum into it."

"Actually, it wasn't very difficult." He moved closer to her. "She thought she had no life left, that she'd spend a couple of months with one of your brothers or sisters, and then a couple with another, and that there was no place left for her in life. She thought they might not even want her, in their crowded little homes. The hardest part was leaving her grandchildren. But I pointed out she had grandchildren here she had never seen—and that there will be more." He smiled. "With Danny coming, and not having seen you in over seven years, it was not so difficult. In fact, she spent all of three or four minutes thinking before she answered," he said, chuckling. "I wouldn't be at all surprised if the idea hadn't crossed her mind before. Danny's decision to come made the choice easier. But it was a rough crossing." He was searching Hallie's eyes but could not find what he wanted.

"It is kind of you, nevertheless." Her voice was formal. "From your letters it sounded as though Danny had given up on life."

He nodded. "This may be his salvation. While the women were below being seasick or taking care that the children weren't washed overboard, he stayed up on deck, glorying in the wide-open spaces, in the adventure of it. Like his sister, I presume." They smiled at each other with the awkward shyness of two people who had not met in many years and didn't quite know how to behave.

"I'm grateful," said Hallie, moving away from him to return to the porch. "This is still such a surprise, I don't quite know how to behave."

"Nor do I. It's been far too long." He reached out to touch her arm, but she was already gone.

After eight months cooped up in the close quarters of the ship, Pamela and Roger broke forth like Indians. They ran and shouted and wanted to see everything. At first Jamie and Alex stared at them as though they had been invaded.

Hallie took Jamie aside and suggested, "They're younger than you, so you'll have to take care of them. They've never seen a barn or a cow . . . or a creek, so don't dare let them near the edge." Thank goodness it was low; the rains hadn't begun. "You're in charge." She saw him straighten up, square his shoulders. "They're our guests, so you and Alex be nice to them."

Rising, Susan said, "I'll go see if I can help Beth."

"Beth cooks for us," Hallie explained to the others.

"You've a maid?" her mother asked, her voice incredulous.

"No, she's a friend who lives here with us. But we've divided our duties, and she's in charge of the kitchen."

"You don't cook?" asked Tess, her eyes round.

Hallie laughed. "I don't think I've cooked in years. I imagine I could if Beth got sick, but it's been a long time. I—I have other duties."

Chad, leaning against a pillar of the porch, alternately stared at her and gazed out at the landscape.

"What do you do?" Danny leaned forward, excited. "If you don't cook . . ."

Hallie smiled. "I don't clean the house, or wash the clothes . . ."

Mum stared at her. "Don't you do anything, then?"

It seemed that Chad was waiting for an answer, too. Hallie smiled to herself. The life she lived could not even be imagined back in England. "I help round up sheep, and see what fences need mending—sometimes even help. I breed the cow and help deliver foals. I see that twenty-two men—including free men and convicts—are kept busy. I ride out to the shepherd—"

"Shepherd? Twenty-two men?" Chad interrupted.

Oh, so much to tell him.

"I help deliver lambs, and sometimes help with the shearing, though not much anymore. I have ten men who are trained to do that now. I see that the gardens are kept tidy, and the hay—"

"Ten?" Chad asked.

Hallie smiled, enjoying letting him know of her progress. "We also have a multitude of sheep." And as she talked on, Ben was suddenly there.

He looked surprised, though he had seen the wagon pass and wondered where they were going. Ah, the lord of the manor come home. Looking at Chad, Hallie said, "This is Ben Lambert. Ben runs the store."

"The store?" He'd guessed that the building he'd passed was a store, and he knew it was on his land, but he hadn't known it was *his* store. Was the smithy his, too? And what looked to be a pub? He felt alienated, as though he were the only one who had no knowledge of what was going on, yet he imagined he owned it all. He would wait until he and Hallie were alone. After all, he should have recognized that things could not have stayed the same for over five years. In some ways, it seemed half a lifetime. But he had held in his mind the image of life as he had left it, of Hallie cooking and cleaning, of her spending time with the children, and Brian doing the men's work. He had imagined the small house he had built when it was large enough for just the two of them. He should have known better. He had

359

worried, also, of time passing him by, of the sheep not increasing, though heaven knew Hallie's fleeces had brought him thousands of pounds. But he had no way of knowing how many were from what year and how many sheep . . . He sold by the kilo, not the number of fleeces. How many did they have? he wondered. From the looks of things the flock had increased to more than five thousand . . . way more. Well, he would bide his time for all the questions. They didn't have to be answered right now. There was tonight, when he and Hallie would be alone, and there was tomorrow, and there was forever. He vowed never to leave again; he had missed too much. His children, to whom he had crooned lullabies, did not know him.

Molly and Beth brought steaming platters of food to the porch. There was a side of beef, red and velvet smooth, sweet baby carrots, small new potatoes drowned in butter they'd churned that morning and sprinkled with parsley, Yorkshire pudding dripping in gravy, and—for dessert— rhubarb pies. The table was not large enough for everyone, nor were there enough chairs, so the children sat on the stoop.

Beth said not a word and ate very little and didn't even smile when everyone commented on the food after so long at sea. Of course all of it disappeared quickly.

Chad . . . Amidst all the noisy conversation, of hearing how beautiful and clean and warm Australia was, what a beautiful house, what the eight-month trip was like, how wonderful it was to be here at last—amidst it all Hallie thought, Chad . . . Her mind stopped there.

It was not until later—after boxes were taken down from the wagon, after Danny and his family had been distributed in the unfinished bedroom that as yet had no beds or even enough blankets for them all, after Mum had already gone to bed and Molly had put the children down, and as she and Susan and Beth and Chad sat around talking—that the first realization of what was happening hit Hallie.

She said to Chad, "You might be more comfortable in the bed in the barn rather than the sofa here in the drawing room."

He looked at her as though she had lost her mind. It wasn't until Susan said, "Beth can sleep in with Molly and the children," that Hallie realized her husband was home.

Beth had slept in the bed with Hallie longer than Chad ever had. Now she was being displaced. They had had no time to prepare themselves for this intrusion into their lives, these people whose presence would change them forever. At the time, only Susan had the premonition that life as Hallie and Beth had known it would not be the same, that something would be gone from their lives . . . lost forever.

Thirty-five

With her hands under her head, Hallie lay staring up into the darkness. Beside her, Chad's breathing was even. Once she was sure he was asleep, she'd taken the arm that was spread across her and put it by his side.

She was overcome with an unbearable urge to weep.

The first years they were married, Chad had denied himself to her when she was pregnant, telling her that making love would, in all likelihood, kill the baby growing inside her. Had these few moments of his homecoming murdered Tristan's child?

Tristan—oh, God! What was to become of them? It was all too clear that she could not have him. After all the years they had loved each other, now that they had permitted it to flower, was it over?

Chad's hands had not excited her; the touch of his lips against hers had made her want to shiver. She might as well have been deaf, for all that the words he whispered in her ear meant to her.

"I've missed you. I've dreamed of holding you again, kissing you, feeling your body against mine."

"You've grown even more beautiful."

"I want to see the farm, hear everything, every detail of what I've missed, but I couldn't tear myself away from looking at you. I wanted to reach out and touch you, feel your breasts, kiss them."

But she could not respond. She lay motionless as he tried to bring her to life. At last he stopped, in the midst of lovemaking, and asked, "What's wrong?"

She said, "I wasn't prepared. I didn't expect you. You're a stranger."

"That didn't stop you the first time."

When she made no answer, he rocked back and forth, doing to her the things that once had set her afire; and she lay rigid. When he was spent, he moved beside her, his head on her breast, and said, "I'm home. I'll never leave you again, Hallie. I know how unfair it's all been. I'm home to take care of you, brave girl."

Brave girl! She bit her tongue not to burst forth with, "I don't want to be taken care of." Nothing inside her moved. He did not know that her mind was locked, too. Locked on Tristan and filled with despair.

She slid from between the sheets and padded to the window, open in the warm summer night. She walked onto the veranda and looked up at the stars, and the first she saw were those that formed the Southern Cross. She had not thought of it in years, except as an indication of direction in the southern sky.

Her melancholy was dispelled when she recalled her joy at seeing Mum and Danny again. Yet she realized that this very happiness was what would put her into bondage, what made any thought of Tristan impossible. Oh, Tristan!

And what about the baby? She thought she must be nearly a month pregnant. What could she tell Chad? But perhaps it wouldn't matter. If he was right, their lovemaking tonight would abort the fetus. But she wanted Tristan's child!

She began to cry, softly. How could she have Tristan's child and stay married to Chad? How could Tristan stand that? And Chad . . . Chad would never forgive her.

She did not think of Chad's thoughtfulness in bringing her mother and brother. All she could think of at the moment was her anger and resentment at the intrusion he represented. Damn him! Why had he come home? Yet at the same time she was engulfed with guilt. Her husband was here and she was pregnant with another man's child.

In the morning she was out of bed before Chad awoke. Beth was already in the kitchen, and Susan was with her. When Hallie appeared, Susan walked over and wrapped her arms around her.

"Oh, my dear," was all she said.

Beth kept her eyes averted as she put a tray of biscuits in the oven.

"I think," said Susan, "it would be best if Molly and the children and I leave."

"You'll do no such thing. If you're any kind of friend, you'll stay till Harry comes out in ten days; you'll stay and give support to both Beth and me. I need you. I need you both." Hallie's eyes were hard, the substance as well as the color of sapphire. Hard and bright.

Hallie spent the morning showing Chad and Danny around. Chad didn't say anything about the new additions, either to the house or to the barn. He nodded at the second barracks, which was an exact replica of the first one. Hallie introduced him to the more recent convicts. Danny, who had never ridden a horse before, was excited at the prospect of riding.

"We'll find you a gentle one this afternoon," Chad promised, "and start your lessons right away."

Since Danny wasn't experienced on a horse, they used the wagon to ride to the store. Inside, Danny was effusive as he looked around. "This is yours, too, Hallie? You started this?"

Hallie looked over at Ben. "I got the idea, but it's Ben who's made it work. I don't even know all that he does."

Ben chewed on a piece of straw and looked at Chad the whole time. Chad studied the shelves and walked through the big empty back room with its unused bed, now that Emil was in his own cottage. "Make money?" he asked.

Ben nodded. "Enough." He expected that he would now be responsible to Chad as well as Harry. The thought did not give him comfort.

While they were at lunch in the house, Jock came riding in from the hills. Except for shearing time, he seldom came down. He'd send for supplies a few times a year, but he and the two men who had been assigned to work with him were nomads of the hills. Hallie never quite knew where they were, though when she would ride out searching for them, she always found them.

Hallie introduced him to Chad, but Jock scarcely blinked at him. He addressed himself to Hallie. "We've got trouble, ma'am. Got dead sheep."

In all the commotion, Hallie had forgotten that yesterday morning Brian had told her he'd found six dead sheep. Jock told her which pasture, and it was beyond the one where Brian had made his discovery. "They have convulsions, too." He scratched his head. Hallie knew it had to be important to bring her shepherd down from the hills. "Think it may be black hair."

"Black hair?" she repeated, puzzled.

Chad jumped up from the table. "My God! That could destroy the whole flock."

Jock nodded. "Could kill every damn sheep for miles around."

"Black hair?" Hallie repeated again.

"Anthrax," Chad explained. "It can ruin livestock raising. Come on," he said to the man he had just met. "Take me there."

"It's a half day's ride." Jock glanced at Hallie.

"I'm coming, too," she said.

"No." Chad put a hand on her shoulder. "This isn't work for you. This is man's work."

Irritated, Hallie said, "What do you think I've been doing all these years you've been away? What if it were this time yesterday and you weren't here? Don't you think I've been coping with everything that's come along for nearly five years? Men's work! Mum"—she turned to the women at the table—"we have years to talk and catch up. I've got to go up in the hills. We'll be back tomorrow."

Beth packed food for them while Chad saddled Thunder and Princess. He felt a stranger in the land he had chosen as his, knowing it was only right that he should. Life had not stopped while he was away, but he guessed he had thought it had. Of course Hallie had done men's work. What had he been thinking, that it had all just magically gotten along by itself?

As they started toward the hills, following Jock, Chad asked her, "How many sheep do we have?" He was expecting the hundred he had brought with him, superior breeding stock, to arrive tomorrow.

"I don't know for sure," Hallie replied. "About three thousand were killed in the flood."

"Three thousand?" The flock must be depleted, he thought.

"Then there are various flocks in different pastures. Jock takes all the young ones each spring, all the superior stock. How many do you have up there?" she called out to him.

He was silent for a couple of minutes. "Don't rightly know. Close to eight thousand, would guess."

"Eight thousand?" Chad echoed, astonished. "Hallie,

365

five years ago we had two thousand. Where did they all come from?"

"Mostly right here, though a couple of farmers left and I bought their flocks. A few left their farms because of the drought. I bought theirs, too. We've tried to cull those from the ones Jock thinks are the best, and he takes care of them."

Chad was still reeling from Hallie's first bit of information. "How do twelve thousand sheep manage on a couple of thousand acres?" He thought that they were heading out to no-man's-land, open pasture that was too far out to be owned.

Hallie said, "We have another ten or twelve thousand roaming over the pastures Brian oversees, and down south. It's not all fenced in yet, so we've had to assign some of the men to watch them." Then she looked at Chad and smiled. It was the first she'd smiled all day. "We don't have just a couple of thousand acres. We have closer to twenty thousand."

"How in the world . . ." He couldn't finish. "Twenty thousand acres!"

"The governor granted us some land, but I bought most of it."

"Where did the money come from?"

"I don't know exactly. But Harry told me I could afford it. His bank loaned me the money, and then each time we shipped fleece or butchered, or sold horses, he wrote it off against the loan."

Chad frowned. "How much in debt are we?"

Suddenly Hallie was exhilarated. All the years of hard work, the years of acquiring more land and sheep, all the years of her decision making, were coming to fruition. "Harry told me recently that we're some of the wealthiest people in the colony. I don't think we owe anything right now. But he and Ben keep track of it, I don't. I don't have much of a head for figures."

Of course not, thought Chad. Women didn't.

His mind reeled. Twenty thousand acres . . . more than fifteen thousand sheep. This was more than he had dreamed of when he began. He had thought seventy-five hundred, maybe ten thousand sheep would be a lot, and maybe ten thousand acres. He had thought he'd have to work a lifetime to achieve those goals. He calculated that if Hallie's last two shipments of fleece—ones that would have arrived after he'd left England—contained half that amount, they'd be wealthy. Harry's bank had loaned money to a woman? That was impossible in England. Risking a loan, or loans, to a woman? He looked at Hallie, riding smoothly in the saddle on the horse ahead of him, her back erect, her hair pulled back from her face and caught in a comb, hanging in golden waves down her back.

This woman whom he had married in order to found a dynasty . . . it was no one's fault but his that he had left and there were not yet other children. But what a woman! He had been afraid that he would never achieve his lifetime dream because of the years he had been gone. He knew already that he had the money, from all the fleece as well as his gambling. He knew he was rich. But now, to be land-rich also! He had come home with grandiose dreams. He would begin a breeding program with the merinos and Af-rikaans sheep he had brought, a scientific breeding pro-gram designed to produce the best fleece in the world. A program that would bring an industry to this continent and make it famous worldwide. He had stared out at the hori-zon for eight sea-tossed months, envisioning how he would petition for another two thousand acres. And now to hear they owned twenty thousand!

In his mind's eye he had built a new home, a baronial estate on the brow of a hill. It would have two, maybe even three stories, overlooking the river and valley. It would con-tain more than a dozen rooms and would be a showplace. Now he had come home not to his three-room house, but to a seven-room estate. He had brought with him, though it had not arrived—for he had arranged warehousing in Sydney until he had room for it—furniture that he knew would amaze Hallie, and probably all of New South Wales. He had brought home chandeliers, and sofas, and four-poster beds, and mahogany tables. He had brought home a piano, and a desk, cupboards, and carpets, thinking to astonish and delight with such purchases.

Reality here was larger than his dreams had been. He had seen his visions as grand and glorious, if sometimes impossible or improbable. Now he learned they had already been achieved. By a woman.

He looked at Hallie's ramrod-straight back and saw none of the softness he remembered. Last night there had been none of the fire he recalled, little that satisfied the hunger in him. None of the electricity that had coursed between them before.

She had changed, he realized. But he would take care of that. Now that he was home, she could afford to be a woman again. She could relax. He would take charge, make the decisions, catch up on all that had been done and all that needed doing. They would have more children, and she could forget the hard work. She might have accumulated the enormous flocks of sheep and the land beyond compare, but he would see to the breeding program that would make New South Wales world famous; he would allow her to lead a life of ease after the years of hard work. He would build her a castle, from whence they could see the distant mountains and the river a ribbon of silver flowing through the valley. They would have stables as well as a barn, and paid servants for the house.

He realized they had had little time to talk, that he knew next to nothing of what had happened in the years he had been gone. His children had shied away from him this morning, preferring Beth and Molly. But he had fences to mend and bridges to build before tackling anything new.

As they rode up into the hills, crossing the river, he made a conscious choice to think of these things later. He was in new country, farther out than he had ever been, and he wondered at its beauty.

"Do we own this land?" he called out.

He saw Hallie nod her head.

After several hours they began to find dead sheep, one here, one there, several rigid. Jock stopped near his covered wagon, and two men rode up on their horses.

"Sheep in convulsions over yonder," one of them said.

Chad, and Jock looked at each other, then rode over to investigate.

It was anthrax. Neither man had any doubt about it. Jock said he had seen it only once. "Had to burn and abandon the fields," he said. "Burned the carcasses of the sheep, too."

"What does it mean?" asked Hallie, watching a sheep foaming at the mouth and jerking spasmodically.

"It's one of the deadliest diseases known to livestock," said Chad.

"What about people?" Hallie asked.

"Not likely," answered Jock, squatting down next to the convulsive sheep. "Sheep, cattle, swine . . ."

Chad said, "Once contaminated, the soil may harbor the germs for years. If anthrax spores are brought to the surface of the soil by burrowing animals, for instance, any susceptible animal may become infected through even an infinitesimal scratch on its legs or feet."

"What can we do?"

Chad shrugged. "You say Brian reported it in another field? Is it near here?"

"Not far. Next pasture northeast of here," Hallie answered.

"Most animals," said Jock, standing up, "die from blood poisoning within twelve hours after the first sign of disease."

"Is it always fatal?" Would they lose more than had been lost in the flood?

"Some recover," Jock murmured. "But hardly ever. Best to shoot them before they contaminate others."

"Some don't die for three to five days," interjected Chad. "Send men out to oversee every flock, wherever they are. Symptoms are dysentery, chills, fever . . ."

"How can you tell when a sheep has a fever?" Hallie asked.

"There's an increase in heart rates," Chad answered. "You can see when one has trouble breathing. There's progressive weakness. They'll begin to stumble, lie down. Convulsions, like this one. This sheep will be dead within hours." He turned to one of the men. "Shoot it. Get it out of its agony, but don't touch it. We'll burn it and the other dead ones."

Hallie wondered how they'd collect the dead ones without touching them. "They can't shoot it," she told Chad. "They don't have guns." No one did, in fact. Chad would have to return for the two he had at the house.

"We can't wait until tomorrow," he said. "We've got to go back tonight. We need help. We need all the men we have. If we don't burn the dead sheep, their hair or wool

369

or dried blood can live in the soil for years, still capable of causing disease."

"How will we know which ones to move? Maybe some have it and don't show it yet," said Hallie.

"That's the chance we take." Chad turned to Jock. "Where can you take them?"

Jock said, "Anyplace between here and there." He pointed westward. "It's all open land."

But we don't want to contaminate open land, Chad thought. Nor do we want to contaminate the land we do own. It would mean we couldn't use it for years, maybe ever.

Adrenaline flowed through his veins, firing his resolve. This was more like it, he thought. An emergency. A crisis for him to take charge of. Just when he'd felt like a guest in his own home, now he had to take command.

He glanced at Hallie. She was waiting for him to tell her what needed to be done.

Thirty-six

It was dark, even in these longest days of the year, when they returned. Both were exhausted; Hallie wanted nothing more than to go to bed, but Chad ate the hot meal Beth had kept for them and then walked up to Brian's. There, he told his foreman what they had learned; in the morning, he said, he wanted all the men called together. This was a priority: nothing else mattered.

The next morning, when the men had been gathered together, Chad explained, "Anthrax has the possibility of not only wiping out our whole flock, but of rendering the fields untenable for more than twenty years. It could spread to the entire valley and wipe out the sheep industry in New South Wales. When anyone comes back from the fields, don't go near the barn. Tether your horses away from the rest of the livestock. Spores may be on your boots. Don't get near the cow, or the horses in the barn, or the pigs. Every bit of livestock can be wiped out if we're not careful."

Six men were to ride around to the other pastures and report back if they found any sick sheep. The rest—most of whom had never even seen Chad before that morning— would come up in the hills with him, to the area where the infected sheep had been discovered.

He turned to Beth. "Boil all the water for at least twenty minutes. You never know if infected sheep drank upstream." Then he turned to Susan and said, "You and your children better go home."

"I'll take Jamie and Alex with me," Susan volunteered. "We don't need help. Between Molly and me, we can take turns driving the wagon." She turned to go into the house, to pack her belongings and prepare to return home.

Hallie followed her. "Don't let Tristan know yet," she said.

"About the anthrax, you mean?"

"About Chad. I want to be the one to tell him."

371

Susan looked at her and then began to gather her clothes together. "I wish there were something I could say or do to help you. Chad, your mother and Danny, now anthrax . . . Oh, Hallie." Suddenly she began to weep for her friend.

"Don't do that," Hallie said, her voice hard. "I can't bear it. I don't have time to think of any of it. I can't think of Tristan, or of Chad, or of anything now . . . not even of myself."

At that moment Chad appeared at the door. "Susan, don't mention anthrax. Let's see if we can stop it here. Maybe no place else has it. No need to set off a panic. *If* you do hear of it someplace else, then contact the governor. Otherwise, I beg you be silent about it."

"I'll have to tell Harry," Susan said uncertainly.

"Of course," Chad said. "And thanks for taking the children. I'll feel safer with them out of here. We should send Sophie, too," he said to Hallie.

Sophie? thought Hallie, astonished. The only times she had ever heard her mother so addressed were by a couple of neighbor women. Her father had always referred to her as "your mum" or, when he addressed her directly, "Mrs. Thomas." Hearing Chad address her as Sophie was something of a shock.

"Mrs. Thomas is welcome to come with us," Susan offered. "So are Tess and her children."

Sophie refused, but Tess jumped at the suggestion. So the three women started off in the wagon, loaded with six children.

Chad told Hallie they'd have to shoot any animal found bleeding. And there might be hundreds. A major problem, he thought, was the fact that they only had two guns: his unwieldy long-nosed musket and the pistol with which Hallie had shot Archie's murderer and without which she never traveled. Convicts were forbidden firearms by law. Brian said he had never used a gun.

"It'll be rough for one person to keep up with them, if there actually are hundreds," Chad said, shaking his head. "Perhaps we'll be lucky and there'll just be a couple of dozen. Maybe I can teach Brian how to use a gun."

Hallie spoke up. "I've shot animals before. I don't like doing it, but I know how to."

Chad barely looked at her. "Hallie, this isn't the kind of work—"

"What?" she interrupted. "That women do?"

"Of—" Then he caught himself. Looking at her he thought, What kind of woman has she become?

"You can shoot?" Danny's mouth was agape. Sophie stared at her, too.

Hallie barely nodded. "I'll have Beth pack us some food. Mum, we may be gone several days. I feel I haven't had a chance to talk with you."

Sophie shook her head. "Don't worry about me. Danny and I will manage."

Danny said, "No, Mum. You and Beth will have to manage. I'm going along."

"You don't even know how to ride yet," Hallie said.

"I guess this is one way to learn," he answered. "I didn't come this far to miss out on excitement."

"You'll get saddle sores," warned Chad.

Danny stood his ground, jaw set stubbornly. "I'm coming."

So, in the middle of the morning, the three of them rode off, Brian and Robbie tagging along behind with the rest of the men. Hallie suggested that Beth take Sophie up and introduce her to Belinda.

They crossed the river just about where Jamie and Ben had been stuck in the tree. No one talked much and they rode slowly. Brian led the way; Chad couldn't have found it after just one visit.

"Seems funny," he said to Hallie. "To think I own this land and I'd never seen it before yesterday."

"You own lots more that you haven't seen," she said.

"We'll have to cordon off pastures where we find even one dead sheep," said Chad, thinking aloud. "Burn carcasses. Kill the sick ones. Set fire to the fields."

"Why?" she asked.

"They've picked this up from some infection in the soil, and it gives them blood poisoning. Sheep can get it from feces of other sheep, from close contact with infected sheep. It takes only one sheep to start an epidemic."

"I sure don't wanna get it," one of the men called out.

"Then be careful," Chad cautioned him. "People hardly ever contact it, but if you don't use common sense—if you walk barefoot and get infected through a scratch on your leg or foot, for example—you *can* get it. And it's nearly always fatal in humans." He wasn't trying to scare them so much as make them careful. "Don't touch the infected animals. We'll burn them on the spot. Don't handle them."

He told Hallie, "We're not safe until there are three days with no new cases." He saw the stricken look on her face. "I doubt that all the land is infected," he said to reassure her. "It probably started with one sheep out there in the western pastures, and one infected another and another. But unless the sheep have had contact, the ones in pastures far from them are safe. The trouble will come when we move sheep to other pastures and find some of them infected."

They passed no dead sheep. There were hardly any in sight, in fact, until they reached the sheep herder's camp. The air from the west was filled with the sickeningly sweet smell of burning carcasses, of fields burning, of death. Of rot.

Jock said, "Better follow me. We've burned the dead ones, but daren't touch the sick ones."

Before Chad followed, he instructed the other men to fan out in pairs into the surrounding pastures. He reiterated, "Don't touch any. Set the dead ones on fire, but report back here with the location of any dying ones." Then he turned to Hallie. "Sure you want to do this? Killing an animal . . . A dead animal isn't a pretty sight."

The field before Hallie was filled with a dozen sheep that oozed blood from their noses, their ears, their anuses. In answer to Chad's question, she took aim and, closing her eyes, squeezed the trigger. She heard the shot and knew it had hit its mark. Her thoughts flew back to a time, a place, two years ago. . . .

She had shot a horse that had stumbled and broken its leg. It could not stand; it had raised its pained eyes to her, pleading. She'd realized, sensed, what had to be done, but could not bring herself to do it. She'd sat with the horse all night, out where it had fallen, where the convict to whom it had been assigned had been forced to leave it.

In the morning she'd known what she had known all night—that there was no choice. She'd ridden back to the farm, loaded the pistol and returned, alone. Its eyes, she

374

had told herself, begged for relief. Yet when she'd pulled the trigger and heard the loud reverberating echo and saw life leave the horse, blood spurting from the hole she had put between its eyes, she'd had to lean against a tree, fighting for breath. Falling to her knees, while Princess nuzzled her neck, she had shaken with dry heaves.

She had done the right thing, but right hurt. It seemed doing what had to be done, taking a life, killed a part of her—a small part, perhaps, but one that brought her own mortality closer.

For nights afterward, in her sleep, she'd flown with that bullet as, in a slow arc, it had hurled itself from her gun into the center of the graceful equine head. She'd felt herself thrust into the black bullet hole as the sticky, thick blood gushed over her, blinding her for eternity. . . .

Now, at the end of four days, deaf from the gunfire that echoed across the hills and down the valleys, Hallie felt nothing when her aching finger pulled the trigger—nothing internally. Her hand, however, was cramped and painful. She had used those muscles over five hundred times. She had shot hemorrhaging sheep, convulsing sheep, sheep that had become rigid and those showing any signs of weakness or stumbling.

She found herself vomiting each morning and knew that she was still pregnant. She'd thought perhaps that riding out in the rough terrain might have aborted Tristan's child, but none of the things that Chad had refused her in her earlier pregnancies had proven detrimental. He had made love to her and it hadn't interrupted the fetus. She'd ridden hard over rocky ground and it hadn't affected her at all. She didn't know whether she wanted it to or not.

In the hours that she was on horseback, scouring the pastures for infected sheep, she had little time to think of anything but anthrax, of what could happen to her flock and her home. Jesus, dear God, she prayed. But she didn't know what she was praying for. She found herself crying. The men thought she was worried about the loss of her sheep.

And, in fact, that *was* a large part of it. It was the only part she allowed herself to think about. She could not face the other problems, could not even bask in the pleasure that Mum and Danny's arrival provided, for she knew it was a double-edged sword. She could not think of Tristan, of bearing his child while married to Chad. She could not think of settling down again to life with Chad, a life without Tristan.

But this, ultimately, was what kept her awake nights after exhausting days in the saddle. She would collapse in a bed-roll and immediately drown in sleep, only to awaken in the middle of the night, knowing she could not bear to be denied Tristan. She would lie there, in the middle of the night, listening to the bleating of lambs in the distance, and fantasize solutions that weren't heartbreaking.

But in the light of day, as she rode off with Chad and Jock, she wondered how she could face Mum. Mum and Danny were obviously fond of Chad. They had uprooted themselves from the only life they had ever known, and dared to sail around the world not only to be with her, but because they trusted Chad, because he had painted the picture of a better life for them.

And how could she face Chad? she wondered. He had absented himself all these years not only in the hope of making a better life for them, but because he felt an obligation to a dying father. And, in the process, had taken care of *her* dying father.

But I love Tristan, she thought, her heart wrenching. I've never known what love was before. I liked Chad; heaven knows I really liked him before. It had been so long ago, she scarcely remembered what she *had* felt for her husband. He had been fun, and he was kind . . . but she had never felt a part of him, as she did with Tristan. Certainly the way he was acting now was admirable. He knew how to take charge, what to do. And even when he was exhausted, he was courteous and thoughtful to the men. And to her. She felt snappish and short-tempered, and was amazed that Chad showed no signs of impatience or irritability.

When they talked, it was simply of immediate concerns. At night she slept between him and Danny, who marveled to be sleeping out under the stars "in February." Chad showed him how to locate the Southern Cross, too. Hallie lay there silently.

On the fourth day they found no new cases—no dead ones, no dying ones. However, a sickly sweet smoke covered the land. It made the sunsets spectacular, purple undersides of gold-and-red clouds that hung low in the skies, lighting the heavens in gaudy splendor. Hallie was torn between wonder and revulsion. On the fifth day the smoke began to dissipate.

Chad said, "Why don't you and Brian take four of the men and go back? If there's no more by tomorrow night, it may be over." Over half the men were building fences in unclaimed pastureland to the west, land that had not had sheep on it before.

They all knew by now that the hundreds of acres that had been burned—thousands, probably—were lost. "They won't be usable for years, probably not in our lifetime," Chad said. Jock nodded; he knew that, too. "We'll have to fence them off, but I don't know what to do about any wild animals or aboriginals who will cross them, not knowing. They could spread the disease across the entire continent."

"Won't burning them kill any germs?" Danny asked.

"I hope that'll be the end of it. But I'm not optimistic. It's a disease that petrifies the heart of anyone who knows what it means." He turned to Hallie. "I'd guess we've lost between two and three thousand."

That was her estimate, too. Her finger could hardly pull the trigger, it ached so from the repetition. "Won't we have to tell our neighbors?" she asked.

"Yes, of course. They must be aware. But I didn't want them to panic."

Hallie, along with Danny and four of the men, returned to the house. They were so tired they couldn't sit straight in their saddles. And saddle sores plagued Danny, who wondered if he would ever be able to walk again.

It was dark when they arrived home. Hallie fell into a sleep from which she didn't awaken until mid-morning. When at last she emerged from her bedroom, Sophie fussed over her as though she were not grown. It was a nice sensation, she thought. She sat on the porch and listened to Mum tell her about people in Newcastle she had almost forgotten, about her brothers and sisters, nieces and nephews, neighbors and girls she had played with as a child. She closed her eyes and felt her mother's hand in hers and listened to her voice and felt safe. She wondered, vaguely, if Mum would still love her when she found out, when she knew what her daughter had done. But she was too tired to think straight.

Danny lay on his bed, stomach down, for two days.

When Chad returned with most of the other men, he said, "There's been no new sign for four days. Someone will come get me if they find more. We moved many of them to western land, where there are no fences. But I think we have it under control." Then he collapsed on the bed and slept for twenty hours.

When he awoke he started coughing. "Inhaled too much smoke," he said, his voice hoarse. He barely made it out to the porch for breakfast.

Sophie and Danny were already there. "This isn't the grand introduction I'd envisioned for you," Chad said, smiling weakly.

Though Sophie didn't say it, she found the smoke that had floated through the valley as bad as Newcastle's persistent coal dust. Except she had grown used to that; here, she found herself coughing and her eyes irritated. But then, they all were reacting that way.

"You look wore out," she commented to her son-in-law.

"I worked no harder than the other men," Chad said. He hesitated a minute. "Or Hallie—" He broke off as another fit took him, causing him to cough as though his insides would come out. Sophie didn't say what she thought—that he sounded like Dada.

Hallie watched him, her entire being in turmoil, wrung out from the events of the past week. Oh, God! Had any woman before her ever been in such a predicament? What was she going to do? She knew that she was going to have to tell Chad. No matter the consequences. She would wait until he felt stronger, until after Tristan . . .

Tears welled in her eyes, and she rose so abruptly from the table that her chair fell over. She headed to the kitchen, and then suddenly realized Beth had not eaten with them. Beth had not eaten with them last night, either. She had placed the food on the table and disappeared.

Beth was standing, plate in hand, eating in the sun-filled kitchen doorway. She looked at Hallie with a level gaze.

"Why?" asked Hallie in a small, choked voice. "Why are you out here?"

"I don't know," Beth responded after a short silence.

Then, placing her plate on the table, she turned to Hallie, who moved into her open arms and began to sob. And Beth—who knew only that Hallie had been happy with Tristan and was now in pain—held her tenderly and cried with her at the realization that five years of security and peace, years of being loved and learning to love in return, had come to an end.

After Hallie had wiped her tears and washed her face, she returned to the porch, but it was empty. Walking out back, she saw Chad, Danny, and her mother standing by the barn door. She followed.

Chad was holding onto the side of the barn, shaking his head as though trying to rid himself of . . ."I'm dizzy," he said.

"Let's go back and you can lie down," Hallie suggested. "Inhaling that much smoke wasn't good for you."

Without objecting, Chad started back to the house. As soon as he lay down, he fell asleep, spread-eagled on the bed. His breathing was loud and sounded as though it came from deep within him.

"He's been such comfort, such strength," said Sophie, from beside Hallie. "All the time Dada was dying, all those years and months, Chad came by. He read to him, and talked with him, and made him laugh. He was the only one who could. He brought us all presents and made life easier." She sighed, remembering. "I don't know that Danny would have gone on if it hadn't been for Chad. Just being with Chad gives one courage. He's a rare fine human being."

"He left me for nearly five years," Hallie said, her voice expressionless.

Sophie looked at her sharply but didn't respond.

Hallie did not wake Chad for lunch. She insisted Beth dine with them, but her friend remained silent. Danny tried to include her in the conversation, but Beth had closed herself off completely and communicated in no way. At last he gave up and addressed himself to his sister.

"I know what's been happening has been awful, Hallie, but I can't help it. Darn, I find it exciting, even if it still pains me to sit. Such a grand, glorious-looking land! Imagine wakening mornings to the song of birds, and the sounds last all day. It's music, that's what it is. They're the prettiest birds I ever saw. What are they?"

"The ones that awaken you, the black-and-white ones, are magpies," she told him. "The laughing, raucous ones are the kookaburras. The—"

"Even the names are different," Danny said, sitting on the porch step. "Kookaburra. Doesn't even sound like English."

"It isn't. It's aboriginal." Hallie sat down next to him.

He looked at her with excited eyes. "Do you have trouble with them? Are they like the Indians in America?"

"No." She smiled. "The few times I've met them they've been pleasant. But there are a lot of people who hate them."

"Why?" asked Sophie, rocking behind them.

"People are scared of them, I guess. They're black. They're different. They have habits unlike ours. They don't believe in our God."

Danny looked at her. "Your God, not mine."

Pain shot through Sophie's eyes and she stopped rocking, reaching forward to put a hand on Danny's shoulder. "You mustn't talk like that."

Just then Chad appeared in the doorway, holding onto it as though he might fall without its support. His eyes were fevered, glassy.

"I have it," he whispered hoarsely. "Don't get near me. I have anthrax."

But when he fell, Danny and Hallie had to touch him, had to pick him up and carry him back to bed.

"Dear God in heaven," Sophie murmured. "What will we do?"

"We'll send for the doctor," said Hallie. "I'll ride over and tell Brian he has to go into Sydney, to fetch the doctor."

Thirty-seven

She told Brian to ride as fast as he could. "Don't tell the doctor that it's Chad," she said, giving him a level look. "Just tell him someone has anthrax and to get out here quick. If you ride fast, you can get to Sydney shortly after dark. Try to start by dawn tomorrow. I want you back here, with Dr. Faulkner, tomorrow afternoon. Tell him I said it's an emergency."

As she rode back to the house, she was aware of the irony of asking her lover to come save her husband. Yet something inside her prayed, with urgency, "Don't let him die. Please—please don't let Chad die."

On the other hand, his death would solve everything.

Hallie and Sophie, and even Danny, took turns sitting with Chad, sponging him off with cool boiled water when his fever made him sweat. Sophie tried to force a weak chicken broth into him, one that she didn't insist on making but about which she gave Beth instructions. Through it all Chad coughed as though his ribs might crack.

Hallie and Sophie looked at each other, wondering if tending him would contaminate them. Hallie wondered why, if he'd gotten it, she hadn't as well. Why hadn't Danny? Were there any men still up in the hills who might have it, who might be sick and dying? Hadn't Chad said it was almost always fatal in humans?

This was the least opportune reunion Hallie could imagine. Not since they'd arrived had any of them had time to assimilate emotions. Sophie hadn't yet had an opportunity to get to know her grandchildren. Hallie hadn't seen the metamorphosis in Danny: to her he seemed as cheerful and filled with good humor as he had when they were growing up together; she saw none of the bitterness Chad had written about.

The man lying in her bed was a stranger, more alien to her than when she had first met him, first seen him on the beach in Sydney town. When she sponged him off or sat on the chair staring at him, he would open his glassy, dazed eyes and try to smile at her, reaching out weakly to grasp her hand. Afterward she remembered to wash herself.

From noon on she listened for hoofbeats. She knew Tristan and Brian could not make the trip in less than eight hours, no matter how hard they pushed the horses. She didn't expect them before midafternoon at the earliest, *if* they had left at dawn, *if* Tristan were free to leave immediately, if . . .

But it wasn't much after one o'clock when she saw two riders rounding the far hill. Picking up her skirts, she began to run. When they met, she knew that Brian could tell by the look in her eyes that she wanted him to go on to the house and leave Tristan with her.

"We came as fast as we could," Tristan said, sliding down from his horse and reaching out to grasp Hallie's hands. Then he saw the look in her eyes. "What makes you think it's anthrax?"

"We've been up in the hills for near a week; Jock knew what it was."

"Give me just a second." Tristan pulled her toward him, but she backed away.

"My mother and brother are here," she told him.

"Good Lord!" he cried, staring at her. Then: "It's not your brother, is it?"

Hallie shook her head, pain evident in her eyes. Throwing her arms around his waist, she held him tight, her head pressed against his chest, her eyes averted. His arms encircled her and he scarcely heard her whisper, "It's Chad."

His arms went limp. Hallie held him tightly and finally raised her eyes to his. "They arrived right after you left. And then we were up in the hills, killing sheep, fencing new pastures . . ."

Tristan stared at her. "Chad?"

Hallie began to cry. "And I'm sure I'm pregnant. I don't know what to do. I want your child. I want you."

There was silence. As she stared at him, his eyes went dead. Then he drew her close to him and she felt his heart beating. "Hallie, promise me that you will never tell me there's a God."

No, she thought. I won't.

They stood, clinging to each other, until she pulled away from him, left his arms, and said, "He may be dying."

"And I'm to save him, is that it?"

They started toward the house.

"The children went to Parramatta with Susan," she told him. "So did Danny's wife. We thought it safer."

"I know next to nothing of anthrax," Tristan admitted. "I've never seen a case of it. I studied my medical texts last night, and found out that human anthrax is either internal or external. Internal is nearly always fatal and tends to localize in certain organs before the bacillus gains access to the bloodstream."

Hallie didn't understand what he was talking about, but she didn't question him.

"It's a massive pneumonia, probably caused by breathing contaminated dust from the wool. Intestinal injuries may develop; it may also be manifested as a tuberculosis."

He sounded as though he were reciting something he had memorized.

"Is there a carbuncle with a black center?" he asked her. "If so, it may be fatal."

"I haven't seen anything like that," she said, torn by her emotions. "But he's breathing from deep in his lungs and he's feverish."

"Sounds like pneumonia," Tristan guessed.

Danny stood on the porch, watching them approach. Hallie wondered how long he had been there. She introduced them, and Tristan stuck out his hand, which Danny shook. "I'd know who you are anywhere," said Tristan. "You two must be identical twins."

Danny nodded distractedly; his mind was with Chad.

Tristan tied his horse to the veranda post and strode inside. Sophie rose from her chair when he entered the bedroom and watched as he sat on the chair she had vacated and studied Chad.

Chad was delirious and sweating profusely, even as his entire body shook with cold. Tristan pulled the covers back and listened to his heartbeat, to the rattle in his lungs. He watched him for a long time.

Hallie stood in the doorway next to her mother and observed them both—the man she had married . . . and the man she loved above all else in the world.

Tristan stayed with Chad all afternoon. Once in a while he would stand and stretch, walking over to the open French doors and staring out at the land. Hallie sensed he was not looking at it, that what he was seeing was visible to no one else. Sophie moved a chair on the veranda right outside the window and sat, fanning herself and looking in at Tristan observing Chad. Once in a while her eyes flicked to the doorway, from where Hallie stared at the men. When Hallie could stand it no longer, she walked out to the barn. She always loved the smell of the hay piled high, the odor of manure, the cozy feeling of animals herded together. Their sounds always comforted her.

She walked to the stall where Tristan had spent his nights, the stall where, perhaps, their child had been conceived. She sat down on the bed, fingering the blanket, and began to weep, great heaving sobs that would not stop.

It was here that Danny found her. He entered the barn, not looking for Hallie but wandering around restlessly. The cries that had threatened to wrench Hallie apart had subsided somewhat, and Danny followed the muffled noises, surprised to find his sister sitting on a bed in the barn. Her eyes, red and swollen, were unfocused, and he watched as she pummeled the bed with her fists, whispering in a cracked voice, "Why? . . . Oh, *why?*"

Instantly he was at her side, kneeling and taking her hands in his. "I'm devoted to him, too, you know," he murmured. Hallie looked at him strangely. "He gave me the courage to come to this land, despite Tess's fear and protests. This is the man who convinced Mum she wasn't too old to dare. The man who gave you, my sister, all this—all this land, this house, this adventure. The man who brought us all together. Hallie, if it weren't for him, I'd still think life had played me a dirty trick. I'd still be clerking in that damn store, still living in that house like every other house I'd ever seen. Still walking a treadmill."

Suddenly Danny buried his head in Hallie's lap, holding her hand so tight it hurt her. "He *can't* die!" he whispered savagely. "He's the only hope I have. Oh, God, Hallie, if I could consider using the word *love* about a man, with any man other than Dada, I love Chad."

Hallie stared at her brother and began to run her fingers idly through his hair, now sun-streaked like hers. After a few moments he raised his eyes to hers. "He has saved this family," he said. "Is this doctor any good? Can he save our savior?"

Hallie put her hands on his cheeks, brushing away the tears that Danny had shed. She stared into his eyes, into the brother who was more a physical part of her than even her children. And she knew that should Chad live, this brother would be partly responsible for her lifelong imprisonment, for the renunciation of the man who meant more to her than life itself. This magnanimous gesture of Chad's—of bringing Mum and Danny to her—designed to please her, would ultimately destroy her by denying her the man she loved, and would love forever.

At last, in answer to Danny's question, she said, "He's a wonderful doctor, as well as one of the best friends I have in the world."

In that moment she sensed that Chad would live.

Tristan, however, was not so sure. He relied more on his medical knowledge than on intuition.

He did leave Chad's room for dinner, and it was only then that he and Hallie's family began to talk. For hours the house had been oppressive with worry and watching.

"His temperature is so high that he hallucinates," Tristan said. "We should know tomorrow, or at least by the day after, whether he . . ." He did not have to finish the sentence.

Then his innate social sensibilities triumphed, and he asked Sophie and Danny about their trip, about their first impressions of this land half a world away. He talked to them of its birds, and its unique animals, and of its climate. All safe topics, yet—on this continent—ones of unending fascination.

After looking in on the still-sleeping Chad, Tristan returned to them and kept talking—far more than was his wont—telling Sophie and Danny of things Chad could not have known: of opening the continent by triumphing over the Blue Mountain pass, of settlements beginning as far as hundreds of miles away, of Macquarie's attainments. In short, a history of Australia of the last five years. And Sophie and Danny, despite their concern about Chad, sat mesmerized, asking questions about this land and its peoples—this place for which they had given up all that was familiar to them.

At ten o'clock—long after the sun had set and twilight surrounded them—Sophie gave in to her exhaustion and excused herself. But Danny stayed up awhile longer, talking until Beth decided it was time for her to retire also. It had been agreed that she and Hallie would share the children's room, since anthrax could be contagious.

Tristan announced that he would sleep on the sofa rather than take up his usual place in the barn. He and Danny picked up the sofa and moved ii to the doorway of her bedroom. Then he told Hallie that since Chad's fever made him sweat so profusely, it would be a good idea to sponge him off with cool water before retiring for the night. They did it together, staring at each other across the sick man's naked body.

When they were through and Danny had gone to bed, Tristan took her hand and led her down by the creek. It was completely dark now, no moon was out. He turned and took her in his arms, burying his head in her hair, holding her to him.

"You're mine," he whispered. "No matter what anyone else thinks, you're mine."

And there, in the blackness of night, while Hallie's husband lay in her bed—unconscious and close to death—Hallie and Tristan held each other beside the soft running creek.

"Tristan, whatever will we do?" He drew his arms tighter around her. "The baby . . ."

"Oh, God, Hallie, all I know is that I feel life has been ripped from me. My insides are bleeding, and nobody but you can see. I am as sick as that man in your bed. I am in as much pain as he. Only he is unconscious and I am not." His voice grew louder, its tone ragged and agonized. "I am going to help him live. And by his living, part of me will die." He laughed; it was a harsh, metallic sound. "What do you think Fate has against us, Hallie? In all likelihood I shall deliver my child so that another man may father it!"

He let go of her and walked a few paces away, leaning his hand against the trunk of a tree.

"All I know is that I have to do everything in my power to keep this man, your husband, alive." And he began to pummel the tree with his fists.

Tristan sat with Chad for three days, just as he had sat by Hallie when she lost her baby, when she, too, was unconscious. At the end of the three days, his fever broke.

"He's still not out of danger," Tristan told Hallie. They were standing on the porch, having just finished breakfast. "All sorts of complications could develop. He could sink into a stupor, seizures might occur. There's a remote possibility of deafness or paralysis. I'm not telling you this to frighten you, Hallie, but to prepare you. As far as I know, there's no specific treatment. My staying would be of little help. Even blindness is . . ." He shrugged.

"Is there anything I can do?" Hallie asked. Her voice was hollow and her eyes empty.

"He's not to get out of bed, he's to be fed liquids, with a weak gruel once a day." His hand reached out to cover hers, and his eyes were bloodshot, as though he, too, had been crying all night. "I'll come back as soon as I can, but in the meantime he is not to get out of bed, whether I'm back in one week, two, or three. I think he'll live, though the convalescence will be long. In his weakened condition, he's susceptible to everything. Even a cold can be disastrous to the pneumonia. There is also a danger of meningitis. Whether or not that period has passed, I don't know. This is probably the first human case of anthrax in this country. It wasn't a part of my training."

He turned away from her. "I have to return to Sydney. I've been away too long. I imagine Susan is in Parramatta. I'll send word to her that it's safe for the children to come back in a week. But you shouldn't let the noise of children interfere with his rest. Let nothing disturb him."

Hallie tried to hold him with her eyes. All she could see—all he would let her see—was his professional manner. "Next week," she said, "I'll send one of the men in with the wagon to bring everyone back."

When Tristan turned and went back in the house, into

Chad's room, Hallie did not follow him, but stood listening outside the French doors. Chad was still too weak to sit up, too debilitated to talk much. She imagined Tristan leaning over, close to her husband, to hear whatever it was that he was saying, and she heard Tristan answer, "Yes, of course we shall be friends when you recuperate." His voice had a hollow ring to it.

When Tristan came back out, his eyes were hooded, lifeless. He thrust his medical kit into his saddlebag, checked the cinch on his horse, and turned toward her. "If you need me for any reason, I shall come, of course," he said.

Taking his hand in hers, Hallie pressed it to her lips, and the pain she felt turned to tears. "I always need you," she whispered, her eyes pleading with him.

He brushed her tears with his fingers and raised them to his lips. Then he turned abruptly and jumped on his horse.

"Tell me it's not good-bye." She looked up at him. "I can't bear that."

His eyes had tears in them. "Of course it's not good-bye. It will never be good-bye. You know that." He was silent a moment as they stared at each other. "We are bound together forever."

"And ever." The tears were flowing freely now. "Oh, Tristan . . ."

He leaned down and put a finger over her lips, driving her to a silence more eloquent than words.

Just then Sophie walked onto the porch. Tristan straightened in his saddle, doffed his hat at her, and said to Hallie, *Auf wiedersehen.* Then he turned and rode off, his back straight. Before long he was cantering, and by the time he had reached the hill, his horse had broken into a gallop.

"What did that mean?" Sophie asked, walking down the steps to put an arm around her shoulder.

"I don't know," Hallie said, her face still wet with tears. "He was just telling me the terrible things that can still go wrong."

But can anything worse go wrong? she asked herself, feeling her heart shatter into a thousand fragments. She would go through the rest of her life as one dead—a woman with no heart, whose emotions had just been scattered to the wind, chasing behind a lonely man galloping north.

388

Thirty-eight

Chad's seizure the next day scared them all; they stood by watching—revolted and helpless. Sophie was sitting with him when his eyes began to roll, when his legs and arms began to jerk spastically. Though seated beside her son-in-law, she called out to him—sensing he was traveling to some far-off place she could not see. Her call brought both Hallie and Danny running, in time to see Chad's arms flailing in the air and his legs twitching convulsively.

The three of them looked on in horror. "He's either going to swallow his tongue or bite it off!" Danny cried.

Sophie reached out for a handkerchief and thrust it into Chad's mouth. He bit hard on it as sweat popped out on his forehead and his eyes rolled. Hallie thought it was like being dead. His body was there, but his mind and his soul had gone elsewhere. Lying on the bed was nothing more than a twitching body they could not reach. None of them had ever seen anyone like this.

It was over in less than two minutes, yet it seemed an eternity. When his spasms ceased, he lay still for several minutes, perspiration running in rivulets down his face and neck. Then he looked at them—truly *saw* them—and smiled in what could only be considered a sweet manner. "I'm tired," he said. "I think I'll sleep." And he did. Instantly.

The three of them looked at each other, frightened not only by what they'd just seen, but by their feelings of helplessness. Sophie and Danny followed Hallie out onto the veranda. Hallie gulped a draft of air, feeling her breathing and heart rate slow down. I need to be *doing* something, she thought, and turning to Sophie, asked, "Do you mind staying here and letting me take Danny out to help with some work? I've been letting things go far too long. Between spending time up in the hills shooting sheep, and now Chad, I've fallen behind in work. And if Danny's going to be part of this life, I'd better teach him to ride properly."

Sophie walked back and forth, relieving the stress she felt. "Hallie, I do want to stay with Chad, but when you teach Danny, include me, will you?"

"We have a carriage for you; you needn't learn to ride a horse at your age."

Sophie looked at her sharply. "I spent every one of those nights, the eight months on that ship, wondering why I was coming to a new world. I'd left all I'd ever known behind me. And I finally decided I was coming not only to a new land, but to a new life. I vowed I wasn't going to live as I'd lived for the past fifty-two years. I was going to begin to experience all that I could before I died. If I have to, I'll cook and scrub and do all the things I've been tied to all my life. But I didn't come to Australia to live like I've lived in the past."

Hallie was taken aback; this strength of will was something she'd never suspected in her mother.

"For beginners, I want to learn to ride a horse," her mother continued. "I don't know what else I want to learn, but I'll find things."

"We'll have a riding lesson after lunch," Hallie promised, smiling.

Chad did not have another seizure. It was almost as though that one had somehow rekindled life in him, and he began to recuperate in earnest. He sat up in bed and was interested in what was happening around him. He asked Hallie about the children. He chatted with Sophie and smiled as he listened to Danny go on and on about how wonderful this new country was.

"To think that I can work out in the sunshine, in the clear air, with mountains in the distance and green grass below instead of coal, to look up at blue sky instead of a low black ceiling! I can hardly believe I'm here."

At night, after Ben had gone to the barracks and Beth, Danny, and Sophie had retired, Chad would say, "Don't go yet, Hallie," and reach out to her. She'd walk over to him and put her hand in his, and he'd draw her down. He wanted her to sit on the bed next to him. "We have so much to catch up on. And I never seem to see you during the

390

day. Tell me . . . tell me about my five lost years. What you have done and . . . tell me everything."

It was thus he learned the details of Archie's death, of Ben's arrival, of how Brian had grown in his job. He listened without questioning, looking at her all the time, watching the dancing shadows on her face, images created by the flickering lamp. When she came to the part about Emil and the vineyard, he stopped her, asking for details, pulling from her that it was a joint enterprise with Tristan.

She explained, hesitatingly, reluctantly, it was Tristan who had saved her life not only when Archie died, but on the ship, when he had taken out her appendix. "I don't know what I'd have done without him." She was silent then, and Chad stared at her. She tried not to meet his eyes.

"He has a habit of saving the lives in this family," she added quietly. "He's the one who rescued Jamie during the flood."

"The flood?" Chad's voice cracked.

Oh, so much he didn't know! She couldn't recall whether she'd written him about any of this. So, she had to tell him about the flood, and the drought. He wanted to hear every detail of Jamie's escapade, and how Ben went after him . . . and how Tristan saved them both.

She did not tell him about learning to dance and the governor's ball, but she did remember the horse race and her witnessing the flogging and hanging. He listened as she told him of the land she had acquired, and he smiled at the friendship Harry and Susan offered.

She told him a bit more each evening, and every day he waited out the long daylight hours with the happy expectation of shared evenings with Hallie, of catching up on his five years, of listening to Hallie's voice and holding her hand as she recited her adventures.

In all that she said, she lied to him about only one thing: Beth. She told him Beth had come to marry a man, and that once she'd met him, she felt she could not go through with it. Since the two women had become friends on the *Charleston*, she explained, Beth had searched for her and had been here since shortly after Chad had left. Chad did not ask why it had taken Beth three years to find Hallie if she had immediately known this man was not for her.

"Her being here has made it possible for me to concentrate on the farm work," Hallie concluded. "She's taken over all the household chores."

When she told Chad of the evening classes, that all of them—including Brian and Beth, as well as the children—knew how to read as well as add, subtract, divide, and multiply, she neglected to mention that Tristan had been their teacher before Ben took over.

She told him of the necessity of adding onto the house, but omitted the pleasure it had given her; told him of building Brian's home and the second barracks, of adding onto the barn.

There were hundreds of things, small things that made up the fabric of life, that she forgot to tell him. There were incidents that seemed so unimportant at the time that she had forgotten them herself. There were dozens of emotions she did not share with him. She told him all that she did—not so much because she wanted to share, but in order to have something to talk about. She didn't unfold any part of her inner self in the telling. When she related the years' events to him, it was as though she were narrating a documentary.

In all her recitations, she never once discussed Tristan other than as a noble savior or trustworthy business partner. She forgot to mention time spent in Sydney, or the fact that the governor and his wife had been out to the farm, or that she had stayed at Government House with them. She did not tell him of the many bushes and shrubs Tristan had planted, or the fact that the landscaping, which now added greatly to the beauty of the farm, was due to the man who had helped save his life. She did not tell her husband that her heart was in Sydney, with a man who was probably riding around in his carriage—visiting patients, performing operations, delivering babies, staring at death, setting broken bones—that her heart was with a man whose own heart was as fractured as her own.

She did not tell him it was Tristan who had given Jamie and Robbie riding lessons, who had brought Gently to the children, who had made love to her, and whose child she carried.

She only half listened when Chad talked of his years in England, when he tried to describe his loneliness without his family, of the deals he made with the woolen mills, of how he was shown the King's own flock and given twelve of the royal sheep with which to upgrade his already superior breeding program. She paid closer attention when he described Dada's last year, his slow, painful death. She really heard him when he talked of Danny's despair at being blinded in one eye, at his depression and frustration with life. She sat up sharply when he told her how Danny and Tess had fought about this move to the new world. For months Tess had refused to consider the move, even though Danny was set on going.

"Would he have left his children?" Hallie asked.

"I don't know," answered Chad. "Having left mine for five years, I know I would never do it again. Oh, Hallie, how often I asked myself why had I done such a thing! Was money worth giving up my family for? Is getting rich worth not knowing my children as they have begun to grow? They didn't recognize me! Was it worth leaving you? There wasn't a woman in England who could compare with you. I would attend parties and balls at my sisters', when I was in London, and every woman made me think of you. I wanted you, Hallie, I wanted you badly. I shall never leave you again. No matter what."

His hand grazed her breast. Without realizing it, she pulled away from him.

"When I am well, Hallie . . ."

No, she thought. When you are well, we won't. Tristan is the only man I want.

But Chad continued in a different vein. "When I am well, I'll make up to you for all the years you've worked so hard. You won't have to do any more of it. You can concentrate on being a lady. When I invited you to come here, I honestly never dreamed you'd have to do what you've done. I'll try to make it up to you."

"I've enjoyed it." She didn't cry out, I don't *want* to stop it! She was finding it difficult to share with Chad anything about which she felt deeply.

"Send for the children tomorrow, will you?" he asked.

Hallie nodded. "Now it's time for you to go to sleep." She leaned over to blow out the lamp, but Chad reached out and pulled her to him, his lips brushing hers.

"Don't go to Beth's room tonight," he murmured. "Sleep here next to me. I want to feel your warmth beside me. I want to know at last I'm home next to you, where I shall stay from now on. Certainly I'm well enough that you can just sleep in the bed with me."

She blew out the lantern. "All right."

Moonlight flickered through the leaves and shed lacy images on the wall. "Let me watch you undress," he said.

She rushed into her nightgown and slid between the covers. When he reached out and took her hand in his, she did not draw away. Soon, she heard his even breathing. For hours Hallie lay unmoving, staring at the ceiling. When he was better, she would tell him she was pregnant, and that should put off any advances until well after the baby was born.

The baby . . . Tristan's baby. How could he bear this? Was he lying in his bed, twisting the coverlet, agonizing that he was not going to be allowed to father his own child? She turned on her side, away from Chad, her pillow wet with tears.

When the children returned, any quiet that Chad might have enjoyed vanished. Danny's children were younger than Jamie and Alex and ran through the house and jumped noisily on the porch, shouting and shrieking with laughter. Hallie was dismayed to discover that she had trouble liking Tess. Her sister-in-law was pretty enough, in a pale, north England way. Even the months aboard ship had not affected her pallid complexion. She had preferred to stay below deck, fearful that the children would be washed overboard the moment they ascended. She was a worrier. Whenever they were out of sight, she became frantic. She knew they were drowning in the creek, that a horse had stepped on them in the barn. Her worst fear seemed to be that some convict wanted nothing more than to behead them or to rape the little girl. Tess dreamed up atrocities daily. A black man might want to eat them. Blacks and convicts sent the fear of the devil into her. She had seen women accosted in Parramatta and heard lewd catcalls from emancipists.

She stared around her at the wide-open spaces and shivered. "Why, tribes of aborigines or bands of escaped convicts could descend on us and hack us all to death, or kidnap us women and take us back to wherever and do all sorts of awful things to us. I heard that had happened up on the Hawkesbury," she told Sophie, referring to the Hawkesbury River Massacre up near Windsor. Some local men had raped two aborigine women, and the tribe had retaliated by knifing and killing three white women and five children.

There was nobody to talk to, she whined. Hallie had to laugh at that. She thought there were too many people around. It interfered with the work she had to do. Someone was always making a request, asking for something, wanting to stop and chat. No one to talk with? She thought of the years she and Chad had been out here alone, with only each other and Archie to talk with. Danny told her that Tess meant she wished her mother and sisters were here.

Gradually Hallie resumed the schedule she'd kept to for the last few years. She rose at dawn and breakfasted with Beth before setting out to oversee work parties. When Danny realized she was gone by the time he awoke, he forced himself to rise early also and rode out with his sister, wherever she was going. He took to riding with relish, as did Sophie. Though Sophie did not go out with them or spend the day in the saddle, she never failed to take a ride into some new section in the afternoon. Beth warmed to Sophie once she realized Sophie had no desire to displace her in the kitchen. She disliked being with Tess as much as Hallie did, so she usually managed to have Jamie and Alex ready after lunch so they could all join Sophie for a ride.

On Mondays Sophie would walk to the creek with Beth and the children, and while the latter splashed around, she would help Beth with the washing. It was such a different chore here in the clean air and sweet-scented countryside! She enjoyed the smell of clothes dried in sunlight and helped Beth spread the sheets in wide patches on the grass.

Hallie oversaw the harvesting of the hay. She had always enjoyed participating in the event, driving the wagon while the men piled it high with forkfuls. After drying the cut hay, they raked and mounted it into enormous stacks. She had Danny drive the other wagon this year. He was like a child with a new toy. Instead of waiting, as she did, for the hay to be piled high in the wagon, he would jump down and help the men. The entire operation took one week.

Hallie wanted to anticipate the March rains and be secure in the knowledge that all her hay was safely stored in the barns.

Every day she found something in her brother that made her smile at his delight at being here. Danny enjoyed digging in the earth, finding the potatoes hidden there; he rhapsodized when he pulled on green feathery tops and tender carrots broke through the earth. He waxed poetic watching the cabbages grow larger, "sitting there right on the ground, where I can see 'em grow." He picked the tomatoes as though he were tenderly touching a woman.

Beth watched him from the porch. "He looks like a man born to the soil," she commented to Tess, standing nearby.

Tess made no answer.

In the midst of the confusion that still reigned as an aftermath of the arrival of so many people, and of Chad's illness, Ben said to Hallie one night at the dinner table, "May I speak to you private-like after dinner?"

Hallie's stomach twisted into a knot. Something's wrong with our money, she thought. We're in debt, or something bad's happened at the store. She'd hardly had time to talk with Ben, except in dinner-table conversation, for weeks. There was no private place for them to talk, so she suggested they walk down by the creek. Ben was silent for a while, and then he stopped by a big rock. "We can stop here," he said, sitting on it.

"What's wrong?" asked Hallie, thinking, Let's get it over with.

"I know I've got three more years to serve." He wasn't looking at her, but reached down to pluck a spear of grass and put it between his teeth. "I'd like your permission to get married," he said.

Hallie tried not to laugh out loud, not knowing whether it was from relief or because she simply couldn't imagine Ben married. He seemed such an isolate, despite the fact that he was always surrounding himself with people.

"There's those two rooms in back of the store," he went on, gazing across the creek into the trees. "I've never used them, you know. We could live there. I mean, I'd still like to eat up here with you all, but . . ." He was having a great deal of trouble.

"Do you have someone in mind?" Hallie tried not to let her amusement be reflected in her voice.

He shot her a look. "I thought you'd know by now. I'd like your permission to ask for Beth's hand."

Hallie wished *she* had a seat to sink onto.

"She's seemed to favor me ever since Jamie and I . . ."

Hallie was astounded. "I didn't know you two had even exchanged two words away from the house."

"Well, we haven't exactly. I'd like some children, a family. Beth's a born mother. We been enjoying each other's company for years. She's a good cook. Besides, she's just what a woman ought to be."

What ought a woman to be? Hallie wondered. Did Ben have any idea that Beth was a murderer, that she had been seduced and raped and burned? "Have you talked with Beth about this?" she asked.

Ben shook his head. "Thought I ought to ask your permission first."

"Do you know how she feels about men?"

Ben looked at her questioningly.

"I have to tell you, I don't think you have much chance. But certainly, if you need my permission, you have it."

"Why don't she like men?" Ben asked, puzzled.

"It's not for me to say. But she once told me"—Hallie wondered how she could prepare Ben without giving Beth away—"that she'd never marry."

"Will you ask her for me?" His voice was low, and he couldn't look at her.

"Me? Why don't you ask her yourself?"

"I don't know how to." Now he looked up at her with pleading eyes. "Please."

It was the first time Hallie had ever felt like putting her arms around Ben, yet she refrained. He had saved her son's life; he kept her accounts with honesty and accuracy; he dined with them every night of his life, and neither added to nor detracted from the evening meal. Once in a while he contributed to the conversation, though he was usually silent, smoking his pipe. He told her when valley people moved in, when they needed credit, when they expected babies. Harry respected him enormously. Yet Ben lacked the kind of warmth that would have endeared him to her. Hallie suspected she needed him more than she knew, but he sometimes seemed bloodless, as though passion were alien to his veins, as though he would go through life doing what he did but without a pulse.

Hallie couldn't imagine any woman really desiring him. She almost laughed when she tried to picture him in bed with a woman. She wondered if he'd ever had a woman, ever made love with gusto or with feeling of any kind.

"Yes," she said after a moment, "I'll speak to her. But I wouldn't get my hopes up, if I were you."

When she did broach the subject, Beth was rolling out bread dough. Flour was spattered over her apron and white powder smudged her cheek. Trying to look at her through a man's eyes, Hallie decided she looked quite adorable—just like a woman ought to look, doing what a woman should be doing.

"Beth . . ." Hallie was not going to beat around the bush. "Ben talked to me last night. He'd like to marry you."

The rolling pin clattered to the floor. Beth stood with her hands on the table for a minute, then leaned over and picked up the utensil. She wiped it off and slowly, methodically, began to roll out the bread.

"He said he thought you'd favored him since he saved Jamie," Hallie continued.

Beth said nothing for a few minutes, merely concentrated on her dough. She folded it over, plumped it into four pans. These she covered with a towel and put on a sunny shelf.

"It's true: he saved Jamie's life. I can never thank him enough for that. And he's a nice person. Maybe that's why I can like him." She looked over at Hallie. "But I never think of him as a man."

Hallie knew what she meant. "He says he thinks you're what a woman ought to be." She leaned back against the wall and waited.

Beth glanced at Hallie, her brow furrowing. "Ben doesn't *know* me. He doesn't understand what beats beneath the surface. He doesn't know the hate and passion that's made me who I am. Once in a while, it's true, I forget. I'm so happy here, and the men here have all been nice. I can relax and not be scared. But I can never get married, Hallie. I couldn't go to bed with a man! I'm afraid I'd kill him if he tried . . ." She paused, and took a kettle down from a shelf. "Ben likes me for the wrong reasons. He sees me as a quiet, even-tempered woman who goes about the household chores like wives should. And I love every minute of it. I like cooking, and I love taking care of Jamie and Alex, and I do little things like wait dinner for him because he saved Jamie. But I'm not going to marry anybody. No man's ever going to touch me again."

Hallie nodded. "I thought you'd feel that way. I'll tell him."

"You won't tell him why, will you?"

Hallie was hurt. "Do you think I'd ever tell *anyone*?"

"Not even Chad?"

Hallie walked over and put her arms around Beth. "I have no need or desire to tell anyone. You are my dear, dear friend. You must know that, must know how much I love you."

"I did."

Hallie backed away. "What does that mean?"

"Oh, I don't know. Nothing seems the same since your husband came home."

Hallie sighed. "I know."

"What are you going to do about Dr. Faulkner?"

Hallie hesitated. They had never discussed Tristan, but . . . perhaps, if she shared her most secret self with Beth, they would be even, tied together. "I'm going to bear his child," she said softly. A part of her felt freed to have said it aloud.

Beth's mouth opened, and her hand went to her throat. "Oh, dear God," she whispered.

Hallie turned and left the kitchen. Later, when she told Ben what Beth had said, he nodded as though not surprised and replied, "I'll wait. I have all the time in the world. But the seed's been planted."

Thirty-nine

In another two weeks Chad was well enough to be out of bed, but not strong enough to work. He spent his time sitting on the porch, watching the March rains, absorbing the land he had been gone from for so long. Sophie usually kept him company, while Hallie attended to the chores that needed to be overseen. Emil and Danny took to each other; it became Emil's custom to ride down to the barn when he was ready to set out in the morning and collect Danny, who would be waiting, his horse saddled. Danny seemed to have little trouble understanding the thick accent of the German vintner and was thrilled to be out in the fields working with his hands.

Tess, on the other hand, never seemed to accomplish anything other than yelling at the children. Her admonishments fell upon deaf ears, but she was satisfied that as long as she had told them not to do something, her job was finished. She never reinforced any of her threats and never volunteered to help wash the clothes with Beth and Sophie. In fact, she never offered to help do anything. But she seldom sat; she paced around constantly, although she rarely left the house. When the women and Jamie and Alex would go to the creek to bathe, she resisted, saying, "It's too cold." She also thought too much bathing could lead to pneumonia.

Hallie wanted to welcome Danny's family with open arms, build them a house, include them in her life, but she soon found herself—as did everyone else—ignoring Tess. The woman chattered constantly, until her voice faded into the background, and no one heard what she said or paid any attention to her. When Sophie and Chad sat on the porch talking in the afternoons, Tess would sometimes barge in on their conversation. They would try to listen, but Tess droned on and on, so they soon continued their talk, and gradually Tess disappeared.

Her conversation was always the same. How could anyone live in the country, so far from other people? All this open space might be fine for the aborigines, but civilized people lived in cities. She missed gossiping with her mother and sisters. She did not write them letters. With an odd sort of pride, she claimed to have no desire to read, repeating her father's homily, "Women weren't meant to read and write. The more they learn, the bigger their brain becomes, the smaller the uterus." Tess knew that her role was to have many children, and she didn't want any written words coming between her and her destiny.

She wanted badly to have another child. But after a day spent in hard work outdoors, Danny was asleep before she even crawled between the covers.

It was three weeks before Tristan rode out again. He pronounced the obvious—that Chad was recuperating nicely—but added that Chad's lungs had been injured and that he should not take on any physical work for several months.

Disappointed, Chad said, "I hope you'll stay overnight, riding this far."

Tristan raised an eyebrow and glanced at Hallie. She felt her face redden.

"Of course," he said. "I always stay overnight when I come."

Chad looked from Tristan to Hallie, a shadow passing over his eyes. Then he smiled.

Tristan stayed not just overnight, but for two nights. He spent most of the time talking with Chad, while Hallie attended to work. She could not leave Chad's bed at night as she had when she was sleeping with Beth. But she lay awake the entire time, her whole being straining, wanting to run out to Tristan, wondering if he were lying awake in the barn, staring into nothingness.

Her few moments alone with him came the morning he was to leave. Dawn streaked the sky when Hallie slid out of bed, trying not to disturb Chad. Dressing in the pearlescent semidarkness, holding her shoes in her hand, she tiptoed out the French doors and ran through the field to the barn. Tristan was just awakening.

"It's torture," she whispered, running to him and kneeling beside his bed. "I can't bear not reaching out to touch you. I can't stand looking at you as though you're—you're not a part of me."

He gathered her in his arms and kissed her. Then he said, "We cannot continue this way. There is such a thing as honor. I will not go around kissing another man's wife when he's right here."

Hallie stared at him. "I'm the mother of your child! I can't let you go this easily. I can't let you go at all! We're part of each other."

He held her close, the beat of his heart pulsing in her ear. "Have you told him yet?"

"No." She shook her head, her hair flying in the air.

He put his hand under her chin and looked at her. "You'll have to. And soon."

"I know. He's getting better and will want to—want to—you know. When I tell him I'm pregnant, that will stop *that*."

Tristan raised her face. "What does pregnancy have to do with *that*?"

She looked at him, bewildered. "I don't want to abort it. I was afraid, the night he came home—that's the only time we did it," she said, as though trying to prove her faithfulness. "I thought then it might kill the baby."

"Hallie, making love has nothing to do with aborting a fetus. Unless it's painful or results in some bleeding, which is only likely to occur with some women in the last trimester, there is nothing to deter . . ."

She was silent a moment, absorbing his words. Then: "Don't let Chad know. He's the one who told me that. I don't want him near me. I don't want him to make love to me."

"It pains me to think of you in bed with him, of his touching you. I wake up in the middle of night in a cold sweat, and I have nightmares of you in his arms. I won't tell him. I don't want him touching you, either."

They clung together for a few minutes, lost to one another in the midst of their pain. Then Tristan said, "But try as I might, I can't dislike him. In fact, as we sat talking, I found myself liking him tremendously. Under other conditions, I would find him a most attractive friend. He has a joie de vivre, an energy even when ill, that shines through. He's an exciting man, Hallie. He was telling me of the mansion he wants to build, of the scientific breeding program he's going to start, of breeding horses not only to sell, but to race."

Hallie stared at him and let go of his hand. Chad had not mentioned all this to her. A mansion . . . ?

"He wants the world to know that Australia is not just a cesspool of the dregs of humanity, but a country to be reckoned with, one with an unlimited future. It didn't seem to matter to him that I'm an ex-convict."

Her eyes reflected puzzlement. "Why did you tell him?"

"I don't know. Does it embarrass you?" It was an accusation.

"Of course not," she said fiercely. "It makes me love you all the more." And then she said, putting her hand on his knee, "Are you really not going to kiss me anymore?"

"Hallie, what would happen if anybody saw us?" he asked, as though imploring her to understand. "What kind of man would I be to seduce another man's wife?"

"We've already done that," she threw at him.

"For God's sake those were not the same circumstances! You know that." Anguish was evident in his voice.

Of course she knew it, but the thought of never being touched again by Tristan was more than she could bear. She stood up and began to unbutton her dress, and Tristan did not stop her. "One last time," she pleaded. "Make love to me one last time. Let me savor every moment so that I can live and relive it over and over again, so I can feel your breath, remember your lips on me, the touch of your hands . . ."

"Oh, God, Hallie!" He reached for her.

Afterward he said, "My love . . . my one true love. I don't know what's going to become of us." Then he dressed quickly, looked in on Chad for a moment, accepted cold biscuits from Beth, and rode off.

After she had watched him disappear around the bend of the hill, Hallie walked back to Chad. "I've thought so for a while, but Tristan just confirmed it. I'm pregnant."

Chad's eyes brightened. "We didn't waste any time, did we?" He reached out for her hand. "After all the years I wanted to get back to you! I've lain here next to you at

403

night and could hardly control myself with desire. I thought I knew the first thing I wanted once I was well. I have fought down my longing, knowing that I should not expend energy; I have yearned for your body, and now I shall be denied it for nearly a year." His laugh had a brittleness to it. "Oh, Hallie, I don't know if I can bear it."

Was it she or Tristan who had just said the same thing? "I thought you'd be happy. On the way to your dynasty." Her voice was flat.

He looked at her. "Of course I'm happy. It's what I want above all else. But there's an irony attached to it." His smile was wistful.

Over the next few months, Hallie thought the farm was the colony's center of social life. They had a steady stream of visitors. Neighbors who had never called before rode over to chat. Governor Macquarie rode out with an entourage, although without his wife. He had heard that Chad was home and knew of his illness. He intended to stay overnight and of course was invited to do so. The men who accompanied him slept outdoors in equipment they'd brought along, but the governor slept in Sophie's bed, for she had volunteered to sleep on the sofa.

When the governor commented on the smithy and pub alongside the store, Hallie said, "It's going to be a town someday. It already has a name." The governor cocked an eyebrow, and she smiled. "Morgantown."

"That sounds reasonable," he murmured.

Chad gazed at her and reached out, bringing her hand to his lips in an unaccustomed public display of affection.

"This wife of yours," declared the governor, "outshines any woman I've ever known."

"All the years in England," Chad said, "and all the months coming back on the ship, I had a dream. I was going to own more land and more sheep than anyone could imagine. And I came home to find I already owned more than double what I'd imagined."

The governor laughed. "Your wife's quite a woman!"

When Harry and Susan came to visit a few days later, Hallie said to her friend, "I never dreamed a four-bedroom house wouldn't be large enough!"

While Harry spent hours sitting on the porch with Chad, discussing with him the state of his finances and holdings—all of which impressed and amazed Chad—Susan and Hallie took a long ride up the river.

"I think of you so often," said Susan. "How are you handling all this, my darling? Sometimes I find myself weeping, knowing of all that rests on your shoulders." She stared out at the ribbon of blue shimmering in the distance.

"I haven't seen Tristan smile once in all these weeks," she continued after a moment. "He doesn't accept dinner invitations, not only to our home but to anyone's, from all I hear. He has disappeared from the social life of Sydney. You must be torn."

"I am," Hallie said, her voice hollow. "I tell myself there are too many things to do to think about it, but at night . . ."

"Yes, what about night?" her friend prompted her.

"Oh, Susan, sometimes it's all I can do to be pleasant to Chad. But other times, he's—he's really so nice."

Susan laughed. "Of all the words one could apply to Chad, 'nice' seems the most bland."

Hallie nudged her horse and they began to trot. "You haven't been around him in his weakened condition. But I suppose even then his dreams fill him with energy. His mind is never still. Even from bed he has ideas that Brian and the men begin. He's itching to get out to the barn with his new sheep. He sits on the porch with paper and pencil and plots a breeding program. He also wants to raise racehorses that will win at Hyde Park; he wants to start racecourses in every small town. He wants his horses and sheep all over the colony, wants people to come from far and near to buy them. He wants to build a mansion on a hill overlooking the river, one that will never fear flood, one that has a dozen bedrooms. . . . Can you believe it?"

"Chad has never thought small," Susan said as their horses slowed.

"I thought the additions to this house were more than enough, that it was more luxurious than anything I'd ever dreamed of, and now I find it crowded."

"Well, when Danny and his family have a place of their own, you'll have more room." Hallie was about to start the men building a house for her brother and his family.

"True. But just one bedroom more. And when the children grow, Chad thinks they should each have a room of their own. And who knows how many children there will be. I'm pregnant; can you tell?"

Susan tried to look deep into her friend's eyes. "How do you feel about that?"

Hallie sighed. "I wish I knew."

"When is it due?"

Hallie hesitated and wondered if Susan had already guessed. "Nine months from the night he returned."

"The end of October, then. Oh, Hallie, I've always thought having babies was the most wonderful thing in the world, not just because I love my children so, but as a reflection of how Harry and I feel about each other." They were silent for a while, listening to the water rushing by, the river swollen by the autumn rains. "This, too, shall pass. You'll love the child, and it will bind you closer to Chad."

Suddenly Hallie began to cry. They had been sitting on their horses, by the side of the river, surrounded by sheep and last spring's lambs munching grass contentedly.

Susan moved her horse closer to Hallie and reached out for her hand. "Hallie, I've never had a friend I loved more. I hurt when you hurt. I hurt when I imagine you're hurting. I don't know how I'd deal—or if I'd even be able to deal—with the dilemma you're caught in. But, somehow, life goes on. If Chad were not as 'nice' . . . but he's wonderful, Hallie. Before he left I always saw him as one of those larger-than-life men, men who made their dreams realities. Also, he's the best-looking man I've ever seen, and that includes Harry and Tristan."

Despite herself, Hallie had to smile. Tristan, indeed, was beautiful to behold, but Harry—by no stretch of the imagination—could even be considered very good-looking. He had a marvelous, solid face to which his oversize rusty mustache lent a rakish air . . . but handsome, never.

"I don't know that looks have anything to do with the person inside," Hallie murmured, thinking of Tristan.

"I agree. Maybe it's not just his looks, but when Chad's in a room, he's the center of attention."

"And"—it was as though Hallie were trying to convince herself—"he's so remarkably kind. He brought Mum and Danny not only for their sakes, but because he knew it

406

would please me. I tell myself I was happy with him before. I know all the good things about Chad, but I have to remind myself of them daily. Because a great part of me resents . . ."

Susan squeezed Hallie's hand. "I know. But you have to surmount that. The happiness of too many people depends on you."

"But what about me? What about my happiness?" Hallie's pained voice mirrored her feelings.

"Hallie, look at me. Happiness is not what life is all about." Susan tightened her grasp on Hallie's fingers. "We have larger duties in life than concern for our own happiness. I know, I know, I'm a fine one to talk. I live inundated with happiness every day of my life." She hesitated and pulled on Hallie's hand so Hallie had to look at her. "But that doesn't mean I can't understand beyond myself. If Chad beat you, or was unkind, or ignored you, or was even just deadly boring, I might not give you this unasked-for advice. But Chad is—is all sorts of wonderful things, and he loves you, too. Remember that."

Hallie freed herself from Susan's grasp and shook her head. "First of all, Chad does not love me. I know he likes me. I even think he respects me." Now, anyhow, she thought. Now that I've done a man's work. "Love had nothing to do with our marriage, you know. We both entered it knowing what to expect." She paused, gazing out over the land. "He wanted someone who didn't mind hard work, who would mother a large brood of children, someone he enjoyed looking at." With pleading eyes, she turned to Susan. "But he has never shared himself with me as Tristan does. He never spent hours talking over future plans with me as he did with Archie. For heaven's sake, he never even told me he was going away! Everyone else in the colony knew it before I did." Her voice grew hard. "Chad has never looked below the surface, never asked me how I feel about anything, never asked my opinion about his ideas, never done anything but admire my looks. I doubt that he sees the real me. Or even knows there's more to me than what he sees."

Susan cocked her head to one side and studied her friend, though she didn't respond. They sat in silence, holding hands. Then Susan leaned over and put an arm around Hallie, an awkward position across the horses. Hallie turned and kissed her cheek.

In that moment she almost told Susan the baby was Tristan's.

"Whether he knows it or not, Chad loves you," Susan said softly. "He lights up when you enter a room. I suspect he's having a hard time now. He—the man who has always been in command—is being waited on." When Hallie didn't respond, she continued, "He's come home to find his wife has exceeded the dreams he's had for himself. He's come home to children who do not know him, to a household and farm that run well without him. I think all of this must be more than his self-respect bargained for. Before he left, his world centered around him. Now, he discovers that in his world he is but peripheral."

"What does that mean?"

"He's not necessary," Susan explained. "He's a spoke, but not the center of the wheel. Men's images of themselves are far more fragile than ours, Hallie, so I suspect Chad is having a hard time with these thoughts he never shares with you. You're the core—not only of his life, but of the lives of everyone on the farm. It all revolves around you." Her horse started walking, and she turned it around so she was facing Hallie. "I imagine he tells himself he's to blame for leaving. Had he not gone to England, of course, he might never have been able to get the prices for wool that the mills have promised, might never have given us the chance of being put on the map. But he was caught in a web of duty, too. His father—your family. He put duty before happiness, my dear."

Hallie let this all sink in before saying, "Susan, never stop being my friend, will you? I need you."

Susan laughed. "I'm flattered. When everyone else needs you, you need me."

"No one ever told me that friendship is one of the most important treasures of life."

Susan smiled. "I suspect friendship like ours is beyond measure, Hallie."

Forty

In the ensuing months Chad recovered, but slowly. His irritation showed now and then, though most of the time he kept it under control. He was not a man used to being waited upon, nor a man used to waiting. At times Hallie found herself the brunt of his anger at his inability to function and to lead. Chad did not take graciously to inactivity.

He often sat with a sheaf of paper and drew diagrams, plans for his proposed mansion. "Bigger than anything in this country," he said. "Something even England will envy." Hallie did not ask how England would envy it half a world away. If it amused him to draw pictures, and it kept him from irritability, that was all right with her. Her more immediate problem was deciding where to build a house for Danny and Tess.

"Beyond the barn," Chad said as if the solution were obvious.

"That's fine for now," Hallie replied, "but what good will that be when you build this fine new home you're planning, over by the river?"

"I don't want to see any other houses from there."

"They might as well live in this one, then." When they talked together, their voices often took on an edge of friction.

Chad glared at her. "For God's sake, Hallie! Get that woman," he meant Tess, "out from under us." He tapped on his drawing paper. "I won't have this place finished for over a year, maybe more. I certainly can't stand her here that much longer."

On this point Hallie agreed. "Why don't you draw a plan for them, then, something that can be started immediately?" she suggested.

"All right," he said, and as he looked at her, one eyebrow arched sardonically. "Except you're so good at getting things done . . ."

She walked out of the room before he finished his sentence.

Danny did not have Hallie's ability or penchant for seeing what needed to be done, and was content to be Emil's aide, learning all he could about the day-to-day operations. It would be another year before the vines began to produce quality wine grapes.

"I suspect every year in this climate will be a vintage year," Emil told him. "We have here all the conditions necessary for good vintage—spring rains for bud burst and shoot growth. Every year I have been here, so have the right amount of spring rains. There is hardly ever the heavy summer rain that sometimes plagues the Loire and Rhine valleys and encourages mold and fungi. Here it is *always* moderate." He smiled happily, showing a gap where he'd lost a tooth.

"It is always been dry in the summer. You never know in Europe if wet conditions and excessive heat in September will upset the sugar and acid levels. We are truly blessed here."

So he and Danny planted yet more vines that year, and pruned them to run along the stakes, reaching sunward. Danny spent weeks helping the convicts dig trenches three feet wide by the same depth, preparing the soil, breaking and loosening it, loving the hard physical work that returned muscles to his arms and gave spirit to his soul.

Tess, however, never stopped fretting. Having a house of her own would be good for her, Hallie thought. She would be forced to clean and do the cooking. Here she left belongings strewn around, and it was Beth or Sophie who picked up whatever clutter she left behind her. Her children, once given free rein to run with Jamie and Alex, stopped whining and became rather likeable. Hallie had to admit that Danny wasn't much of a father. He seemed to think his business was all outdoors and that it was Tess's province to raise the children.

Sometimes she heard Chad talking with the children and telling them stories, and once she even heard him singing softly to them. At such times she hated herself for resenting his homecoming.

Sophie and Beth rode off in the afternoons, often just the two of them, and Hallie never knew where they went.

They had become friends, for the only time Sophie barged into Beth's kitchen was to make cakes, and then she asked permission. "I've no desire to spend the rest of my life in a kitchen," she said once, "but I never had enough eggs or milk to throw caution to the wind and bake cakes. I always wanted to, though." After that they had cakes at least twice a week.

Hallie was also surprised to see her mother sit still without putting her hands to some task or doing something constructive. Sophie sat for hours and talked with Chad, gazing out over the land with contentment. She loved the perpetual sunshine and all the flowers that surrounded them. Hallie showed her how to prune the roses, and Sophie told her she was looking forward to planting flower seeds, something she'd never done before. The only time they'd seen flowers in Newcastle was at the park in spring or summer.

Her mother did not engage in the twice-weekly evening classes that Ben still conducted, but she observed. And her observations were more human than cerebral. She particularly responded to Robbie, who was a handsome lad, looking so like his father one knew in a minute what their relationship was. The black Irish. Black hair, luxuriant and wavy, always falling over his forehead. Black eyes like the coals of Newcastle, with warmth and humor that animated his face; lips that smiled easily—"ones," said Sophie, much to Hallie's amazement, "that'll drive the girls crazy before too long." His stockiness gave way to an easy feline grace as he shot up almost six inches in that year when he turned thirteen. His quick mind and his willingness to work hard made him popular not only with Sophie, but with everyone.

Though his interests were no longer the same as Jamie's and Alex's, he was consistently kind to them and included them in activities he knew would give them pleasure. Ben told him he could be an accountant, so quick was he with math, but Robbie laughed derisively. Not for him the indoor life.

Tristan traveled out monthly, ostensibly to check on Chad's recuperation. He and Hallie stole quick looks at each other when they were sure no one was looking, and managed to brush against each other in passing. But Hallie

411

did not go out to the barn at night, even though she lay awake for hours, all too aware of his nearness.

Tristan spent a great deal of time talking with Chad, who would deny him nothing. Tristan had saved not only his life, but that of his son and his wife's, twice. Tristan took the children riding, one time suggesting that it was time for Alex to have a horse rather than ride in the saddle in front of him. Chad never evidenced any apparent resentment at Tristan's easy familiarity with the children, nor of Jamie's obvious hero worship. Yet he'd watch them with a strange look in his eyes as they'd disappear on their horses.

Tristan seldom laughed; his eyes were masked. There was a formality to him that Hallie had never seen, even in Sydney. She wondered if knowing of his anguish was what exhausted her all the time. As Chad gained strength, she seemed to lose hers. Everything was a chore. She no longer went riding off to help with the outdoor work. She felt ponderous and uncomfortable and couldn't remember if she had been this big in previous pregnancies. Her breathing came harder, and she had to get up in the middle of the night with cramps in her calves. Walking around the room cured the leg pains, but by then she'd be wide awake and stand staring out into the starry night sky.

This awakened Chad, always a light sleeper, and he would lie still, watching her movements in the darkness. The nights were too cool for the windows to remain open, but Hallie would stare out just the same, sighing. Most nights he just watched her and then lay awake long after she had fallen asleep again. But once he reached out, asking, "What is it?"

"Nothing. My legs hurt."

He understood that was the reason she walked around the room, stretching her calves, but he knew it was not the reason she stood staring out into the darkness, sighing. When she slipped back into bed, he moved onto his side and, leaning on his elbow, said, "Is it because you have all of us on your conscience? It won't be much longer, you know, before I can take over again. Before you can relax and do nothing more than be a mother."

Hallie lay there, her body rigid. Talk like this only intensified her frustration. She wanted to scream at him.

But he did not leave her alone. He ran his fingers

through the hair that tumbled about her shoulders, rubbing his face in it, kissing her shoulder. "You never wrote and told me of all you took upon yourself. No wife could be better, Hallie. When I sent for you, I only remembered you were pretty and hated Newcastle, and had a yearning for excitement . . ."

"And that I would be willing to work hard and mother your dynasty!"

He either did not hear or chose to ignore the tone of her voice. "That, too. But I had no idea how fortunate I'd be. I don't know any woman of your calibre, Hallie. I'm aware you've done too much, that you've had to go beyond your role in life, and for this I'm eternally grateful. I shall pay you back, my dear."

He raised her hand to his lips and kissed her fingers, then the palm of her hand. "Oh, God, Hallie, you torment me! I want nothing more at this moment—and so often when I look at you—than to experience the wildness we used to know, to touch you and feel your body against mine, to kiss you places where only I have been. . . ."

There's no part of me like that, she thought. Every place you have touched, Tristan has touched. Every place you have kissed, Tristan has kissed.

"I want to damn fertility," he went on, his voice a whisper. "Every goddamn time I have you, you become pregnant. It shouldn't have to result in that every time. God knows, it doesn't with every woman. I want a year—a whole year—of being able to make love to you whenever I want, of feeling the silkiness of your body against mine, of being able to fulfill this terrible yearning within me when I am with you."

He leaned against her and kissed her, something he ordinarily did only when he was going to make love to her. Don't let him, she thought. My body is too big, too swollen. I don't want him. Don't let him know it would not hurt the baby—maybe it would, it's just two months until it's due, though he thinks three. Dear God, if you're there, don't let him do it.

Chad's lips were soft against hers; his tongue brushed her lips, gently forced them open. When she made no response, he pulled back. "I just want to kiss you," he said, "touch you. I'm not going . . . any further." But still she could not respond.

When he lay back on his pillow he threw an arm across her and she felt imprisoned. Suddenly the baby kicked. Her hand touched her belly, and Chad's covered hers. They lay there like that for a long time. "I feel it kicking, too," he said, his voice drowsy.

When Danny's house was finished, it wasn't possible to tell whether he was prouder to have a house of his own or the others were more thrilled to be rid of Tess.

When Chad had asked Tess if there were anything in particular she wanted, she just said, "People. I don't want a house out here."

Sophie couldn't believe that even in late winter the noon temperature would reach the seventies. "Flowers bloom year round," she marveled. She did not push herself on Jamie and Alex, and consequently they took to her more quickly than they did to Chad. They still acted shy around him, not responding with the enthusiastic abandon they showed Tristan.

Hallie sometimes worried that Jamie and Alex were too perfect. They never fought. Once in a while they spoke sharply to each other, and now and then Jamie purposely escaped from his sister, but they were obedient, mainly because so few restrictions were put on them. They had grown up being constantly hugged and loved by Hallie and Beth. One or the other of the women was always there to respond to either child's current need. They were permitted and encouraged to help with chores, though it was not demanded. They thought that laying the sheets and washed clothes on the grass was a game. They were encouraged in their freedom, given free rein to run in the woods or play in the barn, and they seldom tested Hallie or Beth. There was laughter at the dinner table, and lessons that were like games after dinner. In the last year Alex had joined the evening class, although she quickly felt discouraged because everyone was so far ahead of her.

They never talked back to Beth or Hallie. They would wander up to the barracks and talk with the convicts, and Hallie never stopped them from doing that. The convicts

414

spoiled them to pieces, taking them for rides or playing horseshoes with them, even though Alex could scarcely lift the horseshoes. They showed Sophie how to gather eggs, and it was a game the three of them participated in.

Alex helped Sophie plant seeds when the time came, and Sophie swore "she never lost one of them." Alex was in love with everything alive. Her particular penchants were birds and plants, and before she was six, she could mimic most of the birdcalls. She wanted to ride, but there were always people who delighted in hiking her up on the saddle in front of them, so it was not until Tristan suggested she have a horse of her own that she began to learn to ride in earnest. Horses, the dog, any animal—wild or domestic—Alex loved.

Jamie was a dreamer. He would lie in the field afternoons, his hands tucked under his head, and stare at the sky, his eyes following a cloud when it skimmed along. Flamboyant sunsets enraptured him. He refused to turn his attention to anything else when the sky was a palette of fiery colors. And though he, too, loved any and all animals, it was books that captured him. Everytime Tristan came, he brought Jamie new books. If he had been permitted to, Jamie would have eaten with a book in his left hand. Already he had announced his intention to be a doctor.

When Hallie mentioned this to Chad, he responded, "But he's the oldest. He's going to run this farm. That's why I moved here."

Hallie looked at him. "Isn't that why your father had the coal mine? To leave to his sons? To bind them to his dream?"

Chad gave her a sharp look, but said nothing for a long time. Then he said, "You're right. None of them has to farm. They can all do what they want, spreading their influence over the colony. Jamie doesn't have to stay on the land." He thought to himself, But he would have if I'd been here. It's my fault.

Yet while he considered his distance from his children and wife his fault, he knew that had he not spent those years in England solidifying relationships with the mills, had he not lobbied for Australian wool, this country would not be getting the prices for its fleece that it was now able to ask. He knew that Sophie and Danny would not be here.

He knew that his conscience would not be free with respect to his father. Yet still he was sorry he had gone. He knew that he would be forever denied parts of his family because of that trip. He would make it up, he vowed, to the rest of his children.

It was not that he didn't love Jamie and Alex; it was simply that they treated him like a stranger. They were invariably polite. They kissed his cheek good night. They loved listening to the stories he told them. They delighted in locating the stars he pointed out. But there was a reserve that they didn't show even to the convicts.

At dinner one night in mid-September Ben announced, "Coltons' new baby died."

Hallie was startled. She'd been so caught up in the vicissitudes of her own life that she had not thought of her neighbors in a long time. She now realized that Etta was supposed to have had her baby back in July.

"Two months old and died."

"Oh, dear," said Hallie. "Do you know how Etta's taking it?"

Ben shook his head. "Little girl. Heard it from Will. I haven't seen Etta in months—many months. Not since you were out there last spring, maybe."

Well, she couldn't ride over now; she knew that her own baby would come soon. She was so big that it might come any time. When Chad teased her about her size, Sophie said, "Wouldn't surprise me at all if it's twins. I was that big with you and Danny. Came early, too."

Twins? Why had she never considered that? Even Tristan had not voiced any suspicion of it. She wanted Tristan to deliver his baby—or babies. Yet how could she provide for that? Sophie had delivered at least a dozen babies. Even Chad had delivered Jamie and Alex. What reason could she give for wanting a doctor? The next time Tristan came out, she found time alone with him.

"It's due any time from—"

"I know when it's due!" His voice was sharp. When he saw the look in her eyes, he put a hand on her arm. "I'm sorry. I know this is difficult for you, too."

"Difficult for me, too! Oh, Tristan, do you know what these last eight months have been like!"

"I know too well what they've been. But perhaps I've

416

been so busy being sorry for myself that I haven't considered how difficult it's been for you. I've thought you were out here with everything . . . when I'm here you never seem unhappy, but are surrounded with people who love you, with your children, with—"

She threw her arms around him. "Oh, Tris." She had never called him that before. "I ache for us. For you. For our love. I know it must be harder for you than it is for me, but Tristan—oh, God, how I love you, how I wonder whether this whole thing is driving me crazy! I don't seem to function anymore. I'm tired all the time, my legs ache, I have indigestion, I can't sleep for thinking of you. Sometimes I think I'm going mad!"

He held her close and stroked her hair. "Darling. My darling . . ."

She looked up at him. "Mum thinks it's twins."

"I've already considered that," he admitted. "It would explain so much. Your lethargy, your size . . ."

"Tris . . . I want you to deliver our children."

"Of course," he said, his voice soft.

"But I don't know how to manage it. No one in Newcastle had doctors. With Mum and Chad here . . . I'm sure I'll give birth a month early. What shall we do? I want so much for you to bring them into the world."

"At the first sign of labor, send for me," he said. "I'll come immediately."

So when Hallie awoke two weeks later near dawn, feeling the first faint pains of labor, she lay still, listening to the birds presaging the break of day. She lay, her hand on her belly, knowing that today would be the day. Probably not until nightfall, she decided, remembering what the others had been like. Not time, really, for Tristan to arrive and deliver them himself. But her water had not yet broken, and she was filled with an energy she hadn't felt in days, weeks. Perhaps there would just be time. If she sent Robbie to town, if she admonished him to ride as hard as he could, maybe Tristan could arrive by midnight.

She stared out the window as the sky lightened. Beyond the treetops, to the east, she knew a thin red line would trace the horizon and soon burst into shades of pink and red, vibrant and alive. Beside her, Chad stirred, and she felt pangs of guilt.

But she would not let that bother her now. There were things to do. She tried to creep out of bed, but her movements awoke Chad. "What's wrong?" he murmured, his words slurred with sleep.

"I think I should send for Tristan," she whispered.

He sat bolt upright. "But it can't happen now! It's not time."

"I can't help it," she said, and he didn't question her. "Send Robbie," she continued. "Tell him to ride hard and have Tristan come back right away. It's early, so perhaps it is twins, as my mother guessed." That should allay any suspicions.

All day the energy she felt swept her along. She, who never scrubbed floors, took to scrubbing the porch, singing as she worked. Chad did not go out to the fields, but stayed near the house, finding work to do in the barn or within shouting distance.

Her water broke in mid-afternoon and the pains began in earnest shortly afterward. No, she thought. I won't let it happen until he's here. Until he can deliver his own babies. But the pains became so sharp that she had to take to bed.

Sophie smiled and held Hallie's hand. "When you took off for here, I was sure I'd never be around to deliver any of yours. What a happy time for me."

Just then Chad entered the bedroom, his sleeves rolled up, drying his hands on a towel. "I've just scrubbed up. I'm ready when you are."

Sophie gave him a stern look. "This isn't any place for a man."

"You forget, I delivered Jamie and Alex. I intend to at least assist in this delivery. I want to help bring all my children into the world," he said.

"It's not fittin'," Sophie muttered.

Laughing, he put a hand on her shoulder. "Not much is fitting in this country. Hallie, tell her. Tell her I'm an excellent midwife." He walked over and sat beside her on the bed, wiping the perspiration from her brow with the towel. Then he leaned down to kiss her forehead. "Of course I'm going to be here with Hallie."

She looked up at him, clenching her teeth as a pain seared through her. "My branch," she said without thinking. Her thoughts were centered on holding out until Tristan arrived.

Chad's hand held tight onto hers. He remembered, too.

Sophie shook her head in disapproval. "Birthing isn't a man's business."

Chad glanced at her over his shoulder. "Birthing is every bit as much a man's business as a woman's. Let's have no more about it, Sophie. I'm staying. And I'm helping."

At that moment Hallie let out a moan. "Oh, God," she said. "I can't hold out, I know it."

Chad fell to his knees, his face beside hers. "Darling, there's no reason to hold out. We're here, your mother and I. We'll take care of you. I promise." He rose and strode to the living room, where he found the whiskey decanter. He poured himself a drink before taking one in to Hallie.

"Drink this," he said, holding out the glass.

He sat her up and forced the amber liquid down her throat. For a moment she looked at him and thought, Oh, dear God, Chad, how can I do this to you? Then all she saw was black, and she recognized the voice that screamed as her own.

"The head's in place. I see fuzz. . . . Hallie"—Sophie raised her voice—"push hard."

Hallie breathed deeply. She heard her mother saying, "I'll turn the shoulder now that the head is out—isn't it a beauty. Be ready, Chad, I'll have to hand it to you so I can be ready . . . I'm sure there's another one. Here we are." The baby slid out, and Sophie held it along the length of her arm, holding the little wet mass up by its feet, gently tapping it until a lusty cry escaped. She and Chad smiled at each other.

"A son," Sophie said.

"Let me deliver the other one." Chad's voice shook.

Hallie heard them as though from a distance.

"I think it'll be a few minutes before the other one. . . ."

The first baby's afterbirth, looking like liver, oozed out. To Hallie it felt like another child. It hurt like hell. Pain ripped her open. A black hole in the universe opened and she fell through it.

"Push hard, Hallie. . . ." Chad's voice was tender, coaxing. "Come on, honey. Just one more big push. I know it hurts. Here, hold onto that towel and push. Try, Hallie. Just

419

one more big one . . . That's it. There, now try another little one. You don't have to use all your energy, come on, just one little—ah, there we are.

Suddenly it was over. The pain was gone. It was a few minutes before she could gather the energy to open her eyes. She felt too tired to make the effort, but when she did, Chad and Sophie were smiling at her, each of them cradling a blanketed baby. Chad's tear-filled eyes met hers.

As though from a great distance, Hallie heard her mother say, "Both of them," as she tucked them next to Hallie, in the cradle of her arms, "the spittin' image of how you and Danny looked, blond, fuzzy heads."

Hallie fell asleep.

When she awoke, much later, it was dark and there was no one in the room. She heard voices in the living room and tried to call out, but her voice was only a hoarse croak. Hearing Robbie, she knew Tristan must be here. Oh, Tristan, she cried silently, come see our babies.

She called again, and this time Chad entered, a candle in his hand. Robbie followed along behind him, standing outlined in the doorway.

"Where's Tristan?" she asked.

Chad looked over at Robbie. "He can't come," said the young man.

"Can't come?" she repeated. "Why in the world not?"

Chad walked over to her. "We don't need him now, anyhow. Everything's fine."

"He was getting married," explained Robbie. "I had to wait for them to finish the ceremony, and then he said to tell you he was sorry, but he just couldn't come right now."

Forty-one

The next day, late in the afternoon, Tristan arrived with Molly beside him in a carriage. In fact, she entered the room before he did, dressed as Hallie had never seen her, in a pale green gown with a feathered hat tied in a large bow under her chin, her chestnut curls escaping in a most charming way. Her eyes were shining, and she rushed over to Hallie and threw her arms around her.

"Oh, Hallie, Chad says you have twins. How wonderful! And to think they were born on my wedding day."

Tristan stood in the doorway.

Somehow Hallie mustered a smile. "Why didn't you tell us?"

"We didn't tell anyone, except Susan and Harry," Molly said, her arms still around Hallie.

So the Langleys knew . . . No matter how hard she tried, Hallie couldn't keep her eyes from Tristan.

"I'd no way of knowing, of course, that's the moment you would choose to give birth," he said.

"Of course not, old man." Chad grinned. "No one's faulting you for that. Sophie and I had no problem. Now I've delivered *all* my children."

Tristan's level gaze met Hallie's and did not waver. "I knew you'd be fine. Now, where are they, these twins?"

Chad led him to a large cradle in the darkest corner of the room, Molly following behind him. "Oh, the darlings," she sighed, picking one up. 'What perfectly beautiful babies!"

Tristan picked up the other one. "I'll examine them," he said, "but I know already they're fine. No children of yours could be otherwise, Hallie."

He sat on a corner of the bed and examined first the little boy, then the girl, handing them back to Molly when he was finished. She returned them to the cradle. "Good job with the navel, Chad. You could always be a midwife should your farm fail."

Chad laughed. He was in high good humor.

"What are you naming them?" asked Molly.

"I've always fancied a boy named after me," Chad said, "though I hate the name Chadwick. We'll call him Wick."

You never asked me, thought Hallie, thinking it ironic that he should name Tristan's son after himself. She had thought it would be nice to name the girl Sophie, but she and Chad hadn't talked about it.

Tristan looked at him across Hallie's bed. Chad turned a disarming smile on Tristan and said, "Since you're in the habit of saving members of my family, and have been such a friend to my family over the years, I'd like his middle name to be yours. Chadwick Tristan Morgan."

Tristan's eyes flicked to Hallie. "I'm flattered," he said.

Chad walked across the room and threw an arm around Tristan's shoulder. "And you'll be their godfather, won't you?"

Tristan looked at the father of his children and said, "It's very hard to resist you, Chad."

"Good, that's settled, then. Now, why don't you name the girl?"

Hallie, at first pained, then touched, by the scene, found herself suddenly angry. Had she no say in any of this? She had borne these children; was she not allowed to have a say in naming them? Harking back to the births of Jamie and Alexandra, she recalled Chad had named them, too, but at the time it had never dawned on her to question him. She was sure Tristan would ask what she wanted to name a daughter.

Instead he said, "My mother's name is Julie. I've always liked that."

"Julie?" Chad scratched his head.

"That doesn't have to be her name," Tristan added hastily. He could tell it didn't appeal to Chad.

The thought that his mother would have a granddaughter named after her suddenly pleased Hallie. "I like it," she said. "We'll call her Julie."

"Now," said Tristan, turning to Molly and Chad, "if you'll leave for a few minutes, I ought to examine the patient."

Chad took Molly by the arm and asked, "You're staying the night, of course?"

"Of course." Her voice rang with happiness.

When they'd left the room, Tristan sank onto the bed next to Hallie, who said, "Why didn't—"

He put a finger across her mouth, silencing her. "Try to understand," he murmured. "I couldn't bear it, Hallie—knowing you were having our children and that I would not be a part of their growing up. They can never acknowledge me. There have been times these past months when I thought I couldn't stand it. I timed it on purpose—not the day, mind you, for I really anticipated attending your delivery . . . Hallie, you have everything, and I've had nothing. Do try to understand."

Tears filled her eyes. "Oh, Tristan, of course I do! It's just that it came as such a shock. I guess I've never thought of your marrying. At first I felt betrayed. How selfish of me. I just know that I shall love you forever, and I thought . . . I don't know what I thought."

"I shall never love anyone as I do you. But I need someone, too. I want a family. I don't want always to see my children brought up by someone else." Tears sprang to his eyes. "No other woman feels like you, no other woman kisses like you, no other woman can compare with you. There's not a woman on earth who can equal you, who is as strong and capable and willful."

"Willful?"

"Whatever you set out to do, you do. You're not like other women, Hallie. And know this, no matter what lives we live from here on, I shall love you forever." He leaned over and kissed her, tenderly, softly, without passion. "Can you be nice to Molly?" he asked.

"Of course." She tried to smile but only half succeeded. "I've always liked her. Though it surprises me that you've married her."

"I don't know why. She's a wonderful woman."

"I won't deny that." Hallie felt tired and weak. She knew it was not all due to the twins' birth.

Tristan rose and walked over to the window. "I've been seeing her for many months. I thought Susan might have told you."

Hallie shook her head. "No one did."

423

He turned and looked at her. "Let us be friends, Hallie. Let our families be friends. And only you and I will know we are really one family."

"Tied together for eternity."

Tristan smiled.

Since Hallie was still too weak to get up, after dinner Molly, Tristan, and Chad dragged chairs into the bedroom and sat talking. Apparently they had been discussing education at dinner, for the conversation continued.

"However, I refuse to do what all the other large landowners are doing, and what all the government officials do," Chad was saying to Tristan. "I'm not going to send Jamie back to England for his education."

Hallie drew in her breath sharply. "Of course not," she said, aware that again he was not consulting her.

"We'll have to import teachers and start a school system in this country where all children can find education," Chad went on. "I don't want my son brought up over ten thousand miles away. I've spent five years away from him; I'm not about to spend another fifteen."

"There's an excellent boys' school in Sydney, and a rather good one in Parramatta," Tristan ventured.

"I'll investigate," said Chad, "though even then I'm not happy with his being away all week. But I imagine we can find boarding for him."

Hallie's heart seemed to have stopped. Board Jamie? Cut him off from the farm all week long? Leave him with strangers? "How unfair," she said. "I don't want him to grow up away from us, live with people he doesn't know, who don't love him."

"Better Sydney than London," said Chad.

"Well"—Hallie thought too many new things were happening—"I'll talk with the Langleys. Maybe they wouldn't mind having him. Though they're not always in Sydney, there *is* a housekeeper who remains there. Let me talk with Susan and Harry."

"No," said Tristan. "Let us have him. Let him come to me."

Hallie found it tiring to nurse two babies. Her strength did not bound back as it had with Alex and Jamie. And it

424

seemed they nursed constantly. The babies were in a cradle in the bedroom, and Chad slept almost as little as she did. When she suggested he use Danny's old room, he refused. "I like the sounds. I like watching you nurse the babies. I'm never again going to deny myself a thing about fatherhood, or about being a husband."

The twins arrived at lambing and planting time, the busiest time of the year. Three horses foaled, the cow calved, piglets squealed in the barnyard, and fluffy little yellow chicks captivated Jamie and Alex, as they always did. All of it enthralled Roger and Pamela. Robbie came and woke Jamie up to come watch the calf being born. Alex trailed behind them, and behind her was Beth.

It was the first time in all the years she had lived here that Hallie did not participate in farm chores. It was the first time in five years that she had not directed it all. She not only lacked the energy to participate, but Chad would not hear of her "overextending" herself.

"I'm home now," he said. "You never have to do any of it again."

"But I like it," she protested.

He smiled down at her, watching her nurse Wick. "You'll have your hands full."

But one person still considered her his boss: Ben. After dinner one Sunday he asked, "Got a couple minutes?"

They strolled out to the porch, and he sat down next to her. "The other night at dinner, when the doc and his new missus were out here, they got to talking about schooling. I've been thinking ever since . . . You know those two rooms behind the store I never use, except to store things? I think one of them could be a schoolroom."

Hallie stared at him, her mouth open. Months could go by when she hardly gave him a second thought, and then he'd come up with something like this.

"Lots of children around the valley," he continued. "Ours are the only ones who know how to read and add and subtract." Hallie smiled at his use of "ours." "Of course, only ones with horses, ones old enough to ride alone, could come, I guess. But I imagine there are a dozen children who could do that, all within a couple miles of the store."

"How could we find a teacher?" Hallie asked, warming to the idea.

"Well . . ." Ben took the omnipresent blade of grass from between his teeth. "I thought I might do it. We could just tell people that three mornings—or afternoons, whichever it turns out to be—a week, the store'll be closed. Of course, if there's an emergency I can just go into it, it'll just be the next room. People'll get used to it."

Hallie leaned back, narrowing her eyes to study him. Ben was an enigma.

"If it works out," he continued, absently sucking on the blade of grass, "and we get a lot of students, we may have to consider a full-time teacher. But it's a shame to have a country of blithering illiterates. Like being in the Dark Ages. Sydney and Parramatta are too far for children to go to school, and besides, they cost money. These farmers can't afford anything."

Hallie tried not to smile. "So, you'll do it for no pay?"

Ben nodded, his face serious. "What do I need money for? Everything I need is supplied. I don't know what we'll do about books if families can't afford them."

"I imagine we can figure out something."

"I thought you might." For the first time in all the years she'd known him, Ben's eyes held the hint of a smile.

"Of course. Go ahead. I think it's a wonderful idea. Besides, children should get to know other children."

"My sentiments exactly." He stood up and rubbed his hands on his pants. "I know Jamie is far too advanced. He knows as much as children who've been going to school three or four years. This school's not for him. You're right to be sending him into town. His fine brain shouldn't go to waste."

"What about Alex's brain? She seems to think well, too."

Ben caught the tone in her voice. "I agree. And maybe we should let girls come to school, too."

Hallie had never heard of boys and girls in class together. She didn't know how other parents would react, but it seemed all right to her.

"But just remember that most of the farmers won't expect their girls to read and write," Ben added in a voice that showed contempt for such thinking.

Hallie sighed. She knew her parents had been ridiculed

in Newcastle, trying to "be something they're not, that's what. What's a coal miner gotta read for? And educating them daughters, too." Well, none of them had gone farther than the fourth grade, and she'd forgotten all she'd learned there except how to read, and then she hadn't had access to books. She hadn't even remembered the arithmetic when Tristan began to teach them.

"Should I speak to the mister about it?" Ben asked.

Hallie bristled. "You needn't. I'll tell him. I'm sure it'll be all right with him. It's a splendid idea, Ben."

He nodded and rose, hat in hand, slouching off toward the barracks.

Forty-two

In the months since the birth of Wick and Julie, Hallie had been relegated to the role of mother and wife, and she chomped at the bit. She missed riding out daily with Brian, missed being in charge of Cowarra, missed the outdoor life. Chad was gone all day, so she joined Emil and Danny in the winery, just standing around more often than not. Nursing two babies did not leave her the energy needed for working in the vineyards now that the year of the first harvest had arrived, but the trim brick building that the two men had constructed, with help from convicts Chad had loaned them, attracted her.

"These are the basket presses," Emil told her during one of her visits, pointing to the wooden slatted vats held together with iron-studded bands. Then he looked up, his eyes glowing. "Nothing," he said in his halting English, so slowly that Hallie had the urge to shake the words from him, "can narrow fine wine to a recipe. The most aristocratic grape may, even with the most loving care and ideal growing conditions—once fermentation has started—produce but ordinary vintage. We shall do all that is humanly possible to see that we produce superior wines, ones worthy of the gods." To this, it appeared, his life was dedicated.

Hallie often wondered how he could find fulfillment in this. The only person he really conversed with was Danny, and at night he dined alone in his two-room cottage, where there were no books and nothing that Hallie could see to give him spiritual sustenance. Only on Sundays and Christmas did he come over to the larger house for dinner, though he always had a standing invitation. And even then he had only one topic of conversation.

Hallie herself needed something challenging. It wasn't that she didn't enjoy motherhood. But while it filled her soul, it did not always occupy her mind. And the lack of mental stimulation left her wearier than she could ever have imagined.

Aside from feeling displaced now that Chad had taken over the work, she was also confused. Part of the problem was Tristan. When he looked at her these days, his eyes were never soft; they were impersonal. He made sure they were never alone. He hardly ever spoke to her directly. But by far the greater part of her confusion stemmed from her relationship with Chad. She had naturally resented his homecoming, but she also suffered a gnawing guilt over her own lies and deception. How would he feel if he ever discovered the truth? What might he do? These anxieties were secondary, however, to the self-castigation she endured.

Whenever Chad reached out for her, she thought, It's not me you want. It's who you think I am, and I'm not that woman at all. At the same time she couldn't help but enjoy him. Now that he was well again, he exuded the vitality that had attracted her to him when she'd first arrived. It wasn't that he always talked, but he was always at the center of conversation. Ben eventually stopped deferring to her and began to ask Chad's opinion.

Sophie and Danny conversed with him endlessly. Hallie wondered what they found to talk about; he discussed the children with her, once in a while the store. He talked no more of the events of his daily life or his visions of the future than he had before he'd gone to England. Except for his excitement about his "castle," she knew little of what he thought or felt. But then she never confided in him, either.

When they were alone, he was warm and loving. It had been two months after the twins' birth before he made an overture to her. "I've known how tired you've been nursing two babies," he said. "And Tristan told me you shouldn't have more children right away."

She had just gotten into bed, and she looked up at that. So, Tristan had told Chad to stay away from her, had he?

"I've spent a great deal of time thinking about us, Hallie." Chad sat down beside her and took her hand in his, looking into her eyes. "About how all I have to do is get near you and you become pregnant. Once—once in six years we've made love and it resulted in—in them." He arched his arm toward the cradles on the far side of their bedroom. "But"—he reached over as they lay in bed, to run a finger across her shoulder, down her arm—"all the time I was in England I yearned for you, for your body, for your kisses, for the taste of you. I am not going to be denied you." He leaned over and kissed her neck, running his tongue gently along her skin.

She wanted to turn away, kept telling herself this wasn't Tristan. But a ripple of gooseflesh flushed down her arm. His fingers brushed across her nipples. It *had* been a long time, nearly a year.

"I want you so badly I can hardly stand it. I look at you every day. You're my wife, goddammit, and the great majority of our life together you've been denied me. I want to devour you, I want to spend nights making love, I want . . ." He paused, looking into her. "Hallie, we can make love without your getting pregnant."

His fingers pulled up her nightdress and feathered along her thighs. "I promise," he whispered, bending over to taste the skin where his fingers played. "I promise you won't become pregnant." She felt his tongue flick along her inner leg, felt his teeth sink gently into the soft flesh there, and she heard herself moan. It felt so good.

She parted her legs. Closing her eyes, she thought, I'll pretend it's Tristan. . . . And it became Tristan's lips searching, Tristan's tongue plunging into her, Tristan's fingers on her breasts, Tristan's words, "My darling . . ."

Her body began to gyrate as he moved his mouth up along her belly, one hand under her buttocks, pressing her against his face, the other still exploring between her legs, rubbing softly in a circular rhythm. Reaching out, he unbuttoned her nightgown and slid it off of her. He extended his body against the length of her. She liked the feel of his bare chest against her breast, felt his hardness between her legs. His lips touched hers, gently at first, then with a hunger that awoke the passion she had stifled for so long. Their tongues met. His hands glided down her body, cupping her breasts. When his lips covered her nipples, she blazed with desire. Fire ignited her.

"Touch me," he whispered, guiding her hand.

He was hard and strong; she felt a pulse. As she moved her hand back and forth, she heard him say, "Oh, Jesus

. . ." His lips trailed down her belly, down between her legs again, and he kissed her there. Involuntarily she arched upward, giving herself to him, throwing her legs and arms wide apart, wanting him to be everyplace at once: where he was with his mouth against her—his tongue darting in and out . . . She wanted his hands and his lips on her breasts, she wanted him inside her, she wanted his mouth on hers, devouring her. She moved without control, rising and falling, reaching for him, locking her legs around him.

In tandem they rocked back and forth. Nothing existed but the two of them. And as his tongue thrust harder and deeper, she felt the warm wonderful waves wash across her, knew ecstasy again as though for the first time.

She could not resent him then. Not afterward, as she lay in the crook of his arm, remembering the intense pleasure he had given her. Not as his lips brushed her eyelid. Not as she heard his ragged breathing become even and knew that sleep was upon him. She could not deny the power he had over her at such times, did not even want to deny it. She luxuriated in it.

It was more than animal coupling, but she didn't know exactly what. It *was* confusing, for she did not know what she felt for Chad. But whatever it was, she knew it was not love.

Because she was nursing the twins and had one or the other at her breast every couple of hours, she and Chad turned down the invitation for the governor's second annual New Year's Eve Ball. Hallie didn't feel up to the holiday activities, to packing up all the children, to buying a new party gown—she couldn't fit in any of her others. She didn't think she could go off to the gaiety of Sydney and the governor's and leave Danny's family and Mum out of it. She thought having Christmas at home with all her family around her would be enough to cope with.

But in one particular Chad was not to be deterred. "I'm going in to the New Year's Day races, he announced the day after Christmas. "I've never seen them, you know. I have to take Jamie in to Tristan's anyhow, since the term begins right after the holidays."

Jamie was excited about going to school and about living

with Tristan. He was not yet used to the rough-and-tumble father who had been thrust into his tranquil existence. When Chad saw Jamie lying in the grass, studying the clouds, or with his nose in a book, he'd call out, "Come on, son. Let's go." And it was always someplace connected with hard work and fast riding. Though Jamie loved riding, he was aware that his father's presence attracted others and he did not always enjoy being surrounded by a crowd. There was a fraternal feel and bawdy, joking language to which he was not accustomed. The men had never acted like that when his mother was with them.

Even at seven Jamie was aware that the one who would suffer most by his absence would be Alex. Although a bit scared of the new life he was about to embark upon, he also admitted to an excitement about the aspect of adventure. Alex would be staying at Cowarra. What would she do? he wondered. How lonely might she become? Lately she had taken to reaching across the space between their beds at night and holding out her hand until he clasped it. She fell asleep that way, and he would lie awake, wondering what his sister would do once he was gone. At the same time, he was exhilarated. What would city living be like?

The wonder of it all was that Tristan had invited him to come live with him.

Watching Jamie as he and Alex sat on the grass playing a game of their own invention, Hallie wanted to run over and throw her arms around her son. Soon he would be leaving her; soon he would not have someone to attend to his every whim. He would not have the freedom of the outdoors or the leisure of youth. She had no doubt that he would grow up to be a doctor. Tristan would probably take him on house calls after school, or even to the hospital. Hallie envisioned them sitting together evenings, talking. Perhaps Jamie would grow more from this than from any formal education he would acquire. How ironic it all seemed. She couldn't tell whether the invitation had been a magnanimous gesture on Tristan's part, as Chad surmised, or whether it had been a selfish indulgence: this way Tristan would have at least one of her children to father. Or perhaps, she mused, it was simply the genuine affection he felt for her eldest son.

* * *

When Chad returned from his Sydney holiday he was in jovial spirits. He had no apparent qualms about having left Jamie with Tristan. "If he's going to be a doctor, he might as well be introduced to it now," he said. He had won big at the races, and he caught them all with his energy, saying, "Next year we're going to enter a horse. Hallie, you know the horses. Which yearling should we train?"

"Let me give it some thought," she said, surprised that he'd asked her advice.

As they did every summer evening, they all sat on the porch listening to the cockatoos and kookaburras screeching before nesting in their trees. The sun took a long time setting, splashing its colors across the blue southern sky. Danny and Alex were out in the garden, where they spent the hours until her bedtime. Sometimes, on an afternoon, the two of them rode off together, bringing back flowers that none of them had seen before, cradling them as though they were jewels. Surprisingly, it was Danny to whom Alex turned when there was no Jamie—Danny, who had come to share her love of growing plants and her reverence for all that was wild and wonderful around them. Danny, who never seemed to have time or patience for his own two children, sought Alex's company. "She lights up my life," he told Hallie.

One evening after dinner Chad stood and walked over to Hallie, reaching out a hand. "Come," he said. "Take a walk with me. Just down along the creek."

Startled, she took his hand and he pulled her up. She noticed Sophie gazing after them with an unreadable expression in her eyes.

Chad did not let go of her hand but tucked it in his arm, putting his hand over hers and leading her down by the creek, which gurgled quietly in the evening warmth. When they came to the bend where the women swam afternoons, he stopped and turned to her.

"Hallie, what's wrong?" he asked quietly.

She was so unprepared for the question that she said

433

nothing, unable to think of a reply. She took her hands from his.

"You do that all the time," he said. "Turn from me. From everyone. Pull into your shell. Where do you go?"

She stood with her back to him, not knowing what to say. His arms wound around her, the length of his body against her back. "Where is the Hallie I knew? Where is the Hallie I want?" He hesitated. "Tristan says some women go into depression after childbirth. Is that it? But it's lasted for months, Hallie. The twins are over four months old."

So, he had been talking to Tristan about her.

When she still didn't respond, he continued, "I knew you better when I was in England than I have since returning home. I felt closer to you there than I have since coming back."

"That Hallie no longer exists," she said. "She ceased when you left her to make decisions for herself, when she had to run the farm, when taking care of babies and cleaning a house were the least of her worries. . . ."

"When fighting flood and drought and adding thousands of acres to an empire?" he suggested.

"When I was a whole human being, not just a child-bearing . . ." Words she had not even thought came spilling out, and she began to cry.

Chad searched for a handkerchief in his pocket and wiped her cheeks with it, putting his arms around her and stroking her hair as she sobbed. Hallie was confused. She had thought all of her unhappiness was because Tristan was denied her and because she had committed adultery. Now, she realized the reasons were not that clear.

"Oh, Chad, I feel so useless. I loved making decisions, I loved riding out every day to inspect pastures, seeing and deciding what work needed to be done." She blew her nose on the handkerchief. "It's not that I don't think the babies are important . . ."

"But it's not enough, isn't that it?" His eyes were searching hers.

"It used to be that every morning I'd wake up with more than enough things to do in a day. Now I wake up and there's nothing to do." She stepped away and averted her eyes. "Beth and Sophie take care of the house. Danny—and even Alex—take care of the garden. You take care of—of

434

our life. Tristan's taking care of Jamie. And I'm taking care of the twins. It's as though any meaning I have is in my breasts!"

Chad walked to the edge of the creek, staring into the deepening twilight. "Is this why we don't talk?" he asked.

"Don't talk?" Instantly Hallie was defensive. "It seems to me you talk to everyone but me. Everyone else seems to know what's happening to the house you're building. It's always yours, never ours."

He turned abruptly, facing her. "Hallie, everytime I've ever mentioned the house, beginning with when I was ill, you've dismissed it. You've never shown any interest in it."

"Mightn't you have asked if I even wanted it?"

He was silent for a moment. "So that's it."

Not entirely, she thought. Mainly, it was that he was Chad and not Tristan.

"The first time you've ever—ever!—asked my opinion about anything has been about training a horse for the race next year. You never asked how I've felt about names for the children. You never asked me about sending Jamie to school. You've never even commented on anything I did with Cowarra while you were away. You always—you did this even before you left—you always make up your mind and tell me later. And you seem to think that whatever you decide will either be all right with me or, if it's not, my opinion isn't important."

Chad stared at her before reaching out to brush his hand along her cheek. "How remiss of me not to tell you what I think of what you've done to the farm. All the years I was in England, I was filled with resentment that my dream was not proceeding forward. I came home to find even more than I'd dreamed—and it had all come to pass without my knowing it. Maybe that's been difficult for me, Hallie. But I am also grateful, surprised, elated. It is not easy to have pictured myself a hero, carving out an empire in a new land, only to have a vision of myself outdone by—by a woman."

"Why, what's wrong with being a woman?" Hallie asked, hands on her hips.

Chad laughed, but it sounded forced. "Obviously nothing. You break all the rules, Hallie. But you also make me question my sense of . . . of who I am. I'm more comfort-

435

able with you nursing babies, being a mother. There you don't . . . threaten me."

"Threaten you?" she echoed, puzzled.

"I was far more comfortable when I thought you felt beholden to me. I was the hero, rescuing you from the drabness of Newcastle, of routine." There was a sadness to his smile. "I offered you a new life, excitement, a chance you'd never have had without me. I rather liked the role. I knew when I sent for you that you'd be grateful. And we *were* happy, weren't we?"

Hallie nodded. Suddenly Chad seemed . . . vulnerable, something she had never imagined him to be. "Yes, I was happy. I loved it all."

"But it's not the same, is it? I came back the same person, but you're not the same. And I haven't known what to do about it. You've become a stranger to me, Hallie. I thought bringing your mother and Danny would make you happy. But even they haven't . . . Hallie"—he reached for her hands—"tell me what to do. I will try to do anything in the world to make you happy."

But she had no response. Life was far too complex for a simple answer.

Let's go back in time, she wanted to cry, and don't go to England. Don't leave me alone for five years, to discover my love for Tristan. Don't give me time to be unfaithful, don't leave me to glimpse such a big part of myself. Let's go back and start over and not do any of the things that have hurt us. Let's find innocence again.

But she knew that innocence, once lost, was gone forever.

Forty-three

In the second year after Chad returned, though only a few of them were involved directly, everyone was interested in the grape harvest. It had been a near perfect year, Emil intoned, for grape growing. In February he examined the grapes every morning. The drama of ripening was under way. Actually it had begun in midsummer, when the grapes were scarcely visible, when the long clusters of small hard berries were tucked under wide green leaves. Even then, intense changes had begun. The early concentration of tartaric acid had begun to abate, and every plant was using its photosynthetic ability to generate sucrose. Grapes began to swell as the vines moved the sugar from their leaves to the clusters of fruit.

Danny was at Emil's elbow every step of the way, listening and looking. "Although sugar is the vital ingredient in determining when to pick wine grapes, it is not the only element," Emil said. Often it was as though he were talking more to himself than instructing Danny. "Sometimes one more day of sugar formation will give the perfect wine, other times one extra day will dry it just too much to even be decent."

Machinery had been arriving for nearly a year. Crushers and destemmers, rollers, basket presses. Emil explained their uses time and again. Everytime he passed one of the cumbersome machines, his hand glided over it with the love and tenderness some men reserved for women. At last the time came when he said, "Today. Today we will begin the harvest." Anyone familiar with him could sense his excitement. It was as though he were the leading actor with a case of stage fright. Adrenaline pumped through him, though a casual observer could not have seen it.

Chad, who approved of the winery but deliberately separated himself from it, letting it remain Hallie's responsibility, gave Emil as many men as he needed. Emil instructed them in how to pick the berries, but he did not rest easy for fear they would pick ones that were not yet ready. He flew down the rows and from hill to hill, never resting, admonishing, "Not that cluster yet," and Hallie was reminded of a wild horse, rearing into the wind.

She went out mornings and picked, next to Danny. All the grapes ripe for this first harvest were for Burgundy. White grapes, comparatively few, had been planted just the year before, so it would be another three until they were ready. Though Emil was proud of his Germanic heritage, it was French wines that he loved. "We are going to produce the finest cabernet sauvignon outside of Europe," he vowed. "And we will try a little Semillon, but the Burgundy types will be our claim to fame."

When overflowing baskets reached the winery, Emil announced, "When we get to the whites, they will be crushed differently. The red ones are destemmed before crushing." The fruit was guided into the destemmer by a hopper, which ensured an even flow of fruit. The blades inside the drum rotated and propelled the bunches toward the opposite end, removing individual berries as they caught in the perforated lower half. The berries fell through the perforations onto the rollers and were crushed.

Gallons of the red fruit—rich, bubbly, lustrous juice, thick with smashed skins, "unlike white grapes"—sluiced into fermentation vats, where the color was then extracted from the skins. After three to five days, the liquid was pumped off and the remaining fruit placed in the basket press. Then the basket was raised to the overhead pressing plate and the resultant juice collected. The remains were loosened for subsequent pressing.

Within six hours of crushing the somewhat settled and cool must—the pulp and skins of the crushed fruit—was placed in padded fermentation tanks that would hold the temperatures to about fifty-four degrees and then injected with the purest wine yeast obtainable. This procedure continued, cluster after cluster, from tank to tank, and would not be completed in this, its primary stage, for six weeks. Racking would follow late in April, and thereafter the wine would be stored in the oak barrels until the next summer, when a drum with centrifugal force would complete the process and the wine would be ready for bottling. After a year it would be ready for consumption. This was wine making as it had been done from time immemorial.

Six years, thought Hallie, for a bottle of wine.

It was a pretty scene, the men busy in the fields, shouldering baskets of grapes to the winery. Inside the trim brick building that housed the oak caskets, it was cool. After the heat outside, the wine cellars inside the bowels of the hill made one shiver. Or maybe it was the excitement. A total of six years of labor and dreaming, and there was no guarantee that the result would be more than barely drinkable.

"A gamble," said Emil, his eyes fierce and afire. "Like anything else worthwhile in life."

Emil was a man of great limitations, but within those limitations beat a passion. Nothing but his grapes interested him. His monomaniacal dream was to produce a wine that the world would recognize as superior, that would give Australia the admiration and respect of wine connoisseurs and gourmands all over the world.

Hallie missed Jamie terribly.

When he came home to visit, the boy was always full of tales of his city life. He enjoyed school and talked of his friends and the things they did, of what he was learning. He did not feel alienated from the family and was always affectionate, but his real pleasure lay in the city, where he was being introduced into Tristan's adult world of medicine and politics.

Sometimes, Jamie said, if Tristan were free on Saturday afternoons, they went fishing out in the harbor or found coves where Tristan rowed a boat. Tristan had permitted him to witness an operation, and took him on house calls after school, as Hallie had surmised he would.

"I wish *we* lived in the city," complained Tess, whose husband had come alive in the land where he could be outdoors in the sunshine all year long. "I never get to do anything."

One evening in late March, Ben took Hallie aside and said, "Maybe you should go see Etta Colton. I think Will is beating her."

Hallie's first reaction was one of shock. Why would a man beat his wife? And then she realized she was not surprised at all. She remembered the twisted ear and the haunted look in Etta's eyes.

"Think she might have a broken arm," Ben said offhandedly.

So the next morning Hallie took Sophie and the twins and set out for the Coltons'. It was hot for March, and the autumn rains had not yet started. Looking up at the sky, Sophie commented, "It's as perfect as a day can be. I never know how anyone can help but be happy when there's weather like this. If they have their health, that is."

"You're glad you came, then?" asked Hallie.

Sophie glanced at her daughter, who held the reins of the horse loosely. The babies were asleep behind them in the wagon. "Can't you tell? It's like I'm born all over again, into a new life. I crawled out of something, my skin or my head, something. I'm fifty-three years old, and inside me I know I'm beginning another life."

"What do you mean, beginning?"

Sophie laughed. "I know it doesn't make sense. D'you see the way I sit around nights and have no knitting in my hands? I don't feel I always *have* to be doing something. I think I'm resting, gathering strength for the next step. I don't spend my time rushing around caring for everybody else. No one needs me. . . ."

"Doesn't that bother you?" Hallie asked.

Sophie shook her head, her eyes dancing. "I like it. I have time for myself. I think I never knew me before. Maybe I wasn't anybody yet. I was my father's daughter, until I married Dada. Then I was Mr. Thomas's wife. And the mother of each of you . . . of my nine children. Everything I did, someone else was first. All the women I knew were like that. I didn't feel put upon"—she touched Hallie's arm—"I didn't mind. When Dada died I was scared that no one would need me and that I'd be dependent on my children and they'd get tired of me. That I'd no longer have a place. I missed him so dreadful that first year. It was like I stopped living, too."

She was silent a moment, staring out over the vastness of the land before her. "You know," she said at last, "I really thought I came to Australia to die. For a while, to

440

take care of your children—and maybe you, still—and Danny's children. To be near my youngest ones, and maybe be of more help than if I'd stayed in Newcastle. I do sit on the porch a lot," she laughed, "but instead of just rocking into my old age, I think I'm growing."

Hallie stared in amazement. She'd never heard *anyone* talk this way, let alone her mother. She'd had no idea so much went on in Sophie's head.

"It's nice doing just what pleasures me for a while," the older woman continued. "I like not having to spend every minute of my life waiting on someone else's wishes. I like looking at life, taking the time to smell flowers and watch clouds drift across the sky. I like seeing the sky all the time. I like watching the foals in the paddock—pretty sight. I like not worrying about having enough to eat. I like feeling that I'm a part of—of everything. Learning new things, like riding a horse. Like reading. Getting to know people . . . Beth, Ben, Emil, Brian's family—Robbie, in particular. None of them people I'd know back home. The doctor. Back home no doctor would ever have come to dinner. No banker. I've even met the governor. All things that could never have happened back . . ." Sophie's voice trailed off.

By this point Hallie's mouth had dropped open.

"And next time there's a choice," Sophie concluded, "when I'm ready, *I'll* decide what I want to do with my life." She leaned back on her elbows. "And it's all thanks to that husband of yours, Hallie. He's the most wonderful man I ever met. He's not like other men. Not like other anybodies. But," she gazed upward, "you don't love him, do you?"

The question surprised Hallie. She and her mother had not talked of anything personal since Sophie had arrived. "What has love to do with marriage?" she countered. "I came to marry a man I didn't remember, someone I didn't know. Were you in love with Dada?"

"Ah," said Sophie, "being in love with and loving are quite different. I never was 'in love.' But I loved him. More as the years went by. Though perhaps by the time he died I might have been in love with him." When Hallie didn't say anything, she added, "But I don't miss him anymore, Hallie. You'll think I'm terrible, no doubt, but I'm not sorry

441

he died when he did. Otherwise I might never have begun to find me."

"I think I understand. . . ." Hallie thought of the years Chad had been away. She smiled ruefully. Later she would have to reflect on this conversation, think about it awhile to gain a better understanding of this woman she had known for twenty-seven years.

"Well, I don't understand how you don't love this man you're married to," Sophie was saying. "If he was mine, I'd be 'in love' with him. Head over heels in love and considering myself the luckiest woman in the world."

At that moment the Coltons' cabin came into view.

Despite the fact that there were three children, it was so quiet that a kookaburra's laughter and the grunting of a pig were the only sounds to be heard. Hallie noticed that the fields were neat, the hay was ready for harvesting and looked to be prime. A garden plot was tidy and well cared for. Several pigs rutted about by the barn. Somehow Hallie always associated pigs with Will Colton.

The front door was only slightly ajar, despite the perfect weather. When Hallie knocked there was no answer, so she pushed the door open and there, huddled in a corner, were Etta and her three children.

"My heavens, Etta!" Hallie rushed to her.

Etta seemed paralyzed. "It's you, Hallie," she murmured, her voice filled with relief.

Hallie reached down to pull her up, and Etta held out her right arm. The left hung limply by her side, and Hallie could tell she was in pain.

"My dear . . ." Hallie stared at her, shocked at her appearance. Etta was dirty, her hair hung in clumps on her neck, her face was smudged, and she smelled of curdled milk. Clutching her youngest child, who had thrown up on her, Etta made no move to leave the corner. Mary Ann and the little boy clung to her skirts, peering shyly at Hallie.

"What has he done to you?" Hallie asked, furious.

Etta's eyes filled with tears. "It's my fault, Hallie. I'm not a good wife. I don't—"

"I don't care if you've committed murder!" Hallie cried. "Whatever he's done, he shouldn't have. You need a doctor for that arm." As Etta turned toward her, Hallie saw that

442

her cheek was blotched purple and she had a swollen eye. "Oh, my God!"

The children looked as frightened as Etta. Mary Ann, at six, was thin to the point of emaciation. Just Alex's age, Hallie thought fleetingly. There was scar tissue on the little girl's leg. They were all barefoot.

"I brought my mum and my twins over for a picnic lunch," Hallie explained hastily, "but we're not going to stay. I'm packing you up and taking you home with me."

Etta shook her head wildly. "No, no," she said in a voice that was weak and hoarse. "We can't go. He'd kill us."

"He can't kill you at my house," Hallie said. "Come on, hurry, before he comes home. You can't live like this."

"I can't come," said Etta, shivering. "He wouldn't let me. He'd come get us and . . . Oh, Hallie, if I just learn to clean and cook better, if I just stop asking questions, or stop saying no, even in my head . . . If I learn to be a better wife, he'll stop this. He says he's just doing it to teach me how to be a good wife."

Hallie had a vision of Beth, of what she had gone through. Suddenly Sophie, who had been standing in the doorway, hurried into the room. Without saying anything, she gathered up the young boy and took Mary Ann by the hand. "Hurry up," she said.

"I won't let him hurt you again," Hallie promised. "We'll get your arm fixed, and he won't hit any of you again."

Etta let herself be led outside, and the children, with Sophie, followed. "He'll kill me," Etta kept repeating. "He don't let us go out of the house without his say-so."

She was too weak to climb up onto the wagon, so Sophie pushed her while Hallie pulled. Then Sophie handed the children to Hallie and climbed up, saying, "Hurry, let's get out of here. This whole place makes me nervous."

As they rumbled away, Hallie began to wish she had brought a whole team of horses; there were too many people in the wagon for one mare to pull quickly. She heard Etta's soft crying, heard Etta say, "It's not his fault. He tries to teach me how to be a good woman. I'm bad, Hallie. So're the children."

Hallie turned around to look at the bad children and saw skinny, cowering urchins huddling close to their mother, eyes filled with terror. The little boy had begun to cry, but Mary Ann just stared. Suddenly, in the distance, she saw the flick of a shadow emerge from among the trees, behind the barn.

"Damn," she whispered.

Sophie, who had never heard Hallie swear, turned and spotted the figure heading toward the house that was now a dot in the distance. "Hurry," she urged Hallie.

"I'm going as fast as Sable can pull us." Which was not fast at all. In less than five minutes they could hear the pounding hoofbeats, hear the cry in the air. But Hallie would not stop.

When Will Colton caught up with them, his whip whistled through the air and hit the side of the wagon. Though Hallie jumped, she did not stop. She turned to face him and called out, "Stay away from me, Will Colton! Don't get near us."

He rode his horse directly in front of Sable and halted. Sable stopped, too. "Why, good day, Hallie. . . . He bent over, doffing his hat. "We haven't seen you in a long time. I see you're taking my family for a little ride."

"Will Colton, I'm taking your family to my house," Hallie snapped. "Get out of my way."

He didn't move. His lips smiled under eyes of steel. "No, you're not, Hallie. I didn't give my permission. My family only leaves home with me. Come on, Etta. Get down now." His voice was measured, friendly.

Etta stood up, still holding the baby, and began to climb down.

"No." Hallie grabbed her. "Don't do it, Etta."

"See . . ." Will's voice had a smoothness to it. "See, Etta. That's what I mean. You have to learn, practice so hard, to be good. Your driving off with Hallie shows you haven't been good. Come on, now, get down, you and the kids." He did not talk to the children directly. "And you'll walk back, like a good family."

"No," said Hallie.

"I gotta go, Hallie," Etta pleaded, the panic obvious in her eyes.

"I won't take you back," Hallie said.

"Of course you won't," said Will. "They'll walk. A nice day for a walk."

444

"They all have bare feet. That's a mile through all that sharp grass."

Will's mouth curved. "What ye sow, ye shall reap."

When Hallie saw that nothing she could say would dissuade Etta, she sighed. "Here, I'll drive you back."

"No," said Will. "You will not. Nor will you visit again, Hallie. You have tried to tear my family apart, you have behaved in a most unneighborly fashion. You have kidnapped my children. . . ."

Etta had trouble climbing down from the wagon, holding onto the baby without the use of her left arm.

"She ought to see a doctor about that arm." Hallie thought she might cry, she was so angry.

"What I do with my family is *my* business, Hallie, not yours. The Lord has chosen to punish her for being a bad woman. But she's learning, I do think she is. Aren't you, Etta?"

When his wife looked at the ground rather than at him, he said again in a voice so smooth that Hallie could hardly hear the threat in it, "Aren't you learning, Henrietta?"

She nodded mutely.

"Say it!"

"I'm learning." Etta did not look up. The baby's cry sounded like the mewl of a sick kitten.

Will laughed. "Slow process, but I think she'll make it."

"Will Colton, I'm going to tell everybody how you beat your wife," Hallie said furiously. "I'm going to send a magistrate out here."

"I ain't broke no laws. What I do with my family is no one else's business."

"I'll make it mine."

He looked at her and the smile was gone. "You don't know how sorry you'll be if you do. Go on, Etta, start walking."

His whip tore through the air again; they all jumped at the cracking sound it made. Julie and Wick were crying now, and Sophie gathered them into her arms. "Let's go," she whispered. "Please."

Hallie looked at her and the twins, looked at Etta and her three children beginning to walk through the sharp grass. She heard the little boy crying, already saying, "My foot's bleeding. . . ." Neither she nor Sophie talked on the way home.

It was just noon when they arrived. Hallie paced back and forth on the veranda, waiting for Chad to return home. By mid-afternoon she couldn't contain her restlessness, so she rode down to the store to talk with Ben.

"You were right," she told him. "Will's beating her." She described what had happened. "What can we do? What do you think the law can do?"

He didn't know any more than Hallie did, but he was equally determined to do something. However, when they faced Chad with it after dinner, Chad said, "There's nothing we can do. It's his family. We can send Tris over and hope Will will let him do something about that arm, but there's nothing we can do legally."

"Chad"—Hallie gripped his arm—"we *have* to do something to save that woman and those children."

He looked at her. "My dear, there is absolutely nothing that we can do. The law is on his side."

The next day Hallie decided to ride into Parramatta. When Alex found out, she asked, "May I come, too?"

"Of course, darling." Hallie was delighted. "But we're not going into Sydney, so you won't see Jamie."

"That's all right," replied the little six-year-old. "I haven't been to town in a long time."

"How about me?" Sophie asked Alex, smiling. "May I come, too?"

"Of course, Mum!" Alex had early on adopted Hallie's name for her. She giggled. "You don't have to ask *me.*"

So the little party took off for Parramatta in the wagon, arriving early in the afternoon. Fortunately, Susan was there and not in Sydney. She was with Kara and her youngest. Christopher had started school in Sydney. "When we're here," she said, embracing Hallie, "Christopher stays with the Faulkners, with Molly. He's as used to her as to me. He and Jamie get along well, too. I miss Molly. She's so wonderful with babies."

Harry had walked in as Susan was speaking. Now he put his arms on Hallie's shoulders, kissing her on the cheek, and shook hands with Sophie. "I tell Susan Sydney's overtaking Parramatta. The majority of the bank's business is there now. We'll probably have to move there and just come here weekends." He grinned. "Great to see you, Hallie."

"I've really come to see you, Harry. Tristan tells us you've been made a magistrate." Her voice became brisk.

Harry nodded. "I hope a far fairer one than Marsden is. . . . Do you need some legal advice?"

"Can't it wait until later?" Susan interjected. "After dinner?"

But Hallie would not wait another minute. Pacing around the room, she told them about Etta Colton.

"What do you want me to do?" Harry asked, frowning, when she'd finished.

"Something! Get her away from that man. There must be some way to protect her." She couldn't believe their hands were tied.

Harry pulled at his mustache. " 'Fraid not. It's his family. He hasn't broken a law."

"Breaking her arm isn't breaking a law?" Hallie asked incredulously.

Harry looked at her. "It's his family," he reiterated.

"Harry . . ." Hallie's voice rose. "Do you hear what you're saying? You'll let him beat and maim her and scare those children half to death? What do you have to do, wait for him to kill her?"

Harry nodded. "That's about it."

Susan took hold of Harry's hand. "Surely there must be something we can do." Her voice was soft, pleading.

Harry shook his head. "There's nothing. It's his family."

"I'm going to the governor," Hallie said, her voice strained.

"There's nothing he can do," Harry repeated. "Hallie, understand that it's—"

"His family—yes, I know. For God's sake, Harry!" Hallie's voice was strident. "He doesn't own them, does he? They're not slaves, are they?" There was a tinge of sarcasm in her voice.

"They might as well be," Harry replied, his voice flat. "Etta simply has no rights."

Hallie looked at him for a long time; Susan let go of his hands. "I did. You let me buy land. You lent me money. You gave me the go-ahead for starting the store. You let me buy sheep. You extended credit."

447

"Yes, well . . ." said Harry, not meeting her eyes. "Chad was away."

"You mean I couldn't do any of that now that Chad's home?"

"Not without his permission."

The silence stretched into long, awkward seconds. At last Susan spoke up.

"What if—what if you raped me?" Sophie's gasp reflected her shock at such a question.

"You know I'd never do that." Harry's voice was pained.

"Of course I know that. But what if you weren't you? What if I didn't want . . . and you wouldn't take no for an answer? What then?"

"I would only be asserting my conjugal rights."

"In other words, men can do almost anything they want to women?" Hallie's question sounded more like a statement.

"Stopping short of murder, I hope," Harry said. He felt he was on trial and had been convicted unjustly. "You know, this isn't how I feel. You're asking about the law."

"And you're saying we can't do anything to help save a woman and her children. . . ." Hallie's voice was filled with anger. "Nothing at all."

"That's right," he said. "Nothing at all."

Forty-four

Late the next year, near the end of 1820, Chad's great house was finished. Alex was eight and, along with twelve others of varying ages, attended Ben's school three days a week, until noon. She was one of only three girls.

Emil had pronounced Cowarra's first two harvests to be of excellent caliber. Danny devoted as much time to the vineyard as did his mentor, and absolutely none to the continually complaining Tess. Over Tess's protestations Pam and Roger attended school along with Alex.

Jamie spent one weekend a month and all vacations at Cowarra. He was equally at home in Sydney, where he was not only at the top of his class, but received Tristan's and Molly's devoted attention, despite the arrival of two children of their own, Megan and William.

Julie and Wick were as alike as any two people could be. They defied restraint and authority, even at two years of age. They were wild and irresistible. The only person they obeyed consistently was Alex, who read to them by the hour, took them by the hand, put them on her pony and walked them in circles, awakened them to the joy of seeing a flower open its petals and the song of a bird.

They were offered love and affection from all sources. Beth fussed over them just as she had with Jamie and Alex, and Sophie was never too busy to give them time and a hug. Ben talked to them as though they were adults and treated them with great seriousness. But they were never content with what was offered them.

Chad adored them. One or the other was often in the saddle in front of him. Like Ben, he listened to them with seriousness, but—unlike Ben—he brought gaiety and laughter into their lives, teaching them irreverence for convention and pride in their individuality. He had bought a mate, though of unknown breed, for Gently, and there were now six or seven dogs that romped around and constantly surrounded the children.

A new son, Garth, was four months old. Hallie wondered if she would ever be free of nursing a baby. She could not go jaunting off to Sydney with a baby at her breast, and she had not had a private talk with Tristan in over a year, not since she'd sent him over to the Coltons to see about Etta's arm. And that situation had ended tragically, in Hallie's opinion. Will Colton had refused to allow Tristan to break and reset his wife's arm, so Etta now walked around with it hanging uselessly at her side. Hallie had not gone back after that one incident, though she still dreamed of it at night.

Hallie had to admit that Chad's house looked the way she imagined a baronial estate must look. She had never known that a place to live in could be so large. "We'll get lost in it," she said, marveling.

"I shall look in every room and every closet, then, until I find you," Chad said, putting his arms around her.

The mansion rose in splendor almost a third of the way up the hill, above where the creek joined the river. Three stories tall, it was built primarily of sandstone, interspersed with brick. At the western end there was a circular turret on the second floor, which Chad had designated as their bedroom—large, circular, with mullioned windows overlooking the valley, the river, and the mountains to the west. A long driveway wound up from the valley floor, with young eucalyptus trees planted on either side. "Someday," he said, "there'll be a canopy of them a mile long."

In the reflected rays of the setting sun, the house resembled a sparkling panoply of jewels, in hues of mauve, purple, pink, and blue.

A wide, formal veranda built of large sandstone blocks, with an iron railing running the length of the entire structure, welcomed visitors with planters of flowers and yellow-and-white-striped chairs scattered about. When tall lamps were lit at dusk, Emil said it reminded him of castles on the Rhine.

The giant entry hall, with its shining wide-planked floor covered with Persian carpets, was but a backdrop for the dramatic staircase. Wider than most drawing rooms, the carpeted stairway descended—with arms leading down from either wing of the house—into the middle of the entry hall. At times, a hundred people would gather here and not be crowded.

To the right of the entry hall was a large dining room whose long mahogany table could easily seat thirty. Its six-foot-wide windows overlooked the porch and valley. Beyond that was a smaller dining room, the informal one where the family ate when there was no company. Behind these rooms were the kitchens—which included a pantry and a room just for baking, which housed the cast-iron stove and the wall ovens. Shining copperware hung from the ceiling within reach of the cooks; when not in use, they could be raised to the ceiling by a pull on a rope. Beyond the kitchen door was an herb garden. Finally, just off the pantry, there was one room simply for the storage of china, linen, and silver.

On the other side of the house, to the left of the entrance hall, was the formal drawing room, lushly textured with mauve wallpaper and forest-green carpets. Curved sofas, straight-backed satin-covered teakwood chairs, and a spinet piano graced this room, so obviously intended for pleasant—and decidedly polite—conversation. Beyond this was the family room, with large cushioned chairs and chaises, a few mahogany tables, large lamps for reading, and a rag rug for Gently or any of the other dogs who claimed it. Two colorful little blue-and-yellow budgerigars sang and flitted in a golden cage.

Behind that room, on the other side of the hallway, was Chad's office. Books lined the walls, and a six-foot desk of teak dominated the center of the room, which also contained three dark and very large leather chairs. Here, as well as in the family room, toys were always strewn around. There were several smaller rooms—offices, Chad called them, but over the years they would be used for sewing and mending, for secret games of youth, for birds whose wings needed mending, or for dogs giving birth: in short, for whatever anyone needed them for.

Upstairs, on either side of the stairway, the house was divided into two wings. On the right side, toward the mountains, in the large circular turret, was Hallie and Chad's bedroom, itself nearly twenty feet around. Chad had given it a great deal of thought, and to him, it reflected Hallie.

451

There was a connecting dressing room on either side, and one large bathroom, which housed a massive iron tub. Beyond Chad's dressing room was a small chamber where he kept his more important private papers.

In this wing, too, were Sophie's and Beth's rooms, as well as two large guest rooms. That hallway also contained a bathroom whose cupboards seemed to house at least six dozen towels. Chad had installed a dumbwaiter so that the maids wouldn't have to scurry up and down the stairs with pails of water.

The children's wing, with its own bath, held six rooms—one each for Jamie, Alex, Julie and Wick (who still shared a room), and Garth, and two empty ones "for guests or future brothers and sisters."

On the third floor, also with its own bath, were the maids' rooms, plus an immense square playroom where the children reigned. Built to alleviate boredom on rainy days, it was to be the room each of the children would remember with affection the rest of their lives.

Once Hallie realized she would never be reunited with Tristan, she tried to stop yearning for him. Chad was, after all, an exciting person. His dreams and appetites were enormous, and they became reality. He was affectionate, at least when it led to lovemaking. And he was the most perfect father Hallie could imagine.

She loved listening to him talk of the sheep, of the breeding, and she enjoyed suggesting which stallion should be mated to which mare. But no big decisions were hers. She received none of the satisfaction of doing it all herself, but at least Chad had begun to ask her opinions. And although she was never sure if he was really listening or just humoring her, it didn't seem to matter anymore. He was her husband, and he was able to arouse emotions in her that could not be denied: anger, joy, a sense of fun such as no one else in the world kindled, tenderness . . . And those nights when they made love, he brought her to shivering ecstasy, to peaks of passion.

"We're going to have a party," Chad announced one

morning, his eyes dancing. "A housewarming. A barbecue. We'll dig pits in the ground and roast a pig and a steer. Guess we better include a lamb, too."

"In the ground?" Sophie asked, looking up from her mending.

Chad nodded. "We'll have a party that this colony won't soon forget. We've bedrooms enough, between the two houses, for most of the married couples. For the single men, I'll get tents from the army. We'll decorate them, and they'll never have believed such luxury possible in a tent. We'll have the band come play, and at night we'll have a ball. And champagne for breakfast."

"It's a lovely idea," Hallie said, catching his enthusiasm almost instantly. "How many are you thinking of inviting?"

Chad grinned. "I don't know . . . dozens. Let's make out a list. Governor and Mrs. Macquarie, of course . . ."

"The Langleys, naturally."

"Tristan and Molly."

The total eventually exceeded one hundred. Chad tossed the list at Hallie and asked, "D'you want to make the arrangements?"

It was true she'd been begging for responsibility, yearning to take charge of something. But a party wasn't what she'd had in mind. "No," she said slowly. "I know nothing about giving parties."

"Better learn," advised Chad. "This is just the beginning."

Susan, she thought . . . Susan will know what to do. And she smiled.

"Spare no expense," Chad went on. "I want this to be something no one will forget."

When Hallie, with Garth beside her, rode into Parramatta, she discovered that the Langleys were in Sydney. She stayed overnight in their house with the housekeeper, who told her, "They're only here a couple of days a month now."

The next day she took the ferry downriver. As they pulled in, she was startled to see how much larger Sydney had become since she'd last seen it . . . when?

The gulls screeched. A pelican swooped down, passing not inches away from her before landing gracefully in the water beside the boat. Hallie frowned, lost in thought.

453

When was the last time she'd been to Sydney? she asked herself. It was . . . it was at the governor's ball, three years ago. It was when—perhaps when Wick and Julie had been conceived. Oh, was it so long ago? She had lost Tristan since then. Lost so much. So much gone from her life.

Maybe I can have some time with him today, she thought. Or tonight? See Jamie and perhaps speak alone with Tristan.

Holding Garth close to her, she found a carriage and headed immediately for the Langleys'. Hearing someone call her name, she tapped the driver on the shoulder and asked him to stop. Then she turned around in time to see Tristan in a passing buggy.

"Hallie!" He jumped down and ran back to her. Standing in the dusty street, he looked up at her, smiling. "What brings you into town?"

Her heart beat wildly at the look of pleasure in his eyes.

"I've come to see Susan," she said. "And Jamie, too, of course."

"You're just the person I've been thinking of," he said, and she melted. "Can you spare me a few minutes while you're here? I've a favor to ask and something . . . Well, it can wait. But do arrange some time for me."

"I'll come by about five, if it's all right. I thought I'd invite Jamie to Susan's for dinner. I can pick him up then, if you don't mind."

"We're dining there, too," he said with obvious delight. "But . . ." she sensed his hesitation. "Come by at five anyway. I want us to be alone when I talk to you."

"So mysterious!" She smiled, and her heart turned over. Oh, Tristan!

"Not really. It concerns . . . well, come by at five, that will be fine." Hallie watched as he got into the buggy and rode away.

"What a lovely surprise! I can hardly believe it after so long," exclaimed Susan when Hallie rang the bell. "How wonderful!" She reached out to take Garth from Hallie's arms.

Something about Susan always gave Hallie a feeling of security. "I've really come to have you help me in an enormous undertaking," she said. With Susan she never waited for niceties of conversation, but always burst with what she considered important.

"Well, come in and get settled first. . . . You want my help? Isn't it a coincidence. Jamie's coming to dinner." She looked into Hallie's eyes. "So are Tristan and Molly."

"I know." When Susan looked at her questioningly, she said, "I ran into him on the way here. I'm going over there at five, but he told me they're dining here."

Once Hallie had nursed Garth and put him down to nap, and she and Susan had had a cup of tea in the back garden, Hallie explained why she had come. "Chad wants everyone he knows to see our new house. To see what Australia is capable of, he says. He wants to throw a party that no one will ever forget. And the job has fallen to me to plan it. Trouble is, I've never even been to any parties except the governor's balls. I haven't the faintest idea how to go about it."

"An extravaganza!" Susan cried, clapping her hands.

"I guess so." Hallie nodded. "I thought we could put our heads together and come up with something."

Susan laughed like a delighted child. "Let's include Harry, too. He'll love it. I'll try to remember some of the really outrageous parties we attended in India. Hallie, dear, I think it will be a great deal of fun. I love the idea of our planning something together. It's been far too long."

It had. Hallie had seen too little of Susan and Harry since Chad's return. When she left for Tristan's Susan looked at her and put her arms around her friend.

"I'm only going to be gone an hour," Hallie said.

"It will seem longer, I imagine."

Jamie greeted her with his usual warm affection and then said, "I'll be upstairs. Tristan says he wants to speak privately to you. We can all walk over to Aunt Susan's together afterward."

Tristan was waiting in his office. After she'd seated herself, Hallie heard him walk behind her and close the door. Her body felt warm. "I want to ask a tremendous favor," he said, his voice low.

Hallie waited. She would do anything he wanted.

Hands clasped behind him, he paced around the room.

455

"Two weeks ago one of my patients, a woman named Mary, who lives a mile or so outside of town, sent for me. She's expecting a baby any day and her husband's at sea, but she insists on living in the home they built." He glanced at her. "Thinking the baby was coming early, I rode out, but that wasn't it at all. She led me into her bedroom, and lying in the midst of sheets of caked blood was a young woman, barely conscious."

Hallie felt a sharp stab of disappointment. It's not about *us* after all, she realized.

"She'd arrived at Mary's house the night before, in the midst of rain, one of our dazzling thunderstorms," Tristan continued. "Mary told me she heard knocking and, when she answered the door, this young woman fell into her drawing room. At first she thought the girl was dead. She had been stabbed in the arm and in her thigh." His voice quickened. "Mary washed the girl off and tried to stem the flow of blood. She fed her broth and dragged her to her own bed. There she had to pull the mattress onto the floor, for she couldn't lift the young woman. She slept next to her, trying to warm her. Early in the morning she sent the single manservant who works for her in to get me."

Tristan paused. Hallie heard him sigh. "By the time I arrived, it was obvious the girl's arm had to be amputated just below the elbow."

Hallie put her hand to her mouth, stifling a cry. He looked at her in understanding.

"The thigh wound was not deep, and though it was beginning to fester through the dried blood, I was able to cleanse it. But the arm was another thing. God"—he shook his head—"if there's anything worse than amputation, I don't know what it is. I hate to do it. Each time I think I'm going to be sick. I dream of it for nights—and days—afterward. I thought, before attempting it, I should try to get the young woman into the hospital. As I started to lift her, her eyelids fluttered and she asked what I was doing. When I told her, she said, in a voice so weak I could scarcely hear, 'No. Let me die instead.' Hallie"—Tristan stopped pacing directly in front of her, not a foot from her face—"she's an escaped prisoner. Ran from the man who did this to her. Sometimes"—there was a puzzled and sad expression on his face—"sometimes I feel guilty to be a man, part of the same

456

sex that can do these terrible things to this young woman and Beth. I don't understand what drives men to . . ."

Hallie thought, I know what he wants. I know why I'm the one he's telling this to. Oh, Tristan, I do love you. You care so much. She reached out to touch his arm. "Did you take the arm off?"

"Yes." There was no inflection in his voice. "Mary had a bottle of whiskey and we forced it down the girl's throat until she was unconscious, and I cut it off." His eyes held the pain of recollection.

After a moment's silence, Hallie said, "I know what you want. And of course I will."

He turned to look at her. "How do you know?"

"You want me to take this girl . . . what's her name?"

"Laurie."

"You want me to take Laurie, don't you?"

He knelt beside her. "Oh, Hallie. I've tried to think what to do with her, and it's always the same answer. Yet I don't want to endanger you." He reached for her hand.

"No one has ever questioned about Beth, have they? That's why. You're sure of me, aren't you?" Strength seeped into her.

Tristan's eyes were puzzled. "Doesn't Chad know about Beth?"

"Only you and I know."

He threw his arms around her and buried his head in her lap. "Oh, Hallie, you are so strong! So good. I thought perhaps that with your mother, with Chad, with all the children, you wouldn't want . . ."

His touch warmed her. Happiness flowed through her. "Of course I'll take her. We'll make arrangements. Get her to Parramatta two days from now and I'll take her from there."

"What about Chad?" He took his arms from around her and raised his head from her lap.

"Trust me," she whispered, her face close to his.

"God . . . oh, God, Hallie!" When his lips met hers, she savored the feel of his mouth, the way he crushed her to him. Her arms flew around him, pulling him close, wanting to feel him next to her. Then she heard the pounding of her heart, felt him push her back, crying, "No, Hallie! No."

Before she realized it, he was halfway across the room.

He turned back to face her. "I can't stand it," he said, his voice defensive.

Silence filled the room.

"Tell me, do you love her?" Hallie whispered, her eyes pleading for the one answer she wanted most to hear.

Tristan was quiet for a moment. "If you mean in the way I have loved you, no. In the way that I shall always love you, no." Then his voice hardened. "But I think she is an excellent mother, a fine wife. She is someone I enjoy for the sweetness of her spirit, for her cheerful disposition, for . . . for many things. I can never let go of you, Hallie. You're the unobtainable, part of me now and forever. And we are bound together in a way only you and I know. My passion is at Cowarra, but I feel at peace when I am with Molly."

"Can you stand it?" It was a question she'd always wanted to ask. "Can you bear the knowledge that Chad is fathering your children?"

Tristan hesitated. "It may seem strange, but I can. If anyone's going to be a father to my children, I'd have it be Chad. He's become like a brother to me, he and Harry. And after all, I am fathering *his* son, aren't I? Jamie is with me."

Hallie wondered if he found this a fair exchange. "It's not quite the same. Jamie knows his father is Chad."

Tristan walked over to her. "And you and I know about Wick and Julie. If I did not now have children of my own and expect another, I might not be able to bear it. But I beg you, Hallie, do not feel guilty on my behalf."

He was not nearly so engulfed with self-reproach as she was, it seemed. "So now the only guilt I have left is for what I've done to Chad?" she said bitterly.

Tristan took her hands. "Try not to do that to yourself. You've given him two fine children who he's allowed to love. I take pride in them, too, but I'm content to let Chad be their father."

"And are you content, then, with life?"

He drew her hands to his lips. "I find happiness now and then, but I can never find contentment without you."

Forty-five

By the year 1821, life in Australia was thriving. It was not a country suited to the structured mores of London, but by the second decade of the nineteenth century there were concerts, dances, horse racing, yachting, kangaroo hunts, picnics, even opera. A number of literary magazines had appeared, and a Mrs. Hickey even opened a boarding school for young ladies, instructing them in the writing and grammar of English and French and in geography. Chad, however, had refused to enroll Alexandra. He had no intention of allowing his daughters to leave Cowarra just to get an education. Instead, he sent to England for a governess who would teach them in a house he would build for her in Morgantown. If others out their way wanted their daughters educated, he agreed they might be sent to her, too.

It did not dawn on him, nor would it have mattered on this issue, that Ben considered this a personal rejection. Chad believed that girls should receive an education quite different from that of boys. He was also of the firm opinion that by the age of ten, boys and girls should not spend hours cooped up in the same room with each other even if it was just for half a day three times a week.

Thus, while Hallie was awaiting the birth of her sixth child, Chad constructed a charming house down the street from the store, a house with a covered veranda so that the teacher could walk from the living quarters to the attached schoolroom without getting rained on. Morgantown now had not only the store and the blacksmith's, but a pub named The Black Swan.

When Hallie had brought home Tristan's patient with a stump for an arm, Sophie took one look at her and suggested that she and the ailing woman move together into the first house Hallie had lived in, the one whose coziness she often missed. For many weeks Laurie, the young

459

woman, lay lifeless on the bed in the room that used to be the children's. Sophie left the big house and moved into Hallie and Chad's old room, with the long French windows opening from two sides onto the veranda, the room that was so light it became a part of the outdoors.

She began to cook again, preparing dishes that were impossible for Laurie to resist. She started with weak broth from freshly killed chickens. Putting one arm under Laurie's head, she ladled the bouillon into the young woman's mouth, talking softly to her the whole time, until Laurie gradually began to unclench her teeth and look directly at Sophie. Eventually her eyes lit up each time Sophie entered the room. Sophie would read to her, even when she thought Laurie might be asleep.

And then Laurie began to sit on the porch with her, rocking together, and Hallie was surprised one afternoon to hear Laurie call her mother "Sophie." Sophie came over to the big house every day, riding on the gray-and-white horse Chad had given her, and once in a while stayed for dinner, but she really lived over at the other house with Laurie. One day when Hallie rode over to see how they were doing, she heard laughing from the creek, and following the sound, found Mum and Laurie bathing there, giggling like schoolgirls.

When Hallie was in her last month of pregnancy and Laurie had been there seven months, Tristan rode out in the wagon one day, accompanied by Molly and their three children and another young woman they'd never seen before. Though she was clean and neat, which Hallie suspected was Molly's doing, the pale brown eyes that matched her mousy hair looked upon the world without expression. One tooth was missing, and she kept putting her hand in front of her mouth, hoping to hide the gap.

"You've come to stay several days, I hope," Chad greeted them, riding in from the hills. "Molly, you've never looked lovelier." Molly had acquired a glow since her marriage and motherhood.

Tristan jumped down from the wagon and reached up for Molly. "Of course," he said, turning and reaching out to shake Chad's hand. "You don't think we'd come all this distance and not stay for a visit." But they didn't come often anymore.

Hallie had emerged from the house when she'd heard the arrival of visitors, and—her heart skipping a beat, as it always did when she saw Tristan—she waddled rather than walked down the steps with her arms out, ready to greet them. Then she saw the stranger, sitting still in the wagon, looking at Chad and now Hallie, but with no expression on her face.

Molly, who greeted Hallie with a hug, said, "You talk while I take the children inside. They're dying of thirst, they tell me."

"Here," offered Hallie, "I'll come with you."

Molly, whose foot was already on a step, turned to her. "No, I know my way. Tristan wants to talk with both of you." And she started up the steps, her littlest hanging onto her skirts trying to negotiate so many stairs.

Hallie turned to Tristan, looking up into his handsome face, at his concerned eyes and the crow's-feet that marked the corners now. For a moment he looked directly at her. "I've another favor. . . ." His voice lowered, and he moved away from the wagon several steps, as though he did not want the almost comatose woman to hear them.

Hallie knew what it was before he told her. Someone else to join Laurie. Another abused woman. Another woman Tristan had helped to save. Someone who needed time and a place to recuperate.

"Her name is Melanie," Tristan said. "She's expecting a child."

He paused and looked at Chad. By now Chad knew, too, and he looked at Hallie. "So are half the women in New South Wales," he said.

Something terrible had happened to her, though, Hallie knew.

"Let's take her over to Mum and see what she has to say. It's fine with me"—Hallie moved toward the wagon—"but it's Mum who ends up taking care of them."

Chad climbed back onto his horse, and Tristan helped Hallie, who felt clumsy and awkward in her ripe pregnancy, up on the wagon, saying, "I couldn't think what else to do with her, Hallie."

"I know," she said, pleased that Tristan had turned to her. But they said nothing else to each other during the fifteen-minute drive.

461

And so Melanie came to live at Cowarra, and Hallie wondered how many others Tristan would eventually bring out. Her heart ached for these young women who must have had experiences similar to Beth's. Wasn't there something that could be done to prevent this mayhem?

Tristan had informed the governor where these young women were, and had them remanded into his custody. But Lachlan Macquarie was not a typical governor. And because he was not, catastrophe struck.

He was ordered back to England.

The news shook New South Wales to its core, though many, such as the self-righteous Reverend Samuel Marsden, were pleased. The very elements that history would regard as aesthetic, as humane, as worthy, had brought about the governor's recall.

The ship that came to take the Macquaries back to England brought not only the new governor, Thomas Brisbane, and his wife, but the teacher Chad had sent for, Dorothy Hamilton, and her four-year-old son, Nathan.

"I'm thirty years old, Chad." Hallie lay in bed cradling her three-day-old infant daughter, Chloe. "We have six children. Isn't this enough for your dynasty?"

"I thought you loved the children." It sounded like an accusation.

"I *do*. But I never get to do anything else with my life." She'd been thinking about this ever since she'd awakened at dawn. "As it is now, Chloe will be nursing for another year and a half. I hardly ever get in to Sydney. I'm tied to the house with babies. There are other things I badly want to do with my life as well as nurse babies. And, besides, thirty is old enough to stop having children."

Chad was sitting on the edge of the bed, watching Hallie nurse their new daughter, whose head was covered with pale fuzz. "Seems to me you've done everything a woman could do. You've sailed halfway around the world, worked a farm into a sheep empire, you've a fine winery that can't even begin to keep up with orders—"

"I have about as much to do with the winery as you do!" Hallie snapped. "We listen to Danny and Emil talk about

462

it, and at harvest time I help pick grapes, just to pretend I'm part of it."

Chad looked at her, waiting for her to finish nursing so he could hold his new daughter. He continued talking as though she had not interrupted. "You do more than that. You know and seem to understand about destemmers and why red wines keep their skins and whites don't . . . or"—he smiled—"vice versa."

She tossed her head, and her blond hair cascaded over her shoulders. "Oh, it started out as my project—mine and Tristan's—but along the way he got too busy in Sydney, now that he's married." She tried to keep resentment from her voice. "True, it's some of his money and our land—well, a bit of our money, too, I suppose—but it's no longer my project, really. Aside from tasting it." She held Chloe out to Chad.

He took his daughter and brushed his lips across her head. "Can you tell a good wine from an inferior one?"

"Not really." Hallie buttoned her nightgown and lay back among the pillows. "I don't have what Emil calls a sophisticated palate. It all tastes very nice to me."

Chad held Chloe up so he could study her. "God, she's beautiful," he said, and snuggled her close to his chest. "That may be because Cowarra raises very good grapes and Emil's a very good vintner."

"Danny seems to have found his calling, too. For which I'm grateful. But it's no longer mine." Hallie wondered if Chad were really hearing her.

"Nevertheless, you're responsible for it. Initially, anyway. You set it in motion. But if it's something of *yours* you want, Cowarra is yours as well as mine." He stood and, with Chloe against his shoulder, walked back and forth.

"That may be." Hallie nodded as she handed him a towel, in case Chloe burped over him. "But I never *do* anything anymore. I haven't in years."

"I wonder why you're not content to be like other women?" Now he looked from their daughter to his wife.

"What other women?" Hallie asked querulously. She always felt defensive when he made a remark like this. "Would you like me to be like Tess? Would you prefer I was like Beth, or Melanie, or Laurie? Or Etta Colton? Do those women fall into any category? Or even my mother

. . . she's no longer content to be what she was for the first fifty-four years of her life. She's been reaching out ever since she arrived here. What you really mean is that you wonder why I'm not content to be like Susan and Molly. Aren't they the perfect women?"

Chad sighed and gave her a melancholy smile. "They are the ideal, I admit, particularly Susan—the kind of women men dream of for wives. Who couldn't love them? But, Hallie"—he sat down beside her and fingered the tendril of hair that curled about her neck—"there's not another woman in the world who can hold a candle to you. However, when everything seems to be just right, when I think I can relax for the next year, you bring drama into our lives."

"I can't tell whether or not that's a complaint." She searched his face.

"I'm not sure, either." He grinned. "Let me put it this way. Life without you would be like being in England."

Hallie laughed. "What does that mean?"

"Gray. Now, what is it that you want to do?"

Hallie looked beyond him, out the window, at the jagged lavender peaks in the western distance. Then she turned and gazed around at the opulent bedroom in which she lay. The walls were covered with a creamy satin-textured blue wallpaper. Their four-poster bed, more immense than any she could have imagined, seemed large enough for an army, and indeed sometimes contained not only her and Chad, but all the children at once. A handwoven canopy of the finest cotton hung above it, with a matching bedspread and the same flowered fabric on the chair in front of the large fireplace. The bureaus and closets were of the same cherrywood as the bed, and Persian carpets adorned the highly polished wooden floors. Yet despite the luxury of the impressive estate, there were times she yearned for that other house, where Sophie now dwelt with the two women.

Chloe burped onto Chad's shirt. He smiled and jiggled her, then turned his attention back to Hallie. "Well? What is it you want to do?" he repeated.

She watched him as he patted the baby soothingly on the back. "What a nice father you are," she said, speaking her thoughts aloud.

He walked across the room and put Chloe into her bassinet. "Don't you know, or are you afraid to tell me?" he asked as he returned to her, his eyes now intent on hers.

"Afraid?" What a strange word to use, Hallie thought. I'm not afraid of him.

"Afraid I'll say no?"

"You've never done that," she said, reaching out and pulling him down beside her. "You're quite tolerant of me, I think. But I'm not what you expected, am I? When you sent for me?"

He drew her hand to his lips and kissed her palm. "Not exactly."

With this birth she felt no postpartum depression, at least not yet. She was filled with contentment, and now stretched like a lazy cat. Watching her, Chad added softly, "But you were, our first years here. Far more than I'd hoped for." He sounded wistful and faraway.

Hallie noted the past tense. With a self-conscious vulnerability, she said, "I want . . . to change the fate of women in Australia."

Her words startled and then amused him. "I should have known better than to ask a question like that, shouldn't I? 'Hallie, what do you want to do with your life?' and the answer comes back that you single-handedly want to change the lot of women."

She felt her cheeks grow warm. "I didn't say single-handedly."

Chad laughed. "Oh, my dear, how peaceful my life might have been had I married someone else." But he wasn't complaining, she could tell. "Improve the fate of women? Is yours so terrible?"

"No," she said. "I am marvelously fortunate, and you know it. Well, a little bored now and then. And that's why. Look at Laurie and Melanie and Beth." She could have cut her tongue out. Beth . . . But Chad seemed to accept her statement without question.

"I figured that something must have happened to Beth to make her shy away from marriage." He nodded. "Any woman can get married in Australia."

Hallie interrupted. "That's just not true. Convict women are rented out—"

"Rented?" Chad's voice rose.

"Well, that's what it might as well be. They're used in

whatever way the man who has them wants. If they complain, they're sent back to jail. They're raped, a lot of them, and manhandled—"

"Well, now, I doubt that's the—"

Hallie raised her hand to shush him. "After seven years of that, of being used in whatever way a man wants to use them, no decent man will marry them. *Not* every woman can get married, Chad. There's lots no man will have. And many of the men wouldn't think of marrying them when they can get them for nothing—no responsibility except to feed them. You know marriage doesn't cure it all, either. Look at the Coltons."

Chad continued to stare at her in silence.

"Most women get off their convict ships and are hired before they even get to jail," she went on, warming to her subject. "And some of the free women who've come hoping for a better life, they don't stand a chance, either. On the docks, men propose to them, but once they get them home and in bed, refuse to marry them. You've heard the stories."

"Still, if all you say is true, how are you going to change it?" Chad said. "It seems to me that turning over our other house to those two young women is already doing a lot."

"But not enough." Hallie's voice rang with conviction. "I don't know what I'm going to do. I can't do much of anything while I'm still nursing Chloe. But I'm going to think about it."

Chad smiled. "I wonder if a peaceful life would be dull." He stood up and walked to the door. He hesitated, then turned around and asked, "Do you find men so terrible, Hallie?"

"Some of the nicest people I know are men." Hallie smiled at him. "Present company included."

Chad looked at her. "Sometime, Hallie, you may find out I haven't always been so nice, either," he said, and left her to ponder his words.

A month after Dorothy Hamilton and her small son, Nathan, settled into the cottage Chad had built for them, not more than two weeks after Alex and two other little girls from nearby started school there, Ben said to Hallie in that taciturn way of his, "Don't think a woman ought to

466

be alone in a town. Someone ought to be nearby in case she needs help." And he picked up and, at last, moved out of the barracks and down to the room behind the store that had been built for him years before.

Attached to the end of the small house was the classroom, which had walls painted white and large windows that overlooked a huge cork tree as well as gold-dust wattle. The fresh-faced young teacher won Alex's heart immediately by saying, "I want to start a garden out back. Do you know how I'd go about getting some plants?"

Alex reported to Hallie that "Mrs. Hamilton is the prettiest woman in the whole wide world." At first glance Hallie thought the teacher attractive, but in no way pretty but within five minutes of meeting her she, too, thought Dorothy beautiful. Her auburn hair was brushed smoothly across her forehead, pulled back into a shining copper chignon. Freckles dotted her alabaster skin, and emeralds glowed from her eyes. Her heart-shaped face had too determined a jaw, a nose that was not quite straight, and lips a trifle too full for conventional beauty. Her voice was quiet, so much so that in a classroom the children had to be silent to hear her.

Alex rode around the countryside collecting flowers for Dorothy. Schoenia, that pink papery flower with such a seductive aroma; the blue tinsel lily, with its spectacular blue-purple flowers. Leafless orchids growing in the she-oak forests. Pine heath with its crowded pinelike leaves and elongated yellow flowers. Plants that grew nowhere else did not yet even have names. Everytime Alex found a new flower, she would draw a picture of it in a notebook she kept for just such a purpose and describe it as well as she could, giving it a name she'd dreamed up after long, careful thought.

Every afternoon Ben wandered across the dusty street, walking across the large expanse of lawn that was Dorothy's front yard, and asked, "Need anything?"

"Well, you might bring a pound of flour when you come to dinner," Dorothy would say. And once in a while, on Tuesday and Thursday mornings when he taught nine boys, she'd go over and walk through the store and stand in the doorway, watching him. He acted as though he never saw her, but everyone knew better.

In the evenings, after he'd dined with her and Nathan, they'd sit and talk about teaching and about the people in the valley, and on Saturdays Ben, who still hated horses with a passion, could be seen teaching Dorothy and Nathan how to ride.

Now that Ben no longer dined at the main house, Hallie and the rest of the family missed much of the valley's gossip. Hallie had never dreamed that his absence at the dinner table would create such a void. He had dined with them for so many years, long after his term of service was over and Chad was paying him a wage. She was surprised at how much she missed him and how much they'd relied on him for news. To her, Ben had always been a presence, someone who was just there and who didn't really add to her life. When he was no longer there she realized how wrong she'd been.

Two months after Chloe's birth, on a Tuesday, Ben came riding up to the big house, looking for Hallie. "Mary Ann Colton's disappeared," he announced. "We're rounding up some men to go looking for her. Not been seen since Saturday night." The little girl was nine, the same age as Alex. Hallie hadn't seen her since she'd tried to rescue Etta. "Thought you might want to go comfort Miss Etta."

Hallie imagined how she'd feel if Alex had disappeared, but she said, "I don't know that Will will even let me on the place."

"There's that about it, too." Ben scratched his ear, the ubiquitous blade of grass between his teeth.

Hallie decided not to go; the memory of the last time was still too sharp. So Sophie volunteered and rode out immediately to see if she could help. But she didn't stay long. It wasn't Will who ran her off, it was Etta. The distraught woman was crying and screaming, shouting, "Don't no one come near, hear?"

Sophie asked Will if he'd any idea what could have happened. Will gave her a level look and said, "I been suspicious of that big handsome kid over at your place. The one with the black hair. He been riding over and staring at us from afar."

"Robbie?" Sophie couldn't believe it. What was Robbie doing over here?

"He been staring at Mary Ann," Will said in his even

468

voice. "Don't trust him. I seen him over at the store. He been lookin' at us funny even then."

Brian came to see Chad and Hallie that night. Hat in hand, he scuffled his feet. "Been hearin' what Will Colton's saying about my boy. Not true. Robbie wouldn't harm the hair on the head of any woman."

"Have you talked to Robbie?" asked Chad.

"Yes. But I didn't need to." Brian's dark eyes smoldered.

And Hallie knew that was true. Robbie couldn't possibly have anything to do with Mary Ann's disappearance. At sixteen Robbie was a strapping, handsome lad who'd stolen the heart of every young woman who saw him. No one in the area could rope a horse like Robbie could or fleece a sheep. Young and old alike respected his ability. There was a gentleness about him that endeared him to all who knew him. He did not shy away from fights, but he did not seek them either. Robbie was innocent of any wrongdoing; Hallie knew it in her heart. She knew that Chad knew it, too.

However, the next morning men found Mary Ann's body in a ravine, a creek washing over her feet. She was naked, there were scars over her body, and her face was swollen and purple.

"It was Rob Daugherty," declared Will Colton. "He been lookin' at her from afar for a long time."

All eyes turned to Robbie, who denied it. He did admit to riding over to the Colton farm and seeing Mary Ann. He'd been doing that for a couple of months, he said, but he'd never spoken to her, never been near her.

When Parramatta heard about it, the citizens shook their heads and said, "What do you expect? The son of a convict. It's in their blood." Even emancipists were prone to believe, sight unseen, that the son of one of theirs had done it.

By the time Tristan could examine the body, there was no way for him to tell if Mary Ann had been raped, but he doubted it. He said the scars had nothing directly to do with her death; they were from old wounds. The community chose not to believe him. Why else would someone murder a nine-year-old girl?

"It's ridiculous," said Sophie, riled as though Robbie were her own. "He could have any girl he wants. Why such a young one?"

"Well, why'd he ride over there?" Chad asked.

"For heaven's sake, do you think he did it?" Hallie turned on him in anger. "You know that boy better than to believe that."

"Of course I can't imagine him doing anything like that." Chad's frown reflected puzzlement. "I'm trying to ask questions that the magistrates no doubt will ask."

"Oh, my God, do you think it will come to that?" Hallie's hand clutched at her throat.

It came to that two days later, when Harry—in his role as magistrate—rode out to Cowarra. "I've come to arrest Robbie," he announced, reluctance obvious in his voice and face.

"You can't do that," Hallie pleaded with him. "He didn't do it."

"He'll get a fair trial," Harry reassured her. "I'm sorry, Hallie. This isn't my doing. I'm but a representative of the government."

Fire leapt into Hallie's eyes. "You're going to take Will Colton's word? A man who beats his wife and doesn't associate with anyone in the valley—or in town, either? Who doesn't let a doctor set his wife's broken arm?" Hallie's voice was abrasive. "You're going to take his word?"

"Hallie, we hear the boy's admitted to being over there, to sitting and staring at the house for months," Harry said, looking to Chad as if for understanding.

Hallie bristled. "That doesn't make him a murderer!"

Chad put a hand on her arm, but she threw it off and glared at the two men.

"The valley's scared, Hallie. They don't want a murderer of young girls on the loose," Harry implored her.

"Nor do I. But it's not Robbie!" she shouted.

"It'll come out at the trial, then," Harry said.

"A trial!" Hallie spit the words out. "A judge and two magistrates. What do they know of that boy?"

In desperation, Harry turned to Chad. "Chad, tell her . . ." When Chad stood silent, he turned back to Hallie. "Don't be angry with me," he pleaded. "If not me, it'll be some other magistrate."

470

"Let him stay here, then. I'll promise he won't leave Cowarra. Let him stay here." For a moment Harry thought Hallie might fall to her knees, begging.

"I can't do that. You know it."

Hallie sank onto a chair, her whole body sagging. "How can you possibly believe Will Colton?"

"Just because you don't like him doesn't make him a liar," said Harry, his voice uneven.

Hallie began to sob. "I'm going up there when you get Robbie. I'm going up to their house with you. I want to be there when you tell them. I'm not going to let them stand there alone."

"I'll come, too," said Chad, his voice quiet.

Forty-six

The wheels of justice did not grind slowly in the early days of the colony. While Robbie was incarcerated in Parramatta, Harry rode over to the Coltons to talk with Will.

"Did you speak with Etta?" Hallie asked him when he returned to Cowarra.

Harry shook his head. "She's distraught. I didn't see any reason to add to her pain."

"Didn't it dawn on you that she might have some insight?"

Harry looked at Hallie and then at Chad, who merely shrugged. "Will says he saw Robbie sitting on his horse, or riding around the perimeter of their land, at least half a dozen times. Once he even saw him heading toward Mary Ann, but the boy rode off when he saw Will approaching."

Hardly anyone had ever seen the Colton children and only a few knew what Etta looked like. She hadn't been in town, or even to the store, in years.

"What about Walker, their convict?" Hallie asked Harry. "Did he see anything?"

"They haven't had anyone working over there for a long time, he says. Not since before their last baby was born."

The entire family was turned inside out by Robbie's indictment. Alex was so disconsolate she couldn't go to school. Belinda was out of her mind. Brian didn't talk, simply walked around almost in circles. Both of them had driven into Parramatta to visit their son. When they returned, Hallie decided to go see the boy. She stayed at the Langley house, although they were still in Sydney, and left Chloe with the housekeeper while she went to the jail.

"I didn't do it," Robbie said, his black eyes pleading with her for reassurance. "I swear to God I didn't."

"I know it." Hallie reached out to take hold of his large hands. "Is there any way to prove where you were that night? Anything we can do to help show you're not guilty?

Robbie, I know—I know you wouldn't, *couldn't* do such a thing."

"That Saturday night"—Robbie dropped his gaze to the floor—"that Saturday night I was—I was with a woman."

Hallie pulled her hands away. Robbie, with a woman? He was still but a boy! "For heaven's sake, Robbie, who? Why hasn't she come forth to tell you were with her?"

"I don't know who she was." He sounded miserable. "I wouldn't even recognize her if I saw her again."

Stunned, Hallie stared at him.

"It was the first time I'd ever done such a thing. I . . . I got drunk and went to find a woman." Suddenly he jerked his head up defensively. "All the men do it! They tease me, so I thought . . ."

"Did you ever tell your parents this?" Hallie continued to stare at him, but he averted his eyes.

"I might have told my father, but not with my mother along, too." Yes, thought Hallie. Belinda would be as shocked as I am.

"Is it true you were often watching Mary Ann?" Her voice softened.

Robbie nodded, in obvious pain.

"Why?" she urged.

When he didn't answer, Hallie took a deep breath. "Robbie, look at me. I think I know why."

He did look up at that.

"It's because she looks so much like you, isn't it?" Her hand again touched his.

Tears sprang to the young man's eyes and he nodded. "I felt like I was looking into a mirror every time I saw her. I knew it couldn't be, but at the same time I knew it had to be. I told myself my father was over here a long time without us, not even knowing if he'd ever see us again. But wouldn't Will Colton have killed him? It would kill my mother to know. Yet I couldn't stop from thinking, wondering if she . . ." He paused.

"If she's your half sister?"

He nodded. "I never said this out loud before."

"I know. Neither have I." Hallie leaned over to kiss his cheek.

"And"—his eyes held hers with a plea of desperation—"I'd rather die than have my mother know."

473

When Hallie put her arms around him, she barely came up to his shoulder.

From Parramatta she rode to Sydney, foregoing the more leisurely ferry, and went directly to Tristan's new house. Molly answered the door, so delighted to see Hallie that she embraced her, immediately taking Chloe into her arms and cooing over her.

"Oh, I do hope you'll stay overnight," she said warmly. "You never have stayed with us, you know."

Hallie nodded, too preoccupied with her thoughts to respond to Molly's pleasantries. "I've got to see Tristan," she said.

"You'll have to wait. . . ." Molly kissed the top of Chloe's fuzzy head. "Oh, this is the most beautiful little girl I've ever seen! I'm going to reserve her for our Jason," she said, referring to their month-old son. "Tristan's out making calls. He won't be home until dinner. In the meantime, why not freshen up a bit? And please, Hallie, stay overnight with us. Jamie will be pleased and surprised to see you. So will Tristan."

Hallie had yet to see the inside of Tristan's new home, so as she waited impatiently for him to arrive, she examined her surroundings . . . and her hostess. Both, she decided, were gracious and beautiful.

The house, built of substantial blocks of sandstone, was two stories tall, with large, square rooms. It looked more like a government building than houses she had seen. It was not as imposing as Chad's, of course, but it was a far cry from the little house where they'd made love in his bedroom with the sloping eaves and long windows.

Molly herself seemed positively luminous; marriage and motherhood obviously agreed with her. No doubt everything about her life agreed with her. Yet all that Hallie envied her was having Tristan. That alone would transform any woman. . . .

When at last Tristan arrived, his eyes lit up at the sight of Hallie in his drawing room. She would have explained the reason for her visit at once, but Molly begged her to wait until Tristan had had time to relax, until after dinner, when the children had been sent to bed. Reluctantly Hallie agreed, forcing herself to make light conversation when her mind was on saving Robbie's life.

When the children were finally in bed, she began: "Tristan, Robbie did not murder Mary Ann Colton. He rode over there because—because he thought she might be his sister."

Molly gasped. Tristan tamped his pipe, striking a match several times before he lit it successfully. "I would imagine," he said slowly, "that anyone who had seen the two of them would have had that thought."

"You, too?" Hallie wondered why she was so surprised.

"Of course."

"Well, anyone knowing that would know Robbie wouldn't rape and kill her." She paced back and forth across the room, unable to be still.

Tristan looked at her. "I don't think she was raped, Hallie."

Hallie's eyes narrowed as she reviewed the likely possibilities behind the murder of an innocent nine-year-old child.

"You think Will did it, don't you?" Tristan asked, watching her. Molly sat, her eyes intent on whoever was speaking.

"Of course." Hallie replied. "He's a hateful, spiteful, cruel man. Maybe he did it and placed the blame on Robbie as a way of getting back at Brian—I mean, if Brian and Etta really . . ." Her hand grasped the back of a chair, the knuckles white.

Tristan nodded. "That thought has entered my mind, too."

"Well, what are we to do?" she demanded.

"You expect *me* to come up with a solution?"

Hallie leaned forward. "You've got to. We have to save that boy."

Tristan rose from his chair and walked over to stare out the window. After a minute he asked, "Can he prove where he was that whole weekend?"

"No." Hallie's voice broke. "He came into town and spent it drunk with some woman he doesn't even remember."

"Robbie did?" Molly's voice revealed her surprise. She, too, had known him since he was a child. To both women, the sixteen-year-old was still a young boy.

"The rites of manhood . . ." Tristan's voice was soft. "Don't judge him too harshly."

Both women stared at him.

"Proving that Robbie thought Mary Ann was his sister will not exonerate him," Tristan continued. "I think it might be used against him. He killed her so that his mother would never know. He thought she was the result of evil. He did it because he could not forgive his father. There are any number of reasons that would make his killing her believable."

Hallie thought for a minute. "I think Will Colton killed her to get back at Brian and compounded it by blaming Robbie," she said firmly.

Tristan looked at her, an eyebrow raised. He still stood with his back to the window. "I agree Will's capable of any amount of evil. But how are you going to prove it? Men simply don't kill their children."

"What if we could prove Mary Ann wasn't his child?"

"What? Make it public that Brian and Etta . . . ? Tear Belinda apart?"

Hallie turned to Molly. "Wouldn't you rather know your husband had been unfaithful when you'd been apart for over six years than have your son hang for murder?"

"Of course." Molly's expression was one of pain.

"If I learned my husband had fathered a baby with some woman when we'd been apart for six years, I certainly could understand." Her eyes met Tristan's. "But Robbie *does* think he's protecting his mother by remaining quiet."

Tristan raised his voice. "Dammit, Hallie, even if Robbie admitted that he thought Mary Ann was his sister, that doesn't prove he didn't kill her. Public sentiment is already against him."

"The public doesn't even know him."

Then the three of them were silent. Finally Hallie said, "The trial is in five days."

"Have you discussed this with Chad?"

She shook her head. "I came here right from seeing Robbie in jail."

Tristan walked over to her, stood in front of her, put his hands on her arms. "You have to get to Etta, talk to her alone. Appeal to her. She's probably scared to death of Will. Look at what he's done to her before. If he killed Mary Ann, he'd have no compunction about killing her.

476

She must know that. She's terrified. Do something, Hallie, to force her to tell the truth."

Hallie stared at him. How could she possibly do such a thing? "Will won't even let me on his property."

Tristan's hands on her arms tightened and he spoke forcefully. "Find a way. Get Chad to keep Will busy while you get into that house."

"Just getting into the house doesn't mean I can get her to tell the truth."

"Maybe," suggested Molly from her chair, "she doesn't know the truth."

Tristan let go of Hallie. "If not, she suspects it, I'm sure. And if Mary Ann really was Brian's child, she knows who Robbie is. Of course, maybe Will doesn't know Etta and Brian—" Tristan stopped.

Now Hallie grabbed his arm. "You have to get this information to Harry," she said urgently. "Whether it's legal or not, whether it's helpful or not. Harry *has* to work on Robbie's behalf."

"I'll see to it. But how much Harry's hands are tied—"

"Harry's as fair as any man I know," said Hallie. "Once he has this information, he won't let Robbie hang."

"Let's not let it come to that," Tristan said, and his eyes bored into Hallie. "Get to Etta."

Hallie calculated. "It'll take me a day and a half to get home, with Chloe along. The trial's in Parramatta, so that's half a day back from Cowarra. That gives us three days to get to Etta and plead with her to tell the truth. . . . Oh, God, Tristan, what if she won't? What if she's too afraid to? What if Will won't let her?"

"Will Colton will be at the trial. He'll be away from home that day."

Hallie sighed. "That day may be too late. . . ."

Two days later Chad and Hallie rode over to the Coltons'. Will stood rigidly by his front door.

"Morning, Will." Chad nodded. "Came to see if you need anything. See if we can help in some way."

"Right neighborly of you." He did not look at Hallie. "No, we're gettin' 'long fine."

"Hallie thought Etta might need some woman comforting, losing a child. Another woman—"

"Etta don't need no one," Will interrupted. "We're fine."

"She can't possibly be fine," Hallie said, her voice tight with anger. "Losing a child—"

"Losing *our* child ain't none of *your* business," Will said evenly. "We'll handle it our way.

"I'd like to see her anyway," Hallie said, though Chad touched her arm in a cautionary gesture.

"Sorry, Hallie. She don't want to see you or no one."

"Ask her!" Hallie challenged.

To her surprise, Will walked to the open door and called out, "Etta. Come here."

A zombie showed itself in the shadows. Etta, her greasy hair matted and her skin so pallid it looked like chalk, stared out at Chad and Hallie with dead eyes.

"You wanta see Hallie? You want her to come in and talk to you?" His voice held that level calmness that Hallie found so unsettling.

Etta stared at them silently, with no expression in her eyes.

"Etta." Will talked very slowly. "You want to talk with Hallie? Fix her some tea?"

"No. I don't want to see anyone." Etta's voice was hollow as she stood in the doorway, staring into space.

Will turned to Hallie. "There's your answer. Then, to Etta, "You can go back."

Like a trained dog, Etta turned and stepped back inside.

Chad said, "Will, if there's anything we can do at this troubled time, don't hesitate to call on us." He turned Thunder around and jerked his head at Hallie. "Let's go."

Hallie was seething. She waited until they were half a mile from the house and then burst out, "Chad Morgan, what earthly good are you? For heaven's sake—"

"Calm down, Hallie! What do you think you'd have gotten from her if you had gone in? Will had an invisible musket in his hand. She doesn't even breathe without him telling her to."

Hallie halted Princess. "Is Robbie going to die?" she asked, beginning to cry.

Chad sighed. "I wish I could tell you no. I don't know.

478

Etta's our only hope . . . and maybe Brian. If we get him to admit Mary Ann was his child, maybe that will slow down the trial, give us time, make the magistrates realize Will had a vindictive reason."

"I hate that man," Hallie said, kicking Princess so hard that the horse reared. They raced back to Cowarra.

When Hallie stopped at the house, Chad said, "I'm going to ride over to the Daughertys', talk with Brian."

He rode down the hill, slowing Thunder to a snail's pace. To himself he admitted that he was as fearful for Robbie's life as Hallie was. He knew that boy like a son. Better, really, than he knew Jamie. Loved him, if not like a son, like a nephew, like he wished he could feel for Danny's children. He, too, was convinced that Will Colton was lying.

When he knocked at the door, Belinda answered. Her eyes were bloodshot. Hat in hand, Chad asked, "May I come in?"

Belinda stood in the doorway, staring at him. Her voice low, she said, "Brian's in the kitchen."

Chad followed her to where her husband sat staring into a cup of tea. He turned to Belinda. "I've just come from seeing Will Colton. Mind if I talk alone with Brian?"

There was a moment of silence. Then: "I know. I've always known. Brian told me a long time ago," Belinda said.

Surprised, Chad cleared his throat and sat down opposite Brian. "If you tell the magistrates about—about you and Etta, it may help Robbie. They'll at least have to consider this an act of vengeance on Will's part, a way to get back at you."

"Get back at me?" Brian raised pained eyes. "For Christ's sake, he *made* me do it! Sat right there and forced us, holding a gun across his lap."

Forty-seven

The trial was to begin Tuesday morning. Chad couldn't imagine its taking more than one day, if that. However, he took off on Sunday for Parramatta, to try to convince Harry to use his influence to draw it out to two days so Etta might be persuaded to testify against her husband. Will was to take the stand on Tuesday morning. They reasoned he would rise early, while there was still moonlight, and ride into town; that way he would not have to spend money on lodging. Etta would then be alone.

Hallie and Belinda rode over to the Coltons' early Tuesday morning. As she and Belinda approached the cabin, Hallie swore she could hear the silence. There was no breeze; no colorful birds flew from tree to tree with their raucous calls. The sun beat down as heat waves shimmered mirages in front of them. Hallie could taste the dust. Looking around, it seemed to her as if everything had died.

The door to the small house was shut, and there was a lock on it. Hallie knocked, but there was no answer. Had Will taken Etta and the children? She and Belinda walked around the house, straining to see through the dusty windows. Hallie tapped on one. Silence. And then came the faint mewling cry of a baby.

Belinda tried to open the window but could not. In the shed behind the house, Hallie saw an axe. She grabbed it and ran back to swing it against the window; rainbow prisms colored the air as shards of glass flew in all directions. Careful not to cut herself on the jagged edges of broken window, Hallie leaned in and saw Etta sitting on the bed, holding her youngest child; the little boy stood behind her, his arms around her neck. The baby was crying, but neither Etta nor the older child made a sound.

With blank eyes, Etta stared at them.

Hallie climbed through the window, followed by Belinda. She walked over and knelt in front of Etta, thinking, I won-

480

der if she's insane, if she's lost her mind. . . . There was no emotion evident and hardly any life.

Belinda, who had never seen Etta, stared in fascinated horror. Her matted hair hung in greasy hanks. There were hollows so deep that her eyes were large orbs protruding from sunken sockets. Her neck was scrawny, and her ear— the one that had been mangled years ago—looked like nothing human. Her left arm hung limp, useless, dead. Her dress might not have been off her for months. Her dirty feet were bare, and Belinda saw no shoes anywhere. The entire house was filthy beyond words.

"Etta, we've come to help you," Hallie said softly.

Silence echoed off the walls.

After a few minutes, in a voice that spoke of death, Etta said, "No one can help."

"Do you know who I am?"

"Hallie . . ."

"Yes. Do you know where Will's gone?"

There was a hesitation. "He's not here. He went to town."

"Yes. Do you know why?"

Etta nodded. "Yes . . ."

"Why, Etta? Why did he go to town?"

Etta stood up and walked over to the dresser in the corner. There she picked up what might have been the only clean thing in the room, a fresh diaper. Returning to the bed, she laid the baby down and changed it. Then she looked up at Belinda.

"Who's that?" she asked, lifeless eyes swiveling back to Hallie.

"Do you know who Robbie is?" Hallie persisted, determined to go slowly.

Etta shrugged.

"Do you remember who Brian is?" There wasn't a sound, not even of breathing.

Etta sat down. A tear gathered in the corner of her right eye. "Yes . . ." Her voice was a whisper.

"Who is Brian?" urged Hallie.

Etta's mouth trembled. "He was kind to me. He was very nice to me. It was a long time ago."

"Etta, Belinda is Brian's wife, Robbie's mother." Hallie waited a moment for that to sink in. "Will has gone into

481

town to testify that Robbie killed Mary Ann. I don't think he did."

Frightened eyes, like those of a sparrow, darted to Hallie.

"Did Will kill Mary Ann?" Hallie whispered, taking hold of Etta's dead hand.

Etta remained silent.

"Etta, you can help save Belinda's son." She knelt next to the frightened woman. "You've just lost a daughter." Again, she paused. "You know how terrible it is to lose a child. Nothing in the world can be worse. Her son will die if the truth isn't told. Do you know how Will killed her?"

"He took her in a sack out into the woods."

There had been no hesitation, no emotion in her voice. Yet it sounded like an explosion.

Belinda leaned forward. "Did you see him kill her?" It was the first she'd spoken.

No movement from Etta.

"Why did he kill her?" Hallie asked. Her stomach was knotted with apprehension, and her heart pounded. She could hear Belinda's breathing as a little moan escaped her. "Etta . . . look at me," she persisted. "Is Will doing this because Brian is Mary Ann's father?"

Etta stared straight ahead.

"Is he punishing you, and Brian?"

And then the words came pouring out—inexorable, inescapable . . . as though they had a life of their own. Etta opened her mouth, but the resulting flood of sound was beyond her control.

"We'd been married six months," she began. Her eyes focused on some distant spot, and her voice was a monotone. "Will never touched me."

Belinda and Hallie exchanged glances.

"He'd stare at me all the time, and he liked . . . he liked to watch me undress. But he never touched me. Never kissed me. . . ." Her voice trailed off.

"Go on," Hallie urged gently.

"I used to think he was disappointed in me."

Hallie remembered her back then: gloriously beautiful, sweet.

"I was scared to ask him if he was sorry he'd married me. I didn't know what I'd do if he said yes. I tried real hard." Her eyes came back from somewhere and focused

482

on Hallie. "Tried real hard to be pretty for him. Kept the house real clean, you remember?" It sounded as though she were imploring Hallie to reaffirm her. Hallie reached out and patted Etta's skirt.

"I fixed nice meals. I'd go out and chop wood and plant seeds, even when he didn't ask me. I'd ask questions, or comment on the weather, but he'd hardly talk to me." A tear slipped down her cheek. "Except at night, after dinner. Then he'd say it was time for lessons. He'd lecture me about how to be a better wife, a good person. I'd done something wrong, like hadn't folded a napkin the way he liked, or his eggs had been runny, or I'd done something . . . naughty, that's what he called me. I'd done something without asking him. And"—she began to cry quietly—"he'd make me pull down my drawers and lie over his knees and he'd spank me. If I didn't cry, he'd take off his belt and whip me until I couldn't sit for a week."

Hallie felt Belinda's hand on her shoulder, felt Belinda's nails dig into her.

" 'Now,' Will'd say, 'next time you won't do that, will you? You'll learn to ask, won't you?'" Etta was quiet. "But every day he'd find something different. I don't know how I kept on being so stupid. I never seemed to be able to keep track of the things he didn't want me to do." A sigh escaped her. And then she was quiet.

Even though Hallie knew time was of the essence, she couldn't make herself force Etta to go faster. She reached up and put her hand on Belinda's, and Belinda loosened her grip on Hallie's shoulder.

"When Chad sent over a convict to help plow, it was her husband." She nodded at Belinda, but her eyes remained on the floor. "I heard Will telling Brian when he was a child he'd caught a disease that left him unable to ever have children, but that I wanted them mighty bad. I heard him saying in a real low voice, 'I'd consider it a favor if you'd bed my wife. Get her with child.' " Etta's hand went to her mouth and balled into a fist.

"I heard Brian say no, he couldn't do that. Over and over. But Will kept begging. 'It'd make the missus mighty happy,' he said. 'You'd be doing us both a favor.' And then I heard Brian say, 'I haven't had a woman in over four years. Let me ask Etta how she feels about it.' "

Hallie heard Belinda sob.

Etta looked up from the spot on the floor, at Hallie, and said, "I'd never heard him talk of a disease. I didn't believe it. It didn't explain why he never touched me. And I was scared. Bedding a man other than my husband? But he was so nice-looking. Despite being so big, he was gentle and had such sweet black eyes. And I hadn't been held or touched in so long." She drew out the "so," and it sounded like forever. Then she raised her eyes to Belinda, as though offering a reason. Belinda wiped her eyes on her sleeve.

"I thought no man wanted me. I could tell by the way he looked at me, he liked my looks." Hallie felt Belinda's hand on her shoulder again and reached up to touch Brian's wife. "And I did so want a baby. Someone to love."

Hallie drew her head back and looked up at Belinda. Tears drenched her face.

"And then we got on the bed and he undressed me." Again, Belinda's nails dug into Hallie's shoulder. "And just as he entered me—God, I can remember it like it was yesterday—just then Will burst into the room, laughing fit to be tied." Etta started crying again, and her body heaved with sobs. Hallie got up and put her arms around Etta, sitting next to her on the bed.

"He had a gun with him. . . ." Etta's voice sounded like a little girl's, a scared child's. "He sat down on the chair and told Brian, 'If you leave that position, I'll shoot you.' Will sat there for what must've been hours, making Brian do terrible things to me." Belinda's ragged breathing filled the room.

"When finally Brian began to cry, Will let up. He'd been licking his lips and his eyes were glazed." Etta talked as though she still saw it, all these years later. "Every once in a while he'd cry, 'Oh, yes.' Then, when finally Brian couldn't stop crying, Will said, 'Okay, you can stop,' and he told me to get dinner. He wouldn't let either of us put on our clothes. Brian just sat on the floor, with no clothes on, and kept crying. We ate . . . I don't remember what. It's the only thing about that night I don't remember."

Belinda collapsed onto the chair where Hallie had been sitting.

"He told Brian to sleep on a blanket he threw on the floor, and he lay down next to me, and all three of us were naked there together. And he kept asking me what I liked best. And I began to cry, and he said, 'Tell me what his touch felt like . . . tell me what hurt the most.' And while I cried and answered his questions, he kept rubbing himself until at last he moaned and then he let me sleep."

Etta stopped, exhausted. Hallie wondered if she could bear to hear more. She looked over at Belinda, whose hands were shaking.

"The next morning," Etta continued, "Will was in a good humor. He said to Brian, 'I don't expect you've had such a good time since you come here, have you?' But Brian wouldn't answer him. After Brian left, Will left me alone and didn't mention it.

"But a few weeks later, when Brian came back, he told me he'd come back mainly to see if I was all right. But Will pointed his gun at Brian, this time threatening to tell the magistrate that Brian had raped me unless he did those things to me again." Etta looked at Hallie and wound her fingers around Hallie's arm. "He made me crawl on all fours as though I were an animal, and made Brian attack me."

Belinda's cries filled the room.

"I don't remember what else. It was so awful. Then Will went out to the barn and Brian sat with me and we cried together and he said, 'You know I can't come back again. But if you ever need help, you know where I am.' He apologized for all the things he'd been forced to do to me, but he told me how nice I was and how pretty and then he cried again, like a hurt little boy."

Oh, Brian, thought Hallie, and I never knew. I never knew how much you hurt inside. And she remembered his saying, "Don't send me back there again."

"When Walker came"—and Hallie interrupted to explain to Belinda that Walker was the convict—"Will made him do those things to me. At first Walker seemed to like it. He and Will would sit at the dinner table and discuss what Walker'd do to me that night. They'd laugh when I cried out in pain. Will made it clear that if Walker ever touched me without his say-so, he'd kill him. That's how David and my baby came along. They're Walker's."

It seemed Will was fascinated with anything sexual and exhilarated by anything sexual *and* painful. "Yet he never touched me except to beat me or twist my ear or my arm. He told me over and over he couldn't touch me because I was 'defiled'—that was his word. I took too much pleasure in being a wanton whore, he said. He couldn't touch me 'cause I wasn't a lady, because I wasn't neat, because my dinners weren't good, because I didn't sweep the house clean enough, because I was disobedient, because I cried all the time. Or threw up too much. Or was too friendly to neighbors . . ." And absentmindedly she patted Hallie's knee. "He told me if he ever caught me telling family business to anyone, he'd punish me for sure." As it was, he'd beat her on the legs with his belt, he'd broken her arm, turned her ear into a vegetable, and lashed her derriere until it was leathery welts.

"Then it was the children. If they cried, he took his belt to them. If they spilled something, they received the back of his hand. He threw Mary Ann across the room, where she hit the wall"—Etta pointed to the wall—"and slid right down it, unconscious. He picked on her in particular, I guess, 'cause she was a girl. I remember the night"—and now they could hardly hear Etta's voice—"he burned three of her fingers."

Belinda got up and went outside and vomited beside the door.

"She didn't feel nothing anymore," Etta waited to say until Belinda had returned.

Hallie and Belinda could hardly look at each other. No one said anything for a long time. Hallie heard rattling and saw Belinda cleaning up the table, saw her back heaving with sobs. Hallie took a deep breath and turned Etta's face to hers, looking her straight in the eyes. "Are you going to let the man who was so nice to you, the father of your dead daughter, are you going to let his son die for Will's sins?"

Belinda stopped the clatter, standing with her back ramrod straight.

"He'll kill me . . ." Etta gave a low keening cry, like the sound a wounded animal might make.

"He killed your daughter."

Unbroken silence. It must have lasted five minutes. Not even the children made sounds.

Then, in a voice that sounded as though it were coming from far away, Etta said, "He was beginning to look at Mary

Ann funny like. It scared me, and I didn't know why. Everything scared me, though. And then he said, 'It's time Mary Ann got lessons in how to behave like a woman.' I lay awake nights unable to sleep. And then one night, after dinner, instead of giving me lessons, he turned to her and said, 'Today you were talking to that boy. That big boy on the horse. I told you never to speak to strangers.' Mary Ann, she just looked at him and put her thumb in her mouth. 'What'd you tell him?' Will asked her. 'My name," she said. 'Anything else?' he asked. She shook her head. Will reached across the table and put his hand over hers, and I was dreadful frightened, and he said, 'Now, how many times, do you think, have I told you not to talk to no one?' Mary Ann began to cry, and he told her to take off her clothes, and then he poked her in places, and when she cried, he slapped her until her nose began to bleed. Then he said, 'That's just a beginning. I see you talkin' to anyone again, this won't seem like nothin'.' "

Hallie and Belinda listened, mesmerized. It's like being caught in a nightmare, Hallie thought.

"That night I took a pillow and held it over her face until she didn't breathe no more," said Etta, her voice a monotone.

It was a bolt out of the blue.

And then Etta began to cry, sobs that became hysterical, convulsive. Belinda put her arms around the wounded woman and held her close, stroking her hair. Hallie gathered the children into her arms.

"If I'd just been a better wife, he wouldn't'a done it," Etta moaned. "I did all I knew how to. I couldn't think of no more to do. He told me—"

Hallie wanted to shake her. "Etta," she said sternly, "listen to me. Nothing you did or didn't do made you deserve that kind of treatment." But she knew Etta didn't hear her. She may have heard the words, but one statement couldn't overcome years of listening to Will.

"Hallie . . ." Belinda's voice was so quiet that Hallie had to strain to hear her. "How can we ask her to admit to that?"

"Robbie is not going to hang," Hallie said, eyes flashing fire. "We'll take her, and we won't even have her testify. We'll say that it was—it was an accident, that it happened in trying to protect herself and the girl." She stared at Belinda challengingly, daring her to object.

When Belinda merely nodded, Hallie knelt down beside Etta. "Will you come with us, Etta?" she asked softly.

Etta stopped crying, although she was still shaking. "He'll kill me."

"No, he won't. We'll see to that. You'll never have to see him again, ever."

With the face of an innocent child, Etta looked up at them. "I don't have no way to make a living. Will's the only way I can feed my children. I'll starve out here without him."

"I'd rather starve!" Belinda exclaimed.

"But my children . . ."

"Look what you had to do to one of your children to escape him." Hallie realized then that no amount of intelligent discussion would have any effect. Etta was too afraid. "All you'll have to do is stand in court, and let people look at you. You won't have to say anything."

It took over an hour to bundle up Etta and her children, to get a horse saddled, to get a wagon ready. Will we be in time? Hallie wondered. They won't hang Robbie today, certainly. Can they change the verdict if he's already been judged guilty? Was Harry able to stretch it out to two days? Do we have time?

Leading Belinda's horse, Hallie rode alongside the wagon while Belinda tried to make the cart mare go as fast as possible. By the time they arrived at Cowarra, it was past noon.

There they left the two children with Beth, and with Etta in front of Hallie on Princess, the three women took off at a gallop for Parramatta. Etta kept saying, "I'll never see my babies again. He'll kill me." It was after four by the time they arrived, but they could tell by the circling mob of people that the trial was still in progress.

Their entrance created a commotion.

With a quick look at Hallie, Harry rose. "Your Honor, I believe these women have some vital information that would effect the verdict of this trial."

Hallie was about to seat Etta next to her, but the other woman pulled away and walked down the aisle, staring at Will Colton. Hallie reached out for her, afraid that one look from him would inhibit her, but Etta was not to be stopped.

The crowd gasped at the sight of the battered, grotesque automaton.

"Please be seated," intoned the judge.

But Etta merely stood staring at her husband. Then she turned and looked at Robbie, the image of her dead daughter.

"Judge . . ." Hallie's voice quivered. "We have evidence that Robert Daugherty did *not* kill Mary Ann Colton."

"Order in the court—" began the judge.

Hallie saw Etta shaking. Dear God in heaven, she thought, don't let her back down. Without realizing she was going to say it, Hallie heard her own voice, loud and clear: "Will Colton killed his daughter."

Etta turned to stare back at Hallie. Their eyes locked.

Hallie took a deep breath. Forgive me, God. But even if you don't . . . She felt Belinda's hand squeeze hers. She turned to gaze at Belinda, and only she saw the nearly imperceptible nod.

"Look at this woman," Hallie continued. The judge and magistrates were already staring with open mouths. "Will Colton beat her. Will Colton broke her arm. Look at her ear. Not only is it disfigured, but she can't hear in that ear. Her body bears marks of repeated beatings. Dr. Faulkner can examine her and verify that, and that the dead girl's body bore marks of beatings—not fresh ones, either." She paused for a space of three beats to allow her words to sink in. Then, slowly and deliberately, she said: "He did the same thing to his little girl as he did to his wife—and the beating killed her."

Will Colton leaped to his feet. "I didn't kill no one!" His eyes burned into his wife. "Tell them, Etta. Tell them!"

Raising her right arm, Etta pointed it straight at Will. "He done it," she said in a loud, clear voice. "I saw him. He done killed my daughter." She turned to look at Hallie and then Belinda. "I told them so," she said. "Didn't I?"

In a state of exhaustion and shock, Hallie and Belinda looked at each other. "Yes . . ." Belinda's voice was but a whisper; she was pressing Hallie's hand hard. "That's what she told us. Mr. Colton killed their daughter."

Will didn't say anything. Etta smiled at him.

Forty-eight

Governor Thomas Brisbane decided to throw *his* annual gala on the King's birthday, and Hallie and Chad—without the children—went in to Sydney for the parties. Not only was there the governor's ball on the King's birthday, but for a whole week the city would be buzzing with picnics and yachting races and a band concert, as well as numerous other dinner parties. People had come from as far as 150 miles for the festivities. Chad had entered their prize two-year-old, Timor, in the Saturday race. He and Hallie stayed with Tristan and Molly so that they could spend time with Jamie, though they already had received invitations to dine each night at different houses.

When Chad had suggested that they leave the children with Beth and Sophie and go into Sydney for a week of merrymaking, take the first holiday they'd ever taken together, Hallie's initial thought was that she no longer fit into either of her ball gowns. It wasn't that she had even become plump, but six children had taken their toll on her—she no longer had a twenty-two-inch waist, and her bosom now curved so voluptuously that the early, girlish gowns no longer suited her.

Chad, who delighted in shopping with her, insisted on buying her an absolutely stunning scarlet ball gown that would undoubtedly scandalize all of Sydney. He ordered slippers dyed to match, and laughed when he saw the expression on her face. "My heavens, Chad," she exclaimed, "I can't wear this!"

"Why not?" He grinned. "Show them that we country bumpkins can set the style."

Then he had waited until that evening, as they were dressing, to say, "Close your eyes."

She was pinching her cheeks, trying to get them to match her dress, and looked over at him. "Why?" she asked.

"I have a present for you."

490

"Another? This dress, these slippers . . ."

"They're for the party," he said. "So that people will look at you and envy me. This is . . . well, close your eyes, but stay there, in front of the mirror."

She felt him slip a chain around her throat, felt his fingers playing with a clasp. Felt him kiss her shoulder, then run his tongue along her neck.

"Now. Open your eyes." He was smiling.

Encircling her neck was a thin gold chain, but slipping between her breasts was an immense square-cut diamond. It sparkled in the candlelight. Chad, filled with anticipatory pleasure, watched her.

"Oh, Chad!" Delighted, Hallie pirouetted in front of the mirror. "But why?"

He shrugged. "Must I have a reason for giving a jewel to my wife? Well, if so, let's say it's—it's a thank you for six lovely children. For all that we have built up *together*. For your being like no one else in the world."

Hallie laughed. "How you do exaggerate." She had heard "our six children" and, as usual, experienced a twinge of conscience that kept her from complete enjoyment of the diamond. "Why, everyone will just die of jealousy," she said, turning back to the ornate cheval glass. "I do believe they will."

"You've never had any jewelry before, have you?" Chad asked, his eyes narrowed.

"No," she said. "How could I have?" Again, uneasy stirrings of guilt . . . for hidden in the back of a drawer, tied in a handkerchief, were the earrings that had belonged to Tristan's mother, the other Julie. She had not taken them out, not even looked at them, since Chad had come home.

The Brisbanes' ball was even more lavishly decorated than those of the Macquaries. Hallie knew that despite being thirty-two, despite having six children, heads often turned to look at her. Tonight, however, no one could fail to notice her—and, she observed, not everyone eyed her flamboyance with approval.

Chad introduced her to Governor Brisbane, who bent slightly while holding her hand and said, "I see the things we've heard about you are true."

Chad smiled at her proudly. "The most beautiful woman in New South Wales."

491

Embarrassed, Hallie wondered why Chad always put so much importance on having everyone acknowledge her beauty. Damn! Sometimes she wished she were plain, just to know for certain if it were she he admired or merely the superficial trappings. For some reason she suddenly recalled the phrase Chad always used when referring to Timor or one of their prize merinos: good breeding stock . . . Was that how he saw her?

A moment later Captain Merriwether of the New South Wales Corps approached and offered her his white-gloved hand. "May I have the honor of this dance?" he asked.

Hallie moved into his arms as the music began, praying she could remember the steps to the minuet.

"You're the most exquisite creature I've ever seen," he murmured as they danced.

Was that supposed to impress her? Hallie wondered. Should she find *him* irresistible because he liked her looks? She didn't answer, merely gave him a polite smile . . . and was relieved when the dance was over and another partner claimed her.

Then it was one after another. Hallie found that she was enjoying herself immensely. It wasn't until supper was announced that Chad walked over to her. She had watched him, all evening, staring across the room at her. He had danced but twice, once with Susan and again with Mrs. Brisbane.

"When did you learn to dance?" he asked, bringing her supper. "You never told me."

"I told you I've been to governor's balls before, while you were away. Susan and Harry taught me." And Tristan . . .

"Well, the next one's mine," Chad declared.

All her life, Hallie would associate Tristan with the governor's New Year's Eve balls, but actually he would no longer be invited to them. She had known he would not be attending tonight, but she kept looking for him anyway. Lord Bathurst, the secretary for the colonies, and the new Governor Brisbane had agreed that emancipists should neither be appointed magistrates nor be invited to dine at the governor's. Redeemed they might become, but invited socially into homes of the free immigrants, no. Thus, one of Sydney society's richest citizens—and certainly one of its most respected, the one who had saved their lives and seen their private parts and heard their innermost secrets—was now officially a social outcast.

That night, Hallie was unquestionably the most glamorous woman at Governor Brisbane's ball. But without Tristan there to mirror what she saw in the eyes of strangers, it was a hollow triumph.

On their way back to the Faulkner household after the ball, Chad announced that he would leave her off but then was going on. Merriwether and some of the others were gathering for a game of cards. "I probably won't be home until nearly morning," he announced. Hallie caught the enthusiasm in his voice.

"What would you do if you lost everything?" she asked idly.

"I'd never wager *that* much," he said. "I never bet more than I can afford to lose. But as an academic exercise? By 'everything' you mean financial, don't you? You mean Cowarra and all the sheep and horses and . . ."

Hallie looked over at him, beside her in the carriage.

"My dear, I would still be the richest man imaginable. I have you, and our children, and we would simply start over. Somehow it is not something that greatly worries me. We'd go over the mountains and start anew." He squeezed her hand, then laughed. "You'd probably like that, wouldn't you? A new challenge. You'd have to work hard again, and every day there'd be excitement."

"It does have allure," she agreed, smiling. "However, it would pain me deeply to leave Cowarra."

"I know," he said. "But you asked."

When they arrived, he helped her down from the carriage. Bringing her gloved hand to his lips, he murmured, "I'm not sure why I'm going when the most exciting thing I could do tonight is make love to you."

No, she thought, not in Tristan's house. I couldn't. "You can have me any night," she said as they approached the front door.

"After all these years, that idea still excites me," he said, gazing at her in frank admiration.

She felt a sudden warmth toward him. He really was an awfully nice man, she reflected. She leaned over to kiss him lightly. "I'm very fond of you, too, Chad Morgan."

"Why, Hallie . . ." He laughed self-consciously. "I have

493

a mind not to go to that game. You never say such things to me." He put his arms around her and kissed her lingeringly, hungrily.

But after a moment she held him away from her, saying, "You can kiss me anytime. Go, have fun at your cards. Win enough to pay for my necklace."

"Will you be fond of me even if I lose?" he asked teasingly.

"I'll have no way of knowing, will I?" She no longer knew anything about their finances. She no longer knew how many sheep they had or how many pounds of fleece they sent to England. Sometimes she didn't even know how many convicts they had.

Chad grinned. "I may wake you up when I return, if I feel like I do now," he said, and opened the door.

Tristan stood there.

He had not been home when they left, as he had been performing emergency surgery at the hospital. He had not dined with them, nor seen Hallie in her red dress. He had not seen the diamond necklace.

"Hello, old man," Chad said, reaching out to shake hands. "Didn't expect anyone to be up at this hour."

"I've not been home long," Tristan answered, his eyes on Hallie.

Chad noticed the look and laughed. "She might have been the Queen herself for all the attention she received tonight."

"I remember"—Tristan's voice was soft—"another dance, many years ago, when the same thing happened."

Chad clasped Tristan's shoulder and was off. Hallie waved at him as the carriage rumbled away, then turned back to find that Tristan still had not taken his eyes from her. He stepped back several paces, the better to survey her. "Turn around," he said, twirling his hand in the air, "so I can see all of you."

She did.

"Oh, Hallie . . ." It was scarcely a whisper. His gaze fastened on the diamond, and when his eyes again met hers again, it was as though they were magnets. He moved toward her slowly—giving her time to back away, time to say no. But she could not. Did not want to. She wanted to feel him against her, feel his lips on hers, his very breath mingling with hers.

She leaned back against the door, and he stopped but an inch away from her. She could see the hunger reflected in his eyes as his lips met hers. Their bodies did not touch. His hands were on either side of her head, palms flat against the door, and his lips were soft against hers, his tongue running gently along her mouth, pressing hers open. And in that instant, five years melted away. They were one again. When he moved the length of his body against hers, she could feel his heart beating, hear the pounding of her own, and she threw her arms around him.

"Oh, Tristan," she breathed, holding him close. "I miss you so."

"It's been torture to keep away from you all week," he whispered. "So many times I've wanted to reach out for you, touch you, kiss you. Even look at you, look at you and tell you I love you—that I shall never love anyone as I do you."

"Yes. Yes. I love you, too. I think of you . . ."

Abruptly he backed away, his eyes tortured. "God, Hallie, we must stop this. It's just that you look—I saw you there . . ." His voice trailed away and he stood staring at her.

She tried to control her rapid breathing. He was right: they must not let themselves. It was wrong. Tristan had a wife who loved him; he had children, responsibilities. And she . . . she had a husband who gave her scarlet gowns and glittering jewels. It was an impossible situation.

Tristan went over to the cupboard and poured himself a drink. Hallie took off her gloves and sank onto a nearby chair. Tristan drank quickly and stood where he was. Then, in an instant, he was across the room, kneeling next to her. "There's only one problem with Molly. She's not you. I lie next to her at nights, Hallie, and sometimes I'm angry at her because she isn't you."

She nodded. "I know. It's the same with Chad. A really nice man whose main fault is that he is not Dr. Tristan Faulkner."

"But Chad is much more than Tristan Faulkner. He's a man of vision, of action, of marvelous temperament—"

"I've never seen you lose your temper," Hallie said.

He shook his head. "I've become disgustingly moody."

"But you have a gentleness Chad doesn't." She put her hand on his.

"And he generates an excitement I lack."

"Whatever you are or aren't, I love you," Hallie said, taking his hand. "I have never been happier in my life than the years you rode out to Cowarra, when we shared our ideas, when you brought plants and grapevines, and taught us all how to add and subtract. I have never been happier than in those years—those years when Chad was away."

"If only Molly and Chad weren't such fine people," Tristan said, rising, "It might be easier. I would like to dislike Chad, because he has you. But I like him, and if I can't father my children, then he's the one—"

"I know," said Hallie, standing also. "Life is a puzzle, isn't it?"

Tristan smiled wistfully. "I'm not sure I believe in God, or an afterlife," he said softly. "But I do feel that someday our dust will mingle. And then we shall be together for eternity. And that will have to suffice."

Tears sprang to Hallie's eyes. She held out her hands, and Tristan took them and drew her close. "Know, always, that I love you, and have never stopped for one minute. Know that you are always in my heart." He kissed her with tenderness.

She lay in bed for hours that night, awake until nearly dawn. She was in that half-dream state between sleep and wakefulness when Chad returned, at nearly five.

She didn't open her eyes, even when he turned back the covers and said, "Why, Hallie, I've never known you to go to bed without your nightdress." And then he laughed, as though to himself. "Have you been waiting for me all this time?" Then she turned toward him, her eyes still closed, and opened her arms. He came to her with passion, aroused at her quick response, at her legs around his waist before he barely was in bed. He made love to her with a wildness that had been lacking lately from their love-making.

With her eyes closed, Hallie responded to Chad as never

before. For it was Tristan to whom she made love, with whom she had been making love all night long as she lay alone.

Forty-nine

Now that there was a road between Morgantown and Parramatta, most women rode in buggies or wagons. Hallie only did so when the children were with her or when she was taking a wagonload of goods one way or the other. She far preferred riding on Princess. On this trip to attend the festivities in Sydney, she had told Chad she wanted to ride through the beautiful valley, cantering with the wind in her face. Molly packed them a picnic lunch.

It wasn't until they stopped for lunch by a clear fast-running creek that they had an opportunity for conversation. Chad was in high good spirits. Timor had won, for the first time since Cowarra had entered horses in Sydney's races—a long shot. Not only had Chad made a great deal of money on the race, but he had also sold prospective breeding rights by Timor for an unbelievable sum.

He had tried to explain to Hallie that it was not so much the money that counted, "though that is fun. It gives me enough to spend on baubles like your necklace. But it's pitting oneself against chance that excites me. I like betting on my instincts and finding them right."

"I don't understand the desire to gamble at all," she said, though she didn't mind his penchant for wagering.

Chad leaned back against a large she-oak. His still-luxuriant chestnut hair never quite looked trim. Five minutes after he brushed it, a lock would fall over his forehead. Hallie thought he always looked slightly windblown. The sun, dappling through the leaves, danced shadows across his rugged face. His gray eyes smiled at her.

"My dear, you are as much a gambler as I," he told her. "You gamble on many things, though perhaps not with money. You've taken many chances. The store, buying thousands of acres, all those sheep. Look at the chance you took coming halfway around the world to marry me."

"That didn't seem like much of a gamble," said Hallie.

"You've never been sorry?"

She smiled. "Have I ever seemed so?"

"I mean sorry to have married me."

There was just a second's hesitation. "Have I ever seemed so?"

He gnawed on a chicken leg and then tossed it across the stream. "Hallie, we need more of the socializing we've had this week. You've enjoyed it, too, haven't you?"

"It's been wonderful. I feel invigorated."

"I've been thinking—let's build a house in Sydney. No, now listen," he said as she opened her mouth to interrupt. "Not to live there, but to have when any of us wants to be in town. For weeks like this one and other holidays. When we go to the races. For times when you miss Jamie. For times when anyone at Cowarra wants to go to town. Nothing grand, just a nice house."

He couldn't have known, of course, but it went along perfectly with an idea crystallizing in her mind. She wouldn't talk to him about it now, however.

"The other boys will be going in to Sydney to school before too many years," Chad continued. "We can't impose on the Faulkners to take care of all our sons. Wick will be going in another year, and two years later, Garth. I go into town often enough that a house there would be a viable financial investment.

"I think we also ought to build a mill next to the store. Grind flour and corn for the valley's farmers. And a kiln. Ours at the farm isn't large enough to supply all the building needs of the valley."

She looked at him with envy. Obviously he had been busy with plans for the future. And Tristan was right when he'd said that Chad was exciting. But he was no longer as invigorating or overpowering for her as he had been before his long sojourn in England. Ever since she'd had the chance to be in charge of her life and the lives of so many others, to be the one who could answer all the questions that needed answering, she'd seen life from a different perspective. And there could be no turning back. Never again would she be content to be just a mother and dutiful wife. She had to have more.

But how? Chad was always brimming with plans and schemes for his precious dynasty. What motivated him, kept him interested and excited with life? Idly, she wondered if he had ever been in love, truly in love, as she loved Tristan. Without realizing it, she voiced her thoughts aloud. "Have you ever been in love?"

Chad, in the act of peeling a banana, looked at her. He stared for a long time before answering. "Why do you ask that?"

Hallie shrugged, gazing through the lacy foliage up at the cobalt sky. "I don't know. I just wondered."

He was silent for so long that she thought he might not answer. She watched the stream rush over smooth stones.

"When I was in my teens, I thought I was in love with . . . an older woman. I couldn't think of anything else for two years. Nothing else mattered at all. Is that what you mean?"

"I don't know."

He arched an eyebrow and stared at her with an indecipherable look on his face, appearing vulnerable to Hallie. It surprised her. Suddenly she was frightened, sorry she had asked such a personal question. What if he, in return, asked her?

She stood up abruptly, brushing crumbs from her skirt. "We'd better get going if we hope to be home for dinner." She waited for him to place his hand under her foot so he could boost her onto her saddle.

By 1824 Chad's "nice house" was finished. It resembled an Italian villa, with six bedrooms on the second floor, and—like the big house at Cowarra—even a bathroom with a cast-iron tub all its own. The drawing room was not ostentatious—about the size of the first house they had built at Cowarra—but there was also a ballroom with a marble floor. The drawing room and ballroom faced the harbor, on either side of a large foyer with wide stairs leading to the other floors. The third story contained the maids' rooms. Hallie and Chad's bedroom overlooked the immense veranda, with its marbled columns, and manicured lawns sloping down to the harbor, sparkling in the sunlight. Hallie and Alex took upon themselves the planting of thousands of plants, bulbs, shrubs, and trees. Chad again chose all the furniture without consulting Hallie. She did not mind, however, for she knew his taste was far more sophisticated than hers. She'd always liked whatever he had chosen, in all three of their homes.

The smaller children—Wick and Julie were now six, Garth four, and Chloe three—loved the variety of two homes, of added playmates in the city, of the change in environment. It was Alex who resented having to divide her time. She set her jaw and proclaimed that she didn't want to miss school, that she hated the city. Hallie lured her to town only when she asked for horticultural advice and help. At twelve Alex knew more about plants than anyone except Tristan. Thus she came in to help plant the spacious grounds and visit with Jamie, who continued, at his own request, to reside with the Faulkners. Otherwise, she stayed at Cowarra with Beth. Hallie also suspected it was to be near Robbie.

"Three, *three* homes." Sophie couldn't get over it. Nor could Danny and Tess. They came into the city one weekend and Tess's eyes lit up. She prowled the streets happily and stopped to talk with people she'd never seen before.

Hallie was embarrassed to overhear a conversation her brother and his wife were having in the dining room Sunday afternoon. She knew she shouldn't listen, but it riveted her to the spot.

"I want to stay here." Tess's voice had a hardness to it. "I don't want to go back to the country."

There was silence for a minute, and then Danny said, "But that's where my life began."

"And where I died," hissed his wife. "I haven't felt alive since we left England."

"You've made no effort to become part of my family."

"Your family! Sure, they live up in that big house and lord it over us! You work just as hard as Chad does. Harder'n Hallie. And they're up in that big castle . . . instead of giving us that house they used to live in, they give it to sinful women. Women who have illegitimate children and no arms! And leave us in that little five-room house to show us we're not important."

Have I done that? Hallie wondered, guilt surging through her. Why did I not see? Certainly I should have let Danny have that house and put Melanie and Laurie in

501

their little one. She heard Danny's sigh, even from the next room.

"It's bigger than any house we'd have had in Newcastle," he said defensively.

"Sure, you're never there. But I'm cooped up all day with no one to talk to."

"There're lots of people at Cowarra. Lots of women. You mean they're not your mother and sisters! You just don't try to talk with them."

Then Tess began crying, a whiny sound. *"You* never talk with me. You never even answer my questions. You don't pay attention to the children. All you want to do is play with grapes. For heaven's sake, drinking spirits is evil, and here's my husband doing that kind of work. Work of the devil!"

"You think everything's the handiwork of Satan." Danny's voice sounded resigned. "You thought creating children was evil."

"I don't notice you've wanted more children since we moved here."

"My God," he cried, "everytime I ever tried to touch you, you acted like I smelled! Even when you didn't push me away I thought I was doing something horrible to you. Why the hell would I keep trying?"

"It's true," she cried, "I hate it. But I'm smart enough to know I have to do it to have children. You make me feel useless, not a real woman, when I don't have children. But I do hate it; it's evil."

Danny's voice was quiet, so low that Hallie had to strain to hear him. "What's so evil about creating children? About a man and woman who're married touching each other?"

"Touching? Is that what you call it? Wet, slobbering lips, being grabbed . . ."

"Yes, even when you nursed the children, you couldn't stand to have them suckling you."

Tess began to sob. "I hate the smell of sweat. I hate the things men do to you to have babies. I hate—"

"You hate kisses and you hate touching another person's body and you hate how men look . . ."

"I wish I'd never met you." She'd stopped crying and sounded like she'd pounce on him, wanting to claw at him.

In a tired voice, Danny said, "I know. I've known that for years."

"I wish you'd died in the mine. Wish I were back in Newcastle with my mother and sisters. Wish I were a widow and could leave here, get away from this dreadful country."

With that Tess swept out of the room, past Hallie, who was glued in the hallway, brushing her as she passed, her eyes afire, and spitting at Hallie, "And it's your fault!" Tess propelled herself up the wide stairway, and in a minute Hallie heard a door slam upstairs. When she looked in the dining room, Danny had put his head on the table, his hands over his ears.

He left for Cowarra the next morning. Tess stayed on in town, just moved herself into one of the big upstairs rooms and didn't return to the farm even for Christmas. Roger and Pamela, with no one to oversee them or feed them, moved into the children's wing of the big house at Cowarra, and Danny lived alone in the little house Chad had built for him. Once or twice a week he ate with Emil, but otherwise he dined at the big house, and no one made any mention of the new housing arrangements.

One Sunday afternoon, Hallie was reclining on a green-and-white-striped chaise, at Cowarra, watching Sophie, Chloe, and Garth play a game at the far end of the veranda, when she heard Beth say, "I killed a man. At least I think I did. . . ."

The words hung there in the air. There was no vocal inflection. It was a flat statement.

Quietly, Hallie rose and walked soundlessly toward Beth's voice, but before she could descend the porch steps and peer around the side of the house, she heard Danny's voice.

"It doesn't matter," he said. "He must have deserved it. It doesn't matter at all, do you understand? It doesn't change my feelings whatsoever."

Hallie stopped. She stood there for a moment, thinking, and then backed silently away.

For a long time Beth had not done the cooking. She arranged the menus and spent hours in the kitchen, tasting dishes and overseeing the kitchen help, but she also spent time supervising the two maids who were necessary in the upkeep of such a large house. They slept in rooms over the stables that were behind the great house.

She never went into Sydney, never left Cowarra for any reason, even though it was now nearly twelve years since she'd arrived. Sometimes she could be seen out in the vineyards with Alex and Danny and Emil, or riding with Sophie or Alex across the hills. And she was nanny to all the children, to Danny's as well as Hallie's and Chad's. Recently Hallie had noticed a new look in her eyes, one she now thought she understood.

Sometimes Beth spent the night over at the old house with the women. Etta and her children had taken up residence there, along with Melanie, Laurie, and Sophie. Sophie told Hallie she thought it was time for Melanie and Laurie to stop sitting around and start doing things. Maybe get jobs in Sydney or Parramatta, something to bring them into contact with people and away from such a restricted life.

Etta, on the other hand, who was slow coming out of the shell she had been thrust into and who cringed whenever she saw herself in a mirror, was finding solace in living at Cowarra. Several months before Will Colton had been killed in the prison up at Coal Town, strangled by two other prisoners who were then hanged. It was only upon hearing that news that Etta began to visibly relax. Hallie wondered, however, if Etta would ever fit back into society after her years with Will.

"They're becoming like nuns," Sophie said to Hallie about the two younger women, the ones Tristan had brought out to them. "Separated from the world. If we don't get them back into society soon, they'll be too scared to talk to people again. Time to let them learn that all men aren't bad, too."

Yes, thought Hallie. And it's up to us to see that they aren't treated like they were. For this purpose the new house in town was exactly what she needed. Now that it was completed, she found herself dividing her time between Cowarra and Sydney.

She spent a long time thinking of Etta, and of Laurie, Melanie, and Beth. It made her look at every woman she passed on the streets of Sydney. She began haunting the docks when new ships were sighted, watching the women

504

come ashore, waiting to see both the free women and the women prisoners and to study as well as question them. All the time the new house had been under construction, she made excuses to be in Sydney but spent more time at the docks than in overseeing details of the house. She visited the Women's Prison Factory in Parramatta over and over again. Once in a while she succeeded in persuading Susan to join her on these excursions.

An idea had been evolving in Hallie's mind. "Why can't we find a place where these women arriving can be housed?" she asked Susan one day.

Susan looked at her, raising her perfect eyebrows in question. "Come, Hallie, you're thinking beyond that, I can tell."

Hallie smiled. "We could meet them at the ships, offer them shelter and find decent jobs for them. Not let them take the first ones offered. See that men don't offer them marriage, use them, and then renege on marriage. See that they're not carted off to thankless jobs at next to no pay. Have someone—us—to guide them and take care of them in a new country."

Hallie's enthusiasm was contagious. "Be marriage brokers, too, couldn't we?" Susan said, her eyes sparkling.

"Wonderful idea!" Hallie threw her arms around her friend. "Yes, not let them be taken advantage of. Get them decent wages or husbands instead of having them end up on the streets, used . . ."

"Dis-used, you mean!"

Hallie nodded in agreement. "Dis-used. I've been thinking of how we could get money to finance a home for them, someplace that would house . . . oh, fifty to sixty women."

"More than that arrive with each ship. How about ninety?" Susan got up and began to pace across her living room. "And what of the young women convicts? Some of those should be given chances, not just arbitrarily assigned to any man who wants to use them and then throw them out seven years later, when they're unmarriageable."

Hallie gazed at Susan with admiration. She'd been thinking along such lines for months, while Susan had jumped right in with gusto, full of ideas.

"Let me talk to Harry," Susan continued. "He may know how we could raise funds for housing . . ."

"I think we could approach the wives of all the city's leading citizens," said Hallie, "not the men. Involve the women, and make this a project in which they can participate."

"Of course the money *will* have to come from their husbands."

"Of course." Hallie smiled.

At this, Susan broke into laughter. "What a wonderful idea, Hallie!"

The two women agreed that it would take tact and time to approach their husbands. Hallie waited while her mind churned furiously.

Sophie began to accompany her into Sydney and found city life invigorating. "I'd forgotten that I liked living with neighbors in sight," she said, "I love the country so. But there is something exciting about a city, isn't there?"

Unlike the squalid, ramshackle colony of Hallie's arrival, Sydney was now clean. Its streets were symmetrical, all houses had neat patches of gardens, and ducks and chickens waddled around the streets, but this added a charm lacking in English cities. Porches abundant with bright geraniums and nasturtiums were swept mornings, and pride was evident in the public and private buildings of the city.

The Rocks, that open peninsula to the left of Sydney Cove proper, was a notorious hangout of prostitutes and ex-convicts who did not have steady jobs; murders were rampant there, and raucous carousing continued until the early morning hours. Sewage clogged its streets, and its houses were already in states of decay. But in 1825 the solid citizens of Sydney ignored this part of their city that was so readily visible from the docks and harbor.

Nevertheless, Hallie and Sophie visited it in the light of day, clutching each other's arms for reassurance. They ignored the catcalls and innuendos, the drunken leers, and though they spoke to no one, they looked around them carefully.

At dinner one night, when he'd come in from Cowarra for several days, Chad said, "What's this I hear about you two wandering around the Rocks? Every person I meet tells me—it's the first thing I hear."

Sophie and Hallie looked at each other; they hadn't thought anybody had even noticed. Then, with a slight nod,

506

Hallie looked to her husband. This, she decided, was as good a time as any to tell him her plans.

"Chad . . . do you remember when Chloe was born, I told you I wanted to change the fate of women?"

"I remember. I hoped you'd forgotten. You must have enough to keep you busy."

"Busyness isn't always enough," she remarked sharply. "There's more to life than just being busy."

"Are you going to tell me that running two homes, the farm, the vineyard, six children, and your mother and brother is not enough for you?"

Hallie turned on him. "Enough? Are you measuring quantity? What do you mean, 'enough'? Ever since you came home I've been relegated to the typical role that all women are supposed to find satisfying. And a great deal of it I do find fulfilling. I love being a mother. It's fun to have two homes. But dammit, Chad, you allow me no dreams, no goals. Nothing that comes from within me. I do follow a role, and often it pleases me. But I need more. I need to *do* something. I need to have *my* mind active, be planning things, make things happen. You robbed me of that when you came home, and I miss it!"

Chad sank onto a chair, staring. "I robbed you?"

Sophie stood up. "Excuse me," she said, and left the room.

"Yes," Hallie continued. "You sent me back to days with no challenges except changing diapers or deciding what to eat for dinner."

"You don't even do that now!" he exclaimed.

"I know. There's absolutely *nothing* I have to do. And it doesn't make any difference that we're rich. If we weren't, I'd be cleaning and cooking and doing all the things Sophie was imprisoned by for years." She began to pace. "Drudgery. I do thank you for rescuing me from that. But ever since you came back from England, I've felt that I was playing a role. Mrs. Chadwick Morgan. Mother Morgan. I haven't been able to be the me I discovered and liked, the life I loved while you were away!"

"Hallie, I didn't know—" He looked up at her, perplexed.

"Oh, yes, you've known. How many times have you said to me, 'I don't understand you'? You've sensed there was something deep down that wasn't satisfied, but you didn't want to see it." She pointed an accusatory finger at him. "You've thought I ought to be grateful, coming from the grime of Newcastle—where my life would have been drudgery forever—to a clean land and to riches, to homes and to servants, and to wide-open spaces, to being invited to the governor's, to lovely clothes—which I admit are very pretty. You've thought I ought to thank my lucky stars that you sent for me and that you give me so much!"

"Have I ever said that?" Chad sounded lost.

"No. You're much too much a gentleman for that."

"Hallie . . ." He was silent a moment before continuing. "Maybe I have done that, though not so as I was aware of it. I have enjoyed buying you things, giving you homes—"

"You haven't done those things for *me,*" she interrupted. "You've done them for yourself. For the pleasure you think you've given me. For the pride you feel when others make comments about the homes and clothes and carriages and diamond of the wife of Chad Morgan."

The air hung heavy with tension as Hallie turned her back on Chad and gazed out at the expanse of lawn, at the harbor in the late afternoon sunlight. Her heart pounded. Where had all this anger come from?

"Susan and Mum and I . . ." She was being a coward, she knew, to include two women whom she knew Chad respected. But she couldn't help it. She watched his face as she told him of their plans, still in the dream stage. Told him they hoped to build a house, "one where women newly arrived here can stay until we find them well-paying jobs or reliable husbands. They can stay there until we are as sure as we can be that they find men who won't beat them or won't bed them without marriage, or won't misuse them or pay them incredibly low wages or make them lowly servants and nothing more. We'll meet ships and urge these women not to wander around Sydney alone, tell them not to believe the men who offer them marriage or jobs with good wages. We'll tell them they have a choice and that they needn't take the first man who makes them offers, but they can take their time and choose who and what they want. And we shall include women recently released from prison, or from servitude with men who have misused them, so they needn't turn to prostitution or to hopeless lives."

Chad's mouth had dropped open in amazement. "How are you going to pay for all this? A house takes money, you know. Feeding them will take money, too."

Now Hallie turned from the window and met his eyes. "You don't have to put money into it; we're going to raise the money ourselves. From the women of this community."

Chad continued to stare at her. "You are the damnedest woman in the whole world." She could not tell whether it was a compliment or a complaint . . . until he smiled.

In the next six months there were raffles for quilts, a strawberry social, a dinner dance that cost fifty shillings a couple, and a dozen other money-raising activities. The men smiled at each other over the women's heads, convinced they could never raise enough money. Harry had volunteered to keep track of their funds and opened an account for them at the bank. The women raised barely a quarter of the money to cover the cost of a three-story home that could house ninety women. During a visit, Chad told him, "Let them think they've done it by themselves. But let me know what's needed."

That night Harry lay with Susan in his arms, listening to her enthuse over the project. The next day he donated land on George Street. Tristan announced a donation of over three hundred pounds, earmarking it for the first year's expenses. The women never knew that three quarters of their money, the difference between what they needed and what they had raised, came from a check that Chad gave to Harry.

509

Fifty

While Hallie and Sophie were tramping around the Rocks and scandalizing Sydney's finest with their bold ways, Ben Lambert was in the process of wooing—and winning—Dorothy Hamilton. Though no one knew for sure which had come first, Dorothy's pregnancy or Ben's proposal of marriage, it all worked out for the best, and Hallie returned home for the wedding. She and Chad agreed upon a handsome wedding gift with which to launch the happy couple: one-half interest in the store, from Hallie, and from Chad, a half interest in the kiln and mill that was being built.

Shortly after his wedding and formal adoption of Nathan, Ben came up to the house to speak with Chad. "Been thinkin'," he began. "Now that I'm part owner in the store, I'd like to expand."

Chad smiled. "I was wondering how long it'd take you to start thinking along those lines. What exactly did you have in mind?"

"All these little towns sprung up could use a store like ours. And I want a big one in Sydney. One that carries everything. One where I can buy things right off the ships and store them in a warehouse. One that can supply stores directly in the towns, an operation that'll rely on no one else but ourselves."

"What do you want from me," Chad asked, "approval?"

"Well, that, too." Ben shifted the ever-present blade of dried grass from one side of his mouth to the other. "But money, mainly. Won't be cheap. You put up the money, I'll do the work and . . . and the planning," he said, and Chad could have sworn Ben puffed up like a rooster. "If we're going to be partners in Morgantown, I may as well cut you in on all the rest."

"Tell you what," Chad said. "If any of my sons wants to

510

participate when they're older, you let them. They'll have my partnership then."

Ben scratched his head. "Same, then, for mine. If Nathan wants. Or if the baby's a boy."

Chad held out his hand. "I'll tell Harry to give you a line of credit. Keep me informed as you go along."

Ben shook Chad's hand. "I need help in this store, though. I'm going to have to be in Sydney a lot. And go over to Windsor and Richmond, Parramatta. I'd like Charlie."

Charlie was a nondescript convict whom they'd had about two years, a skinny young man who worked hard but was too frail to keep up with the others in farm work.

Chad nodded. "Start training him tomorrow. How is he with figures?"

"Better'n I was at his age." Ben turned, ready to leave.

Quietly Chad said, "Partner."

Ben turned, a smile on his face. "You know what? I'm going to be somebody. I have a family I'd never have had back there, and I feel it all over me—I'm going to be somebody. I guess I already am if I'm *your* partner, huh?"

"Ben, tell you what. From the minute I returned from England I've known you were somebody."

Ben blinked quickly and said, "Thanks, Chad." It was the first time he hadn't called him Mr. Morgan.

At around this same time, Tristan told them it was time for Jamie to return to England to study medicine. Hallie protested.

"Certainly you can teach him all he needs to know. All that you know," she said.

"I can't let my limitations be his. Jamie should go to the Royal College of Surgeons."

Hallie looked at her son. Despite his spending the school year with the Faulkners, she saw a great deal of him, especially now that she was often in residence in Sydney herself. He still spent summers at Cowarra, and when he came home, Alex had eyes for no one else. "Is this what you want?" Hallie asked him. "It means not only five years of school, but a year and a half coming and going."

Jamie's eyes sparkled, although he tried to remain calm. "I know, Mama, but I *do* want to be a doctor."

"He can stay with my sister in London," Chad said,

though he didn't like the idea of Jamie's being away any more than Hallie did.

And so it was decided that the following year, Jamie—at fifteen—would head for England. The year 1826 would also see the end of the short reign of Governor Thomas Brisbane. He had been an ineffective governor, more interested in the stars and in living a life that would assure him a place in heaven than in governing the colony. To Hallie, however, he would forever be remembered as the legislator who held office when she began the project that had captured her heart and overtaken her dreams.

By the time Brisbane's replacement was announced, the sanctuary Hallie had conceived had become a reality. The long, rectangular three-story residence she had built contained mainly dormitory-style rooms that would house six women each, and six rooms that would accommodate two each, in case of illness or other problems. An enormous dining room led into a spacious kitchen, and there was a great room downstairs where the women could congregate. Off of that was a bedroom/sitting room for Sophie, who had long ago appointed herself custodian of the women who would come and go.

On December 20, 1826, the same day that Hallie officially opened her women's residence, Lieutenant General Ralph Darling, the new governor, arrived in Sydney. Hallie had made plans to meet his ship, though she did not know he was on it. She was running late, however, and for a reason that disturbed her deeply: she could not find the fifty pounds she had withdrawn from the bank the day before. She'd had it in mind to buy clothes for all those who came back with her to the women's residence that night. She still remembered how Beth had looked on the *Charleston,* how the captain had used burlap to replace the clothing of the women convicts, and how filthy and raveled the coarse material had become by the time they'd arrived. New clothes would make a nice Christmas present for the new arrivals, a welcoming gesture from this new land. But now the money was gone. She tried to dismiss the unpleasant thought that either Melanie or Laurie, who had recently moved to the town house as maids, had robbed her. She knew she had put the money on top of her dresser while she bathed, but now she could not find it.

512

She was far too busy to confront either of the women before she rushed to her carriage. She could see from the sails that the ship was rounding Bennelong Point and turning into Sydney Cove, and she knew she must hurry. In her heart she was certain neither Melanie nor Laurie could have taken the money. They would have given their lives for her. Still, the thought sat gnawing at the back of her mind while she waited on the dock for the passengers to disembark.

Whenever she saw young women alone, obviously not waiting to be met, she approached them. If they knew no one and had no job awaiting them, she talked them into accompanying her, taking them over to a bench where Sophie was sitting. In all, on this ship there were thirty-three young women who had come to Australia with no knowledge of what might be waiting for them.

At last, too impatient to remain on the dock, she picked up her skirts and started up the ship herself. A familiar voice called to her from below, and she turned. It was Tristan, carrying his black bag and hurrying after her. Oh God, she thought, he's never less beautiful. Age is gracious to him.

"I thought if a doctor accompanied you, the ship's captain might be more receptive to you," he said when he'd reached her side.

Neither of them knew that on the second ship, which was waiting for all the passengers and convicts to be dispersed, their new governor was a passenger. The captain, therefore, was trying to dispose of his passengers as quickly as possible. Already men were pacing in front of a row of women prisoners, pinching their arms or sometimes breast, lifting a skirt. Some of the women flirted outrageously, making obscene gestures themselves.

But it was the frightened ones Hallie searched out, the young ones looking like scared rabbits, who had obviously not been the street women of London, Liverpool, or Dublin. These were the ones who had not yet had time to learn a life of hardened crime, who looked at the men with fear in their eyes or anger in their stances.

Hallie recruited twenty-seven of them that afternoon. After the holidays she would visit the Women's Prison Factory in Parramatta and see if there were others.

Thus, with her band of sixty women, Hallie made her way to the home waiting for them.

For the next two days there was seldom time to think. Hallie fell into bed each night exhausted. Chad and the children returned to Cowarra, leaving early on the morning of the twenty-second. Hallie promised to be home by the evening of the twenty-third. She was enormously pleased with what had been accomplished. Her dream was well on the way to fruition.

On the morning of the twenty-third she set about preparing to return to Cowarra, then knocked on Tess's door to tell her to be ready to leave by ten for Christmas at the farm.

Tess was not in her room, but a large envelope lay on the bed. "Thanks for the fifty pounds," it read. "It's the only thing of value I ever got from you. Pamela and I are returning to England. No one here will even know I'm gone, I'm sure. I won't miss you, either. This isn't a country fit to live in. I have already wasted far too many years of my life here." It wasn't even signed.

No word for Danny. The room was as neat as if it had never been lived in. There was no trace of Tess, nothing left behind to remind anyone of her. Hallie's reaction was one of relief: now she would not have to accuse either Melanie or Laurie of thievery. She should have known better all along.

Hallie's big surprise that Christmas came not from Chad—though he did present her with a bay mare to replace the aging Princess—but from Beth.

"I'm in love," she announced shyly to Hallie on Christmas morning. "With Danny. I was sure you knew already. You can't be so blind."

Hallie just looked at her, mouth open.

"It's happened so gradually, over the years," Beth went on. "I think it began because—because he looks just like you. And he's gentle, and kind, and . . ." She raised her eyes to meet Hallie's. "Oh, Hallie, it's been going on for years! Like it seems forever."

Hallie realized she had been so concerned with her own dreams that she never considered Beth's, or Danny's. Beth continued, "He knows all about me, knows all that happened. All this between us happened so slowly . . . little by

514

little . . . I've never been afraid of him, Hallie. I've even wanted him, wanted him to want me—for years."

"Does he know?" Hallie's heart sang for her friend.

Beth laughed. "Of course, though the only time we've touched is when our hands brush."

"It must have been torment for you."

Beth shook her head. "It's been wonderful. It's given me time to get ready. Now that Tess has gone, we're free . . . I want to have a baby."

Hallie continued to stare at her. Beth would have a baby at the age of thirty? It seemed almost indecent. It also seemed wonderful, as though it could atone for all the past.

"I love him so much, Hallie." Beth smiled and blushed. "I look at him and ache with the sheer beauty of him."

Yes, thought Hallie, that's what love is. "I take it for granted that he loves you, too?" she asked.

Beth nodded. "I think that he's loved me from the minute he arrived. We've worked and eaten and talked together for almost nine years. Yet he's a man of honor. And I love that about him, too. As long as Tess was here, even though I know he didn't love her, he wouldn't, couldn't—" She stopped, and a little frown puckered her forehead. "That's not quite true. Years ago, I don't know how many, he kissed me. Once. Over the years we've accepted it . . . just being together has been enough."

"What are you going to do now, now that Tess is gone?"

"I'm not sure. But this afternoon, after Christmas dinner is over, I'm going to him. And, if he, wants, we can be together."

Hallie walked over to her friend and embraced her. She would never have believed Beth could come so far. "Now, you will truly be my sister in all ways," she said softly.

And holding each other, they wept with happiness.

After Christmas dinner was over, and the lethargy that follows such a feast had settled over everyone, Hallie followed Chad into his office and sat on the big chair across from his desk. Chad could tell she had something on her mind, and reached into his humidor for a cigar.

She told him about Beth and Danny.

515

"Well, I'll be damned!" he exclaimed, grinning. "Have you talked to him about it yet?"

She shook her head. "I wonder if they can even marry. Is it possible for him to divorce Tess?"

"I'll find out," he offered. "But legally possible or not, I doubt Tess will ever return to this part of the world. I shouldn't think there will be any complications."

An idea had been jelling in Hallie's mind ever since dinner. "Chad . . ." she said.

"I can tell by your tone of voice." He smiled apprehensively as he lit his cigar. "You're evolving some sort of plan."

"You once said the winery's mine, that you're not involved with it at all."

"That's true." He nodded, waiting to hear what was coming next.

Hallie rose from her chair and walked from the room, leaving him to stare after her. Then, as he realized what she must be thinking, a grin spread over his face.

He knew before he looked out the window that Hallie was running down the steps, that she'd head to the stables and probably saddle Princess rather than her new horse. That she'd ride over to Danny's.

And she did. When she reached his cottage, she jumped down from Princess and called, "Danny!" He'd left the big house as soon as dinner was over and was waiting inside. Waiting for Beth, she thought, happiness engulfing her.

When he appeared in the doorway, she threw her arms around him. "Oh, Danny. Beth must have talked to you. She told me she would. I'm so happy!"

His arms encircled her and he said, "I wondered. I mean, I'm still married . . ."

Hallie backed off and held him at arm's distance. "I want to give you a present. I want you and Beth to move over to that first house Beth and I shared together. I'll have Etta and her children move over here."

Danny raised his eyebrows. "Hallie, you don't have to . . ."

But Hallie would not be dissuaded. "I'm sure Beth would love to live there again." It brought back happy memories, and she knew it would to Beth, too. "And something else . . ." She couldn't hide her smile. "Oh, Danny, I don't know when anything's made me so happy!"

He grinned. "Me, either."

"Danny . . . you love the winery, don't you?"

He started to answer; then, looking into Hallie's shining eyes, knowing his sister better than anyone else in the world, he held up a hand and said, "Now, Hallie, you can't—"

"Don't tell *me* what I can or can't do. I want to. I want to give it to you. My half of it, anyway." She brushed away any objections. "I'll have a legal deed drawn up. Let me, please. More of your work than mine has gone into it. I have so much. I want you to have a part of this new world, too. You've earned it. You really have."

He reached out for her hands. In a low voice he said, pulling her closer, "Do you remember, once back in Newcastle I asked you what else life could offer, what you were searching for? I couldn't understand, then. And yet somehow I've come along on this journey. Oh, my dear—" He kissed her forehead, wrapping her in an embrace. "You're the most wonderful person in the world." His choked voice brought tears to Hallie's eyes, too.

"Imagine," he murmured, "a coal miner from England owning Cowarra Wines." His voice held wonder.

"Do keep the name, won't you?" She smiled up at him.

"Of course. Now I, too, am part of Cowarra."

We are all part of Cowarra, she thought. Chad and I, our children, Danny, Mum, Beth . . . even the part of Tristan that owns the other half of the winery.

All the people she loved most in the world.

Fifty-one

In the two years since she'd opened her halfway house, Hallie began to spend more time in Sydney than at Cowarra. And, while in Sydney, she found herself missing the green valley, the hills, the wide-open spaces, although the view of the harbor from her bedroom window sometimes made up for it. But she was aware that even though she was busy and always surrounded by people, she experienced great loneliness.

Alex would hardly ever come into town. Now that she was sixteen, her schooling was finished. Her thoughts, as they'd always been, were of Robbie.

Late each afternoon Alex took herself to the creek and bathed, shampooing her hair and towel-drying it as the shimmering waves, caught back by combs, tumbled down her back. And then she'd dress, humming to herself, pirouetting before her mirror. After dinner she'd rock on the porch, her eyes always alert, until she'd see Robbie come into view.

With unladylike eagerness she would dash from the porch, the chair she'd left behind rocking wildly, and run to greet him. Sometimes they'd walk, hand in hand, down the hill to the creek. Other evenings they'd sit on the steps together and talk endlessly. If Alex saw Robbie on his horse, instead of rushing to him, she'd dash for the stables to saddle her horse, and they'd ride off together—to the top of a hill to watch the sun setting over the western mountains, or along the river, where they'd dismount and watch each other's reflections in the clear water.

During the days she'd help Danny and Emil in the vineyards. In just a few short years Cowarra Wines had made quite a name for itself. Emil's thoughts or topics of conversation always centered around grapes and wines. His dream was to ship selected vintages back to England, wines that could compare with the best of the French and German varieties. So far, however, all they had produced had been bought up immediately by Australians. So, each year Emil and Danny added more vines—dotting the lower parts of the hills and undulating valleys throughout the land.

Danny was happier than Hallie had ever known him, though he and Beth had had no luck making babies. They had moved to the original homestead, and Etta and her children moved into what had been Danny's and Tess's house. Young Roger had chosen to remain in the big house with the other children and now went to school in Morgantown. No one ever mentioned Tess or Pamela.

Though neither Chad nor Hallie wanted Wick to leave home, they realized—or, at least, Chad did—that the boys' academy in Sydney was far superior to their little Morgantown school.

Hallie was in town so often that she and Chad had planned for Wick to stay at their big house while he attended school, but in the large chunks of time that Hallie was at Cowarra, he was alone in the mansion with just two maids. Bored even when Hallie was there, because she was seldom at the house, he eventually asked if he mightn't follow in Jamie's footsteps and stay at the Faulkners'. They were right in the midst of the city; with their four children, and surrounded by neighbors, he would not feel as lonely in the long evenings. Even if Tristan were at the hospital or out on emergency calls, Molly always had time for children, talking to them as though they were adults, teaching them games and laughing with them as though they were peers.

Hallie was not surprised at Tristan's and Molly's eagerness when she asked how they felt about Wick's living with them. Life never ceased being a puzzle, she thought. It was but justice that Wick should have a chance to live with his father. Yet as time passed, the guilt that plagued her about her unfaithfulness to Chad deepened. Would Wick's living with Tristan create a separateness from Chad?

When she returned to Cowarra and told Chad of her decision, she saw his eyes darken like storm clouds. "Am I to lose both my sons?" he asked as though to himself.

In that moment Hallie hated herself. Yet she said, "It wasn't Tristan who came between you and Jamie. It was your being gone those five years of his life." That, at least, was true. It was your being gone, too, she thought, that created Wick and Julie.

"I know." Chad leaned his elbows on the table and buried his head in his hands. "I know, Hallie, I'm not blaming anyone but myself. And certainly I would rather have the boys stay with Tris and Molly than board at the school, where they would have rules but no love. I am indebted forever to the Faulkners for their hospitality."

"Don't sound so formal," Hallie said. "You know they love doing it."

"Yes. I think"—Chad raised his eyes to meet Hallie's—"they couldn't love our children more if they were their own."

Does he suspect? Hallie wondered, shaken. It had never dawned on her that Chad might somehow have divined the truth. Both of the twins looked like her, almost replicas of her and Danny.

But in the end, Wick never did take to schooling or city life. Smart as could be at whatever interested him, he refused to concentrate on the intricacies of Latin and math. He didn't mind reading, and wrote rather well, but being cooped up in a schoolroom all day, learning things for which he could see no meaning, was not his cup of tea. There was a wildness to him—and to Julie—that he kept in check in the city. Bored as he was, he found no pleasure in playing tricks on his teachers or other students, so he was not a problem.

He lived for holidays and Cowarra. When he was home, he and Julie were always off on their horses. Usually they rode up to the Daughertys' early mornings with their father and went out with them. Wick could lasso a calf like no one else on the farm. Even Julie did pretty well at that. They could both castrate lambs with no hesitation, something that always hurt Alex to watch or even to think of. They loved sleeping out nights, around campfires, listening to the men talk. They even liked haying. Whatever Wick did, Julie followed suit.

When there was no school, Julie often rose before dawn and rode out with Chad. "Sometimes I think she doesn't even know she's a girl," Chad said over and over again. Not that he minded. Whatever his children wanted to do was all right with him, as long as it was something constructive.

When Wick was at school, Julie attended Dorothy's school, but afternoons she was off somewhere on her horse. Sometimes she'd be out in the vineyard with Alex, but that didn't hold enough variety or excitement for her. She'd talk Alex into taking off, and they'd gallop away, stopping to swim in the river, or bringing back plants, or finding stray lambs, or sitting by a stream and talking for hours. Julie's nature was torn between her two idols, Wick and Alex, though when Wick was home there was no thought of competition. Whatever Wick wanted to do, so did Julie. Not that she was always a follower, for she could induce Wick to do anything she had her heart set upon.

Now that Ben was happily married and had a family of his own, it was ironic that he spent more time away from Morgantown than there. Even after the birth of their daughter, Annie, Dorothy continued to teach. She did not object to Ben's absences, for it gave her the freedom to pursue her calling. Ben took over, without any discussion, the room Tess had abandoned in the Sydney house, but he was not often there, either. They all laughed at the hours he spent in the saddle, knowing how he felt about horses. He not only set up stores in Richmond, Windsor, and Campbelltown, but ventured over the mountains to start one in Bathurst. The wedding present that Hallie and Chad had given him stirred him to dreams and actions even he had not known were within him. His children were going to grow up as the children of somebody, and to that he dedicated his life.

Hallie spent most of her time going from store to office to business, searching out jobs for her "girls," most of whom were under twenty years of age. She would not let them work in pubs, and she established a curfew. If any of the girls wanted to break the curfew, that was the end of their stay at Hallie's George Street house. No one was going to take advantage of her girls if she could help it. By the end of 1828 there were no women available for hire for wages of which Hallie did not approve, there were no women arriving in Sydney—or dwelling in town—who were available for living in a house with a single male unless the man proposed marriage.

One night, when Hallie and Chad were dining at the Langleys', Harry said, "Hallie, I do believe you've become the most unpopular woman in New South Wales, and all within just two years. Unpopular with men, that is. They no longer have easy access to women."

Susan's eyes shot fire. "Aren't you proud?" She loved it that Hallie spent so much time in Sydney now, though she wondered if the work were jeopardizing her marriage to Chad. It never appeared so, but Susan knew too much to ever have her heart at rest concerning her dear friend. And she had begun to involve herself almost as much as Hallie with the George Street house and its occupants.

Harry turned to Chad. "Does that bother you?"

Chad, his mouth full of tender veal, answered, "When you can get the Reverend Marsden to say something kind from the pulpit, one has reason to worry. He has vociferously approved of Hallie, which does make me nervous." He laughed. "When that hypocritical bastard approves of anything, I am skeptical."

"Well," Susan put in, "the governor hails her as 'one who has brought Christian principles into practice in New South Wales.' "

Many of the "Christian" women—even those who donated time and helped in fund-raising—found Hallie treading on dangerous ground. They called her aggressive, thereby robbing her—in their own eyes—of feminine traits that they nurtured. They said she should be home tending her husband and children, not out fighting to see that other women were taken care of, meddling in something that was none of her business and cavorting with "bawdy" women.

As for her children, wherever Hallie was, there were Garth and Chloe. The women at the George Street house spoiled them with attention and affection, and Sophie was always happy to spend time with them. And wherever Garth and Chloe went, so did Jock, a Scottie presented to the family by the shepherd who lived in the hills and who was affectionately named after him. Gently had long since died, and though the farm had several shepherds that ran with the flocks, Jock was the family dog. In a few months, seven-year-old Garth would begin school, and Chloe could accompany her mother for another year. Hallie never felt they impeded her work, but took great pleasure in carting them with her everywhere.

Early in 1827 Hallie had received the first of what would be dozens of letters:

Dear Mrs. Morgan,

I hear you pervide wifes for men in need. I live 80 miles northwest of Bathurst. I have a two rm house, it's not too clean but a women could strate it up. I farm a lot of akres and have a dog named Smith and close to 1000 sheep. I don't drink two much and my naybors think Im helpful I dont sware in front of ladeys and would be kind to a wife. I ben in this country 22 years, and ben freed 16. I never ben in trouble since. I need a wife to help on farm, to be nice to Smith, and one who dosnt need naybors. Id like someone who dosnt talk *all* the time and wants children. I am 41 yrs old and have all my own teeth. I dont have time to git to town. Could you send me a wife?

Chester I. Holroyd

At first Hallie smiled to herself. Later, when she showed it to Chad, he raised an eyebrow and asked, "Why not? All those men alone out there beyond the mountains, and up north. Without women. Why not, Hallie?"

Why not, indeed. Already the seed of an idea was beginning to germinate.

She showed the letter to the women and asked if anyone was interested. Three of the young women raised their hands. "Then let's find out more about him," she said. She wrote asking Holroyd to send her letters of reference from some of his neighbors. It took four months before she had a reply, by which time two of the three interested young women were already married. The two letters spoke of his diligence, his willingness to help neighbors—even though the nearest one was over twenty miles away—when they needed it, that though he was quiet, he was invariably pleasant, and they did not think he had a mean temper. The last was most important to Hallie.

When a troop of soldiers marched out that way on a surveying trip, Mary, the young volunteer, accompanied them. Hallie would not let her travel alone, and there were no roads anyhow. Mary was to let Hallie know as soon as possible if she wanted to stay. Hallie talked the governor into permitting the sergeant major to perform a civil marriage because there was no possible way for a minister or priest to tour the outback. She convinced him that it was far preferable to condoning "living in sin." A civil marriage, in the governor's view, was far preferable to even a Catholic priest, that was certain.

One night when the entire family was at Cowarra, after they'd all played a rousing game of horseshoes and the evening had been filled with laughter, Hallie could tell from the look on Chad's face that he was filled with contentment and a sense of well-being. The younger children had been put to bed, and Alex, Julie, and Wick decided it was a perfect evening for swimming in the river. Wick shouted, "Shall I go fetch Robbie?" thinking he'd get a rise out of Alex.

But she would not be goaded. "He'll probably be over soon, anyhow," she said serenely.

Chad's eyes met Hallie's, and they smiled at one another.

When they were alone, Chad walked over to the sideboard. "How about a brandy?"

Hallie made a face. "I'd prefer a glass of wine."

He brought the glasses and suggested, "Shall we sit outside?"

The veranda here was not as cozy as the one Hallie had wrapped around their first house, and while it was not of marble, it was nearly as ostentatious as the one in Sydney. Its view, though not of the harbor, looked over the valley, at the hills that rose intermittently, and in the distance, at the jagged edges of the Blue Mountains, dark against the last rays of the vermilion sunset, streaked lavender.

"I do love this country," Chad said, putting an arm around Hallie. "Just look at it. I wonder if there's any place here that isn't beautiful?"

"I'd like to find out." Hallie moved away from him and sat on a bench.

He arched an eyebrow. "What does that mean?"

"I hear there are quite a few farms up on the Hunter River."

Chad sipped his brandy and waited.

"I should think," mused Hallie, looking at but not seeing the orange-red that now outlined the mountains, "they'd need women—wives and mothers. I've come to believe that women—mothers, in particular—are the civilizing influence in this world."

Chad laughed, but the sound was like the distant mountains—jagged. "You do this to me all the time, my dear. Lull me into comfort, to total enjoyment of my life and family, and then explode a cannon."

Hallie looked up defensively, just able to make him out in the rapidly fading twilight. "I don't mean to. I don't do it to upset you."

Chad sighed. "I know that. You do it for such grandiose objectives—to civilize a continent, for God's sake! That's what you're telling me now, isn't it?"

"Well, just the Hunter River Valley. I thought I could take about forty or fifty women. Ben wants to go to Newcastle."

"Ironic, isn't it . . . Newcastle?"

Hallie nodded. "And we could go that far with him. He says there are boats on the Hunter, and I thought we'd get one and stop at farms as we go upriver. They may want wives or servants."

"You're planning to lead the expedition, I gather?"

"Oh, Chad, would you mind so? I don't think it will take more than a month, if that. Everyone here can do without me very well, and it would be such a wonderful opportunity to bring women, to begin families, to—yes, you're right, I do mean civilize—parts of this land. And"—it was now too dark for Chad to see her shining eyes—"I *could* see more of this colony that we both love."

"It'll be great fun for you."

Her enthusiasm did not allow her to hear the tone in his voice. "You *do* understand! Of course it will. It makes me feel I'm doing something—something no one else is even thinking of doing. Something of value."

"I imagine"—Chad's voice was dry but not without humor—"that if my name is ever mentioned in history books, it will be as the husband of the woman who brought civilization to the remote reaches of Australia . . . or, at least, made civilized human beings out of barbarians."

"Don't put words into my mouth," said Hallie. "All the men I know are very civilized."

Chad walked over and put a hand on her shoulder.

"There are times," he said, his voice soft, "when being a bit of a savage has its rewards."

She reached up to put her hand over his. They were silent; laughter floated up from the river.

"Is Robbie going to be our son-in-law?" Chad asked, listening.

"I certainly hope so, don't you? They've loved each other for some time now. Alex will be seventeen soon."

"My little girl," Chad said. "Thank goodness she's content with her lot in life. She'll be pleased to spend her whole life at Cowarra."

"I know. And so will Robbie." She leaned her back against him.

His arms went around her. "It's big enough for them all."

Hallie nodded. "But don't clip their wings, not yet."

"I let Jamie go to England, didn't I?" he said, kissing her neck.

"He'll come back. He'll be part of your Australian dynasty." She turned so that her cheek rubbed his.

"I wonder if he'll settle in Sydney?"

"Where else would he?"

"Every month new towns are starting. New explorations are being made. . . . Yes, yes, new places to send your women. Go ahead, Hallie, take them. That's what you're thinking, isn't it?"

So Hallie and thirty-seven women sailed up to Newcastle. There they said goodbye to Ben and boarded a barge that carried mail and supplies up the river. It was three weeks before Hallie and four of the women returned to Newcastle. Three of the four had decided they really couldn't live so far away from towns, and the fourth hadn't been able to find a man she was willing to marry. Five of the women had opted for service with families, and twenty-eight of them had married men who already had erected houses— some of them huts, but at least wooden and not sod. By the time Hallie returned to Sydney, seven of these were already pregnant.

Hallie reported to Chad, "There isn't a part of this country that isn't beautiful, if you don't count Newcastle."

How word got around, Hallie never knew. But within two

years she received over four hundred requests for wives. Along with those came letters from families requesting servants: maids, kitchen help, nannies, and, in some cases, female company.

But before she would send her young women out into the great unknown, far from neighbors and protection, she thought she and the women themselves should meet the men casting their lot in life so far from civilization.

Chad sat with no expression on his face or in his eyes as she told him her plan. "I'm going to take these women over the mountains and find them husbands or jobs. The farther away from towns these people are, the higher the wages the girls can command. These women should be able to see whether they're condemning themselves to isolation with a man they couldn't bear or whether they're willing to take the chance."

"You didn't know me or this country when you came."

"I was lucky."

Raising his eyebrows, he gave her a half smile—nodding his head as though accepting a compliment. "You're thinking of going over the mountains with a handful of women, by yourself?"

She nodded, suddenly remembering Archie and the billabong.

"Then I'm going to ask the governor for some soldiers," Chad said. "Otherwise, I'll forbid it."

Hallie's eyes shot fire. "Forbid it? Am I your child, then?"

Chad shook his head. "I'm sorry, Hallie. But there are chain gangs in the mountains, and escaped prisoners roaming beyond—"

Hallie raised her hand to cut him off. "All right. All right. And I'll ask for a minister to perform the weddings."

"There aren't roads out there. How will you know where to go?" he asked.

"I'm sure people will direct us."

He shook his head. "Aside from you, do any of the women know how to use guns?"

"Oh, Chad, that's so smart of you! I'd not have thought of that. I'll train them to shoot and provide each one of them with a pistol."

He was defeated—and he knew it. "Where are you going to get horses for the women?"

"They'll have to walk. The soldiers and I will ride. But the women will have to walk."

"Have you any idea how long it will take a handful—by the way, how many women are you thinking of?"

She couldn't help smiling. "About two hundred."

Chad burst out laughing. "At first I thought you were serious. No one can walk two hundred women over the mountains into a land without roads, into a land that, from all I hear, goes on forever. How would you feed them? How would you keep from getting lost? How would you protect yourselves? How would you last out there?"

He stopped laughing when he saw the look in her eyes. "Jesus Christ, Hallie, you've done some of the damnedest things of any woman—wait—anyone, I ever heard of, but you can't be serious about this."

Her voice was like ice. "Not only two hundred women, but about fifty children."

"What about *your* children, *your* family?"

"Don't be silly, Chad." She turned away from him, walking over to her closet. "You can get along without me just fine for a couple of months. After all, we managed without you for five years. Besides, I haven't been necessary since Chloe stopped nursing. Beth just about runs the house, the children are all well and happy, and I do think I have very nice relationships with them." She pulled out a green dress, remembering it needed mending. "I've never been too busy to listen to them when they want, or to teach them to ride, or to take them with me, or to answer their questions."

Chad took out his new spectacles and blew on them. "But not to play games with them, or—"

Hallie whirled around. "I'm just not the game-playing type. Maybe Susan and Molly are more what women should be, but you know my family *is* important to me. I don't think any of the things I've done have taken away from my family, except maybe those years when you were away and Beth had more to do with mothering them than I could take time for. I was too busy running the farm, and I felt guilty then, about not spending time with them. But I've never sacrificed them, and time for them, for the other things I've done."

He looked at her across the room, the candlelight flickering on the walls. His eyes darkened. "What about me?" he asked. "What about time with me? Does it never dawn on you that we haven't spent much time together in the last few years? You're in town more than you're here. You're so busy with finding homes and jobs for your girls, you forget you have a husband."

She had never imagined he felt this way. He was out working all day, poring over the account books in the evenings, or talking with Brian and Robbie or Ben. When they were in Sydney, they dined out together or had guests, and if the guests left early, Chad found a card game. He was always busy.

"I don't want you to do this, Hallie," he said softly. "It's too dangerous for women to wander around the continent. You might get lost. A handful of soldiers, should the governor allow them to accompany you, isn't enough to protect you from whoever's wandering around out there."

He had never said no to anything she wanted to do, even when she knew he disapproved. He was not saying no now: he was telling her he didn't like the idea.

"What if I were a man?" she asked, a belligerent tone in her voice.

"For God's sake, we wouldn't even be having this conversation then! But men *do* get lost out there, men *do* get murdered and robbed out there. It's a big empty land, and the sun does crazy things to men's minds after a while. And some of them have been without women for years."

"That's why I'm going. They need women. And remember, we'll be two hundred armed women!"

Chad shook his head as though the very idea were too much to comprehend. Then he smiled. "How long have we been married?" he asked. "Nineteen years, isn't it? Been together fourteen. And it's still like meeting you for the first time. You're certainly never boring, Hallie. That much I'll give you. Why do you have to do it *all*? Why aren't you ever satisfied? You have everything."

She looked at him across the room, sitting in the wingback chair. He doesn't understand, she thought. The man who had seemed larger than life when she first saw him, the man who was a giant those first years they were married, now looked like a puzzled little boy. Hallie had never thought of that before. Never wondered how confused a man might become if his wife did not act like the other women.

"No," she said. "*You* have everything that *you* want. You'd be bored, I know you that well, if everything ran itself so well that you just sat on the porch all day, waiting for dinner, or taking a leisurely hour's ride. Tell me you wouldn't be restless if each day didn't present you with challenges, problems to solve, work you love. You had to invent a second house, you had to have the largest and best sheep-breeding station in the country, you had to have horses that win races. You had to have children whom you think will keep your name in front of the world. And every day you work toward those goals."

She walked across the room and knelt next to his chair, peering into his eyes. He reached out and fingered a tendril of her hair. "Are you ashamed of me?" she asked. "Do people make fun of you that your wife isn't like other wives?"

He permitted himself a small smile. "My dear, if someone made fun of me because of you, they would never do it within my hearing. I have no idea how other people view you, Hallie. No, I am not ashamed of you. In fact, I think—quite often—that I'm inordinately proud of you. I set out to make a dynasty, to see that the name of Morgan would be remembered a hundred years from now, but I never dreamed it might be my wife who achieved it for me."

"But they're already calling you the 'father of the Australian sheep industry.' "

This time he laughed aloud. "And there, it should be my wife again. While I was back in England, you built Cowarra."

"But you've bred the finest sheep in the world." She ran her hand through his hair. "It was your dream, I just sustained it while you were gone. You've made all the decisions for the last eleven or twelve years. You've made us rich. You build mansions. You never consult me. You have *never* asked my opinion on anything that you consider important. You buy my clothes—"

He reached out and stroked her cheek. "You know, just now, this very minute, I think I'm beginning to understand you. Now, as we talk."

She waited. Not a sound could be heard. It was nearly midnight; no breeze wafted through the open windows. It was as though they were the only ones awake in the universe. Suddenly their conversation had taken a strange turn. Hallie felt an excitement, looking at Chad, that she hadn't experienced since the first time. . . .

"What do you understand?" she whispered. She was watching the vein pulsing in his temple, saw the crow's-feet at the corners of his eyes, the graying temples, and reflected that she had lived with this man for a long time. Maybe she didn't know him, either.

"I haven't understood you because I've been looking at you all these years as a woman." His hand dropped from her cheek and brushed along the curve of her breast. "That's understandable. Anyone who sees you thinks of that first. Men must envy me with a wife who looks like you, smiles like you . . ." His voice trailed away.

She put her hand on his knee and rested it there, leaning her chin on it and looking up at him.

He smiled. "It's very hard to look at you and not think of you as Woman with a capital W. Desirable. And I do think that was my reaction the moment I saw you standing on the beach lo these many years ago. I couldn't believe my good fortune that you were the Hallie I remembered. What I do think I remembered had been the fire and restlessness in you. And those qualities have never left you. They are still what make me love you."

Hallie raised her head with a jerk. "Love?" She said it aloud without thinking.

Chad stared at her. "You haven't known?"

She thought of Tristan. That was love. . . .

"But wait. Let me finish this other first. Women make men happy—or unhappy. They give them children and cook their food and clean their houses and wear the clothes and jewelry their husbands buy them so that everyone can see how successful their husbands are. . . ." His voice slowed. He was thinking as he talked, searching for words that reflected the ideas that were tumbling into him. "They smile at banquets and dinner parties, and behave in a ladylike fashion and don't scream at the races, and are quite nice to everybody—trying never to give offense—and spend their time being mothers. Whatever pleases their husbands, pleases them. When their husbands succeed, they succeed. When their children achieve, it proves they've been good mothers. When anyone in the family is ill the woman cares for them. They keep their opinions to themselves, or at least within their homes."

"Saints, in other words." Fascinated with Chad's thinking, Hallie smiled.

"Yes, in short. Living lives vicariously is supposed to satisfy all women."

"'Vicariously?'"

"Through your husband and children."

"Well, there is a satisfaction . . ."

"Of course. But women aren't supposed to have dreams. Women aren't supposed to pursue anything . . . outside the family. And that's where you confound. I imagine it's largely my fault, if that's the right word. Before I left, you were what wives are thought to be. And then, with Archie's death, you were forced to act and think like a man. You succeeded beyond most people's wildest dreams."

Hallie stared at him, astonished.

"And then I came home, thinking you'd be happy to see me, thrilled to be relieved of the work you'd been doing, delighted to be Mrs. Chadwick Morgan again. Content to continue your predestined role in life and have more children."

"I do enjoy my children."

He nodded. "I know. At times, though, I have despaired, wondering why none of that has been enough for you. But I have been looking at you primarily as a woman. My woman. Only now, as we've been talking, do I begin to see my limitations. You are a person who happens to be a woman. Someone with dreams, like men have. Someone with vision, like some men have. Someone who thinks what she does can matter for a larger world than the family. Someone who wants to achieve—who has goals, who doesn't want to follow others' dreams or in others' footsteps."

He fell silent as Hallie stared at him. He had captured in words things she had vaguely felt and never been able to verbalize.

"I have let your being a woman blind me to the inner you," he concluded, smiling at her with infinite tenderness.

Tears sprang to Hallie's eyes.

"Of course I shall not keep you from this journey. I shall worry. I may not spend one night sleeping well. But I cannot keep you from what you perceive as your destiny."

"You make me sound so noble, Chad," she protested. "It's not that I think I have a destiny. It's that I see things that need to be done, and if I don't do them, no one will."

He reached out and pulled her up on his lap, cradling her in his arms. "And now, perhaps, after all these years, it is time to talk of love."

Fifty-two

"Love," Chad murmured, holding Hallie close. A warm soft breeze sprang up, billowing the curtain.

How strange, thought Hallie. I've never thought of love in connection with marriage. The only married people I know who are in love are Susan and Harry. I've never thought of love in connection with Chad; it was always Tristan who meant love.

Chad stroked her hair. "Some time ago, years, you asked if I'd ever been in love. I thought you meant aside from you, so I told you about my young love. I always thought you knew I've loved you from the moment I first saw you on the beach. And I've never stopped, not one minute in nineteen years."

He pulled his head back so he could see her. "Have you not known that, Hallie?"

"I knew you were happy that I look the way I do," she began tentatively, "and I've known now and then that you've been proud of me. I've also known that sometimes I drive you crazy and you've wondered why I couldn't be satisfied with what you've given me. Including those five years. At first I was so angry with you for leaving me like you did. But now, I think it was a gift. I found a part of me I never knew existed."

Chad sighed. "I shall never forgive myself for staying away so many years," he said. "From the first moment I saw you, I was head over heels in love. But it wasn't *how* you looked, the external parts. It was the light."

She frowned. "Light? What light?"

"The light within you . . . the light that shines from inside. I felt like the schoolboy I had been with my first romance. That must have been so obvious those first years. I could hardly wait to get back from the fields to be with you. I thought of you all day, out working. It drove me wild when you became pregnant and I didn't know there were other things we could do to satisfy us. I was mad with desire all those months I denied myself you. I could barely look at you without wanting you so badly it hurt."

Hallie sat up and looked at him as though seeing him for the first time again, on the beach.

Eyes tender, Chad continued. "I didn't know men fell in love with their wives in the crazy way I felt about you. I'd hoped, as with most marriages, that love might grow, but 'in' love—having you consume my thoughts and heart—that was unexpected. I had never really believed such things happened outside of poetry."

Hallie tweaked his ear and leaned over to kiss it. "Here I thought all you wanted me for was to clean your house, cook, and bear your children."

"That was the initial idea," he admitted with a wry smile. "But you carry an excitement within you, generate it wherever you go. It wasn't just your looks, though I do admit that's a delight—I never tire of looking at you, even after all these years. I wake up in the morning, and if you're still asleep, I lie there looking at you, basking in the beauty of you at—my God, what are you, thirty-seven? You're an exciting person. Always have been."

"It's you with your ideas and visions and the way the center of a room seems to follow you wherever you are . . ."

He laughed. "I won't deny that. But look at us—I've always thought we must be the most exciting couple in New South Wales. Maybe in the world!"

Hallie leaned down and kissed him.

"Do you know," he said, "that's the first time ever, I think, that you've done that? Been the one to initiate a kiss."

"Don't let it stop you from talking," she said, resting her head back on his shoulder, leaning against him. She wasn't yet sure what she was feeling, but she hadn't felt this way before. His hand touched the gown over her breast and rested there.

"You want me to talk some more about love?" He was smiling.

"We've hardly mentioned it before," she said. "I never knew you thought that way about me. I've known you liked me and that sometimes I've been a satisfactory wife for you. But you've never mentioned loving me."

"I guess I thought you knew. Have always known. Known from that first night in the billabong." He laughed. "Even all these years later I can recall every detail of that night. D'you remember, I showed you the Southern Cross, and we slept out under the stars? And I thought, My God, I've fallen in love in less than twenty-four hours. I knew, then, that it was forever. As I knew I must be the most fortunate man on earth. It was one of those times I believed in God."

"I remember it," she said, though she'd tucked it out of her memory for so long. The billabong also brought back the nightmare incident of Archie's death at the hands of that horrible man. She could never pass that beautiful, peaceful-looking place without remembering that stranger's surprised look and the way his face had splattered all over her when the bullet went through his head. Even now, recalling it, she shivered.

Chad held her closer, tighter, against him. "On the ship going to England, I saw you in every star. I heard your laughter. I damned every wave that took me from you. I wondered why I could possibly think that getting top money for our fleece would ever be worth a separation from you. I never dreamed it would be five years. Hallie, there was never a night, never a morning, that I didn't curse the distance between us. I missed seeing Jamie and Alex grow— I knew that, yet I was amazed that it wasn't my children I missed the most, but you."

Oh, God, she thought. While he was feeling that way, I was falling in love with Tristan, creating babies with Tristan. She closed her eyes, trying to block it out, but his voice went on, murmuring into her soul.

"I've known ever since I came back that it was not the same. Us . . . life. I had stayed where we'd been, and you and New South Wales had grown. I felt bewildered often, confused by your restlessness. By bringing Sophie and Danny, I'd hoped to please you."

"You did. I love having them here. It makes this family have roots. It's given me Mum in a way I'd never have had in Newcastle."

Chad nodded, his hand gently fondling her breast. "I know that. But the reaction, nevertheless, wasn't quite what I'd expected, and I grew afraid."

"Afraid?" Chad, afraid?

536

"Something had left us in those years I was gone, and I knew it. You had found the strength to live alone, and I had found I couldn't live without you. You didn't need me or anybody, I don't think."

"Of course I do," she said. "If I didn't have my family, I'd be nothing."

"Not quite true," he said. "You had yourself. That's not the way it is for most people. And I knew, to my great shock, that you didn't need me as I needed you. Oh, yes, we have functioned very well. We're companionable. I don't know that we've ever fought, at least not about anything really important, but perhaps that's because there's a lack of passion on your part. I have been afraid, I admit, to let my ardor show. I've far preferred to go along as we have than tell you how much I need you, how much I love you."

His voice was lulling her. "Why are you telling me, then?"

He leaned down and kissed her. "I don't know. Suddenly, it seems like the time has come, the time to take a chance, the time to risk . . . to tell you the truth. I didn't plan it."

He sighed. "Hallie, I love you more now than that first night in the billabong. I haven't pretended that I've understood you, until tonight. Until suddenly you forced me to stop looking at you as just a woman and see you as a human being with dreams and desires and without limitations. And though it does not always make for a comfortable life, one where life centers around me as I'd always thought it would—"

"When have you ever denied yourself what you've wanted because of me?" Hallie interrupted, sitting up.

He thought a moment. "You're right. Maybe it's just that it hasn't always tasted as sweet as I'd hoped, because you've not always seemed totally involved."

"Like with the two houses?"

Chad nodded.

"I'd have been perfectly happy to have lived in our first house forever," she told him, her voice soft. "I still have a feeling for that place that neither of the big ones has for me. I won't say I don't like the luxury, but I haven't needed all of that. I haven't needed the closets full of clothes. . . ."

"Need has nothing to do with it. I wanted to show you how much I care. It's been one of the ways I can tell you

I love you. But perhaps all along I was trying to buy your love, thinking that if I gave you presents . . ."

They were quiet for a long time, breathing in unison, listening to the silence of the night. Hallie was engulfed in a warm glow. She had never felt as close to Chad. To anyone. The things he'd said, not just that he loved her . . . but as though he saw inside her, understood her. He'd told her things about herself that even she had not recognized. Most important of all, he'd told her he loved her enough to permit her the freedom to do what she must rather than try to force her to do what he wanted. He loved her for her, not for his vision of her.

She threw her arms around him, overwhelmed with his sudden insight and his words of love. "Oh, Chad," she whispered. Slowly she began to undo the buttons on his shirt. Then she leaned over and kissed his chest, running her tongue across it. "I've never known you loved me," she murmured.

"Don't put it in the past tense," he said, not moving. "I love you now as much as ever, perhaps more. I shall love you with every ounce of breath and being forever, as long as either of us shall live. You are a woman who could be queen, Hallie . . . And to think that you are mine . . ."

Hallie stood up and reached her hands out for his, pulling him to his feet. He started to put his arms around her. "No," she said. "Let me." She took off his shirt, then unbuttoned her own dress, stepping out of it and kicking it away. She drew off her chemise and stood facing him, dressed only in her pantaloons. She put her arms around him and rubbed her breasts across his chest, loving the feel of their flesh meeting, sensing something different in this lovemaking, knowing she was initiating the moves he had always made, aware that she wanted to make love to him.

She unbuttoned his pants and slid them to the floor, knelt so that she could pull them off one leg at a time. His hands played with her hair. She looked up at him and thought, What a wonderful body for a man forty-two. And she took him into her mouth. Her hands feathered up his legs, around him, pressing his buttocks, and she heard him groan, "My God, Hallie!"

Yes, she thought, that's right. God . . .

Slowly, very slowly, she drew herself up the length of his

body, kicking off her pantaloons, so that they stood naked, not quite touching each other. When he did reach out to touch her nipples, she leaped into his arms, clenching her legs around his waist and kissing him with a wildness she'd only rarely experienced. She wanted to devour him, wanted to do the things to him that he had always done to her.

Holding onto her, he walked over to the bed. But she would not lie next to him. She crawled to the foot of the bed and kissed each of his toes, each leg—working her way slowly up, up, until she took him into her mouth again, her hands under him, pressing him into her. She heard his heavy breathing and flicked her tongue back and forth in rhythm. Finally he pushed her away, panting, "No, not yet. Please, not yet."

He pulled her up the length of him, their bodies undulating rhythmically, in tandem. He circled her breast with his mouth, enveloped it, his teeth biting her gently, his tongue running across the nipple. She cried out softly and arched into him.

"Now," he said, "do it again. But turn around, put your head down there, so I can . . . so we can do it to each other."

She felt him then between her legs, felt his tongue searching, pressing, and she spread wide, wanting him deep within her as she stroked him, as she felt the hardness of him. His hands found her breasts, and she thought she might burst at that very moment, burst wide open like fireworks, lighting up the sky and disappearing into the heavens forever. She began to rock back and forth, her mouth encircling him, moving up and down. She didn't have to die to see the fireworks, to feel the explosion that burst in great shivering spasms until she heard herself crying out into the darkness.

He stopped moving then, let her lie on him for a minute. At last he pulled her up to him, rolled her over, kissed her lips and entered her, rocking up and down, plunging deep within her as she lay there, breathing hard, making sounds that sounded like sobs, crying, "Hallie . . . oh, God, Hallie. I love you so!"

Later, when they lay next to each other, holding hands, Chad said, "If I love you as much as I do, mustn't I allow you the freedom you need to flower and grow?"

Hallie lay there wondering if it were possible to be in love with two men simultaneously. She was aware that her emotional life had been irrevocably tilted. Or had it, at last, been balanced?

Fifty-three

The governor, albeit unwillingly, assigned six soldiers to accompany the women. He was disapproving, but once he realized Hallie was in charge of the excursion, he felt he had no choice but to protect the women. He had ambivalent feelings toward Hallie. Certainly she was one of the most beautiful women in the colony. Certainly she was female. But she spoke her opinion, even at formal Government House dinners when the rest of the women remained silent or talked of the weather and their dissatisfaction with the help they had.

Sometimes there was silence after one of her outbursts, usually about the unfairness of convict treatment, and he could tell everyone around the table was embarrassed for her. But neither she nor her husband seemed to recognize it. Chad even seemed proud of her. No wonder, when you considered her looks. She enhanced her natural beauty with gowns and jewels that found no equal in the colony.

Chad by now was the wealthiest landowner in the colony. The Morgans could do anything and get away with it, which might have been why Hallie was like she was. It wasn't that she had ignored her children, for they seemed made of stern stuff, always polite, well mannered, though each gave the impression of waiting to take off—like eagles, ready to soar; restless—unable to sit for long. He'd not met the son in England, but he'd heard of his courtly manners as well as his keen intelligence. The governor hoped the young man *would* be coming back here to practice medicine, and wouldn't be tempted by the seduction of London, of any-place in England. Though he wouldn't blame him should he choose to stay where there were refinements denied this raw land.

And that daughter, Alexandra, God, what a beauty. He'd only seen her twice, but she, too, was a raving beauty, a mixture of her mother and father. Young men traveled out to Cowarra to court Alex, but he'd heard they had no luck. Eighteen now, ripe. Yet she refused to attend any of the balls for young people that Sydney offered; no one saw her at concerts or at picnics or at regattas, only at the races, now and then, when her father had a horse entered. And then, in unladylike fashion, she and her sister Julie jumped and screamed when the horses rounded the bends. Neither of their parents admonished them; in fact, Chad looked at them with amusement.

Julie—even at twelve . . . Were all the best-looking women in this country Morgans? Julie and that twin of hers were the images of their mother, with her stubbornness and a wildness of Chad's that he always seemed to hold in check. Maybe he wasn't wild. Maybe he just had that air about him, willing to risk, not fitting into the mold of the gentry into which he had been born. Drank like a gentleman, which he was. Liked to gamble, but was never in debt. Seemed to have the Puritan work ethic, which—no doubt—explained much of his wealth. That and native intelligence and willingness to dare. The whole damn family had that quality. Not genetic, because Hallie had it, too.

Of the children he'd met, the governor was most attracted by Wick. The boy had an irresistible charm. Dragging along in the middle of his class at studies, nevertheless he never seemed to shirk hard work—if he liked it. While he was polite, he gave the impression of resenting any authority, that he was waiting to get away, get back to the horses and sheep. He was only twelve, but the governor foresaw great things ahead for that boy, being a Morgan.

He envied the Morgans. Already there was a growing town named after them. He'd like something named after him, something for the history books to say, "See that, the Darling whatever"—maybe a river or a state on this big continent—"named after one of our most renowned governors."

Hallie had acted as if there would be no question whatsoever that he'd assign soldiers to protect her women. "My women," she'd said. Well, maybe they were. He didn't know why he resented her. His wife had pointed out that he'd really respect her if she were a man.

So he'd said yes, and agreed to ask the clergy to send

along someone to solemnize any marriages; then at least he couldn't be criticized.

The one who did criticize, however, was Tristan. Chad had invited the Faulkners to dine a week before Hallie's excursion was to take place. He hadn't been in town himself in the five weeks since Hallie had told him of her plans. Tristan wasted neither time nor words.

"You can't let her do this," he said flatly. "I've tried to tell her it isn't safe." He turned to Hallie. "Certainly you can't have forgotten what happened to you once, even though you had a man around."

"Think of all the times I've ridden around alone since then, though," she countered defensively. "There will be a contingent of soldiers. . . ."

"Yes, six soldiers and a minister to protect nearly two hundred women."

"And fifty children," Hallie said. "Don't forget them."

"My God, how can I?" Tristan turned back to Chad. "That she's doing something foolish, the whole town is aware. But asking hundreds of women to participate in this project . . ."

"Hundreds of *armed* women," Chad said, and smiled. "Have you ever tried to talk Hallie out of anything? I can't say I'm comfortable with the idea, but I'd rather have her go than spend the rest of my life being responsible for her not going. I'm not sure how long our marriage would last with that on my conscience—and in Hallie's mind. Besides, she's not my daughter. I can't forbid her to do anything." His eyes met Hallie's.

Hallie sat looking at the two men she loved. She'd been aware of thinking the word *love* in connection with Chad all month. Once, she had thought she could never love anyone but Tristan. Though they'd hardly spoken privately in years, she had never doubted their feeling for one another. And while she had loved him too long and too steadfastly to doubt it now, before her eyes she saw the shape of that love changing.

It had begun that night with Chad. Every day since then, she had seen her husband through new eyes. Looked at him differently. Become conscious of the expression on his face when he was surrounded by his family—as if he's died and gone to heaven, she thought once.

543

She was newly aware of him, perhaps for the first time—though she had seen it happen over and over through the years—aware of Julie bringing a wounded bird to him, for instance; together they had made a splint for its wing; together they had hand fed it. She watched them train it to fly again, their patience lasting weeks, and the look in Julie's eyes as the bird finally flew back to freedom. But it was the expression in Chad's eyes as he watched Julie—her hand shading her eyes as the bird flew into the sun, westward—that touched Hallie.

And she realized that she had been blind all these years, that somehow she had chosen not to see, to be aware of this aspect of her husband which now touched her so profoundly.

"Speaking of daughters"—Tristan turned back to Hallie, breaking into her reverie—"I hear you're taking Julie."

Ah, so that was it, she thought.

"She's twelve. She thinks it sounds exciting. A chance to see this land. None of the others wants to go. I thought one of the boys, but no . . . And Alex, well, she never wants to leave Cowarra. . . ." Never wants to leave Robbie is what I really mean, she thought.

"Downright craziness," Tristan snapped. "You have no right to do that to Julie—or to any of those women!"

"Now, wait a minute, Tris." Chad lit a cigar. "Hallie's asked for volunteers. She's not doing it *to* any of them, though I do think she's doing it *for* them. As for Julie, we've talked it over. As I said, I'm not crazy about any of it, but if it's going to happen, I am not going to stand in the way. I've been teaching Julie to use a gun. She's as restless as her mother. Anything that's different, anything that's a challenge, that reeks of excitement and maybe danger—"

"Dammit, no twelve-year-old girl should go marching off into the wilderness!"

Chad remained calm, but his eyes grew cold. "Tristan, you've practically brought up two of my sons. Your hospitality not only to them but to all my family has always been of the closest form of friendship. You are someone I respect and admire without peer. You and Harry are my Australian brothers, with whom I feel closer than my blood brother. But I don't want you to tell me what I can or can't do with *my* daughter."

544

Chad held Tristan's eyes with his own, and a moment later Hallie saw Tristan's shoulders sag.

She gazed upon Chad with tenderness, aware that he was supporting her even though his heart was not in it. He was giving her public approval. He did not like what she was planning, but he would fight for her right to do it.

For the last month she had been confused. And now, tonight, with the two of them arguing at the table, she again wondered not if it were possible to be in love with two men, but if the passion she had always felt for Tristan was over the dam, if she had been blind for these last years since Chad had come home, since Tristan had married Molly. She still loved him, she knew, but how? Would she still walk into his arms were he to hold them out to her?

Tristan was looking at her again, his eyes pleading with her, saying silently, Don't endanger our daughter, Hallie. Please.

Instead she said, "We're going to be perfectly all right. I wouldn't attempt it if I didn't think so." Actually she had been delighted when Julie begged to go. It would give them something in common, memories that would be just theirs, forever.

The morning of the day before Hallie and her contingent of women were to depart, a ship's sails were sighted far out in the harbor. What terrible timing, Hallie thought. She was in the midst of preparations and could not possibly take time to meet it. Well, Susan would take care of it. She had promised that, with Sophie, she would meet the new ships, would settle women who might arrive in Hallie's absence. It never ceased to surprise Hallie that her friend had involved herself with the project. Susan always saw that there was never any inconvenience to Harry, for he came first, but she had volunteered to be in charge while Hallie was absent. Hallie had watched Harry pull at his mustache, as he always did when puzzled, but he'd said nothing. That his wife had branched out into civic affairs pleased him, he said, but he hoped it would not interrupt their home life. It would have to now, though, since Hallie would be gone for several months.

Just at that moment, Sophie appeared at the bedroom door, an odd mixture of defiance and awkwardness in her stance.

"I've come to ask a favor." She stood straight, her hair totally gray now, but with a vitality emanating from her. "But first a question . . ."

Hallie looked up from her position on the floor, surrounded by boxes, wondering what she could leave behind. "Would you go on this trip if there were no one to take care of the women here?" Sophie asked.

Hallie glanced at her mother. "But of course. Yes. The ones here could fend for themselves a few months. I don't have to do everything. I'm not a perfectionist, as you know all too well. Are you afraid I'll come home and think you've failed?"

Sophie joined her daughter on the floor. "No. I'm afraid you and Julie will have an unforgettable experience that I won't. I want to come."

Hallie burst out laughing and threw her arms around her mother. "Go pack," she said. "We'll get you a horse."

Her mother kissed her, then stood up and hurried down the stairs.

Susan appeared later in the afternoon with a young girl of fourteen or fifteen in tow.

"This is Lucinda," she said. "She's looking for Chad."

The girl, whose chestnut hair tumbled in curls down her back, whose gray eyes were clear and sure, said, "I have a letter for him, from my mother. He's my uncle."

Whose daughter was she? Hallie wondered. Elizabeth's? Millicent's? She had only a vague memory of his sisters.

"My mother died," said the girl. "She said my uncle would take care of me."

Why not her father or his brother, who ran the mines? Why had they not heard his sister was dead, or ill?

The girl looked around, wide-eyed but with a self-assurance unusual in one so young. Maybe, thought Hallie, that's what happens when you're brought up in London society. "This is all very exciting," she said.

Just then Julie came running in and was introduced to Lucinda. "A new cousin?" she said, delighted. "Come, I'll show you to a room. How awful you've arrived just now when I'm leaving."

The two girls were out on the lawn, looking at the harbor, when Chad returned several hours later.

"Your niece," said Hallie, not at all daunted by one other family member.

He frowned. "My niece?"

"One of your sister's daughters, I didn't ask which one. She's died, and sent the girl to you." She was too busy packing to realize how bluntly she'd announced his sister's death.

Chad raised his eyebrows and stared out the window of their bedroom at the girls on the lawn.

"There's a letter she brought; it's on your desk," Hallie added while she was sorting out which clothes to take. She heard Chad running down the stairs, heading for the letter. When he hadn't returned twenty minutes later, when she'd heard no sound from downstairs, she went to find him. He sat behind his immense desk, his head in his hands. She went over to him and put her arms around him.

"I'm sorry," she said. "Which sister was it? I don't mind, you know, having one more child around. I'm sorry she's arrived when I'll not have time to get to know her, but Alex and Beth and—"

Chad turned to face her, pulling her hand into his. His eyes were filled with pain. "Sit down," he said.

Hallie was frightened. Something awful was coming, she could feel it. Something she wasn't prepared for. Something that would scare her. As she sank onto the chair near him, his hands held hers and he looked into her eyes.

"She's not my niece, Hallie," he said in a strangled voice. "She's my daughter."

Fifty-four

Hallie sat down hard. She did not see the pain and fear in Chad's eyes. She saw nothing for several minutes. Her hand clutched her chest, and she had difficulty breathing.

Chad reached out, but she held up her hands, warding him off. "You told me you've always loved me," she murmured, not realizing what she was saying.

"I have. There hasn't been a minute since I first saw you that I haven't loved you more than anything in the world."

She sat staring straight ahead.

"I know this is a shock to you. I never dreamed . . ."

"Why didn't you tell me?" Her voice held no emotion.

"Tell you? Tell you I had a daughter by a woman I trifled with? Tell you that this child had nothing to do with us?"

She looked over at him, her eyes now fierce. Did he know? Suspect? Was he guilty of any more than she was?

"I beg of you, Hallie . . ." He leaned forward. "Try to find it in your heart to forgive me. I was away two years, and I was twenty-six years old." He stood up and crossed the room, his hands clasped behind his back. "You were ten thousand miles away, and I ached for you. It's not as if I'm a rake or rogue, like Tristan, who's probably bedded half the widows of New South Wales. Not"—he raised his hand as though waving something away—"that that negates the other admirable—aye, wonderful—parts of him. But except for Edythe and those years of loneliness, I've never been unfaithful to you, even mentally."

Her mind was frozen. All Hallie could hear was, ". . . bedded half the widows of New South Wales."

Chad was continuing, ". . . how awkward for you to be faced with Lucy every day, to remind you of my transgression. I have always loved you, Hallie. Know that."

Bedded half the widows of New South Wales! Her hand flew to her forehead. Dizziness swept over her and she

548

thought, I'm going to be ill. "I must get outside. . . ." Her voice sounded fuzzy. "I think I'm going to faint."

In one step Chad was beside her. Lifting her in his arms, he strode down the hallway and out onto the veranda. The spring air was cool, but Hallie didn't notice—her mind was paralyzed.

Her husband had fathered a child in England, and Tristan, if she could believe Chad, had bedded other women. Women, in the plural. She knelt in the grass and threw up.

"Oh, God," she heard Chad whisper.

He had spent the last month proclaiming his love but had been dallying with another woman for months, or years, while in England.

While she was dallying with Tristan.

Dallying? While her heart had been engulfed with love.

Had Tristan been entangled with other women, or had Chad—knowing the truth about Julie and Wick—merely thrown that at her? Had Tristan been involved—bedding half the widows of New South Wales—in those years he came out regularly to Cowarra, in that time when the twins were conceived?

Surely not. That must have been before she and Tristan had discovered each other again. He could not have had other women in those years when he helped them learn to read, when he brought her plants and taught Jamie to ride. In those years when he'd brought Ben and Emil to her. He had shown in so many ways how much he cared for her.

He loved her, she knew it. He couldn't have been making love to other women then.

Chad was stroking her back and talking, confessing to her. "I can't even justify it as a moment of passion," he was saying. "She was a friend of my sister's, a young woman married to a very old man who was unable to perform his marital duties. Edythe was a lovely young woman. I danced with her, she smiled at me, quite dazzlingly, and said, 'I really think it's you.'

"Of course I didn't know what she meant, and asked her as we whirled around the floor. She looked at me sideways, her eyes sparkling, and—smiling still—murmured, 'I think I'd like you to be the father of my child.'

"Before I even knew what was happening, though I give you no excuses, it was out of hand. Weekends in Scotland, at her husband's hunting lodge. Days spent in a castle in Cornwall. Nights in her London house when her husband was out of the city."

Why was he telling her every detail? she wondered. He was talking in a rush, as though finally cleansing himself of the guilt he had contained all these years.

"I knew it would be years before I saw you again, before I could return home. It had already been years since I had made love to you. I knew, too, that all the time with Edythe Leigh was wrong. And yet I could not stop myself. I would lie in bed nights and see your face and yearn for you so much—but all I could reach out for was Edythe."

Hallie turned to stare at him. She wanted to cry, Stop, but she was unable to.

"Edythe knew I would return to New South Wales, knew I loved you. And when she conceived Lucy, that was the end of it. I have no idea what she ever told her husband, but he apparently did not object. I never did meet him. But around London hats were taken off to him, jokes made that at his age it was remarkable that he had fathered Lucinda.

"I offered to set up a fund to support the child, but Edythe assured me she had more money than she could ever spend. And, Hallie, I felt unable to control myself. I went every day to see Lucy. I kept thinking I was not seeing Alex growing the way I saw Lucy. When I did finally leave England, my only regret was that I would never see my daughter again, the daughter whom I then knew better than Jamie and Alex, the daughter who also made me ashamed of myself. It is the one act in my life for which I am conscience stricken."

She understood that. She had felt that way herself for years. And yet she was furious at him, crushed, hurt.

"Edythe said she would tell Lucy about me, but tell her I was her uncle, the adventurer of the family. I asked her not to write, knowing at the same time it would tear me apart not to hear about my daughter. But I did not want you to know. I wanted nothing to jeopardize my relationship with you.

"I thought not knowing about Lucy was a price I was willing to pay. Now I see I am being forced to pay another price, after all. Hallie, I cannot lie to you. I am through with that. It has been the one thing that has come between us all these years, even though you have not known."

Oh, no, she thought. It has been my guilt, too, that has separated us.

"No matter what else you feel, know that never for a moment have I ever stopped loving you. I don't ask your forgiveness. Forgiveness comes from within. Only I can forgive myself, and right now I am not able to do that. What I do ask is that you try to understand. Search your heart, I beg you!"

Hallie stood up, pushing away his helping hand. "Make my excuses for dinner. I'm going to bed. I have a frightful headache," and she walked away from him, into the house, up the stairs and into her room. Stripping off her clothes, she pulled the curtains and fell into bed, tossing and turning—unable to think.

Had she been but one of many to Tristan?

No, she couldn't have been. She knew—had always known—she was his great love. Yet her mind would not stop. Had he been bedding other women in those years he had come to Cowarra so often? Did Wick and Julie perhaps have half brothers and sisters in Sydney? Had Tristan told those women that he loved them, too, that their skin was like velvet? Had he touched them in ways he had touched her?

Chad's footsteps woke her. "Shall I light a candle?" he asked.

"No."

He sat on the edge of the bed. "Hallie, it seemed a part of another life, one that had nothing to do with us," he said, his voice soft. Leaning over, he reached for her hand.

"It was so long ago. Haven't the years since then shown you how I feel? I won't ask you to treat Lucy like a daughter, but can you not find it in your heart to be kind to her? It is not her fault. And I do feel responsible for her."

Hallie's only response was, "Please sleep in another room."

* * *

She was up and out of the house before breakfast, driving to Tristan's.

A servant showed her in and told her that neither Dr. nor Mrs. Faulkner was downstairs yet. Hallie said she would wait.

Molly appeared first, exclaiming, "Why, Hallie, what a surprise! Is anything wrong?"

"I must see Tristan." Hallie stood by the door to his office, rigid.

"Are you all right?" asked Molly. "He'll be down in a minute."

Hallie, not caring what Tristan would eventually explain to Molly, answered, "I must talk with him."

"Have you had breakfast? Some tea, perhaps?"

Hallie shook her head just as Tristan appeared.

"Hallie . . ." His eyebrows rose. "What brings you here so early in the morning? Aren't you just about ready to depart on your big adventure?"

"I must talk with you."

He glanced at Molly. "Of course. Shall we go into my office?"

"No. Not here. In my carriage, perhaps."

"I'll get my coat," he said. He was back in a minute.

Neither said anything as the horse clopped through the street. It was not until Hallie took the road out past her house, out to a promontory overlooking the harbor, that she stopped.

"Tell me," she said, turning to him. "Have you loved me?"

He cocked his head, looking surprised. They had not used the word or talked intimately since before the twins were born, over ten years ago. "Of course. I have always loved you."

"Do you love Molly?"

He nodded. "Yes."

"As much as me?"

"How does one measure love?" asked Tristan, obviously bewildered. "A teaspoonful? A cupful?"

"An oceanful," said Hallie, her lips tight.

"What's this about, Hallie? It's not yet nine o'clock in the morning, and you've driven me out in the country to talk about love. What is it you want?"

"I've loved you all these years," Hallie said.

552

"And I you," responded Tristan.

"But I am not the only one you've loved?"

"I gather that's a question. Hallie, please, tell me what this is about." He reached out to take her cold hands in his. "What is this anger I see in you? Is something wrong?"

"Wrong?" she cried, wresting her hands from his. "I may just have wasted my life, that's what's wrong!"

"What do you mean, wasted your life?"

"Spending it loving you."

"Is love such a waste?"

"Oh, dammit, Tristan!" She began to cry. "Were there other women before me—here, in this country?"

His eyes held hers with a level gaze. "I don't know what brought this on. Of course there were other women before you. It was nearly three years from the time we landed until I saw you again. I'm a doctor, not a celibate priest. But what has that to do with love?"

"Did you love any of them?"

The look he gave her was still puzzled. "No, Hallie. And if you're asking, I have never loved anyone as I loved—and still love—you."

Hallie jumped down from the carriage and walked over to the water. Tristan followed her, reaching out to put a hand on her shoulder. "Are you upset about so long ago? What is bothering you?"

"What about when—those years you came out to Cowarra. Those years Chad was away."

"What about them?"

"Were—were there other women then also?"

Tristan took his hand away. "Hallie, what is it you're wanting from me?"

"I need to know some things. I need answers."

"Why?"

"I think we—I've been living a lie."

"You mean because Chad doesn't know about Wick and Julie?"

"That's part of it. But only a part."

"Then what is the rest of it?"

"Chad said"—Hallie began to cry again—"that you'd bedded half the widows of New South Wales."

Tristan looked as if someone had hit him. "So it's true,"

553

he murmured as if to himself. "What ye sow, so shall ye reap."

"Did you? Were you bedding other women those years Chad was gone?"

He tried to reach out for her again, but she moved away. "Hallie, my dear. I had no idea you would ever . . . ever be mine. You were a married woman, a respectable married woman. Of course I loved you, as I have always loved you. You fed my spirit and my soul. You've touched parts of me that no one else has even neared. But you could not feed my body, my immediate physical needs. What was so wrong about my finding women to supply those needs at that time?"

"Oh, Tristan!" she cried. "If you loved me, how could you have?"

"What has love, pray tell, to do with what goes on in a bedroom? I will not deny that it heightens the ecstasy. In fact, I will admit there is little if any ecstasy when one beds just anyone. And it has never been better than with you. No one has ever been as passionate, as giving, as alive. I have never felt as close to anyone as those years with you, those years when I came out to Cowarra."

Hallie was staring at him, her mouth open, tears dried on her cheeks. "Do you have other children born out of wedlock?" she asked softly.

He hesitated. "If so, I never took advantage of a woman. I have supported any children of mine who needed it. And I never, ever, made the initial advance. If Chad thinks I've bedded only widows, it's probably because they've been lonely. They've been the ones who made the overtures. I never have taken advantage of any woman. If you'll recall, that night of the governor's ball, it was *you* who suggested we go to my house. It was you who wanted to be made love to."

Hallie closed her eyes and forced herself to breathe normally. She waited until the pain that shot through her chest had eased before she spoke again. "Had I been free, you would have married me, wouldn't you? It was not being able to have me that forced you to Molly's arms, wasn't it?" Her eyes implored him.

"Oh, my dear, why are you doing this to yourself? I would have loved to have had that courage. I don't know

554

any man but Chad who's strong enough to take on a woman like you. I would have faded next to you.

"You thrive on challenges and would never have made me feel rested at home. The cares of the day would not have rolled away were I to return to you each night. Hallie, I am not a big enough man to have taken you on. . . . Love you? How could I not love you? You are excitement and passion and everything we'd all like to have the courage to reach for. You are not serenity, nor peace, nor comfort. And these are all things I need at night when I come home. Oh, I would never have been strong enough to have married you. You are the fantasy tucked away in my heart. You were the closest I ever came to having what I could never have the courage to take. Why did I marry an ex-convict? A woman with the most equable temperament on earth, who worships me and anything I do? If I think something, she thinks it. If I want to do something, she does, too. I don't think we've ever had an argument. She is content to be my wife and the mother of my children. She has no dreams beyond that. She is grateful to be the wife of a doctor, to be my wife. This is what I have the courage for, Hallie. To know that in this relationship, I am superior. I don't think I'm that much different from most men.

No, she thought. That's what Chad envisioned in the beginning, too.

The pain in her heart returned, compounded now with a blinding rage—and this time it did not go away.

Fifty-five

They hadn't yet been able to go over six miles a day. The first day they'd made only four miles—women who were not used to walking, dozens of small children. But there were five wagons, four to carry enough supplies for 250 for over two months, and one for those who couldn't go another step or for tired children or those who might become ill. Rather than hold up the whole procession, women would jump on that wagon for an hour or so and then, somewhat rested, would rejoin the march on foot, giving room to someone else. The wagons were drawn by oxen, which also were slow. Chad had pointed out that speed was not a consideration, and that oxen could pull heavy loads indefinitely.

Chad rode as far as the mountains with them. Ben had volunteered to go over the mountains and as far as Bathurst. He could attend to business there and reassure himself that Hallie had made it to the other side of beyond.

That morning, before Chad left to return to Cowarra, before the women started the steep ascent up the Blue Mountains, he had said to her, "I wish this hadn't happened just when you're leaving."

They had been on their horses, facing each other. He stretched in his saddle and, leaning over, kissed her cheek. Then, in a louder voice, he'd said, "Have a good trip," then turned and rode off to kiss Julie good-bye. Hallie had stared after Chad as he'd cantered away, her mind dulled. She had been unable to think for the last three days, merely going through the motions of packing. Even now she found it impossible to focus on the conversations she'd had with Chad and Tristan, to ponder their implications.

She and Sophie were to bring up the rear of the group, on their horses. Four or five of the other women had found horses; altogether, eight of them were on horseback. Ben and the soldiers had already started up the mountains, which had been dreamlike blue in the gradually closing distance. They did not just look blue from far away. Little beads of eucalyptus oil shimmered from the crowded gum trees, refracting in the sunlight, forming a blue haze. These were no mountains that ascended gradually, but crags that rose straight up. The entourage was forced to stop nearly every half mile for those who were out of breath and out of shape. One of the women said, "I can't go on," and, indeed, did turn back, walking off alone. They watched until she'd become a speck in the distance, heading eastward.

From the time they left Sydney, it took them two and a half weeks to reach the summit of the craggy mountains, until they could look down and see the other side. They passed along steep, perpendicular cliffs, stopped to bathe in narrow, plummeting waterfalls, walked through fern-filled gorges. It was a different world from that just forty-five miles to the east. And when they came to the point where they could view the western lands, see the lush green plains stretching into infinity, see the streams running full in early spring, reflecting ribbons in the bright sunlight, nearly all of them thought they had been right to choose this path. A few, however, gazed out at the infinite distance and were dismayed.

"Enough grass out there to feed cattle for a hundred years," Ben said. He never once complained about the time involved. Alone, he could have been to Bathurst and back in the time it had taken this group to reach the crest of the mountains.

"It's beautiful," breathed Hallie, feeling life surge into her. "I wasn't prepared for this." I want to get away, a part of her thought. I want to try unknown land. Start anew. I want to be one of the first. Think what cattle and sheep could do out here. What a challenge it could be!

"Gets dusty," said Ben, "in summer. But for them that likes being away from crowds, for them that wants to be on their own, it's as close to paradise as they're likely to get."

Julie rode up. "Oh, Mother, it's lovely, isn't it?" she cried. Each day she found a new adventure, and Hallie was thrilled that her daughter was following Sophie's example, riding back and forth to see that those with sore feet or other ailments had their turns riding on the wagon. Julie and Sophie would reach down from their saddles and gather up infants in their arms so mothers could march unimpeded.

At night—and the nights were colder than any Hallie had known since Newcastle—they sat around campfires, huddled in their blankets, with a spirit of camaraderie that was new to her. Ben would say to Julie, "Remember that song I taught you, the one that begins . . ." and he and Julie would start singing. Before long, a chorus of voices echoed in the empty night.

After the fatiguing days spent outdoors, however, sleep overtook the women early. Soon after dark all was quiet. The soldiers took shifts staying awake, but they saw nothing and heard nothing except the rustle of the wind through the trees.

Each night Hallie lay there after everyone else was asleep and tried to sort out her thoughts. Tried to sort out the bundle of emotions that simmered within her, to untangle her jagged nerves. But she never succeeded. She would lie on her back, locating the Southern Cross, feeling the closeness of Julie snuggled next to her, and tell herself, Now, I have time to think. But, always, the next thing she knew it was dawn.

Most of the women had experienced adventure only on the long trip from England, but that lacked the variety and excitement this trip engendered. This was different. Freedom leapt in the air. Exultation. And much laughter.

"I've climbed a mountain," one of the women said with wonder in her voice.

"That's how they all feel," Sophie said. "They're proud of themselves."

Hallie smiled. "Well, aren't you?"

Sophie laughed. "I am that. Sixty-two years old and I'm out climbing mountains with my daughter and granddaughter. Who'd have ever thought it? Just smell that mountain air. It clears out one's head, don't it? My, just look at that view! How lucky Julie is. When we were her age we never even had hope, did we?"

"Well, I had dreams, I think, but no hope."

"Reckon that's what always made you restless. I thought you wanted more than a person had a right to expect, and that you were due for such disappointment. Instead, look

558

at what's happened. When you were her age, you'd already met Chad, hadn't you? But didn't yet know that he was the answer to your dreams."

The answer to my dreams, thought Hallie.

"Wouldn't Alex love all these," Julie said, stooping to gather a flower with large red bracts. "I'll gather some and take them home to her."

"They won't last," said Hallie.

"I know, but she can see them dried."

What really fascinated Julie the most were the koalas and the roos. Her goal was to get close enough to see the babies in their mother's pouches, or to touch the lazy-looking koala, which always seemed to be asleep in the crotch of trees. She would sit with infinite patience, when the women had stopped for the night, scarcely moving, with a crumb in her hands, waiting for a kangaroo to approach her. Shy animals that they were, she seldom succeeded, but every once in a while either their curiosity or their hunger drove them forward, never quite close enough for Julie to touch them, but enough so that she felt her heart thumping.

"I've never seen the child so patient," Sophie commented. "You'd never know this was the girl who can't sit still at home."

"She's not sitting still," Hallie observed. "She's having an adventure. One that few others have ever had. She'd be real surprised to hear us say she's sitting still. She thinks she's in the act of discovery."

Sophie looked at Hallie with a bemused expression on her face. "Maybe if I'd taken the time to look at you like you look at her, I'd have understood your restlessness, understood you."

"Don't blame yourself," Hallie said, hobbling her horse in the midst of a sea of green grass. "You never had a minute when you weren't busy working. You had nothing else to compare life with except what you and your parents had always known. You didn't know more than what you lived."

"You're always busy, too," Sophie said quietly.

"Ah, but my life's so different." Hallie put an arm around her mother. "Mine isn't drudgery. Mine doesn't drain my energy and dull my mind. Mine feeds me. There's such a difference. Poverty imprisons as badly as real jail.

559

In fact, I think most convicts are there because they've been in the poverty prison first. These people that have come to this country appreciate freedom more than anyone I know. They've never known it before. Poverty imprisons the mind, too, I've come to realize. Oh, Mum, do you realize what we're doing? We're leading these women to free lives!"

Sophie shook her head. "Not necessarily, my dear. Some of them are going to marry into poverty."

Hallie was silent for a moment. "I hadn't thought of that. Well, at least they're making the choice. They're going to do it in wide-open spaces instead of crowded cities with sewage running in the streets."

"We never had sewage. . . ."

"Oh, I know. And I don't suppose if you're really poor that it matters if it's in a crowded city or under wide-open blue skies. At least one can grow food out here and not be afraid of being murdered and robbed."

Sophie smiled, letting Hallie ramble on. There *is* some truth to what she's saying, she thought. Look at us. We're prime examples. How different our lives are for having taken chances, having had the courage to say no to the lives we had, for having the guts to venture into and out to the unknown. Pride flowed through her.

A crimson rosella flew in front of them and perched on a nearby branch, its bright blue wings and tail accentuated by the vibrant red of its body. Hallie and Sophie, more accustomed to cockatoos than parrots, stared at the bird. The tree was covered with other parrots, green ones, yellow ones, multicolored birds.

"Actually," said Julie, "it's birds I love. Let Alex have her plants. I never get tired of watching birds."

And each day they saw birds new to them. Birds that nested in grasses. Waterbirds, ducks, black swans, the emu—which one of the soldiers informed them could not fly, but stalked around on long stilted legs that could carry it as fast as fifty miles an hour. Hallie loved the budgerigars and the ubiquitous magpies, songbirds whose melody was matched by the beauty of their dramatic black-and-white feathers.

There were galahs on this side of the mountains, too, with their bright pink breasts and silver-pink crested heads, noisy and spectacular when flying in wheeling flocks. Great wing-spanned eagles soared out of the sky to capture some unsuspecting rodent in their claws; owls *whoo*ed in the night. The band of women saw all of these as they came from the mountains into the plains, green-gold with spring.

Every sixth day they stopped. A day to rest, to launder, to wander around, to do whatever it was each wanted to do. There were no restrictions placed on the women. And it was usually on these sixth days that an outsider could have seen the changes taking place, not so much within the group as within each woman.

Surprisingly enough, there were only three whiners within the entire complement of travelers, only three women who complained. One was constant, the other two intermittent. There were but two who had short tempers. Hallie had seen those two evidence explosive moments back at the house, and she had had her worries about them. But except for brief moments, these two held their tempers in check. No one judged them harshly if they were too tired to walk and opted for a wagon ride. Fewer and fewer women did that as time went on, and only the very small children chose to ride. They did not march, anyway, but rather ran away from the group to explore, to pick wildflowers. Sometimes some of the younger women ran with them.

They stopped fur lunch in the shade of trees or by a running stream, where—when the days were hot—the women and children went swimming. Sometimes they stayed long enough for short naps. The only things that scared the women were snakes, slimy and dark, which slithered away from them quickly. And aborigines, who also ran from them or stared at them from the branches of trees, always at a distance.

When some of the women seemed in conflict, Hallie suggested they move to another part of the parade; friendships that would last lifetimes were formed. There were fewer than twenty women who did not eventually take to the outdoor life, to the slow, easy pace Hallie set for them. Their skins burned, then peeled, then tanned, until some of them looked nearly black themselves.

There was no one to scold them, no one to tell them what to do, no one to stand in judgment of them. Sore feet gave way to calluses, exhaustion to a sense of physical well-being. Six of the women stayed behind at Bathurst. Ben offered to employ someone in his store, but no one jumped at his proposition. After a while, they reasoned, if they had not found husbands or better jobs, they might accept the offer.

One of them took a job at the first homestead to the west of town. It was a large square house standing in the midst of grassland, and had a front porch. The disheveled woman of the house held a baby in her arms, and four other children, no older than five, ran around yelling. But Abigail, the woman who chose to stop there, said, "She needs help, anyone can see that. She's young and looks kind, and they could be my family, too. I need a family more than I need another man." Abigail was a good-looking young woman of even temperament who felt in her heart that she had found a home. "No one in my whole life has ever needed me. I been in the way most of the time. I suspicion they need me here. Maybe God sent me. And if he didn't, I just be plain lucky." And it wasn't too far from town, such as it was.

That night they camped beyond the homestead, along the Macquarie River, swollen by spring rains and the melting snows on the mountains.

Once in the middle of the night Hallie awoke. Lying there, sensing danger, she listened. But all she heard was the far-off cry of a bird or a small animal whimpering. Then silence. Only the rustle now and again of leaves high up in the trees. She fantasized a band of aborigines creeping along low to the ground, ready to attack them. She envisioned a troop of escaped convicts from the work gang they had passed high up in the mountains. She imagined all manner of monsters, wild animals, and snakes roaming the land, ready to devour whomever might be in their path.

But there was no sound.

No convicts, no aborigines, no snakes attacked. She saw the dark outlines, eventually, of two soldiers, exchanging tours of duty—one to go off to sleep, the other to warn of any danger. But he warned of nothing, and eventually Hallie fell back asleep.

Shortly after dawn they were all awakened by the cry of a young woman searching for her two-year-old daughter, calling, "Sara!" By the time Hallie shook herself awake, the young woman was hysterical. Everyone started searching for the child.

"She's gone," cried Mary, the young mother. "Oh, God, it's my fault. She woke me in the night, and I told her to go out in the field and hurry back. I was too tired to get up. Then I must've fallen asleep. She's gone."

"Sh," said another of the young women. "She's all right."

Hallie wanted to shake her. How did she know the child was all right? A shiver passed over her as she remembered the feeling of danger that had awakened her, the cry she'd taken for a bird or young animal. Dear God in heaven, she thought.

They fanned out across the fields and up and down the riverbank. No one said it. They tried not to even think it.

It was over an hour later that they found her, facedown in the river, caught between two rocks. A soldier said, "She must have fallen in and the river just carried her along until she stuck here."

Mary was inconsolable. "It's my fault!" she screamed as they tried to quiet her. "If I'd just wakened up and gone with her. Oh, God! This is my *real* punishment. I should never have come." Kneeling, she beat her head against the sides of the wagon. "Let me die!" she screamed.

Hysteria finally exhausted her and she crumpled in a heap. They picked her up, gently, and laid her on the wagon while they dug a hole and made a cross from two branches. Alden Reed, the young minister who had accompanied them in order to perform weddings, had as his first task to bury a child and wish her Godspeed toward heaven. Reed wasn't past twenty-four himself and felt awkward surrounded by so many women. He preferred the company of the soldiers.

The soldiers themselves had changed considerably in the past several weeks. None had come willingly. "Sissy duty," they called it. But they enjoyed the food and found themselves responding to songs around campfires, to having women sew buttons on their uniforms, and darn their stockings, and listen to their stories. They enjoyed those who flirted with them, and they enjoyed the easy pace and lack of competition. They relaxed. And it felt good.

At first they eyed the women, the young pretty ones in

particular, lustily. But Hallie wasted no time in telling them, "My girls are coming to find husbands. If you want any of them, it's in marriage. If you abuse any one of them I shall have you court-martialed. I hope that's understood." They settled down soon enough after that.

For her part, Hallie did not discount these soldiers as matrimonial candidates. Already Alice, one of the youngest and prettiest of the girls, seemed to have captured the heart of young Lieutenant Charles Godwin. It was Alice who sat on the wagon with Mary in her arms when the procession proceeded again that afternoon. It was Alice who stayed with the distraught mother over the next few days, making sure someone was always at her side, feeding her when the woman refused to eat, wrapping her in her arms at night. And Lieutenant Godwin watched it all.

It was not easy deciding which woman would stay with what man. Shortly after Bathurst, they came upon a one-room shack. In it lived two men, unshaven, dressed in dirty clothes. Their cabin smelled, and tin dishes were piled high. Whiskey bottles littered the yard, but there was a well-fed dog who jumped over everybody, wagging its tail with joy. The two men looked at the caravan with glee, but none of the women volunteered to stop there. They could have made better bargains in Sydney.

In the next place there was just one man, again with a dog. He, too, was unshaven, and his clothes needed mending and washing. But fences dotted his pasture, and there was a small barn, nicer than the house. Pigs and piglets no more than a week old rooted in the earth behind the barn; a horse stood tethered to a post by the barn. And here any number of women were willing to stop. But the man wasn't interested. "I come to find freedom," he said, scratching his ear. "Not to be nagged forever."

The third place—a two-room house—was empty. The women camped here overnight. There was a neat garden, newly planted, with pale green shoots sprouting. One of the women, Lila, said, "Let me wait here. You'll be coming back this way, won't you? If the mister don't want me, or I don't like him, I'll catch you then."

They left her, waving at them from the kitchen door.

At the next ten homes they came to, they left ten women. It was not always an easy choice. Men would look at the mass of femininity in front of them and point, always at the prettiest and the youngest. But the prettiest often held out for more. They wanted to see what was ahead, what more they could be offered. Hallie insisted on talking to each of the men, learning something about them, hoping her instincts would tell her whether to believe them or not, who might beat their wives, or who drank, or who had an evil temper. It was not a hasty thing. Sometimes it consumed the better part of a day, sometimes just a few hours.

In the third week out of Bathurst, when they were heading northwest, and were ready to stop for the night—though it was but four in the afternoon—Julie came riding up to Hallie to consult with her about Eliza, one of the women. "She's bleeding, Mama. She's doubled over in pain. She's been on the wagon most of the day, and I think you better look at her."

Eliza's dress was matted with dried blood. The color was drained from her face, and she lay pale, not quite unconscious, on the hard floor. Once the procession had stopped, the children had jumped down and gone running off to play, so she lay alone on the bleached boards, the sun creating rivulets of perspiration on her forehead.

Hallie bent over the moaning woman. She was curled up in her bloody gown in the fetal position, emitting soft, broken sobs of pain. "What is it, Eliza?" she asked.

Tears had left tracks in the dust on her cheeks. Eliza lay with her hands thrust between her bent knees, shaking her head and crying. She did not talk until Sophie brought her some tea and forced her to drink. Then the color seeped back to her cheeks, but the bleeding did not stop.

"I tried to do away with it," she gasped.

"Do away with what?" asked Julie. Hallie flashed her mother a look, and Sophie put an arm around Julie's shoulders and drew her away.

"I've been suspecting I was with child," Eliza went on, turning to look at Hallie. "I knew no man out here would want me. Not soiled goods. A used woman."

Hallie put her hand on Eliza's thin arm. "What about all these women who are bringing their children?"

Eliza shook her head. "That's one thing. But the rest of us . . . They want us to be virgins. I knew none would want me. So last night last . . . night I tried to get rid of it."

"What about the father?"

"Oh, he was just at me for a few minutes of fun. I didn't even know what he was doing. I never did it before. He said pretty things to me, and we drank some ale, and he said he'd been wanting to get married, and how pretty was . . . And before I knowed what he was doing, he done it. Then he just up and left. He pulled on his pants and left the room and I never saw him again. Not even on the street."

Hallie closed her eyes and let out her breath in a ragged sigh.

"So when I was late, I began to suspect, but that wasn't till we'd already started," Eliza continued. "I been sick with worry every day. Until by yesterday I knew a baby was growing, and if I wanted to get married, I had to get rid of it. My mother told me no man wanted anything but a virgin less'n it was a widow. But I'm not a widow. No man would ever want me."

Hallie wanted to shake her. "Do you think all these women with their children are widows?"

The woman looked at her with glazed eyes.

"Every one of these mothers has had the same thing happen to them, more or less, as has happened to you. Oh, my dear Eliza! Only two of these women have ever been married." Hallie leaned over and put her cheek next to Eliza's.

Through her shudders, the young woman told Hallie, "I stuck a stick up me. Thought maybe I could wiggle the baby loose."

Hallie's eyes widened as she shot up, gazing about her with one hand across her forehead to shield her eyes from the sun. With this many women, maybe someone will know what we should do, she thought.

But even though some of the women had suggestions for how to abort, they all agreed that every method was chancy and could result in the same thing that Eliza had brought on herself. None knew what to do to alleviate Eliza's hemorrhaging.

That she had "brought it on herself," Hallie could not accept. That some selfish man who cared for nothing more than a few moments pleasure had brought it on her was more like it. Kill her with bleeding to death or ruin her life in another way, with a baby to take care of and no way to feed it.

The women took turns ministering to Eliza, applying first hot packs and then cold ones, cloths washed in the icy water from a nearby stream. They made her lie with her feet higher than her head. By morning her fever had increased and she was hallucinating. "Soiled goods," she kept repeating over and over. "No one wants soiled goods." She was too ill to travel even on the wagon, for there were no roads and the wagon lurched and swayed. So they stopped by the stream for the day. No one really did anything, just sat around and walked over every little while to look at the pale, unconscious Eliza. She died at two in the afternoon.

Two deaths . . . two burials, and we've been gone not quite five weeks, thought Hallie.

She was not the only one thinking this way. Clara, a pretty, pale blonde in her mid-twenties, said, "Look what these wide-open spaces do. I'm not going to stay. Nothing could make me live out here." She didn't complain, she walked with the rest, but she would return to Sydney with Hallie.

One afternoon, on the brow of a low hill, a horse and rider appeared, silhouetted against the sky. He rode along with them all afternoon, and when they stopped for the evening, he rode toward them. He approached the group, which, having been aware of him for hours, eyed him covertly.

Hallie saw him lean over in the saddle and say something to one of the women up the line, saw the woman point at her, and watched as the man jogged closer. He was well dressed; there were even creases in his trousers. His wide-brimmed hat hid his face, but he had the body of a man in good shape, who was used to outdoor work. And he certainly rode a horse well. When he reached Hallie, he doffed his hat and she could see he was about thirty with a well-trimmed beard, leathery skin that bespoke a life spent outdoors, and eyes that smiled even when his mouth did not.

"You're the head of this group, I'm told." His voice was polite.

Hallie introduced herself.

He slid from the saddle and stood in front of her. "Samuel Phillips, ma'am."

Hallie nodded again.

"Word's gone like wildfire that you're making the rounds of the countryside looking for husbands for your ladies. I've come to look."

Hallie smiled at him. "Where do you live?"

"About eighteen miles that way." He pointed northwest. "Thought I'd ride along with you for several days, see who I like the looks of."

"What sort of place do you have, Mr. Phillips?" Hallie asked.

"Big one," he said, looking at the women. "Have a hired hand, too. Free man. Don't want a convict, not out here."

No, landowners wouldn't be safe with prisoners out here, Hallie mused. She doubted that the governor would even assign convicts this far from town.

He had arrived in New South Wales three years before, he told her, and decided that Sydney and the towns along the Hawkesbury were already too crowded for him. Within three weeks of his arrival in this new world, he had loaded supplies on a wagon, hired a carpenter, and headed west. He'd not been across the mountains to the east again. All the supplies he needed he bought in Bathurst, coming in once or twice a year to load his wagon. He had over ten thousand sheep, he told her, and he and his hired man took care of the entire flock. Now he was ready for a family. He'd been building the house in expectation of a wife and children.

Hallie recalled with fondness the house that had been waiting for her when she'd first arrived in New South Wales. "Look around, Mr. Phillips, but first I'd like to see your place."

He smiled crookedly. "Don't believe me, is that it?"

"I didn't say that. But I'm particular where my girls go. Do look around, however."

In the days that followed, Samuel Phillips rode beside the group, pacing his horse back and forth along the long line, studying the women. Nights he unrolled his sleeping bag and slept under a tree, apart from the group. He did not join the soldiers.

Like Lieutenant Godwin's, Mr. Phillips's eyes kept stray-ng back to Alice. When he sought her out at evening meals, Lieutenant Godwin realized that he had better show his hand or risk losing the lovely lady. Nearly two hundred women searching for men, and one woman had two vying for her attentions. One or two of the women were able to muster jealousy, but Alice had been too loving to too many of them, had cuddled their children or rubbed the feet of women who had not yet developed calluses. Lieutenant Godwin and Mr. Phillips watched as she ran, her arms spread wide, across the meadows with the children, laughing with them, waving to the birds that circled above them.

The two men brought their tins of supper and sat next to her each night. On the third night she said, "You gentlemen had better know, I'm not much of a cook."

"I am," said Sam Phillips.

"I can afford to hire a cook," Lieutenant Godwin said.

On the fourth day Alice sought Hallie's advice. "They're both more than I could have had in Sydney, I think, and certainly much more than I'd have found back home in Nottingham. Which would you take?"

"Oh, no," said Hallie, smiling, "I'm not falling into that trap. I'm not you. Do you find one more attractive than the other?"

"I find them both exceedingly attractive," Alice admitted. "I'd seen Lieutenant Godwin eyeing me all this time, and though he hasn't done more than take a walk with me of an evening, I thought I might have him, if I should want. But being a soldier's wife doesn't appeal to me all that much." She bit her lip and narrowed her eyes as though thinking hard. Then she grinned. "But he is terrible good-looking, isn't he? And he could hire servants, he said. My, my. Back home I might have been a maid, and now he says he could hire me help."

Hallie nodded. "Yes, how different our lives are here than they'd be where we grew up. It's a wide, wonderful world out here, Alice. I might have been a maid back home, too, or the wife of a coal miner. That and nothing else."

"You?" Alice's eyes were large. "Why, you're the wife of one of the richest men in New South Wales!"

"That I am," Hallie acknowledged. "Though let me tell you a secret. I helped make him that. It wasn't all just him. And that's where the fun's been. Helping to make it more than one's fanciest dreams—more than one ever had the nerve to dream—more than one ever had the knowledge to dream. That's what's so wonderful about this place."

Alice stared at her. "Don't make up your mind yet," advised Hallie. "We're heading toward Mr. Phillips's place. Study each of the men, wait and see what his house is like—maybe it'll give you a clue to what your life would be like with him. See if either of them gets short-tempered while they're both wooing you."

Alice giggled. "I never thought all this could happen to me." She reached out and squeezed Hallie's hand. "I'd like to be like you. Just like you."

"No," Hallie said, returning the pressure of her hand. "Be you. I'd love to be your age again. You're a year younger than I was when I came here. How wonderful to have it all ahead! I envy you. New horizons. New challenges. Be sure that whoever you choose will let you accept challenges, if that's what you want . . . will let you be part of it all."

Alice yawned. "I guess I'd better get to sleep or I'll be no good tomorrow." She stood up. "Coming?"

"Not yet," Hallie said, leaning her head back against the tree. "I think I'll just sit here and look at the stars a bit longer."

As she gazed up at the heavens, following the trail of stars to the Southern Cross, a sense of depression overwhelmed Hallie. Chad and I have been unfaithful to our marriage, she thought. All these years I tried to tell myself that love had justified my action.

But it's all been lies. My marriage is a lie. Tristan's a lie.

My life has been a lie.

And she began to sob.

Fifty-six

When her mother found her the next morning, Hallie was still leaning up against the tree. Sophie bent over and, reaching down to grasp her hand, pulled her up. Hallie was stiff from sitting in the same position all night. In fact, she dragged through the entire day, stiff and tired.

One of the soldiers who had been riding ahead rode back to report hundreds of aborigines congregated about a mile ahead. Hallie knew this was unusual. Aborigines seldom traveled in bands of more than a few dozen. It would take several tribes together to amount to as many as several hundreds. Lieutenant Godwin, having spent two years fighting in Africa, was sure this boded ill.

"They've seen us coming and are preparing an attack," he warned. "Know where your guns are and be prepared to shoot."

Sam Phillips approached them and held up a cautionary hand. "Abos don't attack without provocation. There aren't enough English out here to have intimidated them so far. We have good relationships with them. There aren't fences yet to keep them from their habitual watering or hunting places. I've never had trouble with them."

Godwin glared at the person he already considered the enemy.

"Actually," continued Phillips, ignoring him, "I find them rather gentle people. This many may mean they're having a corroboree."

"A what?" asked Julie.

He smiled down at her. "It's a celebration. They paint themselves all sorts of colors and have dances, ones we'd consider quite wild. They chant. It's all quite unintelligible and fascinating. Can last for hours sometimes."

"You've seen some, then?" asked Hallie.

"Just part of one once. I was out hunting and camped

for the night when I heard a commotion. I crept through the woods to look. It was something I'll never forget."

"Weren't you scared?" asked Alice, her eyes shining with excitement.

"I'd like to sound heroic and say that I was. But the abos have no desire to hurt us. I can understand why the ones near Sydney, where they're being denied their traditional lands, are rebellious. And someday the ones here will be, or will retreat farther into the back of beyond. But right now—I've eaten with them out in the bush, and they've offered me their women—whom," he added hastily, "I have found polite ways to refuse."

Charles Godwin glared but said nothing, his irritation obvious.

"They won't start dancing or chanting until dark," Sam said. He looked over at Julie, but he was really talking to Alice. "Would you like to take a look? I assure you it will be perfectly safe."

Julie's eyes sparkled. "Oh, Mother, may we?"

Hallie thought it sounded fascinating.

"I suggest we keep it down to no more than half a dozen," said Sam. "We don't want to alarm them or interfere with their ritual."

"You won't catch me watching heathen dances," muttered Lieutenant Godwin. "My soldiers and I will stay here to protect the rest of the women in case you're wrong and they do attack."

Sam smiled easily and turned to Alice. "Are you willing?"

In that moment the three of them knew their future hung on her response. If Alice chose not to go, Sam would undoubtedly decide that he did not want a wife who was afraid to live so far from civilization and so close to savages. If she did go, she would be disagreeing with—and embarrassing—Charles Godwin.

"I'd love to see it," Alice said, sealing her fate. On such decisions does life hinge.

When asked, Sophie said, "I'd like to go, but walking another inch tonight is more than I can manage."

So Sam Phillips set off shortly after dinner with five women—Hallie, Julie, Alice, Emily—another adventurous woman—and Mary, whom Alice never let out of her sight.

The soldier who had spotted the aborigines rode a ways to lead them in the right direction, but Godwin had given orders he was to return immediately. The lieutenant was in ill humor.

The land was studded with eucalyptus, which dotted the landscape of the continent. Here they were not towering silver majestic trees, like the ones east of the mountains, but scrub trees—later to be called red gums. They offered shade, if one sat directly beneath them, and made the terrain seem less desolate than many thought it was. Rodents scurried along, and kangaroos—like the gum trees—were red here. They were large, about six feet when standing, and could leap nearly twenty-five feet in a single bound.

As the sun sank below the horizon, leaving misty pink trails that stretched out like long fingers, they could see eagles. "And those are hawks, and over there are falcons," Sam said, pointing. Their wingspans were enormous, and they soared and glided high in the sky, swooping down suddenly to grasp a small reptile or rabbit in their sharp hooked claws. Once the little group even heard the tearing of flesh as the bird glided away.

At this time of evening large whirling flocks of cockatoos and budgerigars swarmed onto the branches of the trees, where they would nest until dawn, turning the branches into limbs of feathers. Three large emus, each at least four feet tall, trotted along in their customary straight line, their speed steady but not fast, their feathers looking for all the world like bouncing bustles.

"D'you know anything about emus?" Sam asked. "They're not like other birds. The female lays the eggs, of course, but then she's through with them. The male incubates them, anywhere from five to twenty eggs, and the young follow him about for a year after hatching. Look at them. Big sons of guns, aren't they?"

"If you were a bird, would you like to be an emu?" Julie asked.

Sam laughed and smiled down at her. "Maybe."

It's a shame he's so much older than Julie, Hallie thought. This is what she'd like—pioneering. And a man like Sam. She found Sam Phillips most attractive. Alice would be lucky . . . *if* his home wasn't a hovel and he wasn't just on good behavior now. But Hallie believed him; he seemed completely at ease.

Gradually they could hear voices. For a quarter of a mile they'd been following a swift-flowing brook about three feet wide and six inches deep. Shouting and unintelligible sounds echoed into the night. It did not sound like hundreds to Hallie.

Sam put his finger across his lips, signifying silence. They followed him and crept up a little hill just as a scream that rendered every nerve end raw reverberated from beyond the hill. Eerie wails haunted the night air.

Down below them, centered around a fire, were perhaps three dozen aborigines. The men had decorated themselves with red paint, or blood, and gray clay. They had either cut or painted ridges into their faces and legs. Gray streaks circled their eyes, jagged lines cut into their cheeks. Several had gray lines crossing their foreheads and running down their noses, meeting at their chins. These continued onto their shoulders and down the middle of their bodies and their legs. Others had painted their ribs, and still others had smeared themselves with scarlet and an earthy yellow-gold. They looked like demonic skeletons.

A group of women appeared as though from nowhere, beating their breasts and tearing out their hair by handfuls. Forming a circle that surrounded the men, the women sat cross-legged, clutching at tightly rolled-up rugs. At some invisible signal they simultaneously stretched these rugs between their knees and began to beat upon them.

An old man in the center of the circle raised his arms heavenward and all was silent, except for the unintelligible sounds he cried into the night. Then, like percussion instruments, the women began to beat their skin rugs again, the men dancing in a ring around the old man, beating their sticks together and keeping in perfect rhythm with the women.

It was a frightful noise, like none Hallie had ever heard, yet it stirred her strangely. Julie's hand crept into hers and pressed tightly. Glancing at her daughter, Hallie realized it was not from fright that Julie had reached out, but to share a moment of indescribable elation. The child's eyes were shining.

Children appeared, and together with the men they

formed a straight line, marching forward and backward to the rhythm of the women's drumbeats, chanting sounds that had to be music.

This continued for close to an hour. Then without warning, it stopped. The men rushed forward and doused the fire so quickly and thoroughly that Hallie could see nothing.

There was not a sound.

The little group on the hill strained to see where the several dozen bush people had been, but they saw nothing, heard nothing. It was as though they had never been.

"Where have they gone?" someone whispered.

Hallie sensed they were observing something that few other people in the world had seen. People still in the Stone Age celebrating their religion, their beliefs, paying homage to their gods.

As she lay on the ground, watching, she thought what Lieutenant Godwin was missing by not being open-minded enough to witness another people's rites. He said, as would many of the people she knew, that they were heathens, practicing pagan rites. But she wondered how he could be so sure that his God was more omnipotent than the gods to whom these black people were paying homage. Was there but one God who refused into heaven all those who did not believe in Him? Perhaps these people were more attuned to real gods. Was there not a god of rain, and of sun, and of fertility, and of who knew what? Or . . . were there gods at all? A God?

Sam turned and began crawling back down the hill. The corroboree was over, and he didn't want to be discovered. He glanced up at the stars, dazzling jewels tossed against the night sky, and Hallie realized he was searching for the Southern Cross so that he could find his way back to camp in the dark.

"There . . ." She pointed to it. She realized where south was but could not tell where they'd been before they'd started. Sam, however, took one look and set off at a good clip. He did not let them talk until he was sure they were far from the band of aborigines.

"I wouldn't have missed that for anything," said Alice.

Sam smiled in the darkness and took her hand. "I wouldn't have had you miss it."

Watching them, Hallie felt a profound sense of contentment.

Later, when she and Julie lay under their blankets, Julie threw her arms around her mother and whispered, "I'm so glad you let me come." Then, a few minutes later, her voice heavy with sleep, she asked, "Do you think often of Father?" Without waiting for an answer, she went on, "I think he would have enjoyed tonight, too. Don't you think so?"

"Yes," replied Hallie. And Chad would have. He would have lain under the star-studded sky and reached for her hand, perhaps not saying anything, just aware, really aware, of what they had seen that night and shared. Just as Julie had.

Two days later they came to Sam Phillips's home. A murmur arose from the women, whose numbers had now shrunk by seventy. It was the first two-story house they'd seen out in the bush. Large and square, it looked as if it had been built for the ages. And it was painted.

"Yellow," breathed Alice. "It's a yellow house."

There were even curtains at the windows, and vines twining up the side of the wide porch, which was shaded by a graceful overhang. Buds of what would soon be purple flowers peeked from the green vines.

Behind the house horses and a colt roamed the pasture, which was dominated by a large barn. Fat brown chickens pecked in the earth next to a neat chicken coop, and a brood of chirping chicks waddled after one of the hens. Sheep dotted the red-earthed landscape as far as the eye could see. Ten thousand, Sam had said.

A smaller house sat on the other side of the barn, one about the size of Hallie's first house. No shack for Sam's hired man, obviously. Everything about the place looked tidy, as though expecting company, as though it were waiting for someone. A cat curled on the wooden rocker on the porch.

Sam shouted, and from the barn walked a man who limped slightly but moved quickly. He raised a hand to his forehead to shade the sun, then approached the group, smiling pleasantly. Clean and neat, freshly shaven, he looked more like the owner than a hired hand. Sam introduced him as Martin, his foreman.

"It's too perfect," muttered Lieutenant Godwin. "Something's wrong here. Men don't live like this alone."

Hallie hoped he was wrong.

They'd camp here tonight, she told the others. Sam offered a barbecue. "We'll kill a few sheep and roast them on spits," he said. "You can wash in the creek, if you want." He invited Alice, Hallie, and Julie into the house.

Inside, the three women looked at each other in astonishment. They'd have thought they were in Sydney, if not London. Shining wide-planked wooden floors outlined the oriental carpeting. The dining room, painted a soft green, contained a long, narrow mahogany table and twelve matching chairs. In the drawing room was an inlaid desk, a spinet piano, chairs comfortably arranged around the room, and the largest sofa Hallie had ever seen.

"Who plays the piano?" asked Julie, pressing a key and listening to the tinkle.

"I dabble at it," Sam admitted.

When they arrived at the kitchen, even Hallie had to admit that neither of her homes surpassed it. Gleaming china stood upright in shelves that surrounded the room. An enormous fireplace, with an oven, filled one side of the room. Next to the sink was a pump, the first indoor one Hallie had ever seen outside of Sydney itself. Even at Cowarra they didn't have an indoor pump.

"If you'd like"—Sam's eyes had not left Alice—"we could ask one of the women to stay as a companion for you. Then you would not feel alone in this vast land. Would you like that?"

Tears formed in Alice's eyes. What she was seeing was more than she had ever envisioned. Sam himself was better than she could have imagined.

And, before they left the next day, Emily—with her child—had volunteered to stay with Alice. "Maybe," she said, "someday marriage. But for now, to stay with Alice and to live in this house . . . that is more than I dreamed of."

Alice had hoped that Mary might remain, but Mary had not come out of her depression. She refused to consider staying on this side of the mountains, and would have nothing to do with thoughts of marriage.

"If you have a friend, you will not be lonely," Sam said, "and will not then be sorry you have chosen to live so far from other people."

Alice looked up at him. "I don't think I should be sorry anyway."

That afternoon, shortly before the barbecue, the Reverend Alden Reed married Alice to Sam Phillips, and the two women and one child settled into his big house. Hallie believed that before long Emily and her child might move up to Martin's house, up behind the barn. He was a solid young man with a hearty laugh, and he kept the women amused with anecdotes of life out in the bush.

The next morning Alice was beaming.

Lieutenant Godwin, who had realized defeat the night of the corroboree, was gallant. As they rode away he said to Hallie, "I should have spoken up sooner, I guess."

At the end of three months, when the group again returned through Bathurst, there were still eighteen women with Hallie. One woman had lost her mind and muttered to herself, fingering invisible beads around her neck and counting them over and over. Every once in a while she would stumble and crawl on her hands and feet, picking up nothings and crying when she could not find what she was looking for. She refused ever to look up. The wide-open spaces had unhinged her. Hallie hoped that once they were back in the city the woman would regain her senses, but Sophie doubted it.

An epidemic of diarrhea and vomiting had waylaid them for nearly a week. Though many lost weight and took days to recover, none died. One woman, whom the Reverend Reed had married to a man with a neat hut, raced after them the next day, her eyes wild with terror and her hair disheveled, clutching at her breasts and screaming, "Wait for me. Don't leave me!" Whether the husband had really been cruel to her or she had been overcome by the particulars of marriage, Hallie never could determine. But the woman swore that no man would ever touch her again.

There had been a thunderstorm wilder and more beautiful than any Hallie had ever seen. Lightning seared and sizzled, then split open the heavens, and she swore they could see to the center of the universe. White bolts shot down, setting fire to hundreds of trees even in the midst

578

of the torrential downpour. Whipped by wind, the fiery landscape looked as though it would devour the world, yet it was miles away. Sophie, Julie, and Hallie sat huddled together; nothing kept them dry, and they shivered all night long, even after the thunder and rain had stopped. The next day dawned clear as crystal, and they placed all their belongings in the sun, amazed to find them dry in less than an hour.

One morning Hallie was awakened by a woman shaking her, whispering, "Wake the lieutenant."

Apparently the woman's companion, Cecilia, had awakened with a large snake coiled on her chest. Unable to stop shivering, she was nevertheless afraid to move. Lieutenant Godwin dared not shoot the reptile as it lay upon the woman, and they all knew that if it was frightened, it might lash its poison into Cecilia. Cecilia lay there, scarcely breathing, her eyes wide with panic. Not for over an hour did the snake move its large brown body; even then it uncoiled with maddening deliberation and stared around before it began to slither down Cecilia's arm, unwinding itself while its hooded eyes stared straight ahead. At last it flicked its tail and slid into the brush. Cecilia broke into hysterics. After that, nothing in the world—no Sam Phillips, no beautiful house, no gold—could have lured her into staying on this side of the mountains.

Another incident occurred when one of the soldiers developed a toothache. He moaned in the night. He cried aloud in the day. He sat down and attempted to hit his head against a rock. Finally Sophie said, "Let's pull it."

She found some string and wrapped it around the poor man's tooth, tying the other end to a horse's leg. Then she slapped the rear of his horse, which took off at a gallop with the sore tooth of the soldier, who screamed, *"Shhee-it!"* Sophie wiped up the blood, and by evening the soldier was able to function again.

There had been no other men and no other homes like Sam's. But there had been huts and small houses, and families who wanted servants and men who were willing to marry the women. By the end of the journey the only women returning with Hallie were doing so of their own volition. Either they could not stand the wide-open spaces or they had not found men they were willing to marry.

Every woman with children had found a destination. Men seemed to want children around as much as they did wives.

One of the women did remain behind to work at Ben's store in Bathurst, thinking that if she didn't like it or couldn't find a husband, she could easily come over the mountains with someone.

Now that they were on their way home, Hallie was aware of a deep depression overtaking her. She was going to have to face all that she had swept from her mind these last three months.

Fifty-seven

Since there was only one road across the mountains, the band of women and soldiers knew they had been this way before, but it seemed different somehow going back—like new territory. Hallie especially found it hard going. Now that her obligation to all the women was done, now that they were returning home, the adventure successful and behind them, she had to fight off despair. It was all she could do to put one foot before the other as they climbed the mountains. From this side the ascent was not as steep, but it seemed next to impossible to her, even though she was in much better physical shape than she had been three months before.

Streams had already dried up; grass was brown. But as they climbed higher, the air was brisker and dust wasn't blowing across the plains. Trees protected them from the sun, now hot in mid-December. They would be home for Christmas, Hallie mused. How could she possibly rouse herself to prepare for the holiday? Her heart would not be in it.

They stopped that night at the peak of the mountains, where the view westward showed endless horizons and the rocky cliffs dropped straight down to a valley thousands of feet below. The evening was blessedly cooler than in the plains below.

After dinner, Lieutenant Godwin walked over to Hallie, who was sitting staring out at the horizon. He leaned against a tree and slid down slowly. "Mind if I sit, too?" he asked.

"Of course not," she answered, hugging her knees.

"Couple more days and we'll be out of the mountains. I don't too much look forward to it," he commented.

"I gather you weren't anxious for this assignment," she said.

He nodded. "It's the truth. And I'm not sure I'm going

to admit how much I've liked it—to my captain, that is." He lit his pipe, tamping it for several minutes before continuing. "It's an experience like none I've ever had."

"I guess that's true for all of us," Hallie said, staring at the valley floor below them.

"I guess I've always thought a bunch of women would fight and bicker, that they couldn't keep up the pace. . . ."

"Despite the popular myth, women really like each other." They don't have to pretend with each other, Hallie thought. Not after they get to know each other. Not like they often have to with men. "And we didn't set much of a pace to keep up with."

"Not at first," he admitted. "Maybe you didn't notice, but halfway through the trip, everyone kept up a good clip. Even those who had already decided to come back. I don't think even they are sorry they came."

He looked at her and then at the distant horizon. They were silent together for a few minutes.

"I think you were very gallant about Alice," Hallie said at last, turning to smile at him.

"I learned from it," he said, puffing his pipe. "I guess what I learned mainly is that when we try to impress someone, the only one we're really trying to impress is ourselves. Tell ourselves we're stronger or harder-working or righter-thinking. Puff ourselves up so that the other person will think we're better than we really are. But all that does is show the other person what we really are. Vain . . . small."

Hallie looked at him. He would never have talked this way three months ago. "You're a very nice young man," she told him. "There are many women as nice as Alice. Whoever gets you as a husband will be lucky."

He laughed self-consciously. "That's another thing I learned. Though Alice is as pretty as they come, so were a bunch of the ladies. It wasn't her looks that attracted me, but the way she was with Mary and with all the children. She was what I'd call . . ." He searched for a word.

"Loving?"

He frowned. "Why do I have such trouble saying it? Yes, of course. And it's shown me that maybe that's what I'd better look for in a woman. Not just her looks. I'd about melt every time I saw Alice mothering someone, giving part of herself to make someone feel better."

"Oh, I don't think it's so much that she gave part of herself. She got something from it, probably more than she gave. That's what made her so beautiful to everyone. You're right: she's pretty, but so are many others. Alice has a beauty that comes from loving so freely."

Again, silence.

"I wasn't ready for her," he said abruptly. "I think I may be for the next woman I find who's like that. It also showed me that I want to resign my commission. I don't want a soldier's life. I want to settle down, though I don't know a thing about farming."

"There are other things you can do. It needn't be a farm," she said.

"Well, actually I've never done anything but soldiering. Not since I left Sandhurst."

"I'm sure there are many things you could succeed at, Lieutenant."

His pipe and the setting sun extinguished themselves together. The last vestige of gold glowed in the purple sky. "What'd you get out of this trip?" he asked. "The same sort of pleasure Alice got, I bet. I've never known women like you two. You didn't get anything out of it for yourself, did you?"

"Oh, but I did. More than you or anyone else can ever know. Besides"—she smiled, now her turn to feel self-conscious—"how many women have crossed the Blue Mountains with two hundred women in her charge? Don't you think I'll fit into a history book, Mr. Godwin?"

"That's not your reason, though."

But that may be part of it, she thought. I hadn't realized it, but it may be a big part of it. Hallie Morgan, who single-handedly . . . "Lieutenant, is there any of your whiskey left? Although I don't know how there would be after three months."

"I've still got a bottle of prime stuff," he said, getting up. "And rum, too."

"May I have some?" she asked. "I feel in particular need of a drink tonight."

"Of course," he replied, smiling. He left, and returned a minute later with a half-filled bottle.

"Join me?" she asked.

"Don't mind if I do . . ." He unscrewed the bottle and

offered it to her. She took a healthy swallow and grimaced as the liquor burned the back of her throat.

They sat there watching the horizon slowly dissolve, feeling the chill night air set in. Then he rose and held out his hand to her.

"No," she said. "I'm going to sit here for another few minutes."

"Come back to camp before it's dark," he said, "so you don't fall off the cliff."

She was feeling better than she'd felt in days. "I'm all right. I'll be along. I'm not going to fall off anything."

A thin red line indicated the horizon. The harder she stared, the more stars glittered into the darkening sky. One of them shot across the heavens, trailing gold dust behind it in an arc before disappearing.

In a week, she thought, I'll be home. Home. Cowarra.

Part of her wanted to stay here or try new horizons. Start a new life. Stop living a lie. She could forgive Chad Lucinda, but could she believe he had truly loved her all along? She had thought Tristan had, thought that their love had been pure and therefore Julie and Wick were not conceived in sin. But to Tristan she had been just another woman. No matter that he told her he'd loved her the most.

Part of her passion for him, she admitted, was his love for her. And now she had discovered she was but one of many. So she had been in love with what she wanted to see rather than with what was. She had loved someone she had believed in, now to discover her belief was fantasy.

Did that mean the last fifteen years had been a waste of her love?

She wanted to focus on Tristan, but her mind kept flowing to Chad. She had understood from the moment of Lucinda's arrival that she had to face questions within herself, come eye to eye with issues of the heart that she had not faced before.

The last month before she'd left on this trip had given her an inner harmony she'd never known before. A peace that was, nevertheless, fulfilling and exciting; a sense of awareness of her daily life and her spiritual being that she had not taken the time to examine. She had sensed, from the night Chad told her he had always loved her, that she was—after nineteen years—falling in love with her husband.

When he entered a room, she came alive, and it was not just a sexual titillation. Sex with him over the years had nearly always been thrilling. Why, she wondered, had she not connected that with love?

She was crushed when Tristan had asked, "What does love have to do with what goes on in the bedroom?"

She was hurt that Chad, so soon after proclaiming how long and deeply he'd loved her, had had to admit he'd been in bed with another woman.

Why, then, had she never connected love with the excitement—often, ecstasy—that she found in bed with Chad?

Because her heart had been tied to Tristan.

Maybe that's what she'd better examine—her concept of love. As the youngest of the children, she'd watched her older brothers and sisters "fall in love," only to have it end in marriage and complacency or bickering, or just become a daily part of a life that was always dull, if not throbbing with poverty and grayness. She had watched her parents and seen the emptiness in their lives, the sameness of one day being exactly like the next. There had been so little joy or cause for exultation in the relationships she had been part of. Joy, usually in the anticipation of a birth, yet so little hope for the life of the newborn.

As she was growing up, when she would witness one of her sisters beginning to show interest in a particular boy— begin to giggle a little more often when he was around, begin to pinch her cheeks in the one scratched mirror they owned, begin to watch out the window for him—sadness would overwhelm her. For she knew this was the end of her sister's childhood, the beginning of a life of burden.

With the invitation to come to New South Wales, she had realized freedom from dullness, from life as she had always known it. She'd sensed the possibilities even before knowing them, had known the moment Chad had sent for her that she could escape and begin to live. Marriage was inevitable, there was no other choice, and she would have the babies just as she would in Newcastle, but she would not endure a hopeless existence covered with soot, or a life governed with worry about whether her husband would be caught below ground one day. She would not be limited by gray horizons.

And each day did fill her with wonder. Her life was not

bound by damp cobblestone streets and a tiny room under the eaves in a bed scarcely wide enough to turn around in. Instead, she'd dug food out of the rich brown earth and felt the wind in her face as she galloped on her own horse.

In those early years of marriage she had not participated in the dinner table conversation much more than her mother had, for Chad had talked mainly to Archie. She realized now that it was partly because she and her husband hadn't known what to say to each other or what they needed from or could give to each other. Even though they had committed themselves to lives together, even though they came together with passion at nights, even though they created children together, they did not know each other or how to talk together. But she was too young and too limited in her perception of life to have understood that.

And she had fallen in love with Tristan on board ship. Love . . . What did that mean?

That's what she'd thought she felt when she had awakened from her appendectomy and seen Tristan's warm eyes, what she'd felt also when he found ways to be with her and spent hours talking to her as she recuperated. She had never known that with a man. Known the trembling anticipation that shot through her when his hand touched hers. It was then that she had irrevocably, she thought, given her heart to him and thus found it impossible to envision love with Chad.

She had not known then that she could love two men. That love for one could even recede and make room for another to grow larger. That she could fall in love with a man who had been her husband for nearly twenty years.

She had never seen what he had felt for her. Part, a great part, of the reason she had responded to Tristan in the years Chad had been away was that she knew Tristan cared, knew he loved her. It was not just her looks, or her ability to bear children, that attracted him. He saw into her, into the person who lived beneath the surface. It was his understanding to which she had reacted; his gentleness and those parts of him that gave so freely.

In the years that Chad had been away, she could lie in bed and fantasize about Tristan. She spent years dreaming of him, whether asleep or awake. Their relationship contained no sense of duty, made no demands on her, but floated somewhere just off the ground, like a mist.

She could look at Tristan, over the years, as the only man in her life when Chad was gone, and yearn to kiss him, to reach out and touch his hand, to dream of his hand on her breast, to wonder what he looked like standing naked in the moonlight. The knowledge that Tristan was forbidden to her fed her passion. She had been in her early twenties, her passionate nature denied with no husband around.

She had thought because she'd lived with Chad for so many years that she knew him. Now she saw she knew little about the inner man. She had ignored much of what he had showed, taking his attitude toward the children for granted. Now she saw that he too gave love, though it was usually in action rather than words.

Why had she not realized years ago what she had with Chad? She suspected her love for Tristan had blinded her. Perhaps she had loved Chad, as well as Tristan, for many years. She might have fallen in love with him as readily as she had Tristan, had not the latter been entwined in her heart, and had their forced leave-taking not still been like a raw wound in her. Her heart had been too full of Tristan for her to open wholeheartedly to Chad. He had come too soon after she'd left her first love.

Besides, Tristan had vowed undying love. Chad had never mentioned love—not once in all their time together, until the month before this western journey had begun.

Ever since he'd told her he loved her, had always loved her, there had been a new tenderness to their relationship. They would reach out, even during the day, to touch each other, even if it were just brushing their fingers together. She found herself laughing more, smiling at nothing in particular, or maybe life in general. They began to sleep without nightclothes, not necessarily to make love more often, but to feel close to each other during the night, to have nothing between them. Yet Chad always acted as though he were waiting for something, listening for something far off, as though he anticipated something that had not yet arrived.

Now she realized he had been hoping to hear her say she loved him, too.

She sat bolt upright. Suddenly she thought, He knows.

She didn't know how, but she was sure of it. He knew about Tristan. Maybe he always had. He had never, ever given any indication that he harbored suspicions that Wick and Julie were Tristan's. Had his intuition told him so from the beginning? He had never withheld love from them because they were not of his seed, never acted as though she were to blame for what she had done. Never kept it from allowing his friendship with Tristan to flourish and deepen.

And now she was having difficulty dealing with his fathering a child while he'd been in England. He had been telling her he had loved her every minute since she'd arrived in Australia. How could he, then, and have been unfaithful while he was away? This was the question that had been gnawing at her. If he'd never told her he loved her, she thought she could have handled his infidelity. Could easily have understood. Could, in fact, have found them equal; it might even have alleviated her own guilt.

But now—on the same day to learn that both men in her life had turned to other women! That neither had loved her enough.

That's not true, she thought. Chad's affair with Lucy's mother had nothing to do with her. About that he was right. They had been ten thousand miles and five years away from each other.

It was Tristan, all along, who had not loved her as Chad had. It was her allegiance to this love that had blinded her to Chad. Chad had never kept her from doing the things she wanted. If, after the twins' birth, she wanted to ride out as she had in the years he'd been gone, he would not have said no. She had done that to herself—seen that she wasn't needed as she had been and withdrawn. Chad had not done that to her. Just by his presence, she'd lowered her expectations of herself.

She'd been unfaithful, true, but she had told herself it was all right, because she hadn't loved her husband, and besides, he had left her for so long. She had loved Tristan, always loved him, and had fought her passion for him for nearly five years. She had been left alone by her husband, left alone to rediscover the man she had first loved, the man who gave her the support she should have been getting from her husband. Damn Chad, she thought. If only he hadn't left.

She would never have been unfaithful had Chad not gone away. Had he been around.

Those first years of marriage had been exciting, she remembered. She'd admired Chad and been responsive to him. She had yearned for his touches, his soft words, his kisses, when she'd been pregnant with Jamie and Alex. How would she have reacted to Tristan had he reentered her life and Chad not left? She knew she would never have permitted her feelings to surface. She certainly would never have made love with him. Maybe she would not even have allowed herself to be in love with him had Chad not left. Damn Chad!

Why was she out here in the middle of the night, on the other side of the mountains, in the great, vast emptiness of the never-never, wondering what to do about her marriage and what to say to Chad when next she saw him? Because, she told herself, everything externally will be the same, but things between us will be different, and it's up to me what direction the rest of our lives will take.

Up to her? She had taken for granted that the emotions and actions of her life were circumscribed by her husband and her lover. She was only in charge of the women, and had been in charge of Cowarra only when there was no man around. But when men were around, life was different. She was not in control of her life as completely as when men were absent. And to think that now her life with Chad would be determined by what she felt and did! That he would react to her actions!

Now, their life would be her decision.

Fifty-eight

"I want to see Father and Wick so bad," Julie said. "Alex, too, of course. Everybody. I've had the time of my life, but I want to see them. Do you know how lucky we are? We have the most wonderful family in the whole wide world."

Sophie smiled. She was ready to stop traveling, too. Ready for the comfort of a real bed, yearning to sit on a cozy chair and put her feet up. She tried to remember what sweet tender carrots and baby onions and small new round potatoes would taste like. And raspberry pie. It would be just the season for raspberries. Freshly churned butter and high loaves of bread warm from the oven. But she wouldn't have traded this trip for anything.

The two of them had chosen to ride ahead of the others. The path was still steep and they wanted to reach the top before noon. They'd promised to wait there if the others hadn't caught up. Get a glimpse of where home was, see the ocean stretching into infinity, like the sea of grass on this side. But here it was now brown, and when they reached the top, they would see the Pacific, blue-green and faintly visible forty-five miles to the east. They would be able to pinpoint Sydney, but Morgantown would be too small to see from this height and distance. Nevertheless, they could look in that direction and know where home was.

"I wish Wick had come," Julie said. "Now he'll never quite know this part of me."

"You can tell him about it."

"But that'll be hearing, not feeling. And Alex, too. Do you think she'll marry Robbie soon?"

"I wouldn't be surprised. She's loved him all her life. As he has her. They're farmers at heart, both of them. The land and all that's on it. That and a family, and they'll be happy."

At least Cowarra will go on, thought Sophie. Even if Julie

marries some city man and Wick decides . . . Alex and Robbie will take over the farm.

Thank heavens Chad and Hallie encouraged all their children to think and act for themselves, she mused. "Do whatever it is you want," they'd emphasized time and time again, "but do it well and enthusiastically. Do it to the best of your ability. And don't let what other people think influence you. Do what feels right to you. Care about something enough to dare! Then you'll always know you've lived."

Yes, Julie was right. How lucky they were. She didn't know how much better life could ever get.

"Look," cried Julie, pointing upward. "There's a work gang of convicts. What do you think they're doing?"

"Repairing the road," Sophie replied. "I'd guess it takes constant upkeep if carriages go back and forth."

Catcalls emanated from the leering, unshaven, surly-looking men in their ill-fitting, tattered clothes. One leaned on a pickax and stared at them. No one seemed to be in charge, and Sophie felt a slight nervousness course through her. When none made any overtures toward them, she was ashamed of herself for the automatic reaction. After all, she told herself, some of the nicest people I know have been prisoners. Why should I be so frightened of a bunch of tattered-looking men?

"Isn't it dreadful, to think of them chained together nights?" said Julie. "Having to pound rock all day. Never having a choice or able to do anything that's fun. How awful it must be to be denied freedom."

Oh, my dear, you *are* indeed lucky, thought Sophie.

About fifteen minutes farther up the hill, with the horses breathing heavily, Julie pointed. "Look, there are two of them up here. They're smiling at us." She waved at them.

"Poor souls," said Sophie.

For the first time since she'd undertaken the trip, Hallie brought up the rear of the procession. She wondered whether she had chosen the position because she didn't want to reach home and face reality, face Chad and Lucy, face the years she had wasted loving Tristan.

After hours of agonized soul searching, she'd come to

591

realize that she'd been wrong about several basic assumptions, and this discovery had shaken her to the core.

Tristan . . . not the undying love she had believed him to be, who'd as much as told her that he would not have married her even if he'd had the chance, that she was "too much" for him.

And Chad . . . her husband, the man who had supported her every inch of the way, even though he admitted he did not always understand her.

Even after all this time Chad found her exciting. Would he have been happy with her if she had not had her restless nature? If she had been content to respond to him? No, it was exactly that—her yearning for involvement, her need to lead and to decide, to try new things, to face and even invent challenges—that fascinated him.

Oh, Chad, she thought. Why didn't I see long ago that we were meant for each other? With others, we might not get what we need, and life would be incredibly boring.

Now, she felt she must open herself to him. Admit that he was not Julie's and Wick's real father. Tell him of her unfaithfulness and ask his forgiveness. She would accept Lucy as he had accepted the twins. Start anew with him. Tell him that she now recognized how much he meant to her. That . . .

She was conscious of passing a work force of convicts, who looked up from their labors, most of them with eyes that had lost life, gaunt faces that were vaguely frightening. They leaned on their shovels or held their pickaxes over their shoulders as the little group passed. She heard Lieutenant Godwin call out, "Did two women—one old and one young—pass this way?"

" 'Bout an hour ago," one of the men called back. There was no other way to pass. It was the only road up the mountain.

It was getting hot, and the sun was not yet overhead. Hallie suspected it must be after eleven. They had not gotten an early start that morning. Her horse still had spirit, would have gone dancing up the mountain had she been at the head of the group.

She turned to look behind her. The view was spectacular. Yes, it might be fun to try it out here, but she really didn't love the desert country; she much preferred the land where

592

it only turned golden in late winter; Where there was never snow, and dust did not constantly cover your face and become ingrained in your hair. It was simply the idea of starting anew, beginning a new project, a new life, that she found exhilarating. Turning back to face the mountain, she realized how ridiculous the thought was. After all, she was thirty-eight. Far too late to begin anything anew.

"I've done everything anyhow," she said aloud to no one.

As the sun rose high overhead, indicating the noon hour, the crest of the mountains came into view. Another hundred feet and they'd be on top, Hallie mused. Another hundred feet and the trip would be nearly over. Suddenly she wanted to be the first to reach the peak. She kicked Coolinda, her bay mare, urging her to push past the straggling group ahead of her, up past Lieutenant Godwin. "I want to look down at the land that is home," she called out as she passed by.

In a clearing at the rim of the mountain she saw two men, one much taller than the other. The tall one shaded his eyes with his hands, reminding her of the Chad she had seen when she'd first landed on the sandy shore at Sydney. The shorter one began to jump up and down, waving wildly, starting to run toward her. Hallie's heart beat so wildly that she thought it might burst out of her chest. Running toward her was Wick.

She jumped off her horse and, with arms outstretched, awaited her son. But all the while she looked beyond him at the tall figure, who had not moved.

Then her arms encircled Wick, whose clothes were dusty and whose eyes were bright and shining. "Mother!" he cried, and she realized as his arms went around her that he was the same height she was. Then he was gone, running toward the riders, calling, "Julie!"

Yes, where was Julie? she thought distractedly. Then the dissonance that clanged within her evaporated as she looked at Chad. Neither of them moved for a moment, and then each began to walk toward the other.

I don't know how to act, Hallie thought. It was as though he were a stranger, someone she had not lived with for all these years.

He would not know what she had been thinking, not know that she was ready to give her heart to him. That the tears springing to her eyes were those of exquisite joy. That her heart was singing at the sight of him.

She opened her arms and began to run. And as soon as she did, his pace quickened. His arms surrounded her and he whispered, "Hallie . . . Hallie."

"What are you doing here?" she asked. He smelled good, of wood fire and leather and horses.

He grinned. "I figured you had to be about ready to come home. You'd said mid-December. And we knew you had to come up here, there's no other way. So Wick and I rode over and have been here for two nights, waiting. We've a tent over there in the clearing. We'd about decided to ride down the mountain and wait for you there. God, it is so good to see you!"

He let go of her as the small group of women and soldiers came into view. Wick was running back, crying, "Where's Julie? I don't see Julie!"

"Isn't she here?" Hallie asked Chad. "She and Mum were about an hour ahead of us. They should have been here by now. A band of convicts along the way said they'd seen them go by."

"We haven't seen anybody," Chad said. "Not today, anyhow. Not coming from the west."

They looked at each other in sudden bewilderment and fear. "The road's as clear as can be," Hallie said. "They can't have wandered off it by mistake. If anything were wrong, they would have waited for us. Oh, Chad!"

Lieutenant Godwin rode up to them and lifted his hat. "Good to see you, sir. Checking to make sure we're all safe?" He laughed.

"We're not," said Chad. "My daughter and mother-in-law . . . they're not here."

The lieutenant's smile faded. "What's that? Not here? Where could they be? Not an hour ago those convicts said they'd seen them go by an hour earlier; they—Oh, good Lord, two women and those convicts!"

Gooseflesh rippled down Hallie's arms. The image of that man in the billabong blazed behind her eyes. She could still see, even after seventeen years, that O of a toothless smile, the sound of his laughter, the look in his eyes, as the bullet ripped his face apart.

But neither Mum nor Julie had a gun with her.

"I'll ride back down to those convicts," offered the lieutenant. "I'll leave two of the men here with the other ladies, and I'll take three—"

"No," Hallie interrupted. "Take them all. There are guns in the wagon. I'll arm the women. With nearly twenty of us, we should be quite safe."

"Wick and I will come. We'll search the woods as we go."

Hallie heard the urgency in Chad's voice. She couldn't wait here with the women while these men searched for her daughter and her mother. Turning to one of the women, she said, "Get the guns from the wagon. Form a circle and stay right here." Her own pistol was in her saddlebag. To Chad she said, "I *have* to come."

"Of course," he said, heading for his horse. "Come, son," he called to Wick, who wasted no time running after him.

As Hallie remounted Coolinda, she saw Julie's frightened eyes, saw toothless men leering at her daughter, saw Mum kicking out at the men and one of them knocking her down, saw a man rip the bodice off Julie's gown. Though she made no sound, inwardly she felt herself sobbing.

She should never have let them go off alone! But three months and no real danger . . . All those weeks out in the back of beyond, miles between homesteads, and no danger from other human beings. Now, back in civilization, where there were dangerous convicts, where greed and desire . . .

She trotted after Chad and Wick, who were pacing their horses as fast as possible down the mountain road. Every fifty feet or so Wick called, "Julie!" and Hallie would follow that with, "Mum!"

The soldiers took up the cries, and the woods echoed with their calls. Without the walking women and the ox-drawn wagons, they made far better time. In barely half an hour they found the convicts, still crushing rocks.

Both Chad and Lieutenant Godwin questioned them. They denied any knowledge of the women, swearing that they'd seen them heading up the mountain about mid-morning. Then one of the men said, "Charlie and Tom're missing, gov'ner. Haven't seen them since early morning. They was uphill a bit, earlier."

"Where?" Chad asked.

"Just about ten minutes farther up. Maybe not that. But that was hours ago. Ain't seen 'em in a while."

"Let's try to find them," said the lieutenant. "Come on men. Circle out into the woods, going uphill."

"Want us to help you, gov'ner?" one of the convicts asked.

"Who's in charge here?" Chad demanded.

The men looked at each other and shrugged. "Cap'n Hunter, sir. He'll be back later today, he said."

No wonder they were working so half-heartedly, Hallie thought. No one in charge of a cadre of convicts.

"I'll give fifty pounds to anyone who finds them," offered Chad.

Instantly the men dropped their shovels and axes and headed out into the woods, calling, "We'll go on this side of the road, you take that."

Chad, Hallie, and Wick fanned out together. Each had a pistol in readiness.

There was still no sign of them by dark, eight hours later.

None of them had eaten since morning, they had ridden all day, their emotions were spent. By the time they made their way back up the mountain, the women had dinner waiting and were themselves in states of near hysteria at the thought of anything happening to Julie and Sophie.

"I can't sleep," said Hallie. Her stomach was knotted, but she forced down some food.

"Try not to think about what might have happened," Chad said, putting an arm around her.

"Can you?"

"Of course not." No one could. They all knew what had happened. The remaining question was, Were the women still alive or had they been left for dead? In the morning would they find their bodies? Would they ever find them?

At last Hallie did fall asleep, lulled by the warmth and strength of Chad's body close to hers. It took him much longer, but when he did sleep, it was so soundly that he did not hear Wick crawl out of his bedroll while it was still dark, though the boy could tell from the bird sounds that dawn would not be long in coming. He crept through the sleeping bodies to the meadow where the horses were hobbled. Several neighed at his coming, but their sounds woke

596

no one. Wick felt the smooth metal of his pistol, which reassured him.

"I'll kill those bastards," he muttered to his horse as he led it quietly from amongst the others.

The woods were alive with soft sounds—little animals running over leaves, chirping at each other, birds awakening in chattering groups, leaves dripping dew. Wick found the road in the dark and continued walking until he was sure he was far enough from the camp so that he could not be heard. Then he climbed onto the horse's back and, in a trot, headed downhill. His eyes had become accustomed to the dark, and he could see the sharp precipice to the side. Soon it gave way, however, and there were trees on either side of the steep incline. He began to shout, louder as he got farther from camp: "Julie!" He knew they weren't within the sound of his voice. They wouldn't be that close to the road. They had to be back beyond where they'd searched yesterday.

What would I do, he thought, if I were those men? He pictured himself, in ragged clothes, no hope of freedom, slamming a pickax into rock, jarring his entire body. He felt the pain shoot through his head. Every time his ax hit the rock, the impact sent him reeling.

What would those two women mean to me? he wondered, trying to get inside the heads of those men. Their hungry heads. Bodies with no blankets during the cold nights on the mountains. Beings that held no hope. Obeying orders, always obeying orders. Never making a decision about anything. Never hoping. Bored as much as anything else. What would he want to do?

Escape.

It wasn't women that interested them. He didn't know why women would be *that* important. That would be the last thing he'd want.

It was the thought of escape.

Get away. Get to someplace where no one told them what to do. The convicts might be cold and hungry, but there'd be no one to imprison their minds and bodies. They could decide what to do for themselves.

It was the horses they wanted. It wasn't Julie and Mum. But had they killed the women to get the horses?

No. He was almost sure of that. Murder was a hanging

offense. Yet maybe they felt death was preferable to the life they were living. Unless they knew someday—maybe years away—they'd be freed. Did that hope keep them from killing? He refused to think Julie and Mum had been raped— he knew what the word meant—but imagined them tied up someplace, left perhaps to starve, to freeze, to die of thirst . . . but not actively murdered.

Julie was there, alive. He felt it. She was out there somewhere, unable to move, unable to get away, but she was there, on the mountain someplace.

He heard her. No one else might hear her, but he did. The woods were silent, but in the back of his head he heard her voice, calling out.

Fifty-nine

"C'mon, Hallie. Wake up," Chad whispered.

She sat bolt upright before her eyes were even open. 'What is it? Is Julie—"

"Shh, no . . ." He put a hand on her arm. "Wick's gone."

"Oh, my God!"

"*Shh,*" he whispered again.

The sky was bleached with morning. In the west glimmered a single bright star. A wedge of pale moon shone high above them.

"He's all right. I'm sure of that."

"How can you be?" She could not keep her voice down.

Chad took her hand and drew her up, putting a finger across his lips to indicate silence. There was no sense in waking all the sleeping women.

Chad unhobbled their horses and led them to the road. Hallie followed quietly, still groggy with sleep. When they'd gone down the road a few hundred yards, he handed her Coolinda's reins and jumped on his own horse. Hallie mounted, and she and Chad began to talk.

"He must've awakened during the night. It must have been sometime after three, for I don't think I got to sleep till then."

"Where could he be?" Hallie's voice reflected her fear. Two of her children and her mother missing.

"He's looking for Julie. You know how they are. It was like part of him was gone the three months you've been away. But he's known you were all safe because he didn't have 'feelings' that there was any danger. Each night I'd ask him if you were all right, and he'd smile. I believed it, too. Every night I rested easy—well, relatively—because Wick's 'feelings' said you were. Now, it's like he's out searching for part of himself."

Hallie nodded. "Remember that time Julie cut herself

on a nail and Wick came home from another direction with a sore finger?"

"Exactly," said Chad.

There were other times, too, Hallie remembered, when the twins had been like that. Maybe if anyone could find Julie, it would be her brother. If she were someplace where they could find her.

"How will we know where to look?" she asked Chad.

He shook his head, but his eyes studied the sides of the road. Bird songs filled the early morning air, a brown snake slithered across the road in front of them, making Coolinda rear. A wallaby leapt from one side of the road to another, back into the forest. An eagle soared out of a dead treetop, its graceful wings hardly fluttering, its hooked beak visible as it circled higher and higher. An animal screeched.

Then a gunshot rocked the air.

"Wick," was all Chad said. It had come from down the mountain and to the left. "Again," Chad urged. "Come on, Wick. Shoot again. Let me hear the direction again."

As though answering his father's plea, another shot ricocheted through the woods. Chad spurred his horse down the road, hoping the steepness would not throw him over its head. Hallie was right behind him.

Then they left the road, fighting their way through the thick undergrowth, until Chad said, "We'd better dismount. We can't ride here. The horses can barely make it through all this."

Holding the horses' reins, they skidded downhill, their hands in front of their faces to ward off the swinging branches. "Son!" Chad called.

Son, thought Hallie. He *is* Wick's father, isn't he? More than Tristan's ever been. But then Tristan had been more Jamie's father. What made a father—or a mother? Was it blood, semen, biology? Or was it an indefinable, intangible gossamer thread? Was it an unreeling of a part of yourself, ever unfolding so that the child caught on, and you became an anchor, something to which the child could attach itself in the vast, measureless space of the world?

And from a distance there was a voice, calling.

Chad clasped his pistol and aimed into the trees above them. The discharge was deafening, and in less than a min-

e there was an answering echo. Wick was sounding them
e way.

When they came upon them at last, both Wick and So-
ie were curled around a crying Julie.

Chad was off his horse in an instant, running to them
d calling, "Good job, son!"

Hallie sat for a moment, tears streaking her cheeks, say-
g over and over, "Thank God. Oh, thank God. They're
ive!" Then she too ran to them.

"Julie, my baby . . ." Chad cradled her in his arms, but
e winced and cried out in pain.

"I think her arm is broken," Sophie said. "When they
arted tying me to a tree, Julie kicked at them and one
rned around and whacked her. She fell down and twisted
r arm under her. He tied it behind her when he tied
r to the tree."

"I was right," said Wick, proud of himself. "They didn't
ant Mum and Julie. They wanted the horses."

Julie's arm hung limply at her side, reminding Hallie of
ta's arm. The pain must have been awful. "We didn't
ink anyone would find us way back here," Julie said, cry-
g. "They didn't hurt us, but they left us tied here."

"I thought we might die of thirst before we were found,"
id Sophie, who was shaking now that the ordeal was over.
allie put her arms around her mother, gathering her
ose. She stroked her hair while Chad picked Julie up in
is arms and headed toward his horse.

"We've got to get you to a doctor and get that arm set,"
e said.

Wick was dancing on one foot and then the other, unable
keep still. Hallie leaned over to kiss him. "I don't know
hat made you know where to look, but heaven knows they
ight not have lived to tell the tale if it weren't for you."

Wick grinned.

Hallie boosted Sophie onto Coolinda and climbed up
ato the saddle behind her.

"You lead the way, Wick," said Chad, "and clear the trees
or us." He leaned down and touched his son's shoulder.
Vick looked up at his father and their eyes met. The boy
welled with pride.

"Thank God for Wick," murmured Sophie.

What would have happened, thought Hallie, had n?
Wick and Chad been waiting for them at the mountainto?

When they returned to the group, all of whom had hear?
the gunshots, Lieutenant Godwin and his soldiers were ju?
mounting up, ready to begin a search.

"We're going ahead of you, Lieutenant," Chad a?
nounced. "I want to get this girl to a doctor."

"It'll take over two days of hard riding, sir," said Lie?
tenant Godwin. "I can set it, maybe not like it should ?
permanently, but so's it won't hurt as bad while you g?
into Sydney. And I have enough whiskey left . . . just so?
she won't feel the pain while I set it," he added hastily ?
Sophie's disapproving look. "The doctor will probably ha?
to break it again, but I can help ease the pain for now."

Funny, thought Hallie. He's listened to me, deferred ?
me, been ordered by me for three months. Now that Chad?
here, I'm invisible.

Julie's frightened eyes met Chad's. He held her clos?
"It's not going to hurt any worse than what you've bee?
through already. Two days of bumpy riding and you'd prob?
ably be unconscious from the pain. I'll hold you, honey. ?
won't let you go."

"Where's Wick?" she asked.

"Here, right here." The boy ran over to her. "I'll hol?
you, too," he said staunchly. He wondered why everyon?
laughed.

Tristan took one look at the arm in a sling. "Man did?
good job, but I *will* have to break it again and set it righ?
We can do it in my office. No need to go to the hospital.

Julie began to cry, and Tristan put his arms around her?
his eyes meeting Hallie's across the room. She stared bac?
at him without expression. How many of his children ha?
he treated? she wondered. How many of his children dotte?
the landscape of New South Wales?

Maybe a friendship would evolve later, but for now sh?
did not feel much of anything for him. The anger that ha?
gnawed at her these last three months had dissipated. No?
there was not even sadness. No reason to feel sad for Tris?
tan. His life was full and happy. No reason to feel sad fo?
herself, except for the years she had wasted not realizin?

602

hat she had with Chad. Now that she could open her
eart to him completely, she would make up to him for the
ast. Give him what he needed from her. Discover the com-
leteness they could have together.

She looked at them both now, hovering over *their* daugh-
r.

"I want to help," Wick said. His right hand was under
is left elbow, holding it as though his left arm, too, were
n pain. Hallie couldn't help smiling.

After he'd finished resetting Julie's arm, Tristan eyed
had and said, "If they'd never gone—"

"If you never dare," Chad interrupted, "if you never
ance the possibility for pain, or death even, you never
ar. I wouldn't wish that on anyone. I imagine Julie
ouldn't have given up this trip knowing of the outcome.
on't talk that way, Tris. It happened. After all, the roof
f your bedroom could cave in on you and you could die
n your own bed."

Tristan's shoulders sagged. "I wish I had your courage,
y friend," he said to Chad. "I've always admired you more
an anyone I've known. You"—his eyes met Hallie's across
e room—"and Hallie."

Chad walked over and put an arm around her. "We are
omething, aren't we? And so's our family. Wick here's a
ero, by damn. And these three women are nothing short
f heroines. They did what people said couldn't—
houldn't—be done. I couldn't be prouder of my family."

Julie called weakly from across the room. "Father . . . ?"

Both men started toward her. Then Tristan stopped, his
yes meeting Chad's, and let him go to their daughter.

"I'm here, honey," Chad said, his hand enfolding hers.
I'll always be here for you."

"Me, too," said Wick.

Sixty

The next day they headed to Cowarra.

Sophie said she would wait at the halfway house unt[il] the women returned but would join them at Cowarra fo[r] Christmas. Hallie decided to come back into town later t[o] do her Christmas shopping. She had to get home to Ale[x] and Garth and Chloe. She also wanted to see Beth an[d] Danny and Robbie. She even found herself thinking o[f] Ben.

Despite the fact that her arm was in a sling, Julie insiste[d] on riding a horse rather than traveling in a carriage. S[o] the four of them cantered across the fields and valleys an[d] were home in time for dinner.

Hallie's heart lurched a bit as they passed her first home[,] now mellowed with age and surrounded by the flowers an[d] shrubs Tristan had planted so long ago. The veranda stil[l] looked inviting. It would always be her favorite home.

But as they approached the great house, whose lawn[s] were emerald green at this time of year, and she saw th[e] late afternoon western sun reflecting rainbowed prisms i[n] its dozens of mullioned windows, saw its spires rising u[p] from the hill, pride surged through her. Home, sh[e] thought.

This was where the people she loved most in the worl[d] lived. The place she had helped to create. The place sh[e] had named.

Chad, who had ridden ahead of them across the miles[,] now turned in his saddle to look at her. She had watche[d] the way he sat in the saddle and the tenderness he exhibite[d] not only to Julie, but to Wick. And she thought, I wasn'[t] free to love him before, and not only because of Tristan[.] It's taken us all these years to get to know and understan[d] each other. He's let me find my way, given me the freedom I've needed, and encouraged me to be me. He's listene[d]

604

me more than I've listened to him. He's given me what e's understood I've needed. Now, it's my turn . . .

They'd really had no time alone since their reunion. After two days of hard riding from the mountains, they'd rrived at Tristan's, where Molly had insisted on feeding hem. They had spent the night at the big house on the arbor, but it had been late when they'd arrived, and they'd ken turns sitting up with Julie and had left in a flurry hat morning. She hadn't even stopped to say hello to usan. Mum would let her know they were home.

As they rode up the hill, on the driveway bordered by rees that had grown taller than Chad, he slowed his horse nd waited for her to catch up to him. "In all the excitement, I forgot to tell you. Beth and Danny are expecting."

"A baby?"

Chad laughed. "What else? And they're very happy. Even Roger is pleased."

Beth was thirty-four years old. Old enough to be a grandmother. And just as she was thinking "grandmother," Chad continued, "And Robbie's gotten around to asking or Alex's hand. They'd like to marry at Easter."

"So soon?" she said. "Alex is not yet seventeen."

"She and Robbie have waited all their lives for her to be old enough," he answered, and she knew it was true.

Wick gave a whoop and raced past them, shouting, "We're home. Hey, where is everybody? Yoo-hoo! We're home!"

Alex, with Lucy at her side, came running out on the porch, and Garth dashed down the stairs, falling and rolling over and over in somersaults, shouting, "Mother, Mother, Mother!"

Chloe trailed Beth, whose arms were outstretched before he even got outside. "Oh, Hallie . . ." She began to cry. "I missed you so. My heavens, Julie, what in the world happened to you?"

"I rescued them," cried Wick. "I saved her life—hers and Mum's."

The next few hours saw a whirlwind of activity. Julie fell asleep before Beth had dinner ready, but all the other weary ravelers had to suffer through an endless round of questions and a cacophony of noise: "There's a new foal!" "Are there lots of abos out there?" Then silence descended a everyone listened, wide-eyed, to Wick tell his story.

Hallie managed a few minutes alone with Alex and wit Beth, and she told Lucy how much she was looking forwar to their getting acquainted. At last she announced that sh was going to follow Julie's example and go to bed. "I'v never been so tired in my life. But first a bath. I haven' bathed in ages."

One of the maids ran up and down the stairs with ho bathwater and Hallie sank into the cast-iron tub, gratefu for the luxury after months of bathing in cold runnin streams. It was just dusk when she went into the bedroom

Chad sat in a large rocker, his feet on the windowsil looking out the open window as the curtains danced in th lazy evening air. "Are you too tired for me, Hallie?" Hi voice was low.

She was. She was too tired for anything, but the bath ha made her lazy and comfortable. It was time for her to think of her husband's needs. Besides, ever since they'd knowr Julie was safe, she'd wanted him. Lying under the star near him, she had thought, I want his arms around me. want to tell him he's more beautiful than I remembered. want to tell him I love him. But she had not been able to . . . then. Now it was time.

She dropped her robe, letting it slide to the floor at he feet. He didn't move but stared at her. "Oh, God, Hallie you can't know how much I've missed you," he breathed.

Hallie walked over to him slowly and, bending down began to unbutton his shirt. "I don't think I shall ever be too tired for you," she whispered, drawing him from his chair to the bed. "You've never looked more beautiful to me."

"Men aren't beautiful," he murmured into her ear.

"This one is," she said as his lips met hers.

She still did not tell him she loved him. Later, as she began to fall asleep, he said, "Tomorrow you can read Jamie's letter."

Jamie had written that he was already contemplating a practice somewhere other than in Sydney. "We hear marvelous stories of the new development at Melbourne," he id in his letter. "If it holds as much promise as everyone ere seems to think, perhaps being a doctor in a new city— nd everyone thinks it is sure to become that—would hold ore excitement and chance for success. And while it is ot New South Wales, it *is* Australia. We could get together r Christmases, certainly. Well, I'm not sure, but it does und alluring. I've written to Uncle Tristan about it, too. d like to know what he thinks."

"Melbourne? Where in the world is it?" Hallie asked, owning.

"A couple of days by ship, I think," said Chad. "To the uth. One hears great tales of it. Like Sydney was in 1790, suspect. I've heard it's beautiful sheep country around ere. It has all the earmarkings of success."

"Jamie, a doctor, in wild country?" She looked up at im. "Does sound sort of fun, doesn't it? Remember how e started? I wouldn't deny that to anyone."

"That's good, because Robbie and Alex are talking of it, o."

"Alex? I thought she and Robbie would be content to ay at Cowarra forever."

"They'll be content to farm forever, I think. But they'd ke to start out new. Build up for themselves. Alex doesn't ave your drive, but she would work side by side with Rob- ie."

"My babies, leaving home . . ." She wasn't quite pre- ared for that. She'd always envisioned her children at owarra forever. "Certainly there's enough land for every- ne here."

"That's not the point," said Chad, grinning. "Besides, I ather like the idea of Morgans all over the continent. Help- ng new endeavors to get off the ground."

"What do you want, a whole series of Morgantowns?" Hallie laughed. This morning she wanted anything he did. ut she did not relish Alex moving away, seeing her chil- ren but once a year in a land that was unknown to her.

When she'd awakened, lying next to Chad, she'd known hat she wanted to get him for Christmas. And what she vanted to give Tristan, too. The next day she returned to ydney, to shop for the family and to pick up Sophie. She nd her mother dined with Susan and Harry, who were ager to hear details of the trip. Susan was tired from running the halfway house by herself and said she needed vacation. Sophie announced that she was ready to take u the reins again.

Before returning to Cowarra, Hallie went to see Tristar waiting for him at the hospital rather than at home. Whe he saw her she could tell he didn't know whether to smil or not. Their last private meeting had been fraught wit trauma.

"I'm only staying a minute," she said. "I've somethin to return to you. I thought perhaps you could give ther to Molly for Christmas." She held out the handkerchie that had lain in the bottom of her bureau all these years

Tristan didn't even unknot it. "They're yours, Hallie They were my mother's. I gave them to you."

"I don't want them." Their fingers touched as sh handed him the earrings. It did nothing to her.

"Hallie, I love you. I have always loved you. I shall alway love you."

She shook her head. "I'm sorry," she said. "I don't lov you any longer. Not that way. Maybe I don't love you at all in any way. I'm sure these would mean a great deal to you wife." Was he still pleasing lonely widows, or was he faith ful to his marriage? It didn't matter anymore.

She saw the pain in Tristan's eyes. "Are we not even t be friends?"

"I don't know. Time will answer that." She turned to go and did not look back when he called her name. In tha moment she knew she would never tell Chad he was no father to the twins. He was.

It was the afternoon of Christmas Eve when she and Sophie arrived back at Cowarra. Chad and the children had decorated "the biggest tree in the world," as Chloe called it, holding tight to Lucy's hand. The child had taken fancy to her "cousin" and followed her everyplace.

Hallie looked at Lucy, such a pretty girl, and thought Well, if I'm going to lose one daughter, I've gained another

"Let's go swimming," cried Wick. "We've just time be fore dinner, and it's too hot to do a lick more on this tree!' All the children whooped and hollered and ran en masse down the hill to the river.

Belinda, Brian, and Robbie, as well as Danny, Beth, and Roger, all came to Christmas Eve dinner with the Morgan family, and would come tomorrow, too, for roast goose and plum pudding. Presents were piled so high that half the tree could not be seen. On it burned candles in little holders, and Chad kept glancing at it every few minutes to make sure it was not afire. It would take all morning for the presents to be opened, one at a time. Over the years Christmas had become a long-drawn-out process that kept them all on pins and needles for hours, with stops for little fancy sandwiches and egg nog, and dinner at three in the afternoon.

Everyone was allowed to open one present on Christmas Eve, and they each spent a long time trying to decide which one it was to be. Chloe left a plate of cookies for Father Christmas, then she and Julie and Lucy, who had decided they all wanted to share a room that night, walked up the stairs together.

Hallie said, "I'm going up, too." It had been a long day for her. In fact, all the days had been long. She thought after Christmas she might just not do anything for a while, maybe weeks.

When Chad came up, she said, "I have a present I want you to open tonight."

His eyes smiled at her. "You do?" It was he who always gave the fun presents. "Your being home is enough."

"I'm never going to leave again." She held her arms up, and he walked over to her.

"Then you'll ruin my present," he teased.

"What is it?"

"Oh, no, yours first." He laughed, sitting down on the bed next to her and leaning over to kiss her.

She drew the little box out from under her pillow and handed it to him. Suddenly she felt shy, as shy as the first night he had made love to her in the billabong.

He tore off the paper with obvious delight. "It's such a small box," he said, "it must be a big present."

"Important, anyhow," she said, waiting to see his reaction.

Inside the box was a wide gold ring. "It's a wedding ring," she explained. "I know men don't wear them, but I thought you would. Look inside, at the engraving."

He turned it to the light. "Read it out loud," she said.

He looked at it, then at her, and she saw his eyes glisten. " 'I love you', it says."

Hallie felt her own eyes well with tears. She thought there weren't enough words to tell him how overflowing she was with her love for him.

Handing the ring to her, he said, "You slip it on me." She did. It fit perfectly.

"Since it's a wedding ring," he said, his voice breaking, "I promise again to love you till death do us part."

His kiss was more tender than any she could remember.

"And now yours," he said, smiling. "You say that you're never going to leave home again. Hallie, my dear, I'll give you five weeks, until February first, to come up with an idea that may galvanize your energies. So, to save you time and energy"—his smile was broad—"I've done it for you. If you want, that is. I don't want to be the decisive factor in this. I got the idea, but it's only with your approval . . . I thought we could take a trip."

"A trip? I've just come back from one." But before he had time to say it, she knew. "Oh, Chad, you mean Melbourne, don't you?"

"Well, I thought we could look it over. Maybe find land for Robbie and Alex. Build them a little house." Hallie smiled; she knew what his *little* houses were like. "Not leave Cowarra forever, mind you. Just for a couple of months. See what it looks like—a new city, new land to be developed, new challenges. Right after Alex and Robbie's wedding; a honeymoon for them. See if they like it there. But take all the children. Be able to write to Jamie about it."

Her mind began to whirl. See if it was good grape country. See how the women getting off ships were being treated. Sharing a new life with Chad.

"Oh, darling!" She opened her arms.

"You've never called me that before."

"There are many things I haven't called you before. Funny, I thought we had done everything people could do. But there are still so many things for us to try, aren't there?"

He looked at her and laughed.

AFTERWORD OR A NOTE TO AUSTRALIANS

When I decided to write about early Australia and began research, both in order to learn more about this island continent and to look for a story path, I came upon information about people I had never heard of, but of whom I subsequently would learn much.

I read that at the turn of the nineteenth century Captain John MacArthur founded the first large sheep ranch in Australia at Camden, and he is called "the father of the Australian sheep industry." I then learned he was sent to England to stand trial—for participating in the Rum Rebellion—and took his young son with him so that he could gain an English education. Mrs. MacArthur was left with the other children at home in Australia.

He returned acquitted four years later in 1805 with a handful of sheep from the King's own flock and some Afrikaans sheep he had acquired when the ship stopped in Cape Town, he also had a land grant for another two thousand acres. Four years later he returned to England and stayed for eight years, meaning that from 1801 to 1817 he spent only four years in Australia. During this period of time his wife Elizabeth increased their Australian landholdings to sixty thousand acres and the number of their sheep by many thousands. And, I thought, *he* is called the father of the Australian sheep industry! This seemed an inaccurate and patriarchal view to me, so I began to construct a story of a woman who achieved much of the same.

As my story formed, the characters changed and grew so that they became not at all like my original thoughts. Though, I must admit—with no apologies—that there are some similarities here and there with what the MacArthurs did—*only* in emigrating to Australia, starting the first large sheep farm, living in the Camden area, and in the husband's returning to England for a lengthy time—my characters are not based on the MacArthurs' lives or personalities (or anyone else's). I discovered that John MacArthur, while one of the founding fathers of Australia, was a most strange, unlikeable man. His wife Elizabeth was a remarkable woman and deserves more credit in the history books. But since he was more bombastic and historically colorful and was, after all, a man, he is the one mentioned more often. In the last two years of his life he lost his mind and refused to speak to his beloved wife or of his beloved sheep. He died insane in 1834. Elizabeth lived on to be a grande dame of Australian society until 1850, when she was in her eighties. Australia never daunted her as it did many of the gentlewomen who came with or for husbands. And, in this, my heroine is similar. But their few similarities in no way make them alike. My characters all come quite completely from my imagination.

Another colorful character, Carolyn Chisholm, who changed the course of the fate of women in Australia, lived there for six years in the 1840s. I have based Hallie's involvement with the women convicts on the exploits of Mrs. Chisholm. Mrs. Chisholm was so horrified at the treatment of women arriving in Sydney that she talked her husband into building a large home for them, found them jobs and husbands, protected them, and—leading a large band of women on her big white horse, Captain—crossed the mountains to find them husbands and well-paying jobs. Many women were kept from prostitution. She saw to it that men did not hire women for sexual use, but insisted they marry the women. She refused to permit the women to take low-paying jobs. Pretty soon men from all over Australia were writing to Mrs. Chisholm for wives. In her six years on the island continent she found jobs and/or husbands for eleven thousand women! I fell in love with her accomplishments, and I use these only and not her persona. When she returned to England, Charles Dickens met her and satirized her as a do-gooder in one of his novels, one who cared about causes but whose own house was dirty and whose children ran around in soiled clothes with runny noses and were generally ignored. I chose to capture only her heroic deeds but in no way her personality or private life. Mrs. Chisholm's picture is on the Australian five-dollar bill—the only historical woman of gigantic proportions in that country.

In Chapter 25 the quotes I have ascribed to Governor Macquarie were actually written in letters by him. I think I have quoted him verbatim. The names of Simeon Lord, William Shelley, the explorer Evans, Francis Greenway, and Henry Fulton, mentioned in that chapter, were real people. The flogging scene in that same chapter I owe largely to

Roderick Cameron from his book, *Australia, History & Horizons*.

Mary Reiby, mentioned in Chapter 30, was the actual person I describe. So, in later chapters, were Mr. Bigge, Reverend Scott, Reverend Samuel Marsden, and Governor Brisbane. I have been as faithful to the rendering of them as my research has permitted me.

In dealing with anthrax, I have taken one liberty. It was not thus named until 1850, when the bacterium was first seen. However, it has been a disease since time immemorial and alternately called splenic fever, black hair, charbon, malignant pustule, and murrain. So that present-day readers may understand what I am referring to, I have chosen to use the name anthrax thirty-five years earlier than it actually came into existence. All other details of the disease are accurate.

Australia's recorded history is all so recent that it is readily available and visible. In Sydney and Parramatta I visited the actual buildings of which I write. In Parramatta I visited homes from that era that still stand, and I explored the Camden countryside to determine its topography, flora, and fauna.

I knew that the justly famous Australian wine industry began in 1832 in the Hunter River Valley, but I also learned that vineyards were started in the vicinity of Sydney as early as 1790. When I visited the Camden-Parramatta area I was delighted to see vineyards there. There is no Morgantown, however. I must admit to describing terrain in the Camden area. Also, I founded Melbourne four years earlier than it actually was.

None of this will matter to anyone but Australians. I hope they do not think I have perverted their history or geography. I have tried to be as faithful as I could to both description of the land as it was and the spirit of the times. For the latter, though I read and studied more history books and pictures than I could keep track of, I wish especially to cite C. Manning Clarke's impressive, scholarly, and readable five-part *A History of Australia,* and to tell the Hyde Park Barracks and the New South Wales State Library in Sydney how grateful I am for the lithographs, copies of paintings, and maps of Sydney in 1807, 1810, and 1821.

I spent the summer of 1988 touring over 5,500 miles of

this wonderful land. I went for research, and ended up falling in love with both the friendly, effusive, and generous Aussies and their unbelievably varied and beautiful country. I hope that some of the passion I developed for this land and its peoples comes across in my book.

I shall return!

HISTORICAL NOTE

By 1821 the population of New South Wales, excluding the aborigines, was twice that of 1810: there were 17,629 males, 3,707 women, and 5,668 children. Turnpikes dotted the colony, townships had been incorporated, the Blue Mountains had been crossed, and the land beyond had begun to be explored.

Governor Lachlan Macquarie was probably the single most important force in shaping the Australia that was to come. Significantly, Macquarie pursued prison reform, abolishing the treadmill and the prison on Norfolk Island. He had concluded that the majority of convicts, through many years of forced industry and reformation of deplorable habits, became respectable by degrees until they had become upstanding members of the community. Further, he believed that holding out hope for a life of quality and equality would encourage them to become exemplary citizens. He and his wife, Elizabeth, never hesitated to invite emancipists to Government House and to encourage them in their endeavors. He even appointed Dr. John Redfern, an emancipist, as magistrate, incurring the wrath of the more self-righteous and religious.

In instituting these "radical" reforms, Macquarie sowed the seeds of his own downfall, for the Secretary of State, Lord Bathurst, believed that any change in policy was for the worse, particularly since change implied that previous policies must have been in error, and he was never a man to admit to error. Bathurst believed religion was the cornerstone of society and a moral education a necessity. Like the early American Puritans, he did not take into consideration that giving the populace sufficient education to read the Bible also endangered the status quo, which was then threatened by the curious, the intelligent, the questioners.

Bathurst denied Macquarie's request for trial by jury, stating there weren't enough settlers to undertake jury duty. He wanted nothing that would arouse people's passions. Ironically, when the Blue Mountains were crossed in 1815, Macquarie named the first town to be founded in the west Bathurst.

In 1819 Bathurst sent John Thomas Bigge to investigate the penal system. Bigge reported that leniency was being displayed toward prisoners, who, instead of being confined to jails, were out helping to build most of Australia's early beautiful public buildings and its roads. He took umbrage with Macquarie's appointment of a former convict as magistrate and told the governor to rescind the appointment. Macquarie refused, saying, "My years here have convinced me that many of the most meritorious men in the colony are emancipists. Nine tenths of the population have been convicts. They have built homes, worked the land, built ships, learned how to handle livestock, helped explore the land, they are our manufacturers, our brick builders, our carpenters and merchants. I beg you, do not deny them full citizenship and participation in this land to which they have been sent and have now given so much. It is a chance for human redemption."

Macquarie's attitude toward the aborigines provided Bigge with his final salvo in what had become a battle of political will and public policy—according to the illustrious governor, Australia's "natives" could—and should—be civilized and Christianized!

In his report to the Secretary of State, Bigge recommended that Macquarie be replaced. London agreed.

Here is an excerpt from
Barbara Bickmore's *The Back of Beyond*.
A Zebra hardcover in April, 1994

THE DREAMTIME

A spiny anteater in reds and ochres stared down at them from the huge rock. In yellow ochre and white there was a fish, reminding Cassie of those painted in her long-ago first grade class. There were primitive line drawings of crocodiles; dark handprints against white backgrounds.

"This land has been continuously inhabited for over twenty-three thousand years," Blake said. "This," he pointed to the paintings on the immense rock, "is the world's earliest known art. It's the world of the Dreamtime."

"Dreamtime?" Cassie asked, basking in the warmth of Blake's hand around hers.

"The Dreamtime," said Blake, leading Cassie closer to the painted rocks, "is the aboriginal way of recounting how the land was given to them at the beginning of time, of creation."

"Like Genesis?" asked Cassie.

Blake smiled and squeezed her hand. "Pretty much so, except they don't tell of so much begatting. They tell of how their ancestors rose from the earth in animal and human forms and created earth as it is now.

Cassie reached out her hand and feathered it along the gigantic rock.

"Once upon a time," Blake smiled. "Well, actually before time began, the world was unformed and malleable. Then the Warramurrungundji arose from the sea. She was a woman with a human body, and She created the land and gave birth to human beings. Here," he pointed, "she's represented as a white rock. Along came other creators: Marrawuti, the sea eagle—see, there—who captures a person's spirit when he dies. He also brought water lilies from the sea, dropping them from his claws so they were planted over the floodplain. This crocodile represents Ginga, who became so misshapen because he was blistered in a fire.

617

Ginga made this country, the rock country. The bowerbird here is Djuway, who is caretaker of the sacred initiation rites.

"All living things," Blake said, and Cassie thought his voice took on a reverent tone, "are as One. Tree, eagle, grass, earth, water, people. We are all one. When Creation was finished, the people were told by the ancestral beings that they had made everything necessary, now it was up to the people to keep them safe for all time. They were admonished not to change anything, but to revere and treasure the land and each other."

"So," Cassie said, fascinated with all she was hearing and seeing, "they were made custodians of the land."

Blake leaned down to kiss her cheek. "Exactly. But not only the land. Of each other as well. Of all animals too. The Dreamtime is the glue that's supposed to hold the environment and humans together in harmony. It has succeeded here, for two thousand generations. Because aboriginals are part of the land, part of nature, they can't understand us. Why, they wonder, do we want to change it, destroy it."

Cassie looked up at him. "You have the soul of a poet, you know that?"

Blake grinned. "I don't mind your overestimating me. But it's not true. Look what I do. I graze tens of thousands of cattle on the land. Each day I help to forever change the landscape."

Cassie stared at him. She had never heard anyone talk like this.

"Come on," he pulled her hand, leading her up higher on the rock formations. "Be careful of your step, but I want you to see the view from way up there," he pointed to the top of the escarpment, "where we can see into forever, where you'll never forget the view for as long as you live."

They'd seen no other white people for two days, ever since leaving Darwin. They'd stayed there only long enough to buy food. Tonight they were camping along the Mary River; tomorrow they'd be at that part of the ocean called the Timor Sea.

"We can't swim in the river," Blake said, "it's filled with crocs." But he took her out in a boat, staying out until long after dark, watching the glorious sunset. Red, fiery rays lit up the sky.

"Now," Blake said, "we'll look for crocs. You said you've never seen one."

"I don't have to," she said.

"But you do have to."

They paddled quietly through the turgidly flowing river, heading back south, toward their camp. Blake paddled near the banks of the narrow river, using his flashlight to search for the prehistoric water beasts.

"Okay," he whispered. "Don't paddle. We'll just float along." The moon had not yet risen and the millions of stars gave little light.

Cassie had never felt such contentment yet such excitement. She didn't even know what name to put to her feelings, deciding it was more than love. Blake's touch electrified her. His kisses set her afire. Looking into his eyes gave her a feeling of belonging.

It was something more than love that she was experiencing, unless it was discovering another kind of love simultaneously. A love of the land. Of this wonderful country that had been hers all along, this land she had never known. Every mile of the journey had been discovery. She was so used to flying over it that driving through it awakened new reactions in her.

In Alice Springs they had stayed overnight with an old friend of Blake's, the minister of the Congregational Church, someone from his university days. Further along, in Katherine, he knew someone else with whom they spent the night. Salt of the earth people, ones with whom she immediately felt comfortable. She met no one with whom she felt ill at ease. And Blake's friends welcomed her as though they'd known her forever.

But it was up here, up in the far tropical north that they were at last alone. Blake pointed out landmarks, telling her the history and geography of the land, tales that fascinated her, laughing as he told her humorous stories. As they sped along the highway north he would reach out for her hand, holding it unless he had to shift gears or point out something of interest. They drove mile after mile, hands entwined.

He asked her so many questions about herself that by the end of the third day, when they'd left Darwin heading east to the Mary River, she thought there was nothing else to tell him. She'd never had a man so concentrate on her, urging her to share herself. She'd never known such an open man, one who didn't seem embarrassed by anything, who hugged her in front of his friends with a total lack of self-consciousness.

Once he put on the brakes so sharply she nearly hit the windshield. There wasn't another car in sight, nothing to slow them down. Just an endless straight road whose monotony was broken only by the conversation. He didn't turn the motor off, but reached over and pulled her to him. "I need to kiss you," he said. And, having done so, sped on.

Remembering this as she sat in the fore of the boat, she sighed contentedly, thinking of the wonderful four days they'd had so far.

Suddenly, Blake said, "shh" and slid into the water. "Shh," he repeated, his flashlight aimed at reeds on the river's bank.

He handed her the flashlight. "Keep it exactly on that spot. Don't move it." He glided through the water, barely making a ripple. Now Cassie was aware of two red eyes reflected in the beam of light, not moving, staring, unblinking. Blake reached out to grab the small crocodile, lifting it into the air, holding it by the neck, saying, "Keep the light on its eyes. Light hypnotizes them."

It was small. "Weighs about sixty pounds," he said.

"Could it bite you?"

He nodded. "Could take a big bite out of me. Out of you too." He held it out to her. She didn't let herself shrink away. "Now you can never say you haven't seen one," he said, starting back toward her. Then, grinning, he tossed it back into the river as he leaped into the boat.

How he knew where they were heading she couldn't tell. She couldn't even see the banks of the river, but unerringly he took her down narrow winding channels so that they arrived at their camp.

He'd set up a tent, though they had slept outside last night. "We'll keep the food in the tent," he'd said. "There are no dangerous animals to assault us if we sleep outside. I imagine it's the only continent in the world where it's always safe to sleep outside." He had placed their swags

620

beside each other, a foot apart, and they had fallen asleep holding hands.

"Tomorrow night," he said, "we'll go to a corroboree. We'll move camp tomorrow, go to the sea. You'll like that. I do."

The moon was opaque.

Blake said, "We can't sit together. You'll have to go over with the lubras and I'll join the men."

Cassie nodded and headed toward the black women, in front of their own small fire, not nearly as large as the men's. She and Blake had arrived just after dark, when the tribe was still chanting its prayers . . . to the rain spirit and to the great Mother of fertility. Their voices rose and fell together, rising to a high falsetto, filling the night air.

Through the darkness came the hollow lonesome deep moan of the didgeree-du, a hollowed oboelike instrument. Chiming in were the gil-gil sticks, their high treble sounding like thousands of crickets. Then, softly, voices broke in, rising gradually to an extraordinary crescendo. In unison, torsos undulated rhythmically to the music. The same words were repeated, again and again, the cadence never breaking. Cupped hands beat a tattoo upon glistening thighs, and in the distance tom-toms could be heard as yam-sticks beat the dry earth. Boomerangs—crimson with blood—rattled as they were clicked together. An old man on the edge of the circle beat two tins, breaking into a wild, excited cry, sounding like a dingo wailing at the moon.

The throbbing rhythm rose to a frenzy.

Then, suddenly, unexpectedly, stillness. Not a sound.

Silent echoes pulsated in Cassie's ears. She heard her own breath.

One voice began to sing, a high tenor coursing through the night, and the music began to pound again, quickening, the throbbing of the didgeree-du insistent.

Eyes now accustomed to the dark, Cassie saw dancers emerge from the trees, wending their way to the circle in the center of the group of men. Blake had told her that they timed the dancing to the rising of a particular star.

The faces of the dancers were reflected from the firelight. Painted grotesquely, their frightening visages were topped with silver-white cockatoo feathers, iridescent in the firelight. To these elaborate crowns were added a bizarre medley of ochred sticks and quivers. The white paint on their bodies made them look like skeletons floating in limbo. They stamped upon the ground in unison, making noises like chalk scraping over a blackboard.

Forming a line, the dancers twisted like snakes between the fires lit beyond the circle, their feet pounding, the leaves—fastened at their knees and elbows—rustling like whispers in the night.

Shivers ran up Cassie's back as the throaty, thick, rasping sounds of the savage music wound into her. Lifting their feet in unison, the dancers pounded the earth in such force and momentum that the ground shook under them. The lubras around Cassie hit their thighs, and the men joined together in singing. The dancers wound around the large circle of men, returning to the center of the circle, imitating daily events. An iguana frantic to escape dogs that yelped after it, the ecstatic jubilation of a man finding water in the desert, the slithering of a snake, the willowy sashaying of a brolga in its minuet.

Then a frenzied dance, the feral vaulting of the pursued, the chase, the capture, the culmination with the kill.

The dance continued, repetitively. The staccato sound of the music, the eternal duplication of action and sound pummeled into Cassie's nerves until she felt caught as in a straitjacket, emotionally unable to escape. She wanted to scream, to flee, thinking she could not bear it another moment, when a high-pitched "ai-ee" came from the crowd as the dancers pounded one last time, the stomping of their feet seeming to flatten the very land under them.

Silence. The dancers, moving in a column, snaked out of the circle and sprinted back into the woods, disappearing in the night.

Cassie wasn't aware that she'd been holding her breath until she heard Blake say, "Come on." He reached a hand down to help her up.

Holding her hand tightly, he walked ahead of her in the darkness. "Careful not to trip over tree roots," he said.

Cassie's body was alive, electrified by the music and the dancing, by the lubras slapping their thighs, by their bare breasts glowing in the firelight, by the men's dancing, naed except for their head dresses, beckoning her, luring her soul.

As the sounds faded behind them, their walk through the palm trees slowed, Blake beside her now instead of ahead of her.

"We're nearly at the beach," he said, his hand around her shoulder, holding her close.

The trees ended. Only sand now stretched ahead of them, into infinity. There were no forceful crashing waves, just the pat pat pat of barely lapping water.

Blake stopped, bending down to take off his shoes. Cassie followed suit. The warm sand squished between her toes.

They strolled for over a mile before arriving at their tent under the palms, at the edge of the beach.

"Let's swim," Blake said, peeling off his shirt, turning, gathering her in his arms. She kissed his chest. His hands fiddled with the buttons of her blouse, until he slipped it off her. She put her arms around his chest. She felt her breasts against him, their skin touching for the first time. Oh, God, she thought, closing her eyes. It feels so good.

He let go of her, unzipping his trousers, letting them fall onto the sand, kicking them away. "I want to see you," he said. "I want to see you for the first time this way, by the light of the heavens, see you . . ." His voice thickened.

He walked to her, not touching her, bending over to kiss her breasts. "You're as beautiful as I knew you would be."

He stood looking down at her, then turned from her and ran into the water, diving so that she could not see him. She walked to the edge of the water, so alive that she wanted to shout.

She submerged herself slowly into the ocean. It was as warm as bathwater. Blake's head bobbed to the surface, far out. He swam toward her, long slow strokes, his legs slicing smoothly through the water. A cloud covered the moon and she lost sight of him.

"You're not afraid, are you?" His voice came from beside her.

No, she shook her head. No.

He reached for her hand and pulled her down in the water with him, kissing her wetly, his tongue thrusting into her mouth as though searching for answers there. She felt his hand between her legs, touching her, opening her.

623

She lay back in the warm wetness, feeling his kisses on her, his touches. His lips feathered across her belly, and he pulled her legs around his waist, his mouth devouring her, kissing her neck, his tongue finding her ear, his breath coming hard.

He picked her up and carried her to the sand, kneeling down, cradling her in his arms. He kissed her, and she wound her arms around his neck as water lapped their feet.

"I want you," she said.

"I know. And I've wanted you from that night at the dance."

He leaned down to kiss her again, and his body melded into hers. He rolled over, pulling her on top of him, his mouth finding her breasts, kissing them as she rolled against him, their bodies undulating together in a rhythm that picked up the frenzy of the corroboree.

He rolled her over again. As she arched her back, he thrust into her, pressing her so tightly against him she thought they were one.

The stars above her blazed like fireworks; she felt the ocean rushing into her, over her.

"Oh, dear God," she whispered. "I think I'm falling in love with you."

He arched his back. "Think? You *think*?" His voice cracked. "Goddamnit," he held himself still. "Tell me. Tell me you love me."

"I love you."

He gave one final lunge, and the water washed over them. Opening her eyes, Cassie saw a star shooting across the sky.

ABOUT THE AUTHOR

Barbara Bickmore taught English for twenty years and raised three children before turning her considerable talents to writing novels with her first book, *East of the Sun*.

To research the early days of Australia and its settlers for *The Moon Below*, Barbara Bickmore traveled extensively in Australia. A prodigious traveler, she also spent two months journeying 3,600 miles through China.

A longtime New Yorker, Barbara Bickmore now lives in Mexico.